To So Few

Explosion

by

Cap Parlier

To So Few
Explosion
by
Cap Parlier

SAINT GAUDENS PRESS
Wichita, Kansas & Santa Barbara, California

Saint Gaudens Press
Post Office Box 405
Solvang, CA 93464-0405

Saint Gaudens, Saint Gaudens Press
and the Winged Liberty colophon
are trademarks of Saint Gaudens Press

Print edition ISBN: 978-0-943039-27-5

Library of Congress Catalog Number - 2015911226

Printed in the United States of America

The TO SO FEW series are works of fiction. Any reference to real people, objects, events, organizations, or locales is intended only to give the fiction a sense of reality and authenticity. Other names, characters and incidents are the products of the author's imagination and bear no relationship to past events, or persons living or deceased.

Dedication

—

To all those who have gone before us, and given their last full measure of devotion to the cause of freedom and the defense of those freedoms.

See other great books available from Saint Gaudens Press
http://www.SaintGaudensPress.com

Visit Cap Parlier's Web Site at http://www.Parlier.com

Acknowledgments

—

To John Richard and Roger Benefiel for research assistance.

To my wife, spouse, partner, sponsor and cheerleader, Jeanne, who tolerated the hours, days, weeks, months and years of research, writing and discussion. She has and continues to tolerate my love of flight and the need to tell a story about the greatest event in human flight.

To my reviewers: my wife, Jeanne; John Richard; and Leta Buresh, for their patience, reflection, opinions and suggestions. I believe they made it a stronger story.

A special recognition must be offered to numerous individuals who provided their knowledge, experience and precious time to assist my historical research.

Imperial War Museum – Dr. Neil Young, Research and Information Office

Royal Air Force Museum – Mr. Mungo Chapman, Research & Information Services

Duxford Aerodrome Museum

R.J. Mitchell Memorial Museum – Mr. D.G. Upward, Director

National Railway Museum – Mr. Philip Atkins, BSc, Librarian

Churchill Archives Centre – Ms. Carolyn Lye

House of Lords – Mr. D.L. Prior, Record Office

If there are errors in the representation of historical details, the responsibility rests solely with me and must in no way reflect upon the experts acknowledged above.

Prologue

—

Thursday evening, 31.August.1939, a carefully chosen team of Nazi *SchutzStaffeln* (SS) men executed a precisely planned "attack" on a small radio station in Gleiwitz, Upper Silesia, Germany, to make their actions look and sound like Polish soldiers had attacked Germany under the pretext of a continuing border dispute. Early the following morning, major units from all branches of the German *Wehrmacht* (armed forces) launched a well-planned assault on Poland across a broad front. France and Great Britain issued an ultimatum for Germany to cease and desist, and return to the pre-incursion border, which the Germans summarily ignored. Two days later, with no meaningful response, France and Great Britain declared war on Germany; so began World War II in Europe.

The Battle of the Atlantic began in earnest within hours of the declaration of war, as German *Unterseebooten* 30 (U-30) fired the first shot, as she torpedoed and sank the British merchant ship RMS *Athenia*. The desperate naval battles at sea would rage unabated for years and nearly bring the United Kingdom to her knees, as the *Kriegsmarine* choked off vital supplies from Britain's empire and distant but friendly nations like the United States. The early successes of the German Navy left little doubt this would be a different war. The British were not without success during those dark days. Three cruisers of the Royal Navy's Force G engaged the solo *Panzerschiff* DKM *Admiral Graf Spee*, off the River Platte estuary between Uruguay and Argentina, cornered the German battlecruiser and eventually led the German captain to scuttle his ship in the estuary to avoid a loss to the perceived superior Royal Navy Force G.

Using their new, combined arms tactics – *Blitzkrieg* (Lightning War) – the *Wehrmacht* subdued Poland in one month of combat. The speed of the German victory shocked the world's military leaders and diplomats. The coordinated, highly mobile warfare rendered the Allied defense planning virtually null and void. The Allies were not prepared for this new form of warfare.

The Soviet Union used their treaty with Germany to invade Eastern Poland, as the two "allies" carved up and consumed Poland. The tidbit offered up by Hitler along with the non-aggression pact between the two countries on the eve of war lulled Premier Stalin into a false sense of security that would soon enough prove to be nearly fatal.

Despite the mutual protection treaty with Poland, *L'Armée de Terre* and the British Expeditionary Force sat in defensive positions in Northeast France, virtually impotent to come to the aid of their ally Poland. The Western Press soon labeled the winter of 1939/40 as the Phony War, while the Germans jokingly called it *sitzkrieg*. The Germans were under no illusions and used the valuable months of comparative quiet to consolidate, rearm, redeploy, and prepare for the next phase of Hitler's grand plan for empire – the self-proclaimed thousand-year *Reich*.

The Germans were not the only ones who used the respite to advantage. Air Officer Commanding-in-Chief, Fighter Command, Air Chief Marshal Sir Hugh Dowding honed the skills and equipment that would soon defend the United Kingdom against the German attack sure to come. He deployed the new Hurricane and Spitfire monoplane fighters as quickly as British industry could produce them, and he trained his ground and air crews in the use of the newly deployed radio detection and ranging equipment that would be vital and integral to the command and control of the network at the heart of the Air Defense of Great Britain system. All too soon, the efforts of Fighter Command would be proven in the crucible of aerial combat.

—

Prior to the outbreak of war in Europe, the young protégé of World War I veteran and aerial ace Malcolm Bainbridge – Brian Arthur Drummond – demonstrated his instinctive aptitude for flight as well as some of the aerial skills necessary for aerial combat. Brian believed as Malcolm did that the dark clouds on the eastern horizon meant war was coming and was virtually inevitable. With the assistance of Malcolm, and his brother-in-arms and nephew of Winston Churchill, now Royal Air Force Group Captain John Spencer, Brian left his parent's home soon after he graduated from high school in Wichita, Kansas, and travelled to Windsor, Ontario, Canada, where by prior arrangement, Brian joined the Royal Air Force to answer his generation's call to duty in defense of freedom.

Less than a month before war was declared, Group Captain Spencer orchestrated a visit to his uncle's Chartwell Manor estate in order to introduce Brian to the veteran and outcast Member of Parliament. The connection to Spencer and Churchill would serve Brian well during his service.

Brian progressed quite rapidly through the pilot training curricula. During his training, Brian acquired a new mentor in the form of Flight Lieutenant Lord Jeremy 'Mud' Morrison, Esq., who adds to Brian's flight skills by teaching him the ways of the world in which he now lives.

As the war began, Prime Minister Chamberlain invited Churchill to rejoin His Majesty's Government, returning him as First Lord of the Admiralty, a post he had held 25 years earlier. Churchill's warnings of Hitler's menace during those dark wilderness years had finally come to fruition. He now held the awesome responsibility for the Royal Navy in those early months of the war.

By the late fall of 1939, along with his new friend and brother-in-arms Jonathan Kensington, Brian became a pilot officer in the Royal Air Force, assigned to Fighter Command and No.609 Squadron stationed at RAF Drem aerodrome on the south side of the mouth of the River Forth estuary in Scotland. The new pilots saw their first combat as the *Luftwaffe* probed the northern defenses of Great Britain. They promptly learned the ways of the brotherhood of which they were now a part.

And so, here begins our story.

—

Chapter 1

Everyone pushes a falling fence.

-- Chinese proverb

Saturday, 6.April.1940
No.21 Queen Anne's Gate
Headquarters, Secret Intelligence Service
Westminster, London, England

The urgent knock did not wait for a summons. "Sir, a courier is here with an urgent message," announced the executive assistant.

"Show him in," answered Colonel Stewart Graham 'C' Menzies, DSO, MC, installed as Director General, Secret Intelligence Service (MI6), less than six months ago.

A young man dressed in a nondescript, conservative, business suit carrying a leather satchel with an over-the-shoulder strap entered his office, closed the door behind, and opened his case as he approached C's desk.

"Sir, I was asked to deliver this to you personally," the man said as he handed the single piece of paper to 'C.'

MOST SECRET – C EYES ONLY

A series of messages received this morning from operatives in Wilhelmshaven, Kiel, Hamburg and Bremerhaven reporting the general embarkation of infantry, armour, logistics and communications units on numerous merchant ships. Collation of various reports suggests a multi-division force to be deployed within the next few days. Unreliable sources indicate force bound for Norway. Combatant vessels set sail during the night. Several agents report significant counterespionage operations by security forces and began evasion process.

Sensitive sources and methods. No dissemination recommended.

```
                    L.S.P. Fortman
                    Lieut.Colonel. G.S.
        MI6.
        1040 hrs.
        6.4.40.
        Distribution:
        Single copy.
```
MOST SECRET – C EYES ONLY

'C' looked into the courier's waiting eyes. "Thank you," he said. The man did not move. "I will see to the destruction of this message," he added. The man nodded and departed.

Stewart lifted the handset for the direct line, scrambled, telephone to the Director of Naval Intelligence.

"Yes 'C,'" answered Vice Admiral Sir Geoffrey Ian 'Jumper' Pike, KCB, DSC.

"We just received information regarding the embarkation of troops in several German ports."

"I was about to call you. We have received similar reports confirming your information."

"What do you think it means?"

"Norway."

"Can you see any other signs or possible objectives?"

"No. Everything since the ULTRA message a month ago has pointed directly at Norway."

"What actions is the Navy taking?" asked 'C.'

"The First Lord has placed the Home Fleet on alert. However, interdiction orders have not been issued. He has also requested photo reconnaissance of the German coast as well as Bomber Command missions to disrupt their transportation."

"Thank you, Geoffrey. It sounds like you have things well in hand. I will keep you informed of anything new."

"Likewise, Stewart."

Sunday, 7 April 1940
Air Intelligence Section
Air Ministry
Whitehall, London, England

The windowless, colorless, nearly empty room existed for one purpose only – the supervisory review of photographic material and the correlation of each with one specific spot on the maps that covered the walls. The Air Intelligence Section of the Air Ministry occupied and guarded this interior room along with five others nestled in the basement of the old building.

The three middle grade officers came to attention when Air Chief Marshal Sir Cyril Louis Norton Newall, GCB, CMG, CBE, AM, entered the room alone. A wave of his hand placed the junior officers at ease.

"What have you here?" asked the Chief of the Air Staff – HMG's senior air force officer.

"Sir, these are the latest photographs to be processed and analyzed. They were taken, at some cost I might add, over Wilhelmshaven yesterday morning," the wing commander stated.

Newall immediately began examining the photographs declining the proffered, large, hand magnifying glass. The objects shown in the photographs did not need magnification to be recognized.

"Yesterday you say."

"Yes sir."

"When is the next recce mission?"

"Wing Commander Cotton landed a short time ago. His target was Kiel, which we believe from MI6 information is the main embarkation port. The film is being processed at Heston as we speak. We have one of our men waiting there as soon as the PDU has finished their work."

The Photographic Development Unit under Wing Commander Frederick Sidney Cotton operated a small force of two, twin-engine, Blenheims and two newly acquired Spitfires specifically modified and dedicated to high resolution, photographic reconnaissance. The unique group produced aerial photographs from all the various intelligence units of His Majesty's Government.

"I don't think there is much doubt about the meaning of these ships?" observed Newall.

"No sir."

"Let's get these photos and Cotton's photos from today's mission over to Bomber Command as soon as possible. We will task them for a series of missions to at least let the Gerries know we are watching them. How soon can we have your report?"

"This afternoon, sir."

"Very well. As soon as you can complete it, get copies to the Air Staff, Admiralty and Bomber Command. Do not wait for me."

"Yes sir."

———

Monday, 8.April.1940
No.10 Downing Street
Whitehall, London, England

"This is most unusual for you to be up so early, Winston," said Prime Minister Arthur Neville Chamberlain, FRS, MP, as the two men shook hands.

Chamberlain's staff secretary closed the door to the Prime Minister's office leaving the two politicians to themselves. The mid-morning hour was indeed early for Winston Leonard Spencer Churchill, CH, TD, MP, who usually did not venture beyond his study until late morning or early afternoon, but often extended his workday into the late night and early morning hours.

"Extraordinary times, Prime Minister," responded the First Lord.

"I presume you have seen the latest intelligence from Germany?"

"Yes. The Phony War, as the tabloids have dubbed it, is coming to an end. I wanted a short chat with you prior to this afternoon's War Cabinet meeting."

"Anytime."

"Thank you, sir." Churchill paused as Chamberlain slowly lowered himself to the cushioned chair, and then joined him in the chair directly across the small table from the prime minister. "The U-boats continue to bedevil the Navy's efforts to protect our shipping. We press forward with research to find some tools to bring success. The fast convoys offer a modicum of protection but not enough, and there are certainly insufficient numbers of fast merchant shipping to sustain us. Hitler's widening of this conflict portends worse times ahead."

"Great stress on our industry?"

"Yes. As you know, I have informally corresponded with President Roosevelt. I know he is sympathetic but seriously constrained by the large isolationist faction in the country. This latest evidence of what lies ahead must convince the American people to change."

"Not likely from what I gather. Ambassador Kennedy remains quite emphatic on the U.S. will to remain out of this war."

"The bloody bastard has been a fan of that German maniac from the beginning," barked Churchill.

"That is quite unfair, Winston."

"I suppose it is, Neville. My apologies. But, he has been a little too supportive for my liking."

"Perhaps. However, I believe he does represent America."

"In name and title, but I do not believe he represents Franklin. The President's correspondence has been much more supportive."

Chamberlain paused to consider his words with their eyes still connected. "Winston, you shall occupy this seat soon enough."

"Nonsense."

"We have discussed this before. Hitler is on the verge of consuming Denmark and Norway. Holland, Belgium and maybe even France are next. If he attacks France, he knows he must subdue the British to be successful. My health is rapidly failing me, and I am not the one to lead the Empire in the struggle before us. That heavy mantle shall soon rest on your shoulders. Be prepared."

Churchill reluctantly nodded his head. "I think it is time to make our request for American logistic support on behalf of His Majesty's Government."

"I cannot. I would support your efforts within the confines of the unofficial communications you have established. Continue to nurture your relationship with Roosevelt. When you assume the premiership, an official request would be appropriate."

"It might be too late."

Chamberlain slowly shook his head in disagreement. "We have no choice."

—

Thursday, 11.April.1940
RAF Drem
Drem, Lothian, Scotland

"**D**amn, Nazis. Why is it that horse's arse Hitler feels he can take whatever he wants?"

"I really wouldn't know, 'Angle.' I'd say the bastard thinks he is doing everyone a favor. You know, provide some good German discipline for all of the unruly masses," answered Flight Lieutenant Robert 'Sparky' Morrow – leader of Red Section.

Since the news of the German invasion of Denmark and Norway reached the airfield in Scotland, the discussion in the No.609 Squadron Dispersal building took consistently the same course. The Phony War, as the press and nearly everyone called it, was essentially over. They all expected a new, higher intensity to the air war over Great Britain. Uncertainty remained the only common thought regarding what the Germans would do next.

"Why don't we call off the war today?" asked Flying Officer Reginald 'Organ' Foxworth – left wing of Yellow Section.

"What is the matter, 'Organ?' Life in the fast lane too much for you," jabbed Pilot Officer Stephen 'Mongo' Strickland. – right wing of Green Section.

"Too much beer."

"No such thing as too much beer."

Every morning-after was the same for Pilot Officer Brian 'Hunter' Drummond, still the only American in Fighter Command, so far. Gatherings at the local pub provided the most popular outlet for the pilots. Most often, they met at The Sword and Stone pub in the tiny village of Drem. All the pilots attended. The Officer's Mess, while a convenient place, excluded the flying sergeants, 'Junior' Carrolton and 'Fog' Johnson, since technically they did not hold a commission and therefore proper military decorum prohibited such intermingling. Brian still did not accept the distinction. They all flew the same aircraft, the same missions, and they withstood the same risks. At The Sword and Stone, they drank the same beer, flirted and danced with the same women and enjoyed the camaraderie of fellow brothers in arms without rank. The visits to the pub were more the norm than the exception. Without any overt recognition by any of the fighter pilots, nights of beer drinking some-times to the point of knee wobbling intoxication, laughter, jokes and pranks, and women of various levels of interest, enthusiasm and promiscuity offered the primary release mechanism for the tensions of aerial patrols and combat.

Since Squadron Leader Horatio 'Spike' Darling's announcement of the German move, the speculation regarding the expected movement of the squadron to the South gave everyone plenty of fodder for discussion. Everyone felt the German invasion of Norway as a tightening of the noose. Everyone seemed to point toward France and the Channel as Hitler's next logical step although many could not believe Hitler would be so foolish to attack the largest standing army in Europe, if not the world, *le Armée de Terre*, supplemented by the British Expeditionary Force in Northeast France. The warning order for No.609 Squadron to make preparations for a possible move to RAF Northolt brought the doubters back to the sensations of the tightening noose. The pilots wanted to be wherever the action was going to be. They all shared to varying degrees the same ethos, they wanted to fly the best fighter against the best adversary and win. Some among them felt the weight of patriotic, nationalistic principles, but they all lived the excitement of high-speed flight.

The telephone rang its now notorious bell. "Scramble Green Section," shouted Corporal Jennifer Warren.

There was no hesitation as the section leader, Flight Lieutenant Roger 'Jackstay' Beamish, and his two wingmen, Pilot Officers 'Mongo' Strickland and 'Hunter' Drummond, grabbed their flying kit, bolted from the Dispersal hut and ran toward their fighters. The ground crews were several yards ahead of them from the Maintenance Control building.

They had practiced and exercised the rapid launch routine quite well. From the scramble command to light under the wheels with the undercarriage on its way to the wheel wells took 3 minutes, 22 seconds by Squadron Leader Darling's watch, not the fastest launch but certainly respectable.

"Sorbo Green airborne," announced 'Jackstay' Beamish over the radio.

The response was waiting for them. "Sorbo Green, this is Rooker. Bandits at angels three, heading two seven five. Vector to intercept, oh eight seven, climb to angels five. Bandits appear to be a raid of less than five aircraft on another low level attempt."

Beamish turned the flight of three Spitfires to 087° magnetic as the words were spoken. By the time the controller finished his instruction, they were leveling off at 5,000 feet. Brian rechecked his switches ready for combat – guns armed, gunsight set, engine instruments normal. The guns were charged and fully armed. Brian touched his thumb on the firing button at the eleven o'clock position on his control column hand circle as if he needed to make sure it was still there. The simple metal circle with its small ball for an aiming sight did not need much attention. He did look forward to getting the new, illuminated, reflex sight that would give him better stadiametric range information. The young American volunteer sensed this flight was different from all the others, although probably just a reflection of his first launch since the Norwegian invasion.

A scattered layer of small cumulus clouds lay below them. The sky above and all around them was bright and clear. There should be no problem finding their targets today. Three Spitfires against up to five bombers. Brian remembered all the stories from the other pilots about the gunners on the bombers. Even though their targets would be bigger, slower and less maneuverable, they were not easy targets. He expected and was prepared for the sting. Interlaced fire from a tight formation of bombers had to be respected.

"Sorbo Green, this is Rooker. Vector for intercept, three four five. Target is five miles. Good hunting."

"Roger, Rooker." They turned to their initial attack heading. The morning sun would be directly behind them. As their wings leveled, 'Jackstay' announced, "Tally ho. A 'Vic' of three Dornier One Sevens, spot on. Here we go lads. We will take them as we are. I have the leader. 'Mongo,' you have the right, and 'Hunter,' you have the left." They peeled off in quick succession toward the three bombers still lumbering ahead apparently unaware of the now diving Spitfires.

Brian pushed his throttle up to the emergency seal. The dominant, throaty, purr of the Merlin told him everything he wanted to know about his powerplant. Speed began to build. The sound of the rushing air confirmed his acceleration toward his target. He adjusted the long nose of the Spitfire to place his sight pipper on the tail of the bomber. As he had trained and practiced so many times, Brian would begin his engagement from maximum range trying to walk his eight streams of bullets smoothly up the fuselage to the cockpit.

The bomber grew quickly within his sight circle. The stream of tracers spitting out from each of the bombers toward 'Jackstay's fighter imprinted on his peripheral awareness as the Green Section Leader made his first attack. The red balls flowing up toward the attacking Spitfires shifted to 'Mongo' Strickland as 'Jackstay' dove past the raiders. Brian concentrated on his pipper. A quick glance at his slip ball showed a slight ball out to the right. He added a small amount of right rudder to correct. Ball centered. In range. His right thumb smoothly depressed the red firing button.

The Spitfire shuddered as all eight Browning 0.303 caliber machine guns erupted. The familiar, loud, shaking sound with the rapidly growing planform of the Do17 squarely in his sight pumped additional adrenaline into Brian's blood stream. Pieces flew off the tail. The left Do17 tail gunner never responded to Brian's attack. He was aware of the red balls streaking past him as his pipper moved up the fuselage. Before Brian could get his stream to the cockpit, the hapless Do17 exploded in a bright orange and black ball. The flash surprised Brian but did not cause him to miss a beat as he rolled and pulled hard to avoid the inevitable debris of the disintegrating bomber.

The impacts of metal fragments hitting his aircraft as he flew through the edge of the expanding ball of what used to be a German bomber jolted and staggered his fighter. The sharp report of high energy, metal-to-metal contact instantly produced a sickening feeling in the pit of Brian's stomach along with a flash of anticipation whether his aircraft would soon stop flying.

As quickly as he was into it, he was out of it and the Spitfire was still flying quite well. Brian continued to pull his fighter around into a long, upward arc. He strained to look back through the top of his canopy at the scene. The white circle on the surface of the North Sea marked the tomb of his target. The lead bomber's right engine was smoking badly as he turned back the way they had come. Bombs began exploding in the sea sending geysers up toward them. The third bomber completed a tighter turn and was now ahead of his leader, and apparently undamaged. Brian quickly scanned the sky above the bombers.

'Jackstay's fighter was diving straight for the lead bomber. 'Mongo' approached the perch for his re-attack. Brian adjusted his position extending his flight path for an attack on the faster right wing bomber undoubtedly at full power, much lighter without his bomb load, and diving toward the thickening cloud layer below them. Again, the tracers rose from the beleaguered lead bomber in a desperate attempt to defend itself. 'Jackstay' managed to inflict fatal injury to the Do17 as large chunks of the fuselage and wing blew off. The German raider began a slow roll as the left engine burst into flame. The nose dropped abruptly. Brian did not waste time watching the dying bomber. Neither did 'Jackstay' Beamish who pulled his fighter up in a high climb to curl back into the attack on the remaining Do17. 'Mongo' Strickland completed his second pass at the sole surviving bomber without consequence.

Brian rolled his Spitfire to begin his attack dive. The speed of the Do17 was now significantly higher than it was at the start of the engagement. Brian pushed his throttle forward past the emergency seal to get the full +6 inches of boost from his Merlin II engine. The closure rate with his new target was slower than he would have liked. The Do17 gunners would have more time for him. As he approached still well beyond his maximum range, the red balls began to rise up at him, this time seeming to float, then falling away below him. As he moved closer, the red balls tightened up and moved more vigorously. Brian concentrated on his sight, trying desperately to ignore the angry red balls reaching out toward him. Again, a quick look at his slip ball – perfectly centered. As his right thumb began to press forward, the Do17 disappeared into a cloud.

Brian pulled up sharply but briefly, not wanting to follow the bomber. His throttle came back about an inch, which he knew without looking would give him slightly less than zero boost. His approach had been from the right side. He smartly jinked his fighter to go around the left side of the cloud. He pulled back his throttle a little more as he skirted the edge of the cloud not wanting to get ahead of the bomber.

The Do17 popped out of the cloud slightly below Brian and to his right about 600 yards ahead. The throttle went full forward as he smoothly brought his sight to the target. The gunners must have been looking where Brian was as they had entered the cloud. It took them several long seconds to open fire. Brian squeezed off a short burst as the retreating raider entered another cloud.

His throttle came back again as he dove to get underneath the cloud layer. Instinctively, Brian knew the pilot was probably desperate to escape and would try anything to succeed. Below the floor of the clouds about 1500 feet above the North Sea, he waited. A gap in the clouds exposed the bomber now several hundred feet above Brian and directly ahead. The Merlin roared again to full power. As he closed with the target, there were no red balls coming down to greet him. The tracers rose up. Looking up, the PR-D insignia of Beamish's Spitfire dove past the bomber. The right engine gushed a black cloud and stream of what had to be oil before it erupted in fire. The target's wings waggled as if slammed by a mighty blow from an invisible fist. As 'Jackstay' cleared, Brian opened fire directly into the belly of the wounded bomber. He held his firing button down until the Do17 pulled up sharply as if the pilot wanted to loop the big bomber. Brian pulled up rolling into a circling turn as he watched the bomber straighten out into what would nearly be a hammerhead stall. All three Spitfires now occupied nearly the same circle as the bomber fell off on his right wing into a tight spiral toward the beckoning depths of the North Sea. Only one man escaped the plummeting coffin. A full, round, white canopy indicated a successful bale out by probably one of the gunners.

Another white circle of foam among the gentle waves marked the final resting place for the remainder of the German crew. They watched the German descend in his parachute. 'Jackstay' made several slow passes waving his wings. Brian saw the man wave back. At least he was alive.

"There we go, lads. Work's done. Let's join up," Beamish commanded as they climbed to 4,000 feet above the tops of the cloud heading back to Drem. "Rooker, Sorbo Green."

"Sorbo Green, this is Rooker. Go ahead."

"Rooker, we've splashed three Dornier One Sevens, no losses. We have only one chute about two miles behind us. The bloke is alive. Please, alert Rescue."

Brian knew, as he was certain they all did, that the likelihood of the rescue boats being able to reach the downed German before he died of hypothermia in the cold, dark waters of the North Sea was remote to non-existent. It was an unwritten, unspoken rule among the pilots that every effort must be made to save a downed pilot no matter what nationality. It was their way of believing the same effort would be given to them. For the first time in his life, despite all the words from Malcolm Bainbridge and others, and the extensive training by the RAF, Brian felt a nauseous sensation deep within him as they flew back to Drem. Eleven human beings had just died. Their parents, wives, girlfriends and comrades would soon be mourning their loss. All his dreams, thoughts, images and desires took on an ugly, dirty tinge to them. The war was now very much real for Pilot Officer Brian 'Hunter' Drummond.

The return to RAF Drem was uneventful. As he taxied back into his place in the line, Brian noted the men scurrying about. They obviously recognized the open, blackened gun ports and probably knew about the successful engagement. Pilots appeared from the door of the Dispersal hut. Without hearing any words, jubilation was quite evident among the welcoming crowd. Brian did not share the same elation although he knew he had been very successful on his first actual aerial combat.

Brian's propeller was the last to stop. Leading Aircraftman Bernard 'Bernie' Gordon was up on the wing promptly, as usual, pulling back the canopy and opening the access door. "Good hunting, sir?"

A strange, obscene mixture of excitement, satisfaction and revulsion filled Brian's gut. He swallowed hard, and then sucked in a deep breath of oxygen before pulling up his goggles and disconnecting his mask. He could not let anyone know how he felt. "You betcha," Brian shouted with as much enthusiasm as he could muster up. "Got one of the bastards. Maybe another half with Flight Lieutenant Beamish."

"Congratulations, sir. We'll get the paint ready," Gordon said referring to the tradition of painting a white swastika to symbolize his aerial victories once the intelligence staff confirmed his results.

"Thank you, Bernie. She's running great, but I'm afraid I may have taken some fragments as the bomber exploded."

A large, appreciative smile blossomed across Leading Aircraftman Gordon's rugged face. "We'll give her a good look see and get the damage repaired lickedty split." He turned to get to his work and abruptly turned back around. "By the way, boss, your bird is next up for the mods."

"Great." The modifications to the Vickers Supermarine Mark I were all significant improvements especially the new, three bladed propeller, the armor and the new reflex sight. No more scuffed knuckles raising the undercarriage. Everyone liked the modifications. "When do we get them?"

"They'll take her in tonight. Should take about six days."

"All guns fired. No jams," announced Aircraftman Colin Jenkins with discernible pride that his guns worked perfectly. Brian gave his armorer a thumbs-up acknowledgment.

"We'll get the bird turned around in a flash, sir."

Brian gathered up his flying gear leaving the crew to tend to his mount. He looked over his shoulder at the large white letter 'F' designator for his aircraft. A jagged-edged, dark hole broke up the otherwise clean, white surface. He began to feel better as he walked toward the smiling faces of the other pilots.

As with others before him, 'Hunter' Drummond was greeted by slaps on the back, punches to his shoulder, ruffling of his hair and a variety of congratulatory words as he entered Dispersal. The excitement and reinforcement made the last vestiges of his nausea disappear. Brian wondered if the other pilots had felt the same thing after their first victories.

The intelligence debriefing went quickly as each of the Green Section pilots recounted the elements and sequence of the engagement individually and in private. The debriefers compared notes, and then joined the pilots outside Dispersal.

"Three up, three down. Flight Lieutenant Beamish credited with one and a half. Pilot Officer Drummond gets one and a half. Congratulations to both of you," announced Flying Officer James Royster, the squadron intelligence officer.

Another round of celebratory gestures and words concluded the mission. The mood in and around Dispersal acknowledged as much a reflection of Green Section's success as the squadron's mounting successes.

Jonathan started to ask Brian about his experience when Flight Lieutenant 'Sparky' Morrow returned to Dispersal from the Operations building. "Just received word from HQ. The Norwegian Air Force apparently gave the Huns a run for their money. Made them pay the price, they did."

"What do they fly?"

"Gloster Gladiators, for Christ's sake," he answered with astonishment.

"Gladiators against Willie Messerschmitt's best?" asked Flying Sergeant Miles 'Fog' Johnson.

"So, they say."

"I'll be damned."

"Maybe these bastards aren't as invincible as they are made out to be."

The telephone rang instantly killing all conversation. "Scramble Red and Yellow Sections," announced Corporal Warren.

"Lord have mercy . . . must be a good one," joked 'Sparky' Morrow, as the pilots grabbed their flying kit. As the senior of the two section leaders, Morrow would lead the bottom half of the squadron into combat.

"Give 'em hell, lads," 'Spike' Darling said, as the first of the Merlins fired up.

Within minutes, the magnificent roar of six Spitfires filled the air as they left the ground, turning back to the east. Brian's mind focused on his experience earlier in the afternoon and wondered if Jonathan felt the same things. He would know within an hour or two.

As silence returned to the airfield, routine picked up where it left off. The aviator's conversation took the longest to regain normalcy. The situation in Norway and the experience of the Norwegian Gladiator pilots against the *Luftwaffe*'s Bf109s occupied their thoughts. Brian knew German fighters would be an entirely different problem than a lumbering bomber even with its bristling guns. Having flown mock aerial combat against a variety of aircraft and a spectrum of pilots, an agile, fast, well-armed fighter in the hands of an aggressive, skilled pilot would be a much greater challenge. From everything he had been told, the Bf109 was essentially comparable to the Spitfire, which meant it would be a formidable adversary in the hands of a competent pilot.

The telephone rang several more times before the six Spitfires returned. One call told them the fighters of No.609 Squadron were engaging a raid of ten He111s. The second call told them the Germans lost two bombers. None of them reached their target before turning back.

"Mister Drummond," called Leading Aircraftman Gordon, leaning into the Dispersal building, "you got a little more damage than we thought. I'm afraid you're out of play. We're going to take your bird into the mod cycle now."

Without directly responding to his crew chief, Brian turned to his leader. "Would you mind if I take a look, skipper?"

Squadron Leader Darling smiled. "You're not going to do much flying without a machine. The reserve birds are all down as well. I think you can call it a day."

"Thank you, sir."

Brian walked with Bernie Gordon down the line to the fabricated maintenance hangar. His crew chief described the damage as they walked. Bullets damaged several structural items and creased his coolant system. As Gordon told the story, he had landed with almost no coolant remaining. The big Merlins did not run well without ethylene-glycol coolant or lubricating oil. As Bernie pointed out each injury to his aircraft, Brian thought back to the sounds and feel of the engagement, and tried to determine when he had taken each hit. Ten distinct bullet trajectories had penetrated his aircraft. The physical evidence of combat gave Brian a chill although he tried to hold all his emotions deep within him. He had to make jokes about the damage. Fighter pilots had to have nerves of steel and no apparent fear of death. It was not an easy facade to maintain when you were surveying ten bullet holes all less than twenty feet from where your body had been strapped to the seat.

The tones of the landing Spitfires gave Brian the perfect excuse to leave the wounded aircraft. Six Spitfires took off, and he counted six with their flaps and undercarriages down. Another successful mission. They were all beginning to feel pretty good about their performance against the *Luftwaffe* even if they were unescorted bombers.

Jonathan had a broad smile on his face as Brian joined him. Without asking, he instinctively knew his best friend had tasted his first blood, as the Plains Indians were famous for saying. "I think I got one, Brian."

"I thought so. A smile that big could only mean one thing."

"It was amazing. Kind of like you described it."

"We'd better wait until you've been through debriefing, and then I want to hear all about it."

"Yeah, sure. We must be proper, mus'n't we?"

The squadron pilots celebrated yet another time at the Sword and Stone. To the casual observer and listener, the clutch of men in RAF uniforms guzzling beer with robust enthusiasm had just won a football match, or soccer game as the Americans would say. Laughter, jokes, strong words and exaggerated motions punctuated the scene. From a more distant time, they could be described as celebrating the successful hunt. The clan would be well fed for several months. Brian and Jonathan would wait to share their more personal feelings about the events of this Thursday in the spring of 1940.

———

Monday, 15.April.1940
RAF Drem
Drem, Lothian, Scotland

For Brian Drummond, the glorious spring day with its clear skies, light, warm breeze, and the delicate, tantalizing fragrances of the blooming foliage made this day out of the saddle more tolerable. Progress on the repairs and modifications to his aircraft moved along well. Bernie Gordon, working with the modification team, estimated completion in another couple of days. Watching his mates take-off and land whether they engaged or not added to Brian's frustration. Maybe one of the reserve aircraft would come up soon.

The lengthening days added more flying time. Pilot Officer Jonathan Andrew Xavier 'Harness' Kensington was returning from his second sortie of the day when the telephone in Dispersal rang.

"Mister Drummond," Corporal Warren called from the interior. As Brian entered the building, she continued, "a Group Captain Spencer for you."

Brian wondered why his RAF mentor, Group Captain John Henry Randolph Spencer, DFC would be calling him on a Monday afternoon in the middle of a war. "Pilot Officer Drummond, sir," he said, wanting to be proper for Corporal Warren.

"Brian, has that embassy chap, Slaughter, been to see you, yet?" John Spencer asked with some urgency.

"No, sir."

"Good, then I'm not too late." Fears of the past erupted as John took a deep breath. "Listen carefully, Brian. I thought we had this completely settled a few months ago, but apparently not. A friend in the Foreign Office tells me the U.S. Government has issued a warrant for your arrest under the provisions of the American Federal Neutrality Act."

"God damn it!"

"Hold on a moment and please listen carefully. They can do nothing to you, Brian. As long as you are in this country and especially while you are in the service of the Crown, they can only give you the appropriate papers. I have been assured that extradition proceedings will take a very long time in your case and should provide us sufficient time to work things out. I intend to ask my uncle for assistance even though I know he is a very busy man, at the moment. Now, assuming you want to continue flying with us, you must meet Slaughter when he comes. He will have an FBI agent with him and probably a British constable. They will not be allowed into the facility at Drem, but you must meet them at the gate. Be polite, listen to what they have to say, and refuse to go with them. Remember, they cannot take any immediate action. Do you understand?"

"Yes, sir."

"Do you have any questions?"

"I guess not, sir."

"Excellent. Now, Brian, if you have any problems, ask the gate guards for assistance and call me immediately."

"Yes, sir."

"Whenever you do meet this sod Slaughter, please call me to let me know what happened. We will take care of you and get this mess straightened out quickly. Trust me, Brian."

"Thank you, sir."

"Good luck, Brian. Sorry this must happen with everything else going on right now."

"My apologies to you, sir, for getting you mixed up in this crap."

"No problem. Talk to you soon." The telephone line went dead.

Brian could not believe this was happening and especially at this very moment in time when the situation was so obvious. The concerns must have etched themselves across his face.

"Is everything OK, sir?" asked Corporal Warren.

"Not really but that's life." Brian looked to the status board as Jonathan and the others returned to Dispersal. "Where's the skipper?"

"In his office, I believe, sir."

"You missed another good one," said Jonathan with pride.

Brian ignored the statement as he knocked on the squadron leader's door.

"Enter."

"I need to talk to you, sir. I'm apparently in some trouble."

"What is it?"

Brian relayed the information provided by Group Captain Spencer. He thought he had correct and appropriate answers to all the questions. Squadron Leader Darling remained supportive in every way. When Brian told the other pilots what was about to happen, they united as he had never seen before. Even the usually caustic 'Mongo' Strickland stood on Brian's behalf. The entire pilot staff wanted to go with Brian for his impending meeting with Assistant Commercial Attaché Arnold Slaughter. The camaraderie and uniformity of purpose impressed Brian so much he had to fight back tears of thankfulness and appreciation. It was 16:35 when the call came.

"Mister Drummond, you have several visitors at the front gate," announced Corporal Warren.

Every pilot wanted to go with Brian, but Squadron Leader Darling told all of them to stay since the squadron was still at available status. Darling offered and Brian accepted his companionship for the dreaded meeting.

Three men waited on the other side of the barrier. Brian recognized Slaughter immediately. A rather ominous man in a dark suit had to be the FBI agent. A smaller, more amicable appearing man was probably the British policeman. Darling walked with Brian past the guards toward the Edinburgh Police sedan parked along the roadway.

"Mister Drummond," began Slaughter, "I'm sure you remember me. This is Special Agent Mike Tower of the Federal Bureau of Investigation, and this is Inspector David Galloway of the Edinburgh Police." Brian guessed correctly. He shook hands with each man including Slaughter although he did not want to.

"This is Squadron Leader Darling, my commanding officer."

With the introductions and cordialities dispensed with, Slaughter went right to work. "As I told you last December, Brian, you have violated federal law, namely the Neutrality Act. As such, I'm to inform you that your passport has been revoked, and Mister Tower, here, has a warrant for your arrest."

The big man handed Brian a folded paper that he read, and then handed it to Darling. Brian stared at Slaughter with a scowl and an occasional glance at Tower and Galloway. He waited for 'Spike' Darling to finish reading the papers.

"What do you expect me to do?" asked Brian.

"We expect you to come with us peacefully to be repatriated," said the FBI man with a deep, stiff voice.

Brian swallowed hard as he felt the sweat dampening his shirt. Why did it have to come to this? All I ever wanted to do was fly, he said to himself. Fortunately, John Spencer's words of strength buoyed the young fighter pilot. "I intend to stay here until I am no longer needed," Brian said as firmly as he could although his voice cracked several times in the face of law enforcement.

Mister Tower moved a step toward Brian raising his right arm as if to forcefully take the young American by the arm. Squadron Leader Darling stepped between the two Americans.

"I would not advise taking any physical action against one of my pilots," Darling said with calm, cold strength. The two, armed guards at the gate came to readiness, immediately. Tower was nearly a foot taller than Darling but knew better than to cause a confrontation with two armed and ready guards close at hand. "I trust the inspector has explained your limits under British law." Inspector Galloway nodded his head. "Then, I do believe your business at this Royal Air Force establishment is concluded."

"We shall seek extradition as soon as possible," Tower said harshly, "and, since you did not come voluntarily, we shall prosecute you to the fullest extent of the law."

"Why don't you animals leave the man alone? You want to throw the law at him because he is enough of a man to stand up for the principles we all believe in. I do presume you believe in freedom and the rights of the individual." Darling's sarcastic tone was appreciated by Brian, but not by either Slaughter or Tower. Inspector Galloway displayed an indiscreet smile that conveyed his allegiance. "I suggest you leave now before I ask the guards to escort you off Defense property."

"This is not the last you've heard of this," interjected Slaughter. "We will be back when we have the proper papers." First, Slaughter, and then Tower and Galloway turned to leave.

Brian Drummond and Horatio Darling stood silently until the black sedan moved out of sight. Darling turned to return to the squadron area. Brian quickly caught up but chose not to talk until they neared Dispersal.

"Thank you, sir."

"It was an honor, Brian. I am terribly sorry the American government has chosen to harass you in this manner. I will discuss this with Air Vice Marshal Saul. We will do whatever we can to preserve your right to serve. You are an important member of this team, and we want you to stay with us. We need you."

"Thank you, sir. I appreciate your words and assistance. As I told them, I intend to stay." Brian stopped before they reached the Dispersal building. Several of the pilots sat in chairs outside enjoying the late afternoon weather. "I told Group Captain Spencer I would call after I talked to them. May I, sir?"

"By all means," he responded. "Brian, thank you for staying with us."

—

Wednesday, 17.April.1940
Headquarters, Fighter Command
Bentley Priory
Stanmore, Middlesex, England

Group Captain John Spencer listened intently to Air Commodore James Hogan, DSO. The intelligence data from Scandinavia seemed to get progressively worse with each passing day. Listening to the details about the consumption of the Norwegian Air Force produced a sickening empty feeling deep within his gut. He had not felt the sensation in 25 years. The thought that kept coming back to him revolved around his recognition of the morose, inevitable return of the sickness. The dark, thunderous clouds of the approaching war would soon reach his country with a vengeance. The German Zeppelin attacks during the Great War, the only real combat involving British civilians, would soon pale to insignificance when compared to what the Poles, Danes and Norwegians had already endured.

Beside the looming concern for his countrymen, John could not help letting his thought dwell on the pilots. The War Cabinet wanted to support the Norwegian resistance in the rugged Nordic terrain. They needed air cover to keep the German bombers and strafing fighters in check. The Air Ministry directed two RAF fighter squadrons be sent to Northern Norway.

The discussion this morning centered on Fighter Command Staff positions regarding the directive. The futile operations of the Norwegian Gladiators divided the staff into two factions; those who advocated sending the best and those who wanted a minimal response to satisfy the directive.

Air Officer Commanding-in-Chief Air Chief Marshal Sir Hugh Caswall Tremenheere Dowding, GCVO, KCB, CMG, leaned forward in his chair at the head of the conference table. "Gentlemen, this is not a choice. We have our orders. I need your recommendations."

"We should send two Spitfire squadrons. They'll be able to hold their own."

"One Gladiator squadron."

The other members of the staff fell into one camp or the other. To John Spencer, no RAF squadron was the correct choice, but it was not available to them. He figured Dowding would eventually get around to ask him. What was he going to say? Listening to the arguments for one position or the other convinced him to recommend what his gut told him.

"What about you, John?" asked Dowding.

"I realize it is not a politically acceptable solution, but I would not send any fighters."

"I would be interested to hear your argument as well as the rationale you would recommend I present to the Air Ministry and War Cabinet for refusing to obey our orders."

Group Captain John Spencer could not deny his regret with his instigation of his leader's resentful and edged words. "My apologies, sir. I meant no disrespect or disloyalty."

"No, John. Not so easy. I still would like to hear your argument."

Spencer considered his words. "Simply stated, unless we are prepared to commit a comparable force, we would be sending our crews into the meat grinder. To an even greater extent, sending a few Gladiators into a fight with One Oh Nines, and especially a superior force, is not . . . ," he hesitated. John wanted to speak the words on his mind. Gladiators had no chance against the higher speed, armored, and heavy cannons of the Bf109. ". . . is not . . . reasonable."

The staff fell silent as everyone's eyes turned to Air Chief Marshal 'Stuffy' Dowding. "Well, yes, no one can say you are sitting on the fence, John, now could they? So, what would you suggest I tell the Air Ministry?"

"Sir, despite my view, it would not seem to be a tenable position. I suppose if we must respond," he did not want to say the words because he knew what the result would be, "our best choice is a minimal response. One squadron is the smallest unit that would be viable. If we must send something, then Gladiators would be better than Spits or Hurris. We must reserve our best fighters for the defense of the Home Islands."

The discussion continued for another twenty minutes as they considered logistics, choices, orders and objectives. The tone and mood of the deliberations took on a decidedly more subdued and one might say morose facade. The decision became obvious although the commander's conclusion was rather stark.

"Then, issue orders to transfer Two Six Three Squadron from Filton to Narvik under the command of the BEF. Coordinate the transport with Admiralty and HMS *Glorious*. God be with them."

The blessing sent a chilling shudder throughout the length of John Spencer's body. The Phony War was definitely over.

—

Chapter 2

Let the black flower blossom as it may!

-- Nathaniel Hawthorne

Wednesday, 17.April.1940
RAF Drem
Drem, Lothian, Scotland

The fourth section of Spitfires from No.609 Squadron had their wheels in the wells. Brian watched the last three of eleven aircraft climb away from the airfield. He was the only pilot observing the friendly side of the day's action. Although not much comfort, he knew his aircraft would soon be out of the modification period.

The bite of a spring chill made Brian's observation uncomfortable. He reentered the relative warmth of the Dispersal hut. Corporal Warren, busy with her task of maintaining the squadron's operational diary, was the only occupant. Brian felt left out as if someone had forgotten that he should have been invited to the party. A strange irritation kept annoying him. The others had been flying the Mark IA modified Spitfires with effervescent enthusiasm and praise. The changes gave the pilots an airplane with significant performance improvement, better protection, and easier, quicker operation . . . and a more sexy appearance. The big, bulky, ungainly, two-bladed, fixed pitch, airscrew was replaced by a more appropriate looking, three-bladed, variable pitch, de Havilland propeller that gave the pilot better control, more responsive acceleration, and most importantly, more speed. They never had enough speed, but more was always better. His best friend, Jonathan Kensington, was on his second patrol with his new Mark IA. Jonathan could not stop talking about the added performance of his nimble fighter. All the squadron pilots, for that matter, had nothing but praise and great hopes with the refurbished machines. Brian wanted his turn.

'Sparky' Morrow's Red Section had been the first to scramble. The three Spitfires were also the first to return. All the gun port covers were broken. The hunt had been joined. Brian wondered if his best friend had been successful.

"How's hunting?" asked Brian as Jonathan returned with Morrow and Carrolton.

"Brilliant, Brian. I think I got number two, a Yunkers Eight Eight. 'Sparky' got his third."

"Maybe."

"I saw it. It was pretty clear to me. Anyway, just wait until you get your 'A' model in the air. There is no one who can touch us now."

The intelligence staff shepherded the three aviators into the debriefing room to take their notes and details from the mission. The information would be combined with the data from Sector Control to arrive at a patrol summary statement.

"Mister Drummond," called Leading Aircraftman Bernie Gordon, "your moment has arrived. Your mount is ready."

"Great," Brian responded as he retrieved his flying kit. "Corporal Warren, please tick me out for a check flight."

"Careful, sir," she answered, as she wrote the requisite information on the operations chalkboard. She was not much older than Brian and the other pilots, but she looked after them like a mother.

As Brian walked toward the freshly painted camouflage, PR-F Spitfire with the large white letters bracketing the concentric red, white, blue and gold colored roundel. The fighter – his airplane – truly looked faster. The smaller diameter, thinner, contoured blades of the propeller and the smooth, unobstructed, bulge of the new single piece, bubble canopy accentuated the lines of the machine.

As they walked, Bernie Gordon described one more time each of the modifications completed in this major modification effort. The most notable to the changes revolved around the addition of 150 horsepower in the Rolls-Royce Merlin III supercharged engine using 100 octane fuel although it was still prone to negative 'g' cutout; the new airscrew; and the improved field of view of the new 'Malcolm' canopy. The changes also included the new reflex gun sight, a gun camera triggered by the firing button, armor plating, the undercarriage hydraulic system, and a variety of other system enhancements. Brian was eager to feel the added thrust and responsiveness of the new engine and propeller.

As he radioed for takeoff instructions, he heard the returning call of Blue and Green Sections. His thoughts remained focused on the power he would soon feel when he would throttle up with his crew draped across the empennage for the magneto checks. He wanted the rush of acceleration the thrust would soon produce as his mod IA Spitfire would bounce across the field in its takeoff surge. The ground checks seemed to take an eternity this particular time. With everything satisfactory and clearance received, Brian checked the new propeller pitch lever full forward, mixture rich, and advanced the throttle slowly forward releasing the brakes allowing the takeoff roll to begin. As speed increased, Brian felt the resistance of the emergency power seal at the top of the throttle arc. Plus nine inches of boost. He knew immediately he had a faster airplane.

The sheer, seductive, sensual pleasure of flight, in and of itself, returned to Brian Drummond that chilly spring afternoon. The scattered cumulous clouds over Southern Scotland gave him the temptation he needed. The flirtation with the puffing bulges of clouds took him back to the plains of Kansas just one year earlier. The requirement to complete the necessary evaluation of his aircraft's modifications called him up and away from the cloud layer. Advancing the throttle to the emergency seal, Brian pulled back on the control column to achieve a maximum performance climb. The brilliant sun helped to dull the sharp edge of high altitude cold. Brian put his machine through a methodical series of tests to run the engine and airscrew through their full range of capability including breaking the emergency seal jumping the power to +12 inches of boost, nearly 1100 horsepower. The feel of the renewed and enhanced Spitfire gave Brian even more confidence to face the gathering storm.

Alone with his aircraft, Brian kept his eyes and head moving as the imprinted habits of the fighter pilot reminding him of the eight loaded, charged and armed Browning 0.303-inch bore, machine guns within his wings. The new reflex gun sight with its lighted, adjustable range marks tempted him to find something to shoot . . . to try out the refined sight.

Brian remembered the combat cockpit routine developed for the new configuration – Power, Guns, Camera, Sight. He repeated the litany several times as he performed each action. Throttle up to full POWER; don't break the emergency seal; and, check the instruments. Charge and arm the GUNS. Check gun CAMERA switch ON. Check gun reflex SIGHT switch ON; sight illuminated; and, adjust the range knob. Brian practiced the routine several times committing it to memory and trying to make it habit. In actual combat, there would be no time to think and a fighter pilot can never afford to miss a step. There would most likely be no second chance. Before he moved to other tasks, Brian placed his thumb on the red firing button. The temptation to squeeze off a burst was nearly irresistible, but he did not want to explain why his guns had been fired on a maintenance check flight.

Brian checked all the other new systems, and then resorted to general-purpose enjoyment. Each set of maneuvers was punctuated with clearing turns to ensure no aircraft, friend or foe, approached him. Stalls, a few spins, and a maximum speed dive helped him descend into the thicker air. As he came down to the growing layer of clouds, Brian executed a fragmented series of aerobatic maneuvers to complete his impression of the performance of the aircraft. Even with the weight of his unexpended wing ammunition, the Spitfire danced like a prima ballerina among the clouds, over, under, around and through. His fuel gauge told him the 'check' flight was over.

"How did she do, sir?" asked Bernie Gordon, as the propeller stopped and canopy came back.

"Like a dream, Bernie."

"Excellent. We'll give her a good looking over and get her ready for duty."

As he returned to Dispersal, the jubilant mood told him without words the squadron had enjoyed added success. Jonathan had his second victory, and 'Sparky' Morrow picked up his third. Two fighters had serious damage from the guns of the bombers, but fortunately no one had been injured. Everyone seemed to be pleased with the 'A' modifications. Only two aircraft remained to be altered. Jonathan heard from friends in the South that Jeremy Morrison had achieved his fourth victory, one short of being an ace. Brian wanted to hear more about Jeremy's experience, but the discussion kept returning to tactics, success and the possibilities.

Among the success, the frustration of their outmoded tactics accentuated the limitations and inadequate performance of Blue and Yellow Sections. Several passes were made at their target bombers before the intruders evaded their attackers. The growing examples of dissent came as a complement to their own experiences. The modified tactics advocated by 'Sailor' Malan, 'Bobby' Stanford-Tuck, 'Tin Legs' Bader, as well as other accomplished fighter leaders mixed well with the *Luftwaffe's Jäger Schwarm* and *Geschwader* tactics used in Spain with deadly precision. Squadron Leader Darling, while certainly not as prominent as his more renown peers, recognized the mounting evidence against Fighter Command's Fighter Area Attack tactics developed between the wars before high-speed fighters. Brian wanted to support the direction of his leaders, but the logic to the contrary brought him to concede. The spirited debate among the pilots focused their energy toward improving their ability to deal with intruders. They all knew they would eventually face the massed guns of the bombers, but more significantly, the skilled, experienced and aggressive cannons of German fighters. None of the No.609 Squadron pilots had yet engaged enemy fighters. They all wondered when the situation would change. All, some more robustly than others, said they were ready and eager to prove their capability against a comparable adversary.

The post orderly delivered the afternoon mail. Corporal Warren quickly looked through the items, extracted the official letters, and then called out the names. "Stockard. Foxworth. Carrolton. Mister Drummond, you have one from the states."

"It must be your mother pleading for your return," jabbed 'Mongo' Strickland. The assemblage laughed at the now familiar topic of humor.

"Some day, she'll give up."

"Mothers never give in, Brian," added Roger Beamish. "You have so much to learn about the fair sex. Mothers are relentless until they get what they want."

Roger's comment touched off another round of laughter and ribbing. Brian knew he was not the only pilot with a mother, wife, sister or lover straining to remove them from harm's way. The pilots liked to joke about it and talk tough, but in the end, they appreciated the fact someone cared about their safety. It was part of the game, part of what made them fighter pilots.

Brian looked at the envelope. He recognized his mother's handwriting immediately which meant Stephen Strickland was probably not far from the truth. He wanted to read the letter, but he did not want to feel his mother's disappointment. Although the pilots joked about the interference, Brian wanted his family's support. He reluctantly opened the letter as the jokes continued.

March 27, 1940

Dear Son,

For this letter, I will put aside my pleas for your safe return from this tragic affair in Europe. I want you to know that we love you very much and our concern for your safety is undiminished. We are proud of your conviction, but disappointed with its application. However, this is not the purpose of my letter. I feel ill-prepared to write further. I do not know how to choose the words, but I will do my best.

Brian, I have been asked to pass some very tragic and unfortunate news. Your friend, Malcolm Bainbridge, was killed in a freak aircraft accident two days ago. Gertrude Bainbridge asked me to tell you. She tried several times to write you, but her grief has crippled her. We are helping her as well as other friends. She will be OK once she has dealt with her pain. So, please do not worry about her. We will take care of her.

We know, maybe not fully, how important Mr. Bainbridge was to you, Brian. I know you will grieve his passing, but rest assured, as Gertrude *says, he died doing what he loved best, for that we should be thankful. Our greatest concern is for you. We have tried to follow events in Europe and imagine what you may be involved in as part of these events. This news cannot be helpful to you, but we felt it more important that you know. I must bite my lip when I tell you not to jeopardize your dream trying to return for Malcolm. By the time you get this letter, he will be long buried and there is nothing you can do anyway.*

Brian, please seek the comfort of a minister, reverend or whatever religious figure maybe support to you. We know you must have friends, let them help. Don't keep your grief bottled up inside when you are involved in trying to survive.

We are terribly sorry about your loss, Son. Just don't let this affect your will to survive. We love you very much, Brian. We want you home safely as soon as possible. Remember, the good Lord never gives you more than you can handle. Your grief will pass. Take care of yourself and be careful.
Love,
Mom

P.S.,
Although we do not agree with your actions, the State Department and Senator Capper tell us there is not much they can do. I want you to know we have stopped all our efforts to bring you home and we have asked Senator Capper to stop any government actions. I know your dream is important to you, Brian, and we want you to follow your dream, Son. We love you and miss you terribly.

Brian felt an overwhelming need to be alone. He walked outside in the late afternoon cold and melted into a puddle on the ground. What could have possibly killed an accomplished, expert pilot like Malcolm? What happened? He wanted more information, but was paralyzed.

He sat there slumped over for a long time until Jonathan opened the door to see his friend on the cold ground. Brian did not respond to Jonathan's words as he stared into the grass to some distant point in the universe. Jonathan shook Brian's shoulder. Eventually, he looked up to the worried face of his best friend, but his eyes did not focus.

"Now, you are not going to tell me everything is OK," said Jonathan. "What has happened?"

Brian lifted his Mother's letter slightly. Jonathan took the cue and read the letter. He placed a hand on his friend's shoulder.

"I am terribly sorry, Brian."

The American volunteer pilot nodded his head. He felt the urge to let his tears welling up in his eyes flow freely, but he fought for control of his emotions.

"Do you want me to get the skipper?" Brian shook his head. "What do you want me to do?"

Brian finally focused on Jonathan's concerned eyes. "Nothing. He's gone. There is nothing any of us can do."

"I know how important Mister Bainbridge was to you, Brian, and I know your grief must be great. I lost an uncle who was very special to me a few years ago. I can imagine how you must feel. Do you want me to talk to Squadron Leader Darling to get a bereavement leave for you to go home?"

"No," he answered feebly. "That won't do any good. He is gone. There is nothing I can do, now. I'll pay my respects to him and his wife when the time is right. We've got a mission to perform, and I think I am needed here."

"That may be, Brian, but you won't be much good until you can overcome your grief."

"I'll be OK by takeoff time."

"We'll see."

Several other pilots noticed something was wrong and joined the two friends in the cold air. The others acted like brothers offering words of support and condolence as well as pats on the back. The affected few gave their apologies for their friendly joking over the letter. They ruffled his light brown hair as a big brother would an injured younger sibling. Brian gathered strength from the concern.

Jonathan lifted his friend to his feet and guided him toward the line of fighters. Jonathan stayed with his friend as they let the smooth, curvaceous lines of the Spitfires work their magic. Gradually, color began to return to

Brian, and then, a smile. Brian felt his energy growing with each step, glance and aircraft detail.

The image of Malcolm Bainbridge came to Brian. He heard the words of his teacher, his benefactor, his mentor, tell him 'death is part of life' and 'the best way to remember those closest to you who have gone before is to be the strongest and best you can be and to remember.' Brian knew in his heart that Malcolm would not want his passing to affect the young pilot's flying especially in combat.

Jonathan stopped and turned to Brian as they reached the last Spitfire, PR-A, the commanding officer's fighter. "Are you all right?"

"Yes, I suppose. You know, Jonathan," he paused to swallow hard the emotions he felt. "I just thought about what Malcolm would want me to do right now. The best tribute I can make to one of the most influential men in my life would be to fly the absolute best I can, to be as successful as I am able to be."

"It sounds like a healthy attitude, but do not let your grief consume you."

"Malcolm would not be happy if I let that happen."

"As you say."

"I'm not going to think about not seeing him again physically. I think I will always see him in my thoughts, memories and dreams."

"Quite right," Jonathan said and raised his hand with an extended forefinger as if he was about to make a debate point. "I just remembered . . . do you think you should call Group Captain Spencer. As I recall, your teacher and Mister Spencer were close squadron mates in the Great War."

"Thank you for remembering, Jonathan. You are so right." Brian looked up to the few stars burning through the darkening sky. "I should be able to use the squadron phone."

"I'll go with you."

They walked to the Dispersal building. The telephones would not be critical since they were no longer on alert. The small building was empty but the lights were on. As the door closed behind them, Squadron Leader Darling came out of his office.

"Are you all right, Brian?" he asked.

"Yes, sir. I'll be OK."

"My sincere condolences for your loss. I know he was very important to you. Live for him."

Brian smiled. Darling was a good leader who cared about each of them. "Malcolm would say something like that. Thank you, sir."

"Brian thought he should call Mister Bainbridge's squadron mate at Command, if you don't mind, sir."

"By all means," Darling said motioning toward the telephone. "Group Captain Spencer will undoubtedly still be at the throttle," he added with a broad smile.

Brian returned the expression feeling his facial muscles tighten for the first time since he received the news. Squadron Leader Darling left the building leaving the two friends alone. Brian retrieved a small notebook from his tunic pocket, looked up and dialed Group Captain John Spencer's office number.

"Office of the Staff Secretary," the female operator answered.

"This is Pilot Officer Drummond calling for Group Captain Spencer."

"The Group Captain is unavailable at the moment. Can I take a message?"

Brian thought for a moment whether to leave just a message. "It is very important that I speak to him in person as soon as possible."

"Hold for a moment, sir. I will see if I can find him."

The process took what seemed like several minutes, but then he heard John Spencer's voice. "What can I do for you, Brian?"

"I'm afraid I have bad news, sir." Brian paused, but received no response as his mentor waited for the message. "I just received a letter from my Mother informing me that Malcolm was killed in an aircraft accident several weeks ago."

Light static connected the two men as neither man felt the urge to speak. After a few minutes, Brian felt the urge to ask if John was still there. He knew John Spencer must have been feeling the same things he did a few hours ago, in maybe a far more intimate level – as brothers in arms whose very lives had been dependent on one another.

The strong voice of John Spencer returned. "Are you holding up reasonably well?"

"Yes, sir. I know Malcolm would want me to."

"Quite right, Brian. He was a good man, the best I have ever known. He holds a very special place in my heart. He shall be missed."

"Yes, sir."

"Do you need some bereavement leave?"

"Thank you, sir, but I don't think there is much I can do. I remember one time when Malcolm and I were landing, I hit a dog and cartwheeled a Stearman. Malcolm dragged me from the machine before it caught fire and threw me into his prize Sopwith Camel to get me back in the air. That is what I think he is trying to do for me now."

Brian heard the choked words of a man fighting his own emotions. "You are wise beyond your years." Both men waited for control to return. "Are you managing?"

"Yes, sir. Jonathan and the graceful lines of the Spitfires outside the door have helped me. I'm ready."

"Good lad. Things are going to get quite busy soon, Brian, so I do not know when I will see you again, but rest assured I think of you a great deal, and I wish you the absolute best of luck. Remember to constantly, check six."

"That's what Malcolm always told me."

"Good words that will save your life. Until the 'morrow, cheers Brian." The telephone went dead as Brian responded in kind to his departed mentor.

They turned out the lights and closed the door behind them. A slow, silent walk in the chill had a refreshing quality to it. Neither showed any concern for the passing of the evening meal. Brian was not particularly hungry, and they knew they could probably scrounge up a sandwich when they were ready.

Squadron Leader Darling joined them in the small bar adjacent to the dining room. "Are you up for a pint of bitter?"

"Yes sir. That would do me well, I think."

"Here you go," Darling said handing both young pilots a pint of dark beer. "I have lost friends, Brian, other flyers. I always remind myself, if he was like us, he was doing what he loved most."

"Yes, sir. I agree. It hit me kinda hard . . . he was very special to me . . . but, I'm OK."

"Good. Again, my condolences for your loss. Do you need any bereavement leave?"

"No, sir, but thank you for asking."

"Do you need a warm-up flight?"

Brian thought about taking the opportunity to give himself and his fighter a good workout against another practice adversary. "No, sir. I'm OK. I'll be ready in the morning."

"Very well, then. Don't drink too much. I will see you in the morning," he said, finished the last swallow of his beer and departed, probably to join his wife.

The routine joviality of the fighter pilot's drinking establishment took hold of Brian's thoughts. The laughter, jokes, friendly gibes and camaraderie soothed the wound. In a quiet moment between beers as their numbers thinned, Brian thought of Anne Booth – the woman he had met in London last year and become rather attached. He wanted the comfort of her touch and caring.

The miles between them forced the young pilot to resist the longing that could not be satisfied tonight.

—

Friday, 19.April.1940
Headquarters, Fighter Command
Bentley Priory
Stanmore, Middlesex, England

For Group Captain John Spencer, the invasion of Norway and continued resistance of their diminutive, but potent, military made the hours turn to days, and the sting of his recent loss blend into memory. The demands of the Air Ministry and War Cabinet as well as the increased attention of the *Luftwaffe* meant there were more tasks to perform than people to perform them. Staff meetings as well as ad hoc gatherings to deal with one problem or another filled the gaps between visits to the Operations Room. There was no way to find solace or even a glimmer of light in the darkening picture before them.

This particular meeting blurred into all the others before it in the last ten days. The large maps of Great Britain and Europe, some with new markings, the Command status board and the projection screen covered every available wall and did absolutely nothing to define this meeting as any different from its predecessors. One, probably the only, notable difference was the absence of their leader.

Air Marshal Geoffrey Leonard, CBE, Fighter Command's Chief of Operations, chaired the meeting supported by Air Commodores Herbert Maple, DFC, his deputy, and James Hogan, DSO, Intelligence, and a variety of staff officers populated the underground bunker conference room. The group commanders joined the meeting: Air Vice-Marshal Keith Rodney Park, MC, DFC, No.11 Group at Uxbridge; Air Vice-Marshal Trafford Leigh-Mallory, CB, DSO, No.12 Group at Watnall; and Air Vice-Marshal Richard Ernest Saul, DFC, No.13 Group at Newcastle-upon-Tyne. Air Vice-Marshal Sir Christopher Joseph Quintin Brand, KBE, DSO, MC, DFC, the newly selected AOC-in-C of the soon to be constituted No.10 Group at Box in Wiltshire, completed the list of attendees.

The latest situation report by Air Commodore Hogan set the mood. No.263 Squadron with its antiquated Gloster Gladiators had lost four aircraft and three pilots in the three days of its operations from Narvik. The fact that they had inflicted more losses than they had sustained offered a mere sliver of consolation. The pilots of No.263 Squadron possessed the dubious distinction of being the first RAF fighter pilots to face their counterparts, the *Luftwaffe*'s

Bf109 and the twin engine, H tail, Bf110 Destroyer, as Göring called them. The reports coming back unfortunately confirmed what they all expected but prayed would not be true. The German fighters were very impressive, but it was the quality and skill of the German fighter pilots that held everyone's attention. The tactics the Germans used against the outnumbered and ill-equipped British and Norwegian fighters validated the need to change tactics to those espoused by Bader, Townsend and the others.

"Well, gentlemen," said Air Marshal Leonard in his gravely, thick, Norfolk accent, "not a pretty picture. Nonetheless, we have been ordered to reinforce Two Six Three Squadron. The boss has given us the task. As some of you know already, the AOC is in the City with Sir Cyril . . . ." John thought of Air Chief Marshal Sir Cyril Newall, Chief of the Air Staff, 'Boom' Trenchard's worthy successor and the most ardent supporter of 'Stuffy' Dowding. John Spencer knew as few others did that Dowding was on a most urgent mission to dampen the enthusiasm of the War Cabinet and consequently the Air Staff to pour more of their scarce fighter resources into Norway. They all saw depletion of the less than fifty squadrons of Fighter Command as their greatest risk. They used terms like conserve and husband to describe what needed to be done. Dowding was nearly the lone voice preaching the gospel. Sir Cyril at least listened to the sermon; not all did. "Suggestions?"

"Do we think the boss will be successful?" asked Keith Park.

"We must assume the orders will remain valid."

"Another Gladiator squadron?" suggested Richard Saul.

The suggestion precipitated another round of discussion. The thoughts swiftly distilled down to mostly negative consequences although the choice of another Gladiator squadron would conserve their most capable fighters for future air battles. No one seemed to have the stomach to sacrifice another Gladiator unit.

"Since there does not appear to be much support for Gladiators," began Sir Quintin, "we could use a Hurricane or even a Spitfire squadron to gain some insight into our capabilities against the One Oh Nines and the One One Ohs."

"There is a thought."

"What about Defiants or Blenheims?" offered Herbert Maple.

John Spencer could not hold back his reaction. "No offense meant, sir, but I trust the suggestion was offered in jest. If the Krauts are chewing up Gladiators, they will decimate Defiants or Blenheims. They are even less maneuverable and armed than the Gladiators. If we must send something, I believe the Hurris are our best bet. I like Sir Quintin's view. We can gain some knowledge of the capabilities of the Hurris against the One Oh Nine. The

Hurri is much closer to the Spit, the translation would be more direct. Plus, at present, we have more Hurricanes than any of the other types."

"Now, John, do not hold back," interjected Park. "Let us know how you truly think."

"My apologies, sir. I just have a hard time wasting our precious few pilots."

"No apologies necessary," answered Leonard. "War is nasty business. I'm afraid we'll have plenty of opportunity for strong words. So, gentleman, reasonable argument. Unless there are objections, let's make the most of the experience with a Hurricane squadron." Maple looked around the room. Everyone nodded their heads. "Is the status board accurate?"

"As of this morning," answered James Hogan.

"Right, then. It would appear we have several choices, squadrons at full strength, reasonable training and ready to deploy. I suppose I would take Four Six at Acklington."

"Given the Channel as the most likely axis of attack?" asked Richard Saul, whose group would give up No.46 Squadron.

"That is our best estimate," stated James Hogan.

"Agreed then. The lads are up to the task."

"If that is the case, when do we begin shifting to the South?" asked Keith Park who would bear the brunt of an attack across the Channel.

"The AOC's position remains the same. We won't shift forces until we see signs or intentions from the Germans."

"Most of the signs point to the North," said Saul.

"On the contrary, sir," responded Hogan. "We have numerous indicators that suggest the Low Countries."

"Based on what?"

"Special intelligence."

"Such as?"

"Signals intercepts and SIS."

"What else do we need?" asked Park, always eager to gain additional resources for the fight he was convinced would soon be upon his No.11 Group covering the Southeast.

"We have been over this several times, Keith. The conditions have not changed." Leonard waited for Park's concurrence. "Right, then. James, if you would prepare the orders. Richard, if you would be so kind, please give your lads an advanced notice so they can prepare."

"Yes, sir."

"That should do it, then," Air Marshal Geoffrey Leonard said as he gathered his papers and departed.

The other officers departed in quick succession. Group Captain John Spencer remained and stared at the map of Great Britain. It was only a few years ago that John would not have dreamed of fighters engaged in mortal combat over his country. He did not like the thought and yearned for those more peaceful feelings. Someday, he told himself, someday those feelings would return.

—

Tuesday, 23.April.1940
The Admiralty
Whitehall, London, England

"How was the journey, Bill?" Winston Churchill asked before the door to the office of the First Lord of the Admiralty closed.

"Long and bumpy, Winston. While riding in a flying boat is faster than a ship, it always seems to be a rougher, more tiring mode of transport."

"I can certainly agree with you." Winston wanted to move quickly to his questions. "How did the President respond to the ULTRA messages?"

"With somber resolution," William Samuel 'Bill' Stephenson, MC, DFC, responded. "He recognizes what is coming. He has vowed to help wherever he can and however we can determine a means that will not conflict with the mood of the American citizenry."

"Understood. We can certainly agree to that condition for the moment. *Herr* Hitler will undoubtedly take care of the rest."

"It would appear to be the case."

"Did he have any information for us?"

"Not at present, Winston, but he did promise to keep an eye and an ear out for us."

"He is a good man."

"Yes, indeed, that he is."

"Mark my words, Bill. The Americans will have to come to Europe once again. Franklin Roosevelt is a friend."

"Do we have any more information regarding Hitler's next move?"

"I'm afraid not. 'C,' 'Jumper' and the others have been trying every source to fill in the enormous gaps. The French aren't much help, either."

"Are we ready?"

Winston Churchill, elder statesman of the Conservative Party, laughed a rare cleansing laugh. "Strange, you should ask me such a question."

Bill Stephenson, the Canadian businessman, friend and confidant, realized the ridiculousness of his question to the lone voice of alarm in the early '30's, and he laughed as well. "My apologies, Winston. The question slipped out."

"Not to worry, Bill. The simple answer is, no. We are not ready. We are making progress, but we need at least another year to achieve . . . a distant possibility. The more aggravating piece is, Neville still holds onto the notion, peace is achievable with this madman."

"I thought fighter production was up."

"It is, but unfortunately five years too late. Dowding says he needs more than fifty squadrons of Spitfires and Hurricanes. We have 46 total fighter squadrons with only 39 equipped with our top performance fighters. Dowding demands quite a bit, but I believe he is correct. Somehow we need Hitler to hold off any action against France until at least the following summer."

"Not likely."

"Unfortunately, you are probably quite correct. We still have the Case Yellow documents looming before us." Winston paused descending into his own thoughts. His mind considered so many things especially now that he was back in the service of His Majesty's Government. Everyone knew to leave him alone in contemplation. Before his mind returned to the office, his office interphone buzzer shocked him back. He lifted the handset. "Stewart is here."

The Chief of MI6 joined them. 'C,' as was his characteristic, waited for the door to close and a few moments to pass for Churchill's secretary to reach his desk. "Good afternoon, First Lord, and to you, Bill."

"The best to you, Stewart," answered Stephenson for both of them. "Anything?"

"Not much, I'm afraid. Heydrich changed the code sequence just before the invasion. We are still having some trouble sorting the wheel sequence for Enigma. We have the plug combinations rather quickly, but they have modified their routine for the wheels."

"How long until you break it?" asked Winston.

"We thought we had it, yesterday, but the trial message was too simple, and the sequence did not produce. I suspect Bletchley should have it within a few days, perhaps a week."

"What about other sources?"

'C' looked directly to 'Intrepid' Stephenson. "Do the Americans have anything?"

"Not yet. Roosevelt has promised to give us whatever he can, but no fruit so far."

"We've been through the available information from our agents. We believe it is significant the enemy committed a relatively small force to the conquest of Denmark and Norway. They seem to be content to let an adequate group grind away in Norway. More importantly, they hold an enormous number of units including one entire air fleet on the Western border. A Panzer corps has been moving to Northwest Germany. It sure does look like France is next and reflects the Case Yellow thinking."

"Does it appear they will attempt to breach the Maginot Line?"

"While there are those who disagree with me, it would seem you may be proven correct once again, Winston. Our assessment based on the current picture is they will make a fast armor assault across the Low Countries and flank the Maginot defenses."

"Such a waste," Stephenson commented referring to the enormous resources expended on the monumental French defensive fortifications that did not extend to the English Channel, the only gap from the Alps north being the border with Belgium and Holland.

"Indeed," added Winston. "More importantly, the BEF is the principal deterrent on the Northern flank. With their inferior armor and marginal artillery, I am afraid their teeth are not particularly sharp, especially compared to the quality of German armor they will probably face." The First Lord considered the question he did not want to ask. "When?"

"Within a month or two," 'C' solemnly answered. "Certainly before mid-summer."

"What do the French think?"

"They believe the Germans are simply posturing. *Le Armée de Terre* and *le Armée de l'Air*, supplemented by the British Expeditionary Force and Advanced Air Striking Force, comprise the largest military force in the world. They refuse to accept the possibility the Germans are not impressed."

"A fatal mistake . . . underestimating your adversary. Have Lord Gort and Air Marshal Barratt been briefed?"

General Lord Gort, VC, KCB, CBE, DSO, MVO, MC, held the position of Commander-in-Chief of the British Expeditionary Force in France. He was born John Standish Surtees Prendergast Vereker and became the 6th Viscount Gort of Galway, Ireland, with the passing of his father. Gort also held the Victoria Cross, the equivalent of the Medal of Honor in the United States, for combat valor in action during the crossing of the Canal du Nord, near Flesquieres, France, on 27.September.1918. Air Marshal Arthur Sheridan Barratt, CB, CMG, MC, held the position as Air Officer Commanding-in-Chief, British Air Forces France, which included both the Advanced Air Striking

Force and Air Componet – the tactical and support aviation organizations. His assignment was solely to provide air support to General Lord Gort and the British Expeditionary Force.

"Yes. They both find no comfort in the information, but they have brought the BEF to the fullest readiness and tried to prepare unfortunately rather meager defenses."

"Add to this, the break-out of the battlecruisers *Scharnhorst* and *Gneisenau*, we have a particularly ugly situation. What is more, the fast battle-ship *Bismarck* is making final preparations for sea. I think we are in for a long, hard, hot summer." Winston Churchill accepted the probability none of them fully comprehended nor appreciated the severity of what lay ahead. He felt sick, but knew he had to redouble his efforts to ensure the Royal Navy was as ready as it could be and more critically to convince the Prime Minister and the remaining dissenters in the War Cabinet they needed to prepare the country for what was about to be upon them.

—

Thursday, 25.April.1940
Cabinet Room
No.10 Downing Street
Whitehall, London, England

"Gentlemen, may we please come to order," pronounced Cabinet Secretary Sir Edward Ettingdene Bridges KCB, MC. "We have a full agenda to complete this afternoon."

Prime Minister Arthur Neville Chamberlain looked at Sir Edward, nodded his head in recognition, and concluded his quiet conversation with the First Lord of the Admiralty. The members of the War Cabinet took their seats as the Prime Minister slowly lowered his gaunt frame in the leather chair at the head of the long table in the Cabinet Room. The other members of the War Cabinet broke their conversations and took their seats on either side of the green felt covered, truncated oval, oak table. The military chiefs of staff, invited ministers and cabinet support administrative staff occupied the chairs along the walls behind the cabinet ministers.

The full War Cabinet attended this crucial meeting. Beside the Prime Minister were:

-- Chancellor of the Exchequer Sir John Allsebrook Simon, GCSI, GCVO, OBE, PC, KC, MP;

-- Lord Privy Seal Sir Howard Kingsley Wood, Kt, PC, MP, who preferred Kingsley as his knighthood name;

-- Secretary of State for Foreign Affairs Edward Frederick Lindley Wood, KG, GCSI, GCMG, GCIE, TD, PC, 3rd Viscount Halifax of Monk Bretton;
-- First Lord of the Admiralty Winston Churchill, MP;
-- Secretary of State for Air Sir Samuel John Gurney Hoare, Bt, GCSI, GBE, CMG, PC;
-- Secretary of State for War Oliver Frederick George Stanley MC, PC, MP;
-- Minister for the Coordination of Defence Alfred Ernle Montacute Chatfield, GCB, OM, KCMG, CVO, PC, DL, 1st Baron Chatfield of Ditchling, the former Admiral of the Fleet and First Sea Lord, and
-- Minister without Portfolio Maurice Pascal Alers Hankey, GCB, GCMG, GCVO, PC, 1st Baron Hankey of the Chart, Surrey. Lord Hankey was Sir Edward's predecessor as Cabinet Secretary.
Also in attendance were:
-- Secretary of State for the Home Department and Minister of Home Security Sir John Anderson, GCB, GCSI, GCIE, PC, MP;
-- Robert Anthony Eden, MC, PC, MP;
-- Permanent Secretary to the Treasury Sir Horace John Wilson, GCB, GCMG, CBE; and
the military chiefs of staff:
-- First Sea Lord and Chief of Naval Staff Admiral of the Fleet Sir Alfred Dudley Pickman Rogers Pound, GCB, GCVO, who preferred Dudley as his knighthood name;
-- Chief of the Air Staff Air Chief Marshal Sir Cyril Newall; and
-- Chief of the Imperial General Staff General Sir William Edmund Ironside, GCB, CMG, DSO, who preferred Edmund as his knighthood name.
In addition to Sir Edward, the Secretariat Staff in attendance included:
-- Major General Hastings Lionel 'Pug' Ismay, CB, DSO;
-- Captain Angus Dacres Nicholl, RN;
-- Lieutenant Colonel Vivian Dykes, Royal Engineers; and
-- Wing Commander William Elliott.

Sir Edward waited for the movement and shuffling of papers to quiet. "Our first agenda item is the naval situation."

The eyes of everyone turned to the First Lord of the Admiralty. Winston cleared his throat. "I can now report, we have accounted for all of the Norwegian warships. They managed to keep them all out of the German's hands. The last warship, a frigate, entered Scapa Flow anchorage yesterday."

"God bless them," whispered Oliver Stanley.

"The U-boat menace to our supply lines remains our greatest concern. We need more destroyers for convoy escort duty. The Admiralty's convoy operations center has done an exceptional job given the vast dispersal of operations and our scant resources. The building program is progressing . . . just not fast enough. Naval Intelligence Branch has established that German surface transports are hugging the coastline under constant air cover from their air force, which in turn makes interdiction inordinately risky. We can continue to supply our troops in the Narvik pocket; however, the German Navy remains capable of major surface action. As yet, we have not located the German battlecruisers *Scharnhorst* and *Gneisenau*. Until we do and can eliminate them or render them impotent, they remain very serious threats to our shipping. The hunt continues."

"Any questions for Winston?" asked the Prime Minister. Hearing none, Chamberlain nodded to Sir Edward to continue.

"The next item is the air situation, Sir Samuel."

"Our state remains stable for the moment. I must remind the War Cabinet our estimate of 60 fighter squadrons for the defense of the Home Islands should be considered a minimum level and is of course predicated on Holland remaining unavailable to the German Air Force."

"What is our current inventory?" asked Lord Chatfield.

"We now have 50 operational fighter squadrons, of which 15 are equipped with outdated Gladiator, Defiant and Blenheim aeroplanes. As Winston noted, our building program is progressing rapidly, but not fast enough to cover the Norwegian operations and the BEF, as well as maintain our air defense system."

Lord Halifax interjected, "MI6 continues to accumulate bits of intelligence that suggest the Germans are moving significant ground and air forces from Poland to the west."

"Perhaps the winter case yellow nonsense is not so farfetched after all," Churchill added in a low grumbling tone, as they considered the captured German war plans last January. Winston remembered well the bitter debate that ensued as a consequence and the resultant conclusion the captured plans were most likely a disinformation catalyst.

"Gentlemen, please," Sir Edward said, "the Prime Minister has a full diary today, and we must stay to the agenda. Let us move along."

"I have nothing further," added Sir Samuel.

"Next item, the military situation, Mister Stanley, if you please."

Oliver Stanley looked down at his notes on the table before him, and then engaged the Prime Minister's tired eyes as he began. "First, I must say, the Norwegians have put up a tenacious defense and given a laudable account of themselves. The defensive lines are holding, for the moment, south of the

Narvik enclave. Yet, even with our meager reinforcements, we are only buying time with blood and treasure."

Chamberlain raised his hand to stop the army situation report. He looked down, swallowed hard, and then looked his ministers in their attentive eyes. "We agreed at last week's meeting that we must have fresh, adaptive, withdrawal plans ready for execution should the need arise. Has everyone completed their task?" The Prime Minister looked at each War Cabinet minister and waited for a confirmatory head nod or response. "I think we will all agree, the Norwegians, even with our assistance, have little hope of stopping the overwhelming German forces."

Winston could not resist. The urge to swim against the tide simply proved too great. "Those mountains south of Narvik are rather treacherous. A small band of determined fighters, well placed, can exact an enormous price from a conventional force like the Germans have deployed." A few muffled grumblings caused Winston to pause. "I know it is not popular, but we must fight the Germans – better there than here. The terrain favors the defense. Let us not forget the lesson the valiant Finns taught us in their punishing resistance of the vastly superior Red Army last winter. It can be done."

"Yes, quite so," responded the Secretary of State for War.

"May I," interjected General Ironside from behind Oliver Stanley. The Prime Minister nodded to the Chief of the Imperial General Staff – the top general. "The First Lord is quite correct. The terrain does favor a spirited defense. However, I must remind the War Cabinet of the information Lord Halifax provided. The Germans are moving west, not north. We must ensure the BEF is able to stop the Germans if they should attack the Low Countries. I need not state it, but invasion of the Home Islands would surely be more likely, if the Low Countries were to fall."

"Would it not be better to tie the Germans down and command their attention in the North Country rather than allow them to focus on the west?" asked Churchill.

"Yes, certainly," responded General Ironside.

The Prime Minister again raised his hand. "We agreed last week to have evacuation plans ready, should they become necessary to execute. If our combined forces can hold south of Narvik, then we shall support them. If the line breaks, we cannot reinforce them. Oliver, what is the status of the BEF?"

"Lord Gort reports his forces are at full readiness and prepared should the Germans attack west."

"Excellent. Then, let us stick to the plan." Chamberlain pronounced, and then nodded to Sir Edward.

"Mister Stanley, do you have anything else to report?"

"No, Sir Edward."

"Lord Halifax, what does the Foreign Office have to report?"

"We have from several reliable sources confirmation that Hitler has anointed *SS-Obergruppenführer* Josef Terboven as *Reichskommissar* for Norway, which is not a good sign. Terboven is a long-time and loyal Nazi; he is not a diplomat, bureaucrat or administrator. Terboven's assignment does not bode well for Norway. It also appears they are moving quickly to install the collaborator Vidkun Quisling as the titular president of what will be at best a puppet government. Quisling has set the bar very low for the betrayal of collaborators." No one reacted. Lord Halifax continued, "We also have confirmation the Germans have sealed up a ghetto in Lodz, Poland, and have begun relocating Jews from the surrounding area into confinement in that ghetto. Further, we have confirmation the Germans are building a very large camp in southwest Poland, outside the village of Auschwitz. There is no industry or mining in the area, so it cannot be a labor camp, as they have tried to persuade others they have done at their German camps like Dachau and Buchenwald. The term they use is *konzentrationslager* – concentration camp. We continue to ask, concentration for what purpose? Lastly, we have what can best be classified as rumors of massive killings of captured Polish military officers, diplomats, scientists and intellectuals in the Katyn Forest, west of Smolensk, Russia, likely carried out by the Soviet NKVD."

"This war will likely establish a new infamous and disgusting standard for savageness, as if the last war was not quite bad enough," Prime Minister Chamberlain added.

"Quite so, I'm afraid," mumbled Lord Halifax.

"Anything further?"

"No."

"The last item on the agenda was raised by the Home Secretary. Sir John, if you will."

Home Secretary Sir John Anderson spoke from behind Sir John Simon. "The question of the technical exchange with the Americans continues to grow. As you know, A.V. Hill presented his proposal for the technical exchange to offer our advances to gain access to American scientific knowledge. Numerous leading members of our scientific community believe we can help the Americans and we can gain access to critical technology."

"I might interject here," said Lord Halifax, "Lord Lothian replied yesterday to our query. He confirms the receptive spirit of the U.S. Government to such a technical exchange. Several American scientific and military advances, not least of which is the Norden bombsight we have discuss previously, have been suggested. They continue to avoid the topic and deflect any discussion on the bombsight. Lothian, along with Hill, Blackett, Chadwick, Oliphant and others confirm that the Americans have begun feasibility studies into the potential for atomic explosives."

Lord Lothian was born Philip Henry Kerr and became the 11th Marquess of Lothian in 1930 with the passing of his father. He now held the vital diplomatic position as His Majesty's Ambassador to the United States of America, the posting he admirably fulfilled since June of the previous year.

"Indeed!" exclaimed Sir John. "That is my primary reason for raising this item before the War Cabinet. I think most of you are familiar with the so-called Frisch–Peierls memorandum sent to Marcus Oliphant at the University of Birmingham, by refugee physicists Otto Frisch and Rudi Peierls. With Sir Henry Tizard's sponsorship, the notional MAUD Committee was formed to evaluate the viability of the conclusions in the Frisch–Peierls memorandum."

"What is the significance of Maud . . . someone's sister, or mother, or aunt?" asked Oliver Stanley.

Sir John chuckled softly. "No, I'm afraid nothing quite so innocuous. MAUD is an acronym for Military Application of Uranium Detonation."

"Oh my!"

"Indeed, quite so," continued Sir John. "Until the MAUD Committee completes its work, we shall not have a definitive statement from the scientific community with respect to our assessment of atomic explosive feasibility. My question to the War Cabinet, do we include atomic explosives in the list of technology for a possible technical exchange with the Americans?"

Winston added his opinion. "I have mixed feelings about this proposed technical exchange. These are highly sensitive and vital technologies. We cannot risk disclosure to the enemy – intentional or inadvertent. Yet, one element seems to override all others. We need access to the industrial capacity of the United States, especially with respect to the MAUD work."

"What do you suggest, Winston?" asked Chamberlain.

"One, we should heed Lord Lothian's unique insight and continue to evolve the Hill plan. Second, until we have reason to withdraw the item, we should not exclude the MAUD work."

The Prime Minister scanned the Cabinet Room. "Are we agreed?" He again waited for an approving head nod or words from each member of the full War Cabinet. Neville again nodded to Sir Edward, "Record it so."

"Do we have any further items for the War Cabinet?" asked Sir Edward. No one spoke up. "Hearing none, we are adjourned. Have a good day, gentlemen."

—

Chapter 3

Despair is the conclusion of fools.

--Benjamin Disraeli

Thursday, 2.May.1940
Headquarters, Fighter Command
Bentley Priory
Stanmore, Middlesex, England

The paper mounting on Group Captain John Spencer's desk convinced him he could no longer ignore the least glamorous of all the tasks he needed to do. The various staff reports, logistics status, aircraft production figures and personnel issues invariably made him yearn for the invigoration and re-juvenation of flight. It had been more than a month, before the invasion of Norway, since he had managed to take time to fly. Fortunately for him, he still had friends who were station commanders, often with several reserve fighters in the maintenance pool supporting the squadrons at their stations. John was becoming itchier to fly the new 'A' modified Spitfire. All the reports reflected well on the work of the Supermarine engineers.

A knock on the frame of his open door announced the arrival of Air Commodore James Hogan. "You will not believe the message we just received from my counterpart in *le Armée de l'Air.*"

"And good afternoon to you, commodore," he answered with a smile and outstretched hand to receive the paper.

John quickly read to himself the message from the chief of French air intelligence. A hapless *Luftwaffe* captain enroute to a *Luftflotte* 3 staff briefing landed his Bf109E-3 fighter at the French airfield at Amiens, which he mistook for his destination. The German officer was apparently unaware of his error until he turned from the small storage compartment below and behind the cockpit, and faced the rifle muzzles of several French soldiers. In his hand, he held a leather case containing letters, maps and other data still being analyzed by the intelligence experts that appeared to be operations plans, orders and other communications.

"I'll be damned!"

"Quite, dear boy. Seems the good Lord is trying to look after us."

"The message indicates the aircraft was captured in Amiens."

"Correct."

"That's more than half way through France to Le Havre."

"Correct, again."

"That boy was severely lost if he got that far into France."

"Quite right, once more. Several other subsequent reports indicate why he was lost. There were multiple cloud layers, virtually down to the surface in places. Based on the reports we have, our friend got lost in the clouds, low on fuel, found an aerodrome and landed. He convinced himself he was at Strasbourg."

"Anything wrong with the machine?"

"Needs a little petrol, so I hear. Other than fuel, the aeroplane is fully armed and in fairly pristine condition."

"What are they going to do with the bird?"

"My, my, chappie, you certainly are interested in our find." They laughed. "We do occasionally get things right. MI6, as well as several other agencies, have moved quickly to 'trade' for the captured fighter. The French intelligence types are fortunately very professional, and more importantly, they are pragmatic realists. They have already transferred the aeroplane to No.1 Squadron in Eastern France. We expect to promptly move the sample to Farnborough for proper analysis and exploitation."

"How soon can we get the aircraft out of France and over here?"

"The process has already begun. Considering the ominous situation just to the east, we have convinced the French to give the aircraft to us for safekeeping, just in case the Germans do attack. If everything goes according to plan, the fighter should be at Farnborough in three to four days."

"Why so long?" challenged John Spencer as his mind considered the risks.

"This is a French find after all. They want a few days with the machine. Then, they will hand it over. No.1 Squadron will provide a pilot to fly it to England."

John Spencer anticipated the experience of flying the best and latest model *Luftwaffe* fighter. As he wondered how it would handle, how it would feel, how precise it would be in an attack, John slapped himself to the present. He was not twenty, and he would not be the first choice of the RAF to fly the captured fighter. "We need to get some of our pilots into her as soon as the test blokes have had their go at her." He thought of Brian Drummond. The knowledge of the subtleties of an adversary's aircraft could and most probably would provide an exceptional pilot with an edge. He wanted Brian to have every tool he could. The young man would need every tool for his survival. John wanted every pilot in Fighter Command to fly the Bf109. The captured machine was reported to be an 'E' model, the latest, which made the prize even more valuable. "We need to get a few key pilots, some young, some old, some experienced, and some new." He thought again of Brian. "I know a few I think should fly it."

"Not so fast, John. We are not to that stage, yet."

"I know, but when we are ready."

James Hogan smiled at his enthusiastic friend. "I am afraid, old boy, you are not one."

"Why not? I could fly the piss out of that sodding machine."

"Not your job anymore, old chap. I'm afraid our combat days are behind us."

"You are such a stick in the mud sometimes."

"Yes, well, right you are, John, but I believe I have hit the proverbial nail on the head, as they say."

The disappointment was, the head of Fighter Command Intelligence Section was indeed correct. He would have to leave the young man's work to the young men. "I would still like to get a few key pilots into the bird when RAE is finished."

Hogan grinned knowingly at John Spencer. "I shall do what I can. I will keep you on step, John."

Fighter Command's Staff Secretary nodded his head in agreement and appreciation. Maybe he would have an opportunity to get a few squadron pilots into their principal adversary aircraft. He moved his pencil across the paper pad sketching a familiar silhouette of the *Bayerische Flugzeugwerke* model 109, Willie Messerschmitt's finest piece of aeronautical design work to date. He remembered vividly the harsh lines and menacing edges to the fighter. Next to the sketch, he wrote the names that came to mind, Tuck, Malan, Deere, there were several exemplary pilots who would become better, knowing the intimate details of the Bf109. While Brian Drummond had not been fully tested or demonstrated his skills to the level of the more renown fighter pilots, John Spencer knew the young protégé of his best friend had the touch, the eye, the skill, the instinct to be equally as good if not better than the others. John wanted him to survive his first few fighter engagements. Once he had the taste and knew what to expect, he knew the young pilot's probability of survival would increase substantially. Brian needed the benefit of flying the captured Bf109, and more importantly, to fly the Bf109 against the Spitfire and Hurricane. By knowing his opponent's aircraft, he would know the *Luftwaffe jagdflieger* – the enemy's fighter pilot. He had to find a way for Brian Drummond to join what would be a very small group of pilots.

—

Tuesday, 7.May.1940
House of Commons
Westminster, London, England

As the reports on the growing, now conclusive, evidence of German invasion intent droned on, First Lord of the Admiralty Winston Churchill felt a sad, heavy regret he had not been more successful in showing his colleagues Hitler's evil designs . . . if they had only understood and done something about it. All that time wasted. All the time that could have been devoted to preparations and even preemptive action when it might have stopped German expansion and saved humanity from another world war. The Siren's song of appeasement was truly seductive and fatal.

The Members on this day took on a more hostile, resentful mood. Churchill always marveled how quickly politicians, including himself, could change their stripes. No more than three, maybe four, years earlier he had been virtually the lone voice of caution, of preparedness, of suspicion. Now, those words of criticism, of ridicule, of humiliation were not focused at him. They were aimed at the frail man sitting three places to his right on the Government Bench. It was Prime Minister Chamberlain, despite his sincere, well-intentioned, and earnest efforts to preserve the peace, who had become the most public and visible representative of appeasement. Chamberlain would be seen as the leader who set the course that had brought the world to another war. Winston knew the blame did not rest with Chamberlain entirely. Unfortunately, regrettably, he would be the one history would hold responsible.

He knew Chamberlain as a good man who wanted only good things, who wanted to do the right thing, who took his responsibility as prime minister, as a world leader, very seriously. As a careful student of history, Churchill knew before the words were written how his friend, colleague and antagonist would be remembered. The thought gave his stomach a sharp twist. There was no satisfaction in being right.

Winston listened to the angry words. The questions to the Prime Minster, and Foreign Minister, *in absentia*, left no doubt as to the mood of the House. A few feeble attempts to defend Chamberlain came from those members most supportive of the Prime Minister and the policy of appeasement. The few among them who had advocated joining Hitler were present, but notably and thankfully silent.

The Speaker of the House recognized the veteran conservative backbencher Leopold Stennett "Leo" Amery, Member of Parliament for Birmingham South. Winston knew how his friend felt about the worsening situation. He could imagine what he was about to say and winced to himself

in anticipation. Among the continuing words of anger, challenge, and resentment, he stood waiting for some diminishment of the ruckus. As the House
approached quiet, Amery spoke in a strong, confident voice. "You sat too long
here for any good you have been doing." The roar of the Members became
deafening. "Depart, I say," he shouted as loudly as he could, "and let us have
done with you. In the name of God, go!" Nearly every Member was on his
feet shouting, cheering, objecting, or wanting to be recognized. The Speaker
fought for control.

Amery's choice of Oliver Cromwell's scornful words to the Long
Parliament touched a sensitive and exposed nerve in the House. Winston
remembered his history and knew the sentiment was strongly felt both in the
past and the present. In many ways, Winston felt sorry, even pity, for Chamberlain. All those years of believing in the inherent good of man, the honesty
of Hitler, were now coming back in the form of a terrible price.

Chamberlain stood slowly to address the onslaught. "These are difficult times for all of us. It is in difficult times that friends should not desert
friends." The words had no strength and as such seemed to encourage the
scorn. The shouts against him seemed to sap his remaining strength like the
wounded Wildebeest beginning to wobble in front of the lion. Winston wanted to reach for him, to brace him against the immerciful attack. "Honorable
gentlemen, please, this is not the time for retribution. It is a time for friends
to stand together." Winston wanted to stand in his leader's defense, but he
could not. With the now virtually certain invasion of the Low Countries and
undoubtedly France as well, Neville Chamberlain's time had passed.

Hitler's ambition threatened to consume all of Europe. Japan's territorial acquisitions over the last two years left no doubt what was in store in the
Far East and probably the entire Pacific region. Possibly the strongest nation
on Earth stood idle in steadfast neutrality despite the diminishing circle of
safety around her. Winston could only thank the good Lord that the President of the United States held a more global view. America was not entirely
unprepared for what was about to happen. They stood on the doorstep of
the first truly global war, a world war of unprecedented proportions. Yes,
Chamberlain simply had to accept the consequences of his policies and take
his place in history as the master appeaser. Churchill meant no malice in his
thoughts, simply recognition of world events.

The lions and hyenas of the House tore at the flesh of the fatally
wounded Wildebeest standing before them waiting for the end to come. It was
never a pretty sight, but it was life. Churchill knew the realities of life. Some
things could not be changed.

The *coup de grâce* came from the aging, Right Honorable David Lloyd George, OM, PC, Member of Parliament for Caernarfon Borough, the former prime minister and leader of the Liberal Party. The venerable and highly respected gentleman of the House stood ever so slowly from the opposition benches and faced the Prime Minister. The House fell silent. "I say solemnly that the Prime Minister should give an example of sacrifice because I tell him that there is nothing which would contribute more to victory in this war than that he should sacrifice the seals of office."

The feeding frenzy continued a short time before the motion to adjourn was made. As Winston moved through the corridors of Westminster Palace, old friends as well as new friends found in the fickle tide of political fortune stopped to pledge their support, or offer words of encouragement. The effort to find a successor had begun several days earlier when the mounting evidence of Nazi intentions became quite clear and undeniable. Winston Churchill knew he was a contender to lead a coalition government, a war government. Lord Halifax, the Foreign Minister, had substantial backing among the still powerful appeasers. Winston made no effort to deny the daunting quantity of opponents and antagonists he had managed to build up over his forty years in Parliament. His political stands on South Africa, Ireland, and India as well as the debacle at Gallipoli had produced a large, vocal, influential and determined body of Members who could never support him even in the face of war and possible invasion. He always took the philosophical view, amazingly quite similar to his father, Lord Randolph Churchill, that principle always produced opponents. His position now gained strength predominately from his singular voice against all odds, the clarity of his message, and regrettably the precision of his premonition.

As friends informed him over the remainder of the day, it looked like Clement Richard Attlee, Member of Parliament for Limehouse and leader of the Labor Party, would never support a member of the House of Lords standing as the prime minister. Although Attlee had not yet endorsed Churchill as his choice to lead the nation in war, the action was near. The view Winston had, pointed toward a decision being taken in the next few days and implemented when the Germans executed their invasion plans. Winston knew his time was near. He was ready for destiny.

—

Friday, 10.May.1940
RAF Drem
Drem, Lothian, Scotland
05:45 hours

Pilot Officer Brian Drummond was growing to resent the northern latitudes and the long days common to summer. The morning meal serving time in the Officer's Mess had been moved forward to 05:00, to allow the pilots time to reach Dispersal by 06:00 to 06:30 at the latest. The monotony of waiting was grinding on all of them. They waited for the call to action far more times than they flew. Several of the pilots would conspire with their crew chiefs to find reasons to fly, a maintenance check flight or something. None of them liked the waiting.

This breakfast had been like all the others. Only a couple of the pilots could find anything to complain about regarding the food. They were certainly well fed. Brian appreciated the meals. Many things were different, like black pudding, but more things were like the breakfasts his mother made – bacon, eggs, toast and jam. There was never much discussion at the morning meal. Whether the reason was the aftermath of a 'pub crawl,' or a day or two with a girlfriend or other female companion, they respected one another's need for silence.

"Skipper," called the squadron sergeant major, "my apologies, but I think you should take a look at some messages which just came in from Command."

Several sheets of paper were handed to Squadron Leader 'Spike' Darling. The expression of his face and the shaking of his head meant the information was not good. While several pilots continued to eat, nearly all watched their leader.

Darling raised his head, and then stood to establish he had everyone's attention. "Well, lads, if there was any doubt about the Phony War being over, we can put that discussion aside. At dawn this morning, a major force of German armor and infantry crossed the border into the Netherlands, Belgium and France."

"Dear God almighty," said 'Sparky' Morrow. "So, it is going to be France and the Channel."

"Right, then. I must call Sector for clarifying instructions. I shall need all officers at Dispersal in fifteen minutes." Darling left promptly without finishing his breakfast.

They all were silent and seemed to be thinking about what might be happening. Brian thought about Derek Langston, his colleague at OTU7, whose uncle was a sergeant in the BEF in France. He wondered what must be going on just across the English Channel. Everyone had talked about the enormous size of the French and British armies, and the horrendous conflagration of a major land war in Europe with modern weapons.

The talk around the table now centered on the involvement of No.609 Squadron in the boiling combat in Northern France. While none of them knew what was going to happen, they all knew they had a part to play in it. Brian and Jonathan exchanged expressions of recognition. He knew at least two of them were scared about what would undoubtedly soon be upon them although none of them could utter any words other than enthusiastic anticipation of the real aerial test.

'Jackstay' Beamish brought them back to reality. "The Skipper wants us in Dispersal in a few minutes. Let's not disappoint the boss." The sound of wooden chairs scraping across the oak floor along with the rustle of moving humans punctuated the direction.

Darling was still in his office with the door closed when the last of the pilots entered the Dispersal hut. "What do you know, Corporal Warren?"

"Only that the Germans have invaded France, sir."

"The Skipper's been in there since he arrived?"

"Yes, sir."

Subdued words provided the background within the small building. Several of the pilots took chairs outside in the cool, but comfortable Scottish morning, presumably to enjoy the early morning sun now well above the trees to the east. The predominate words remained attached to speculation although the strong language of the Officer's Mess had been replaced by a more contemplative mood.

"What do you think, Jonathan?" asked Brian, leaning toward his best friend.

"I think we are soon to be in a pile of shite, if you want to know the truth."

"Really?"

"Come now, Brian. I am certain you must comprehend what is happening in France."

The American considered objecting to the jab, but knew Jonathan did not mean it the way it sounded. The gravity of the invasion seemed to be adding progressive weight to all of them. "Do you think we'll go south to get in this thing?"

"Probably. Some of the talk is we do not have enough fighters to protect Great Britain from the *Luftwaffe*. If that is true, I would say we are all going to be in it no matter where it comes. The Channel looks like the logical place to me. So . . . yes, I think we will be going south."

Squadron Leader Darling reappeared with a strange mixed expression on his face, as if he was stretched across the thin boundary between pain and pleasure. He walked over to the status board without speaking. Darling stood close to the board, as if he could not read it otherwise and stared at the listing of the available aircraft and pilots. The outside pilots rejoined the group.

"Do we have everyone?" A quick inventory produced several head nods. "Right, then. The word from Sector is, this is it. The Germans appear to have initiated the full-scale invasion everyone has been anticipating since Denmark and Norway. Our orders are to prepare to move to the south. The expectation is, Gerry will soon be deep into France, and we will be involved in a variety of support operations for the BEF and le Armée de Terre. It is still not clear what that means, but we should know more this afternoon. I have been ordered to Northolt for a commander's conference. I will take two sections, Blue and Green. 'Sparky,' you shall operate Red and Yellow with Rooker. Sector is not expecting much business today, at least not up here, with all the action in France, but they want to retain sufficient strength. 'Jackstay,' we will depart within the hour."

"How are we doing, Skip?" asked Flight Lieutenant John 'Waggle' Davies – leader of Yellow Section in Morrow's division and flew the PR-H aircraft.

"The information to us is still rather thin, but what we do have does not look good. The Luftwaffe has hit almost everything so far this morning, and the Panzers are advancing quickly through Holland and Belgium. It would appear we are going to have our hands full quite soon."

"When do we go south?"

"Again, I will know more this afternoon after the conference. We have been asked to be prepared to move within a fortnight, maybe sooner."

"Where will we go?"

"Look, lads, I do not really know much more than you do at this point. Let us see what they tell me at the conference. There is really no point guessing about what might happen. The current thinking is RAF Northolt." Darling turned to Beamish. "While we are down there, Roger, I would appreciate you and the others to look around, and get a feel for the place. I have been told to expect to spend the night, so if you would, please make arrangements with the Mess."

"No problem, Skipper."

"Brilliant, then let us make ready for the transit south. 'Sparky,' if you are ready, call in your status to Sector."

"Are we going down armed?" asked Pilot Officer Roland 'Boxer' Stockard with a twitch of nervousness. Stockard flew the right wing position in Darling's lead Blue Section in the PR-E aircraft.

"Dear God, man," jumped in 'Jackstay' Beamish, "we are at war. Of course, we are going down armed."

"Roland," Darling said with more compassion, "the days of flying unarmed are over for a while."

The remaining two sections quickly fell into the routine of waiting, so familiar to the fighter pilots. 'Junior' Carrolton and 'Fog' Johnson, the two flying sergeants, started their usual game of chess. The others picked up the banter of frustrated fighter pilots on alert.

Darling decided to have some fun during the flight south. People seemed to appreciate the appearance and sound of the Spitfires, so they would burn more fuel, run the engines hotter than the maintenance crews liked, and fly on a straight line, high speed, low level path from Drem to Northolt. At their fully loaded, top cruise speed of 350 miles per hour, the flight would take slightly more than an hour. It had been many months since Brian enjoyed the exhilaration of high-speed, low-level flight. Passing within feet of the treetops, racing past a locomotive, or watching people on the ground wave to them as they flashed by, the pleasures and sensations of speed offered its own reward to pilots.

As he watched Leading Aircraftman Gordon check and recheck every item on his aircraft, Brian memorized the landmarks of the route to Northolt. As he studied the map, they would fly near Carlingon Castle, Leeds, Bedford and into the Northwest section of London. Mid-spring meant nearly everything would be green or various shades of blooming color. As he waited for Squadron Leader Darling to signal the start-up for the six Spitfires, Brian thought about Anne Booth. If he had no commitments, he would call Anne. He hoped she would be free. The thought of her being with any other man did not sit well with him although they had agreed to the terms of the relationship. Anne did not expect any remuneration or favors, and Brian had to accept the means of her income. Brian often wondered, as he did now, why Anne did what she did, and more importantly, why she accepted their relationship. He felt a debt to Anne for what she had taught him, for what she had enabled him to experience, for being a friend willing to listen and not to judge, and for permitting his most intimate queries. In many ways, Brian Drummond felt he loved her. He wanted the relationship to develop further.

"Ready up," shouted Darling.

The six pilots mounted their aircraft, started their engines, completed their checks and took off turning toward the south. The beauty of Lammermuir Hills attracted his attention once Brian had his aircraft set for low level, high-speed flight. They would all watch the coolant temperature gauge to ensure their powerful engines did not overheat. They flew in two wide Vics with Green Section slightly behind and to the right of Blue Section. Spread out, each pilot could keep his eyes out for obstacles and other aircraft while enjoying the scenery. Brian grinned broadly when he saw people on the ground smiling and waving. The sight of six sleek, curvaceous Spitfire fighters skimming across the countryside announced by the melodic tone of their Rolls Royce Merlin III engines had to be impressive and buoyant for the populace. The RAF was indeed on duty above them.

Their flight path took them several miles to the west of Carlingon Castle. Brian checked his map, and then pushed his throttle up to the emergency seal as he slowly swung wide across the back of the flight as they approached the area. He gained a little altitude to help him locate the castle while he kept an eye on the flight. He saw the distinctive features of Jonathan Kensington's home just to the right of his track. Brian adjusted his path to pass through the clearing immediately to the east of the castle, and then dove to gain speed. Several people were outside although at his speed he could not recognize them. His PR-F Spitfire passed below the height of the structure not ten feet above the grass through the clearing. He pulled up smoothly as he approached the far treeline. With a good rate of climb, Brian pushed forward slightly on his stick to decrease the airplane's angle of attack, and then put full left stick in rolling the Spitfire 2½ times. He stopped his roll in the inverted position, and then pulled back on the stick to bring his nose below the horizon. That should have been a good show for whoever was outside, he thought. He would find out later either from Jonathan or his parents on his next visit to Carlingon Castle.

It took Brian forty miles to catch up to the rest of the flight. Fast Spitfires at low level among the trees, hills and fields were not easy to find. He used emergency power until his coolant temperature rose toward the red line. Eventually, he found the five Spitfires and rejoined the flight.

"Good to have you join us, 'Hunter,'" broadcast 'Spike' Darling over the radio.

Brian did not respond because there was no response that could have altered the lecture he would receive upon landing. Darling tolerated solo stunts, but made sure the transgressor knew he had done wrong. Brian tried to convince himself that what he had done was not a stunt, just a friendly exhibition. He would also undoubtedly receive an admonishment from his section leader to complement the squadron leader. As long as it did not affect his ability to fly, Brian figured he could take the verbal whipping. Maybe the skipper was not as angry as his words.

—

Friday, 10.May.1940
RAF Northolt
Northolt, London, England
08:10 hours

The landing at RAF Northolt was uneventful, as aviators liked to say. The most impressive sight as they taxied to their assigned parking spaces was the number of Hurricanes and Spitfires. Five squadrons, sixty plus fighters with an array of squadron designators, as well as various other transport aircraft, Hudsons, Blenheims and Hampsteads, filled the parking apron of the aerodrome. While RAF Brize Norton had more aircraft in numbers, they were all trainers. These airplanes were fighting machines.

True to Brian's expectation, Squadron Leader Darling did not wait to let Pilot Officer Drummond know he had made a mistake. The words were strong, direct and sharp. Although it was a transit flight in friendly territory, they were at war and breaking up a flight meant weakening the unit. Brian had heard similar speeches given to others, but none were as rough as the dressing down he received. The end of the Phony War and the more vigorous real war made everyone more edgy. Fortunately for Brian, 'Spike' Darling needed to leave them for the commander's conference. Where Darling left off, 'Jackstay' Beamish picked up and amplified. The admoniishment from Beamish was more personal, but meant to temper rather than break. Brian took his tongue-lashing with stoic indifference and quiet resolve. The fly-by Carlingon Castle had been worth it.

While Darling was off with the other squadron leaders, Beamish led the gaggle of No.609 Squadron pilots on a walkabout, first down the flight line to take in the details of aircraft some of them had not seen before. The RAF base was much larger than RAF Drem. They figured out where everything was, including the Officer's Mess for a light lunch of a lamb and cheese sandwich with tea. The afternoon excursion took them to the Operations building that held the control tower and served as the terminal building for visiting dignitaries. There was excitement in the air everywhere they went. As the afternoon waned, the pilots returned to their aircraft to make sure they had been properly serviced and were ready for departure whenever ordered to do so by their leader.

With the day's tasks completed early, the five No.609 Squadron pilots returned to the Northolt Officer's Mess bar at 17:30. The facility was already rather crowded with the diluge of RAF Fighter Command pilots. None of them had finished their first beer when Squadron Leader Darling entered the room with several other squadron leaders. Darling introduced his colleagues: Squadron Leader Roger Joyce Bushell, No.92 Squadron, Spitfires, Pembrey, and his number 2, Flying Officer Roland Robert 'Bobby' Stanford-Tuck; Squadron Leader 'Tin Legs' Bader, the legless legend, No.242 Squadron, Hurricanes, Duxford; and, Flight Lieutenant Adolph Gysbert 'Sailor' Malan, the quiet South African, No.74 Squadron, Spitfires, Hornchurch, Lord Jeremy Morrison's squadron. Other famous names among the spring 1940 RAF Fighter Command would join them later at Shepherds Pub in Mayfair. While Brian was impressed with the fighter notables and the possibility of seeing Jeremy, he wanted Anne. It had been too long since he had seen her. It looked as if it would be a little longer.

"How did it go, Skipper?" asked 'Jackstay' Beamish.

"We will talk about it later, Roger. It is time to toss down a few pints of bitter."

"When do we head back?"

"In the morning. We will avail ourselves of the hospitality of the house, then we are heading down to Shepherds."

"All of us?" asked 'Hunter' Drummond.

"Of course, all of us, you twit. Last time I checked, we were trying to be a squadron. Besides, we at least have something to celebrate in all this."

"Like what, Skipper?"

"I take it you blokes have not heard the latest news." Darling waited to confirm all the blank stares. "Winston Churchill, himself, will soon be prime minister. We were informed before the conference adjourned that Churchill was to visit the King . . . in fact, probably doing so as we speak."

"I'll be damned," said 'Mongo' Strickland.

"I should hope not. We received confirmation this afternoon. The King is expected to ask him to form a unification coalition government, apparently Churchill has the bloody bunch of them already lined up, and the King should accept our Mister Churchill."

"Hell of a time to take up the leadership when the whole soddin' world is coming apart at the seams," observed Beamish.

"If anyone is up to the task, it is our Mister Churchill," responded Squadron Leader Darling. "What's more, we have an added bonus. Our own 'Hunter' is bosom buddies with our new prime minister."

"I only met him once," protested Brian.

"Right then, all you blokes who have sat down to lunch with Mister Churchill at his home in Kent, no less, please be so kind to say, aye." No one responded. "There you have it, bosom buddies."

The light-hearted jabs at Brian kept the tone on a very high plain. To Pilot Officer Brian Drummond, the predictions of his mentors, both Malcolm Bainbridge and John Spencer, had come to fruition. The war had turned ominously more serious, and Winston Churchill had been chosen to lead the nation through troubled waters. An incredible transition had occurred from less than two years ago when Churchill was still an outcast ostracized publicly by many on both sides of the Atlantic to this point where everything was failing and the elder statesman was asked to make it right. The intoxication and addiction of appeasement had numbed everyone except Churchill to the mounting menace.

Brian listened with interest and participated circumferentially, but the image of Anne Booth kept returning to him during lulls in the conversation. Dinner passed quickly with laughter, jokes and strong talk. Brian noted with enthusiasm the popular acceptance of virtually everyone as the news of Churchill's ascendancy passed among the crowd and was assessed.

The camaraderie of the fighter pilots continued through their journey into the city, with fellow travelers watching and listening to the jovial band of RAF officers among them on the Underground. Their fellow travelers, mostly civilians, seemed to draw broad appreciation that if these pilots could laugh at the situation, then they could as well. Smiles, salutes, and various hand signs, like a thumbs up, a 'V' for victory, or a simple wave, greeted them throughout the short trip. Without question, the early stages of alcohol intoxication added to the comical mood of the transit.

—

Friday, 10.May.1940
Buckingham Palace
Westminster, London, England
18:00 hours

The King's orderly stood in the open doorway to the White Drawing Room – the ornate, voluminous, formal state reception room of the palace. The shaded, incandescent lights gave the white walls a golden glow amid the gilded details of the room décor.

"Your Majesty, the Prime Minister, the Right Honorable Neville Chamberlain, the First Lord of the Admiralty the Right Honorable Winston Churchill, the Leader of the Labor Party the Right Honorable Clement Attlee, the Deputy Leader of the Labor Party the Right Honorable Arthur Greenwood, and the Secretary of State for Foreign Affairs Viscount Halifax of Monk Bretton."

The five political leaders entered the reception room. King George VI stood at a position of attention, ramrod straight, dressed in full regalia as monarch and admiral of the fleet, before the fireplace opposite the entryway beneath the massive portrait of Queen Alexandra. He held a grim expression and sadness in his eyes. The visitors assembled in line three paces in front of the King with Chamberlain in the center and Churchill to his right.

Prime Minister Chamberlain spoke first. "Your Majesty, it is with a very heavy heart I must tender my resignation as your first minister."

The King responded, "It is with an equally heavy heart I am compelled to accept your resignation, Mister Chamberlain. None in the realm can claim you did other than your utmost to preserve the peace."

"I am sorry I failed you, Sir."

The King stepped forward, extended his hands and grasped Chamberlain's right hand in both of his gloved hands. "Nonsense, my dear Mister Chamberlain, you did not fail me or the Kingdom. You were betrayed by an insincere and dishonorable man."

Chamberlain nodded his acceptance of the King's compliment.

"Before we move to the formalities of forming a new government, perhaps we could have a bit of a chat regarding our situation," King George VI said, as he motioned toward the golden colored couches on either side of the other fireplace opposite the large exterior windows. The King sat in the middle of the closest couch. Winston sat in the middle of the identical couch opposite the King with Attlee on his right and Greenwood on the left. Chamberlain and Halifax sat in two comparably upholstered chairs between the couches.

The King nodded to Winston.

"Your Majesty, major mobile units of the German Army crossed the border into the Netherlands at dawn this morning. They rapidly overwhelmed Dutch defenses. Their attack has been aided by massive air and artillery bombardment. Unconfirmed reports indicate their assault has also been aided by parachute troops landing behind the Dutch lines to take key objectives to aid their advance. General Lord Gort, in command of your Majesty's troops in Northern France, has advanced quickly into Belgium toward the Dutch frontier to meet the German onslaught per our operational plan. We expect the main engagement tomorrow."

"Thank you for the report, Mister Churchill." The King held Winston's eyes for several seconds before continuing. "It is no secret I favored Mister Chamberlain's exemplary efforts to preserve the peace," he said and nodded to Neville. "I must also confess my support for Lord Halifax's commitment to peace and diplomatic solutions. That said, I understand, appreciate and accept the reality of our situation. The time to rend has come to us, now. If I am properly informed, as leaders of your respective political parties in Parliament, you believe you can promptly form a government in service of the Crown."

"Yes, Sir," responded Winston. "We shall propose a coalition government for the duration of the present war, with your War Cabinet to be comprised of the five of us. With your assent, I shall assume the awesome responsibility as your first minister, as well as minister of defense, first lord of the treasury, and leader of Commons. The former Prime Minister Mister Chamberlain shall assume the role of Lord President of the Council. Mister Attlee shall become your Lord Privy Seal. Lord Halifax has agreed to remain as Foreign Secretary, and Mister Greenwood shall be Minister without Portfolio. These men," Winston said, gesturing to the others, "shall be your sturdy, coalition, War Cabinet until victory is achieved and peace has been restored."

"I presume you have sufficient support among your members to carry on the terrible duties before you."

"Yes, Sir," Winston responded, and then motioned for each man to offer his personal confirmation, which each of them dutifully gave. "I must add, Sir, Archie Sinclair has brought along his Liberal Party members and has agreed to serve your Majesty as Secretary of State for Air."

The King nodded his head. "I do not envy the task before you, Mister Churchill. Yet, I must assure you I have the fullest confidence you are worthy to carry the burden as your ancestor did during the reign of Queen Anne and the War of Spanish Succession. You have an admirable guide in the service of Sir John Churchill – 1st Duke of Marlborough."

"Thank you for your confidence, Sir."

King George VI nodded his head several times as he patted both his knees. "If you would, Mister Churchill, please stand." Winston stood, and the others followed suit, as the King stood. "I charge you with the solemn responsibility to form a new coalition and leadership of my government. I trust you are prepared to accept my charge."

"Yes, your Majesty, I am."

"Very well," he paused to lock upon Winston's eyes, "godspeed Prime Minister Churchill."

"Thank you, your Majesty. By your leave, Sir?"

The King again nodded. The five new ministers stepped clear of the seating area and waited as the King left the White Room by the door behind him. Prime Minister Churchill received the congratulations of his colleagues as they turned to carry out the heavy charge now upon them.

—

Friday, 10.May.1940
Shepherds Tavern
50 Hertford Street
Mayfair, London, England
20:25 hours

Shepherds Pub, the gathering place of RAF fighter pilots in London, was crowded, heavy with the usual thick cloud of smoke choking every room of the establishment. The cacophony of voices each directed at one person or another reverberated among the exposed, dark, wood beamed, ceiling supports as well as all the walls. It took several minutes before the new arrivals could enjoy the earthy taste of a full pint of dark English bitter. The conversation had continued as one natural stream from the Northolt Officer's Mess through the London Underground into Shepherds Pub. Once in the familiar setting, Brian took the opportunity to search out Flight Lieutenant Lord Jeremy 'Mud' Morrison. If he was in London, he was probably either here or with Virginia North.

Brian located Jeremy's squadron leader, 'Sailor' Malan, the quiet, compact, chiseled, South African commander of No.74 Squadron. He seemed to be listening to several other officers and not deeply involved in the conversation. Brian made his way toward him.

"How are you, 'Hunter?'"

Pilot Officer Brian 'Hunter' Drummond was immediately impressed the accomplished leader of fighter pilots remembered his name. "I'm just fine, Squadron Leader Malan. Thank you, sir."

"Just call me, 'Sailor.' We are all in the same boat in here."

"Right, then, 'Sailor' it is."

"What can I do for you?"

"Actually, I thought you might know if Flight Lieutenant Morrison is here."

"You mean, 'Mud?' Sure, he is here somewhere unless he sneaked out to be with his lady friend. Last time I saw him, he was in the back trying to get some darts into the right places."

"Thank you, sir."

"Hold up there," Malan said not finished with the exchange. "Two things, I think you will find most, if not all, of us that fly these machines do not get into rank. We are more impressed with your skills in the air than what you wear on your sleeve. So, from here on out, I would suggest you drop the rank. As I said earlier, in this business we are all the same. We all die just as easily with simple mistakes, and we all want to kill as many Gerries as we can. It is real simple. Do you understand?"

Brian started to respond in the military manner he had been taught but caught himself. "Sure."

"Second, you are the American, as I recall."

"That's right."

"It is good to have you with us, 'Hunter.' From what I hear, you deserve your moniker."

"Thanks."

"Off you go, then. See if you can find 'Mud.' If you find him, tell him to keep it in his pants tonight. And . . . good hunting. See you in the sky."

"Thanks, 'Sailor.'"

As Brian worked his way through the thickening mass of pilots, young women and occasional male civilians, he could not help being even more impressed by 'Sailor' Malan. He seemed to be everything his reputation presented. Brian remembered the stories told by Malcolm Bainbridge recalling the camaraderie of the pilots of his squadron, No.43 'Fighting Cocks' Squadron, in the Great War. The same feelings came to him more with each introduction, with each discussion. It was a small group of men banded together in a mutual struggle with extraordinary leaders who stimulated even more extraordinary feats. There was a feeling of security, not safety, among these men. Brian liked the seductive feeling of this sophisticated, and yet most basic, characteristic among men.

Brian heard Jeremy Morrison's voice before he could see him. The sound told him his friend was well down the road to intoxication and enjoying every minute. Several other similarly affected pilots were gathered around him. First sighting went to Brian although Jeremy was not far behind.

"Brian Drummond, you bloody Yank," Jeremy shouted as he pushed through the crowd. Everyone turned to see who Morrison was referring to. Brian felt a bit awkward like a freak in the circus. Jeremy embraced him as he gave him a quick kiss on his cheek. "It is great to see you again, 'BAD.' No, wait, ah yes, I heard they changed your callsign to 'Hunter,' is that right?"

"Yes."

"Well, good to have you with us. How did you know I was here?"

"'Sailor' told me you were back here."

"Good man, 'Sailor.' I'd follow the bastard to hell and back."

"Yes, well, he told me to tell you, to keep it in your pants tonight."

"He did now, did he? Well, we will have to see about that. Where is the nearest wench I can have without getting my head knocked off?" He looked around the room pointing to each of three women within sight as if he were selecting a suit, and each time drew back in recognition of their attachment to various pilots. "No such luck, it would seem."

"What about Virginia?"

"Good woman, 'Virgin.' She takes good care of me. I love her you know, Brian, but she is a working woman." A somber, sober shade passed over him as he probably considered the vision in his head. The mood changed as quickly as it had come. "Kind of like you and Anne. The two of you have sure hit it off, Brian. She is a good woman, too. I think she loves you. I have never seen her become so attached to a man. You must be good between the sheets, old boy," he said, giving Brian a punch in the shoulder. The reference flushed Brian with some embarrassment although no one could notice.

"Yes, she is a good woman, Jeremy. I like her a lot."

"Maybe it is more than that, my friend," he said with instant sober diction.

"Maybe."

Jeremy Morrison returned to character. "Listen up, you sods." He waited for just a reduction in the din. "I want to introduce a special fighter pilot among us." He slapped Brian on the back. "This here is none other than the very first Yank to join our little band of merry men." Various shouts, greetings and other more colorful words rose out of the mass. "May I introduce to you, Pilot Officer Brian 'Hunter' Drummond, one of the best stick and throttle jockeys I have ever seen. This man can think bullets to his target."

"Big words among this lot," someone responded.

"He is a big man in more ways than one," Jeremy said.

"I will take one of those," shouted a female voice from the back of the room.

The resulting roar grew to deafening proportions. Brian's embarrassment grew substantially. He was not accustomed to the public attention, and quite preferred, as Malcolm so often told him, to let his actions speak for him.

"Do not be so modest, you bloody sod. Bask in the adulation due you," Jeremy said.

Brian wanted to change the subject quickly. "How do you like Spitfires?"

"How do we like Spitfires, the man asks?" he shouted.

"Best damn fighter ever made." "Friggin' beautiful death on wings." "The savior of life as we know it." The shouts from the crowd gave him unsought responses to his feeble attempt to change the subject.

"What do you think? I think they like the bloody machine," laughed Jeremy.

The effects of alcohol clearly defined his demeanor, voice and thought. Brian knew there was no hope of constructive conversation with his drunk friend.

"'Jackstay' Beamish, you sodding Scotsman," shouted Jeremy Morrison. Brian turned to see his section leader working his way toward them. "What are you doing here?"

"I've come to retrieve me lad here." Beamish grabbed Brian's left elbow. "We must be off, laddie. Skipper wants to be off early."

"You can't leave now. We've just got the pump primed."

"Sorry old bean. Duty calls."

Jeremy led the gathered crowd in a resounding chorus of raspberries, hoots and admonitions hurled at the deserters. It was after midnight when they stepped out into the reduced night traffic of the now darkened streets. No one would have ever known the time based on the still teeming occupancy of Shepherds Pub. The journey back to RAF Northolt was filled with the collective gathering of Fighter Command's personnel status. The news from the various corners of Fighter Command brought them all up to snuff with who was where, who was doing what and how each squadron was performing its tasks. The most amazing aspect of these nights was the closeness of the small organization. They truly seemed to be brothers. They had their differences, but the elements in common far exceeded the differences among them. The feelings made Brian feel stronger, more capable, than he had ever felt in his life.

—

Monday, 13.May.1940
House of Commons
Westminster, London, England

The weekend had been days without much rest, a blur of endless conferences, small and large, of negotiations, as well as the personal, intimate moments of finely balanced diplomacy among erstwhile political adversaries. The other members of the newly formed War Cabinet were both contributory and enormously helpful in convincing the disparate political leaders in both the House of Commons and the House of Lords to put their political differences aside and joint His Majesty's Government in vital assignments of ministerial rank but outside the decision-making group, despite rapidly blackening clouds gathering on the southern horizon. The service of these widely varied men became all the more poignant with the looming reality that if they were unsuccessful in defending the Home Islands, they would surely be prime targets for the Nazi SS.

Prime Minister Churchill nodded his head that it was time to stand before their brethren in the House of Commons. Lord Halifax was missing, as a peer he was not allowed in the lower chamber. Chamberlain, Greenwood and Attlee entered Commons in that order. Winston heard muffled encouragement for the former prime minister, and resounding and raucous cheers as the Labor Party leaders as they entered the chamber. Winston took a deep breath, as he stood alone, exhaled, and then entered the House of Commons with a confident stride to the Government bench. Conservative Party members remained seated with only a fraction offering tepid claps, while all the remaining members were on their feet cheering and shouting boisterous words of encouragement to the new prime minister. Churchill did not respond to the applause. He walked directly to his seat on the government bench and sat to await his moment.

"The House will come to order," pronounced Speaker of the House Edward Algernon FitzRoy, DL, MP. "Order, order." The House settled down quickly. "I have the privilege to introduce His Majesty's new first minister, the Right Honorable and Gallant Winston Churchill."

The House remained eerily silent as Winston stood to the Prime Minister's Dispatch Box on the House Table. "I beg to move that this House welcomes the formation of a Government representing the united and inflexible resolve of the nation to prosecute the war with Germany to a victorious conclusion."

"Here, here," numerous members offered. Winston waited for silence.

"On Friday evening last, I received His Majesty's commission to form a new Administration. It as the evident wish and will of Parliament and the nation that this should be conceived on the broadest possible basis and that it should include all parties, both those who supported the late Government and also the parties of the Opposition. I have completed the most important part of this task. A War Cabinet has been formed of five Members, representing, with the Opposition Liberals, the unity of the nation. The three party Leaders have agreed to serve, either in the War Cabinet or in high executive office. The three Fighting Services have been filled. It was necessary that this should be done in one single day, on account of the extreme urgency and rigor of events. A number of other positions, key positions, were filled yesterday, and I am submitting a further list to His Majesty tonight. I hope to complete the appointment of the principal Ministers during tomorrow. The appointment of the other Ministers usually takes a little longer, but I trust that, when Parliament meets again, this part of my task will be completed, and that the administration will be complete in all respects.

"I considered it in the public interest to suggest that the House should be summoned to meet today. Mr. Speaker agreed, and took the necessary steps, in accordance with the powers conferred upon him by the Resolution of the House. At the end of the proceedings today, the Adjournment of the House will be proposed until Tuesday, 21st of May, with, of course, provision for earlier meeting, if need be. The business to be considered during that week will be notified to Members at the earliest opportunity. I now invite the House, by the Motion, which stands in my name, to record its approval of the steps taken and to declare its confidence in the new Government.

"To form an Administration of this scale and complexity is a serious undertaking in itself, but it must be remembered that we are in the preliminary stage of one of the greatest battles in history, that we are in action at many other points in Norway and in Holland, that we have to be prepared in the Mediterranean, that the air battle is continuous and that many preparations, such as have been indicated by my honorable Friend below the Gangway, have to be made here at home. In this crisis I hope I may be pardoned if I do not address the House at any length today. I hope that any of my friends and colleagues, or former colleagues, who are affected by the political reconstruction, will make allowance, all allowance, for any lack of ceremony with which it has been necessary to act. I would say to the House, as I said to those who have joined this government: 'I have nothing to offer but blood, toil, tears and sweat.'

"We have before us an ordeal of the most grievous kind. We have before us many, many long months of struggle and of suffering. You ask, what is our policy? I can say: It is to wage war, by sea, land and air, with all our might and with all the strength that God can give us; to wage war against a monstrous tyranny, never surpassed in the dark, lamentable catalogue of human crime. That is our policy. You ask, what is our aim? I can answer in one word: It is victory, victory at all costs, victory in spite of all terror, victory, however long and hard the road may be; for without victory, there is no survival. Let that be realized; no survival for the British Empire, no survival for all that the British Empire has stood for, no survival for the urge and impulse of the ages, that mankind will move forward towards its goal. But I take up my task with buoyancy and hope. I feel sure that our cause will not be suffered to fail among men. At this time I feel entitled to claim the aid of all, and I say, 'come then, let us go forward together with our united strength.'" The Prime Minster stepped back and sat, as the House stood and displayed its approval.

The unanimous vote of confidence for His Majesty's new War Cabinet completed the day's parliamentary action. The House adjourned for one week to allow the government to complete the task of filling the myriad ministerial positions, as the Battles of France and the Atlantic raged on around them.

—

Tuesday, 14.May.1940
Headquarters, Secret Intelligence Service
No.21 Queen Anne's Gate
Westminster, London, England
14:30 hours

"**W**hat do you have for us today, Alastair?" asked 'C,' Director General – Secret Intelligence Service.

Commander Alastair Ignatius Denniston, Royal Navy, the Head of the Government Code and Cypher School at Bletchley Park, opened the locked and manacled message case and extracted a small stack of papers. "I am afraid none of it is good news." He leafed through the stack until he found the message he wanted first. "The situation in France and the Low Countries is nearly catastrophic. The German assault is only four days old and General Heinz Guderian's Second Armor Division has advanced rapidly toward Abbeville. At his current rate of progress, he will effectively cut off the BEF from *le Armée de Terre* trapping them against the sea."

Menzies looked to his large map of Western Europe to ensure he understood the ramifications of the information. "Does the War Cabinet know?"

"Yes, sir."

"What are the current plans?"

"As best I know, the BEF will continue to resist in an effort to prevent separation from the French. The probability of success given the current situation is quite low, I should think."

"What do we have from ULTRA?"

Denniston leafed through the stack of papers once more. "I suppose that is the only good news. We have been working on about 1,000 Enigma messages per day since the invasion. The productivity of ULTRA has been quite good." He handed 'C' the top message. "That is Hitler's Directive Number One One issued this morning by OKW ordering an all-out assault to end Dutch resistance. Göring translated his piece and ordered a mass bombardment of Rotterdam."

"Dear God."

"What is worse, we intercepted a message from the Dutch High Command; they are preparing to surrender. They have already contacted the *Wehrmacht* XXXIV Corps."

"Dear God Almighty."

"The bad news continues *ad infinitum ad nauseum*. I think you can get the flavor of the situation."

"Unfortunately, yes." 'C' thought about the plight of British youth in Northern France. More than a million precious soldiers needed for the defense of the British Isles were now in grave jeopardy. He instinctively knew their only salvation might lay with little bits of assistance provided from any quarter. "Are you processing all the traffic you are receiving?"

"We are trying to sort the intercepts to concentrate on the most likely gems. We are dreadfully short of staff to analyze all the traffic, and we still takes us far too long to find the correct wheel keys."

"Where can you get proper additional staff?"

"There are various candidates, mathematicians mostly, who could be drafted to help with the decryption. We could also use a handful of military intelligence analysts who understand what they break."

"Then, make it so. I shall clear it with the War Cabinet. Assume approval for the moment and proceed as though you have full approval. Get the very best people you can. This is obviously a question of the highest priority. We may find the one piece of information, which could save those poor lads in France. We must find it. We cannot accept less."

"Yes, sir. I shall get right to it."

"Thank you, Alastair. Good Luck."

Stewart did not like the feeling of impotence that came to him as Denniston departed. The peace and quiet of the No.21 Queen Anne's Gate building seemed so shameful in contrast to the desperate fighting in France, Belgium and Holland. He wanted to do more. He wanted the SIS to do more, but there were limits. This was essentially a military show now, although the signals intelligence work of GCCS could have a positive effect on the outcome. The key had to be the timely decipher, analysis and secure dissemination of results. Maybe they could help the beleaguered British Expeditionary Force before it was too late.

'C' made two telephone calls, one to Carl Acton his head of operations, and the other to the Prime Minister.

Carl was instructed to judiciously withdraw all their agents from the Low Countries and Northern France to avoid capture. He was also asked to initiate the final phase of setting up clandestine networks that would be the nucleus of the resistance movement in the occupied countries. The thought did come to him that he had issued the same order just a month earlier. The boundaries of safe countries continued to constrict around them. Something had to change.

The Prime Minister, once again, was in France trying to bolster the government to hold the line and not crumble. He asked for and received an appointment to see Churchill tomorrow before the afternoon War Cabinet meeting. The Prime Minister's support for staffing GCCS to improve productivity had to be obtained. The use of ULTRA products warranted a strategic discussion. The yield was improving, the benefit would be enhanced and the risk to compromise would rise as well. The future had to be brightened. 'C' was one of the few in the world who recognized that events would most likely get substantially worse before they began to turn, if they ever did.

There was one other task Menzies needed to check on. Winston gave the execution order once he ascended to the premiership, now he needed to ensure the task had been completed before he talked to Winston.

Menzies raised the secure telephone to MI5, the Counterintelligence Branch.

"Yes, 'C'," answered Major General Sir Vernon George Waldegrave Kell, KBE, CB – the aging Director General, Security Services (MI5).

"Have we completed our house cleaning activity as requested by the Prime Minister?" Stewart asked having waited for the proper moment of authority and political coalescence.

"I was just about to call. You saved me the effort. The answer, you can assure the PM, is, yes. Anna Wolkoff and the other prostitutes have been arrested and will remain for the moment in solitary confinement under charges of treason. We have taken into custody Sir Oswald Mosley and other Fascist Union leaders. *Pro forma*, we notified the Palace Chancellory Office since Mosley is officially the 6th Baronet of Ancoats. We have not captured William Joyce, however. He must have smelt something on the wind. We have some indications he has taken flight, quite probably to Germany via Ireland."

"Excellent."

"I must say, 'C,' we found some disturbing evidence in Wolkoff's flat. We may have happened upon a leak in the U.S. Embassy Communication Center."

Menzies stared at no particular point on the far wall, waiting for the rest of the story and not wanting to disturb his train of thought.

"We are developing the information as quickly as we are able."

"Should we notify No.10?"

"Not yet, I'm afraid. We do not have sufficient evidence to believe what we have seen, and we do not have a link to anyone in the Embassy. The two messages could be a disinformation plant to create doubt. I will meet with the Embassy's Legal Attaché tomorrow in our effort to ferret out the leak, if there truly is one. As you may know, the Legal Attaché is FBI Director Hoover's man in this country."

"Yes," "C" responded. "I do know the connection. Please keep me informed. The Prime Minister communicates with the President of the United States through that embassy communication facility."

"We did not know that until now. I should also add," continued Kell, "we are in the final stages of cleaning up this mess. We have arrested seven other co-conspirators, mostly other prostitutes. We believe we have the majority of the principals in this seedy little affair. However, we are continuing our investigations since we have found connections to numerous senior diplomats, ministers and military officers."

"So, I can tell the Prime Minister, we have a firm grasp on this unseemly issue?"

"Yes, sir."

"Brilliant. Thank you, Vernon. Keep the eyes open," 'C' said, as he always did to his counterpart.

"Always, sir."

Menzies did not smile or feel any sense of satisfaction . . . only nausea and conclusion. He knew several of the women would hang and probably the Irishman as well. The legal niceties would be handled quietly and efficiently. He could not ignore the fact they did not need this complication in their state of affairs at this moment in history.

—

Tuesday, 14.May.1940
Cabinet Room
No.10 Downing Street
Whitehall, London, England
21:15 hours

"Thank you for coming at this advanced hour," Prime Minister Churchill said to the assembled members of the Defense Committee. The appropriate defense ministers and the military chiefs were all present as well as General 'Pug' Ismay. "I understand we may have experienced a serious setback today. What happened exactly?"

Everyone turned their heads toward the newly appointed Secretary of State for Air Sir Archibald Henry Macdonald Sinclair, Bart, PC, CMG, Member of Parliament for Caithness and Sutherland, 4th Baronet of Ulbster, and his military chief of the Air Staff Air Chief Marshal Sir Cyril Newall. Both men were discernibly uncomfortable.

Sinclair was the first to speak. "Sir Cyril . . . if you will."

"Certainly, Minister." Newall cleared his throat. "Yesterday, the Germans launched what now appears to be their main assault through what we thought was the impenetrable Ardennes Forest, for armor operations of this magnitude. Their engineers quickly deployed a series of pontoon bridges across the River Meuse near Sedan of sufficient size to accommodate their largest tanks, tracked artillery and myriad of support vehicles. Appropriately, Lord Gord ordered all out air strikes on those bridges to stop or at least slow down the German armor advance on the flank of the BEF and French Northern Army. Air Marshal Barratt ordered the Striking Force to hit those bridges. The sorties began just after dawn this morning. By late afternoon, we lost over half of our entire strength of light and medium bombers in France."

"In one day?" asked Churchill.

"Yes, sir."

"Did they at least knock out those bridges?"

"No, sir, not a one."

"What happened?"

"Our Battle and Blenheim bombers are no match for the German 109 fighters."

"Where were our fighters to protect them?"

"We had insufficient numbers available. The Germans put up overwhelming numbers. Our fighters were hard pressed to defend themselves, set aside defending the bombers. The bombers tried dive-bombing as well as low level approaches. They tried everything they could. The Germans clearly anticipated our attacks. I must say they deployed exceptionally effective anti-aircraft gun fire around the Sedan bridges."

"What are you going to do tomorrow, Sir Cyril?"

"Our air strike capability in France would not survive another day like today, Prime Minister."

"So, you are giving up?"

"No, sir. However, it seems we must recognize reality here. We need more fighters."

"Then, deploy more fighters."

"It is not that simple," interjected Sinclair.

"Why not?"

"Supporting those fighters logistically alone exposes not only those fighter squadrons to greater risk but ultimately risks the air defense of the Home Islands."

"And the Royal Navy," added Churchill's replacement as First Lord Albert Victor 'A.V.' Alexander, PC, Member of Parliament for Hillsborough. "Our ships may well be dependent upon local air superiority of those fighters for them to protect our shores."

"Quite so," First Sea Lord Admiral Sir Dudley Pound said.

Churchill slammed the table with his hand. The sharp repor startled most in the room. "Surely, we are not as bad as this debacle makes us appear," barked Churchill. "Am I the only one who sees those bridges for what they are?"

"No, Prime Minister, you are not," said General Sir Edmund Ironside. "Those bridges have exposed Lord Gort's flank, and the Germans are exploiting that vulnerability."

"Exactly," barked Churchill, again, "and exploiting that vulnerability quite well I must say." The Prime Minister took a few moments to calm his anger. "Our choices are simple. We must stop the Germans. We either do it over there or here."

"Precisely the point," Anthony Eden said. "So the question before us is where best to conduct that fight. The Germans appear to have superior equipment and numbers for the moment. If we do not find some miracle on the battlefield in France, we shall be called upon to defend our precious island."

"The decision may be made for us by the Germans," Ironside said.

Sinclair leaned forward and looked directly to Churchill. "It would take us several days to move additional squadrons to France along with the necessary logistics support to sustain them in combat. They cannot get their fast enough to make a difference. We cannot risk losing what precious few bombers we have left to support our soldiers fighting on the ground in Belgium and France. I am afraid we took our shot yesterday and we failed. Air Marshal Barratt has already moved forward his Air Compoent fighter squadron, his reserves so to speak. As the situation lays for the moment, my recommendation is that we inform Lord Gort and Air Marshal Barratt they must fight with the resources they have. We cannot reinforce them fast enough, even if we wanted to do so, and it is not clear to me that we have the reinforcement resources available as it is, if we are to maintain our defenses for the Home Islands."

"Is that it then?" asked Churchill.

"For now, it appears so," Sinclair answered.

Prime Minister Churchill shook his head in disbelief. "Until we find our way through this mess, what happened at Sedan yesterday will be classified most secret by His Majesty's Government. We do not need to be inflaming the naysayers with the tragedy of yesterday's debacle. Am I clear?"

Everyone in the room nodded their confirmation. The Defense Committee of Great Britain adjourned for the evening. Churchill remained in his chair, brooding about what he had just heard and considering what he must do about it.

General Ismay stopped at the door. "Is there anything I can do for you, Prime Minister?"

"An army and an air force to stop the Germans would be nice."

"If it was but mine to command."

Churchill managed a smile to Ismay. "Have a good night, 'Pug'."

—

Chapter 4

He that lives upon hope will die fasting.
-- Benjamin Franklin

Wednesday, 15.May.1940
The White House
Washington, District of Columbia, U.S.A.

The brilliant illumination of the Oval Office with the afternoon sun and clear skies made the colors all the more vivid. The blue-green rug and the dark green drapes with golden eagle valances burst with vibrancy against the gray-green walls of the presidential office. The President of the United States Franklin Delano Roosevelt sat pensively in his custom, low-profile wheelchair between the opposed golden upholstered couches. Secretary of State Cordell Hull sat to the President's right. Secretary of War Harry Hines Woodring and Secretary of the Navy Charles Edison sat on the couch opposite Hull. The President's ever-present, Mr Fix-It, Harry Lloyd Hopkins sat in a straight back chair pulled up, and situated behind and to the left of the President.

"OK. Where were we?" asked the President.

Hull cleared his throat. "Ambassador Kennedy sent along his assessment of the situation in Europe."

"Oh, do tell, Mister Secretary. I wait with bated breath to hear from our illustrious Ambassador to the Court of Saint James's."

Hull ignored that jab. "Ambassador Kennedy is convinced the British have found themselves in an untenable position in Belgium."

"So, he has become a military expert as well as all his other self-anointed accolades has he?"

Again, Secretary Hull ignored the President's clear disdain for their ambassador to Great Britain. "He indicates the signs of French collapse are mounting, and the British are likely to find themselves surrounded and trapped in Belgium."

"Joe Kennedy's tone is decidedly darker than Ed Murrow's evening reports from London. What makes you believe Kennedy is correct and Murrow is wrong?"

"He is a reporter, Mister President. Joe is our ambassador, who has far greater access to relevant information than a reporter for CBS News."

"You may well be correct, Cordell, but I dare say Ed Murrow is no slouch or slacker."

"As you say, Mister President."

"What does he propose we do?"

"Urge the French and British to seek terms and an armistice before they are defeated on the battlefield."

Roosevelt stared intently at Cordell Hull, who remained stone-faced and equally focused. "I must confess my doubts," the President proceeded. "The British government fell in on itself less than a week ago. The BEF is clearly in danger of being cutoff from the preponderance of the French Army. And, Churchill is trying to organize a new coalition, unity government, which is not an easy task even in the best of times." He turned his attention to Woodring and Edison. "What do you fellows think?"

Woodring was the first to respond. "Mister President, I tend to agree with Ambassador Kennedy. The French do not appear to be well organized, or well commanded. We have fragmentary reports. One of the most disturbing appears to be what, if true, would be an indicative and terrible tragedy. The Germans installed a series of pontoon bridges across the River Meuse at Sedan to facilitate what now seems to be their main assault through the Ardennes Forest region. Yesterday, the British Advanced Air Striking Force carried out an all-out series of bombing sorties on those bridges. They lost more than half of their entire strength in one day due to exceptional anti-aircraft battery fire and literally overwhelming German fighter attacks. None of the bridges were destroyed. German armor forces are flooding across those bridges."

"How accurate is your information?" asked the President.

"Sketchy, I would say," the Secretary of War responded. "The British are understandably reticent to paint too gloomy of a picture, even if that is the true situation."

"We need first hand information. We are being asked to take critical decisions without knowledge whether there will be any friends remaining to receive our support."

Secretary of War Woodring ignored the President's point. "They are much better than their showing so far. As you noted, the British Expeditionary Force is of insufficient size to stop the Germans, and they are likely to be surrounded in short order. Their choices will be surrender the bulk of the British top-tier units of the Army or be chewed up by a relentless *Wehrmacht*." Woodring waited for a response or Edison to pick up the lance. The President stared at him, as if waiting for the rest of the story. Woodring took the meaning of the President's gaze. "As you know, Mister President, I pull no punches with respect to my considered opinion that we must remain out of the conflict in Europe. We lost far too many precious men in France the last time. The British and French must preserve what they have left. Peace terms would appear to be the only way to achieve that and keep us out of the war."

The President had heard enough from his Secretary of War. He turned his eyes to Charles Edison, the son of famed inventor Thomas Edison, as if he was saying, you are next.

"To be blunt, Mister President, we need time. The naval rearmament legislation is working its way through Congress, but we do not yet have the funds to execute our rearmament plan. We are not prepared to take on the modernized German navy, ignoring the potential conflation should the warships of the British and French navies fall into German hands. However, we do it, Mister President, we need time."

"Your counsel presumes war is inevitable," interjected Woodring.

"I do not see that fellow Hitler being satisfied even with all of Europe and the United Kingdom under his control. We would undoubtedly be next . . . well perhaps after he dispatches the godless Soviets."

"He would be foolish in the extreme, if he attempted to subjugate the United States of America."

"Are you and your generals prepared to fight this highly mobile, new form of warfare!" snapped Edison.

"Now, gentlemen," interceded Roosevelt. "No need to fight amongst ourselves." The President scanned his ministers. "The wild card in all this is Winston Churchill. The Secretary of State is aware, but I do not think you fellows are," he said nodding to Woodring and Edison, " I have been communicating directly with Churchill since last summer before he returned to the Admiralty. We have kept these communications close hold for obvious reasons. Harry," he said extending his left hand. Hopkins retrieved a single sheet of paper from the folder on his lap and placed it in the President's outstretched hand. "This is the latest message received from Churchill, now the new Prime Minister of Great Britain. Please have a read, if you will." Roosevelt handed the message to Secretary of War Woodring first.

MOST SECRET AND PERSONAL

```
35
15.V.1940
FOR: POTUS
from: Former Naval Person.
Although I have changed my office, I am
sure you would not wish me to discontinue
our intimate, private correspondence. As
you are no doubt aware, the scene has
```

darkened swiftly. The enemy have a marked
preponderance in the air, and their new
technique is making a deep impression upon
the French. I think myself the battle on
land has only just begun, and I should like
to see tanks [masses] engaged. Up to the
present, Hitler is working with specialised
units in tanks and air. The small countries
are simply smashed up, one by one, like
matchwood. We must expect, though it is not
yet certain, that Mussolini will hurry in to
share the loot of civilisation. We expect
to be attacked here ourselves, both from the
air and by parachute and air borne troops
in the near future, and are getting ready
for them. If necessary, we shall continue
the war alone and we are not afraid of that.
But I trust you realise, Mr. President, that
the voice and force of the United States may
count for nothing if they are withheld too
long. You may have a completely subjugated,
Nazified Europe established with astonishing
swiftness, and the weight may be more than we
can bear. All I ask now is that you should
proclaim nonbelligerency, which would mean
that you would help us with everything short
of actually engaging armed forces. Immediate
needs are:
first of all, the loan of forty or fifty of
your older destroyers to bridge the gap
between what we have now and the large new
construction we put in hand at the beginning
of the war. This time next year we shall
have plenty. But if in the interval Italy
comes in against us with another one hundred
submarines, we may be strained to breaking
point.
Secondly, we want several hundred of the
latest types of aircraft, of which you are

now getting delivery. These can be repaid
by those now being constructed in the United
States for us.
Thirdly, anti-aircraft equipment and
ammunition, of which again there will be
plenty next year, if we are alive to see it.
Fourthly, the fact that our ore supply is
being compromised from Sweden, from North
Africa, and perhaps from northern Spain, makes
it necessary to purchase steel in the United
States. This also applies to other materials.
We shall go on paying dollars for as long as
we can, but I should like to feel reasonably
sure that when we can pay no more, you will
give us the stuff all the same.
Fifthly, we have many reports of possible
German parachute or air borne descents in
Ireland. The visit of a United States
squadron to Irish ports, which might well be
prolonged, would be invaluable.
Sixthly, I am looking to you to keep that
Japanese dog quiet in the Pacific, using
Singapore in any way convenient. The details
of the material which we have in mind will be
communicated to you separately.
With all good wishes and respect.
    WSC

MOST SECRET AND PERSONAL

Woodring passed the message to Edison, who in turned read it and passed it across to Hull. The Secretary of State took a quick look to confirm that it was the same message he had seen yesterday, and then he handed it back to the President.

"Does his message change your opinion?" asked President Roosevelt.

"No, sir," responded Secretary of War Woodring without hesitation. "It reinforces my argument. They are desperate."

"Perhaps so," Roosevelt answered in a rare, subdued and muffled voice.

"If we respond to Churchill's request with anything like the materiel he suggests, we will prolong our preparation time and would most likely antagonize the Germans, bringing us even closer to war with them."

The President nodded to Edison.

"As you know, Mister President, we have begun activating the mothballed, World War I, flush deck, four stacker, Wickes-class destroyers for our use. Even with passage of the naval rearmament bill now before Congress, it will take us several years at least to modernize our escort fleet and build the capital ships necessary should war arrive at our shores. I am afraid we cannot spare any of those old destroyers."

"Nor the aircraft and ammunition he requests," added Woodring.

"Do you have anything to add, Cordell?"

"I will simply complement Secretary Woodring's assessment with respect to the antagonism of the Germans should we decide to resupply the British, especially in the quantities requested."

Roosevelt stared into the distance as he considered his words. "As you know, I speak to a joint session of Congress tomorrow, to present our request for the largest increase in defense spending in our history. Our work with Congress suggests we shall obtain the funds we are requesting. I trust both of you are prepared for the flood tide that is nearly upon us."

"Yes, sir," both Woodring and Edison offered in unison.

President Roosevelt glanced at each minister, and then over his shoulder at Harry Hopkins, who nodded once to the President. "I would like each of you to quickly study the British request in this message," he said as he help up Prime Minister Churchill's latest communiqué, "and provide your considered recommendations. Further and in conjunction with your feasibility study, I would also like to see your plans for execution of Churchill's request as quickly as humanly possible." The President again connected with each set of eyes to convey his earnestness. "Any questions?"

"No, sir," they answered in unison.

"Very well, then. Have a good day, gentlemen," President Roosevelt said concluding his defense staff meeting. He wheeled himself back to the large, dark, mahogany desk, as the three secretaries departed. The President shuffled some papers on his desk until the door closed and he was alone with Harry Hopkins. "What did you think, Harry."

"They stayed true to form."

"Yes, they did. I cannot sugar coat my serious apprehension regarding the viability of the British. From what we see, the French are finished. It is only a matter of time, and there is nothing we can do in any timely or mean-ingful manner. I do not share Joe Kennedy's defeatist perspective, however."

"I am not so sure it is defeatist, Franklin. He has been anti-British and pro-German for quite some time . . . largely his Irish heritage, I suppose."

"Regardless, I need to know what the real situation is and more impor-tantly what the prognosis is for the British. Given Hitler's professed and now proven megalomaniacal appetite, I cannot see how we can avoid this war and stop him. Without England, taking on the Germans on a subdued continent would be monumentally more difficult and consuming."

"Quite so, I should think."

"We need an independent and reliable assessment upon which to make our decision whether we can afford the risk of resupplying the British. Depleting our stores is not the answer either."

"No."

"Why don't you poke around and see if you can find a capable and trustworthy agent for such an assessment. It is at moments like this I am so damn frustrated with this juvenile in-fighting and paucity of coordination among our disparate intelligence agencies. We need a master like the British MI-6 organization."

"I will as quietly as possible," Hopkins acknowledged. "No need to poke the hornet's nest at this critical juncture." He looked at Roosevelt, who did not look up from the papers on his desk. "Is there anything else, Franklin?"

"No, Harry. Thank you for your contributions."

Harry Hopkins left the Oval Office and closed the door behind him.

—

Saturday, 18.May.1940
No.10 Downing Street
Whitehall, London, England
10:30 hours

The three military chiefs of staff along with General Ismay stood quietly in the Prime Minster's conference room adjacent to his study on the ground floor. Prime Minster Churchill joined them and motioned for them to be seated.

"I asked for this meeting to discuss your military perspective regarding the proposed technical exchange with the Americans. However, before we get to that topic, I would like a brief update on the situation in France."

General Ironside began, "Lord Gort has initiated a counter-attack this morning against the extended supply lines behind the German armor vanguard.

He has tried to coordinate his action with General Gamelin for a comparable attack from the south by the French; however, communications between north and south are fragmentary at best."

The Prime Minister interjected, "I shall report to the War Cabinet this afternoon on my journey to Paris. Suffice it to say, the French government seems even less organized than General Gamelin." Churchill nodded to Air Chief Marshal Newall.

"Air Marshal Barratt's air forces are hard pressed. They spend more time defending themselves than they are able to support Lord Gort's ground forces. I suppose the positive side is, at least we are keeping the Germans occupied."

"Not enough, I'm afraid," interjected General Ironside.

Sir Cyril nodded slightly to acknowledge Sir Edmund's poke. "We are flying air cover over the beaches to relieve Barratt's forces from that duty. Neither the Hurricane or Spitfire fighters have sufficient combat endurance over the Continent, which in turn is stretching our home defense forces quite thin as well."

Prime Minister Churchill impatiently nodded to his First Sea Lord. "We continue to move merchants through the Channel. The Germans have been fairly well occupied from the Navy's viewpoint. We have dealt with an occasional marauding fighter's cannon fire, but nothing serious so far. We have not yet detected any immediate threat from German warships or E-boats, and the U-boats have remained clear of the Channel approaches both east and west, presumably as a consequence of our enhanced patrols."

"Very well." Winston again displayed his impatience. "I have a full diary today, and I am afraid we must move on. As I indicated earlier, I want your personal counsel before this afternoon's War Cabinet meeting. What are your positions regarding the technical exchange program?"

Sir Dudley responded first this time. "The Navy's principal concern in this question sprouts from our worry about compromise of critical technology like the underwater sounding equipment and the electronic range finder development. The Americans are not always careful with highly sensitive information, or they have been penetrated by *Abwehr* agents," he said, referring to the German military intelligence apparatus.

"That is a valid concern," Churchill acknowledged.

"Beyond these concerns, I would say the Navy is in a somewhat neutral position. We see positives as well as negatives, being in roughly equal proportion."

Sir Cyril picked up when the First Sea Lord stopped. "The ingenious cavity magnetron is the heart of the Chain Home radio direction and ranging system that is so vital to our air defense system. We are reluctant to share that technology, however, the Americans are accomplished engineers at transforming technology into usable equipment of adequate size. We have struggled to miniaturize the RDF equipment into an airborne unit. When the air battle comes, we expect to dominate the daylight hours, which will in turn force the *Luftwaffe* into night bombing. All of our night intercept experiments have been far less than satisfactory. We are vulnerable at night. The Oslo Report and other intelligence indicate the Germans have been working on an electronic night and all-weather aiming system that they may have perfected by now. We need an RDF unit that can be operated effectively on a night fighter. Our engineers will solve the problem eventually, but the Americans might well produce a usable airborne unit faster and produce them in far greater quantity than we would be able to do. We need the Americans, I'm afraid."

"That very well may be, but the risk is simply too great," Sir Edmund interjected rather gruffly. "The Army is simply opposed to such an exchange with the Americans. As we bear witness on the Continent, our fight with the Germans will be a close run thing at best. We simply cannot afford to take the risk of exposure to our vital technical advantage."

"To further your rather pessimistic view, Sir Edmund," said Churchill, "what if we are overrun like the Poles, Danes, Norwegians, Dutch and Belgians? They will have our technology without our consent."

"Surely you are not suggesting we are defeated," responded Sir Edmund.

"No! Wouldn't the sharing of our technology with the Americans be something of an insurance policy should the unthinkable happen?"

"Perhaps so," answered General Ironside. "However, the Army is still against the technical exchange."

"Pug, do you have anything to add?"

"No, sir," answered General Ismay.

"Anything else?"

"Yes, sir," Sir Cyril answered. "We cannot overstate our desire for access to the Norden bombsight. The American bomb aiming system has repeatedly demonstrated accuracy far superior to any other aiming system we have or are aware of, quite frankly. If we must give up our technology to gain access to that device, it would be well worth the price."

"You cannot be serious," growled General Sir Edmund Ironside.

"I most assuredly am . . . stone cold serious, I must say. The bomber is going to feature heavily in this war. That bombsight may well be the decisive edge for our bombing campaign."

"As you know, Sir Cyril, the Americans have not been particularly eager to share that device or the engineering in it. Would it not be very costly for us to refit our bombers, even if we did get it?"

"Unbeknownst to many, Prime Minister, for several years now, our bomber specifications have all contained provisions for the Norden bombsight – space, mounting, power and such. The Americans have at least allowed us that information . . . presumably in anticipation of the future."

"Well done, Sir Cyril," said Churchill. "The Norden sight shall be at the top of our list should the technical exchange be approved by the War Cabinet." The Prime Minister searched each man's eyes. "Once again, anything else I should know on your behalf?" He waited a few seconds, scanned each man again, and then said, "No? Then, we are adjourned. Thank you, gentlemen." Prime Minister Churchill rose and left the room promptly.

—

Saturday, 18.May.1940
Cabinet Room
No.10 Downing Street
Whitehall, London, England
17:00 hours

"**I** thought I would begin today's meeting with a brief report on my mission to Paris," began Prime Minister Churchill to the assembled War Cabinet. "I can probably sum up the situation with one sentence. Premier Reynaud is despondent and the military command structure is disorganized." He paused for emphasis. "The French are like a powerful but rudderless battleship. The military resources of the great country are being squandered, and we appear to be powerless to stop it. I asked General Gamelin just yesterday, '*Où est la masse de manœuvre?*'" he said in the original language. "His answer was, '*Aucune.*' None. Gentlemen, they have no reserves. I find this entire situation absolutely incredible." He paused again this time to consider his own words. "Mind you, I will not rest until we have turned the situation around. The combined strength of the British and French forces can defeat the Nawzees."

"Prime Minister, have you seen the latest reports from France?"

"Yes. 'C' has given me a quick briefing earlier this afternoon. The Dutch capitulation three days ago added to the abysmal condition of *le Armée de Terre* made for a rather unpleasant picture. The situation does look bleak, however it is not irretrievably lost. I intend to continue my efforts to support Premier Reynaud and his government."

"If I may, Prime Minster," said Air Chief Marshal Newall. He waited for recognition and a nod from the PM. "Have you received Dowding's letter?"

"Yes, and I have read it with dismay."

"Nonetheless, Prime Minister, we must husband our scant resources in anticipation of the onslaught that will surely follow the debacle on the Continent."

"You may very well be correct, Sir Cyril, however, I, for one, am not ready to concede defeat." Newall started to respond but stopped when Churchill held up his right hand. "You will have your time. We will discuss Dowding's letter, and I noticed he is waiting in the anteroom, presumably to address the War Cabinet on this issue." Newall nodded. "Good, then we will address it then. First, we must dispense with today's order of business. I have taken the liberty to ask 'C' for an abbreviated version of his situation report. If you will, 'C?'"

The Chief of MI6 rose from his peripheral seat to stand at the podium at the far end of the room from the prime minister. The intelligence briefing portrayed a broad overview of the military conditions in the Low Countries and Northeast France. He made no reference to or indication of Hitler's Directive No.11, nor any other information derived solely from ULTRA.

A lively discussion ensued over conflicting information from the combat area. Some felt the situation was recoverable with reinforcement, mainly fighter cover to protect the bombers that could stop the Panzer assault. Churchill listened carefully to the words, mood, intensity and confidence of the various participants. There was no question in his mind that the conditions in France were desperate, and the only hope of reducing the combat burden on the BEF was through stiffening the French government and military. The majority of the War Cabinet advocated the defense of Great Britain being executed in France and Belgium. The situation in Holland, especially in light of the imminent execution of Hitler's Directive No.11, was virtually unrecoverable. The Allies needed to concentrate on that which they could affect.

Churchill became impatient with the lack of closure to the discussion. "Other than reinforcement of the BEF, are there any other items requiring our immediate attention?" he asked.

The usual dispensing of logistics, production and routine Royal Navy deployments took twenty minutes, less than previous times. The assembled group seemed to be equally impatient in anticipation of the reinforcement question.

"With that," said Churchill, "let us proceed to the issue of reinforcement. The most immediate action relates to the request for ten additional fighter squadrons. As most of you know, we have received requests from Lord Gort and Air Marshall Barratt. I believe their requests are valid and warranted. I am inclined to honor these requests."

"With all due respect, Prime Minister," began Newall with a calm, cool, confident voice, "as you may know, in the early hours of yesterday, General Billotte, commanding the French Army Group One, telephoned Air Marshal Barratt and literally begged for an air attack on the bridges across the River Meuse. Yesterday afternoon, the Advanced Air Striking Force launched every aeroplane that could fly. The ensuing engagement was a fiasco and a massacre of high order. It was the heaviest loss in any operation of similar size ever experienced by the RAF, and all that was achieved was the temporary damaging of two of the six pontoon bridges. This incident is indicative of the situation we face."

"Are you prepared to abandon our boys on the continent, Sir Cyril?" asked General Ironside.

"No. I am not suggesting we should withdraw. It is possible I suppose that the situation is recoverable, although I must add, the picture is not particularly bright at the moment. What I am suggesting is that conditions in France are likely to deteriorate further. Throwing more men and our precious few fighters into the breach may not stem the tide."

"I'll be damned to hell, if I will agree to that," said General Ironside.

"The situation is grave, I will agree. However, it is possible with fortitude and conviction to hold the line," offered Winston.

"That very well may be, Prime Minister, however we should weigh the total consequences of any action we consider now, against the potential for the critical defense of the Home Islands in the not too distant future," responded Newall.

"If we lose in France, we should nearly guarantee the prospects of invasion," barked General Ironside.

"Invasion is not a foregone conclusion," interjected the First Sea Lord. "The Royal Navy shall see to that."

"Gentlemen, please, let us come back to Lord Gort's request," Churchill said. "Furthermore, I would like to remind everyone, I have promised Premier Reynaud just yesterday the ten additional fighter squadrons, contingent upon War Cabinet approval. Now, I would like to address Dowding's letter and hear what he has to say. Has everyone had the opportunity to read the letter?" Several people shook their heads. Churchill motioned for the Cabinet Secretary, Sir Edward Bridges, to distribute copies of the letter to the ministers.

**HEADQUARTERS, FIGHTER COMMAND
ROYAL AIR FORCE,**

BENTLEY PRIORY, STANMORE, MIDDLESEX

Telephone Nos.: BUSHEY HEATH 1661 (6 lines)

BUSHEY HEATH 1646 (4 lines).

Telegraphic Address: "AIRGENARCH STANMORE."

Reference: -- FC/S.19048

SECRET

16th May, 1940.

The Under Secretary of State,
Air Ministry
LONDON, W.C.2.

Sir,

1. I have the honour to refer to the very serious calls which have recently been made upon the Home Defence Fighter Units in an attempt to stem the German invasion on the Continent.

2. I hope and believe that our Armies may yet be victorious in France and Belgium, but we have to face the possibility that they may be defeated.

3. In this case I presume that there is no-one who will deny that England should fight on, even though the remainder of the Continent of Europe is dominated by the Germans.

4. For this purpose it is necessary to retain some minimum fighter strength in this country and I must request that the Air Council will inform me what they consider this minimum strength to be, in order that I make my dispositions accordingly.

5. I would remind the Air Council that
the last estimate which they made as to the
force necessary to defend this country was
52 Squadrons, and my strength has now been
reduced to the equivalent of 36 Squadrons.

6. Once a decision has been reached as to
the limit on which the Air Council and the
Cabinet are prepared to stake the existence
of the country, it should be made clear
to the Allied Commanders on the Continent
that not a single aeroplane from Fighter
Command beyond the limit will be sent across
the Channel, no matter how desperate the
situation may become.

7. It will, of course, be remembered that
the estimate of 52 Squadrons was based on
the assumption that the attack would come
from the eastwards except in so far as the
defences might be outflanked in flight. We
have now to face the possibility that attacks
may come from Spain or even from the North
coast of France. The result is that our line
is very much extended at the same time as our
resources are reduced.

8. I must point out that within the last
few days the equivalent of 10 Squadrons have
been sent to France, that the Hurricane
Squadrons remaining in this country are
seriously depleted, and that the more
Squadrons which are sent to France the higher
will be the wastage and the more insistent
the demands for reinforcements.

9. I must therefore request that as a
matter of paramount urgency the Air Ministry
will consider and decide what level of
strength is to be left to the Fighter Command
for the defences of this country, and will
assure me that when this level has been
reached, not one fighter will be sent across

the Channel however urgent and insistent the
appeals for help may be.

    10. I believe that, if an adequate fighter
force is kept in this country, if the fleet
remains in being, and if Home Forces are
suitably organised to resist invasion, we
should be able to carry on the war single
handed for some time, if not indefinitely.
But, if the Home Defence Force is drained
away in desperate attempts to remedy the
situation in France, defeat in France will
involve the final, complete and irremediable
defeat of this country.

    I have the honour to be,

    Sir,

    Your obedient Servant,

H.C.T. Dowding
Air Chief Marshal,
Air Officer Commanding-in-Chief
Fighter Command, Royal Air Force.

SECRET

"Sir Cyril, do you have any preparatory remarks before we invite Sir Hugh to join us?" asked Churchill.

"I believe I have had my say, Prime Minister."

"Very well, please invite Dowding to join us, if you will," Winston said to the Cabinet Secretary.

Air Chief Marshal Sir Hugh Dowding, Air Officer Command-ing-in-Chief, Fighter Command, entered the Cabinet Room with Group Cap-tain John Spencer, Staff Secretary, Fighter Command. Both men appeared to be quite at ease in the exalted surroundings. Churchill always admired his nephew, his accomplishments as a fighter pilot in the Great War of 1914 and his cool presence. The younger officer set up an easel adjacent to the speaker's podium and placed a covered board in the holder. Both men began to sit in the open chairs next to the podium.

"Marshal Dowding," Churchill said, "we have distributed copies of your most recent letter to the Deputy Minister for Air. The question before the War Cabinet is Lord Gort's request on behalf of the BEF and *le Armée de Terre* for ten additional fighter squadrons. You have the floor"

"Very well, sir." Dowding moved to the podium. "My letter, I believe, states a simple, cogent, succinct position regarding further depletion of our fighter resources in France. I remain gravely concerned about our ability to defend the Home Islands against a concerted air assault by the *Luftwaffe* even if we send no reinforcements."

"I am afraid, Marshal Dowding," began Lord Halifax, "some of us are not able to see the problem from your perspective. If you would be so kind, please give us the facts that substantiate your concern."

Dowding nodded to Group Captain Spencer, who in turn, lifted the cover from the chart board. "We have plotted our losses of both fighters and pilots since war was declared. Fighter losses are represented by the blue line. Pilot losses are the red line. Our fighter production in green." He paused to let the audience absorb the implications of the chart. "As you will note, our loss rate since the beginning of the Battle of France is precipitous. If we continue to sustain these losses, within ten days, there will not be a single Hurricane left, either in France or in England. Fighter Command will be rendered ineffective in," he moved the pointer across the chart to the blue line, and then down to the date line, "about a fortnight." Not a whisper of sound could be heard in the Cabinet Room. Dowding traced another line across to the red line. "Our pilot resources will reach the critical level in little more than a week." Again, he paused to let reality sink into his audience. "These losses are the core of my concern."

The assemblage of nearly thirty men, the political and military leadership of the United Kingdom, sat motionless and shocked silence. Winston Churchill, one of the most positive and optimistic among the group, recognized the staggering message in Dowding's chart. He now understood why his head of the RAF Fighter Command chose to take the extraordinary step of writing such a strong, blunt letter. His level of respect for the stoic Dowding increased substantially at that moment.

The Prime Minister was the first to speak. "Lord Beaverbrook," he addressed the newly appointed Minister of Aircraft Production, the former William Maxwell Aitken, the first Baron Beaverbrook, and his friend of many years, "do you agree with Marshal Dowding's aircraft production figures?" Churchill glanced to Dowding to ascertain whether any offense may have been taken. The Chief of Fighter Command remained unruffled.

Lord Beaverbrook did not hesitate with his response. "Marshal Dowding's production figures reflect the current output of all fighter aircraft.

However, they do not include Spitfire production from Castle Bromwich. We are redoubling our efforts to bring Castle Bromwich to rate production as soon as humanly possible. The objective given to Vickers Supermarine is to double the current rate by the end of June."

Numerous heads returned to Dowding's chart. Churchill mentally calculated the effect of the increased production levels. He arrived at the obvious conclusion. Even if production of all fighter plants doubled instantly, the added numbers would only extend the point of criticality by maybe a week or two. "Sir Cyril, do you have a view of the pilot training rate?"

Newall agreed with Dowding's information and took the opportunity to establish a clear position relative to the unique qualities required of a fighter pilot and the barely adequate current level of training. Sir Cyril's statement sparked a discussion around the pilot supply process from duration to quality and selection. A variety of points of view as well as several rather strong reactions gushed forth. The interchange among the military officers was informative, but in the end, did not offer a clear picture or sense of direction.

The Prime Minister held up his hand again. Silence took a few moments to be achieved. "I suspect this lofty subject is ripe for further debate." Several politicians laughed while none of the military officers saw the humor. "Now is not the time. Sir Edmund, as Chief of the Imperial General Staff, and in association with Sir Cyril, I trust you will ensure a proper evaluation and implementation of the most aggressive, practical pilot training program."

"Yes, indeed, Prime Minister."

"Good. Now, back to Marshal Dowding's chart. You make a compelling argument, but how can you be so sure the line of defense should not be in France instead of Britain."

Dowding contemplated the question for a few moments as most of the audience was undoubtedly doing as well. "There is no surety in warfare as you well know, Prime Minister. Based on German progress and Allied losses in the first seven days of combat, it is certainly my opinion that further wastage in France will only move toward assurance of our own defeat. Air defense over the Home Islands would give us the maximum advantage possible under these conditions. It is my adamant belief our only hope of defending these islands against the Nazi war machine lies in a vital and durable air defense system. I must have at least fifty, fully functional fighter squadrons to have any hope of defense against a concentrated air assault."

The words sank in like a prisoner watching the hangman reach for the trap door lever. Churchill felt a strange, repulsive nausea he had not experienced since his days in the soggy, fatal trenches of the Somme with the Lancaster

Grenadiers before being appointed by General Sir Douglas Haig to command the Sixth Royal Scots Fusiliers near Armentiéres. Winston Churchill once felt the futility of wasted youth. "What about my promise to Premier Reynaud of ten more squadrons?" asked Churchill, not knowing whether Dowding was aware of his verbal commitment to the French.

Air Chief Marshal Dowding looked directly into the Prime Minister's eyes and did not blink. "If you are asking my opinion, Prime Minister," he paused to receive an affirmative nod from Churchill, "I would respectfully suggest you call Premier Reynaud and tell him we cannot spare one more fighter aeroplane."

"Dowding, you are quite out of line," snapped General Ironside.

Sir Cyril Newall sensed his fighter leader's vulnerability. "Maybe, but he is not wrong."

"Damn you, Cyril," snapped Ironside back at his colleague.

Churchill held up his right hand once again. "I take no offense, General Ironside. I did ask our chief of fighters his opinion. Sir Hugh, I commend you in this not so public forum for your courage, forthrightness and integrity. While I do not agree, I believe you have offered sound advice. Is there any other discussion?"

Several people in the room must have sensed the history that was being made in the Cabinet Conference Room of No.10 Downing Street, this afternoon. Questions, answers and debate continued for another twenty minutes until the same arguments arose. The tension in the room among the professional politicians, diplomats and military leaders was undeniable. The outcome was not.

"Sir Cyril," interjected the Prime Minister, "I offer you concluding remarks."

"I do not believe that to throw in a few more squadrons whose loss might vitally weaken the fighter line at home would make the difference between victory and defeat in France. It can, however, be said with absolute certainty that while the collapse of France would not necessarily mean the ultimate victory of Germany, the collapse of Great Britain would inevitably do so," concluded the Chief of the Air Staff.

"Any more discussion?" the Prime Minister looked into each set of eyes to receive his answer. "Then, so be it. We will not transfer any additional fighter aircraft to France. As we discussed yesterday, the Admiralty is directed to prepare a general evacuation plan for the remainder of the BEF from any available Channel port. The execution date shall be held in abeyance for the moment. The War Office shall cable Lord Gort requesting he consider strongly the withdrawal of his forces from the port of Dunkirk. I shall go to Paris tomorrow to present our position to Paul Reynaud," he paused to allow for any objections. There were none. "I had hoped to discuss the technical exchange program proposal, but it shall have to wait. We have other more pressing matters to be dealt with at the moment. Sir Edward, please ensure the technical exchange program is on the agenda for our next meeting. We are adjourned, gentlemen," commanded the Prime Minister without asking if the meeting was truly concluded. As the assemblage made their way out of the large room, Churchill turned to his staff secretary, "Please find Bill Stephenson and ask him to come immediately."

As his request was being carried out, Winston dictated a quick, succinct note to the President of the United States. The message was typed and edited twice before 'Intrepid' arrived at No.10 Downing Street. The two friends met again in the Prime Minister's private office.

"Bill, I am afraid I must ask you to make another trip to America immediately. I am still not fully confident in the security of our communications system and Franklin must have this message as soon as possible." Winston handed the open, single piece of paper to Stephenson.

MOST SECRET AND PERSONAL

```
37


18.V.40
TO: POTUS
THE SCENE HAS DARKENED SWIFTLY.  THE SITUATION
IN THE LOW COUNTRIES AND FRANCE CONTINUES TO
DETERIORATE.  I MUST EMPHASISE AND REINFORCE
THE URGENCY OF THE REQUEST IN MY PRIOR MESSAGE
OF THE 15TH OF MAY.  I SHALL BE OFF TO FRANCE
TOMORROW IN MY PERSISTENT EFFORTS TO BOLSTER
THE FRENCH DEFENCE.  YOUR TIMELY RESPONSE
REMAINS VITAL TO THE SITUATION.  THANK YOU IN
ADVANCE FROM THE BOTTOM OF MY HEART, ON BEHALF
OF A GRATEFUL NATION, FOR YOUR CONTINUED
SUPPORT.
```

SIGNED,
FORMER NAVAL PERSON

MOST SECRET AND PERSONAL

"Is it really this bad?"

"Yes, and possibly worse. We must prepare ourselves for what is about to happen, and probably more importantly, we must prepare the Americans. They may be our only hope."

"Were you able to decide on the technical exchange program?"

"No, we did not get that far. The Chiefs are divided, and we have not yet received the position studies from the defense ministries. I directed Ed to place the program issue on the next War Cabinet agenda, but I suspect the swiftness of events on the Continent may delay that discussion further."

"Lord Lothian is certain the time is ripe with the Americans."

"Indeed."

"What is the likelihood of invasion?"

"Regrettably, I dare say it is approaching inevitable. It is far from clear whether the French will summon up the mustard to stop the Germans. The BEF is of insufficient size to thwart the assault, and the War Cabinet just now decided to withhold sending more fighter squadrons to France."

"Dear God!"

"Quite so, I'm afraid. Our singular focus will soon fall upon evacuation of as much of the BEF as we are able before the Germans overwhelm all the ports and beaches on the coast. Then, we must gird ourselves for the German invasion sure to come. The Nawzees cannot rest with a free and combative England." Churchill stared at the portrait of his late father – Lord Randolph Churchill – on the far wall. He could only imagine what his father might think of their current predicament. "That said, please convey to Lord Lothian, I am not yet convinced we can afford the risk of potential exposure of our most vital technical advances given our rather precarious position."

"I might say, Winston, perhaps we cannot afford to abandon such an exchange. It would certainly show our good faith commitment to U.S. security and our enduring alliance."

"Yes, of course. I am inclined to agree; however, I need the War Cabinet including myself to be convinced beyond any reasonable doubt."

Stephenson looked at his wristwatch. "I'm afraid I must be on my way, Winston. I have an early morning flying boat journey back to New York leaving from Liverpool. Do you have anything else for me?"

"No, Bill. You are a godsend. I know you are doing your utmost to bring the Americans along. We need them to beat these bastards."

"Thank you, Winston. The pleasure of service is mine."

"Please give my regards to Mary."

"I will."

"Godspeed and following winds, my friend."

"Thank you, Winston. And, good luck to you in the coming weeks."

Stephenson left the Prime Minister alone as he departed and closed the study door behind him.

—

Sunday, 19.May.1940
RAF Drem
Drem, Lothian, Scotland

"Looks like we're going to get into it, now," said Brian.

"I should say," answered Jonathan.

Brian thought about what the move to RAF Northolt meant to all of them. Until now, they had faced only bombers without fighter escort. While heavily armed, the bombers were vulnerable especially in the small numbers the Germans had been sending against the North. They all knew those days would probably end with their movement south to one of the airfields near London.

Brian remembered his mentor and preeminent flight instructor, Malcolm Bainbridge, telling him that the realization of one's dream did not always bring happiness. He had been playing at aerial combat for more than two years. The early experience with Malcolm in the Stearman over Kansas bore no resemblance to the high-speed flashes, to the heavy weight of 'g' forces pulling blood from his brain, and to the lethal hail of bullets of an aerial enfilade of modern bombers. The squadron had practiced against themselves and other fighters, Hurricanes and Spitfires, but none of them shot back. From now on, their business would become something other than sport. They would be hunted as they had hunted the German bombers among the clouds.

Brian looked around to see if anyone was within earshot as they continued to pack their belongings. "Are you scared, Jonathan?" he asked in a near whisper.

"Sure, I am. Aren't you?"

"Yeah, it's really strange."

"How so?"

"I've dreamed of flying the fastest airplanes in a grand event since I first held a stick in my hands. I marveled at Malcolm's stories of dogfights over

France. I learned from him. The more I learned, the more I wanted it. Now, here I am, I've got one victory, you have two, and we are about to jump into our own dogfights with German fighters over France. It all seems so strange."

"I think I can understand what you mean."

"If you think about it, I learned to fly from a man, an American, who flew with the British over France in 1915, and here I am, an American, flying with the British over France in 1940. Twenty-five years, that's all that's changed."

"The aeroplanes have changed."

Brian laughed which triggered Jonathan as well. "You bet, twenty-five years and two hundred miles an hour." Brian Drummond returned quickly to his contemplative state. "I've dreamed of this. I've got it in hand, and it's almost too hot to hold onto."

"For me, it is not quite the same, but I know what you mean." They both fell silent, lost in their thoughts for a few minutes. "I just love flying. Flying fighters has been the most fun."

"Have you ever thought about being killed?"

"I suppose, but it does not last long."

"I crashed once, flying one of Malcolm's airplanes . . . right wheel hit a dog. Destroyed the machine, but I never thought much of it, well maybe a little. Everyone else was scared to death. My girlfriend at the time, Becky, was screaming at Malcolm that he was trying to kill me. Malcolm got me back in the air immediately. I never thought I might be killed." Contemplation filled the room, again. "I still don't think I'm going to be killed. I think I'm more afraid of why I'm not afraid of being killed."

"Strange logic, Brian."

'Boxer' Stockard and 'Angle' Ashcroft entered the pilots' quarters. The conversation between the two friends stopped. It did not end. It just stopped. Pilots did not talk about feelings or thoughts of their own mortality. They only talked about flying or women. The subjects contracted to one with any female in the vicinity.

"Are you two about ready?" poked 'Boxer' Stockard. "Bags go on the lorry outside. Skipper wants to take-off in about an hour. By the way 'Hunter,' I picked up this letter for you from the mail clark. It appears to be from your embassy in London. Important, I should think."

Brian sensed it was one more attempt to get him back to the United States, maybe even confirmation of his imminent extradition. He did not want to read the letter, so he slid it into the inside pocket of his uniform tunic. He decided to delay the depressing news until after they arrived at RAF Northolt.

Being closer to John Spencer would make any counteraction easier to deal with. "We're ready," responded Brian as he closed his duffel bag.

"Aren't you going to read such an important letter?" asked Stockard.

"Not now," responded Brian.

Roland Stockard stood in front of them with an expression of surprise. Either he wanted to know what was in the letter, or he could not believe anyone would ignore a letter from one's embassy.

"'Hunter,'" shouted 'Jackstay' Beamish as he entered the room as well. "Rather smart dolly bird askin' for you outside."

Brian instantly thought of Anne Booth and wondered why she would be in Edinburgh. There was an excitement of anticipation since he had not been able to see her the last time he was in London. Maybe she heard from Jeremy about him being at Shepherds and decided to come up to Scotland to see him? Maybe she was worried about him?

Rosemary Alice Kensington did not wait for Brian to descend the two steps in front of the pilot quarters. The flurry of her golden mane and the penetration of her blue eyes made her lunge seem like a starving, crazed animal. She leapt into his arms, which instinctively wrapped around her. The press of her small but hard breasts against his chest reminded him instantly of their nights of exploration at Carlingon Castle. Her kiss was full and deep with her tongue darting into him like a snake.

"Rosemary," shouted Jonathan incredulously. The challenge did not stop his sister although Brian felt the rush of growing embarrassment. "What are you doing here?" her brother persisted.

The disengagement of the two lovers took several more long seconds. "Hello, Jon," she said finally without taking her eyes away from Brian."

"So?"

"I'm on break. Mum told me they were sending you south, and I thought I should say good-bye properly."

"That is one hell of a good-bye," observed 'Jackstay' Beamish. A small audience had gathered behind them although Brian could only sense their presence. He found himself locked into her gaze, riveted by the probing of her cool, blue eyes.

"Damn, Rosemary. This is embarrassing and most improper."

"I don't know, laddie. I'd say, 'Hunter' here should consider himself lucky," laughed Beamish.

While still looking deep into Brian's eyes, Rosemary Kensington said, "Aren't you going to introduce me to your mates?"

"If you will let go of Brian for a moment, I will." Jonathan waited for his sister to break eye contact with Brian and look at him. "Thank you."

The introductions and related conversation took several minutes as Brian danced around like he needed to urinate, and the others absorbed and appreciated Rosemary Kensington's plain and simple beauty. She did have a distinct comfort and confidence around men that added to Brian's uneasiness and embarrassment. He was glad to feel the touch of an attractive woman, but not in front of his fellow pilots.

'Jackstay' Beamish chose the opportunity to expound on the accomplishments and mythology of 'Hunter' Drummond including the genesis of his callsign. Rosemary seemed thoroughly intrigued by the stories and information encouraging more from the clutch of blue uniforms around her.

"Pilots to the flight line," shouted one of the sergeants from several buildings distance.

The other pilots took the cue each shaking hands with Rosemary Kensington as they departed. She hugged her brother and gave him a kiss on the cheek. "Please be careful, Jon."

"I will, Rose. Let's go, Brian," he said trying to avoid another embarrassing joining between his sister and best friend. His effort was to no avail.

Rosemary Kensington practically wrapped herself around Brian once more and kissed him deeply. This time he looked to Jonathan saying with his eyes, what am I supposed to do? She stopped to whisper in his ear. "I want you right now, Brian. I want to feel you inside me, but I know you must go." A flood of hot lava burned Brian from within, as small beads of sweat descended along his covered skin. Rosemary noticed immediately the affect her words had on him. She drew back just far enough to look into his eyes. The enormous, full bloom, smile and the satisfaction in her eyes told the whole story. She leaned forward to his ear, again. "That's my boy. I will never forgive you if anything should happen to your beautiful body, so be safe. I want to enjoy all of you the next time we meet."

"Dear God, Rosemary. Let the poor man go. We must man our aeroplanes."

Rosemary Kensington finally released him. The lump in Brian's throat nearly choked off his air. The two young pilots walked toward the flight line and their waiting aircraft. Several times before they turned between two buildings Brian looked over his shoulder to see Rosemary standing where he left her. The smile and wave accentuated the attraction that tugged at him.

Jonathan's PR-K Spitfire came into view. "You are bonking my sister, aren't you?"

Brian stopped and stared at Jonathan. His mouth fell open, as he tried to respond, but no words came out. He wanted to tell him but could not bring himself to do it.

"Right, you two," shouted Flight Lieutenant 'Sparky' Morrow, "the skipper told us to mount up. Let's knock off the gab and get to it."

Seeing Leading Aircraftman Gordon and his PR-F aircraft separated Brian from the confrontation. As he strapped into the seat, he closed off the subject by committing himself to telling Jonathan when they arrived at Northolt, what had happened with his sister. The instruments and switches focused in attention.

The flight south was flown at altitude and moderate cruise speed to lessen the strain on the engines and save fuel should they become engaged in air combat while en route. The activity at RAF Northolt possessed an odd frenetic energy and edge to it as they parked their fighters, found their new Dispersal building and completed the process of settling into the rhythm of the airfield. Once their professional tasks were completed, they moved to the Officer's Mess and received their room assignments.

In a lull before the evening meal and the inevitable bar time, Brian remembered the damnable letter from the embassy. Ignoring the message could compound his problem. Reluctantly, Brian retrieved the letter from his tunic and opened it. Even the letterhead looked ominous.

The White House
Washington, DC

April 2, 1940

```
To:  Mr. Brian A. Drummond
No.609 Squadron
Fighter Command, Royal Air Force
RAF Drem
Drem, Lothian, Scotland, United Kingdom
c/o:  The United States Embassy
London, England, United Kingdom


Dear Mr. Drummond:


By order of the President of the United
States, you are hereby granted a full and
```

absolute pardon from prosecution under the provisions of the Neutrality Act. You retain full rights and privileges of United States citizenship. Any legal action, past, present or future, against you under the Neutrality Act is hereby declared null and void.

Please retain this letter in your personal records. Should any necessity arise regarding this pardon, please contact the Office of the Attorney General, Department of Justice, Washington, DC.

The President wishes you the best of luck in your perilous endeavor in hopes you will be able to return home as soon as possible.

By order of the
President of the United States of America
Franklin D. Roosevelt

Brian sat at the desk in his room nearly in shock. The questions came to him faster than he could consider possible answers. He wondered about who, how and why he had become so fortunate to have the threat of criminal prosecution removed from over his head. He did not know whom to thank other than the President.

"At least that bastard Slaughter won't bother me anymore," Brian said aloud before he walked down the hall to Jonathan's room.

He showed his best friend the letter.

"Bloody hell, Brian. This is from the bloody president of the bloody great United States of bloody America."

Brian bounced up and down, like a crazy cartoon character.

The relief gave Brian a welcomed sense of renewal and hope, as well as an energizing commitment to his dream. He knew there was nothing that could stand in his way. Brian and Jonathan joined the others at the evening meal with a great smile on their faces, each for different reasons.

The men and women of No.609 (West Riding of Yorkshire) Squadron were now part of No.11 Group under the command of Air Vice-Marshal

Park, the highly regarded New Zealander and leader of fighters in Southeast England. Although they were closer to the ground combat and inevitably aerial combat with hordes of Bf109 fighters, none of the pilots seemed to show any concern for the changing conditions. It was called, keeping the face, much like a poker player in a high stakes game. The normal rowdy conversation of the fighter pilots came to an abrupt halt when the radio volume was turned up.

"This is the BBC World Service bringing you a special address by the Prime Minister. Ladies and Gentlemen, the Prime Minister, the Right Honorable Winston Churchill."

The characteristic, slightly lisping, clear voice of the new Prime Minister became the only voice heard in the RAF Northolt Officer's Mess. "I speak to you for the first time as Prime Minister in a solemn hour for the life of our country, of our Empire, of our Allies, and above all of the cause of freedom. A tremendous battle is raging in France and Flanders. The Germans, by the remarkable combination of air bombing and heavily armored tanks, have broken through the French defenses north of the Maginot Line. And strong columns of their armored vehicles are ravaging the open country, which for the first day or two was without defenders. They have penetrated deeply and spread alarm and confusion in their track. Behind them there are now appearing infantry in lorries and behind them, again, the large masses are moving forward."

"It's kinda magnetic listening to him," Brian whispered to Jonathan as Churchill continued his broadcast.

"Yes, it is."

Brian Drummond looked around the Officer's Mess bar to see every face, set of eyes and attention riveted to the radio and mesmerized by the words of the Prime Minister. The delivery of these words had far more impact than any he had ever heard. The thought conjured up an enormous array of experience in the last year, more, it seemed, than the rest of his life combined. As the Prime Minister's broadcast continued, the pilots became more animated although they remained silent and attentive.

"Having received His Majesty's commission, I have found an administration of men and women of every party and of almost every point of view. We have differed and quarreled in the past; but now one bond unites us all – to wage war until victory is won, and never to surrender ourselves to servitude and shame, whatever the cost and the agony may be. This is one of the most awe-striking periods in the long history of France and Great Britain. It is beyond doubt the most sublime. Side by side, unaided except by their kith and kin in the great Dominions and by the wide Empires which rest beneath their shield – side by side, the British and French peoples have advanced to rescue not only Europe, but mankind from the foulest and most soul-destroying tyranny which has ever darkened and stained the pages of history. Behind them – behind us – behind the armies and fleets of Britain and France – gather a group of shattered States and bludgeoned races: the Czechs, the Poles, the Norwegians, the Danes, the Dutch, the Belgians – upon all of whom the long night of barbarism will descend, unbroken even by a star of hope, unless we conquer, as conquer we must; as conquer we shall.

"Today is Trinity Sunday. Centuries ago words were written to be a call and a spur to the faithful servants of Truth and Justice; 'Arm yourselves, and be ye men of valor, and be in readiness for the conflict; for it is better for us to perish in battle than to look upon the outrage of our nation and our altar. As the Will of God is in Heaven, even so let it be.'"

The melodic gongs ended the Prime Minister's statement. "We now return you to regular programming."

—

Monday, 20.May.1940
No.10 Downing Street
Whitehall, London, England

Prime Minister Churchill waited impatiently in his ground floor study. General Kell insisted upon a private conversation before the scheduled War Cabinet meeting, and he was now officially late. The knock on his door relieved some of his tension. His Assistant Private Secretary John Rupert "Jock" Colville opened the door.

Before Colville could speak, Churchill asked, "Yes, Jock, what is it?"

"Prime Minister, Director General of the Security Service Major General Sir Vernon Kell is here to see you."

"Yes, yes, show him in."

Kell entered and waited for the door to close. "My apologies for being late, Prime Minister."

Churchill waved his hand dismissively. "What have you? The War Cabinet is waiting for me."

"To the point, the Metropolitan Police arrested an American this morning."

"So?"

"His name is Tyler Gatewood Kent. He is a cryptographer for the U.S. Embassy, specifically the communication center." Churchill stopped his fidgeting, stopped breathing for a moment, and then motioned for him to continue. "I believe you are aware of the unseemly prostitution spy ring we collapsed a week ago." Churchill nodded his acknowledgment. "During our resultant searches, we found some evidence that we simply had to corroborate. We have worked closely with the U.S. Embassy's Legal Attaché and the FBI in Washington. We received the appropriate confirmation in the early morning hours this morning. An FBI special agent accompanied the Metropolitan Police team that arrested him at his flat before dawn. Further, the Americans have given us *carte blanche* to deal with this Kent fellow."

"What has been compromised?"

"I am sorry to say, Prime Minister, your personal communications with President Roosevelt among other secret material."

"Damn it all to hell. We do not need this now."

"Quite so, but it is a reality that must be dealt with."

"Yes, yes, I am well aware of that reality. What are you going to do with him?"

"My inclination is take him out into the courtyard of Brixton Prison and shoot the bloody bastard as a spy." Churchill did not react. "The American ambassador has waived diplomatic immunity in this case. Kent will be tried for espionage and incarcerated for the duration of the war. The Americans have concurred. At the end of the war, he will be repatriated to the United States and most likely tried for violations of their laws."

"Then, you are aware of my communications with President Roosevelt."

"Yes, sir."

"How long has he operated for the Germans?"

"He joined the embassy staff last October. Neither the American investigators nor our experts were able to determine when he began passing sensitive material, and he has been uncooperative. Thus, we must assume his betrayal reaches back to at least October."

Winston's mind churned over the content of his communications with Franklin Roosevelt. "I assume the Americans have initiated the appropriate changes to their encrypted communications systems."

"Yes, sir, they have."

"When will proper security be reestablished?"

"They estimate a few days."

"Very well. Anything else?"

"No sir."

"Thank you General Kell."

As the MI5 chief left his office, Churchill shouted, "Jock!"

Colville appeared in the door. Churchill motioned for him to come in and said, "Shut the door. I need you to collect all of my communications with President Franklin Roosevelt, both to and from, since last October . . . make that September, for safe measure. How long with that take?"

"Perhaps an hour."

"Very well, I would like to see the material as soon as I conclude the War Cabinet meeting."

"As you wish, sir."

Colville departed, leaving the door open. Winston Churchill stood still for a moment as he gathered his thoughts before joining the War Cabinet meeting. Cabinet Secretary Sir Edward Bridges stood just outside the Cabinet Room.

"Do we need to amend the agenda?" asked Sir Edward, his delicate manner of inquiry regarding the status of events.

Churchill held out his hand, into which Sir Edward placed a single sheet of paper with the meeting's planned agenda. "Yes, I am afraid so, Ed. Let us move the technical exchange yet again. I have recent news from General Kell that must be dealt with first. We can retain the status of forces, and last our supply request to the Americans, if we have time. That shall be enough for this afternoon."

"Very well, sir," responded the Cabinet Secretary, and then he motioned toward the door.

Churchill entered the Cabinet Room scanned the various small groups of leaders in conversation to ascertain whether the complete War Cabinet was in attendance. They were all here.

"Gentlemen," Sir Edward announced strongly and firmly, "please take your seats quickly. We are late and the agenda has changed."

Prime Minister Churchill did not wait for everyone to find their seats or for quiet. "General Kell has just now informed me of a serious breech in communications security at the U.S. Embassy." Muffled words of shock and grumblings followed Churchill's announcement. Winston did notice a smirk expression and slight shaking of the head from General Ironside, as if his doubts in the Americans had been vindicated. "We must inform the full Cabinet," Winston said, nodding to Sir Edward, who acknowledged the order, "and take appropriate precautions with respect to any communications with the Americans. Lord Halifax, if you would be so kind, please coordinate with Ambassador Kennedy and notify the Cabinet when the Americans can assure us that proper communications security has been restored. Also, please ensure Lord Lothian uses only our diplomatic means for the time being." Halifax nodded his acceptance. "Now, with that distasteful business behind us, I understand we have had serious developments with His Majesty's Forces in France."

The newly appointed Secretary of State for War Anthony Eden spoke first. "German forces have reached the Channel at Abbeville. The enemy pushed back Lord Gort's counterattack and they have consolidated their hold on much of the ground they have traversed. The BEF is cut off from the preponderance of the French Army. The French counterattack from the south has also failed to stop the German armor. The enemy's infantry is several days behind the armor and struggling to catch up, so their armor forces are somewhat vulnerable, although we have yet to find an exploitable weakness."

"Will the French deploy sufficient army forces to stop the invasion?" asked Lord Privy Seal Clement Attlee.

Eden did not hesitate. "Not likely, I'm afraid. The French are disorganized, uncoordinated and still suffering from the shock of it all. Lord Gort has masterfully integrated remnants of French, Belgian and Dutch forces in his area of operations. However, as I said previously, he has not been able to stop the German armor advance."

"Then, are you telling us the BEF is doomed?" asked Attlee.

Churchill loudly slapped is right hand on the table. "No! We shall have none of that talk. The BEF is not doomed. Lord Gort has a lot of fight left."

"That may very well be, Prime Minster," responded Eden, "however, the facts from the field suggest His Majesty's Forces are in dire straights."

Churchill turned to Alexander. "I know you have only just returned to the Admiralty, A.V., and it has only been two days since you and Sir Dudley received the charge of the War Cabinet, however, I must ask the status of the evacuation plans?"

"Sir Dudley assigned Vice Admiral Bertram Ramsay, Commander Dover Area, to develop the plans for the possible evacuation," began Alexander. "The First Sea Lord and I reviewed his progress this morn . . . ."

"Good man . . . Ramsay. When will the plans be ready to execute?" interjected Churchill. "How long will it take to complete?"

Alexander continued, "As I was saying, we reviewed his progress this morning. Ramsay believes he should be ready by the end of the week. As to how long an evacuation will take depends upon the Germans, now doesn't it, Winston."

"What is the essence of the plan?" asked Attlee.

"He has considered ports and beaches from Boulogne to the Antwerp Estuary. At the rate of German advance, we may lose the use of Boulogne, Ostend, and perhaps even Calais before we can mount an evacuation campaign.

The center of that coastline is the port of Dunkirk. Those ports are not sufficient for deep draft transports, and other debris of war has fouled most of those remaining ports. The larger vessels will stand off shore along with the destroyers we can spare. Admiral Ramsay's staff have already contacted shallow draft ferry companies and such, but he will most likely put out a general call for all small boats in the area to make their way to the French coast and move as many troops as they can safely carry to the larger ships off-shore. All of the Channel ports from Dover to Plymouth have been alerted to make preparations to receive large bodies of evacuees by day and night until this is done."

"What about their equipment?" asked Eden.

"We have no lift capacity in the area. I am afraid the BEF's heavy equipment must be abandoned."

"Let us not fret over the tanks and cannon. They can be replaced in short order. It is the men we must save, for they are not so easily replaced," pronounced Churchill.

"Indeed," Alexander added. Silence occupied the Cabinet Room as all of them considered what was about to happen. "Admiral Ramsay has labeled this Operation DYNAMO, for the underground room they are using at Dover Castle during the planning process."

"I should visit them," Prime Minister Churchill said.

"Winston, I urge you in the strongest possible terms to leave them be. We do not have much time to gather up the resources and complete the planning for the resources we have. Admiral Ramsay has sent his men to Lord Gort as well as the Admiralty and Fighter Command. Everything is being done that can be done."

Churchill looked to the First Sea Lord Admiral of the Fleet Sir Dudley Pound, who simply nodded his concurrence. "Very well, I shall leave them be, although I must say it is against my most basic instinct. I have known Admiral Ramsay for many years and seen his work first hand. He is the man for this vital task."

The First Lord continued, "I might add, the Home Fleet will dispatch two cruiser squadrons to block the approaches both east and west to the area. Air Chief Marshal Sir Hugh Dowding has committed Fighter Command to do its utmost to keep the *Luftwaffe* off our backs."

"Do you have anything to add?" the Prime Minister asked, looking at his three military chiefs. Each of them shook their head in the negative. "Ed, anything else on the agenda?"

"No, sir. We have already moved the exchange program. We are complete," Sir Edward responded.

"Very well, then, we are adjourned. Lord Halifax, if I may have a word."

Winston waited until they were alone in the Cabinet Room. "I know I do not need to say this, but I do not trust Ambassador Kennedy as far as I can spit. Do you or your lads have good contacts within the American Embassy to perform an analysis of our exposure regarding the compromised communications?"

"Yes. I am certain we do."

"I have asked Jock Colville to gather up my communications with Roosevelt. We need to have a clear view of what the Germans might have and how they might view our situation as a result."

"Quite so."

"Will Wednesday be sufficient time for your assessment?"

"I should think so, actually."

"After you have had a quick look-see, set a time with Colville for our discussion."

"As you wish."

The two men shook hands. The Foreign Minister departed. Winston went to one of the windows overlooking the garden as he ground through the afternoon's events. He held no illusions regarding the difficulty of what was before the British people. He also knew that despite his words of bravado, his precious England was far too vulnerable, more so than in the days of Queen Elizabeth I when England was threatened by the powerful Spanish Armada. Winston felt the enormous weight of history and empire.

—

Tuesday, 21.May.1940
Oval Office
The White House
Washington, District of Columbia, U.S.A.

"Mister President, Attorney General Jackson, as you requested," announced Marguerite Alice 'Missy' LeHand, Roosevelt's personal secretary. As the 57th United States Attorney General Robert Houghwout Jackson entered the Oval Office, Roosevelt motioned for him to take the chair beside his desk, so he did not have to move from behind the desk, and 'Missy' asked, "Do you need anything, Mister President?"

"Coffee, Bob?"

"No, thank you, Mister President."

"That will be all, 'Missy.' Please close the door. Thank you."

Jackson took his seat and waited for the President.

"I understand Edgar is not happy with his legal position regarding warrantless wire taps."

Jackson cleared his throat. "So, Henry Morgenthau has carried Hoover's water around me." Roosevelt dismissively waved his hand. He was not particularly interested in the bureaucratic politics. Jackson continued, "I have had this conversation with Edgar several times, now, and he is clearly not satisfied with the decision." This time Roosevelt did not react. "As you may know, Mister President, the Supreme Court issued its ruling last December in the *Nardone* case."

"Yes, a rather narrow criminal procedure decision, as I recall."

"That is the one."

"Hardly a repudiation of the 1928 *Olmstead* decision, now was it?"

"Technically, no. However, the majority made clear their discomfort with the Fourth Amendment concerns that warrantless wiretapping presents to the Court and to the law."

"We are not talking prosecutions or other judicial proceedings here, Bob. The ability of the government's intelligence assets to ferret out spies and saboteurs in our midst has suddenly taken on far more serious dimensions. After the embarrassment and debacle of the Rumrich-Grieb case, I was sorely tempted to fire Hoover as FBI Director. Now, we have this unfolding Sebold affair. Hoover believes this is just the tip of the iceberg, so to speak."

"I am aware of the Director's assessment."

"Yes, well, we are serously behind the Germans in their damnable espionage activities in this country. No telling what the Japanese are doing. The FBI needs all the tools we can give them to prosecute these spy cases before they do irreparable damage to this country."

"Are you suggesting we should set aside the Constitution of the United States?"

President Roosevelt smiled broadly as he held Jackson's earnest eyes. "Now, Bob, no need to get high and mighty with me on this." Jackson did not flinch. "You know perfectly well the Court gave government considerable latitude in the *Olmstead* case, and they have not overruled that decision."

"They were wrong in 1928, and they will eventually make it right, as they implied in *Nardone*."

"You are stretching your indignation, given the reality of what we face in the world today. Implications will not help us win the coming war."

"You have not dissuaded me, Mister President."

Roosevelt considered the delicate line he now walked. He liked Jackson's legal mind and certainly did not want to lose his expertise over this issue.

"I will issue a presidential memorandum for the record to authorize the investigating agents in suspected espionage cases to use listening devices as they deem appropriate for the identification of threats. Clearly, the information derived from such devices would be inadmissible in criminal proceedings. The development of evidence of crimes beyond a reasonable doubt shall have to be produced by other means."

Jackson considered whether such a presidential authorization would be sufficient under the Constitution and judicial scrutiny. "How far do you intend to go with this, Mister President?"

"J. Edgar Hoover and his special agents must have the tools to find these spies and saboteurs that have already done enormous harm to our national defense. We are not yet in this fight, but we are already in it, as we bear witness with the Rumich and Sebold cases. We have strongly suggestive information that some of our most vital secrets have already been betrayed and the Germans continue to operate against us. We are dreadfully behind our likely adversaries, and we must get ahead of the threat by whatever means we have available."

"Including suspending the Constitution?"

President Roosevelt felt the warmth drain from his face as he shook his head in disapproval. He did not take kindly to even a backhanded accusation of violating the law. Yet, he was also a realist and recognized the fine line he had been walking with respect to the law and the constitutionality of his action since his original inauguration. This would also not be the first or last tussle he would have with the Supreme Court of the United States before these crises abated, of that he was certain. Roosevelt swallowed hard, took a deep breath and exhaled to calm his anger. "I shall not dignify that unfounded and inappropriate rhetorical question."

"It was not rhetorical, Mister President."

"History shall judge our actions, Mister Attorney General. I am prepared for such judgment. Until then, the decisions needed to protect this nation and our citizens rest upon my shoulders alone – not yours or anyone else's. The *Nardone* ruling focused solely on criminal prosecutions and does not apply to counter-intelligence operations in the performance of the President's Article II responsibilities. Can you work with a presidential memorandum to that effect?"

"With prejudice, yes, Mister President. I shall promptly discuss this new authority with Director Hoover. We shall do our best to ferret out the vermin among us."

"Thank you, Bob. I know this is not easy, but extraordinary times demand extraordinary measures."

"As you command, Mister President."

"Thank you for coming, Bob. Now, would you be so kind to ask 'Missy' to join me, so we can craft your memorandum. I expect to have it to you by this evening."

"Thank you, Mister President. Good day, sir."

—

Chapter 5

No testimony is sufficient to establish a miracle.

-- David Hume

Sunday, 26.May.1940
RAF Northolt
Northolt, London, England
18:00 hours

"The bloody bastards are everywhere," the anonymous, English voice shouted over the radio. "Dear God Almighty, can't somebody get these sodding Huns off me." Before the pilot released his transmit button, loud bangs of what were probably exploding 20mm cannon shells hitting his aircraft could be heard over the radio, and then silence.

Pilot Officer Brian 'Hunter' Drummond, left wing of Flight Lieutenant Roger 'Jackstay' Beamish's Green Section, No.609 (West Riding of Yorkshire) Squadron, listened intently as he had on every patrol in the last two weeks. The frustration mounted as he sat nearly motionless in the cold confines of his Spitfire fighter cockpit flying extended orbits at 20,000 feet over the South coast of England waiting for the Germans to cross the Channel. The section of three Spitfires flew maximum endurance patrols lasting two to three hours, waiting, watching and listening. The agony of bearing silent witness to the losses of the grossly outnumbered Hurricane pilots fighting Germans in the sky over Northeastern France tempted them like the Devil's seductive offer to violate their rigid orders not to cross the Channel. None of the Spitfire pilots found any satisfaction in the restrictions. None of them cared a sliver about the Air Ministry holding back the best air superiority fighter the Royal Air Force possessed for a cataclysmic aerial battle they all believed to be ever nearer with each passing day.

"Let's go after the frigging bastards," said Pilot Officer Stephen 'Mongo' Strickland solemnly.

Before their leader could respond, the sector controller broadcast with a steady, calm voice. "Sorbo Green, this is Timber calling. Maintain your patrol orders."

'Jackstay' Beamish kept silent but looked off his right wing and held up a fist signaling Strickland to hold his position. Brian could see his compatriot make a slashing gesture across his neck. Steve had always been a somewhat angry person. He was Brian's most ardent antagonist within the squadron, but Brian had convinced himself Steve meant no harm. On this issue, Brian shared Steve's feelings. The cacophony of confused, desperate and pleading radio transmissions from the other side of the Channel begged for help. Each Spitfire pilot knew he could add weight to the battle. They could make a difference. The Hurricane was an impressive fighter, but the Vickers Supermarine Spitfire Mark IA was more closely matched to the growing image of the Messerschmitt Bf109E-4, single seat, fighter flown by the *Luftwaffe*.

Brian wondered what happened to their target. Fuel was no different from ammunition, aircraft and pilots. The Royal Air Force was trying to save everything it could. The altitude of the patrol indicated interception of a probable reconnaissance flight. The fact that they spent the last 90 minutes in a 20-mile long racetrack orbit probably meant the Radio Direction Finding, RDF, folks lost contact with the inbound target. They had not seen another aircraft since takeoff.

"Sorbo Green, this is Timber calling. Return to base," came the command from the sector controller.

"Sorbo Green, roger," Beamish responded. "Let's take 'em down, lads," he added.

Brian watched the PR-D tail markings as Beamish's aircraft pulled up and rolled left over the top of Brian's aircraft. Strickland, in his PR-J designated Spitfire, followed his leader. As soon as Steve cleared, Brian pushed the control circle, the spade to the pilots, hard to the left rolling his PR-F Spitfire. The three fighters dove toward the scattered layer of cumulous clouds below them as they headed back north toward RAF Northolt.

The gentle, rolling terrain of Southern England contrasted distinctly with the hills of Northern Wales near RAF Hawarden, Brian's advanced flight training base, and the jagged, foreboding, rocky, mountains of Scotland. The descent from their patrol offered Brian an opportunity to work on his geographical recognition to improve his navigation skills. The unique terrain of Scotland and Wales made finding your way easier than in the South. The lack of straight lines whether roads, hedgerows, fences or streams made the identification process more challenging and in some ways more pleasant. It was beautiful countryside. The expanse of London enabled terminal navigation for RAF Northolt nearly effortless, especially on a clear, spring day. They landed without incident at the fighter base.

"No joy?" queried Flying Officer Reggie 'Organ' Foxworth, as the three Green Section pilots returned to the squadron's Dispersal hut.

"The bloody bastards are chewing the hell out of our blokes in France, and the frigging controllers won't let us help," growled 'Mongo' Strickland.

"I take it that means, no."

The laughter broke the mood. They all shared Strickland's feelings but chose to let the feelings pass. He always seemed to be in a knot about something. The tighter Steve Strickland wound up, the more relentless the ribbing he received from the pilots. As many times as Steve jabbed at him, Brian found some satisfaction in watching his cohorts wind up Strickland.

The intelligence, post-mission, debriefing took only a few minutes. Brian told the debriefing sergeant they took off, reached their assigned patrol position, loitered for nearly two hours listening to the depressing radio traffic from France, and then they returned – not one of the more stimulating flights. The Green Section pilots returned to an open set of chairs among the squadron pilots basking in the late afternoon sun. The lengthening days added time to the waiting of the fighter pilots.

'Mongo' Strickland broke the melody of birds, crickets and beat of an idling Merlin engine across the airfield. "Those bloody bastards are kicking the crap out of our boys over there, and we simply sit here on our bums. When in frigging hell are they going to let us into this thing?"

For a few moments, everyone seemed to ignore Strickland's admonition. Flight Lieutenant Robert 'Sparky' Morrow, Red Section leader and second in command, responded first. "Don't get your knickers in a bunch, 'Mongo.' You will have all the fight you can handle soon enough."

"You have heard the radio calls. Our blokes are getting the stuffing knocked out of them over there and what do we do – listen – fucking listen. Hurricanes are over there and some of the Hurri squadrons are flying sorties from here. Why are we sitting here on our back sides just because we fly Spitfires?"

"We have been through this several times already," said 'Jackstay' Beamish, deciding to join the conversation with his right wingman. "We are being held in reserve to defend the Home Islands."

"Most of the Hurris are being held back as well," added 'Sparky' Morrow.

The telephone bell stopped the conversation instantly as every set of eyes turned toward the interior even though most could not see Corporal Jennifer Warren, the moderately attractive, Woman's Auxiliary Air Force operations clerk with curly, short, brown hair, as she answered the call. The telephone bell, along with the air raid klaxon and general broadcast loudspeaker, always added tension and spurts of adrenaline like a Pavlovian response in the pilots – combat came from those signals and could be near.

"Skipper, it's for you," she announced.

Squadron Leader Horatio 'Spike' Darling rose from his chair and disappeared into the interior of the small Dispersal building. Brian rose along with his best friend, Pilot Officer Jonathan 'Harness' Kensington, and Flying Sergeant Miles 'Fog' Johnson, the youngest pilot in the squadron at 17 years of age, to stand at the doorway to watch Darling's expression for any signs of good or bad. It was a short message.

"Group called a leader's conference," Darling announced to ease the anticipation. "'Sparky,' you have the squadron. Let's stay on our toes, lads." Darling walked around the Dispersal building to take the only automobile assigned to the squadron and drove off to his meeting.

"Maybe Group is going to move us across the Channel," speculated 'Mongo' Strickland.

"Maybe," responded 'Sparky' Morrow, "but, let us not get carried away trying to guess what is happening. The Skipper will tell us soon enough. We need to keep our minds on the job."

The sputtering and occasional backfire of the engines of landing aircraft naturally drew the attention of the pilots. The markings on the single Spitfires, Hurricanes, Blenheims and one Defiant indicated the gathering of No.11 Group squadron leaders at RAF Northolt. The last time a conference of this type was held marked the invasion of Holland, Belgium and France. The signals pointed toward something big, or important, or both.

The telephone rang again producing the same response. "B Flight to Standby," announced Corporal Warren.

"There we go, lads," said 'Sparky' Morrow. "Let's snatch your kit and man 'em up."

Jonathan Kensington, the medium built, rather Nordic looking man from Newcastle-upon-Tyne and Brian's closest friend, looked at Brian and gave him a wink as he pulled his leather helmet, oxygen mask and Mae West floatation vest off his wall peg. The six pilots walked to their aircraft. They would wait for the signal from Dispersal commanding their launch. Standby status usually meant they were within five minutes of takeoff and rather than run to their fighters. They commonly took the warning to allow a little more time to strap in and prepare the aircraft for combat.

The others waited silently as half the squadron's complement of pilots settled into their cockpits. Each man was now lost in his preparatory thoughts and actions. Brian Drummond stepped through each step in his mind as if he were mounting up. The pilots likened the mental preparation to that of an athlete preparing for a big race or match. The excitement or enthusiasm of the scramble when they flew from RAF Drem in Scotland did not exist here. The waiting and unproductive patrols while listening to the slaughter in France ground down their enthusiasm. They all felt the cobwebs of routine suck energy from them. They knew this alert was no different from those of previous days.

"What the bloody hell are they waiting for?" challenged 'Mongo' Strickland.

The wait for launch approached twenty minutes. The waiting, so close to launch, worked a particularly corrosive depletion in the pilots. They resented the uncertainty.

The phone rang. 'Angle' Ashcroft, left wing of the skipper's Blue Section, jumped as if shocked by an electric charge. All eyes turned toward the interior of Dispersal.

"Standdown. The squadron is released."

"The sods can't quite get it right," Strickland continued with his little tirade. "Why don't those bastards at Sector come down here and try their hand at waiting?"

'Jackstay' Beamish had enough. "Put a cork in it, 'Mongo.' Waiting is what we do. We must save fuel, and you bloody well know it."

Steve Strickland did not respond to the admonition. Instead, he quickly placed his flight equipment on his assigned wall peg and walked briskly off toward the Officer's Mess. B Flight, the Red and Yellow Section pilots, returned to deposit their kit. The two flying sergeants, 'Junior' Carrolton and 'Fog' Johnson, departed for an unspecified gathering off base. Most of the pilots remained in their chairs as if they needed to savor the afternoon sun a little longer. It was five minutes after seven o'clock, and the Sun was still well above the western horizon with barely a few clouds left to spot the sky.

Squadron Leader Darling returned from his conference. "Where are 'Mongo,' 'Fog,' and 'Junior?'" he asked.

"We were released a quarter of an hour ago, Skipper. They had some-thing else to do, I suppose," answered 'Sparky' Morrow.

"They will get the news eventually. I am to inform you, in an hour or so, the Admiralty will order the commencement of Operation DYNAMO – the evacuation of the BEF from Dunkirk." The groans, curses and words added weight. "Air Vice-Marshal Park confirmed what we all suspected. The situation in France is grim. Our boys are surrounded by the Gerries," he paused to let the meaning sink in. "We will be going over to France tomorrow."

"Where?"

"Not relocating. We will have missions over the evacuation beaches to provide air cover. The *Luftwaffe* appears to be having their way with our blokes. We are to see if we can turn that around and give the Tommies some breathing space. The Hurris will have low cover while Blenheims and Defiants will provide ground support. The Spits will have high cover. We must keep the fighters occupied and prevent the bombers from getting to our lads on the ground."

"Why don't we go over now and give the bastards a taste of their own medicine?" said Pilot Officer 'Boxer' Stockard.

"Only two hours of daylight left," answered 'Sparky' Morrow.

"What, do we fall out of the sky after dark?"

"In time, lads," interjected Darling. "We will have more than we can handle soon enough. The German advance has been swift and precise."

The sounds of Merlin engines starting up stopped the conversation. Brian wondered, as probably they all did, whether those Merlins were under a scramble against an inbound raid. The different tail designators told him it was just the other squadron leaders taking off to return to their squadrons.

"What is the plan?" asked Flight Lieutenant 'Sparky' Morrow.

"We will be given patrol orders tomorrow morning. We are in the second wave and should take off about seven tomorrow morning, so it will be a long day for all of us. I suggest we get something to eat and call it an early night."

Brian Drummond and Jonathan Kensington trailed behind the other pilots as they left Corporal Warren to close up Dispersal for the evening, and headed toward the Mess. "What do you think, Brian?" Jonathan asked as they walked slowly.

"Smells like a pile of shit, if you ask me." They both laughed more to relieve the tension than respond to any perceived humor. The laughter did not last long. "Maybe we can make a difference."

"I sure hope so. The Germans are doing whatever they want to do. They may be here next."

Brian felt an undeniable urge, a need to separate himself from the gloom in front of him. "I'm going over to Anne's tonight. You want to come? Maybe we can get Linda to meet us there?"

"No. I think I'm going to do what the skipper said."

"Suit yourself."

While the other pilots sat down to the evening meal, Brian dialed the telephone number he knew by heart. Anne and he had agreed several months ago that a confirmatory call was required to ensure she was not otherwise engaged. Brian still did not like the fact Anne Booth was a high-class courtesan, even if she was very selective and quite handsomely rewarded for her expertise.

He was thankful for her companionship, the extra attention and caring, as well as the continuing education in matters of passion and flesh. He did not like her profession, but he accepted it as the price of her company. When he considered all aspects, he loved Anne, and for the moment, he would ignore the parts he did not like.

A female voice he did not recognize answered the telephone. The woman sounded warm and friendly although a bit impersonal. She indicated Anne was indisposed at the moment, but he should come over as soon as he could. Indisposed? Did that mean she was freshening up, at toilet, or with a customer? Each possibility stimulated uniquely different emotions. The woman's words seemed reasonable enough.

Brian Drummond quickly showered, changed uniforms and found a ride to Hillingdon Underground Station for the journey along the Metropolitan, Jubilee and Piccadilly lines to Knightsbridge Station. The vision of her well-endowed, petite frame dominated his thoughts. Her light brown, almost blond, curly hair did not match the deep blue pools of her seductive eyes. For some strange reason Brian could not determine, he needed Anne's caress, the comfort of her arms and bosom. Tomorrow would be a watershed day. Fortunately, this night, Anne was apparently able to juggle her commitments. For that, Brian was immensely thankful. He would spend the night in her embrace and return to RAF Northolt early to have breakfast with his squadron mates.

—

Sunday, 26.May.1940
Headquarters, Secret Intelligence Service
No.21 Queen Anne's Gate
Westminster, London, England
19:30 hours

"I'll be damned," exclaimed Colonel Stewart 'C' Menzies. "This cannot be true," he added raising the single sheet of paper above his head as if it were some divine edict. The hurriedly called meeting Sunday evening did little to alter the near continuous work in the intelligence community since the invasion of Denmark and Norway not quite two months ago. The urgency of their efforts stepped up several notches as German armor forces rolled through the Low Countries and France.

"I am afraid so, 'C,'" said Alastair Denniston, Head of the Government Code and Cypher School, the cryptographic unit of His Majesty's Government. "We have corroborating evidence from multiple sources. The Germans have stopped their advance," he paused to retrieve a sheet of paper from the metal case chained to his left wrist. The security precaution meant the paper probably contained an ULTRA code message, deciphered using the captured German Enigma code box. "This ULTRA message matches with the information on the ground. Apparently, von Rundstedt wants to preserve his armor resources for the push toward Paris. They must believe they will have a difficult fight, draining their resources, trying to finish off the BEF."

"How long do we expect the lull to last?"

"Without further information, it is difficult to say, actually." Denniston considered other information in his head. "My guess is, it will last only as long as it takes them to realize the objective of Operation DYNAMO. Guderian is redeploying his 2nd Armor Division as well as allowing his logistics tail to catch up to his front-line units. I should think a few days, to maybe a week at the most."

"That may be just enough time for the Navy to complete the task or at least most of it."

"What are the current estimates, if I may ask?"

"The Admiralty contends they will have most of the BEF and the remnants of the Allied forces in the vicinity of Dunkirk off the beaches within a week, given sufficient protection by Fighter Command to minimize the losses due to air raids."

"We might actually make it."

"It would appear so. Any dissemination on the OKW message, as yet?" he asked regarding the communication from the German Armed Forces High Command – *Oberkommando der Wehrmacht.*

"No, sir."

"Have Operations assist you in scrubbing the message. Let us get the contents to the War Office, Admiralty and Air Ministry as well as the War Cabinet as soon as possible. This could be just the impetus we need to finish the evacuation."

"Yes, sir."

"If you were a believer in divine intervention, this must certainly be an instance of miraculous outcome."

"It is almost too good to be true."

"Yes, well, the evidence, as you say, indicates to the contrary, thank God Almighty. Let us make the most of it while we can. Anything else?"

Denniston considered the question, and then remembered one other item. "My apologies, sir. We recovered a short note informing the *Luftwaffe* of an operational meeting of all Air Fleet Three fighter corps commanders day after tomorrow. We know the time and place," Alastair Denniston said with uncharacteristic excitement verging on delight.

"Will the wonders ever cease?"

"We should get the essence of the information to the Air Ministry. Perhaps Bomber Command can offer up a tidy little gift for our adversaries."

The temptation for Menzies brought a broad range of considerations and possibilities. It would be easy to allow this little gem of information to be transformed into real, beneficial, offensive action. He knew better. "Let me have the message. I think we should obtain a War Cabinet decision regarding any action. It is tempting to bomb the bloody hell out of the place. A target of four fighter group commanders is very tempting. If there is a means of making an attack without giving confirmation of our prior knowledge, they might make the attempt."

"It would be nice to have a bright moment in all this disaster around us."

"Leave it with me," said 'C' as Denniston gathered up his material for the train ride back to Bletchley Park. 'C' considered his next move. The first step had to be a private meeting with the Prime Minister. He set the steps in motion.

—

Sunday, 26.May.1940
Cabinet Room
No.10 Downing Street
Whitehall, London, England
20:00 hours

"Thank you for coming," Prime Minister Churchill offered, preempting the Cabinet Secretary Sir Edward Bridges. Winston noted that Greenwood and Chamberlain were missing, yet they had a quorum for the business at hand. The defense ministers, military chiefs and cabinet staff were also present. "Events on the Continent dictated this evening's meeting. Anthony, if you please . . ."

"It appears the hour-glass has run out. Boulogne fell yesterday; Ostend the day before; and, the Calais garrison is cut off, probably surrounded, but they are fighting on for the moment . . . well, as long as their ammunition lasts. Lord Gort has carried out a masterful withdrawal under fire. Surprisingly, the German armor has halted their advance. Yesterday afternoon, they just stopped and went into defensive positions."

"Why?" asked Attlee.

"We do not know. Perhaps the intelligence lads can get a whiff."

A knock on the closed Cabinet Room door interrupted the discussion. Sir Edward went to the door, cracked it open just enough to see who it was and receive a whispered message. He closed the door and turned to the Prime Minister. "Perhaps fortuitously, Colonel Menzies has arrived with the latest information from France."

"By all means, show him in."

Secret Intelligence Service, Director General Colonel Menzies entered, stood next to the door, and waited for the door to be closed behind him.

"What have you for us, 'C'?" asked the Prime Minister.

"We have a reliable source that German fighter commanders will gather at an identified chateau in Northern France tomorrow for some big confab. We suspect but cannot confirm they may be in the final planning stages for a major air operation. We also suspect but cannot confirm that Göring himself and the other Air Fleet commanders may be in attendance as well."

Churchill stared at 'C,' as he considered the intelligence chief's information. Of those present in the Cabinet Room, he was the only other person who knew "a reliable source" was an Enigma decrypt. Winston considered whether to pursue the topic and face the inevitable questions regarding that reliable source. "Let us come back to this topic, 'C.' The issue before the War Cabinet is the pending evacuation of His Majesty's Forces from Northern France."

"As you wish, Prime Minister. In that arena, we have some interesting news as well. The Germans have halted their advance."

"We know that much," Churchill interjected impatiently. "Where?"

"They have assumed defensive formations to the east of Calais on the west flank and west of Ostend on the east flank. The French are putting up a spirited defense on the west bank of the Somme."

The river's name alone sent shudders through several of the men in the Cabinet Room, including Winston Churchill. The battles of the Great War along the River Somme were legendary in their brutality and slaughter.

"Why and for how long?"

"We do not know the answer to either question," 'C' said.

Churchill knew that meant Enigma has revealed nothing as yet, and MI6 had no other reliable sources upon which to form a view. "What is your best guess?"

Menzies took a moment to consider his response. "It appears the German High Command may be concerned about the vulnerability of their armor forces. Our best estimate is their infantry is one to two days behind the armor. They may be running low on fuel and ammunition as a consequence of their seriously stretched supply lines. The RAF has managed sufficient interdictions to slow the supply transport, which has helped exacerbate their supply situation. We can imagine the armor commanders, Guderian and Rommel, are not pleased with the break in their momentum, especially so close to collapsing the BEF and the northern army. However, they have complied, it appears. As to how long . . . as short as a few days to perhaps a week or two, but not longer. They clearly cannot move on to the rest of France until the threat of the BEF is eliminated."

No one spoke for a couple of minutes. Menzies stood rock steady as he waited.

The Prime Minister broke the silence. "Please have a seat, Stewart," he said, motioning toward an open chair along the wall, "we may need more information from you. Please keep a keen ear out for any information as to why they halted their advance. It may give us vital clues." 'C' nodded his acceptance. Winston looked into the eyes of his colleagues on the War Cabinet. "I do not believe the new information alters the decision point before us. I dare say, the time has come to execute Operation DYNAMO, if we are to save any of His Majesty's Forces on the Continent.

"I think we can all agree Lord Gort's situation is not recoverable," Churchill added. "What matters now is saving as many of those troops as we are able in the short time we have left. A.V. and I reviewed Admiral Ramsay's plan two days ago. It is not what we had hoped, but it is a sound plan given our circumstances and resources. Has Ramsay made any more progress?" he asked of the First Lord.

"Yes, Sir Dudley and I reviewed the planning again yesterday afternoon. He needs another week to collect the ships he needs."

"He does not have another week, A.V." Churchill solemnly pronounced. "For some miraculous reason, perhaps divine intervention, the Nawzees have pulled up short. We have a very narrow window."

"Yes . . . well then, we must go with what we have."

"Unless anyone else has anything better to offer," Winston said, as he motioned with his hand and looked into each man's eyes, "I dare say we have arrived at our moment of reckoning. Clement, Lord Halifax, we are about to make a momentous decision. What say you?"

"I am with you, Winston," answered Attlee.

The Foreign Minister simply nodded his head in consent.

"Very well, then, Sir Edward, please record the decision of the War Cabinet. A.V., Admiral Pound, please promptly issue the order to execute Operation DYNAMO. May God be with our men in this dark hour."

Several men stood.

"Do you want to do anything with the fighter commander's conference?" asked 'C.'

"What can we do?" the Prime Minister asked the Air Minister Sir Archie Sinclair.

"It is a tempting target, I must say. Sir Cyril, your counsel?" he asked over this shoulder to the Chief of the Air Staff Air Chief Marshal Newall.

"Quite so, minister. It is an extraordinarily tempting target. However, I noted in Colonel Menzies disclosure he referred to a singular source. I must ask the risk of compromise of such a valuable source?"

Winston felt the urge to stop the path of the discussion

"Excellent question, Sir Cyril. To act upon the information we have, it would certainly be necessary to strike other targets in the area to disguise the principal target."

"Therein lies the rub, I am afraid to say," answered Air Chief Marshal Newall. "We would need several days at a minimum to find those other targets and plan such a raid."

"The meeting is tomorrow," 'C' added.

"Yes, and to mount such a raid through or around the enclave as we are trying to execute Operation DYNAMO would be fraught with unknown and perhaps unacceptable risk to the bomber force, and our window of opportunity is likely a matter of several hours. As tempting as the target is, the risks appear to be simply too great."

Archie Sinclair nodded his head in agreement, and then turned back to the Prime Minister and said, "I concur."

"I agree," Winston added. "Do we need to discuss this further?" Attlee and Halifax shook their heads. "Thank you, Archie, and thank you for the tantalizing information Colonel Menzies. I believe we are adjourned. We have important work to do tonight."

The various ministers and chiefs rose and departed after their historic decision.

—

Sunday, 26.May.1940
No.14 Beauchamp Place
Chelsea, London, England
20:15 hours

Brian's heart rate jumped a few levels as it always did when he saw the large, heavy, black, oak door with polished brass numbers on it. He simply enjoyed Anne Booth, and she seemed to enjoy him. So far, the image of their first meeting arranged by his initial British flight instructor and now friend, Flight Lieutenant Lord Jeremy 'Mud' Morrison, never failed to come back to him as he anticipated seeing the sensual form of Anne. The excitement of tomorrow's impending battle made his anticipation all the more pronounced.

He rapped the brass knocker as he usually did. An average looking, moderately dressed woman answered the door. He introduced himself, but her only response was to open the door and invite him inside. Brian walked into the familiar parlor only to find four serious men standing to greet him. He looked over his shoulder to seek an explanation from the woman only to find another, much larger, serious man who had apparently entered surreptitiously behind him.

"Please do come in," said the oldest man, a short, bald man with a round face and frayed tweed coat. "And, your name is?"

"Who are you?" snapped Brian, feeling like a trapped lion.

"Well, now," the older man said, "I am afraid we shall be asking the questions for the moment."

"Where is Anne?"

"In due course."

Brian stiffened in anticipation of a fight, not really knowing whether there would be a fight at all. "Not until I know who you are, and where Anne is?"

"Dear boy, I am certain you do not know the trouble you are in here, so let us make this as simple and painless as possible. We shall identify ourselves in due course, but for now, I am afraid I must insist you provide us with your name."

"Brian Drummond."

"An American, I should think?"

"Yes."

"And a pilot officer in the RAF . . . with which unit?"

Brian did not like this questioning. The possibilities seemed beyond his grasp. Were these angry, powerful clients of Anne's, meaning to harass and scare him? If so, they were doing a rather good job of it. He did not like the one-sided conversation and the uncomfortable position. Brian decided to test his inquisitor. "I'm a pilot with Three Six Five Squadron at RAF Hornchurch."

The short man chuckled softly as he looked around the room. None of the other men showed the slightest humor or reaction. "So, you wish to play games. Let me give you a taste. You are Pilot Officer Brian Arthur Drummond with Six Oh Nine Squadron at RAF Northolt presently," he said without referring to any notes or taking his eyes off Brian. "You are an American volunteer pilot, 19 years of age, who violated the U.S. Federal Neutrality Act to join the RAF on the 5th of June, 1939, in Windsor, Ontario, Canada. And, I might add, there is no Three Six Five Squadron at Hornchurch or elsewhere." Brian swallowed hard. He suspected this man knew quite a bit more information about him than he had just recited. "Now, if we can dispense with the games, I should like to see your credentials, if you please."

This did not sound like angry clients. This sounded like the police. Was Anne in trouble? Had she done something wrong? Jesus, Brian said to himself thinking back to his experiences with his mentor and primary flight instructor, Malcolm Bainbridge. Had she been arrested for prostitution? Brian produced his identification card along with his current assignment orders as he had always been instructed to do when asked.

The man reviewed the papers then said, "I shall hold these for the moment." He placed them in the left, waist pocket of his tweed jacket.

The older man who appeared to be in charge motioned for a chair. One of the other serious men moved a straight back, wooden chair from the dining room and placed it in the middle of the parlor. The older man motioned for Brian to sit in the chair. Two of the men stood behind him on either side. The others sat on Anne's sofa.

"Now, then, I should like to know about your relationship with Miss Anne Booth."

"She is a friend."

Several muffled chuckles came from the others.

"How close of a friend?"

Brian considered how much he should say. He decided to keep it as simple as possible. "A good friend."

"Are you a client of hers?"

Brian bristled. "That's none of your damn business," he spat.

The man smiled and lowered his head like a bull about the charge. "Oh, my little neophyte, it most certainly is my business. Now, I am losing my patience with your impertinence. I shall not tell you, again. Either you answer my questions directly, or we shall do this the hard way, and I can reasonably guarantee, you will not like the result. Now . . . ," he said motioning with his hand for Brian to answer his earlier question.

Brian had little doubt something serious had happened, and he did not doubt the determination and power this man held. "No."

"You never paid her or compensated her for her womanly services?"

The sharp stabbing pain in his gut stimulated him to react, but he fought his emotions to concentrate on the battle before him. "No."

The man looked toward two of the men on either side of him. Both men nodded their agreement. They obviously knew much more about him and his relationship with Anne than he thought. Brian swallowed hard. Maybe he was in far more trouble than he was aware.

"Good. How did you meet Miss Booth?"

Brian told them about Jeremy's well-intentioned connection as well as his own embarrassment when she told him what she did for a living. He remembered her words clearly telling him she wanted to be friends, not client and service provider. They asked about the number of visits, times as best he could recall, and other meeting places. They wanted to know about his relationship with Virginia North. He told them everything he could remember except the one night of pleasure as a *ménage à trois*. They did not seem to be interested in his intimate relations, and he was not about to volunteer such information. They also asked many questions about Jeremy that he answered completely.

"Have you ever discussed your line of work with either woman?"

"Only in a general sense."

"How so?"

"That I fly Spitfires, and I enjoy it very much."

"Did Miss Booth or Miss North ask you specifics about the aircraft, the air defense system or your tactics?"

"No," protested Brian. "She knew what flying meant to me, but they never showed any interest in what I did, or how I did it."

"Did you tell them about your visit to the Drone Hill Chain Home Station?"

Brian stared at his inquisitor. He now began to wonder what they did not know? Only a handful of people outside his squadron knew of his visit to the Drone Hill Radio Direction Finding site near Cockburnspath in February. Brian could feel the sweat descending over his back and chest although the room was not hot. These people knew precisely what they were doing.

The questioning about his work, and what he did or did not say went on the longest. Brian guessed it was an hour. He tried as hard as he could to think about what he might have said to Anne or Virginia. Neither of the women showed much interest in the fighter business although they did show more interest in just flying. He even told them about offering to try to fly them in a two-seat airplane. Neither woman actually pressed to fulfill the offer.

The older man looked to each of his colleagues including the woman who remained in the background. They appeared to be satisfied with his answers.

"Now, since you have been forthcoming and honest with your answers, I will offer a brief explanation. First, I am Inspector Dunwoody of Scotland Yard, and these," he said sweeping his arm around the room, "are investigative colleagues from MI5, the Counterintelligence Branch, and the Metropolitan Police, who shall remain nameless for the moment. Your dolly-bird friend, Anne Booth, along with several others of her ilk were arrested a fortnight ago for treason and espionage. They were spying for the Germans."

"Spying!" shouted Brian, not believing what he was hearing.

"I am afraid so, dear boy."

"What? How?" asked Brian in a reflex response.

"Sorry, chappie. We are not at liberty to discuss any of the details. Suffice it to say, we have all of them dead to rights, and they shall pay the price for their treachery."

"Not Anne?"

"The King's Bench shall dispense the appropriate justice."

"Can I see her?"

"Afraid not, old bean. Security risk, you see."

"Is she all right? Is she in jail?"

"Yes, considering the circumstances. She and the others are being held incommunicado at an undisclosed location. You will most likely not see her again . . . ever. So, I would suggest you leave this place, get her out of your mind as quickly as possible, and concentrate on the task at hand. As we understand our military situation, your skills are in high demand." Inspector Dunwoody reached into his shirt pocket and withdrew a small card. He handed it back to Brian. "If you should think of anything else or anyone should contact you regarding Anne Booth, Virginia North or any of their friends, you are to call me at that number immediately. Do you understand?"

"Yes, sir."

"As long as you do what you are told and you do not discuss this entire situation with anyone, we shall not mention your involvement to the Air Ministry. Now, leave here and do not look back."

Brian hesitated. He had more questions, many more questions, but the serious men still looked serious. He started to leave, and then remembered that Inspector Dunwoody still had his identity papers. "May I have my identification papers back?"

"Ah, yes," the inspector said, reaching into his pocket and returning Brian's papers. "So sorry. I did not intend to be so absent-minded."

Brian took the papers and placed them in his shirt pocket inside his tunic. He could not imagine the inspector being absent-minded. He wondered what the man's real purpose was, wanting him to leave without his identification papers. Without the papers, any policeman could arrest him on the spot. There was no point in worrying anymore. Brian did as he was told.

As he made his way back to RAF Northolt, a million questions, thoughts, worries, concerns and fears came to him. Would this jeopardize his flying with Fighter Command? Would he be expelled from Great Britain? Could he face prosecution in the U.S. despite the presidential pardon he received? What had she done and why? He thought about calling Jeremy when he arrived at Northolt, but decided to keep everything to himself for the time being.

—

Monday, 27.May.1940
No.10 Downing Street
Whitehall, London, England

The Prime Minister's personal office or study was modest in size and appointment by executive standards. A wall of bookshelves with books that belonged to the residence occupied one wall. A rather small window to the rear courtyard, bounded by medium yellow curtains, allowed a nice, natural illumination to the room, although the Prime Minister used a table lamp to assist his vision. Winston Churchill sat comfortably in a large, dark brown, leather, swivel chair as he and his administrative staff tended to the morning's dispatches.

Private Secretary to the Prime Minister John Miller Martin stood beside to the left of the Prime Minister's chair with a stack of papers cradled in his left arm, all arranged in priority order decided by him, although the individual papers offered clues like urgent, most urgent, critical, or some other primal notation from one minister or another. Martin was handing letters, memoranda, notes and other correspondence to Churchill like he was some industrial strength paper shredder. Two pool stenographers, one male, the other female, both in their mid-twenties, sat on the other side of the desk taking down the prime minister's dictation at a frenetic pace.

The knock on the study door broke the process and gave the overtaxed stenographers a most welcome break. Jock Colville opened the door.

"Mister Eden is here."

Churchill waved away the administrative staff.

As John trailed the stenographers, Jock announced, "The Secretary of State for War the Right Honorable Anthony Eden."

Churchill barely waited for the announcement, as he motioned for the door to be closed. "What hear you?" asked Winston.

Eden knew the unspoken topic and waited for the door latch to close. "The evacuation has started . . . rather modest recovery, I must confess. A.V. indicated they have only managed a few thousand troops so far, but it has been less than 24-hours since the order was issued."

"Yes, yes, indeed. We have a long way to go in this affair. Let us hope the Germans give our lads a chance." Eden nodded his head in agreement. Winston changed subjects. "We need to make a change."

"What sort of change and to what?"

"We need to move Ironside. We need a younger, more energetic CIGS," he said, referring to the Chief of the Imperial General Staff – the Army chief of staff.

"He is rather long in the tooth, I should say."

"Who would you recommend for CIGS?"

"Sir John, without question or hesitation." Sir John was Deputy Chief, General Sir John Greer Dill, KCB, CMG, DSO.

"My thoughts precisely; then, Sir John it shall be." Churchill went to the window to observe the dreary but not yet dripping mid-day sky and consider the next portion of the move. "Ironside has had a long and venerable service to the Crown. I do not think it appropriate to dismiss him or force him into retirement, and I think we can still utilize his experience. I was thinking commander-in-chief Home Forces."

"Do you want me to handle it?"

"No. It must come from me, so there is no question in his mind."

"He is a professional. He will take it, as the gentleman he is."

"Certainly." Eden departed. Jock Colville returned. "I shall take lunch, now, and then my nap. I wish to see General Ironside, and then General Dill before the War Cabinet meeting this afternoon."

"I shall make the arrangements, sir."

—

Prime Minister Winston Churchill returned to his office on the ground floor at half past three. Jock Colville was waiting for him.

"Do you need a few minutes, Prime Minister?"

"No, Jock, we have no minutes to spare. Show the general in."

A few seconds later, Jock returned. "Chief of the Imperial General Staff General Sir Edmund Ironside."

General Ironside entered and saluted. Churchill returned the salute, and then motioned for Sir Edmund to take a seat opposite the Prime Minister.

"The War Minister informed me earlier DYNAMO is off to a slow start."

"Yes, sir. Slower than expected, I am afraid."

"Invasion may well be closer than we think."

"Yes, sir."

"We need your experience to prepare and lead the defense of the Home Islands, Sir Edmund. The people need the name and face of a general in command of the home defense they recognize and respect. I can think of no one beyond you who meets these requirements and is better qualified for this challenging assignment."

"I serve the King's first minister."

"You shall be commander-in-chief, Home Forces."

"As you wish."

"Who would you recommend succeed you as CIGS?"

"General Dill, sir. He is an experienced, highly capable, and respected leader. He handles the staff exceptionally well."

"Then, we are agreed. The War Minister and I concur. Thank you for your service, Sir Edmund. You have a most daunting task ahead of you."

"Thank you, Sir." Sir Edmund stood, saluted and departed the office.

Colville returned and asked, "Are you ready for General Dill, Prime Minister?"

"Yes, show him in."

Again, a few seconds later, Jock Colville returned and announced, "Deputy Chief of the Imperial General Staff General Sir John Dill."

General Dill entered the Prime Minister's office and saluted. Churchill motioned to Sir John to take a seat in front of the desk. "We do not have much time, Sir John. To be direct, I would like you to assume the duties of Chief of the Imperial General Staff."

"Yes, Sir, it would be an honor."

"We have a scheduled War Cabinet meeting in a few minutes. If you are able, please attend."

"May I ask of Sir Edmund?"

"Certainly, I have asked him to become Commander-in-Chief, Home Forces, to lead our ground defense of the Home Islands, for the invasion that is sure to come from all this. Will you have any difficulty working with Sir Edmund in your new assignment?"

"No, Sir. None. He is a brother-in-arms and has been a friend for many years."

"Quite so. We have dark days ahead, Sir John. We will need every man pulling his oar to the same stroke. Both the War Minister and I have great confidence in you. The assignment is yours, Sir John."

"Very well, thank you, Sir."

General Dill stood and saluted. Winston moved around the desk and extended his hand. As the two men shook hands, Dill nodded slightly. Winston patted Sir John on the back as the general left the office. Sir Edward and Jock Colville returned to complete final preparations for the pending War Cabinet meeting.

—

None of the usual muffled conversations preceded this particular War Cabinet meeting. A solemnity hung over the ministers and chiefs. They all sensed the worsening situation across the English Channel and remained introspective as to what the future held in store for the British people and more personally for the leaders of His Majesty's Government.

"The situation at sea is our first order of business on the agenda," announced Sir Edward.

First Lord of the Admiralty A.V. Alexander cleared his throat with the soft cough. "The results of the first day's evacuation have not been as good as we expected. We managed just over seven thousand by the preliminary count from Admiral Ramsay. We expected the recovery numbers to improve as more small boats are deployed to the beaches. Several attempts were made to clear the harbor at Dunkirk without success. We shall make further attempts for the next few days; however, it does appear we shall be relegated to the near shore transfer process currently in operation."

"Is there any thing you need from us?" asked Clement Attlee.

"We ask ourselves that question incessantly." Alexander glanced at the First Sea Lord Admiral Pound, who almost imperceptibly shook his head. "We have broadcast our call for small or shallow draft boats by every means to our knowledge. The response has been overwhelming, quite frankly. We have deployed every available officer in our attempt to coordinate instructions to these boat captains, owners, fishermen and operators to maximize the productivity of the small boats. We are moving supplies of fuel, rations and water to keep them on station as long as possible. These are civilians who are braving the rigors of combat to save our troops. Yes, the first day results were meager in the light of the daunting task before us, but we expect great things from these little boats of Dunkirk."

"What of the Germans?" asked Attlee.

"German E-boats have made numerous attempts to breech the destroyer screen without success so far. I dare say we must remain prepared for an onslaught as the German High Command realizes what we are attempting to do."

"E-boats?" Greenwood asked.

"The Germans call them *schnellboot*, meaning fast boat, or *S-Boot*, as in Type S-100 torpedo boat, and they are very fast – upward of 50-knots. They have two forward-facing torpedo tubes and carry four, perhaps six, full size torpedos. They are also armed with 20mm and 57mm cannons. These are lethal boats, Arthur."

Greenwood nodded his head to acknowledge the information.

Alexander scanned the group to see if there were any other questions, and then continued his report, "We never have sufficient air cover. Fighters and bombers manage to reach the beaches despite the efforts of the Air Force."

"We have deployed all available fighter assets," Air Chief Marshal Newall added. "We have also directed fighter squadrons in Western France to engage as their supplies last, but to preserve sufficient fuel to get those aeroplanes to England at the end of the day."

Churchill and Attlee nodded their heads.

"The bomber will always get through," mumbled Arthur Greenwood.

"Quite," said Attlee.

"German armor remains in defensive positions," added Eden. "The Air Force has managed to interdict several of their lorry and rail supply convoys to slow down their refit process. However, as A.V. noted, this respite in ground combat operations will not last much longer, perhaps a day or two, if we are lucky."

"What of the army's heavy weapons?" Churchill asked.

"As A.V. reported, the Navy has made and continues to make attempts to open the harbor at Dunkirk, without success so far. It appears we shall not be able to recover any of the heavy weapons. Orders have been issued by Lord Gort to destroy or render inoperable everything that must be abandoned – armor, artillery, lorries, all of it. We shall look for opportunities to save what we can, but our focus is on the men."

"Quite so!" Churchill said with emphasis. "Do not allow anyone to be distracted by the equipment. We need those men to come home."

"I must say," interjected Lord Halifax, "the French are not pleased with our decision to execute DYNAMO. They are saying we are deserting them on the battlefield. They have stopped just short of accusing us of cowardice before the enemy."

"Damn them!" exclaimed Greenwood.

Churchill pushed his left palm out as a signal to stop. "I shall tend to the French in the next few days. Let us not be distracted from the task at hand. We have a larger fight before us and we must preserve our strength."

"Perhaps we should use this lull in ground combat operations to seek armistice terms, to seek an accommodation," Lord Halifax offered. "Perhaps the Germans pulled up their armor vanguard to give us a distinct opportunity to seek peace and an understanding."

The statement froze the Cabinet Room, except for Prime Minister Churchill, who quickly scanned every man in the room. "No!" Winston said firmly. "We shall fight on as along as there is fight in the bulldog."

"Winston, an armistice might well save the BEF and save England."

"As long as the Nawzees occupy our neighbors, there can be no peace."

"So, you would rather risk destruction of the Army and subjugation of the United Kingdom to maintain your honor?"

Winston Churchill glared at the Foreign Minister. His lowered forehead and the scowl on his face, nearly baring his teeth, made Winston appear ready to explode or charge. Muscles in his jaw twitched quite prominently. "I shall not take the bait, Ed," Winston said, using Lord Halifax's given name, and then offered his own challenge. "If you believe you have the numbers, call for a vote of confidence in Commons to have done with me. Until then, there shall be no question of our objective."

"Which is?"

"As long as I remain the King's first minister and the leader of this coalition government, our objective shall remain as I stated in Commons over a week ago. It is victory, whatever the cost, over the forces of tyranny unleashed by Hitler and his Nawzees. Our situation may be rather grim at the moment, but we shall never surrender and we shall ultimately prevail in this conflict."

"Yes, well . . ."

"We stand with Winston," Attlee interjected in a clear, firm voice, to punctuate the Prime Minister's position. Greenwood nodded his head in agreement. Chamberlain remained silent and still.

Churchill smiled slightly and motioned with his hands, as if to say, your move.

Lord Halifax shook, and then lowered his head in resignation.

"I might remind the War Cabinet that . . ." Eden paused as he considered his words, ". . . that even if we are successful in evacuating the BEF, which is not a given I must say, we shall not have sufficient heavy weapons to equip, support and field an army to defend England."

"Are you joining Ed?" snapped Churchill.

"No, Winston," Eden said softly. "I am only stating the facts."

"We shall find the path with the resources we have," Churchill responded in a more control tone. "We are not defeated and we shall not countenance defeatist rhetoric. The Royal Navy remains the most powerful naval force on the planet. Just a week ago, we took the very painful decision to withhold deployment of additional fighter squadrons to the Continent to protect the Navy should the Germans attempt a crossing or to dominate our skies."

"Winston is correct," added Clement Attlee. "Let us not lose sight of our assets, our determination to prevail in this struggle. Whether the Germans attempt an invasion of the Home Islands is not yet a reality."

"Thank you, Clement."

The First Lord of the Admiralty added his perspective. "The Home Fleet is fully armed and prepared for the fight."

"Fighter Command will do what must be done," Sir Archibald contributed.

"They haven't yet," grumbled General Sir Edmund Ironside.

"We cannot be everywhere at once," Sir Cyril responded.

"Now, now, gentlemen," Winston said. "This brings me to a defense personnel action taken of which the War Cabinet must be informed. As you may have noticed, I asked General Dill to join us this evening, as he has agreed to relieve General Ironside as Chief of the Imperial General Staff. Concomittantly, I have asked General Ironside to take up a new, critical assignment as Commander-in-Chief, Home Forces, to prepare our defenses."

Broad congratulations passed among the attendees to both generals. The War Cabinet meeting concluded. The ministers and military leaders dispersed quickly, as if a reflection of the urgent times in which they worked.

—

Tuesday, 28.May.1940
Headquarters, Fighter Command
Bentley Priory
Stanmore, Middlesex, England

The blackout curtains over the large, French doors eliminated any last threads of connection with the way things were – with peace and tranquility.

John Spencer knew the curtains were only the most immediate manifestation of things to come. Outside the walls of the old monastery, only the waxing quarter moon illuminated the countryside. London was no longer visible at night. The late night meetings, which were now a matter of routine, did not have the distraction of twinkling city lights.

As the senior staff waited for their commander, Air Chief Marshal Sir Hugh Dowding, John Spencer's mind ran through the day's events. So far, the night brought a respite in the action. So far, neither side carried out offensive operations on the ground or in the air. During the days since the beginning of the Battle of France, events moved too fast to allow time for meetings. These days, meetings occurred after sunset, which as they neared mid-summer night, the Summer Solstice, meant staff meetings at 22:00 or 23:00, and often a short, fitful sleep on a cot or sofa at the headquarters building to be ready for the next day's action. It had been more than six weeks since John Spencer had a day off to spend with his wife, Mary, who was likewise becoming more and more frustrated with the demands of the war.

Dowding finally entered the conference room adjacent to his office looking tired and gaunt from the long hours necessary to deal with the operations of Fighter Command as well as the political burden of defending his understrength force. Both the War Cabinet and the Air Ministry, despite the agreement a fortnight ago, still wanted to send more fighter squadrons to France. They all shared the desire to help their comrades in action to the south. Only a few key individuals shared Dowding's steadfast insistence that no more squadrons should go to France.

"Here we are once more, gentleman. I am afraid I can no longer offer apologies for the late hour. The enemy seems to dictate our working hours these days." Dowding paused to allow several derogatory remarks to pass. "Well, then, shall we begin," he added nodding toward Air Commodore James Hogan, Chief of Intelligence for Fighter Command.

Hogan uncovered a map board of the Dover Straight area including a variety of markings to establish the front surrounding the Dunkirk enclave as well as the shipping routes from the Dunkirk beaches to virtually every English port from Southampton to Norfolk. "Operation DYNAMO continues to progress exceptionally well thanks in large part to the lack of offensive ground action by the Germans. We have received no information as to why General Guderian's Second Panzer Division halted their advance two days ago, but the situation remains stable for the time being. We have all asked the question . . . how much longer? No one knows since there is no logical reason we can find for halting the advance, especially with the enormous vulnerability of the BEF in the evacuation area."

"What are the current estimates for the conclusion of DYNAMO?" asked Air Marshal Geoffrey Leonard, Chief of Operations.

"The current estimates indicate, under the present conditions, namely no armor offensive and moderate air action by the Germans, we will need another week to complete the evacuation."

"Incredible, absolutely incredible," said Leonard. "The Germans have our boys in a bad way, and they let us snatch them off the beach from their grip. Just incredible."

"Let us hope they do not change their minds," commented Dowding. "It adds to the importance of our air cover for Operation DYNAMO. We have had one day's operations under the Air Staff's instructions. How did we do?"

Air Marshal Leonard moved toward the intelligence map. "As agreed, we have kept at least a squadron overhead Dunkirk from dawn until dusk," he said pointing to various key areas on the map. "The last sorties landed just over an hour ago. The One One Group squadrons flew three and in a few cases four sorties today. Our judgment is, we were quite effective. German fighters have not risen to engage in large numbers, as yet. We stopped far more bombers than got through, but they are still able to bomb the harbor. Psychologically, the worst element, according to the War Office, is the occasional section of Messerschmitt 109s that come in low down the beaches strafing the troops in the water or waiting to board."

"Losses?"

"We lost six Spitfires, twelve Hurricanes, two Blenheims and seven pilots. We have four pilots missing along with one known captive who strayed inland and was observed being taken captive."

Dowding sank into contemplation. The losses, while they did not seem great for all-out combat, were unacceptable to the maintenance of the air defenses of Great Britain. John Spencer could feel Dowding's agony. The need to support the evacuation of some of the best ground forces in the service of the King had to be saved, but the risk was depletion of scarce fighter resources not easily replaced.

"Prepare plans to redeploy our resources as necessary to maintain the daylight cover over Dunkirk. We must take the risk. Sir Cyril issued an instruction in the wee hours this morning. He felt this day would be the most critical for the stability of the British Army and the evacuation of the British Expeditionary Force. As I am certain each of us would agree, he was precisely correct. The daylight fighter cover is considered crucial to the success of

Operation DYNAMO. He feels it is probably more important for national morale than it may be for the physical defense of the evacuation."

"Yes, sir."

"Geoffrey, please call each of the group commanders. Make sure Keith Park knows what we want, but ask him to instruct the pilots not to take unnecessary chances. They are not to move inland even if in pursuit. We cannot allow added losses with our lads being tempted into the offensive. This is a desperately fine balance. I know Keith will do his best. The other groups should prepare to transfer assets, as required."

Air Marshal Geoffrey Leonard nodded his head in solemn consent.

"I have one last announcement before we adjourn," Dowding said calmly. "The War Cabinet announced this afternoon, effective immediately, General Sir John Dill is to replace General Sir Edmund Ironside as Chief of the Imperial General Staff."

The staff discussed the change. Some of them knew one or the other of the two senior Army officers. The Fighter Command staff seemed divided over the change. John knew the reputations of both men – General Sir John Dill, an inventive, respected and accomplished officer – General Sir Edmund Ironside, an equally successful Army officer in the more traditional vein. Dill would take risks while Ironside would rest on the conservative, cautious course of his experience in France. Group Captain John Spencer saw the change in Army leadership as a positive move.

"Any other business?" Dowding asked to end the conversation and the evening meeting. Everyone shook their heads. "Well, I am certain tomorrow will be another big day. Let us stay the course. I would suggest our most earnest prayers for the salvation of the Army, gentlemen. We need a miracle."

—

Chapter 6

They make a wilderness and call it peace.

-- Tacitus

Friday, 31.May.1940
RAF Northolt
Northolt, London, England

'Hunter' sat motionless in the cockpit of his Spitfire after the big Rolls-Royce Merlin III engine and three blade, de Havilland propeller stopped. This had been the second, long, flight of the day. He landed with no ammunition remaining and barely ten minutes fuel left in the two tanks between the cockpit and the engine. He was tired – mentally and physically – from engagement after engagement above the columns of black, ugly smoke rising from the Dunkirk beaches.

His canopy moved back over his slumped head and the access door opened. "Are you all right, sir?" asked Leading Aircraftman Bernard Gordon. Brian heard the question and felt the concern but still did not move. He had not removed his gloves, helmet and oxygen mask. Gordon touched his shoulder. "Mister Drummond, are you injured?"

Slowly, Brian began to take off his flight equipment. As he unsnapped his mask, he looked into the worried eyes of Bernie Gordon. "Yeah, I'm OK." Brian soon progressed more rapidly toward reality. They had been told before they landed to turn around as quickly as possible and standby. "We need a quick turnaround, Bernie."

"Right, sir. We already got the word. Jenkins and Toldson are working the guns. I shall load some petrol into her and give her a good look-see. Can I do anything for you?"

Brian knew he needed to exaggerate his action, now, to dispel his crew chief's worry. He quickly unstrapped, jumped out of the cockpit and hopped a few times as if to get blood back into his legs. "I'm OK, Bernie, really. I'm just tired, and apparently we're going again." Brian started to walk toward Dispersal. "I don't think I took any hits and no squawks. She's runnin' great."

"Excellent. I will get her ready for you."

Each of the pilots took turns in the mission debriefing. Brian was in the middle. He did not have much to say on this sortie. By the time they reached the Channel, the black smoke mixed with white cumulous clouds up to 10,000 feet. When they saw the French coastline, the aerial battle was underway and confused. The squadron entered the fight with Bf109s and Bf110s tangled among Spitfires and Hurricanes. Targets came and went faster than clear shots could be taken. Brian knew he hit several enemy aircraft. Parts of his targets flew off along with flashes of fires and smoke trails, but none of the aircraft went down. He could not claim a single victory. His ammunition ran out before his fuel. He used some fancy maneuvering as well as the assistance of his buddies to disengage for the return to RAF Northolt. The debriefing sergeant asked several questions without clear focus.

As Brian left the debriefing room, Jonathan Kensington stood to take his turn.

"You get anything?" Jonathan asked Brian.

"No. Not that I could tell. Enjoy your little chat."

"Thanks," Jonathan said with the same fatigue Brian felt.

The telephone rang. Everyone froze. "Scramble the squadron," shouted Corporal Warren.

The shot of adrenaline reanimated the pilots. Hands grabbed flight equipment as legs ran toward the waiting aircraft. Engines started as Brian strapped in. He hurried to catch up. They were airborne in under three minutes, climbing at full power with the throttles straining against the emergency gate wire. Brian went through the litany. Power – full and engine instruments normal. Guns – charged and armed. Gun camera switch – on. Sight – illuminated and set. Without looking, Brian's right thumb touched the large, red button at the 11 o'clock position on the spade.

Sector Control gave them vectors south and an initial altitude of 20,000 feet. Fighters. They were probably headed toward fighters. The controller eventually told them a squadron of Hurricanes was being pursued by German fighters. They were not able to disengage, and they needed assistance. The vectors put them to the west of the mêlée. Brian spotted the ball of fighters before Squadron Leader Darling called, tally-ho.

"Here we go, lads. It's show time," the skipper said as he rolled toward the targets. "Let's make sure we sort them out before we shoot."

As they dove toward the twisting fighters, several of the gray and black camouflaged Bf109s turned into the diving Spitfires. Brian moved off to the left from 'Jackstay' Beamish as he scanned the sky above and below. Events moved with lightning speed as the No.609 Squadron Spitfires joined the fight. The Hurricanes recognized the assistance and quickly disappeared into the clouds below.

A Bf109 fired head-on at 'Spike' Darling, and then pulled up turning in front of the descending squadron. 'Jackstay' pulled up to chase. Brian followed his leader looking over his shoulders to pick up other opponents. The yellow propeller spinner of a turning Bf109 caught his peripheral vision. He saw the gun flashes from the 20mm cannon and machine guns with tracers arcing toward Beamish.

Brian rolled sharply, brought his sight on the attacker and squeezed off a quick burst. The two fighters passed in an instant. Brian pulled back hard and rolled his fighter onto its back straining his neck to reacquire his target. Before he could reacquire his target, another flash under him caught his attention.

This time, it was the green and brown of another Spitfire with two Bf109s in close pursuit. Brian flattened his roll and pulled his nose down to engage the two attackers. The menacing edges of a Bf109 nearly filled his sight recticle. Check ball – slightly right – nudge the right rudder pedal – back in. Squeeze the firing button. Brian felt the guns fire as he held the firing button down and watched the Bf109 grow further in his sight. He dove past. The control column came back hard to regain altitude. Airspeed fell off . . . the whistle of the rushing air washed away into the melodic tones of the Merlin . . . the altimeter wound up. Brian rolled inverted to pull his nose back down.

"'Hunter,' you've got one on you," someone shouted over the radio.

Brian pulled back on the spade as hard as he dared. The Spitfire shuttered near stall. He released some backpressure to eliminate the buffeting. Just as he turned his head over his left shoulder, the loud bangs of 20mm shells exploded on his aircraft. Brian slammed the control column to full left. The last impact struck the engine. It sputtered and shook, but kept running although it was no longer firing on all twelve cylinders.

A flash of fire leapt out of the hole, and then disappeared to be replaced by a stream of black smoke. Brian kept pulling the control column as he maneuvered to avoid any further hits.

"He's gone, 'Hunter.' Head north. We'll cover you," came the voice of 'Jackstay' Beamish.

Brian checked his compass, which fortunately agreed with the afternoon sun. He turned his wounded Spitfire toward the north-northwest, which would be close to a direct line back to RAF Northolt. Speed dropped off which did not seem healthy with enemy fighters still in the sky. Brian checked his instruments.

16,500 feet.

He lowered the nose to gain speed. He was nearly over the French coast that meant he had at least 25 miles of water to cross.

"Keep her flyin'," coached 'Jackstay.'

Brian checked his instruments. The engine's oil pressure was falling. The engine kept turning over although it was running rougher by the minute. An agonizing, scraping, metallic sound gradually gained intensity. The wounded engine was consuming itself. Halfway across the Channel, he could finally see the famous white cliffs through the broken clouds.

"'Jackstay,' bandits six o'clock," shouted someone over the radio.

"Keep going, 'Hunter.' Be back in a moment. 'Mongo,' split. We shall take 'em head-on."

Brian craned his neck to see what was happening behind him. He wanted to maneuver. He still had ammunition. The dying engine needed no further antagonism. He had to reach England.

A few tracers passed him although thankfully not close. The German was probably trying for the easy kill. Brian twisted and turned in the cockpit, but could not see anything behind him other than the trail of grotesque black smoke from his mortally wounded fighter.

A horrific wrenching of steel preceded by an instant the stoppage of the Merlin. Seeing the clear edges of the propeller blades while he was still in the air gave Brian a sickening, nauseous, sour feeling throughout his core. 5,500 feet.

He pointed the nose down more to keep some precious airspeed against the now greater drag of the stopped propeller. The light strip of sand marking the boundary between the blackish-green water and the alabaster cliffs was about five miles away. He was going for a swim.

"'Hunter,'" came the calm voice of his leader. "Listen to me carefully. You must bail out. Do not take the Spit into the water. You are not going to make the coast. You must jump."

Brian considered the words. He had never parachuted before. Something told him he was safer in the still flying aircraft with a dead engine than he would be falling through the air hoping a silk canopy would inflate above him to slow his fall. Brian did not want to jump.

"Brian, you must jump. We shall get the rescue boys out to you. Now, jump lad. You do not have much time."

The altimeter spun counterclockwise showing steadily decreasing altitude.
3,000 feet.

He did not have much time.

"Jump, damn you," shouted Flight Lieutenant Roger 'Jackstay' Beamish.

At that instant, Brian stopped thinking and simply responded as he had been taught. The canopy came back. The rush of air felt good. He unplugged his oxygen mask and radio cords, released his harness, stood up and pushed himself away from the dead machine.

The sensation of falling did not last long as he pulled the silver, steel, loop handle freeing his parachute from his seat pack. The white, silk canopy opened with a jolt knifing the crotch straps into his tender flesh. Brian felt a gush of air forced from his lungs.

"Damn," he said aloud in recognition of the shock. He looked up to see a perfect, white, creased circle of material above him with 32 thin lines attaching him to it. So far, so good, he told himself.

Brian looked down to see the choppy water beckoning to him. He glanced up. More than a mile to the shoreline. Actions raced through his mind. He wanted a boat to be beneath him, to catch him. There were no boats close by, only in the distance. He remembered his water landing procedures. He had to get out of the harness and out from underneath the canopy immediately to keep the sinking parachute from dragging him under with it. Next would be his Mae West. An inflated Mae West would keep him on the surface, then all he needed to do was swim to shore. The thought of swimming a mile or more added substantially to his apprehension. Fortunately, he told himself, he could swim, but he had never swam anywhere near that distance before.

As he waited for the water to swallow him, he finally became aware of the melodious tones of the most successful product of the Rolls-Royce Aeroengine Company. He twisted his parachute risers to see the elegant curves of a Vickers Supermarine Spitfire Mark IA roll toward him as it passed. He looked into the cockpit to see the smiling face of 'Jackstay' Beamish grinning at him and holding up his raised left thumb. Brian waved to signal he was uninjured. As the Spitfire pulled up, Pilot Officer Brian 'Hunter' Drummond caught sight of at least three additional Spitfires circling over him. They looked like angels hovering over him to protect him from evil. His eyes watered as he swallowed hard choking back tears of pride. Brian Drummond knew he would be safe. He felt safe.

Brian plunged into the water. He moved quickly, while he was still underwater, to release his harness buckles. Once free, he thrashed his way to the surface. A slight breeze blew the deflating canopy away from him.

"Damn, this is cold," he shouted, as the first recognition jabbed through part of his body.

He knew he had to move quickly. He felt for the red ball and pulled, inflating his Mae West flotation vest. The cold water brought a surge in his heartbeat and a quickening to his breathing. He remembered his buddies. The large white letters of 'Jackstay' Beamish's PR-D Spitfire passed near him in a slight turn with his inboard wingtip nearly touching the water. Brian waved to his section leader to tell him he was all right. What signal would he use to tell 'Jackstay' he was very cold? The wings rolled level, the nose came up and the glorious sound of the Merlin engine throttling up to full power made Brian smile. He needed to move, to generate some muscle heat. Brian started swimming toward the enormous white cliffs beyond the swells.

It seemed like it took Brian days to approach the beach. The cold pain in his hands, feet and face washed away under a heavy blanket of numbness. The cliffs did not move closer despite his struggles through the constant swells and choking gulps of salt water. The numbness crept further up his extremities. He wondered if he would lose consciousness when the advance of numbness up each limb met in his chest. The sky was darkening quickly, and it made Brian feel even chillier.

A hand grabbed his left shoulder. Startled, Brian turned to look in the concerned eyes of a soldier. "Thought we'd lost ya there, mate," the man said as another pair of hands grabbed his right shoulder. The two men lifted Brian nearly out of the water and continued to talk to him with words of encouragement, comfort and survival.

Once on the shore, they wrapped him in blankets, hustled him into a waiting horse-drawn cart. The soldiers turned out to be Home Defense Force volunteers who spotted Brian's smoking airplane slash into the Channel water and then his parachute descent. They transferred him to an ambulance and transported him promptly to the nearest medical clinic. While the doctors evaluated his condition, they disrobed him, warmed him and notified the RAF of his rescue and safe condition.

It was nearly dawn by the time Brian reached RAF Northolt and the smiles, thankfulness and camaraderie of No.609 Squadron. He recounted his story several times before 'Jackstay' Beamish banished everyone from the residence hall, so Brian could get some much-needed sleep. This ordeal became history.

—

Sunday, 2.June.1940
Brighton, East Sussex, England

Brian appreciated the ease of travel manifested in the British rail system. The Underground ride to Waterloo Station on the South side of the River Thames did not take long. The train south toward Brighton had given him plenty of time to think, to consider what he was doing. Part of him wanted this meeting, but most of him resented the coercion Rosemary Kensington used to convince him to make the journey. Her threat to expose their affair at Carlingon Castle, the family home, over the Christmas holiday break during the Phony War, to her brother and his best friend, was certainly not the basis of a great relationship. Brian had told Jonathan the basics, but certainly had not gone into the details of the affair. Rosemary's rather lame threat of exposure sparked his curiosity. Why would Rosemary Kensington resort to such methods to establish a Sunday meeting at the coastal resort town in the middle of a naval evacuation of the British Army from the Continent?

He remembered the torrid passion enveloping them and her aggressive, uninhibited nature. Her lack of self-conscious propriety gave her a mysterious, curious quality. Although he had seen her several times since Christmas with the last time at the squadron's departure from RAF Drem outside Edinburgh, Scotland, neither of them recaptured the heat of those few nights surrounding the celebration of the birth of Jesus despite a few attempts. Brian liked Rosemary for her passion, enthusiasm and freedom. He loved Anne Booth although he knew he should not. He should love Rosemary, but he did not, at least not yet.

The telephone call from Rosemary Saturday afternoon as he returned to the Officer's Mess from flying his new PR-F Spitfire, replacing the one he lost over the Channel, seemed to be fortuitous. Squadron Leader Darling was able to give him two days recuperation although Brian felt fully recovered from the ordeal of being shot down and nearly freezing in the chilly water of the English Channel. The telephone call from Rosemary convinced him to take the two days.

The walk from Brighton Station down to the shoreline Boardwalk, and then east to the Seasprite Inn where Rosemary was waiting would give him some fresh sea air in the warming late spring morning.

What he actually found was not what he imagined. The air was not of the sea, but of smoke, dust, oil, blood and gunpowder. The streets were crowded with soldiers. The water was covered with small boats of all descriptions. These were the Dunkirk survivors, the British Expeditionary Force soldiers evacuated from the German encirclement. A large group filled the street before him. Several bandaged men were helped by others as they made their way toward the rail station. Every one of the men appeared exhausted and beaten. Their blood stained, muddy and wet uniforms added to the image of defeat. Only a few carried rifles.

"Where the bloody fuck were you, mate?" shouted one of the anonymous voices from the group.

"Yeah, right you are man, we've been fightin' for our friggin' lives and you bloody junior birdmen in your nice fancy, clean uniforms take a holiday weekend at the bloody fucking beach."

Several of the men refused to allow Brian passage. He remembered the confrontation with the sailors in Liverpool during his advanced training at RAF Hawarden last year. Brian wanted to say words of support, but instincts told him no words would suffice to comfort these men.

"We ought to bloody you up a bit, birdman," growled another.

"Where were you flyboys when we needed you to keep the bloody Huns off our backs?"

The intense anger spawned an unexpected fear. None of the men showed any signs of moving. Brian decided to give it a try. "We have been fighting the Germans in the skies over Dunkirk. We've tried to keep the Germans away from the beaches."

"Isn't that sweet, lads. They've been trying while we've been dying."

"So, why are you in Brighton Beach instead of in the air helping our mates still over there?"

"I was shot down yesterday and nearly froze in the water. I'm recuperating."

"You look fine to me."

"All right, men. Leave the man be," said one of the soldiers wearing sergeant stripes. "Let's not take our frustration out on the RAF. They are on our side."

"Friggin' hell, it surely don't seem like it."

"Come on, now. Split up. Let the man pass."

Reluctantly the soldiers moved aside to let Brian move through the group. Several soldiers sneered at him although most just looked down and trudged forward. With the tattered remnants of the British Army's finest soldiery behind him, Pilot Officer Brian Drummond silently took in a deep breath in an effort to dissipate the heart pumping adrenaline. He felt the anger like a foul odor on the wind. He wondered why they directed their anger at him. Two, three, sometimes four, missions a day over Northeastern France and specifically the beaches of Dunkirk certainly qualified as supporting the evacuation. The contrast between the nearly effervescent support from citizenry and the disdain of the evacuated soldiers could not be more stark, jagged and brutal. Likewise, the contrast between his fresh, crisp RAF blue uniform and the greenish-brown, torn, soiled and bloody, Army uniforms represented extremes of the spectrum.

To Brian's surprise, his thoughts enveloped a multifaceted question. How soon would the greenish-brown Army uniforms be replaced with the steel gray uniforms of the *Wehrmacht* on the streets of Brighton? The British Army looked, felt, sounded and smelled defeated. What defense would they have if the Germans decided simply to follow the remains of the Allied armies into Great Britain? There did not appear to be much to stop them. Hitler and his military had yet to suffer a defeat of even minuscule proportion. Everything they did became victory. What would stop them now?

The white, blue trimmed, nautical exterior of the Seasprite Inn materialized before him just as Rosemary had described it. The small lobby and reception area was well appointed with exquisite watercolor paintings of boats, coastal wildlife and the inn itself blended well with the flowers and leather upholstered chairs.

"Room Twenty-one, please?" asked Brian of the diminutive, silver haired, rather frail looking desk clerk.

"Ah, yes. Miss Kensington is expecting you," he answered with a wink. "You are, I might add, exactly as she described you, sir."

Brian felt a flush of embarrassment. This was obviously not the first time the innkeeper had an unmarried couple as guests. "Room Two One?"

"Yes, right. Shall I ring Miss Kensington?"

"That won't be necessary," said Brian. "Just tell me where the room is, if you please."

"Miss Kensington asked me to knock her up when you arrived, if you don't mind, sir?"

"Very well. Now, where is the room?" Brian wanted to remove himself from the scrutiny of anyone as quickly as possible.

"First floor, first door on the right. It's a lovely room with a view of the beach," the clerk said to Brian's back. He heard the old man announce his arrival as he ascended the stairway.

Brass numerals identified the room. His knock produced the soft voice of Rosemary Kensington telling him to enter. As he opened the door, the shock froze him for an instant, and then caused him to jump into the room slamming the door behind him. Rosemary Kensington lay on the double bed with covers and sheets drawn back smiling at him in her full glory.

"Rosemary, that could have been the maid," Brian protested as he struggled to regain his composure.

She laughed. "I told the desk clark only you should disturb me," she said at the excited discomfort she caused. "Now, doff those clothes and mount up. You have work to do." The giggles of unadulterated enjoyment accentuated her words.

"Jesus H. Christ, Rosemary. What are you doing?"

"Trying to get bonked, actually."

"Rosemary," Brian continued to protest. Neither of them moved. Brian recognized his response to the stimulation but fought against the temptation. Rosemary Kensington had yet to fail to shock, surprise or otherwise keep Brian off balance. "We need to talk."

"No," she snapped. "We are going to fuck before we do anything. Now, get your clothes off and come to me, or do I need to do it for you."

Brian caved in under the weight of visual stimulation. He began to undress with a quickening pace. How could he possibly resist such an invitation?

"That's it. Come to me."

Brian did not find it difficult to make love with Rosemary Kensington. She possessed an exuberant and thorough enjoyment of sex as a free expression of emotion between two people. While Anne's enjoyment was more polished, mature and fully developed, Rosemary's felt more energetic and youthful. They both took pleasure in one another until the fire peaked.

As she lay draped across him caressing his chest, Rosemary was the first to speak any words beyond the red hot, expressions of passion. "What did you want to talk about?"

"What?"

"You said, you wanted to talk. What did you want to talk about?"

"Nothing. It doesn't matter."

"It must have been important enough to nearly keep you from our union."

Brian thought about the topics he had in his mind before he entered the room, but they did not matter, now. She did not seem to expect much from him other than sex. That was enough for Brian. He could accept their relationship.

"I simply have not figured you out."

"That's it," she laughed as if an accomplished comedian had just told the most raucous joke. "Don't you know that is what men and women are all about – mystery, curiosity and passion."

They talked about attitudes, feelings, desires, emotions, wants and needs. They talked about many things until Rosemary Kensington asked him how long he could stay. Brian recounted the confrontation with the soldiers. The desperate situation across the Channel brought a shroud of reality to their idyllic moment of pleasure. Without thinking, Brian told her about his experience Friday afternoon and his need to get back into the air, to help, however he could, in the evacuation. For the first time since Brian met Rosemary Kensington, she turned very serious. Although she tried to camouflage her feelings for Brian, the connection was unmistakable and mutual.

"Brian, I want you to tell me the absolute truth." An inquisitive expression conveyed the message. "Do you really have a girlfriend as you told me at Carlingon Castle?"

"I used to. Her name was, Rebecca. I called her, Becky."

"She is back home in America?"

"Yes."

"You said, used to. Does that mean you split up?"

"Yes. She told me she couldn't stand the separation any more, and she met another guy at the university."

"I am sorry," she said with true sincerity.

"It's OK."

"Don't you have a girlfriend in England?" she asked. ". . . other than me, of course."

Brian considered whether he should mention Anne. The hesitation told Rosemary the answer to her question.

"Tell me about her."

"I don't think that is appropriate."

"Why?"

"I'm lying naked with you. It would not be proper to talk about another woman."

"Why not? I'm here with you. She's not."

Everything about Rosemary Kensington was up front. Brian had yet to see any hidden element from her. He figured he had nothing to lose other than some good sex. "Her name is, Anne Booth. I met her shortly after I arrived in the UK."

"Do you love her?"

"Yes."

"Why are you here with me, rather than with her?"

Brian thought about telling her about Anne's arrest for spying, but he remembered Inspector Dunwoody's admonition. The less people who knew of his connection with an accused spy, the better, as far as he was concerned. Brian chose to keep that aspect of his life hidden for the moment. Rosemary might find out eventually from Jonathan, but he would have to take that risk. "You said you'd tell Jonathan. Your brother is my best friend, and I don't want to injure my relationship with him."

"I am quite glad you are my brother's best friend. He thinks highly of you. I will not jeopardize your relationship with Jonathan." Rosemary paused, became very still and looked away out the window. "He needs you, Brian. You need each other in this desperate time." She rolled away from him. "I fear for both of you, and yet I know we need you to do what you do."

Brian rose on his left elbow and touched her shoulder. He leaned forward to kiss her cheek and noticed a stream of tears. The source of her tears was not readily apparent. A helpless, lost sensation demonstrated his lack of experience in affairs of the heart.

"Rosemary, what's wrong?"

"You have been shot down already. The two men I love the most are in danger. Aren't I allowed to cry for the men I love?"

"Don't worry. We're in one of the best squadrons in the Air Force. We'll beat the bloody Germans."

Rosemary rolled back toward Brian to look directly into his eyes. Her eyes shimmered. "Why don't you quit, Brian. You are an American. You don't need to be in this fight."

"I'm sorry, Rosemary. This is everything I've ever dreamed of and the Air Force says they need my skills."

"But, Brian, I don't want anything to happen to you. I can accept you being with other women, but I could not stand not having you at all."

"They're not going to get me. I'll survive this."

Rosemary wrapped herself around Brian holding him tightly as if he might float away. They remained connected for quite some time without words and only the touch of lovers. They melted into each other several times that Sunday afternoon although there were no more words between them.

It was not until the light outside began to dim that they ventured out of their room. A walk along the beach felt like the right thing to do. The detractor unavoidably became the flood of soldiers pouring across the piers, landings and beaches. The scene was depressing to Rosemary. She said she did not understand what was happening. Brian felt guilty of betrayal walking along Brighton Beach Boardwalk with a beautiful woman on his arm while the survivors of the Battle of France struggled to return home. He could not eliminate the vision of other soldiers still fighting among the burning hulks in a collapsing perimeter for enough of a lull to run to the Dunkirk beaches and hopefully a waiting row boat, fishing boat, trawler, ferry or warship to extract them from the jaws of certain death or capture. The vision extinguished the flame of passion for both young lovers and created a growing urge, need, desire within Brian to return to the cockpit as soon as he could. Rosemary Kensington accepted gracefully Brian's announcement that he wanted to shorten his recuperation and return to RAF Northolt in the morning. They used the remaining hours as lovers should.

—

Tuesday, 4.June.1940
No.10 Downing Street
Westminster, London, England

The meeting of the War Cabinet went well considering the curious mixture of good news and bad news. The downside without question had to be the worst defeat for the armed forces of the United Kingdom since the surrender of Lord Cornwallis at Yorktown in 1783. The embarrassment of the Battle of France made most Britons resent the years of appeasement and lack of preparation. The only good news anyone could find rested in the miracle of salvation represented by the rescue of a sizable portion of the British Expeditionary Force from the beaches and harbor of Dunkirk.

The Prime Minister sat alone within himself in the large, brown leather chair at the head of the long, green Cabinet Room conference table as the others made their way out. It had been a lengthy meeting to assess the statistics of consequence regarding the desperate situation in France. The Admiralty declared the evacuation complete at 14:23, this afternoon, but there were still trickles being plucked from the cold water. The tension among the members of the War Cabinet remained after the near fatal confrontation a week ago with Lord Halifax, the chief spokesman of the appeasers. The thought of seeking peace terms as Lord Halifax had so strongly argued sent a shiver through Winston's entire body. The resentment of him ran deeper than he had estimated, and the direct challenge to his infant premiership had come within moments of success. The strain of those arguments had been replaced by the enormous stress of the evacuation operations.

Elements of General Heinz Guderian's 2nd Panzer Division were at the outskirts of Dunkirk. Any further operations to remove the remaining soldiers would mean certain disaster. Nearly a third of a million Allied soldiers had been safely transported from France to England. Several thousand had been or would soon be captured by the advancing Germans. Winston rejoiced with the saving of his fighting men, but most of their equipment from tanks to heavy artillery as well as a good portion of their rifles and personal weapons remained in France.

"See you in Commons," said Lord Beaverbrook. Winston's friend, now Minister of Aircraft Production, placed his hand on Winston's shoulder. Max Aitken had resigned his seat in Commons upon his elevation to peerage as the 1ˢᵗ Baron Beaverbrook in 1917, thus he would have to observe Churchill's report to Commons from the Peer's Gallery above the Commons floor, as a Peer Lord, he was no longer permitted on the floor.

The Prime Minister nodded his head but did not make eye contact. He knew he had friends, and now many new colleagues who looked to him for leadership, for guidance. Winston Churchill, as a student and author of history, knew how history would view the Battle of France and Dunkirk. The doom and gloom around him, around them all, was a virulent contagion that would soon extract the last vestiges of strength from His Majesty's Government, the armed forces and the population. He knew what he must say to his colleagues in Commons and in his broadcast to the people this afternoon. He knew they had to be inspiring words in the darkest hour in the history of the United Kingdom.

Finally, Winston rose from his chair retiring to his private office. The staff recognized the moment. In less than an hour, he would address Parliament as the leader of the coalition War Cabinet and His Majesty's Government to report on this miraculous minor victory among the gruesomeness of the most tragic defeat. The words he had written looked strange and foreign. Winston told himself the feeling was good. The words were more positive than he felt, but he recognized more than most people that no matter how bleak the situation, success would ride on the shoulders of conviction. Their only hope for survival in the face of the most formidable and now successful army in modern times rested in their faith, their collective will to be victorious. Winston swallowed hard, and then rehearsed his speech one more time as he had done so many times before. This had to be the best, most inspiring speech he had ever given and may ever give. It had to be honest, but uplifting.

The Prime Minister of Great Britain, the Right Honorable Winston Spencer Churchill, MP, folded his notes, placed them inside his coat where they would stay, took a deep breath and said aloud to himself, "And, so into history we go."

—

Churchill walked by himself although he was certainly not alone. Virtually every citizen smiled, tipped his hat, waved and shouted words of encouragement to him as he walked the less than a mile distance to the Palace of Westminster. He intended to deliver his report to Commons, and then, probably more importantly, broadcast to the nation, the Commonwealth, the Empire and the world, his message on behalf of His Majesty's Government.

His colleagues were less ebullient and optimistic than the citizens he passed on the street as he made his way into the Commons Chamber. Friends gave him a smile, a nod, a firm hand on his shoulder as their means of encouragement and support. Winston sensed an air of anticipation in the Members, more so than upon previous occasions of his expected speaking time. His mood improved, drawing strength from the people and the Members who looked to him for leadership in this most desperate period in British history.

The House of Commons filled to capacity. A dozen or more Members stood opposite the Speaker's Chair. Even the Stranger's Gallery could no longer offer standing room. The Speaker called the House to order, proceeded through the formalities of the session, including the invocation and prayer for wisdom and courage. At the appropriate moment as the floor was turned over to him, Winston hesitated with his head lowered looking at his clasped hands. The House fell deathly silent adding to the solemnity and gravity of the occasion.

Winston Churchill, newly appointed Prime Minister of Great Britain, son of Lord Randolph and Lady Jennie Churchill and cousin to the 7th Duke of Marlborough, stood slowly before the Prime Minister's podium. Winston allowed himself to slump slightly as though nearly buckling under the invisible weight on his shoulders and placed his clenched fist before his mouth in contemplation. He lowered his hand, grasped both sides of the podium and looked up just enough to scan the nearly half a thousand faces, mostly familiar to him, returning their gaze and attention in silence. As he had done since beginning his political career forty years earlier, Winston Churchill prepared himself mentally to speak without notes, cues or other aids. He intended to deliver this crucial report and message to Parliament and the people as he had rehearsed it, from memory.

Winston began with a low, solemn, almost remorseful voice. "From the moment that the French defenses at Sedan and on the Meuse were broken at the end of the second week of May, only a rapid retreat to Amiens and the south could have saved the British and French Armies who had entered Belgium at the appeal of the Belgian King; but this strategic fact was not immediately realized. The French High Command hoped they would be able to close the gap, and the Armies of the north were under their orders. Moreover, a retirement of this kind would have involved almost certainly the destruction of the fine Belgian Army of over twenty divisions and the abandonment of the whole of Belgium. Therefore, when the force and scope of the German penetration were realized and when a new French Generalissimo, General Weygand, assumed command in place of General Gamelin, an effort was made by the French and British Armies in Belgium to keep on holding the right hand of the

Belgians and to give their own right hand to the newly created French Army which was to have advanced across the Somme in great strength to grasp it.

"However, the German eruption swept like a sharp scythe around the right and rear of the Armies of the north. Eight or nine armored divisions, each of about four hundred armored vehicles of different kinds, but carefully assorted to be complementary and divisible into small self-contained units, cut off all communications between us and the main French Armies. It severed our own communications for food and ammunition which ran first to Amiens and afterwards through Abbeville, and it shore its way up the coast to Boulogne and Calais, and almost to Dunkirk. Behind the armored and mechanized onslaught came a number of German divisions in lorries, and behind them again there plodded comparatively slowly the dull brute mass of the ordinary German Army and German people, always so ready to be led to the trampling down in other lands of liberties and comforts which they have never known in their own."

Winston stopped to take a drink of water and allow his words to ripen in the minds of his audience. He looked carefully around the large hall to ensure he still had everyone's attention. "I have said this armored scythe-stroke almost reached Dunkirk," he paused for one dramatic moment, "almost but not quite. Boulogne and Calais were the scenes of desperate fighting. The Guards defended Boulogne for a while and were then withdrawn by orders from this country. The Rifle Brigade, the 60th Rifles, and the Queen Victoria's Rifles, with a battalion of British tanks and 1,000 Frenchmen, in all about four thousand strong, defended Calais to the last. The British brigadier was given a hour to surrender. He spurned the offer, and four days of intense street fighting passed before silence reigned over Calais, which marked the end of a memorable resistance. Only thirty unwounded survivors were brought off by the Navy, and we do not know the fate of their comrades. Their sacrifice, however, was not in vain. At least two armored divisions, which otherwise would have been turned against the British Expeditionary Force, had to be sent to overcome them. They have added another page to the glories of the light divisions, and the time gained enabled the Graveline waterline to be flooded and to be held by the French troops.

"Thus it was that the port of Dunkirk was kept open. When it was found impossible for the Armies of the north to reopen their communications to Amiens with the main French Armies, only one choice remained," he said as his voice lowered to a heavier tone. "It seemed, indeed, forlorn. The Belgian, British and French Armies were almost surrounded. Their sole line of retreat was to a single port and its neighboring beaches. They were pressed on every side by heavy attacks and far outnumbered in the air.

"Meanwhile, the Royal Air Force, which had already been intervening in the battle, so far as its range would allow, from home bases, now used part of its main metropolitan fighter strength, and struck at the German bombers, and at the fighters which in large numbers protected them. This struggle was protracted and fierce. Suddenly the scene has cleared, the crash and thunder has for the moment – but only for the moment – died away. A miracle of deliverance, achieved by valor, by perseverance, by perfect discipline, by faultless service, by resource, by skill, by unconquerable fidelity, is manifest to us all. The enemy was hurled back by the retreating British and French troops. He was so roughly handled that he did not hurry their departure seriously. The Royal Air Force engaged the main strength of the German Air Force, and inflicted upon them losses of at least four to one; and the Navy, using nearly 1,000 ships of all kinds, carried over 335,000 men, French and British, out of the jaws of death and shame, to their native land and to the task which lie immediately ahead. We must be very careful not to assign to this deliverance the attributes of a victory. Wars are not won by evacuations. But there was a victory inside this deliverance, which should be noted. It was gained by the Air Force. Many of our soldiers coming back have not seen the Air Force at work; they saw only the bombers, which escaped its protective attack. They underrate its achievements. I have heard much talk of this; that is why I go out of my way to say this. I will tell you about it."

Words of encouragement and anticipation accentuated the growing tempo and confidence in Churchill's voice. "This was a great trial of strength between the British and German Air Forces. Can you conceive a greater objective for the Germans in the air than to make evacuation from these beaches impossible, and to sink all these ships which were displayed almost to the extent of thousands? Could there have been an objective of greater military importance and significance for the whole purpose of the war than this? They tried hard, and they were beaten back; they were frustrated in their task. We got the Army away; and they have paid fourfold for any losses which they have inflicted. Very large formations of German aeroplanes – and we know they are a very brave race – have turned on several occasions from the attack of one-quarter of their number by the Royal Air Force, and have dispersed in different directions. Twelve aeroplanes have been hunted by two. One aeroplane was driven into the water and cast away, by the mere charge of a British aeroplane, which had no more ammunition. All of our types – Hurricane, the Spitfire and the new Defiant – and all our pilots have been vindicated as superior to what they have at present to face."

The Members became more animated and vocal as Winston's words fueled the embers of patriotism, confidence and hope. "When we consider how much greater would be our advantage in defending the air above this island against an overseas attack, I must say that I find in these facts a sure basis upon which practical and reassuring thoughts may rest. I will pay my tribute to these young airmen. The great French Army was very largely, for the time being, cast back and disturbed by the onrush of a few thousand of armored vehicles. May it not also be that the cause of civilization itself will be defended by the skill and devotions of a few thousand airmen. There never has been, I suppose in all the world, in all the history of war, such an opportunity for youth. The Knights of the Roundtable, the Crusaders, all fall back into the past; not only distant but prosaic; these young men, going forth every morn to guard their native land and all that we stand for, holding in their hands these instruments of colossal and shattering power, of whom it may be said that: Every morn brought forth a noble chance, and every chance brought forth a noble knight, deserve our gratitude, as do all of the brave men who, in so many ways and on so many occasions, are ready, and continue ready, to give life and all for their native land."

Winston smiled for the first time as the cheers echoed through the Commons Chamber. His incantation of the heroics and valor of the armed forces gave strength to the leaders of His Majesty's Government, to Parliament. He knew now the same words would be a soothing salve for wounds and injury suffered by the nation in the last few weeks. The sting of embarrassment would disappear as the energies of his countrymen were turned toward the advancing threat. Nodding his head in recognition, he wanted to bring the speech to a dramatic climax.

"When Napoleon lay at Boulogne for a year with his flat-bottomed boats and his Grand Army, he was told by someone 'There are bitter weeds in England.' There are certainly a great many more of them since the British Expeditionary Force returned."

The House roared its approval. Even the jaded journalistic observers seated in the Stranger's Gallery could not resist the waxing enthusiasm in the House.

Winston picked his tempo and straighten himself pulling back his shoulder as if preparing to accept a certain blow. "Even though large tracts of Europe and many old and famous States have fallen or may fall into the grip of the Gestapo and all the odious apparatus of Nazi rule, we shall not flag or fail. We shall go on to the end, we shall fight in France, we shall fight on the seas and oceans, we shall fight with growing confidence and growing strength in the air, we shall defend our island, whatever the cost may be, we shall fight on the beaches, we shall fight on the landing grounds, we shall fight in the fields and in the streets, we shall fight in the hills; we shall never surrender," he said as he pounded his fist upon the podium and once again the House roared, stopping his speech just short of its conclusion. He waited for the relative quiet to return. "And even if, which I do not for a moment believe, this island or a large part of it were subjugated and starving, then our Empire beyond the seas, armed and guarded by the British Fleet, would carry on the struggle, until in God's good time, the new world, with all its power and might, steps forth to the rescue and the liberation of the old."

The applause, cheers and approval was nearly unanimous even from some of his staunchest, perennial opponents in the House. Defiance of the odds, the thunderous storm upon them, the evil force swallowing Europe, buoyed them all against the fight, which would all too soon become quite personal and ugly. Winston Churchill did what he knew he had to do, what was their only hope. He knew the British people would respond. He prayed to himself for God's help in overcoming the vision of invincibility presented by their antagonists.

—

Saturday, 8.June.1940
Headquarters, Fighter Command
Bentley Priory
Stanmore, Middlesex, England

The days and nights blended into one solid mass of intensity, reaction, confusion, and, although he hated to admit it, desperation. Group Captain Spencer sat in the same conference room that had become the nearly permanent living quarters for the immediate staff of Fighter Command. The brief instant of elation associated with the deliverance of Dunkirk did little to brighten the constant stream of discouraging, disappointing, and in some cases, outright depressing news from almost every direction.

It was now not quite a fortnight since he had been away from this converted old monastery for even a moment. Although he tried to talk to his wife, the lovely Mary Spencer, once a day, he missed her. The fact that she occupied their house seven miles away made the separation more intolerable especially during the occasional lull or late at night. The pressure of invasion threats and the lack of preparedness of Fighter Command and the Home

Defense Force created the environment demanding such long, devoted hours. He needed a day or two to replenish and hopefully feel the touch of his wife even though their relationship had been severely strained by the war. Separation would never repair the damage.

"Are you with us?" asked Air Chief Marshal Dowding.

"Yes, sir."

"You appeared to be not entirely here, Group Captain Spencer."

"So, sorry, sir. Long days, I suppose."

Rare laughter briefly occupied the space. "And nights, I'd say," added one of his colleagues.

"Yes, right you are. Now, can we return to our business? Air Commodore Hogan, if you would be so kind," Dowding said of his Chief of Intelligence.

"The evacuation of Norway has been completed."

"Yes, indeed," interjected Air Marshal Geoffrey Leonard, Chief of Operations. "Squadron Leader Kenneth Cross managed to talk the Navy into taking his Hurricanes aboard *Glorious*. They got the barge going as fast as they could into the wind, and Cross led his ten remaining Hurricanes, landing on the carrier. A Hurricane has never been landed on a carrier . . . let alone ten of them. Incredible, actually. Only minor damage to a couple of the last aeroplanes to land. I'd say it must have been some of the fanciest flying I've heard of, actually. The young man's energy and the Navy's appreciation of our problem saved nearly a squadron's worth of our fighters from certain capture or annihilation."

"Did we send a congratulatory message to the Admiralty, HMS *Glorious*, No.46 Squadron and especially Squadron Leader Cross?" asked Dowding.

"Already done, sir."

"Well done, Geoffrey."

"While we accomplished another successful evacuation," continued Hogan, "the situation in France progresses toward total collapse. The French seem to have lost their will to fight. The War Office estimates that Paris will fall in less than a week, and the rest of France will not be far behind. We have evacuated the remainder of the BEF from Western France."

"The Air Ministry has left the tempo of fighter operations in France to be under our control," stated Leonard.

"Is there a reason for us to continue to risk further losses, if the situation is hopeless?" asked John Spencer.

The obvious question halted the discussion as if no one had thought about the topic. Air Marshal Leonard answered, "Bomber Command flies several missions a night. It seems at least one sortie a day needs escort support in the late afternoon or very early morning."

"There are also political reasons," added Dowding. "The Navy calls for fighter cover as they are still plucking off small groups from various beaches. We are all keenly aware of the criticism our lads have taken for the perception by the Army that we were not there."

"They should see the losses," interjected Air Commodore Herbert Maple, Deputy to Air Marshal Leonard.

"Now, now, we all can feel the stress. Let's not add to it."

A knock on the large interior, oak doors usually meant an urgent message or immediate action. Group Captain Spencer glanced at the wall clock – 23:25. It had to be a message, he told himself. He opened the door to a serious expression of a leading aircraftman from the Communications Center.

"Urgent message for the Air Chief Marshal from the Air Ministry, sir," the man said, as he handed John a folded paper marked for Sir Hugh.

"Is an immediate response requested?"

"No sir."

"Thank you," said John Spencer as he shut the door to the man's back. He walked to the far end of the conference table and handed the message to Dowding.

The head of Fighter Command read the note carefully with every set of eyes affixed to his face looking for the slightest indication of the message contents that never came. Sir Hugh Dowding read the note several times providing the only sign of its importance.

Finally, Dowding looked up to scan the faces of interest and concern. "It appears we have more bad news." He paused to glance at the piece of paper one more time. "The *Glorious* has been sunk."

"Dear God above," gasped Air Commodore Maple.

"What the bloody hell happened?" asked Air Marshal Leonard.

Dowding cleared his throat and kept his expression emotionless. "According to the Admiralty, *Glorious* and her escorts, *Ardent* and *Acasta*, were engaged by *Scharnhorst* and *Gneisenau* six hours ago. *Glorious* was sunk in 20 minutes by main battery fire from *Scharnhorst*. Both her destroyer escorts were also sunk. The report indicates there were very few survivors due to the rapidity of the sinking. The Navy intends to continue the search for survivors through the night. They apparently also sank the empty troop ship, *Orama*, and two other ships earlier in the morning."

The tick-tock of the mantel clock offered the only sign of life in the Commander's Conference Room. The loss of the *Glorious* with No.46 Squadron and elements of No.263 Squadron hit each of the officers in personal and professional ways. For John Spencer, the loss of the pilots after their heroic carrier landing accomplishment hurt the most. The ten Hurricanes could and eventually would be replaced, but the experienced pilots represented a greater loss. John ruminated over the fickle character of success and victory. Minutes earlier they nearly rejoiced over the success of Squadron Leader Cross and his pilots, and now they mourned their loss.

"We shall see more tragic losses before this is over. Our men and our nation are depending upon our focus and concentration. Pray . . . let us not disappoint them," said Dowding in an effort to regain the attention of his staff. He allowed several minutes to pass before he continued. "What is our strength, now?"

Air Marshal Leonard and Air Commodore Maple promptly perused their papers and made several pencil calculations. Leonard responded, "Thirty-two full strength squadrons with four or six partial squadrons by our calculations. We have lost about 25% of our pre-war strength, mostly Hurricanes in France and now Norway."

Silence filled the conference room as the enormity of Fighter Command's losses in France and Norway hit home. Put in real numbers the importance of Dowding's obstinate stand against sending more fighters to France seemed like an epistle from the Oracle.

"If we consider the ineffectiveness of the Gladiator, Blenheim and Defiant against the modern German fighters, we have actually lost an additional nine squadrons," added Group Captain John Spencer as he thought aloud.

Dowding considered the meaning of the estimate, and chose to ignore John's observation. "Any ideas on how to make up the shortfall prior to the onslaught?" asked Dowding.

"I might suggest, Sir Hugh," began Leonard, "redeployment of the squadrons to place our strength at the most likely point of attack."

"Which is?"

"With France near collapse, I believe the Southeast, One One Group."

"If we move the Gladiator, Defiant and Blenheim squadrons to the West and North, and put Keith Park's Group at 100% with Spits and Hurcs, we might give 'em a good go," added Herb Maple.

Dowding assessed the options but recognized a more thorough staff evaluation would yield better results. "It would appear we need a commander's conference. Schedule the group commanders in here as soon as possible. Give them the information as we have it and the options as we see them. We must explore every possibility in detail. We need at least fifty, full strength, fighter squadrons to defend the Home Islands, gentlemen. We have our work defined for us. We shall not rest until we have found the way forward."

Group Captain Spencer left the midnight conference wondering for the first time in his life whether the United Kingdom as he had always known it would continue to exist. He feared for his wife and family, and especially his uncle, Winston, who would certainly perish in the consolidation of a German victory.

Every time he thought the enormous burden could not get much heavier, it did. John Spencer told himself he could no longer take the luxury of imagining what might happen. He simply had to banish any thought of defeat, injury or subjugation. The British people had to rise to this desperate occasion.

—

Chapter 7

It becomes no man to nurse despair,
but, in the teeth of clenched antagonisms,
to follow up the worthiest till he die.

-- Alfred, Lord Tennyson

Monday, 10.June.1940
Prime Minister's Office
No.10 Downing Street
Whitehall, London, England

Jock Colville followed Prime Minister Churchill into his office as the busy afternoon schedule began.

Winston did not wait for his assistant private secretary to open the discussion. "Is Stephenson here?"

"Yes, Sir. He is waiting in the Anteroom. Would you like to talk to Sir Edward or Mister Martin first?"

"Do they have any urgent business?"

"Not that I am aware of, Sir."

"Please show Bill in . . . that is urgent."

Winston had just sat down at his desk when Jock returned to announce the Prime Minister's first afternoon appointment.

"Mister William Stephenson, Sir."

Winston nodded and waved his hand to hurry the process up. He moved around the desk to warmly greet his friend. "Great to see you, again, Bill."

"Likewise, Winston."

"Would either of you care for tea?"

Both men shook their heads. Colville nodded and closed the heavy oak door behind him.

Winston motioned for Stephenson to sit in an adjacent, dark brown leather upholstered chair with a small table separating them. "Let me jump right to it . . . very busy schedule this afternoon. You will recall our meeting last September upon my return to the Admiralty." Stephenson nodded his agreement. "With the Germans advancing swiftly through the Low Countries and well into France, the urgency and importance of our relationship with the Americans and President Roosevelt specifically has taken on even greater criticality to our position. You have done everything I asked of you, and you appear to have a trusted relationship with the President."

"I think so, yes."

"The time is now to take this special relationship to the next level, which is precisely why I asked you to work with 'C,' 'K' and the ministers of His Majesty's Government to take on a more permanent position as well as deepen our involvment in the Americas."

"Understood."

"You can be so much more than a courier between me and Franklin, as you have been for the last nine months. This assignment, as I see it, may well be the most important single position in the entire Empire, and I do not think I am overstating it. We need the Americans with us, and I am counting on you to help me make it so."

"You know I will do my best."

"Yes, yes," said Churchill as he waved his arms dismissively and responded impatiently. "I understand from the Home Secretary that you and 'C' have agreed on the arrangements for your new assignment."

"Yes, we have. The British Security Coordination agency shall operate under the cover of the British Passport Control Office. We have entered into a long-term, as in multi-year, lease for office space on the 35th and 36th floors of the International Building, Rockefeller Center, New York City. I believe we have all of the agreements in place with the War Office, Admiralty, Foreign Office, as well as related ministries like Aircraft Production, and with the White House and the Federal Bureau of Investigation."

"Excellent. Stewart was not particularly happy with my decision to send you to manage our clandestine activities in the United States."

"He made that point quite clear to me as well. However, I must say, he has come around quite nicely in the last few days."

"You should know my reasoning here, Bill." Stephenson nodded his head. "I need a trusted friend, as well as someone who understands the Americans, to be my eyes and ears, and to manage our intelligence relationship with the United States. To be brutally frank, we need the Americans on our side. We must have their industrial capacity. We do not have the means to defeat the Germans by ourselves. The Empire will help, but until the Navy can gain the upperhand on this damnable U-boat menace, they can only relieve our burdens in the Dominions."

"Understood."

"I am also quite concerned about the lack of cohesion and structure within their intelligence services. I know President Roosevelt shares my concern here as well. They are going to need our help in that arena."

"Yes, Sir."

"How is Mary? Is she prepared for this move?"

"She is doing quite well. Thank you for asking. She understands the necessity and as you can imagine she is eager to return to the States, and easier access to her family in Tennessee."

"Excellent. I have confidence she will be an enormous help to you."

"Thank you for that. I am sure she will."

"I am certainly you have anticipated the next question. How soon can you get to New York?"

"Yes, indeed! Mary is supervising the closing of our home here and the shipment of our household goods to the dock in Liverpool. We are scheduled to depart aboard the *Victoria Bay* Thursday evening. We should arrive in New York Harbor on the 21st."

"She's a fast ship and should do better than eight days to cross," Winston said, with a tone of puzzlement.

"Yes, quite so. We make a very brief stop at Halifax . . . something about a special cargo for Canada."

"You are the special cargo from Canada, my friend."

"Thank you."

Winston reached for a single sheet of paper on the corner of his desk, and then handed it to Stephenson. "This is my personal and official letter of introduction for you." Stephenson took the letter and read it, as Churchill continued, "President Roosevelt has agreed to see you as soon as you get Mary settled."

"I can head to Washington as soon as we dock. Mary is quite capable of handling our household affairs."

"Very well, then. You have my personal charge. Do not hesitate to use it. If you run into any obstacles that you cannot readily breech, you must inform me immediately. This is an absolutely vital mission to our war effort, Bill. Nothing must get in your way or slow you down."

"I shall do my best, Winston. It is an honor to be of service."

Churchill nodded his head rapidly and waved his hand dismissively. "Certainly. You know our priorities . . . at least for now."

"Yes. Resupply, destroyers, convoy escort, intelligence, and of course the potential for the technical exchange," Stephenson replied.

"Exactly. Franklin is aware and supportive of those priorities. They are working on a large shipment of guns and ammunition to refit the BEF prior to what we believe is an impending invasion. He has indicated he is working on the naval items. Franklin is frustrated with his intelligence agencies, and he is trying to coax them toward a master coordinator on the 'C' model. When that comes, you will be our primary representative, and I am sure you recognize the essential importance of that roll. I am not yet convinced about giving away our most sensitive defense secrets; however, the reasoning for such an exchange is quite sound given our current circumstances."

"Understood."

Winston stood. Time was up. "Unless you object, we will continue to use the moniker 'Intrepid' to identify you in our communications with President Roosevelt.

"Fine by me."

"Excellent. Godspeed and following winds, Bill. You go with our blessings."

"Thank you, Winston."

The two men shook hands. Stephenson let himself out and closed the door behind him. Winston returned to his desk. He picked up the latest report of shipping successes and losses, as well as U-boat sightings and engagements.

—

"Are you ready for your scheduled meeting with Sir John?" asked Jock Colville.

Winston's concentration remained on the Admiralty's shipping report. He held up his hand palm out for ten seconds, and then he motioned with his hand inward to bring his next appointment, without taking his eyes off the report. Colville departed and promptly returned with the Prime Minister's next visitor.

"Home Secretary Sir John Anderson, Sir."

Chuchill did not look up from the shipping report as he motioned toward one of the chairs across the desk opposite him. As Anderson situated himself, Colville closed the office door.

Winston looked up from the report. "We are in one hell of a fight for our very survival."

"Excuse me . . . Dunkirk?"

"The U-boat menace! They are winning at the moment."

"That is not good news."

"Indeed! Quite so! However, that is not the topic we need to discuss."

"Which is?"

"General Kell," Churchill answered, referring to Director General, Security Service, Major General Sir Vernon Kell.

"Is there a problem?"

"He has been in his position since 1909, and has been the only MI5 director the agency has known. It is time for some fresh blood."

"Winston, seriously, is this the correct time for such a monumental change?"

"MI5 has not kept up with the threat from German spies. They were too late on the prostitute and Kent cases, and they mishandled the whole situation, exposing the government to incalculable risk at a critical time in our history. We must make this change now. It is past time for Kell to retire. You must have succession plans in place. So, what is your recommendation for his replacement?"

"Sir Vernon is 67 years old. As you said, he has been the head of MI5 since its creation – 31 years now – so, he is certainly eligible. Knowing Sir Vernon, I believe he saw himself serving until his passing." Sir John paused to think for a moment. "Yes, we have had a succession plan in place for quite some time. However, you may not be aware, I asked David Petrie to conduct a study of MI5 performance. His findings are not due until early next year."

"And, your point is?"

"I think Petrie is the correct man to succeed Kell. It was my intention to spring off his study to affect the change."

"We cannot wait until next month, set aside next year. The invasion is sure to come in the next few months, before the winter weather sets in. We cannot have the complication of spies amongst us, aiding the invader and stirring up the Irish."

Anderson considered their options for another moment. "By our succession plan, Brigadier Jasper Harker is the designated successor."

"Will Harker agree to be the acting director general until Petrie completes his assessment?"

"I have not discussed that alternative with him."

"Why can't Petrie take the assignment now?"

"We discussed the potential, but he insisted that there are likely mandatory changes requisite for his acceptance of the assignment. He believes a clear understanding on those changes is essential to his success."

"You mean to tell me, he would not serve, if the King asked for his service?"

"I do not think that a wise move, Winston. Petrie is a good and capable man. We do not want to start him on the wrong foot. I am fairly certain Harker will agree to assume the responsibilities of MI5 for the interim. Rather than make him a temporary head with the concomitant uncertainty such an action inherently produces, I would recommend Harker be given the assignment outright, with the private proviso that it is a temporary assignment until Petrie completes his study. When we make the change to David, I would strongly recommend we make Harker his deputy."

Churchill stared at Anderson as he digested Sir John's words. "Very well, then. I asked Sir Vernon to meet with me, as soon as we are done here. I will inform him of his retirement and leave you to carry out the transition with Harker. I must insist upon meeting with David Petrie after I have read his study and before his appointment as director general."

"By your command, Sir."

"I will see you at War Cabinet. I will announce these changes this afternoon. We need to move quickly."

"I will talk to Brigadier Harker immediately, as you meet with General Kell."

"Very well, then. Make it so."

Sir John departed, leaving the Prime Minister's office door open. Churchill returned to the shipping report.

—

"Security Service Director General Major General Sir Vernon Kell, reporting as you requested, Prime Minister."

Sir Vernon entered Churchill's office in full military attire with his rank insignia and decorations properly affixed. Churchill motioned for Kell to take a chair opposite him and waved for Colville to close the door.

"I shall move directly to the point, Sir Vernon. It is time for you to retire."

A flashed expression of shock covered Sir Vernon's face, to be just as quickly replaced with his commonly stoic appearance.

"Is there something I have failed to do in service to the King?"

"We are immersed in a new kind of total war. You have been in service of the King for better than four decades and 31 years as chief of MI5. You have served honorably, Sir Vernon, but I am afraid these times demand a fresh approach to counter-espionage, and time is short."

"I do not suppose there is any room for discussion?"

"No."

General Kell locked upon Churchill's eyes, as he considered what had just happened and the ramifications to his perception of the future. "When is this to be effective?"

"Immediately."

"Who is to replace me?"

"Brigadier Harker."

"Good man, Jasper. Is there anything else, Prime Minister?"

"Thank you for your service to the Crown, Sir Vernon. I hope you can excuse the lack of cermmony. We have a war to fight. I also hope and trust you can enjoy some much needed rest in your retirement."

Kell stood, came to attention, saluted, and said, "Thank you, Sir." He performed a crisp, about-face, rarely seen among generals and departed.

—

Colville knocked on the door, opened it just enough for him to step halfway in, and announced, "Sir, the War Cabinet is waiting on you."

Winston Churchill walked the short distance down the hall, waved Sir Edward into the Cabinet Room ahead of him, and went directly to his chair at the head of the long table. As he sat, he found Sir John Anderson on the periphery, nodded slightly and received a confirmatory nod in return.

"We have much to discuss this evening," Winston began without ceremony or procedure. "First, I must inform the War Cabinet, General Sir Vernon Kell has retired from active service." A few indiscernible mumbles conveyed the surprise of some in the room. "He has been replaced by Brigadier Harker."

"What brought this on?" asked Arthur Greenwood.

"It was time for a change in the Security Service."

Greenwood's expression indicated his dissatisfaction with Winston's answer, but he chose not to challenge the change.

Churchill moved on to the next topic. "I understand *Il Duce* has decided on his pound of flesh," Winston said.

"You are correctly informed," Lord Halifax answered. "The Italians declared war on France this morning and sent troops across all of their common border checkpoints. I informed Anthony and A.V. promptly."

"The execution order for the seizure plan went out promptly this morning," A.V. Alexander interjected. "As of half an hour ago, roughly a third of the entire Italian merchant fleet has been seized throughout the Empire, largely without incident. There were a few scuffles and shots fired, but no injuries to our men"

"Well done to the Royal Navy," Churchill proclaimed. "Let us re-flag and man up those ships as quickly as possible. If the cargo they hold is usable, bring it home. I have studied the latest shipping report. We need those ships in service to make good our losses. Whatever must be done, we are losing the Battle of the Atlantic. We must find the means to gain the upper hand against those damnable U-boats."

"Quite so. We have numerous developments that show promise and a few nearing operational status – radio detection, improved underwater acoustic detection, and an improved torpedo. Coastal Command has tested a prototype airborne radio detection unit."

"The engineers must understand and appreciate the urgency in this endeavor," Churchill said.

"I think they do. These projects have the utmost in priority and urgency. We will deploy them as soon as humanly possible."

"I have also sent Bill Stephenson to the United States as our defense liaison. He will have a cover within the Foreign Office and report to 'C.'" Winston did not want any discussion. "Do we have the final numbers from DYNAMO?" asked the Prime Minister.

"We are still collecting the count, but it appears we have recovered over a third of a million men from Dunkirk."

Spontaneous applause erupted among the ministers and generals. "A miracle" was heard more than a few times. Churchill let the brief respite of jubilation continue for a few more seconds, and then held up his hand to stop, so they could continue.

"Others outside the pocket and the German held territory are making their way to the Normandy and Atlantic ports. We have ships loading troops and refugees as we speak, thus we expect the recovery to improve over the next few days and weeks. Of particular note, the Earl of Suffolk is shepharding 35 French nuclear scientists and nearly the entire world's supply of heavy water to the southwest. We have the *Broompark* waiting at Le Verdon sur Mer near Bourdeaux to load him and his charges as soon as they can make their way to the port. We have a squad of Marines guarding the ship. We hope to have them off in a week or so, depending upon the dreadful refugee predicament. They are clogging the roads out of Paris to the south and west."

The 20th Earl of Suffolk was actually Charles Henry George Howard at birth and had become quite the contributor to British defense efforts. In addition to being a rather dapper nobleman, he was also an explosive expert and bomb disposal specialist – an odd combination for a man of privledge.

"We need those scientists and especially that heavy water," Sir John Anderson said. "But, more importantly, we simply must keep them out of the hands of the Germans." In addition to his duties as Home Secretary, Sir John was the ministerial supervision for the British nuclear weapons research group spread out among a half dozen university physics laboratories and secret test facilities.

"Understood," responded Alexander. "Depending upon how fast the Germans turn west and how far they are prepared to go in their occupation of France, we will return more troops, diplomats and citizens over the next few weeks. The problem for the transport crews will be defending their vessels from the flood of refugees fleeing before the German advance."

"Can the Navy provide any protection for our ships in those ports?" Clement Attlee asked.

"We are spread rather thin," the First Lord answered. "However, we shall see what ships we can redeploy to the Atlantic to help out."

Sir Edward did not let the ministers mull over the news for long. "The next item on the agenda is the Channel Islands."

Lord Halifax leaned forward and retrieved a single sheet of paper from his expand-a-file. "The Governor of the Channel Islands as well as the bailiffs of the individual islands are requesting transport for evacuation of non-essential personnel as well as reinforcements for the defense of the islands."

"What capability do we have to support them?" asked the Prime Minister.

Secretary of State for Air Sir Archibald Sinclair cleared his throat for attention. "We took the decision just three weeks ago not to reinforce the BEF, for God's sake. We just managed a true miracle in saving our troops from certain destruction. Surely, we are not considering further depletion of our scant resources . . . all desperately needed for the defense of the Home Islands."

Sinclair's blunt statement of the facts caused everyone pause, including the Prime Minister.

With a somber, nearly muffled voice, Churchill said, "Those islands have been the dominion of the Crown for four centuries." Not that anyone in the room needed the history lesson.

"At their rate of advance," began Anthony Eden, "the Germans will be there in a week . . . two at the most."

"We can see what transport might be diverted for evacuation," A.V. Alexander added.

"It would appear the best we can do is demilitarize the islands and declare them open to avoid unnecessary bloodshed and destruction," Lord Halifax said.

"Four centuries," Winston boomed.

"Is this not the exact same premise we considered with Dowding's letter?" asked the Foreign Minister.

"We cannot give up Crown territory so easily," barked Churchill. No one moved, spoke or even mumbled. "I am going to France tomorrow."

"Winston?" Attlee objected.

"We shall return to the question of the Channel Islands upon my return. Each of you shall have two days to consider our options," the Prime Minister pronounced

"Winston, you must not go to France," said Attlee. "It is far too dangerous."

"Perhaps, but we will not be forgiven by history, if we do not do everything to keep the French in this fight."

"We cannot afford to lose you at this critical time, Winston. Goebbels would be insufferable, and your loss might well be crushing to the morale of the people."

"It is a risk I must take to keep the French in this."

Clement Attlee glanced around the room to see several heads nod in concurrence. "No, Winston! It is not a risk you must take. We can send an emissary, if you think there is any hope of salvaging the French. Frankly, based on what we know at the moment, I think there is none . . . hopeless. At last report, the Germans are within artillery range of Paris."

"I appreciate your wise counsel, Clement, but I do not agree. The French are still fighting and dying. We have already risked their condemnation of desertion on the battlefield. I must show them, convince them, we are still with them in this fight. An emissary will simply not do for that purpose."

Attlee stared intently at Churchill for the longest pause, as he considered Winston's words. He eventually turned his eyes to Sir Edward Bridges. "I think I speak for the whole of the War Cabinet, and at this sitting, the Defense Committee," he paused to see heads nodding and a few "here-here's" before he continued, "we do not approve of the Prime Minister leaving the kingdom and especially flying into a war zone."

"So recorded," Sir Edward responded.

"Very well. Fate shall have my soul. Against the objections of the War Cabinet, I shall fly to France tomorrow afternoon to bolster the French defense. I shall return as soon as possible, and I shall take Inspector Thompson with me."

"Winston, this is serious," added Attlee. "Do not mock us. Despite Inspector Thompson's abilities, he is no match for a panzer division, and neither are you."

"I will order a squadron of Hurricane fighters to escort your aircraft."

Churchill nodded his head in acceptance. "I appreciate the concern of all of you. I shall be as careful as humanly possible."

"Any new items?" asked Sir Edward. Hearing none, he said, "We are adjourned."

—

Tuesday, 11.June.1940
Admiralty House
Whitehall, London, England
09:05 hours

Churchill laid back, nearly submerged in his bath, letting the hot water envelop him. His morning bath offered him just a few moments of quiet, peace, solitude and contemplation. The flight to France this afternoon gave him plenty to consider. What would he find when he arrived? Would there be any leadership with whom to discuss defense plans? What could he offer? Perhaps the War Cabinet was correct; this gesture might well be hopelessly wasted at the risk of his life. As he had done so many times in his past, Winston put those thoughts of danger aside, as if they were trivial in comparison to the weighty matters of state.

A short couplet knock interrupted his thoughts. The diminutive, rosy cheeked, bald-headed person of Frank Sawyers, his long-time valet and personal butler, dressed to perfection as always, entered the bathroom and closed the door behind him. Sawyers always seemed more comfortable and at peace away from Chartwell and the tension of personality with manor house butler David Smithfield. Winston truly appreciated Sawyers devotion and attention to detail, although he tended to take the man's service for granted, as was so often the case with men of his pedigree and station.

"I am so sorry to disturb you at bath, Mister Churchill. However, both John Martin and Jock Colville have arrived with urgent matters."

"Yes, yes," Winston responded. "I still have warmth in the water. Please show them in."

Both of his private secretaries entereed with dispatch boxes in their left hands.

"Sorry to disturb you, Prime Minister," began Martin. Winston waved his hand dismissively, spraying bath water on the two men. "We . . ." Martin stopped, when Winston gave him a stop hand signal.

"First, before you give me the bad news and before I forget, Missus Churchill has become rather eager to move into Number 10. How is the renovation progressing?"

"Quite well, actually," answered Colville. "I have informed Missus Churchill the apartment will be ready for your occupancy on Friday. The workmen are finishing up, as we speak. With your permission, Prime Minister, I would like Sawyers to accompany me on the acceptance inspection. He has coordinated with transport to move your household goods from Admiralty House during your absence. As I understand the process, Missus Churchill intends to stay at Chartwell during your journey to France, and will join you at Number 10 on Friday."

"Very well. Sawyers will be of exceptional assistance in this matter. Now, let me have the bad news."

"The Admiralty has informed us, more Italian merchants ships have been seized in Singapore, Bombay and Karachi. The Admiralty believes the Italians have informed their flagged, ship masters to avoid British or French territorial ports, so I final count of seized ships is likely to remain at 220."

"That is good news, not bad."

"Indeed. The arrangements have been finalized for France. Your aircraft will be waiting for you this afternoon at RAF Northolt, with a planned half two departure. The Foreign Office indicated the French have shown no enthusiasm for your visit."

"Hummm," grunted Churchill.

"We received a message from Malta. The island is under aerial bombardment from the Italians."

"You know, John. They only have three fighters on the island for air defense . . . Gladiator biplanes, no less. They have called them, Faith, Hope and Charity."

All three men chuckled at the levity in the face of what had to be daunting odds. Perhaps, Malta would set the standard for resistance to the naked aggression of the Axis powers. A somber mood returned.

"What else have you?"

"That is the immediate news we thought you should be aware of from the ministries."

"Sawyers," called Winston, as he stood in the tub in his full glory. Neither visitor showed the slightest discomfort, as this was an all too common event in their relationship with Winston Churchill.

Sawyers entered the bathroom, adjusted the bath mat, and spread the bath sheet to envelop Winston.

As Sawyers dried his pink charge, Coville continued, "You have a few, short, personal meetings after lunch time, and then we must get you on your way. I am prepared to go with you, Prime Minister, if you wish."

Sawyers wrapped him in a large, multi-color, floral print, silk robe. He looked like a chubby *geisha*. Churchill walked into the adjacent dressing room.

Sawyers and Churchill transitioned immediately into the dressing process. He would be wearing the uniform of an RAF air commodore for the journey to France and traveling under the alias Frankland.

"I would enjoy having you with me, Jock, but alas it is not appropriate. I suspect what we shall find will be quite disheartening. Inspector Thompson and I shall be sufficient . . . well, and after some consideration . . . I asked Bill Stephenson to make the journey, even though he is within days of his sailing for America, as I believe his first hand witness of the situation in France may be most useful in his new assignment."

"As you wish, Sir," Jock responded.

—

Tuesday, 11.June.1940
RAF Northolt
Northolt, London, England
14:30 hours

The Lockheed Hudson Mark I light bomber in tactical markings sat on the tarmac with its aft hatch open, poised for loading and prompt departure. The tail designation of NQ-V signified the aircraft was operated by No.24 Squadron and configured with comfortable passenger seats rather than bomb racks in what used to be a bomb bay. Bill Stephenson stood calmly and casually beside the entry hatch, as Churchill's limousine arrived.

"How are you this fine afternoon?" asked Winston.

"Quite well, Prime Minister. Thank you for asking. And, you?"

Churchill waved his hand dismissively, and then the two men shook hands.

"I truly hope Mary is not too cross with me pulling you away like this, so close to your embarkation and departure for America."

"To be frank, she was not pleased. However, she is a good soldier and she understands that when the prime minister summons, I must attend."

"Again, if you please, when does your ship cast off?"

"Thursday evening . . . prior to sunset."

"We shall endeavor to return you as soon as possible." Winston paused long enough for Bill's acknowledgment head nod. "I should have mentioned this journey in our meeting yesterday. Given your new assignment, I thought it might be most useful for you to have first hand knowledge and witness of the situation in France."

"Quite so."

Churchill motioned with his arm toward his bodyguard. "Have you met Inspector Thompson?" Detective-Inspector Walter Henry Thompson of Scotland Yard had been assigned as Churchill's armed personal protection since the war began. "Walter, this is Bill Stephenson."

"I have heard the name and reputation," responded Stephenson, "A pleasure, Inspector."

"The honor is mine," Thompson said, as the two men shook hands.

"Is the crew ready?" asked the Prime Minister.

At that moment, an RAF sergeant in a crisp uniform appeared from the interior and descended the short ladder, smartly saluted, and then assisted the boarding of his important passengers. "The pilot and navigator are ready for your departure, Prime Minister."

The pilot glanced back into the cabin. As soon as Churchill sat in his chair, he started the right engine. The sergeant closed and locked the door, ensured his passengers were properly buckled into their seats, and took his seat across from the hatch.

Churchill immersed himself in a small stack of papers he carried with him. They took off within a few minutes and headed south-southwest. As they crossed the West Sussex coastline, a full squadron of 12 Hurricane fighters appeared around the Hudson. The fighters had the tail designator FT in front of the roundel, which meant they were with No.43 Squadron based at RAF Tangmere. Stephenson motioned out the window.

Churchill looked to the fighter off the right wing, and then said, ". . . to make the War Cabinet feel better."

Stephenson grinned.

The flight across the English Channel took 20 minutes. As the flight approached the Normandy coastline of France, all but two of the fighters took stations above and behind the Hudson.

Winston put his papers in a small leather case, and then leaned toward Stephenson in the seat beside him. "I am not sure what we shall find upon our arrival. We have evacuated our embassy staff and other nationals. I understand the French are moving their government southwest from Paris to quite possibly Tours. We shall find out once we meet up with Premier Reynaud."

"Do you think there is any hope?"

"There is always hope, my friend . . . as long as we are alive."

"You are always so optimistic, Winston."

"Not always, Bill. As you know, occasionally the black dog visits."

Churchill's family and close friends knew what he meant – the black dog was incapacitating depression that occasionally gripped the veteran politician.

He has certainly had cause for depression in his life – his dismissal as First Lord in 1915, the financial devastation of the Great Depression, his ostracism and banishment in the early 30's. Those who knew him best protected him from scrutiny when those black dog episodes consumed him.

"To be candid, I dread this journey more than I did the carnage of the Somme trenches. The Germans have captured Le Bourget Aerodrome, northeast of the French capital, in one month. They will likely enter the city in the next few days. We are not sure if the French will fight for the city, but I suspect they will declared Paris an open city to avoid the destruction the Germans meted out in Rotterdam. We shall know soon enough. Hitler managed to do what the Kaiser had not accomplished 25 years earlier."

"With such a stark and gloomy assessment, is this visit wise?"

"The War Cabinet did not think so, and made sure their disapproval was duly recorded."

"Then, why Winston . . . when there is so bloody much to lose in this gesture?"

"It is more than a gesture," Winston said softly, almost inaudibly over the drone of the engines, as he looked out his window.

Churchill remained quiet and pensive for the remainder of the flight across the French countryside. They could see the roads jammed with refugees. As they approached the Orly airfield, plumes of black smoke were clearly visible to the northeast. The Germans were very close.

———

The twelve Hurricanes landed first at Orly airfield, south of the city, as they had less fuel reserve than the Hudson. By the time the Hudson taxied to parking, a group of men in blue overalls swarmed the fighters, refueling each aircraft to make ready for a rapid departure in case of German air attack. A small detachment of well-armed Royal Marines in battle dress awaited the RAF Hudson at the far end of the tarmac, away from the Orly passenger terminal building. An unmarked Renault sedan was waiting for them as they deplaned. As soon as Churchill and Stephenson settled into the back seat, Thompson closed the door firmly, and then took the front seat next to the driver. They drove away. The squad of Marines divided, loaded into two personnel carriers, and took station in front of and behind the prime minister's automobile.

———

Wednesday, 12.June.1940
No.312 Rue de la Fontaine
Paris, France
10:30 hours

Paris was in considerable turmoil. The usual calm, almost slow, pace of the city had been replaced by what could only be described as frenetic chaos like popcorn in a pot. Like the country roads they had witnessed on the flight in, people were moving out of the city by whatever means they had – trucks, automobiles and carts loaded beyond capacity, horses with mules carrying the burden of their fleeing, and even men, women and children walking with suitcases in hand. The columns of black smoke northeast of the city added to the somber scene. Despite the disheveled appearance, Churchill's small motorcade had made the journey to the heart of the city and the nearly vacant British embassy, where they spent the evening. Ambassador Sir Ronald Hugh Campbell, GCMG, PC, eager to evacuate his remaining staff and depart himself, had offered the same admonition as the War Cabinet, but his small personal staff had tended their guests surprisingly well despite the conditions. They also received the latest information about the situation in France and Paris from the ambassador – none of it encouraging.

The distant rumbling of artillery through the night had made for a disturbed night and less than restful sleep. Churchill had risen and prepared earlier than normal. Many of the streets between the embassy and the apartment of Premier Reynaud's mistress had been deserted, except for the uncharacteristic flotsam and jetsom of rapidly departing citizens. The short drive put them at the proper address at the appointed hour. Inspector Thompson nervously scanned the abandon street and lifeless buildings before he opened the rear door.

Churchill took a deep breath and exhaled. "We will make quick work of this and be gone," he said. "I simply could not live with myself, if we did not do our utmost to keep the French in this fight."

"As you wish, then, let's be done with this as quickly as possible."

Churchill led the other two through an interior courtyard to the primary apartment on the first floor that had become all too familiar to Winston in the month since the invasion began, having visited the French leader six times. The door was open. No one seemed to be in attendance. Winston called out and received a faint reply from one of the bedrooms. They entered upon a most incredible scene.

The leader of the French Republic, Premier Paul Reynaud, sat in a simple chair with his head buried in the ample bosom of his mistress, the

Countess Hèléne de Portes, who stood unabashedly before him stroking his head as if she was soothing an injured child. Winston stood in the doorway frozen by incredulity and resentment. He found little tolerance for leaders who could not face the horrible reality of armies fighting for a nation's survival.

"Paul, darling," the countess said in soft, relaxed, smooth French, "we have visitors. Winston is back."

The choice of words struck Churchill. Reynaud's mistress used the same words broadcast to the entire Royal Navy nine months earlier. Somehow, the meaning was not the same.

Reynaud raised his head just long enough to see Winston, and then returned to the console of his mistress. Winston felt a tug on his sleeve. The expression on Bill Stephenson's face replicated his feelings. If this was how the leader of the French people dealt with adversity, then maybe all was truly lost. He wanted to leave just as much as Bill wanted him to, but Churchill knew the outcome of the Battle of France and the war might very well rest on this meeting.

Reynaud mumbled some words that Winston could not hear. The curious, searching expression on his face must have given the Countess a hint. "He said, what do you want?" the Countess said in heavily accented English, as if she was the translator.

Winston Churchill spoke in acceptable, but certainly not perfect French. "I am here, Paul, to ensure the continued support of His Majesty's Government."

"Support of what?" the French Premier said. "All is lost. The Germans shall have our beloved Paris within a few days, and we must leave."

"You must gather your strength, encourage your troops and stop the Germans."

Reynaud looked up from the bosom of his mistress. "Have you ever tried to stop an avalanche?"

"These are just men, like you and me. They can be stopped where the will to stop them exists."

"There is no will."

"There must be," challenged Churchill. "You must rally the Army, Paul. We must stop them."

Reynaud stood to face Winston. The Countess de Portes stood behind the French Premier with her hands on his shoulders, as if she needed to brace him. "Where are the ten additional fighter squadrons I requested several weeks ago?" spat Reynaud.

Churchill swallowed hard and gathered his words. The most recent assessment of His Majesty's Government estimated a total collapse of the French armed forces and the French government itself within days. He was not authorized to send additional reinforcements, and he indeed recognized the futility of the situation in France. However, he also refused to accept the outcome where any maneuvering room or possibility existed. He chose not to acknowledge the remonstration.

"We must stand together, Paul, or there may very well be a great probability *Herr* Hitler will rule the world."

"So, where is your Army? Where is America?" Reynaud dropped his head. The countess embraced him as a mother would an injured son.

The Dunkirk debacle, the refusal of the additional fighter squadrons and the relentless success of the *Wehrmacht* on the battlefield brought a sobering reality to the conversation. The only answers available to Winston could do nothing to soften the hurt, depression and despondency of his friend.

"We must think together of how to strike and strike again, no matter what the cost or how long the trials ahead," Winston continued, trying to ignore the demoralized French premier.

"Winston, General Gamelin has reported that the Army can no longer conduct offensive operations. Its ability to provide a viable defense is nearly depleted. He has recommended that we sue for peace. So, what would you suggest we do to strike at the *Bosche*?"

"We must provide inspiration, to encourage the troops, to move reinforcements from the South and West. If the Army can stall the advance, I will press for Commonwealth divisions to supplement and then drive back the Germans. We simply must prevail."

Premier Paul Reynaud considered Winston's words. "I will do what I can, but I would not hold out much hope. We intend to complete the evacuation of the Government to Tours, this evening." Reynaud looked at the Countess de Portes, as if he needed her reassurance or concurrence, and then back to Winston. "I will do my best to keep things going as long as we can."

"Let us try to remain in contact during this crisis. We will do our best to relieve some of the pressure." Reynaud nodded his head. "Good luck, Paul. May God be with you."

The Prime Minister turned to see Bill Stephenson and Inspector Thompson standing in the doorway. He nodded toward the main exit. The two men led the way down the hallway. Winston felt the urge to say more, to provide more encouragement, but he also knew he had a country and commonwealth to lead, and a beleaguered Home Defense Force to bolster. He left the French Premier, and his mistress, not knowing if he would ever see him again. Winston chose not to look back, but he easily imagined the head of the French Republic returning to the comforts of his lover's bosom.

No words were spoken between the three men until they were airborne in their Royal Air Force Lockheed Hudson Mark I light bomber-transport turning north, only after they were well to the west of Paris. Winston eagerly wanted the distinctive lines of a squadron of Hurricanes around them for some comfort. He contemplated for the first time the consequences of the total collapse and loss of France. To fight a war alone against Germany, soon to occupy virtually all of Europe, without assistance, did not appeal to him. His thoughts turned toward a distant ally across the Atlantic. Feeling the weight of the Americans might cause Hitler to hesitate long enough for the course of the Battle of France to change.

The waters of the English Channel came into view through the clouds. Winston finally looked up into the waiting eyes of Bill Stephenson. "What did you think of that?" he asked.

"It appears the estimates were spot on. They have thrown in the towel."

"Quite right."

"How do you see it?"

Winston did not hesitate. "We must complete the evacuation of the BEF from the West and South of France, and redouble our rehabilitation of the Home Defense Forces. We must prepare for the invasion attempt that is certain to come before summer is out."

"It would appear to be our only choice."

Winston thought about alternatives. Only one possibility came to mind. "Bill, I want you to convey the message of what you have seen, but it must be done in a positive manner. You can best serve the Empire talking directly to Franklin and Harry Hopkins, as soon as you can upon arrival."

"It may be too late. Even if I fly tonight, it may be too late."

Without another word, Winston found a piece of paper and retrieved his fountain pen from the interior of his tunic. He wrote his thoughts down then handed the paper to Stephenson.

49
12.VI.40

To: POTUS
Just a very short note. I am en

route back to London from a visit
with Premier Reynaud. It was not
a successful visit. The situation in
France is dire. As you will know, I
have asked 'Intrepid' to carry this
note to you personally as the Kent
affair is not yet behind us. I would
like him to stay with you until the
immediate crisis is resolved. There is
no pleasant direction to approach this,
so I will come straight ahead.

France is in need of support, the kind
of support His Majesty's Government
is at present unable to provide. I
would like to impress upon you the need
for America's benevolence once more.

If you could see your way through
the political environment in the United
States, your support for France at
this critical juncture might very well be
the deciding factor. Please consider
the possibilities. We must not lose
France.
signed,
Former Naval Person

"Your thoughts?" asked the Prime Minister.

"To be frank, Winston," he paused to consider his words, "do you really think the Americans can have any effect on this dreadful situation at this point?"

"Possibly not, but it may be our only hope."

"France may very well fall before I can hand this note to Roosevelt."

Winston Churchill thought about Stephenson's observation. "Of course, you may be precisely correct." He thought for a moment. "If you arrive in Washington and France has fallen, do not deliver the note and await further instructions from me. If there is still hope, proceed. We must take the risk."

"Very well."

The pilot announced their approach to RAF Northolt Aerodrome. The Right Honorable Winston Spencer Churchill, MP, Prime Minister of Great Britain, 1st Lord of the Treasury and Minister of Defense, turned his thoughts to the task at home.

—

Wednesday, 12.June.1940
Headquarters, Fighter Command
Bentley Priory
Stanmore, Middlesex, England

Air Commodore James Hogan, Chief of Intelligence, Fighter Command, closed the door behind him as he entered the office of Group Captain John Spencer. Immediately, John knew something important had happened or sensitive information had come in from the intelligence community. Hogan sat down before he started to talk.

"The Air Ministry's Department Y established that the *Knickebein* system is active. They picked up the signal last night using both their equipment and the captured receiver. It appears you were spot on with your assessment. *Knickebein* is both a navigation aid, but more importantly, it is a foul weather and night bombing system. Department Y confirmed the process last night. It seems they transmit two highly directional radio beams aimed to intersect over the bomb release point for a particular target. The bombardier simply gets his aircraft to the prescribed altitude and speed, and waits for the two needles to form a cross. *Voilà*, bombs away."

John knew the Department Y unit, the electronic countermeasures organization within the Air Ministry, was rarely wrong once they broke down the elements. "Damn, Germans. Clever little devils, aren't they?"

"Quite."

"Has Department Y determined a countermeasure?"

"Not yet, however, they do believe they may be able to jam the signal at least to create some confusion in the cockpit near the anticipated target area."

"By when?"

"Hard to say, actually. The Y boys estimate a fortnight to several months. It seems the Germans use a variety of alternate beam frequencies and secondary beams. The equipment we captured from the Heinkel was setup for one set of frequencies."

"They are sure this broken leg system of the Germans is not simply a navigation system?"

"According to the reports, John, when the Y boys have found the frequencies, the beams are quite discrete and very precisely positioned as an intersection. While they could be used for navigation, the beams are far too narrow to be of general use. From what I have seen and heard, there is only one real purpose . . . terminal navigation for bombing."

John Spencer thought for a moment about options. Although there was doubt about the ability of the RAF to control the daylight skies over Britain, the *Knickebein* equipment would give the *Luftwaffe* dominance of the night skies. In the winter months, that meant more than half the day would belong to the Germans. Depending on the precision of the German bombing aid, they might be able to operate at will over British cities, factories, airfields or any other site of value. Curiosity also stimulated John's inquisitiveness.

"How accurate is the system?"

"We don't know precisely, as yet. Bomber Command has a small research section that has been working with Y Department. Their best estimate today is, the system is at least accurate to within a mile, and maybe as low as a quarter mile depending on target winds."

"My God. With that accuracy, they could go after anything they want."

"Correct."

"Does the night section of the Fighter Interception Unit have this information?"

"Not yet."

"Bloody hell!" John struggled with the reality soon to be upon them. "The night fighters can't get within several miles of a bomber at night. How the bloody hell are we going to keep the sodding *Luftwaffe* from bombing us into oblivion?"

"Air Marshal Leonard has the best team we have working on this problem and the Air Ministry has designated the *Knickebein* countermeasures as the number one intelligence and operations priority. We need time. We need time to sort this out and find an antidote."

Group Captain Spencer overcame his frustration. "My apologies, sir. I don't mean to curse. It just seems every time we think the situation can't get much worse, it does."

"No apologies necessary. We all feel the same sentiments, John."

"Thank you, sir."

Hogan thought for a moment. "Ah yes, there may be at least one piece of good news in this ugly condition. The Farnborough lads think they will finally have the captured Heinkel One One One flying soon. As soon as the flight evaluation is complete and the *Knickebein* kit has been duplicated, they will reinstall the gear in the bomber and use the captured machine for the countermeasures research. Also, if you recall the One Oh Nine captured at Amiens just prior to the invasion," Hogan paused to get a nod of recognition, "it is safely at Farnborough, and if I am not mistaken, will enter flight evaluation within a few days."

"That is good news of a sort."

"I suspect the best thing for you, at the moment, would be a little hands on time. Why don't you make a visit to Farnborough to see our growing stable. Maybe you could visit Frank Whittle to see how his turbine engine is progressing."

John Spencer recognized the wisdom of Hogan's suggestion. He needed a break from the confines and burden of this staff assignment. "I do think you have something there, air commodore."

"Jolly good, then. I shall make the appropriate clearances and access today."

"Thank you, sir. You are a saint."

"Do not go over the top on me now, John."

They laughed until the telephone rang. Air Commodore James Hogan left John to his work. They all needed a break, and they also knew they would not get one any time soon. The worst was yet to come.

—

Saturday, 15.June.1940
No.10 Downing Street
Whitehall, London, England

The Prime Minister sat with growing frustration over the incessant stream of bad news, and negative observations and views. Couldn't anyone find something positive to talk about in all this gloom?

This particular War Cabinet meeting droned on probably because it was a Saturday and the affairs of state waned just slightly on the weekends. Since the invasion and given the ferocity of the German attack of the Low Countries, the War Cabinet met at least once a day and sometimes several times a day to keep up with the volatile situation in France.

A knock at the door signaled a pause to the current debate regarding options. A messenger entered the Cabinet Room to hand a small note to Lord Halifax, the Foreign Minister. He read it, nodded his head for the messenger to leave without a response, and waited for the security of the closed door. He looked first to Winston, then to the other members of the War Cabinet and the Chiefs of Staff. "Paris has fallen," he announced.

The silence of a morgue snuffed out all sound of any kind as each man grappled with his own thoughts without the slightest motion.

Yet one more defeat befell the Allies. The Germans finally accomplished what they had not been able to complete in the Great War. Winston knew the significance of Paris to the French – the same as London to the British. Without Paris, the fall of the remainder of the French Republic would soon follow. Winston sensed the mood of the War Cabinet and recognized the need for more information.

"It is now," Winston glanced at the clock, "half four. Let us adjourn until six. Please gather up all pertinent information regarding the situation in France. I would like to reconvene at six to assess our condition and identify our possible actions."

The shufflings of papers, the movement of chairs and the muffled comments among friends and colleagues were the only acknowledgments of the Prime Minister's direction.

Winston retired to his private office. John Martin brought messages to him. He quickly read through the latest dispatches from France. Reynaud and the core of the French government were now in Tours. Although every attempt to bolster the French government had failed, Winston committed himself to another visit to support Reynaud and possibly turn the avalanche.

A note from Lord Lothian gave him a little encouragement, as he passed along a few words from a speech by President Roosevelt at the University of Virginia in Charlottesville on the 10th of June.

Winston read aloud for the benefit of himself and Martin. "'We are convinced that military and naval victory for the gods of force and hate would endanger the institutions of democracy in the Western world, and that equally, therefore, the whole of our sympathies lie with those nations that are giving their life blood in combat against those forces.' Rather heady words, I should think."

"Yes, sir."

"Lord Lothian says we shall have the rest of the President's speech within a day or so."

"Very good, sir."

"Anything else?" asked Winston. Martin shook his head. "Then, if you will excuse me, I need some quiet time to compose a missive to our friend. Please fetch Kinna, if you would."

Patrick Francis Kinna had recently been released from service to the Duke of Windsor, as the evacuation of Paris began, and came to John Martin's attention with the Duke's glowing endorsement. Kinna was a civil service employee with a blooming reputation as a stenographer and typist of exceptional speed and accuracy.

With the door to his office closed and Kinna poised with his notepad, Winston dictated his message as he stared out the window into the garden of No.10 and allowed his thoughts to coalesce. Once the Prime Minister finished, Kinna left him alone to perform his magic, and returned with a typed sheet of paper before Churchill broke his pensive gaze.

MOST SECRET AND PERSONAL

```
50
15.vi.40
to:  POTUS
As I am sure you have undoubtedly heard, the
capital of the French Republic has fallen to
the bloody hands of the Nazi dictator.  It is
a sad day in the history of Europe, but we
must not and indeed we will not despair.  Ours
is a noble birthright and we shall not fail to
uphold the heritage passed to us through the
generations.
I must say, it is my private opinion, that
unless America can throw its weight on
the side of right, reason and democracy,
France, in toto, will surely fall to the
Teutonic sword within the fortnight.  As I
have said before, Mr. President, I recognise
and acknowledge the mood of avoidance so
prevalent in America.  I am certain from our
communications your heart rests with us,
however, we need your armaments and soldiery
to stem the tide rising against us.  The
most immediate need appears to be destroyers
to combat the U-boat menace, and rifles and
artillery to replace the materiel lost in
France.
As you now know, upon his arrival in a week's
time, I have asked 'Intrepid' to remain
```

in Washington at your disposal until this
immediate crisis has past. I will endeavour
to protect your anonymity as well as our
communications during this trying time. Lord
Lothian very kindly forwarded to me an excerpt
from your recent speech at Charlottesville.
I am encouraged by your words of wisdom and
support, and trust we may translate those
words into physical deeds soon.
As you are aware, Mr. President, the war
cabinet is considering the dispatch of a
small, high level, delegation to the United
States to meet with their counterparts as
soon as the appropriate arrangements can
be made. The purpose of the visit will
be to share information regarding some of
our most sensitive and treasured national
defence secrets. I have been urged by most
members of the War Cabinet and our scientific
community to protect vital secrets from
capture or compromise by our enemy. I trust
you will share my concern and help us in this
endeavour.
In the interest of absolute candour, I must
say our future without France or America to
stand with us would have to be considered
questionable. Do not however doubt for a
moment our resolve to persevere to the end.
We shall never surrender these sacred Isles
no matter how foreboding the opposition may
become. If our monstrous antagonist should
prevail, I can make no guarantee regarding
the status of the Fleet or other assets of
the British Empire. We must stand against
tyranny. Now is the time.
I hope this note finds you in good health and
spirits. Please, at this difficult hour, do
not doubt the resolute spirit of the British
people. With God's grace, we shall prevail.

```
'Intrepid' will answer any immediate questions
and facilitate the initial discussion
regarding the above issues.  I look forward to
hearing from you at your earliest convenience.
signed,
Former Naval Person
```
MOST SECRET AND PERSONAL

Winston reread his typed note several times before calling in Sir Edward Bridges to cable the message via the most secret means to Lord Lothian in Washington to be hand delivered to the President of the United States of America. With good timing, the message would be in the hands of Franklin Delano Roosevelt by the end of the working day in the U.S. capital.

"Prime Minister," Sir Edward said, "the Director of the National Gallery has just this afternoon suggested and recommended that we move the art work of the gallery to Canada for safe keeping."

Winston pounded his fist on the desk out of frustration, more than anger. "No! We will not. They can bury them in caves, cellars and any other hiding place, but we will not move our most visible and public treasures out of this country. We are going to beat the Germans. Mark my words. We are going to beat them."

"I will inform the Director."

"Please do," Winston said in a far more sharp and caustic tone than he wanted.

Colville entered and said, "Lord Halifax should arrive shortly, sir. He has requested an immediate, private audience with the Prime Minister. He gave no subject."

"Very well," Winston answered in a more calm and measured tone. "Show him in as soon as he arrives."

His tolerant, understanding and supportive assistant left him once more to the privacy of his thoughts and paperwork. Winston knew people were scared, as he was, but he had to find the key to inspiration. He must find the key to girder the government, the military and the people against the worst that was approaching. As he said to the world and he believed, and the people must themselves believe, we shall never surrender. It must be so. It simply must be made to happen.

The interphone buzzed. Winston lifted the lever to hear the message from the outer office. "Lord Halifax to see you, Prime Minister."

"Very well. Show him in, if you will."

The door opened allowing the tall, aging and lanky figure of the Foreign Minister to enter. He was dressed as he always was regardless of the day in a dark, pinstriped suit – always the proper gentleman. The long time servant of the Crown waited for the door to close. Winston nodded to him at the appropriate time, not really wanting to speak.

"Just a short comment to begin," he said pausing to receive a nod from Winston. "The situation in France continues to deteriorate. The best information we have is that Reynaud is preparing to resign within the next day or so, and thus allow Marshal Pétain to form a government with the intention of suing for peace." Halifax waited for a response from Churchill. The leader of the British government wondered when someone would bring good news to him. Was this a death spiral with an inevitable outcome? Winston could only stare at Halifax. The Foreign Minister continued his report. "Fortress Verdun fell this afternoon."

"The Hun could not take that fort in the Great War, but they have now. This will not be the last of our losses before the tide turns."

"Quite so, I suspect." The Foreign Minister paused. "There is some good news among all this darkness."

"Do tell."

"Lord Lothian informed us the President signed the Naval Rearmament Act yesterday. The new law provides massive funding for a most ambitious warship construction program."

"Which take several years to realize . . . but a positive sign. I just hope the American recognition is not too late."

"Also, the Admiralty informed us the *Eastern Prince* departed New York harbor in convoy. The entire ship is loaded to the gunwales with rifles, machine guns, artillery pieces, ammunition, and other material declared surplus to remain within the law. This is part of their cash and carry policy enacted by amendment to the Neutrality Act last autumn."

"Excellent."

"Lastly, we did receive late this afternoon an intriguing proposition."

"What, pray tell, might that be?" Winston asked with heavy sarcasm.

"A member of the French Economic Mission here in London, one Monsieur René Pléven, has presented a most ingenious move worthy of our fullest consideration. The young man suggested a formal union of the French Republic and the United Kingdom." Halifax paused for effect, which he received. Winston sat up and leaned over the desk toward Lord Halifax. The idea caught his interest and imagination immediately.

"They won't have to surrender or sue for peace."

Halifax smiled in recognition. "Precisely."

"Quite imaginative, I must say."

"My thoughts exactly. By joining the two countries, we transfer the resultant capital to London, and the decisions are no longer made in Tours. We evacuate the government, combine the expertise including control of the joint armed forces and continue the fight. We will simply have a portion of our new country occupied."

"Brilliant. Absolutely brilliant."

"Whatsmore, we save the French the humiliation of surrender to the Germans."

"What did you say this young man's name was?"

"Pléven. René Pléven."

"I would like to meet him immediately."

"I shall see to the arrangements, but if this is to work, we must act without hesitation and delay."

"Agreed. I shall call a special session of Parliament tonight. While the arrangements are being made, we shall use the six o'clock War Cabinet meeting to establish our position for presentation to the full House tonight. If we are skillful, we could have a resolution and treaty proposal for me to present to Reynaud tomorrow or the next day.

"Yes."

"Cable Reynaud. Ask him to hold out for at least another few days. I will travel to Tours myself to present the treaty."

"That may not be wise, Prime Minister. The Germans have advanced past Paris and are within two or three days march of Tours."

"My dear Lord, this is a most historic act we are about to take. It is worthy of our greatest sacrifice, effort and commitment. I simply must present this union in person."

"As you wish, then we must maintain the absolute highest secrecy."

"Certainly, certainly. Now, we have much work to do. We have barely twenty minutes until the War Cabinet meeting. Please prepare the proper proposal for the Cabinet, and thence the House. Let us see if we can make this move as quickly as possible before Reynaud resigns."

"Agreed," Lord Halifax responded as he rose from his chair and left the Prime Minister to his thoughts before what would surely become a very long night.

Winston smiled broadly alone in his office as he considered the possibilities. The prospect of keeping the French in the struggle kept his focus. While the French Army and Air Force had been mauled on the battlefield, the French Navy remained near its full potential and would be an enormous complement to the Royal Navy. The combined fleets could quite possibly choke off the Germans from access to the sea. Yes, Winston told himself, the subtlety, breadth and consequence of Pléven's union proposal staggered the imagination.

The Right Honorable Clement R. Attlee, MP, Lord Privy Seal and Leader of the Labor Party, came to Winston's office just prior to the War Cabinet meeting. "Lord Halifax informed each of us about the Union proposal. He should have a draft for us when we start in a few minutes. I thought I should offer my opinion."

"Surely," Winston answered, intrigued about how Attlee might feel about the proposal.

"I was struck, as apparently you were as well, by the ingenuity and simplicity of the union proposal. Lord Halifax indicated you intend to take this through to the House. Simply put, Winston, I do not think we have time. I would suggest we take this as the War Cabinet. We do not have time to find a consensus in the House. Sometimes the hardest decisions demand the courage of our convictions."

"Well, Clement, I am overwhelmed, pleasantly so I might add." Winston Churchill felt a unique, very British, pride in his colleague and often, political opponent. "This fellow, Monsieur Pléven, has offered us perhaps the one tool we have to keep France in the war and out of the enemy's camp. While I am inclined to agree with you regarding time and the need for prompt action, this is one of those historic moments that must be recognized through parliamentary debate."

"What if we cannot quickly find consensus? If a consensus cannot be achieved, are we prepared to use our war powers to take this beyond the House?"

"Cogent and poignant questions, Clement. I am not certain I have answers, but my feeling is, if we cannot convince the House, then maybe this is not quite the idea we think."

Both men stared into the others' eyes as if answers might emanate from them. Clement Attlee was the first to nod his head.

"So be it, then."

"Good. Once we approve the draft proposal, I shall take it to Tours myself."

"Lord Halifax also shared your intentions. I happen to concur with his view, Winston. You, as always, grossly underestimate your importance to our defense. Your words and inspiration have kept all of us going through the worst of the last month. We need to send someone else. Lord Halifax has volunteered, and I think he is the only one with the stature and skills to win the day with Reynaud."

Winston felt humbled by Attlee's words. He did not feel he reached those words. He also knew what destiny demanded. "Not to detract from Lord Halifax or anyone else, but I have tried to keep Reynaud in this thing, and I must see this to the end."

"I shall not argue this point with you, and I shall not resist you. You have my support, Winston. I can only pray our good Lord continues to look over you."

"Thank you again, Clement."

The knock at the door preceded the entry of Sir Edward. "Good evening, Winston . . . Clement. It is time for our meeting."

"Thank you, Ed. I am certain you are aware of the union proposal."

"Yes."

"In the interest of that urgent business and with Clement's concurrence, I should like to dispatch the remainder of any actions from this afternoon's session as quickly as possible, and then go into closed session. Clement and I both agree this union proposal is time critical. We must prepare for the presentation and debate in the House tonight. If you would be so kind, Ed, please issue the appropriate notice to the Members, we shall need an extraordinary closed session tonight. We simply must gain ratification of the union proposal within a day, two at the most. We shall have more time to work out the details of confederation once we have given the French an honorable way out of the mess we are in at the moment."

"As you wish, then."

Bridges performed his task to the letter moving along each topic quickly toward a conclusion. The usual peripheral participants in the daily War Cabinet meetings, namely the service ministers and military chiefs of staff, knew about the union proposal. A brief discussion gave them the essence of the proposal. They also understood the need for the closed session to hammer out the final draft. Before closing the meeting to all but the five War Cabinet members less the gravely ill Neville Chamberlain, Lord President of the Council, Winston asked the Admiralty to arrange for a cruiser to transport the Prime Minister, as the representative of His Majesty's Government, from Southampton to Bordeaux to meet with Premier Reynaud and present the union proposal. The Air Ministry was instructed to provide air cover for as much of the journey as possible.

Numerous parallel actions were set in motion. Naval assistance to evacuate the French Government to Africa or England as well as a meeting of the leadership of both countries to include all three major parties in Great Britain would dominate the activities of everyone for several days. As the concept began to solidify, support grew.

The War Cabinet crafted a draft proposal as well as the arguments to place before the House. They departed No.10 Downing Street and walked together to enter the House of Commons precisely on time to begin what they hoped would be a short session. The veteran politicians knew parliamentary action of this magnitude was never predictable. They were prepared to do whatever was required to obtain ratification as soon as politically possible.

—

Chapter 8

The mass of men lead lives of quiet desperation.
-- Henry David Thoreau

Sunday, 16.June.1940
House of Commons
Westminster, London, England
23:15 hours

The extraordinary session lasted just over 24 hours including several brief adjournments to allow for some rest and consultation. The normal gamesmanship of 'what ifs' had filled the space until minutes prior to the final vote when the Prime Minister assured the Members no alternate arrangements would be made without the consent of Parliament. Winston was amazed and gratified with the support the proposal finally received. While there were a few complaints regarding mostly insufficient pre-session preparation of the Members, the significant majority recognized the importance of the proposal. The final vote 20 minutes earlier was not quite unanimous . . . 23 abstentions or absentees, and 17 nay votes. The Union Declaration represented not just an incredible, historic and unprecedented parliamentary action, it was also an ingenious instrument to ensure the continued viability of the Anglo-French alliance. It would maintain the unified opposition to Nazi Germany despite the devastating losses in the Low Countries and Northeast France. Winston was anxious to make the journey as the messenger of the important agreement.

"Congratulations."

"Good luck."

"Godspeed and following winds."

The words of encouragement from Members from all parties came to Winston Churchill in the Member's Lounge after the historic vote. Parliament gave the Government the mandate it sought. While a few words had been changed during the day of deliberation, the Declaration of Union, as it was now known, remained essentially unchanged from the previous evening's initial presentation to the House.

"Thank you, Clement. Thank you, all," he said to the leadership of the various political parties gathered around him. "We have a historic agreement which shall preserve the alliance."

"Now, we must hope we can deliver the Declaration in time," said Attlee.

"Indeed. The appropriate arrangements have been made. I shall immediately take the train to Southampton. We should sail at dawn."

Well-wishes continued to pass among the Members. There was an unusual mood of optimism among the season politicians. The initiative might just work, they told themselves. It would deny Hitler the victory he sought. Fatigue and accomplishment quickly dissipated among the Members.

Not quite alone in the Lounge, Winston read the document one last time.

DECLARATION OF UNION

At this most fateful moment in the history of the modern world, the Governments of the United Kingdom and the French Republic make this declaration of dissoluble union and unyielding resolution in their common defence of justice and freedom against subjection to a system, which reduces mankind to a life of robots and slaves.

The two Governments declare that France and Great Britain shall no longer be two nations, but one Franco-British Union.

The constitution of the Union will provide for joint organs of defence, foreign, financial, and economic policies.

Every citizen of France will enjoy immediately citizenship of Great Britain; every British subject will become a citizen of France.

Both Countries will share responsibly for the repair of the devastation of war, wherever it occurs in their territories, and the resources of both shall be equally, and as one, applied to that purpose.

During the war there shall be a single War Cabinet, and all the forces of Britain and France, whether on land, sea, or in the air, will be placed under its direction. It will govern from wherever it best can. The two Parliaments will be formally associated.

> The nations of the British Empire are already
> forming new armies. France will keep her
> available forces in the field, on the sea, and
> in the air. The union appeals to the United
> States to fortify the economic resources of
> the Allies, and to bring her powerful material
> aid to the common cause.
>   The Union will concentrate its whole
> energy against the power of the enemy, no
> matter where the battle may be.
>   And thus we shall conquer.
> 16th June 1940

As Winston walked back to No.10 Downing Street along the black-out-darkened street, he considered the next sequence of events. A train would be waiting for him in a few hours at Waterloo Station. The rail journey would take about two hours. He planned to arrive at Southampton prior to dawn. The light cruiser HMS *Argonaut* would depart as soon as he was aboard. Fighter Command would have a squadron of Hurricanes or Spitfires overhead the cruiser for better than half the transit to Bordeaux.

The British Ambassador to France was in contact with the French Premier and other members of the French Government. The situation was deteriorating by the moment. Winston considered leaving immediately by airplane to arrive at dawn, but everyone else vetoed the idea. The risks were far too great with the *Wehrmacht* now well into Western France and nearly to the Atlantic Coast. Winston knew he would not get much sleep this night as he prepared for his next journey to France.

—

Monday, 17.June.1940
HMS Argonaut
Southampton Harbor
07:00 hours

The sleek gray warship sat peacefully at anchor in the harbor under a dull gray, overcast sky of early morning. The launch carried the Prime Minister and several aides to the ship. He looked forward to the short voyage and the opportunity to feel the heartbeat and rhythm of a warship as well as talk to the sailors who protected Great Britain.

With minimal but appropriate fanfare the leader of the British people arrived aboard. The captain of the cruiser met the former First Lord at the quarterdeck. The stern expression and cold eyes could only mean more bad news. Winston Churchill prepared his mind.

"Sir, just moments ago, I received a cable from Admiralty. I am to inform you," he glanced at a piece of paper, "Premier Reynaud resigned at 30 minutes prior to midnight, last night. Marshal Pétain has already formed a government and petitioned the Germans for peace. According to the report at Admiralty, an armistice is to take effect at mid-day, today."

Winston's heart sank like a heavy stone in dark, icy water. It was not just the failure of the Union initiative after so much hasty work that brought the chill. They were now alone.

"There is more, Prime Minister."

Churchill motioned impatiently for the additional news.

"The message also indicates the *Lancastria* was bombed by the German air force as the ship was departing Saint-Nazaire."

"Loaded to the gunwales with our soldiers and refugees."

"Apparently! Yes, sir."

"Damned bloody bastards."

"There is no report of survivors."

"Anything else?" growled Churchill.

"One more item. They say the *Broompark* is loaded at Le Verdon sur Mer and waiting for a score of personnel still on the road. The Admiralty confirmed the dispatch of a destroyer and a corvette to escort the *Broompark*, but cannot leave the escort waiting for the *Broompark* to sail."

"Yes, well, they will wait. That cargo is priceless. You will reply to the message. The escort must provide what protection they are able and ensure the safe arrival of the *Broompark* in Home waters."

"Yes, sir."

"Thank you, Captain. The reason for our little cruise has vanished."

"Yes, sir."

The Royal Navy commander stood before his Prime Minister as though he was patiently waiting orders. Winston actually considered whether he should press his mission in an attempt to recover the situation. In the end, reality decided the question.

"Would you be so kind . . . radio Admiralty . . . I received the message and terminated the mission. I shall, from this moment, release you from your orders."

"Very well, sir. I should like to see you off first, Prime Minister. I intend to weigh anchor as soon as you are clear. I will feel much better in open water."

Winston smiled in appreciation of the warrior's focus. "By all means."

"I am terribly sorry we were not able to fulfill this mission, sir."

"I as well. It is a dark day." Winston truly felt dark and cold. He also knew he did not enjoy the luxury of despair. He had a leadership role to perform. "The bright side is, our task is now clear. The burden of defeating this foul bastard is now squarely upon our able shoulders."

"Yes, sir, and we shall be worthy of the task."

Winston smiled, again. "All will be right in due course."

"As you say, sir."

Winston stood unaided in the harbor launch as it motored toward the landing. He watched the majestic cruiser gracefully steam toward the Solent, the English Channel and the high seas beyond. He kept his few tears to himself as pride buoyed him. The sailors went in harm's way to the certain battles that lay ahead. Yes, indeed, Winston told himself, theirs was a righteous crusade, and they would prevail.

—

Monday, 17.June.1940
RAF Northolt
Northolt, London, England
16:45 hours

Pilot Officer Brian Drummond added up in his head the time he had flown as he walked toward Dispersal from his third mission of the day. By his rough estimate, he had flown more hours in the last six weeks than he had in the previous six months. With the exception of two maintenance flights, one for his new Spitfire to replace the one he was shot down in and one flight to check the control rigging after replacement of a damaged aileron, all his flights had been combat flights. Everything was greater – more gun time, more maneuvering, higher altitudes, and more fatigue.

The intelligence debriefing finished quickly. There really was not much to tell. The long flights over the Channel to support the operations of the Royal Navy only allowed brief encounters when they found something to shoot at among the clouds. This sortie was like all the others in recent days. Short, fleeting engagements as their targets dove for the cloud cover, and sightings but no time to engage, punctuated hours of loitering in the cold of altitude. Frustration mounted. They all knew the situation in France was bad and getting worse. They all wanted to do more to help, to stop the Germans, to save France.

With all the pilots settled into chairs or lying on the grass enjoying the late afternoon Sun as they waited for their next scramble, the conversation soon rose up.

"Why don't they move us to Le Mans, Rennes, Cherbourg or Brest for that matter?" asked Pilot Officer Stephen 'Mongo' Strickland as he usually did challenging decisions around him. "We could achieve greater on station time."

Everyone ignored Steve's question as they usually did. Brian knew, as he surmised most of the pilots would agree, 'Mongo' was correct, but the powers that be must have a greater view. They knew something the pilots did not. There was a reason the squadrons had not been moved further south as they had when the invasion of France began.

"Doesn't anyone have something to say. Don't you blokes agree?"

"Give it a rest, 'Mongo,'" said Flying Officer 'Organ' Foxworth.

"Why? Couldn't we do more if we were closer?"

"Sure we could, but have you considered that Command may be saving us for the greater fight ahead."

Everyone seemed to perk up at the vocalization of what they all thought. They all wanted to do more, knew they could do more, but were thankful for each moment they could relax in the sun. Brian Drummond and Jonathan Kensington shared their thoughts, and they both agreed with 'Organ' Foxworth, but no one talked about what might come, now. It was as if any discussion about the approaching battle would bring it a few steps closer.

The peculiar silence of a squadron dispersal building moved in among the lounging pilots. The tones of aircraft engines, fuel bowsers, the gun-firing pit, and hustle and bustle of a major working fighter base occupied the spaces between them. Jonathan told him the waiting felt like an athlete resting before the finals race.

Corporal Jennifer Warren left her post at the Dispersal desk and stood just outside the doorway. That meant one of two things – either nature called or she had an announcement. "The BBC just broadcast the news that Premier Reynaud has resigned. Marshal Pétain formed a new government, and then promptly sued for peace," she said in a low, solemn voice. Many of Brian's squadron mates visibly slumped with the news.

"Bloody Frogs gave up," barked Strickland.

"Yes, indeed," said 'Organ' Foxworth, "and, where would that have left us if we had relocated to France?"

Steve Strickland had never been known for his humility, but this occasion became the exception. "All right, then, I was wrong."

"There is a lesson here," interjected Flight Lieutenant Roger 'Jackstay' Beamish. "We've got one sodding job to do, lads. The country has given us these machines," he said nodding toward the flight line, "to kill Germans. All the country asks of us is to do the best we can."

"That's all I was trying to say."

"Certainly, 'Mongo,'" said Beamish, "but you always worry about the wrong things, or say it with the wrong words."

Miles Johnson and James Carrolton, the two flying sergeants, by now were totally detached from any of the conversation and snoring loudly. The obvious sounds of deep sleep gave each of them a humorous break from the depressing news.

Brian Drummond thought back to the story's his mentor, Malcolm Bainbridge, told him about operations with the Royal Flying Corps in France. How had he dealt with the waiting, the uncertainty, and the suffocating reality of depressing news? How did anyone keep from going crazy dealing with the extremes of being required to wait under the strain of a very short leash and the intensity of mortal, aerial combat against a skilled and determined adversary? It was during the lulls like this moment Brian wanted the counsel of Malcolm, just to know what others had gone through it and maybe how they dealt with it.

There was also defiance that each of them felt in their own way. A few could vocalize their feelings, but most, like Brian, tended to keep things bottled up inside. He had opened up with Anne Booth a few times and Rosemary Kensington once. The information scared Rosemary and inspired Anne. He touched on the tensions with Jonathan a couple of times, but they seemed to play against one another not wanting to show any weakness.

The fact that France had been done in by the still undefeated German Army and Air Force told each of them without information from the government, their leadership or the press – they were next. They would soon be put to the ultimate test.

The Dispersal telephone rang bringing each pilot to instant, gut wrenching alertness. If they scrambled now, they would undoubtedly have a night return that none of them liked in a blackened countryside.

"Stand down, lads," announced Squadron Leader Horatio 'Spike' Darling. "That's it for the day. Let's get something to eat."

Those that still wore their flying equipment removed the items, and each of them returned their kit to their assigned pegs and places. As they walked toward the Officer's Mess, the conversation turned more jovial and animated. Several would soon see girlfriends or just female companionship. Jonathan considered a run into the city for a few hours of pleasure. Brian agreed to go although he wanted to avoid any action that might draw attention to his relationship with Anne Booth. He still thought he loved Anne, but he could never forgive her, if she truly was a spy. Brian kept telling himself, there had to be a mistake, and that in due course, the misunderstanding would be corrected. Fortunately for Brian's reticence and concerns, their fatigue caught up with them before they could finish their evening meal.

—

Tuesday, 18.June.1940
RAF Northolt
Northolt, London, England

The telephone ring nauseated the bevy of No.609 Squadron pilots. They waited the few extra seconds that told them this call was probably not a run-to-your-fighter launch command. This call might be one of several other possibilities. A release from alert – not likely. It was a sunny day with scattered clouds. A patrol order – more routine than a scramble. A change in alert status – most probable. They were already at Readiness meaning they had to be less than a handful of minutes between scramble and wheels in the wells. Or, the skipper just received a routine administrative call from Sector Control. Half the pilots fained ambivalence although Brian Drummond knew every single one of them were on the knife edge waiting for the outcome.

Squadron Leader Darling joined the basking pilots. "Routine patrol, lads. Blue and Green Sections. 'Sparky,' you have the helm."

Brian retrieved his flying gear as the other designated pilots did and walked toward the line of perched Spitfires.

"What is it this time, Skipper?" asked Flying Officer George 'Angle' Ashcroft, the left wing of the commander's Blue Section.

"We are the reserves as I understand it. We will be overhead South London at 20,000 feet in anticipation of one of several possible attack directions."

"Splendid," said Pilot Officer Roland 'Boxer' Stockard. "More waiting."

"At least we're flying," Brian interjected.

"Right, then, just what we need more flight time."

The flight turned out to be about as routine and boring as they ever got. Ninety minutes of long, racetrack orbits without any radio transmissions of any kind. They saw nothing other than clear sky above, scattered clouds below and the reaches of the capital city of the United Kingdom between the clouds. They heard absolutely nothing other than the deep, monotone hum of the engine, the gentle rush of the air stream as they loitered at maximum endurance airspeed, and finally the words terminating the patrol and returning them to the airfield.

By the time, Blue and Green Sections landed, Red and Yellow Sections were airborne on their own patrol. It would be another hour or more before the squadron became whole again.

"No squawks, Bernie," Brian told his crew chief as he unstrapped from his PR-F Spitfire. "We flew. We heard nothing. We saw nothing, and we did nothing."

"Right you are," Gordon responded as he ran his left hand over the red gunport tape still in tact. "We shall have you refueled and ready to go in a snap."

"Great, Bernie. Thanks."

They returned to Dispersal, debriefed in less than a minute and waited for Squadron Leader Darling to obtain whatever news he could from Sector Control. The result did not take long.

"Red and Yellow relieved us on the patrol, so they will probably have the same conclusion," Darling said. "Sector Control put us at Available status, that should finish us for the day."

"Anything else, Skipper?"

"Like what?"

"Why have we had all these boring patrols lately?" asked 'Angle' Ashcroft.

"Sector said they have had more high altitude reconnaissance flights. It seems Gerry is stepping up his probes of our defenses."

"Then, why haven't we engaged them?" Ashcroft pressed on with his questioning.

"They are apparently having some difficulty with altitude determination. According to Sector, we should see some improvement any day now."

"We haven't seen any action for several days," added Brian.

"Patience, my young colonial. We shall have all the action we can handle soon enough, I'm afraid." Several pilots laughed in the face of the fear they knew would soon haunt them.

Brian Drummond decided he needed a walk. Rising from his lounge chair still wearing his Mae West, he grabbed his helmet with oxygen mask and gloves to walk toward the line of fighters. There was no sense having to run back to Dispersal in the event they received a scramble.

Brian found Bernie Gordon with one of the engine cowling panels open working on something. "Find a problem, Bernie?" he asked.

Gordon stopped wiping his greasy hands on a rag extracted from his overalls pocket. "No, sir. Just cleaning our baby up a little. I like to keep her clean. Makes it easier to work on."

"Brilliant."

"What's our status, sir?"

"We're back to Available."

"Good, then I can tidy up a few more things."

"Hey, Bernie," shouted Aircraftman Colin Jenkins, the team's armorer. "Look what they . . . ," he said as he came around the nose of the Spitfire seeing Brian, "Oh, excuse me, sir. I didn't see ya there."

"No problem, Colin."

"So, what do ya have there, mate?"

"They started distributing these blimey pamphlets," Jenkins said handing Gordon the pamphlet. "Couple of the blokes got 'em in the village. Just started making 'em available on the aerodrome."

Gordon looked through the four-page, long but narrow, pamphlet. "I'll be," he said as he handed Brian the paper.

The Alert Pamphlet described the actions each citizen should take in the event of enemy parachutists landing in the neighborhood. Remain calm. Call your local constabulary immediately, passing information regarding the location, the number and description of the parachutists. Alert your neighbors. Evacuate the area. Keep watch. Do not believe rumors, and do not spread rumors. Able bodied men should report to their nearest police or Home Defense Force station for instructions.

"Sounds like they mean business," said Brian.

"I'd say so, sir," answered Bernie Gordon.

"Does this mean the government knows we are going to be invaded soon?" asked Jenkins.

"I don't think so. Just prepared," Brian responded. "We haven't seen much activity in the skies. They would have to carry out a major air campaign before they would invade according to the squadron leader."

"So, if air activity picks up, we should start lookin' for the Huns to rain down from the sky?"

They all laughed at the image created by Jenkins' words. "You mind if I show the Skipper this thing?" asked Brian shaking the pamphlet between them.

"No, sir."

"Thanks, guys. See ya later."

As Brian approached the Dispersal building, he noticed none of the pilots sitting outside. Everyone was gathered around the old radio inside.

"What's . . . ," Brian started to ask, but stopped as several of the pilots held up their hands signaling him to be quiet. Then, he heard the distinctive voice of Winston Churchill.

"I am happy to inform the House that our fighter strength is stronger at the present time relative to the Germans, who have suffered terrible losses, than it has ever been; and consequently we believe ourselves possessed of the capacity to continue the war in the air under better conditions than we have ever experienced before. I look forward confidently to the exploits of our fighter pilots – these splendid men – this brilliant youth – who will have the glory of saving their native land, their island home, and all they love, from the most deadly of all attacks."

"You tell 'em, Winnie," interjected 'Sparky' Morrow.

"The bloody Prime Minister thinks a few fighters are going to stop the Germans whom, I might add, have just vanquished the largest army in Europe, from invading our little island," added the usually skeptical 'Mongo' Strickland.

"Knock it off," commanded 'Spike' Darling. "If the Prime Minister believes in us, then we had damn well better not disappoint the man." Everyone's attention returned to the radio.

"What General Weygand called the Battle of France is over. I expect the Battle of Britain is about to begin," the Prime Minister said slurring his words somewhat in dire solemnity. His almost hesitant voice continued. "Upon this battle depends the survival of Christian civilization. Upon it depends our own British life, and the long continuity of our institutions and our Empire. The whole fury and might of the enemy must very soon be turned on us. Hitler knows that he will have to break us on this island or lose the war. If we can stand up to him, all Europe may be free, and the life of the world may move forward into broad, sunlit uplands. But if we fail, then the whole world, including the United States, including all we have known and cared for, will sink into the abyss of a new Dark Age made more sinister, and perhaps more protracted, by the lights of perverted science. Let us therefore brace ourselves to our duties, and so bear ourselves that if the British Empire and its Commonwealth last for a thousand years, men will still say, this was their finest hour."

The room fell silent except for the minor radio static. "This has been a general broadcast of the BBC World Service by the Prime Minister, Winston Churchill. We shall now return you to our regular program." Classical music of some kind returned.

The pilots sat as if some mysterious force had stunned them. No one moved or talked for several minutes. Brian knew he had only heard the last few minutes of the broadcast, but he felt tears of pride, patriotism and enthusiasm well up. He looked down at his lap so the others could not see his eyes and swallowed hard to fight back any dripping. Here they were, Brian told himself, on the verge of invasion by a victorious enemy and Churchill talked as though they had just achieved the victory. Individual words told of sacrifice, difficulty and the struggle ahead, but the combinations of words shouted strength, confidence and commitment. Every speech he heard from Churchill seemed to be more inspiring than any before it. Brian Drummond was thankful he was part of this historic event.

"Their finest hour, aye?"

"That is what the man said."

The spits and sputters of idling Merlins in the landing Spitfires broke the trance. Several pilots including Brian rose to check out the returning fighters. The PR letters designated the returning half of the squadron. The gun port tapes were still in place. Red and Yellow Section had not had any better hunting.

"No joy?" Brian asked Jonathan as the returning pilots entered the Dispersal building.

"Same as you, I'm afraid." he answered in a mood of frustration they all shared.

With the intelligence debriefings completed and the squadron released from alert status, the pilots retired to the Mess for a quick meal and a few beers together before they would begin to scatter. There were only two topics of discussion while they were together – the Prime Minister's broadcast and the frustration of waiting. There was universal acceptance of the speech and universal revulsion over the inaction.

"Want to go into the city?" asked Jonathan Kensington of his best friend.

"Not tonight," answered Brian. "I have a few letters to write and some reading to do, and then I want to call it an early night."

"Linda says, some of the ladies are gathering up for a gay old party. They seem to feel the PM's speech made them feel like a party. Don't you want to see Anne?"

Brian, somewhat surprised Jonathan had not heard about Anne, wanted to tell Jonathan about his experience with Inspector Dunwoody, but he convinced himself it was not yet time. He needed to talk to Jeremy Morrison to find out more about what happened and to put a measure on what little he knew. "Naw, not up to it tonight."

"Is there something wrong with you? Do you not feel well? Just a short time ago, you would be crawling over bodies to get to Miss Anne Booth. Has something happened?"

Brian could not answer the question. "No problems. I'm simply worn out."

"Well, I shall give Linda a kiss for you," Jonathan said.

"You do that."

Jonathan departed leaving Brian with his thoughts. Why had Anne betrayed him? Maybe she did not betray him? Maybe she just betrayed her clients and her country? Brian wanted to talk to someone. There was a fragment of regret that he had not shared with Rosemary. She was always so open, forthright and unashamed about anything. He needed to find a different viewpoint on this whole episode surrounding Anne Booth. Jeremy Morrison's name kept coming back to him. He was probably the only one he could talk to about Anne. He was involved, more deeply than himself. After all, Jeremy introduced him to Anne, and he was rather attached to Virginia North.

Brian needed a diversion. He made his way to the Officer's Mess bar. Everything appeared to point toward the monumental character of the events of the last few months, in his life and in the life of nations. Something truly important was happening and edged ever closer with each day, with each encounter, with each meeting of separate souls.

As he entered the Officer's Mess, numerous pilots were still in the bar including two of the No.609 Squadron pilots. He knew he would not be able to go to sleep right away. He ordered a pint of beer and joined his colleagues.

"Did you hear the guns tonight?" asked 'Mongo' Strickland.

"Yeah. What was it?"

"Word has it, the Germans tried to bomb London" said 'Angle' Ashcroft. "An entire squadron of Heinkels flew up the Thames at a relatively low altitude. What the fighters did not get before dark, the guns took care of in the beams of searchlights. Apparently, they got all of them before they dropped their bombs or got away."

"I saw the flashes and heard the guns in the city. Didn't seem to bother anyone."

"Maybe not now, but it will probably get more personal rather quickly, I suspect."

Brian's thoughts turned to the women in his life – to Anne Booth, a woman he loved, but now in prison probably near the center of the capital city; to Mary Spencer, who lived near the headquarters of Fighter Command; and to Rosemary Kensington, who went to the university near the largest pilot training base in Great Britain. If the Germans were going to bomb the cities, there would be many civilians, other than military people, injured in the conflagration. They had to keep the Germans out of Great Britain.

—

Thursday, 20.June.1940
House of Commons
Westminster, London, England
16:30 hours

The War Cabinet meeting lasted longer than planned which forced another, relatively rare, secret session of Commons to start more than an hour later than planned. The Summer Solstice meant they would start the meeting with the Sun still above the rooftops in the West. If they were lucky and the debate did not take long, Winston Churchill thought he might be able to have supper with Clementine before the end of the long summer twilight of the northern dusk. Midsummer's Night was traditionally a time of celebration in Northern Europe. This year, there would be no romping, joyous celebration of the renewal of the cycle of life.

The Prime Minister's report to Commons had gone reasonably well. Only minor shouts punctuated his presentation. It was uplifting but honest. The news from the Continent continued to grow worse. The little dictator rubbed the nose of the French in their own failure by forcing their capitulation in the same railcar that the Allies demanded the Germans sign their surrender 22 years earlier. The losses at sea mounted with no signs of rescue from the United States. All the available intelligence, which he had not shared with any of his colleagues in the House outside the War Cabinet, pointed toward Great Britain as the next target of the *Wehrmacht*. The best estimates set the invasion date in August, or September at the latest, just a little more than a month away. The condition of the Home Defense Force, while placed in the best possible light, was abysmal.

"The Chair recognizes the honorable member from Norfolk," the speaker announced continuing the Prime Minister's Question Time.

"There has been no mention of the extraordinary action taken by this House just four days ago. What happened to our proposal of union with the French Republic, and why could we not make our presentation before Marshal Pétain sued for peace?"

Churchill stood before the Prime Minister's podium. "It is by oversight that His Majesty's Government failed to report to the House on this matter. In short, messages were sent to Premier Reynaud in Tours indicating the importance and urgency of our proposal. We still, as of this moment, do not know what events transpired in those last few hours and days. We shall know as soon as the intelligence services can make contact with the cognizant individuals. In the end, our party was stopped as we boarded HMS *Argonaut* in Southampton Harbor by the news of the French capitulation. On behalf of His Majesty's Government, I should take this occasion to thank the honorable members for their support and timely response in this most delicate matter." Winston sat down at the center of the Government Bench. He wanted Question Time to be over, so they could get on to the new business.

The next question came smartly. "Why must the British people give away to the Americans some of our most precious technology?"

"The Right Honorable and Gallant Member from Manchester surely recognizes the military significance of our present situation. It is in that light His Majesty's Government proposed, the War Cabinet approved, and we are seeking the consent of the House for the unprecedented move to protect the vital secrets of our defense capability. While the enemy may have similar activities in most of the affected areas, we are convinced our technology is superior, and therefore we would not want it to fall into the hands of the enemy without some guarantee of parity for our friends across the water."

"Yes, but, the Americans are also one of our principal competitors. Why should we give away our edge in this industrial competition?"

"As the Right Honorable and Gallant Member knows, we are regrettably on the cliff's edge awaiting the forecast and some would say the inevitable storm. The risk of compromise is in our opinion far greater than the benefit to our friendly competitor. We are talking about the very survival of the freedoms we hold dear. This seems a small sacrifice to ensure our ultimate victory."

The response touched a nerve as numerous Members on both sides of the aisle jumped up asking for recognition. The raucous comments and shouts broadcast the concern. "Order," the Speaker commanded. "Order. We shall have order before we proceed. Order." Gradually, the shouts died down and the parliamentary process continued.

The release of secret information to the Government of the United States occupied the attention of the House for most of the allotted hour of Question Time. The passing of vital information on turbine engines, radio direction finding equipment, underwater detection devices, and several advances in radio communications technology became the touchstone at this moment in history. The release of the defense secrets seemed to be more important than the possibility of invasion. Winston had underestimated the sensitivities of the House, but the tone of the questions did not convey an insurmountable condition.

"Last question," announced the Speaker. "The Chair recognizes the Honorable Member from Liverpool."

"Being half American and a professed friend of America . . ." The Members began to rumble. ". . . I should like to know what other motives the leader of the Conservative Party has for giving . . ." Nearly the entire House jumped in boisterous response. Winston kept his seat and warmed to the implicit defense of his honor.

"Order. The House will be in order," shouted the Speaker. "I demand order. Order." The ruckus gradually died down. "The Chair must caution the Honorable Member to avoid personal offenses against another Member."

"Then, I shall continue." He considered where to restart his question. ". . . for giving our most valuable secret technology to the colonials?"

The House roared once again with shouts of resentment, of objection, toward the meaning behind the question. Winston quickly considered his response, if he would respond, to the implication he was somehow subverting the sovereignty of the United Kingdom. He thought just for an instant about whether he was moving too quickly to safeguard the national secrets. The thought lasted for only a moment. Winston Churchill knew he was absolutely correct in proposing this action for several reasons. It was a move to safeguard national secrets, and it was a good faith gesture to encourage the Americans. The Prime Minister stood before the podium and waited for the rage to die down in the House.

"The Honorable Gentleman is ill-informed," he said and sat on the Government Bench.

A moment of stunned silence preceded the shouts of approval. He chose the high ground and avoided an emotive response. The man simply did not see the severity of the situation.

Question Time ended with a short break.

The debate on the National Secrets Protection Act took another two hours before the Government bench called for a vote. The measure passed by an impressive 127-vote margin. Churchill walked the short distance in the fading evening twilight down Whitehall to the historic residence of the Prime Minister of Great Britain with some sense of relief and satisfaction. Reason had prevailed over emotion, but the enormity of the action Parliament had taken this night would eventually mark history books with the monumental weight and seriousness of this particular instant in time.

Thursday, 20.June.1940
Oval Office
The White House
Washington, District of Columbia, U.S.A.
13:45 hours

"**M**ister President, Misters Stimson and Knox are here as you request-ed," announced Marguerite 'Missy' LeHand.

"Thank you, Missy. Show them in, would you please." Roosevelt wheeled his chair from his desk to the opposing couches in front of his desk. The two men entered and the door closed behind them. "Good afternoon, gentlemen . . . a pleasure to see you both."

"Good afternoon, Mister President," Knox and Stimson said in unison.

They shook hands. The President motioned to the couches. The two visitors sat separately on the opposing couches.

"I do not have much time before the scheduled Cabinet meeting, so I shall cut directly to the chase." Knox and Stimson nodded. "With events unfolding in Europe and Asia, I think it is only a matter of when this nation shall be drawn into war." Franklin looked directly to Frank Knox. "We discussed your service last December. You told me you did not think the situation warranted. Do you now?"

William Franklin 'Frank' Knox, the 66-year-old veteran Republican politician from Michigan and the Republican Party vice presidential candidate in the previous election, knew exactly the conversation to which Roosevelt was referring. "Mister President, do you seriously want two staunch Republican politicians inside your Cabinet? We are not New Deal-ers."

Roosevelt did not answer and let his stern, unflinching expression speak for him. He waited for the response to his query.

"Yes, well, I suppose the situation has changed," answered Knox.

Roosevelt turned to the 72-year-old Henry Lewis Stimson of New York. "And you, Henry?"

"If you truly believe we are your best choices to serve in these trou-bled times, Mister President, then I would be honored to return to my former office as secretary of war."

"Let me be very clear here, gentlemen. This is going to get much worse before we can even hope to see the light at the end of the tunnel. We are woefully ill prepared for what is occurring in the world around us. Our oceans will not offer the protections they once did. Both of you are veterans. You know what it means to fight. You have both argued for defense preparedness in the face a palpable isolationist mentality in this country. We will soon need a unity government capable of waging war successfully. So, yes, Henry, I truly believe you and Frank are the best men in this country to prepare us for what is certain to come."

"Then, I would be honored to serve, Mister President."

"Likewise, Mister President."

"Will you be able to square this assignment with your Republican colleagues?"

Stimson responded for both men, "We Republicans understand far better what is coming."

"We have a presidential election this Fall, as you well know. I do not presume to know who the Republican nominee will be. In fact, I am struggling with reconciliation between some in my party and the two-term precedent in play since President Washington."

"Your cousin managed that reconciliation," quipped Knox.

"Yes, he did, but he did not have continuous service, either; and, he did not win re-election as you well know."

"True."

"Wilkie appears to be making headway."

"Yes," Stimson answered. "He is more internationalist and isolationist, despite the party's presumptive platform. I cannot speak for Frank, but I do see the wisdom in your objectives, Mister President."

"I concur."

"Very well, then. I have already discussed these changes with Woodring and Edson. Fortunately, they appreciate the larger objectives. I shall inform the Cabinet shortly. Your nominations shall go to the Senate this afternoon, and I shall request an expedited confirmation process. I need you both in harness as soon as your nominations are confirmed." The President reached forward, extending his hand to each man. They stood and shook the President's proffered hand. Roosevelt glanced at the large desk clock on the credenza to his left. "I am already late. Lastly, as you will soon recognize, if not already, we are in a sad state regarding our collection and analysis of strategic intelligence. I have seen the consequences of our deficiencies too many times in the last few months. Military intelligence and naval intelligence are good at what they are interested in, but they are far too exclusionary, insular, isolated and parochial. Hell, even the FBI has been caught with their pants around their ankles regarding the infiltration of German spies and saboteurs among us. I need . . . we all need . . . a chief of intelligence to coordinate, collect, process and understand intelligence information that will be vital to defend this nation against the forces of aggression around us. I would like your thoughts once you have a handle on things . . . hopefully sooner rather than later."

Both men chewed on the President's words and perspective. Knox was the first to respond. "I think we have both seen elements," he said, glancing toward Stimson to get a nod of concurrence, "but, certainly not to your extent. It will be a tough nut to crack. I have not known them to play well together."

"Yes, well, we will have a real war to fight sooner than we think, and this nation cannot, will not be able to tolerate such juvenile conduct."

"A Columbia Law classmate of yours may be just the man for such a Herculean task." Roosevelt raised his head and eyebrows in anticipation. "Bill Donovan."

"Wild Bill?"

"One and the same. He is not afraid of the bureaucratic fight, and I know he believes in the need for strategic intelligence. He has many, perhaps countless, international connections."

The President considered Knox's suggestion as well as his personal knowledge of Colonel William Joseph "Bill" Donovan -- holder of the Medal of Honor for combat valor in the Great War; an accomplish New York lawyer; founder and principal partner of the successful, Wall Street, law firm of Donovan, Leisure, Newton & Irvine; and an influential Republican Party member in good standing. "Interesting proposal. We have an immediate need."

"Certainly."

"France has collapsed and seeks an armistice with the Germans. Hitler cannot sustain his conquests as long as the Royal Navy controls the North Sea and English Channel. It would appear to me he must subjugate Great Britain, and Prime Minister Churchill has made it clear the British will not go quietly into the night. We just sent the first of what will certainly be many shiploads of arms to England at considerable risk. We need to know the real situation in Great Britain, and we need an honest, unbiased assessment of their viability in the face of demonstrable German military superiority."

"Are you asking if Bill can make that assessment?"

"Yes, precisely."

"With a letter of introduction from the President of the United States, I do not think there is a man more capable."

"I am not prepared to issue such a letter for a host of reasons, Frank. He would have to operate under the unofficial authority of the new secretary of the Navy."

Knox quickly considered the consequences. "I think we could make that work."

"I do not want Churchill to think or even question whether we believe his position. Yet, somehow, we must have an independent view of whether the British will survive what appears will be an inevitable German invasion."

"Bill can handle that."

"Do you have any suggestions, Henry?"

"Nothing further, Mister President. I concur with Frank's proposal of Bill Donovan. Good man."

"Very well, then." Looking directly into the eyes of Frank Knox, Roosevelt said, "Talk to Bill. Make sure he is amenable to the assignment. We will need a week or so to grease the skids before we launch this mission."

"I will confirm the arrangements to your office."

"He will have to wait until your confirmation by the Senate to make the cover story work."

"Yes, sir, as you wish."

"Excellent. Welcome aboard, gentlemen. I do not envy the challenges you will face, but I have full confidence in your abilities. I expect the Senate to make quick work of your confirmations. Thank you for coming and thank you for your service to the Republic. Now, I am signficantly beyond fashionably late to the Cabinet meeting. Please excuse me, I shall bid you *adieu*."

As both men departed, Harry Hopkins entered to wheel the President into the Cabinet Room. Roosevelt winked and smiled to Harry – mission accomplished.

—

Friday, 21.June.1940
No.10 Downing Street
Whitehall, London, England

Jock Colville knocked twice, entered the Prime Minister's study, and closed the door behind him. Churchill looked from his papers, waiting for Colville. "Sir, the Air Ministry group you requested is nearly assembled in the Cabinet Room."

"Thank you, Jock. Call me when they are ready."

"Yes, sir. If I may, sir, Lord Halifax wished me to inform you, the French have agreed to terms with the Germans. An armistice signing ceremony will be held tomorrow in the Foch railcar at Compiègne. The Foreign Office is attempting to obtain the precise wording and stipulations of the armistice document."

"Tempting target, wouldn't you say?"

"Indeed, sir."

"Idle musing, I'm afraid. What else have you?"

"The Admiralty informed us the *Broompark* sailed yesterday from Le Verdon sur Mer, Bordeaux, without incident. She is under Royal Navy escort and expected to dock at Plymouth in the next day or two. The Earl of Suffolk and his precious cargo are all safe and sound to the moment. The south coast ports are working around the clock to accommodate the continuing, near overwhelming, stream of evacuation ships. A senior Admiralty officer will remain at dockside to ensure the *Broompark* obtains highest priority handling."

"Excellent. Please pass a note of gratitude to Admiralty and the Foreign Office for their continuing exceptional service to the Crown."

Colville jotted down a few notes on his note pad. "That is all I have at the moment, Prime Minister. Would you like me to check on the attendees for your Air Ministry meeting."

"Yes."

Churchill returned his attention to the latest shipping report . . . always a disturbing but necessary activity these days.

Colville returned within minutes. "They are ready for you, Prime Minister."

"Thank you, Jock."

Prime Minister Churchill rose from his desk chair and proceeded to the Cabinet Room. As he entered, he scanned the room. The catalyst for this meeting, his science advisor since reinstatement as First Lord of the Admiralty last year, Professor Frederick Alexander Lindemann stood opposite the door and would likely take the seat at the table to Churchill's left. The expected Air Ministry personnel were present – Sinclair, Newall, and of course Wing Commander Elliott of the Cabinet Secretariat – as well as Minister of Aircraft Production Lord Beaverbrook. Churchill nodded in recognition of Sir Henry Thomas Tizard, KCB, FRS, Chairman of the Air Ministry's Advisory Committee for Aeronautics, whom he had known professionally since the beginning of the rearmament struggle during the appeasement years. The Prime Minister also nodded to the bespectacled Robert Alexander Watson-Watt, the highly regarded creator of radio detection and direction finding technology upon which the air defense of Great Britain now depended. The young man at the far right corner of the room had to be Doctor Reginald Victor 'R.V.' Jones, PhD Physics – the 28-year-old, science officer assigned to the Air Ministry Intelligence Branch Technical Assessment Division, with whom the Professor was so impressed and was the object personage of this meeting. Churchill motioned for everyone to be seated.

"Since you raised this meeting, Professor, why don't you introduce the issue before us," Churchill said.

Lindemann leaned forward and scanned the room. "The question before His Majesty's Government boils down to the allocation of scarce Air Ministry resources on technical problems and intelligence issues. Specifically, the young Doctor Jones," he said, looking at and nodding toward R.V. Jones, "has analyzed the body of intelligence information currently available and determined what he believes is a German system of intersecting, highly focused, radio beams that may well be utilized for accurate night and foul weather bombing of this country. I think that accurately states the problem, Doctor Jones?" he asked. Jones nodded his concurrence. "The Air Ministry's scientific committee chaired by Sir Henry remains unconvinced by Doctor Jones's analysis and argument that scant resources must be deployed more efficiently to higher yield matters. Does that accurately state your position, Sir Henry?"

"Yes, as far as it goes," responded Tizard.

"How much farther do you need to go?" Churchill asked.

"Prime Minister, I am cautious not to offend the excellent work that Doctor Jones performs daily for the Air Ministry Intelligence Branch. However, I must point out that his analysis has a very soft foundation."

"Which is?"

Tizard appeared a bit nerous. "Sir, if you will excuse me, I do not know whether everyone in the Cabinet Room is authorized to know about certain intelligence sources."

"I do, and I believe they are. Nonetheless, I officially inform everyone in attendance here that this discussion is classified most secret and will not be discussed beyond this group. Is that clear?"

Most nodded their concurrence and a few replied with a 'yes, sir.'

"Proceed."

"This whole question of a radio beam bombing system has grown from the Oslo Report," Sir Henry stated, referring to the mysterious German dossier addressed to the naval attaché and deposited under the steps to the British Embassy in Oslo late last fall. "The question as Professor Lindemann stated it hangs fully upon whether the Oslo Report is a godsend from someone very high in the German government's technical research and policy hierarchy, or whether it is a disinformation plant to mislead us."

"So," began Churchill, "if I understand this, you believe the document is false, and Doctor Jones believes it is the godsend of which you speak. Is that correct?"

"Stated in simple terms, yes sir, that is correct."

Churchill turned to the Air Minister. "Archie, why is this a matter for the prime minister?"

"Well, to be blunt, Professor Lindemann believes Doctor Jones in this matter, and the Air Ministry endorsed Sir Henry's scientific recommendation."

"What is involved here? Are we debating the expenditure of millions of pounds sterling on some wild goose chase?"

"Doctor Jones requested several medium bombers be specially equipped and assigned to fly search patterns to find these hypothesized, invisible and probably quite discreet radio beams to prove his hypothesis and help develop counter-measures before the all-weather bombing system can be deployed against Great Britain. Sir Cyril and I are not convinced and we have insufficient aircraft and engineering resources as it is."

"Archie, surely all of your bomber resources are not committed to France or the bombing of Germany," Churchill said with more than a little sarcasm. "What are the conflicting priorities?"

"On going operations and other higher priority projects."

"Such as?"

Sir Henry picked up the lance. "Our highest priority is development of an airborne radio direction finding unit small enough to be carried on an interceptor and powerful enough to detect airborne targets at sufficient range to enable efficient intercepts."

"That is very important, I grant you."

"The problem before us is not just about aircraft and aircrews. It is also about the scientists and engineers who are working around the clock already on a number of technical matters that would have to be diverted to equipping, searching and analyzing the collected data. And, as I tried to point out, the very existence of these beams is highly suspect."

"If I may, Prime Minister," interjected Lindemann.

"By all means, Professor."

"None of the technical programs presented in the Oslo Report have been validated, as yet. However, there are other sources that give us some indication as to the veracity of the document. To be thorough, we also know some projects have either been abandoned, significantly delayed, or were non-existent from the outset. I think everyone here agrees the accuracy of the document is far from conclusive."

Churchill digested the information given as well as his personal discussions with Professor Lindemann. "Doctor Jones, I would like to hear why you believe these beams exist?"

"Yes, sir," Jones answered. "The details in their distance measuring project are technically accurate and rather innovative compared to our work. Last October, a Heinkel One One One was brought down by a Spitfire near Dalkeith in the Lammenuir Hill country. We found a box with a strange label -- *Knickebein*, German for broken leg or dog leg. We suspected but could not determine the purpose of the box. We knew it was a radio receiver but we could not figure out its purpose. Then, nine days ago, MI6 intercepted a *Luft-waffe* operational message that referred to air fleet bombing crews being fully trained on *Knickebein* use before the end of summer. A week ago, with some luck, the Air Ministry's Y Service detected the highly focused, discreet, radio beam, we believe may be associated with the German system. However, it is the gut-check test that leads me to believe the potential for this kind of system. It makes sense to me. Our weather is notoriously ill suited to conventional, visual, daylight, bombing tactics. They need a system like this to carry out any comprehensive bombing campaign. It is within their technical means."

The Y Service was a uniquely configured organization for the collection of signals intelligence – the use of radio energy primarily for communications, but recently expanded to include other uses like radio ranging and direction finding.

"But there is no proof," interjected Sir Henry.

"And how would you go about obtaining the proof you seek?" Churchill asked with a hint of irritation.

Sir Henry Tizard considered his words. "Prime Minister, Mister Jones is a young, bright, ambitious analyst within the Air Ministry, who does not sit at the policy table."

"You did not answer my question," Churchill said, now with mounting anger.

"If you would allow me to finish my . . ."

"Damn it, Tizard," Winston shouted, "it is just this kind of bureau-cratic tripe that will get us all killed. The Germans are not going to wait for our laborious, plodding processes to play out before they decide to invade this country. Mister Jones has presented the facts, as he knows them. There is reason to suspect he may well be correct in his assessment of German tech-nical capability. Now, if you will indulge me, let us assume he is correct and the Germans do in fact have this broken leg system in operational readiness, which in turn suggests the German air force may well have the capability to bomb our cities at night and in bad weather. Do you, or does anyone, have a system to stop those bombers from killing thousands of our people?"

"No, sir," Tizard answered in a subdued, almost inaudible voice.

"Then, I strongly suggest you and everyone else at the policy table damn well better listen to young Mister Jones and help him find those beams as well as develop counter-measures to interrupt them or deflect them. Do I make myself clear on this?"

Sinclair stepped in. "We will ensure Mister Jones gets the support he needs."

"Thank you, Archie. The Professor and I both think Mister Jones may well be onto something that could save countless lives. Let us all take him seriously, find the evidence and figure out how to defeat their bombing system. We just passed the summer solstice. The days are getting shorter and the nights longer. We cannot concede the night to the German bombers. Now, is there anything else?" No one spoke. "Then, we are adjourned here. Good day, gentlemen." Churchill rose and left the Cabinet Room.

———

Three hours later, Professor Lindemann appeared in the Prime Minister's study. "Thank you for taking the time to hear about these beams."

"Certainly."

"If I may say so, Winston, you were a bit harsh on Sir Henry."

"Perhaps so, but we simply do not have time for bureaucratic procrastination and obfuscation."

"Quite so. You might wish to know Sir Henry promptly submitted his letter of resignation and Archie has accepted his resignation."

"That is his choice."

"Indeed. I just mention this because Sir Henry is a very good and capable scientific mind, and administrator, despite our technical disagreements."

Churchill grunted his acknowledgment. "Perhaps we can find something appropriate for him to do."

"If I may plant a seed, perhaps he could lead our team for this technical exchange with the Americans."

"We shall see." Churchill looked up from his papers. "Perhaps you can join me for supper tonight and we can discuss this some more."

"I would be delighted. Thank you for your time. Until then . . ."

Churchill nodded his agreement. Lindemann departed.

———

Sunday, 30.June.1940
Headquarters, Fighter Command
Bentley Priory
Stanmore, Middlesex, England
13:45 hours

Group Captain John Spencer listened to the seemingly endless report by Air Commodore Hogan, communicating the excessive losses of aircraft and pilots in the Battle of France. In the two and a half months since the invasion of Norway, Fighter Command lost 25% of its entire fighter aircraft inventory, and worse yet, nearly 13% of its pilots. Minister of Aircraft Production Lord Beaverbrook had begun to achieve quantifiable results in rebuilding fighter aircraft strength. The aircraft could be replaced within a month or so at the current rates, but replacement of the pilots would take longer, even with the shortened training cycle. John knew, as they all did, the signs pointed directly toward an invasion by the Germans before the close of summer, and they were ill prepared to stop them by every measure possible.

As the reports and discussion droned on, John could not avoid the now, more prevalent, recurring feelings that the only protection the British people had was their spirit, their heritage, the young air force pilots and the English Channel. He was proud of his uncle and the extraordinary effort he expended to bolster a discouraged nation. Everyone he talked to, above and below him, drew considerable strength from the words and message of the Prime Minister. The sad part for John Spencer was . . . it seemed like words were all they had. The Germans had the *Wehrmacht*, the most successful military organization in modern times – *Heere*, *Luftwaffe* and *Kriegsmarine* – they had yet to feel real defeat. The loss of the German Navy's pocket battleship, *Admiral Graf Spee*, in the Battle of the River Platte, last December, was the only substantive loss of prestige the Nazi military apparatus had suffered since Hitler's rearmament began in 1934.

"John, are you with us?" asked Air Chief Marshal Sir Hugh Dowding.

"Sorry, sir."

"If you would be so kind, John, you seem to have a penchant of late for the distance of thought. Please arrange for a commander's conference this evening. Air Marshal Leonard will prepare the agenda. I'm afraid we do not have much time left, gentlemen. Let us use the time wisely."

The staff meeting adjourned with only four hours to make the necessary arrangements. For the convenience of the commanders, the conference would be held ten miles down the A41 roadway at RAF Hendon. Air Vice-Marshal Richard Saul had the farthest to travel from Newcastle. Each of the group commanders still chose to fly themselves with Air Vice-Marshal Keith Park having the reputation for finding any reason to fly. Even though Park could drive to Hendon, John knew the respected group commander would take his Hurricane up for a short, stretch-your-wings flight, and then land at RAF Hendon. The four telephone calls confirmed the arrangements with the four group commanders. John Spencer coordinated the construction of the conference agenda with each of the department heads plus made several calls to the Air Ministry for some of the most recent information.

—

As was usually the case, the requested officers arrived at the concrete and steel building early. The social amenities occupied the few minutes until 18:00 when Air Chief Marshal Dowding entered and started the meeting. Dowding's lack of interest in the social aspects of military life and his serious, let's-get-down-to-business attitude accentuated the poignancy of his moniker, 'Stuffy.' Although he seemed to be distant from his men and those around him, there were very few that did not appreciate his sincere caring.

"Air Commodore Hogan, if you would be so kind to give us the latest intelligence, we shall get started," Dowding said.

Hogan stood, moved to the map placed on an easel, cleared his throat and began. "The Germans continue to consolidate their positions in France. A fortnight after the French capitulation, a few very isolated pockets of resistance remain while most of the military activity has gone quiet.

"We have seen no overt preparations for invasion, as yet, although the Air Ministry believes the Germans will probably attempt an invasion before summer is out.

"Enemy air activity over the UK remains relatively low with only reconnaissance and probing flights. We continue to have some difficulty going after the high altitude Junkers Eight Six P."

"How high are they?" asked AVM Park.

"Best we can tell, between 30,000 and 40,000 feet. Most intrusions appear to be in the vicinity of 30,000 feet."

"Geoffrey, let's pinch the Fighter Interception Unit to see what they need to get some of our fighters up to those altitudes."

"They have been working this problem among others. I shall see where they are."

Dowding nodded in response, and then nodded toward Hogan to continue his report.

"The most significant information confirms the German occupation of the Guernsey Islands today. They landed and parachuted a small force of SS troopers this morning and quickly overwhelmed the meager local defense and constabulary unit."

"I must remind you all," interjected Dowding, "this is the first enemy occupation of British soil since medieval times. Let this be the bitter foretaste, as the Prime Minister said. We must redouble our efforts to protect the Home Islands."

John Spencer watched the RAF officers, the leaders of Fighter Command, look at one another with incredulity as if their commander thought they were not doing enough already. Everyone felt the pressure, the weight of history, and the gaze of generations past. John looked back to 'Stuffy' Dowding and thought he saw a brief expression of unease, and then he waved his hand to continue.

"SIS reports, from multiple sources believed to be accurate, indications the Germans have accomplished sufficient consolidation in France and the strong likelihood a general, high intensity, air campaign for supremacy over Great Britain will begin soon. The report suggests Göring has established the RAF as the highest priority target, and more specifically Fighter Command."

"It is encouraging to know we are appreciated," said Air Commodore Herbert Maple, Deputy Chief of Operations.

A short laugh among the gathering, and even a flash of a smile from Dowding, relieved some of the tension. The struggle would begin in earnest soon, and they were not ready. Fighter Command was making progress in recovering the losses of pilots and aircraft, but they were still well short of full strength. A large portion of the aircrews was young, green and untested. Fortunately, experienced combat pilots from France, Belgium and Holland were in the refugee stream making its way to Great Britain. Also, pilots from Poland and Czechoslovakia who seemed to be in a constant refugee status were among the influx as well as a handful or so of American pilots who had defied their countries neutrality law to fly for le Armée de l'Air. The foreign pilots would be quickly evaluated and taught the doctrine of Fighter Command. The experiences in Norway and France told them in graphic detail the violence of the death struggle bearing down upon them.

John smiled to himself as he realized Brian Drummond was no longer the only American in this fight. The camaraderie of his countrymen would help Brian.

"What do you think is going to happen, sir?" asked one of the staff officers.

Dowding looked sternly at the officer, perhaps wondering whether he should even attempt answering such a speculative question. "I am not clairvoyant. What I think has no real value. However, I suspect we shall go through a testing phase within a few days or weeks – a rather peculiar, get acquainted stage." A number of the officers chuckled although Dowding did not smile or did he probably feel he told a joke. "Then, they shall most probably make a maximum effort to subdue Fighter Command. If they are successful, invasion will surely follow. If they are not," he paused to look at several of the sets of eyes on him including John's attentive gaze, "the Hun will turn his anger and frustration upon London. Our capital city is a ripe plumb, too much to resist. It shall be his undoing." The room remained frozen – not a sound, a twitch or even breathing as far as John could tell. Dowding turned to Air Commodore Hogan. "Is there anything more, James?"

"No, sir, other than details if you would like?"

Dowding held up his hand like a man directing traffic to stop. "That shant be necessary. I do believe we get the picture." A short chuckle from the group punctuated his words. Dowding scanned the conference room before he continued. "I cannot emphasize enough the gravity of our situation. We shall soon be faced with the direct assault of the most formidable air force in Europe, if not the world. But, we have one major advantage. We shall play this match on the home pitch. All the planning and preparation we have been able to accomplish in the last few years will now come to the test. Our success will depend upon our cohesiveness as a team from the RDF operators to the controllers and pilots. We shall succeed together. If we fall, we shall fall together. I urge each of you to take the next few days to visit as many of your facilities as possible and impress upon our team our confidence, faith and support. We are as ready for this confrontation as we can be, and I know without qualification we shall prove ourselves up to the task."

Dowding stood quickly drawing everyone else to stand out of respect and courtesy for their leader. He promptly left the room signaling the end of the conference. The solemnity of the moment captured each of them as they departed without further words. John Spencer knew this would soon be their moment in history, and there was no more they could do to prepare the team for the fight. It was time to do what they all knew they had to do.

—

Sunday, 30.June.1940
Cabinet Room
No.10 Downing Street
Whitehall, London, England
18:30 hours

Among those present for the sabath evening meeting were Foreign Minister Lord Halifax, Home Minister Sir John Anderson, Professor Lindemann along with the other members of the War Cabinet – Churchill, Attlee and Greenwood. Chamberlain was ill and unable to attend. Cabinet Secretary Sir Edward Bridges and the three service representatives to the Cabinet Secretariat – Captain Nicholl, Lieutenant Colonel Dykes and Wing Commander Elliott – were also present.

"Shall we begin? The sole topic on this evening's agenda is the technical exchange program," Sir Edward began.

"Let us make quick work of this, so everyone can attend to their families," added Winston.

Sir John chose to begin. "We have compiled a list of our secret technologies for the potential exchange."

"Let me interrupt there, John. Potential is the operative word. I am not yet convinced this is wise for us to expose our most vital defense secrets to possible compromise when we are so vulnerable. However, the invasion threat is real and expected. I must say to my thinking, given the risk that the Germans might acquire them by conquest, it does seem prudent that our American cousins should have the benefit of our science and engineering, so that they will be better prepared to help us in time."

"If they ever do," grumbled Greenwood.

"Yes, well, that is the premise of this exercise," Sir John continued. "The services are still submitting their candidate items. So far, we have Frank Whittle's turbine engine, the latest mark of the Rolls-Royce Merlin Engine, Watson-Watt's precious cavity magnetron as well as our latest underwater acoustic detection equipment. The most controversial item on the list so far is the uranium explosive research."

"We have discussed this before," Attlee said. "I thought we were in agreement."

"How is the MAUD Committee progressing?" asked the Professor.

Sir John leaned forward to see Lindemann's eyes. "George Thompson informs me they are methodically working through the material they have collected. He believes they will complete their work on schedule next year."

"Let us assume the committee determines such high yield explosive material is feasible," Winston said. "Do we have the capacity to carry out and produce such a device?"

"Professor, please correct me if I get the physics wrong, but as I understand it, just the industrial capability to separate and refine the fissile uranium two three five would take a plant of enormous size and power demand." Sir John looked to Lindemann, who nodded his head in agreement. "The direct answer is, no. I do not think we will have the capacity to undertake such a development, set aside production and sustainment."

"So, we need the industrial capacity of the United States . . . or perhaps Canada," Churchill suggested.

"Yes."

"Then, do we have an option here?" asked Winston. "We know the Germans are conducting research in earnest on this potential weapon. Could we live with ourselves if we did not do everything possible to obtain the atomic weapon first, before the Germans? If that means partnering with the Americans, then so be it."

"I believe the War Cabinet is in agreement, Sir John," stated Clement Attlee, as he looked to the other members to see their nod of concurrence. "Even though the MAUD Committee has yet to complete their assessment, we should share the information we have. The Americans are doing their own research. Hopefully, together we can achieve the objective together, before the Germans get there."

"There you have it," Churchill said. "While I am not yet convinced, as I said, we are in agreement that detailed planning should be carried out *post haste*. I want to see those plans as soon as they are ready."

Lord Halifax added, "Lord Lothian has made numerous informal contacts with the American government, university research facilities and industrial companies working on the periphery. He has seen nothing but encouragement from the Americans."

"Presumably, our experts have or soon will contact their counterparts in North America," Winston added.

"Many have assisted Lord Lothian," Lord Halifax said.

"We must ensure the Americans are ready to receive what we may well give them soon."

"Should we approach this on a *quid pro quo* basis?" asked Sir John.

Churchill did not seek or wait for other opinions. "No! Such a tit-for-tat exchange will simply take too long as the valuation equation reconciliation alone will do. We need the Americans in this fight – the sooner the better.

Their industrial capacity is the only thing that will overwhelm the Germans. Our generosity and magnaminity will go a long way to achieving that objective. Lastly, given our predicament, we must protect these secrets by giving them to our friends for safekeeping and hopefully use on our behalf. I shall communicate with President Roosevelt to ensure this exchange, if it does happen, is received in the spirit it is given."

"Agreed," said Attlee and Greenwood in unison.

"One last item, if I may. I would like to suggest we assign Sir Henry Tizard to chair this exchange team. Are their any objections?"

"Good choice, it seems to me," Attlee responded.

"Here here," added Sir John.

"The generals are here," whispered Sir Edward to the Prime Minister's ear, sensing an end to the discussion. Winston nodded.

"Then, we are adjourned. Thank you, gentlemen."

As the War Cabinet ministers departed, Churchill leaned toward Sir Edward. "Please show the generals in."

Sir John Anderson was the last minister, but he did not leave. "If I may have a private word, Prime Minister?"

Sir Edward waited at the door for a signal from Churchill. The Prime Minister nodded his head, looked to Sir Edward, and motioned for him to close the door behind him. The three Secretariat servicemen, who would have remained, left the room before Bridges closed the door.

"I thought you might appreciate confirmation that the Earl of Suffolk and the *Broompark* docked safely a week ago. It took us a week to inventory what he managed to extricate from France with his rather Herculean effort." Churchill nodded his head impatiently. "First, in addition to the Norwegian heavy water supply we discussed a week ago, he brought out virtually all of the French atomic research team with their papers. They have been linked up with Thompson's MAUD Committee for assimilation into our efforts. He moved and secured five million pounds worth of diamonds moved through France from Amsterdam and ten million pounds sterling worth of gold bullion held in nearly a dozen British and French banks in Paris. Surprisingly, his little band of helpers also moved 600 tons of valuable machine tools, which have been catalogued and distributed to the appropriate defence companies. Mysteriously, a British agent by the codename 'Diamond' accompanied several crates of unspecified material he kept under heavy armed guard. The Admiralty took possession of Diamond's crates and a dozen associated French citizens. They seemed to know what they were doing."

Churchill was fairly certain he knew Agent 'Diamond' was one of 'Jumper' Pike's men about town, and as he recalled, his proper name was Trevor Andersen, also known as Robert Henry Stone Johnston, among other aliases he was confident. Diamond was the field agent who worked with the Poles in February 1939, to capture their first operational Enigma device in a well-executed ambush of an SS transport team. He would check with Pike and Menzies later to confirm what he thought this intriguing bit of news was. Churchill showed no response or interest in the mysterious crates and simply gestured for Sir John to continue.

"Suffolk managed to evacuate most of the embassy staff including Ambassador Sir Ronald Campbell, along with our remaining defense liaison personnel and scores of other prominent British nationals. He managed to pull off his own little Dunkirk, Winston . . . quite miraculous, and I must say bountiful."

"Thank you for the report, John. Would you be so kind to prepare the appropriate application for the King's honors? Suffolk deserves recognition for his efforts, especially in this instance. Anything else?" asked Churchill. Anderson shook his head in the negative. "Thank you again, John. Now, would you be so kind to tell Bridges we need to move along."

Prime Minister Churchill remained in his plump, leather chair at the head of the long, dark, oak table that had been a feature of No.10 almost from the outset. History had been made at this table and more would be made in subsequent days and years. The ebb and flow of people did not disturb his thoughts.

War Minister Anthony Eden entered first, followed by General Sir John Dill, General Sir Edmund Ironside and a new man to the Cabinet Room that Churchill did not recognize. He wore the rank insignia of an army major general on the epaulettes of his crisp, well-decorated uniform. General Ironside saw the expression on Churchill's face as he rose from his chair and moved toward them.

"Prime Minister, may I present General Sir Andrew Thorne. General Thorne, Prime Minister Churchill."

The two men shook hands. "An honor to meet you, General," Churchill said.

"The honor is mine, Sir," responded Sir Andrew.

Churchill recognized the name from many of the Dunkirk dispatches – Major General Sir Augustus Francis Andrew Nicol Thorne, KCB, CMG, DSO, DL. Now, he had a face to the name.

Sir Edmund continued his introduction. "Sir Andrew is currently assigned as General Officer Commanding Twelfth Corps, astride the southeast approaches, which is why I invited him to this meeting."

"Yes, yes, certainly. You were also in command of 48th South Midland Infantry Division that contributed significantly to the defense of the Dunkirk perimeter during Operation DYNAMO."

"Yes, Sir. But, not quite good enough, I dare say."

"Modesty is not warranted with me, General."

"You are most kind, Sir."

"We have much to discuss, so let us proceed," Churchill said as he motioned for everyone to be seated. "What are your plans for the defense of the Home Islands?"

Eden motioned to General Thorne to respond.

"The estimate for planning purposes has the Germans landing up to 80,000 men on the coast of Kent, most likely between Thanet and Pevensey, before the autumnal weather deteriorates."

"Sixty miles from London," said Churchill in a rather subdued, somber voice.

"Yes, Sir. We do not believe they have the ocean transport to move such a force and the logistics support to sustain or reinforce their troops, or move the armored units they certainly would like to have. They will be relegated to using river barges modified for amphibious operations – not an optimal arrangement but probably workable. They can muster up plenty of those barges from the occupied countries. As such, they are most likely to favor the East Channel crossing to minimize exposure of their transport to the Channel swells. They will also need local air superiority and at least naval surface control of the eastern Channel to carry out such a crossing. We have not yet detected signs of barges collecting on the south shore, so they are probably at least a month away. We expect a concerted aerial bombardment effort both to subdue Fighter Command and prepare the landing beaches."

"What about parachute-born infantry?"

"We think such airborne operations far less likely since sustainment would be extraordinarily difficult. We might see diversionary or support landings that could quickly link up, but unlikely the main assault."

"That is what you expect the Germans to do. Now, what are your plans to defend the Home Islands against the expected invasion?"

General Ironside said, "We are organizing and refitting the troops returning from France. We expect to recover small groups ahead of the German advance to the Atlantic ports. Units were rather chewed up during the defense of Dunkirk and Operation DYNAMO, so we are reconstituting units where possible and organizing new units. The arms and ammunition from the Americans have helped."

"President Roosevelt has promised more," Churchill added.

"Thank you for that. We can utilize all we can get. General Thorne has been working on our defense in depth," Sir Edmund said, and then nodded for Sir Andrew to continue his briefing.

"As General Ironside indicated, we are executing our preparation plans as the Army reorganizes and refits. We have already installed numerous beach obstacles to inhibit boat landings, and we will continue to add more fill-in obstacles as time allows. We have conducted a number of field exercises with the remaining artillery units assigned to the Twelfth Corps and constructed a series of camouflaged shelters in layers from the beach boundaries to the outskirts of London, to permit rapid movement of our artillery and ammunition to continuously engage the enemy during their approach. Likewise, breastworks for the infantry have been layered along the likely avenues of advance from the beachheads."

"Do you have sufficient troops for your defensive system?"

General Thorne glanced at General Dill, and then General Ironside, who both nodded for him to answer the Prime Minister's question. "No, Sir. As General Ironside indicated, we are working feverishly to raise new units, and as they are ready, we can quickly integrate them into the plan."

The Prime Minister turned to the Chief of the Imperial General Staff. "We may not have time for 'ready.'"

"Quite so, Sir," answered General Dill. "The new unit commanders have already been notified to equip their troops as soon as weapons are available, to train them fast, and especially to be prepared to move south as soon as we see signs of assembly along the south shore."

"We must stop them at the beach," Sir Edmund added.

"To that end, we are refining our plans daily with the Navy and Air Force to make the mount-up and Channel transit very costly," Sir John said. "As General Ironside said, we must stop them before they get to our shores."

"The Navy is ready," Churchill said confidently. "The Air Force is as ready as they can be, and the greatest uncertainty on this side of the Channel is whether they will be able to withstand what is quite probably going to be an overwhelming aerial attack by the German Air Force."

"We are working together to defend our Island," Eden said. "I might also add that General Ironside has made available veteran non-commissioned ranks to assist and train the Home Guard."

"Yes, I have seen them. Able-bodied men not yet in uniform from puberty to old age," said Winston. "Not a reassuring entity, but fully necessary. We can leave no stone unturned."

"They are quite enthusiastic," General Ironside said. "They are eager to do their part to defend the realm."

"Quite so," added Churchill. "It is just comical to see them drill with pitch forks, shovels and wooden facsimile rifles. That is the disheartening part."

"We will get them weapons once the Army is re-equipped," Eden added. "The *Eastern Prince* arrived in Liverpool a week ago. She has been unloaded and the *matériel* is being distributed to the southern units. We expect General Thorne's Twelfth Corps to be fully equipped by the middle of July. As other infantry divisions approach readiness, we will assign them and move them to the Twelfth Corps."

"I would like to inspect your preparations, General Thorne. I shall have my private secretary arrange a date, preferably this coming week."

"Yes, Sir. We will be honored to host your visit," answered General Thorne.

"Do not worry about hosting. I want to see the beach defenses and the troops working. I will not countenance any ceremonial assembly distracting the troops from their vital tasks at hand."

"Yes, Sir . . . as you command."

"Perhaps you would be so kind to present some more of the details at your headquarters after my inspection tour," Prime Minister Chuchill said.

"By all means, Sir. It would be my pleasure."

"It will be Mister Colville, Jock Colville, who will make the arrangements with your adjutant."

"I shall alert Colonel Lincoln this evening."

"Very well. Thank you for taking your precious time to brief me. I am afraid we do not have much time left to prepare for what is surely to come soon. As we say in the Navy, godspeed and following winds."

Churchill returned to his study. Jock Colville was dutifully waiting for him. Winston gave him his directions for the following day's tasks. It had been a long day. He was in need of a stiff drink and sustenance. Clementine might well be waiting on him, if he was lucky.

—

Chapter 9

Perseverance is more prevailing than violence;
and many things which cannot be overcome when they are together,
yield themselves up when taken little by little.

--Plutarch

Monday, 1.July.1940
No.10 Downing Street
Whitehall, London, England

The Prime Minister looked with some revulsion at the day's page on his desk diary and the name attached to his next appointment. He never liked the man as a person, nor as the principal representative of the United States of America to the Court of St. James's. U.S. Ambassador to the United Kingdom Joseph Patrick 'Joe' Kennedy, Sr., seemed to enjoy antagonizing him and had become quite adept at the game. During his wilderness years, as he liked to call them, Winston had few critics or antagonists who were more effective and influential than Joe Kennedy. They were required by protocol to maintain a relationship now, but he wondered every time they approached a meeting, why on Earth had Roosevelt picked Kennedy to represent the President and his country. The man made his fortune as a rumrunner during Prohibition, defying the law.

The Massachusetts Democrat sustained considerable influence in the politics of his home state, and he was a wealthy man in his own right thanks in no small part to his smuggling business. Kennedy helped Roosevelt win his first two presidential elections, and from all reports, he was also throwing his political weight into ensuring Roosevelt's reelection this year – should the President decide to stand for re-election. Kennedy's own presidential aspirations appeared to be well known but not contradictory. Winston knew, or at least he believed, Roosevelt was much closer to his own views regarding Europe, the Nazi menace and the prospect of a Grand Alliance between the United States and the United Kingdom. Kennedy seemed to be the antithesis of those views. The Irish-Catholic American Ambassador presented an unmistakable and quite public socialist *Realpolitik*, and yet displayed the image of an ardent, outspoken and enthusiastic supporter of Adolf Hitler's brand of nationalistic fascism. His social and some would say collaborative relationships with the appeasers and proponents of the German public image did not make the headlines every day but were certainly well known within political and governmental circles. The involvement of the State Department cipher clerk in the spy ring broken up in May along with the American citizenship of several of the prostitutes' clients compounded dramatically with Kennedy's Nazi sympathies. His public but unofficial support of Irish nationalism added a foul icing to a revolting cake.

The knock at the door was reserved for those visitors that needed to wait. Jock Colville entered the office and closed the door behind him. "Prime Minister," he said, and then stopped with Winston's raised hand and forced attention to the papers before him. After a few minutes, Winston raised his head. "Prime Minister, the American Ambassador, Mister Kennedy, is here to see you."

"Delightful," said Winston with sarcastic excitement that produced a smile from Colville. "Please show the Ambassador in."

"Very well, sir."

In a few moments, Kennedy entered the Prime Minister's office. "Good afternoon, Prime Minister. Thank you for seeing me."

"And good afternoon to you, Mister Ambassador."

"I hope my visit finds you and Missus Churchill in good health."

"It does indeed, thank you."

Kennedy looked around Winston's office as if he was looking for his lost notes, and then back to the Prime Minister. "I have not had the opportunity since May to see you. I offer my congratulations for the successful evacuation at Dunkirk."

Winston wanted to growl at one of the most vocal appeasers for his contribution to the conditions leading to the debacle in France. The urge passed, not wanting to give any satisfaction to Kennedy. He nodded his head in simple nonverbal response.

"I would like to convey the concern of my government for the continuing reluctance of His Majesty's Government to negotiate a settlement. The bloodshed and loss of life are unnecessary. The Germans have perhaps taken their legitimate territorial claims beyond the sphere of reasonableness. However, we remain convinced the only element precluding a cessation of hostilities is the reticence of His Majesty's Government."

The Right Honorable Winston Spencer Churchill, Member of Parliament for Epping, Prime Minister of Great Britain, First Lord of the Treasury, Minister of Defense and Leader of the Conservative Party, listened to each word with exponentially mounting anger. He wanted to let the demons out of their confinement. This man sitting in the chair adjacent to him could not possibly represent the United States of America. His letters, discussions and other communications with Franklin Roosevelt simply did not agree or even hint at this sort of attitude. It was those personal communications with the American President that gave him strength to hold his anger at bay.

"Upon what do you base this view, sir?" asked Churchill with as much calm as he could muster.

Kennedy either ignored or did not sense the tension in Churchill's voice. "The Chancellor has been consistent, clear and communicative regarding the needs and desires of the German people. We would like to see recognition of those needs and desires. I am convinced the Chancellor will withdraw promptly once the threat of war is removed."

Winston stood, walked away from Kennedy and toward the long book-shelf adjacent to his garden window. He stared at a book with his name on it as the author – 'Marlborough' – a biography of the 1st Duke of Marlborough, John Churchill, his grandfather six generations removed and the hero of the Battle of Blenheim. He knew historic events surrounded him as they had his ancestors. This meeting, although individual and private, was equally part of history. He turned to his antagonist.

"First, Mister Ambassador, let me assure you I do not share your ami-cable views of the *Herr Reichskanzler* Hitler. He is a monster of the worst order despite whatever good he may have done within Germany. Second, I do not believe you speak for the American Government and especially the President. Third, it is beyond my comprehension how a man of your education can pos-sibly believe Hitler will withdraw when he initiated a most violent, unprovoked attack upon neutral countries that bore him no malice."

"I object . . . ."

"You may object all you like, Mister Ambassador," the Prime Minister interrupted Kennedy, slurring his pronunciation for emphasis, "but the facts remain the same."

Kennedy paused to collect his emotions. He spoke in the calm tones of the diplomat. "I do not share your view, sir.

"Excellent. Now that we have that out of the way, what else may I do for you?"

"We want to stop the bloodshed, present and future."

"As we do."

"The Chancellor has made an overture of peace. We would like to see a comparable and suitable response."

"Are you asking His Majesty's Government to surrender?"

"I would not word it that way."

"Then, I shall ask you to speak more plainly."

"As you wish," Kennedy paused to consider his words. "The German armed forces have been victorious on every battlefield upon which they have been placed. The Allies continue to wage war despite the overwhelming successes of the *Wehrmacht*. The British Army has been decimated and the Royal Air Force is a mere fraction of the *Luftwaffe*. I believe further hostility toward the German people will only result in additional needless loss of life and will not alter the outcome. You will be beaten within a month, if you persist with this foolishness. What purpose could continued warfare serve?"

The Prime Minister smiled at the American Ambassador. "While your representation of the situation may be, in part, accurate, you failed to recognize the most important ingredient." He stared at Kennedy with his head lowered, as if he was a broad-horned bull about to charge. The pause gave his visitor time to think. "You have forgotten your history, and the will and courage of the British people. We have been tested before and have not been found wanting. We shall not disappoint our ancestors on this occasion."

Joseph Kennedy shifted his position. "Many Members of Parliament and officials within your own government want peace, and do not want more suffering."

"Mister Ambassador, I am terribly sorry, but I have a busy diary yet to serve, as I am certain you can appreciate. I thank you for your candor, but we shall answer *Herr* Hitler with the sword until he returns all of his ill-gotten booty. Now, if you will be so kind . . . ," the Prime Minister said, motioning toward the door.

Ambassador Joseph Kennedy rose, started to say something, and then turned and left. He moved quickly without closing the door behind him. Winston waited for Colville to glance into the office. He acknowledged his secretary's expression of concern with a flick of his hand and a grunt of disgust. The door was shut once again.

Winston Churchill thought about his communications with Franklin Roosevelt. The urge to pen a note to the man he considered a friend, a colleague and a supporter took several minutes and failed attempts before it passed. He trusted his instincts, and they told him Kennedy did not speak for the President or the American people. He wanted to talk to Bill Stephenson, but his confidant was in the United States. Instead, Winston jotted a few notes in his diary to remind him of the content of his most recent meeting.

———

Tuesday, 2.July.1940
No.10 Downing Street
Whitehall, London, England

"Colonel Menzies to see you, sir," announced the intercom.

Winston Churchill reached for the bank of intercom levers depressing the first one. "Show him in." He rose to greet the Director General of the Secret Intelligence Service who entered with another man beside him. The metal case and chain attached to the man's left wrist gave him a clue of the purpose of the early visit. Winston reminded himself each time that the deciphered secret messages from the captured Enigma machine, under the code name, ULTRA, demanded the utmost in security precautions. The War Cabinet meeting would not start for several hours. "Good afternoon, Stewart."

"Good afternoon to you, Prime Minister. You do remember, Alastair Denniston, head of Station X."

Winston shook hands with the two men, and then motioned to the group of chairs. As they sat, Denniston unlocked the case to extract several pieces of paper and looked to his boss for the proper cue.

"We have several interesting ULTRA messages that I thought you should see before this afternoon's War Cabinet meeting." 'C' nodded to Denniston who handed two sheets of paper to the Prime Minister.

MOST SECRET - ULTRA

```
SECRET
DATE:   1 JULY 1940
TO:   OKH, OKM, OKL
FROM:   OKW
THE LEADER'S DIRECTIVE NO.16:
    OUR LEADER HAS DETERMINED THAT THE
DIPLOMATIC SITUATION IS HOPELESS.  ENGLAND
HAS BEEN UNWILLING TO AGREE ON ANY MEASURE OF
COMPROMISE.  OUR LEADER HAS ALSO DETERMINED
THAT A LANDING IN ENGLAND IS POSSIBLE
THIS YEAR AND THEREFORE HE HAS DECIDED TO
PROCEED WITH PREPARATIONS FOR OPERATION SEA
LION.  THE SUBJECT DIRECTIVE ESTABLISHES OUR
OBJECTIVES.  EACH COMMAND IS DIRECTED TO
PREPARE APPROPRIATE PLANS FOR THE CONDUCT OF
OPERATIONS AGAINST GREAT BRITAIN.
```

```
    SEPARATE COMMUNICATIONS WILL SET THE
EXECUTION DATE.  COORDINATION BETWEEN COMMANDS
PARAMOUNT AND MUST NOT BE UNDERESTIMATED OR
NEGLECTED.  RESPOND WITH READINESS AS SOON AS
POSSIBLE.
SECRET
```

MOST SECRET - ULTRA

Churchill hesitated for a brief moment's thought without looking to either man, and then read the next message. He needed to assure himself nothing had been missed in the first reading. The magnitude of benefit and value of being able to read your opponent's highest secrecy communications rushed back to him with each decrypted message.

MOST SECRET - ULTRA

```
SECRET
DATE:   2 JULY 1940
TO: COMMANDERS, AIR FLEETS 2, 3 AND 5
FROM:   AIR FORCE HIGH COMMAND
BREAK
THE LEADER'S DIRECTIVE NO.16:
PREPARATIONS FOR OPERATION SEALION ARE TO
PROCEED AS QUICKLY AS POSSIBLE.  THE SUBJECT
DIRECTIVE ESTABLISHES OUR OBJECTIVES AS:
1.) WE SHALL SWEEP THE CHANNEL OF ALL BRITISH
SHIPPING OF ANY TYPE, AND
2.) WE SHALL SWEEP THE SKIES OF ALL BRITISH
AIRCRAFT.  OPERATION SEA LION DEPENDS UPON OUR
SUCCESS.
    COORDINATION CONTROLS ORANGE AND GRAY SHALL
BE USED UNTIL FURTHER NOTICE.  SPECIAL AND
EXTRAORDINARY SUPPLY REQUIREMENTS MUST BE SENT
IMMEDIATELY.  ALL AIRCREWS SHALL BE BRIEFED ON
IMPORTANCE OF IMPENDING OPERATIONS.
```

```
          NOTIFY THIS COMMAND AS SOON AS PROPER PLANS
          AND COORDINATION ARE READY.  ALL AIR FLEETS
          MUST BE AT MAXIMUM READINESS NO LATER THAN
          CONTROL BLUE.
          SECRET
```

MOST SECRET - ULTRA

Winston reread the two intercepted and decoded messages one more time before returning his attention to 'C.' The meaning of the notes was clear and unmistakable although some of the details remained outside their grasp.

"Combined with other intelligence, we believe high intensity, focused air operations will begin next week. All the available field intelligence indicates they are still mopping up pockets of resistance, redeploying and resupplying their forces, and preparing forward facilities. Although we do not know the commencement date, yet, estimates set the day between the 10th and 15th of this month."

"Please prepare an appropriate notice to the service ministers and chiefs of staff."

"Yes, sir."

"Also," continued Menzies, "we have information from several reliable sources . . . the Japanese, with the assistance of the Germans, forced Vichy France to cede their military bases throughout Indochina to the Japanese. We have not yet acquired the details as to which bases precisely or exactly what they intend to do with them, however, it is safe to say the Japanese will probably move south."

"Singapore,"

"Yes, Sir, that seems the logical objective, and undoubtedly the mineral wealth of the Dutch East Indies. If they are successful, Australia will be within striking distance."

Churchill grunted his dissatisfaction. "Please alert the garrisons at Singapore and Rangoon."

"The Foreign Ministry is doing so as we speak, as well as notifying Australia and India."

"Is there anything else I need to know?"

"Details, Prime Minister, just details. As such, I should think not."

"Thank you, Stewart. I feel the need to say it, although I know I certainly do not have to tell you, the value of ULTRA is absolutely critical. We are so bleeding close to the edge of the abyss. ULTRA and the bravery of our fighter pilots may well decide this approaching battle."

"We understand and appreciate your concern, Prime Minister. We shall do everything we are able to get the messages to you as soon as they are decoded."

"Is there anything you need?"

Menzies nodded to Denniston. "We are making good progress with our recruiting. We eagerly look forward to American involvement. There are several key American cryptographers we would like to talk to about the mathematics of sequences."

"Soon," Winston said.

The two men departed. The unscheduled convening of the War Cabinet plus the Chiefs of Staff was now an hour away. All the service ministers and chiefs were immediately available. Clement Attlee would cut short his present appointment to arrive within half an hour.

Winston thought about his conversation with the American ambassador yesterday, the most recent ULTRA messages and the actions that needed to be taken. The battle would soon be joined, and the time for recovery and preparation would be over. For some strange reason, Winston thought of the young American volunteer fighter pilot he met a year ago just before all this horrific conflict began. The image of the young man fighting in the small confines of a fighter cockpit for his life and the life of the nation he served etched itself in his consciousness. The thought that the very survival of the United Kingdom, as Winston had always known it, would rest on the youthful shoulders of a thousand determined pilots shook him even more. He had seen their faces, heard their stories, and watched them fly. In the privacy of his office, Winston Churchill felt a tear roll down his cheek as the war became steadily more personal.

—

The announcement of the War Cabinet finally being assembled broke his thoughts. He left his notes and proceeded directly to the Cabinet Room.

"Good afternoon, gentlemen. Thank you for altering your schedules to accommodate an earlier meeting," Sir Edward said, opening the meeting.

"We have evidence the Battle of Britain is about to begin. The latest estimates predict the commencement of German air operations against Channel shipping and the Air Force to be less than a fortnight away. This whole affair will soon come down to the ability of the Royal Navy to keep the sea-lanes open and Fighter Command to maintain air superiority over our islands and beaches.

We must find the time for the Army to rebuild. The three summer months are most probably the only window of opportunity this year for the Germans to attempt an invasion. While the signs of preparation continue to mount, it is fairly certain they will not attempt an invasion without air superiority."

Winston looked to the Secretary of State for Air, and then to the Chief of the Air Staff. Both men acknowledged the unspoken concern and challenge of the Prime Minister. Winston saw the expression of commitment he wanted.

"We do not appear to have much time before the *Luftwaffe* begins a general air offensive. The likely targets may be Channel shipping and coastal installations although they must place a high priority on elimination of our fighters. As long as our fighters remain effective, it will be nearly impossible for an invasion attempt."

"We are as ready as we can be," responded Sir Archibald.

"I know you are."

The distinguished figure of Anthony Eden, Secretary of State for War, wanted to add his thoughts regarding the condition of the Army. "We have used the hiatus since the completion of Operation DYNAMO with better than expected efficiency. The rearmament of the Army is proceeding quite well. In another six months, we will reach a minimum strength for defense."

"How long until you can conduct offensive operations on the Continent?"

The question stunned the entire War Cabinet. Many in authority wondered how they would be able to carry out a successful defense of the Home Islands, and the Prime Minister was considering not defense but offense. For Winston, the question had the desired effect.

"We could carry out limited objective raids possibly late next year, but a full scale assault on the Continent will take four," Eden said as he looked to the nodding head of General Sir John Dill, "maybe five years to prepare for, I should think."

"Excellent. Please make plans to achieve offensive readiness in two years."

"Prime Minister," objected Eden.

"I did not ask you to land forces, Anthony. I asked you for some plans. Let us see what it would take to accomplish this before we convince ourselves we cannot do it."

"Yes, sir."

Winston's thoughts returned to yesterday. "I might like to tell a short story," he paused to ensure he had everyone's attention. "I received the American Ambassador, Mister Kennedy, yesterday afternoon. It seems he is of the impression many in Parliament as well as His Majesty's Government believe the German Army is unbeatable, and furthermore, we shall be done in within a month. He has suggested we should seek terms for peace." A discernible rumble of grunts and whispered comments briefly floated through the large room. "I should like to ask how many here share Mister Kennedy's view?" Winston purposefully did not look at any of the Members or invited attendees, but rather concentrated on the portrait of King George VI and the painting of Oliver Cromwell.

"I believe I am the most conciliatory among the War Cabinet," answered Lord Halifax, the Minister of State for Foreign Affairs, "and indeed all the attendees. If I do not speak for all those present, then by all means correct me, but there is not one among us who is not deeply committed to see this to the end. *Reichskanzelor* Hitler sought war, he shall have war."

"Here, here," came the unanimous confirmation accompanied by the pounding of several fists on the table.

The Prime Minister scanned each face in the room and received an affirmative head nod. He felt a sigh of relief within himself that his understanding of the leadership was clear and true. The National Coalition Government forged in the first moments of trial was functioning to the highest standards set and expected by their ancestors.

"One last item before we adjourn," Winston said. "As we have discussed the last few days, we have attempted to find satisfaction through various diplomatic and military means regarding the French Fleet, given the capitulation of the Government. It is most unfortunate for me to report to the War Cabinet, all our efforts have been for naught. As a consequence, I have given the order to execute Operation CATAPULT. The Royal Navy will confront elements of *Marine Nationale* at Oran, Mers-el-Kebir and elsewhere tomorrow morning. They will be given one last chance to provide assurances in some concrete form that their warships will not fall into the hands of the *Kriegsmarine* in any direct or indirect manner."

"Oh dear," said Greenwood.

"It has to be done," Attlee added.

"Quite so," Churchill continued. "We simply cannot tolerate even the potential of those warships turning on us through some sense of noble duty to the collaborators in Vichy."

"The French will not take kindly with what is about to happen, no matter how we couch our rationale," Lord Halifax said.

"Yes, I am certain of that, as we have discussed. What matters are events, not words, especially in this situation. I shall shoulder full responsibility, but as Clement said, it must be done. Also, we shall exercise similar operations, as we did against the Italians, on vessels of the French merchant marine in British and Commonwealth ports as part of this neutralization process."

"May God bless the Navy in tomorrow's action," Lord Halifax said.

Several 'amen' utterances could be heard before the ministers adjourned and dispersed.

—

Wednesday, 3.July.1940
RAF Northolt
Northolt, London, England
10:30 hours

Pilot Officer Jonathan Kensington felt the same frustration they all did with the seemingly endless, fruitless patrols and occasional scrambles against a threatening enemy only to find themselves unable to locate their targets. The only difference between this patrol and the others before it over the last few weeks came in the form of a threatening line of thunderstorm clouds. Flight Lieutenant 'Sparky' Morrow's Red Section, of which he kept the left wing position, managed to land back at RAF Northolt less than half an hour before the heavy downpour blanketed the airfield.

The squadron pilots sat or stood inside the Dispersal building listening to the pounding of the rain, the flash and clap of the occasional thunderbolt, and smelling the heavy, earthy aroma of the storm. The sleek, curvaceous lines of the Spitfires presented a lonely, isolated scene, like seeing your favorite dog sitting alone in the rain not knowing quite where to go. As the rain began to die down, a senior air force officer burst into the doorway shaking his umbrella off then closing it before fully entering the building.

"Group Captain Spencer," Brian Drummond called out to the pilot room. The entire room tensed up and came to attention when they heard the senior rank.

"Hello, there, Brian," he said.

Jonathan immediately looked into the face and eyes of a man he had never met but seemed to know quite well. This man was Brian's benefactor. This was the man who helped Brian join the RAF from the Great Plains of America, and most likely was the man who helped his friend obtain an operational assignment to Spitfires.

The skipper, hearing the commotion, entered the room from his office. "Squadron Leader Darling, sir. May I help you?"

"I am Group Captain Spencer from Headquarters. I am here on official business, which I would like to discuss with you in private."

"Certainly, sir," Darling answered, motioning for Group Captain Spencer to lead them into his office.

Everyone looked back to Brian Drummond. They all knew the stories, knew the name, and wondered why such a senior officer from Fighter Command had appeared at their squadron Dispersal building.

"Who wants to bet 'Hunter's protector has come to save his boy from all this madness?" said Pilot Officer Stephen 'Mongo' Strickland.

"That's it," answered Flying Officer George 'Angle' Ashcroft.

The pilots laughed loudly and added their versions of the friendly jabs at the visit of a senior officer coming to visit one of their most junior officers. Each one of them understood the significance of Brian's relationship with Group Captain John Spencer. Some of them were envious, and a few were jealous, but none of them resented Brian for his good fortune although they did not miss an opportunity to poke at him.

Squadron Leader Darling opened the door. "Pilot Officer Drummond, if you please."

"You're in it now," they said, slapping Brian on the back as he walked to Darling's office.

Several officers walked toward the door accentuating the gesture of putting their ears to the door. Curiosity gripped them. None of them had experienced such a visit and the privacy of the meetings made for intriguing speculation.

"That's enough, lads," chided Flight Lieutenant Roger 'Jackstay' Beamish, causing the errant officers to move away from the door.

The meeting did not take long, lasting only a few minutes. Brian emerged with a stone face. Darling followed him.

"Pilot Officer Kensington, it is your turn," Darling said.

This time the remarks fell upon Jonathan. Brian gave him a wink as he entered Darling's office.

"Group Captain Spencer, this is Pilot Officer Kensington," said Darling. They shook hands, and then he continued. "Group Captain Spencer is here to offer you a rather unique opportunity."

"I understand you are Mister Drummond's best friend."

"Yes, sir. We are pretty good mates."

"He has told me quite a bit about you, and your commanding officer has provided the requisite additional details we needed. Before we go any further, I must be absolutely candid with you. Brian was my first choice for this assignment, but as a non-British citizen, the Air Ministry excluded him as well as several exemplary non-Commonwealth pilots."

"I understand why you wanted Brian," Jonathan said. "He is one of the best natural pilots around, and he is good at the hunt."

"Quite so."

The telephone bell startled everyone including Group Captain Spencer. Darling went immediately to the door. He closed the door behind him as he went to ensure his squadron's performance.

Corporal Jennifer Warren announced, "Scramble Green Section."

Beamish, Strickland and Drummond grabbed their flying kit and ran from Dispersal. The first throaty sounds of the Merlin III engines starting punctuated the launch of three Spitfires. John Spencer and Jonathan Kensington looked out Darling's window until the No.609 Squadron Spitfires were in a maximum performance climb toward the now broken clouds.

"It is still a treat for me, and I have not seen an operational fighter cockpit since the Great War," Spencer volunteered.

"Have you flown the Spitfire?" asked Jonathan, as they watched the three fighters disappear into the clouds.

"Yes, and every opportunity I can find, but never operationally."

"Well, then, I do not need to tell you what an exceptional machine she is." They both laughed.

"No. I am quite aware of her greatness. It is just unfortunate her designer, Reginald Mitchell, did not live long enough to reap the accolades of his vision."

"When did he die, sir?"

"1937 . . . before the first production delivery."

"Tragic."

"Quite."

Squadron Leader Darling returned to the office with a smile of satisfaction. Jonathan surmised the scramble had been executed in near record time.

"Well, he certainly produced a great fighter."

"Right . . . now . . . I suppose we should return to business." They took their seats. "As I was trying to say before our delightful interruption, Brian was my first choice, but for many reasons the Air Ministry would like to offer you the opportunity of a lifetime." Jonathan's expression of curiosity communicated what he needed to know. "We would like you to fly a special aircraft as part of an evaluation team." Jonathan's interest peaked. "We captured an M E One Oh Nine."

"Dear God Almighty."

"That is what we said when we received the news of a hapless German captain landing his brand new One Oh Nine E Three at the French aerodrome at Amiens."

"And, you want me to fly it?"

"Yes."

"When?"

"Tomorrow."

"How? Where? How do I get there? What . . ."

Group Captain Spencer stopped Jonathan's onslaught of questions and explained the status of the Bf109E-3 single seat fighter – Willie Messerschmitt's design, much as the Spitfire was Reginald Mitchell's design – drew its designation from the principal design and manufacturing factory, *Bayerische Flugzeugwerke*, although the popular description was ME rather than BF. The aircraft had been fully evaluated by the Royal Aeronautical Establishment, RAE, but Fighter Command argued for a wider benefit and the Air Ministry agreed. The operational evaluation plan called for a spectrum of pilots to fly the captured fighter in three segments: prescribed maneuvers designed to accentuate capabilities and limitations of the aircraft, free form maneuvers at the pilot's discretion within a defined flight envelope, and mock aerial combat against the pilot's primary aircraft. The Intelligence Section would brief you on known tactics used by the Germans, and the most successful countermeasures identified to date. In turn, the RAE engineers at Farnborough as well as the Air Ministry Intelligence analysts would conduct a thorough debriefing for a final compendium on the Bf109E-3 fighter for dissemination to the squadrons.

"Is all this secret?" asked Jonathan at the conclusion of Spencer's presentation.

John Spencer laughed but was thankful the young pilot was conscious of the concern. "Well, we certainly would not want you to be talking to *The Times*. We would encourage you to convey your experience to the other fighter pilots. The object here is to give our lads as much advantage as possible against the enemy fighters. Simply do not talk about this project outside the sphere of Fighter Command. Agreed?"

"Absolutely," Jonathan answered with uncontained enthusiasm.

"Given the information and the conditions, do you want to do this?"

"You must be joking, sir. Without question, I want to do it."

"Mister Kensington, your manners," chided Darling.

"Sorry, Sir."

"Great. Then, I am certain Squadron Leader Darling will release you from alert tomorrow," he said looking to Jonathan's commanding officer.

Darling nodded his head. "An Anson will land about Oh Seven Hundred to take you to Farnborough for the day. You will have two, maybe three, flights with the machine. You should return to Northolt by early evening."

"I can't wait."

"Excellent. I wish I were in your shoes, young man. We could have benefited greatly from flying a Fokker *Eindecker* or the later Triplane. I only hope this experience makes you all that little bit better. We need all the help we can get." John Spencer smiled with his memories. "One more item of interest to you, Squadron Leader Darling. As I understand the situation this morning, the Air Staff will be assigning your squadron some experienced pilots quite soon . . . recently evacuated from France. A Czech pilot who speaks passable English and flew fighters in Poland and France, and for Mister Drummond's benefit, several American volunteers who also flew combat missions for the French."

Before Darling could respond, a knock came to his door. "Yes," said Darling.

Corporal Warren opened the door just enough to stick her head through. "Sorry, sir. Green Section returning, sir."

"Thank you, Corporal. If you will excuse me, sir."

"I think we are finished here. I shall get out of your way, and let things return to normal."

"No problem, sir. Thank you for the information. We need the help."

The three men went outside with the other pilots to watch the three PR Spitfires land, taxi in and park. The gun port tapes were missing on all three aircraft. There had been an engagement of some sort. Jonathan watched his best friend's expression change from business to a smile.

"Good hunting?" asked Group Captain Spencer.

"Yes, sir. I hit two of 'em, but no victories I could tell. Flight Lieutenant Beamish may have downed one. We chased 'em off nonetheless."

"Brilliant. I must be going, Brian. Keep up the good work."

"Thank you, sir. We will certainly do our best."

Group Captain Spencer returned to a waiting automobile with a driver and departed. The Green Section pilots completed their debriefing before the squadron was released from duty.

"What happened, Brian?" asked Jonathan.

"We jumped a reconnaissance bomber, but this time he had an escort of five One Oh Nines. We managed a couple of bursts at the bomber before the fighters engaged, which was enough to turn him around. The bad guys didn't seem to have their hearts in the fight. They wanted to disengage and stay with their bomber. We gave chase and kept on them as long as we could."

"Five escorts for a reconnaissance aeroplane . . . rather odd, don't you think?"

"Yes, now that you mention it."

"And, you got some hits?"

"Yeah, some bits flew off a couple of 'em, but they kept going."

"Maybe we are getting back into this thing?"

"Yeah. Hey, what about this project?"

"Exciting, isn't it?"

"You bet your booty. When do you get to fly it?"

"It looks like tomorrow, but it should be you, Brian."

"Naw. I understand. Will we get to talk about it when you get back, so we can hear all about it?"

"Group Captain Spencer says that is the point of this evaluation, so yes, I think so."

"Great."

"He seems like a very nice man," Jonathan said, to recognize Brian's benefactor.

"He has been the best for me. I probably wouldn't be here if it wasn't for him."

The telephone rang and everything stopped instantly. "The squadron is released," reported Corporal Warren.

"So ends another day at the office," said Squadron Leader Darling. "Shall we retire to the Mess?"

The resounding chorus of agreement firmly established the answer to Darling's rhetorical question. The friendly and envious ribbing by the other pilots began as the meaning of the senior officer's visit spread and carried on into the night. They all wanted to be in Jonathan's place.

—

Wednesday, 3.July.1940
Cabinet Room
No.10 Downing Street
Whitehall, London, England
17:30 hours

"I have the honor to report to the War Cabinet, and later to the House of Commons, that Operation CATAPULT was executed with precision this morning," Prime Minister Churchill announced. "For the most part, the French naval merchant marine vessels at Portsmouth, Southampton and Alexandria were boarded and successfully subdued. Unfortunately, attempts to negotiate with the French admirals at Dakar, Casablanca and Oran proved unsuccessful. Vice Admiral Somerville initiated a general attack this afternoon on the main body of the French Fleet at Oran and Mers-el-Kebir. Offensive naval and air operations were also conducted at Casablanca and Dakar. Regrettably, the magnificent battlecruiser *Strasbourg* escaped along with several destroyers and reportedly made for Toulon. Most of the remainder of the French Fleet has been sunk, grounded, captured or incapacitated including the battleships *Bretagne*, *Provence* and *Richelieu*. Admiral of the Fleet Darlan feels we have betrayed him and has protested along with the Vichy Government."

"They gave us no choice," commented Attlee.

"The record will show we took all possible steps and measures to neutralize the French Fleet. We are resolute," said Lord Halifax, "that even the remotest possibility of French naval assets falling into the hands of the Nazis was categorically unacceptable."

"We are all in agreement," Greenwood added. "Do we know the extent of damage and losses on both sides?"

"The reports are still coming in," answered Winston. "Other than the regrettable loss of life, Operation CATAPULT appears to have been successful. I shall fully report the results to Commons tomorrow afternoon. I have asked the Ministry of Information to prepare the appropriate release of actions and results to the press the day after tomorrow. I will ask the Admiralty to convey a well-deserved well done to the Fleet for the successful conclusion of Operation CATAPULT." First Lord of the Admiralty Alexander and the First Sea Lord Admiral Pound nodded their heads in agreement. "Now, if there are no further questions, we should complete the agenda."

The logistics of the defense plans occupied the remainder of the two-hour meeting before they adjourned for Members of the House of Commons to attend the scheduled evening session. Winston Churchill looked forward to Prime Minister's Question Time with rejuvenated vigor. Although he intended to avoid any mention of Operation CATAPULT in the open session this evening, Winston felt more satisfaction than regret. Turning the military forces on an ally so soon after their capitulation left a very sour taste in his gut, but as Halifax had said, they simply could not take the risk that the Germans might gain control of the excellent French Navy vessels. The resulting combined French and German Navies would rival and in some cases surpass the Royal Navy. The risks were too great, and the responses of the French naval commanders too vague and in some cases too belligerent to find a peaceful resolution. The British people demonstrated their willingness and commitment to defeat the Germans, and they were prepared to take whatever steps were necessary to accomplish that objective.

—

Wednesday, 3.July.1940
The White House
Washington, District of Columbia, U.S.A.
18:00 hours

"The Navy is here," Harry Hopkins informed the President.

"Let's hear what they have to tell us."

Hopkins nodded his head and invited the Navy leaders to join them in the Oval Office. Soon-to-be confirmed Secretary of the Navy Frank Knox led the small group into the President's office – Chief of Naval Operations Admiral Harold Rainsford Stark, USN and Chief of Naval Intelligence Rear Admiral Walter Stratton Anderson, USN. Harry followed the naval officers, and Bill Donovan trailed Hopkins. Hopkins closed the door as everyone took their seats in front of the President.

"Good evening, gentlemen, and thank you for making time for me this evening. On Frank's suggestion, I have asked Bill Donovan to join us. He had all the necessary clearances from me for this discussion. I understand we have had some excitement today."

Frank was not yet confirmed, so chose to remain silent unless spoken to in this briefing.

Admiral Stark began, "The Royal Navy executed a rather bold operation today to neutralize the French Navy."

"I guess that answers the question as to whether the British are going to fight," Roosevelt said.

"Yes, Sir, I think there is very little doubt remaining about that. Mister President, I have asked our Director of Naval Intelligence, Admiral Anderson," Stark said motioning toward Anderson, "to brief you on today's events."

"Good evening, Mister President," began Anderson. "Various reliable naval sources confirmed the Royal Navy's Mediterranean Fleet under the command of Vice-Admiral Sir James Somerville signaled an ultimatum to Admiral Marcel-Bruno Gensoul in command of the heavy French squadron at anchor in port of Mers-el-Kebir, French Algeria. We believe the British sought solid assurances the French Navy would remain neutral and oppose any move to enter naval operations against the British either on orders from the Vichy Government or at the command of the Germans. Admiral Darlan refused to give the necessary assurances, as did Admiral Gensoul when confronted by Admiral Somerville. The British opened fire at 17:54 hours local time, just before noon here. The French were late in responding and the damage was done in short order. We are still working on a damage assessment, but it appears the French may have lost at least two battleships, several cruisers and a number of destroyers and support ships."

"Rather impressive, it would appear," said Roosevelt with solemnity.

"Yes, Sir. We also have numerous unconfirmed reports the British seized French naval and merchant shipping in Commonwealth ports around the world, most without resistance, but there were a few reports of skirmishes aboard the warships. As you may recall, Mister President, the British executed a similar action against the Italians not quite a month ago with very much the same result."

"Anything else?"

"That is the extent of our knowledge so far, Sir."

"Please continue your efforts to clarify the situation regarding the French Navy and their maritime assets."

"Aye aye, Sir."

"The British are in a very tough spot. They are very much alone now in this fight with the Germans. Churchill has publicly vowed to fight on to the end, whenever that might be. Yet, he has a substantial portion of his own political party and the government who advocate for an armistice with Hitler. Churchill undoubtedly gave the order to neutralize the French Navy."

"Rather ballsy," interjected Knox.

Roosevelt chuckled. "Yes, Frank, very much so, it seems to me. No one has accused Churchill of being a shrinking wallflower. You have to love him for that. He is asking for military *matériel* support from us, and there are more than a few in Congress and even in my administration who want the British to seek terms from the Germans, and thus would not look favorably upon our supporting the British in any form. I know what Churchill says, but the question in my mind is whether he can marshal the strength of the British to fight on. Lord knows, we need the British to continue the fight, at least to buy us time to mobilize." Roosevelt paused in contemplation. No one spoke. "Enough proselytizing. It is approaching suppertime, and I need to let you go. Thank you for briefing me on today's events. Please keep me informed as your information clairifies. I really would like to know what the British accomplished today."

"Yes, Sir," responded Admiral Stark.

"Frank, Bill, do you have anything you want to ask or say?"

"No, Sir," answered Knox and Donovan simultaneously.

"Very well, then."

Roosevelt motioned with his hand for everyone to leave. Hopkins pushed the President back to his desk, went to the door, closed it, and returned to the President's desk.

"We simply must determine whether the British can stay in this fight," he said to Hopkins.

"Churchill is certainly putting up a brave face."

"That may not be good enough to stop the Germans."

"He definitely made a statement today."

"Yes, he did. Knox has proposed we send Donovan to England on a fact-finding tour. What do you think of that?"

"He did not say much this evening."

"He wouldn't. He does not have a charter, as yet, so it would have been out of place."

"He is highly regarded, not just by Frank Knox, but by many inside and outside the government."

"We need to get Frank confirmed, so we can send Donovan. I suspect he will be a bulldog with this information business, and we need a bulldog."

"Information from the Hill indicates both he and Stimson should be confirmed within the week."

"None too soon for me."

"We will see what we can do to speed it up."

"Thank you, Harry."

—

Chapter 10

You can't step into the same river twice.

-- Heraclitus

Thursday, 4.July.1940
Royal Aeronautical Establishment
Farnborough, Hampshire, England

"Pilot Officer Jonathan Kensington, I presume?" asked a flight lieutenant who did not wear pilot's wings.

"Yes, sir."

"Excellent. I am Flight Lieutenant Stemple. I will be your host for the day's activities," he said motioning toward a well-worn, topless vehicle of some sort. "I trust the flight from Northolt was uneventful?"

"Yes, sir, although I would rather have flown myself."

Stemple laughed. "That's what they all say. Unfortunately, these days, we must control traffic rather tightly."

During the drive to the other side of the aerodrome, Jonathan learned that Stemple was an aeronautical engineer with the de Havilland Aircraft Company in Hatfield, Hertfordshire, who volunteered for duty and was assigned to the Royal Aeronautical Establishment as an investigations engineer. He was one of the primary analysts on the Bf109E-3 project. Jonathan also learned from Stemple, the RAF also operated a captured He111 medium bomber that he might get an orientation flight in if the day's tasks were completed in a timely fashion.

The distinctive hard angled shape of a static Bf109 parked in a small hangar told Jonathan they had arrived at their destination. The gray-black camouflage paint and the bright yellow propeller spinner looked threateningly familiar. Only the RAF roundel on the wings and the tail flash dampened its menacing appearance. Jonathan wanted to touch the aircraft, to feel its character, but was shepherded into a specifically furnished briefing room. The drawings of the Bf109, cockpit sketches, performance charts and systems schematics covered all the walls.

A wing commander, who did not give his name, began the briefing with a simple description of the fighter, the circumstances of its capture and the course of tasks to be performed. Several other pilots entered the room but were not introduced. Jonathan would be given a detailed description of the aircraft and the operating procedures in due course. Two Hurricanes would escort them constantly and would not be a part of the evaluation except as protection against some young, inexperienced and overzealous RAF fighter pilot. The first flight would be broken into two halves. The first portion he would fly a prescribed set of normal and combat maneuvers with an assistance pilot flying a Spitfire on his wing. The second segment would allow Jonathan to fly the fighter the way he wanted, to get as complete a feel for the machine as possible. The second flight of the day would be a mock aerial combat exercise against a Spitfire Mark II. Neither aircraft would be armed which also explained the two escort Hurricanes. Jonathan would be asked to fly like a German for the initial element of the flight and would be allowed to fly it the way he thought best for the remainder of the flight. The combat maneuver setups would entail conditions advantageous to the Bf109 and some tilting toward the Spitfire. The third flight, time permitting, would involve switching seats with his assistance pilot and repeating the mock engagements. The purpose of the day's activities was to help him learn how best to use his Spitfire against the Bf109E-3 fighter.

"Do you have any questions at this juncture?" asked the wing commander.

"More than I can think of."

The senior officer laughed. "Let it suffice for now, we shall answer most of your unthought-of questions through the course of the day. I would encourage you to let your curiosity out, to gain as much benefit on the day."

"Yes, sir."

"Right, then, I shall turn over the reins to your assistance pilot. You might have noticed that we have not used names here. It is not poor manners. It is simply a precautionary protection mechanism for our team. I trust you will understand?" Jonathan nodded his head. "Excellent. Then, let the games begin."

The wing commander left the room and one of the pilots, a flight lieutenant, moved to the front of the room. "As the wing commander stated, I am your assistance pilot for the day. The other two pilots," he paused to allow Jonathan to turn to see each with a raised hand, "will provide escort, for obvious reasons, to ensure we get no external interference."

His instructor, as Jonathan thought of him, carried out a quick, but thorough briefing on the capabilities and limitations of the Bf109E-3 as well as the operating procedures. He handed Jonathan an encased card with a strap he could attach to his thigh. The card presented key performance numbers and an abbreviated list of operating procedures. Jonathan listened with object fascination and the constantly recurring thought this was too good to be true. It had to be some kind of elaborate torture to test his mental strength against temptation.

"Any questions thus far?"

Jonathan shook his head and felt the smile grow on his face. He knew he was coming to a key point in this nasty test. They could not keep up the facade forever.

"Brilliant, then let's go fly."

"Oh sure. I can't wait," Jonathan said with as much sarcasm as he could muster.

His assistance pilot stopped and smiled. "This is no joke, or test, or malicious hoax. I trust you will conduct yourself as is the case . . . you are a very fortunate young fighter pilot who is about to fly his adversary's most formidable fighter. I can assure you this is all true, and it is not a dream."

"Sorry, sir, but it does seem to be too good to be true."

"Quite," he said, as he led Jonathan and the two escort pilots outside.

He conducted a quick walk-around pointing out significant features of the captured German fighter and allowed Jonathan the opportunity to feel the leading edges of the wings, the propeller blades, the gun ports he could reach, the flight control surfaces and the smooth aluminum skin. The assistance pilot motioned for Jonathan to climb into the cockpit. He completed a thorough cockpit briefing pointing out each of the controls and instruments. Several of the gauges had paper scales glued next to them showing a green band as well as yellow and red sections to translate the metric indications into normal and abnormal operating readings familiar to the British pilots. The most distinctive features were the simple straight control stick with a rubber grip and red firing button on top, and the almost square, caged canopy. The cockpit felt even more confining than the Spitfire cockpit.

When his assistance pilot went to his Spitfire, Jonathan quickly stepped through all the cockpit controls again and rehearsed the procedures for starting, engine checks and takeoff procedures. He checked the makeshift radio and oxygen mask connections that enabled him to use his RAF flight equipment in the German fighter. For the first time, Jonathan became aware of the peculiar odor in the cockpit, a strange mixture of pickled onions, oil and petrol. Maybe the German spilled his lunch when he realized he had landed at the wrong place.

Jonathan heard the melodic drumbeat of the Merlin starting in the aircraft next to him. He quickly ran through the simple starting procedures before opening the throttle full open to allow the Daimler-Benz DB601C engine's fuel injection controller to regulate the fuel-air mixture and signaled for start. A ground crewman turned the elbowed hand crank just forward of the right wing root. The propeller turned through three blades before it fired off effortlessly. As the engine accelerated, Jonathan pulled the throttle back to the idle stop. The swirling air brought the acrid fumes of partially burnt fuel but quickly cleared the peculiar onion odor. He watched the engine oil pressure rise into the normal range. All the instruments showed what he was told they would. He waited for the coolant temperature to show some warming before he signaled the Spitfire he was ready.

The proper radio calls were made. Jonathan followed the Spitfire snaking their way toward the takeoff area, followed by the two escort Hurricanes. In turn, the ground crew draped themselves over the tail plane to allow the high power engine checks. The magnetos checked good. The propeller pitch control responded correctly. Oil temperature was now in the normal range. Jonathan was ready for takeoff.

"Leopard Flight, this is Leopard One. Readiness for takeoff?"

"Leopard Two, ready for takeoff," answered Jonathan.

"Leopard Three, ready."

"Leopard Four, ready."

Jonathan watched the ground crew for the Spitfire remove the wheel chocks and signaled his crew chief crossing his arms, and then moving his extended thumbs outboard. The crew showed the chocks. Jonathan waited for the Spitfire to move. He pushed the throttle forward about an inch to get the fighter moving. The Bf109E-3 taxied much like the Spitfire although it did not rock quite as much over the small bumps in the grass. With the engine checks completed satisfactorily, he gave the flight leader a thumps up. As they had briefed, Jonathan would takeoff first with the Spitfire right on his wing to make sure everything went right. With a thumbs up from the Spitfire, Jonathan checked the instruments . . . everything was normal.

Jonathan pushed the throttle forward about halfway. As the Bf109E-3 accelerated bumping across the takeoff area, the tail rose like the Spitfire at about thirty miles an hour. As the rudder became effective, he slowly advanced the throttle smoothly to full power adding rudder to counteract the torque of the engine. With the engine purring nicely, the fighter jumped into the air. Jonathan moved the landing gear handle to the up position and listened to the swish of the hydraulic system raise the landing gear until the uplocks engaged, then he raised the flaps as his airspeed passed 100 mph.

The Bf109E-3 accelerated quite well, again much like the Spitfire. As the briefing established, they climbed to 18,000 feet. The prescribed maneuvers included stalls, maximum rate turns, high-speed dives and several aerobatic maneuvers. Typical German attack maneuvers were set up for Jonathan to execute. The most impressive maneuver for Jonathan was rolling the aircraft inverted. It took him several attempts to feel comfortable hanging in the straps and sustaining inverted flight. Flying upside-down felt very alien and was not something the Spitfire could do. The fuel injected engine and the negative g sump in the fuel tank gave the Bf109E-3 its inverted flight capability as well as the most common escape maneuver, the pilot's called, a bunt. Pushing forward on the stick dropped the nose, producing negative g, and gave the pilot the sensation he was being thrown out of the aircraft. The bunt maneuver caused more than one Spitfire or Hurricane pilot to starve his engine of fuel trying to follow his target. The Rolls-Royce Merlin engine used a float type carburetor that shut off the fuel flow when the normal effect of gravity was removed and thus was not capable of negative g maneuvers.

The second flight played more to what excited most of the fighter pilots – testing their skills against another pilot. Jonathan took what he learned on the first flight, plus his thirty odd engagements against Bf109s since the real war started, and used his knowledge in the mock engagements. In the ninety minutes of practice combat, they flew from various initial conditions.

The third flight repeated the sequence with Jonathan flying the Spitfire. It was his first flight in the Mark II with the additional 70 horsepower of the Merlin III engine. The two flights of aerial combat maneuvering provided the most graphic comparison between the two aircraft and left an indelible impression upon his consciousness.

The weather and the machines cooperated in perfect order, thus allowing Jonathan to fly copilot in the captured He111 with several fighters in attendance. He was able to move around the aircraft checking each crew station for field of view, constraints and other peculiarities. He moved the guns to check for gimbal stops or other limits. Jonathan watched numerous mock attacks to get a first hand experience of what the bomber crew might feel when confronted by Spitfires or Hurricanes.

Each debriefing had been efficient, well constructed and thorough. At the conclusion of the bomber flight debriefing, the wing commander who started the day's activities returned to the same room.

"Well, Mister Kensington, I understand you have had a most productive day."

"To say the least, sir, and oh what a day."

"Excellent."

"I am thankful for that," Jonathan said, and immediately wondered about his group. "If I may, sir, how many pilots have flown this One Oh Nine?"

"Four test pilots from RAE, and you are the sixth of ten operational fighter pilots scheduled to fly it."

"It is truly an honor."

"Quite." He paused to look at his wristwatch. "Your ride home should be here shortly. I would like to use the available time to hear your summary of the day's experience."

"Where do I begin?" said Jonathan, giving himself a little thinking time. "I now clearly understand why the One Oh Nine is such a formidable adversary. Its inverted flight or negative g capability is the most notable. The responsiveness of the fuel-injected engine certainly feels to be quicker, better, than our carburated engines. The biggest weaknesses I could see have to be that damned caged cockpit, the high control forces, the lack of rudder trim and the poor roll performance at high speed. All those obstructions in front of your eyes were quite similar to the original Spitfire canopy and makes you appreciate even more the single piece, bubble canopy we have on our Mark One As. The roll performance above 300 to 325 miles an hour was atrocious. The German pilots must be gorillas to overcome such high stick forces."

Everyone in the room laughed as they probably did every time the characteristic was described by a visiting pilot. As the wing commander retold some of the other observations, Jonathan understood the reaction.

The door opened. One of the crew chiefs simply nodded his head and closed the door.

"Your Anson is here to take you home, but I would like just a few more questions or observations." Jonathan nodded his consent. "Overall, has your view of the One Oh Nine changed?"

"Yes, sir, most definitely. While an impressive fighter, it is not monumentally superior, as many Fighter Command pilots tend to think of it. While better than a Spit in some areas, it seems to be quite inferior with regard to other attributes. It is good to know the machine does not give them a decided edge. The pilot makes the difference." Jonathan thought about adding his comments about the Spitfire Mark II, but there were few notable differences other than the newness of the machine.

"Well said, young man. Now, one last question, if I may. What was your general impression of the attack vulnerability of the bomber?"

"Again, a most informative experience for which I am exceptionally grateful, but it likewise is not as prickly as I thought before my flight. It felt like a lumbering leviathan with some teeth to be respected but not feared."

"I say, good show. Could you or did you determine a most vulnerable attack angle?"

"From my experience, the experience of others and confirmed by this flight, I would say he is still most vulnerable from directly head-on or straight up the tail."

"Very good, Mister Kensington. Thank you for your time and observations. You have been quite contributory to this endeavor. In closing, I must say what you have seen and experienced here today is sensitive. We want to protect our knowledge of the enemy. However, the Air Ministry wants Fighter Command to benefit from this godsend. So please, talk of your experience among your fellow pilots, but do not discuss even the very existence of these machines with anyone outside the RAF. Is that clear or do you have any questions?"

"Yes, sir, it is quite clear, and I do not have any questions."

"Brilliant, then your transport awaits you."

Pilot Officer Jonathan Kensington shook hands with the wing commander and each of the pilots before he left the briefing room. He spotted the crew chief who tended to him on the Bf109E-3, and he detoured slightly to shake his hand and thanked him for his expert assistance.

The flight back to RAF Northolt was equally as uneventful as the morning's flight although Jonathan had considerably more to think about on the short twenty-minute flight. This was definitely a day that deserved some extra treatment in his personal diary. He found some paper to jot down many of the key points he would expand later when he had more time.

Fortunately or unfortunately, depending on one's perspective, the squadron had another boring day of waiting and two unproductive patrols. His mates took their frustration out on Jonathan and his good fortune. They all knew what he was supposed to do at RAE Farnborough, but now they had the man himself. The questioning and professional exchange began at Dispersal, continued through evening meal and well into the night with every pilot remaining to complete their interrogation. There was an equal fascination with his experience in the Bf109, the He111 as well as the Spitfire Mark II with maybe a slight edge to the Bf109. They compared experiences, adjusted views, refined their tactics, and in general, made good use of Jonathan's exposure to their principal nemesis. This had been a great day for Pilot Officer Jonathan Kensington.

The other topic that dominated their discussions well into the late evening was the press reports of the Royal Navy's actions against the French Fleet. At first, the announcements were thought to be some cruel hoax. How could the British attack the French? They were allies. What had happened between them? One entire battleship and complete crew were reported lost in the naval action at Oran. French Navy ships being boarded and seized, others seriously damaged or grounded, and a few sunk. It was tragic, confusing and ominous to those beyond the decisions. The whole world had been turned upside-down. Nothing remained normal. Everything became shocking and strange. Brian wondered, mostly listening as an observer, if the world would ever return to normal.

—

Friday, 5.July.1940
RAF Northolt
Northolt, London, England

For Pilot Officer Brian Drummond, there were mixed feelings as the No.609 Squadron pilots continued to examine Jonathan Kensington's experience at RAE Farnborough. He was excited his best friend was able to fly the vaunted German fighter, but he was also slightly resentful it had not been him. He had to be thankful for Group Captain Spencer's candor and honesty with him, but it did not take much of the sting away. Nonetheless, Brian tried to learn as much as he could, to fill in as many of the details about his opponent's primary aircraft as he could. As the discussions continued and new, more incisive questions were presented, Jonathan remembered more of his experience. They all finally admitted, despite their jealousy and envy, it was exceptionally beneficial for them to have one of their own in the small group of chosen pilots.

Squadron Leader Darling returned at about 09:00 from a hastily called, early morning meeting at No.11 Group Headquarters at Uxbridge. They had been at Available status for two hours with no activity or changes of status. Darling called all the pilots into the Dispersal building, which meant an important announcement.

"As you all know, Fighter Command has recently formed a new group, Ten Group in the West, with Headquarters at Box in Wiltshire, near Bath." Groans from many of the pilots punctuated Darling's announcement. They all knew before he said it . . . they were moving again to join No.10 Group. "You have it, lads. We have been reassigned to Ten Group. We will move the squadron this afternoon, at least most of the squadron, to RAF Middle Wallop in Hampshire. We are to stand down from alert availability to make preparations for the move. We will take off at half three with the entire squadron."

"They are moving us further from the action," said Pilot Officer Strickland.

"Not to worry, 'Mongo.' Fighter Command thinks there will be enough for all of us, quite soon."

"Where the hell is Middle Wallop?" asked Flight Lieutenant Beamish.

"A few miles north of Salisbury," answered 'Junior' Carrolton.

"Oh great, they put us in a cow patty."

"And, I was becoming quite accustomed to the dolly-birds of London."

"Now, now, lads. We have business to tend to and Headquarters feels we are best utilized in Hampshire. So, let us quit with the whining and get on with our business. We do not have much time. While the crews prepare the aircraft and begin moving our support equipment, I suggest you proceed to the Mess and get your kit packed up. We will have a lorry parked out front at mid-day to load your baggage."

Some of the pilots kept their flight gear with them while most returned their equipment to the proper pegs to await the afternoon flight. As each of the pilots gathered up their belongings, the discussion of their new base as well as Jonathan's experience yesterday continued intermittently throughout the morning.

The prevailing opinion centered on the notion that any move away from London would be a move away from the action. The pilots of No.609 Squadron anticipated the move south from RAF Drem a month and a half earlier as a very positive event. They were moving closer to the action. This move to Hampshire was a move away from the action. As they usually did, the pilots liked to talk about what was good and what was not so good. They always had an opinion about anything, and this move was no exception.

Brian had all his limited belongings packed in two large travel-all bags and a sturdy footlocker provided by the RAF. He waited in the lobby for the next step in their journey.

"'Hunter,' you have two letters," said Roger Beamish, as he handed them to him.

"Thanks, 'Jackstay.'"

Brian looked at the return addresses. One letter was from Mary Elizabeth Ann Spencer née Armstrong, and the other from RAF Hornchurch. The only person he knew at RAF Hornchurch was Jeremy Morrison. Brian knew he still needed to talk to Jeremy about Anne and Virginia, but he also knew any conversation with Jeremy and especially about Anne would not be a pleasant discussion. He decided to open Mary Spencer's letter first.

2d July 1940
Bushey, Herts
Dear Brian,

As this is my first letter to you, I pray it does not catch you too much by surprise! I thought it best to write rather than some other form of communication.

I have some most urgent business to discuss with you. I have taken the liberty, I hope you will forgive me, to ascertain your next two-day break on the 7th and 8th nearest. Being even bolder, I have booked a suite for you at the Savoy on the night of the 7th. I would like to meet you for lunch at the Savoy Grill at one on the 7th. It is very important to me that I see you soon, Brian. Please honour my request. Unless I hear from you to the contrary, I will see you this Sunday. Until then, please take care.
Yours most sincerely,
Mary

Brian could only guess what Mary's business might be, but the room reservation for the night did not leave him with a good feeling. His last meeting with Mary at the Spencer house four months ago during his visit to Fighter Command Headquarters had scared him. The time made his recollection less vivid, but he could not ignore what he felt certain was an approach by an older, married woman – his benefactor's wife – to have an affair. She was an attractive woman who, independent of all other facts, would be worth a meeting to see what might happen. However, she was not just an attractive woman. Anything more than a proper social contact might jeopardize all he had worked for, dreamed of and sought, by most likely irreparably damaging his relationship with her husband.

"Everything all right?" asked Jonathan, as he sat next to him in the lobby.

"Sure."

"You look like you have seen a ghost. Are you sure everything is OK?"

"It's no problem," Brian said as he folded the letter and tucked it into his shirt pocket. He tried to smile. He thought for a brief moment whether to confide in his best friend and seek his counsel on how to handle the situation with Mary. The risk was too great. "No problem."

"As you say," said Jonathan, as he left Brian to return to his activity.

Brian waited for Jonathan to disappear outside before opening the letter from RAF Hornchurch.

3.July.1940
RAF Hornchurch, London
Dear Brian,

     I have tried to telephone you numerous times, however this bloody war seems to be conspiring against me. I thought about coming to you at RAF Northolt. After all, you are only across town. As I am certain you will understand given the circumstances, I thought you should have some anonymity of distance before we meet. So, I shall resort to the post. I hope this gets to you in a timely manner.

You know why we need to talk. I suspect you have many unanswered questions. I also know I have more information than you at this juncture. I do not want this to come between us as friends. Please call me the next time you are in town. We can meet at Shepherds. This is important, Brian.

Your friend,
Jeremy

Brian quickly refolded the letter and placed it with Mary's letter. He looked around the room to see if anyone had been watching him, so he might be prepared with an explanation if one was needed. Officers moved back and forth like waves against a breakwater. No one noticed him. Brian thought about both letters. Each brought its own darkness to his thoughts. Why was his life becoming so complicated, as if the problems of jumping from Stearman biplanes in Wichita, Kansas, to the cockpit of a RAF Spitfire and fighting extradition for violation of the Federal Neutrality Act were not enough?

Brian decided he would meet Mary in London on Sunday to try to put things straight between them. Maybe he could meet Jeremy in the afternoon after his lunch with Mary. If he was lucky, Brian told himself, he might have everything in proper order by early next week after his 48-hour pass.

The flight from RAF Northolt to RAF Middle Wallop took 15 minutes. Darling kept the squadron low over the countryside and held the throttle back to give the engine coolant system the best condition to prevent overheating in the warmer, denser air close to the ground. The constant scanning for enemy fighters that never appeared reduced the enjoyment of the scenery en route.

They landed, were directed to parking at the far eastern end of the new flightline and hangars, and shut down their fighters. A representative of the station staff, a rather crusty warrant officer, gave them a quick orientation briefing. Squadron Leader Darling, after checking in with Sector Control, gave the pilots the remainder of the day to get their personal business taken care of before taking an orientation flight in the morning. They walked through the orderly but still under construction facility, out the main gate and across the A343 carriageway to the building that would be their residence.

The Officer's Mess was a converted manor house conveniently located across from the main entrance to the airfield. The stone columns, the rich, dark wood paneling, and the oak and marble flooring gave the building a warm, comfortable feel. The smells of fresh cut flowers added to the polishing oils reminded Brian of Bentley Priory – Fighter Command Headquarters.

They checked into the Mess, received their room assignments and weekly allotment of bed linens. Their baggage had not arrived, yet. They rejoined in the bar for a few drinks before the evening meal.

They met many of the pilots from the other squadrons. No.609 Squadron was the first Spitfire squadron to be assigned to the new facility. The other two squadrons already at RAF Middle Wallop were No.238 Squadron flying Hurricanes and No.604 Squadron flying twin engine Blenheims. No.604 Squadron had the distinction of being the first designated operational night fighter unit in the RAF. They continued to work on tactics and techniques that sounded like absolute madness to Brian and Jonathan, but the discussions were intriguing.

Laughter and friendly parries accentuated the deliciously prepared evening meal of lamb, green peas and au gratin potatoes. The other pilots made the newcomers feel as though they had been there all along. It was a unique feeling that he had heard Malcolm describe to him many times. These were truly brothers, and he liked the feeling. It gave him strength.

Several of the No.609 Squadron pilots followed their hosts to what was becoming the favored haunt of the RAF Middle Wallop pilots – the Black Swan Pub in Andover, a few miles up the A343. The pilots jokingly called it, the Mucky Ducky. On the drive up to Andover, Brian finally had a few minutes to think. He thought of Anne Booth. He wanted answers that perhaps Jeremy Morrison could provide. Then, he felt the burn of the letters in his shirt pocket. Mary Spencer. He did indeed have a two-day break starting Saturday night. Should he do as he was requested in her letter? Maybe her request was quite innocent with no illicit intent. Mary Spencer was important to him in a different way, and yet he knew he had to honor her request.

They used the occasion to take full advantage of the services offered at the Black Swan. Although they needed little to drink, they also took every opportunity to drink to excess. For some of the pilots, it was a means to obliterate the fear. For others, it was an excuse to get crazy and stretch the limits of propriety. Brian felt neither urge but stayed with his buddies as they all entered the misty realm of uninhibited alcoholic fog. They laughed at anything and everything. They entertained the locals who seemed fascinated by their lack of any visible concern or fear. That night, the Black Swan swayed to a different rhythm.

———

Saturday, 6.July.1940
RAF Middle Wallop
Middle Wallop, Hampshire, England
07:00 hours

The pounding headache, mouth full of cotton and stale odor of beer that surrounded Brian told him clearly that he had gone too far the previous night at the Black Swan. He wanted to sleep. He certainly did not want to eat, or fly for that matter, but he also knew he could not let the excesses of the previous night interfere with his duty. Brian forced himself to get up, took some extra time in the hot shower and cleaned himself up. The fact that none of the other pilots harassed him about his excess told him they had been just as inebriated.

The morning meal while typically well prepared tasted terrible. The result was not gastronomic satisfaction, but an overwhelming nausea that Brian had to struggle to defeat. Fortunately for Brian, this was an orientation day. The entire squadron would fly an area familiarization flight including several landings at RAF Warmwell near Portsmouth, their primary outlying airfield for dispersion and operational deployment.

The briefing went as usual. The only unusual event was a private question from Squadron Leader Darling asking him if he was ready to fly. The flight was quiet and routine like a sightseeing tour of the countryside of

Southern England. The Salisbury Plain was oddly quite flat compared to the surrounding terrain. They made a low pass over the intriguing circle of large Druid stones called Stonehenge. Brian remembered the discussion he had with Jonathan Kensington on their way to his home, Carlingon Castle, last Christmas. He had to find the time to drive out to the place and see the circle of stones. They also flew along the entire coastline in their sector. He saw the Isle of Wight, the Solent and Southampton, features he remembered upon his arrival in Great Britain a year ago. Brian looked for and finally spotted the Supermarine Works on the Woolston side of the River Itchen. He clearly saw the seaplane ramp and the parking area where he saw his first Spitfire. Seeing these places from the air brought many memories into perspective. Most importantly, he remembered the discussion with Group Captain Spencer during their visit to the Supermarine factory that one day he may have to defend the Spitfire plant against German bombers. While the Southampton area was actually in the Tangmere Sector under No.11 Group, they expected to be tasked with support missions.

RAF Warmwell, farther to the West near the famous harbor and port city of Portsmouth, was the most austere airfield Brian had seen yet. The only permanent building was the Operations building with its squat control tower. All the other 'buildings' were large Army tents. Brian wondered how much time they would have to spend at the rudimentary facility.

With the area flight complete and no operations at RAF Middle Wallop, Squadron Leader Darling formed the entire squadron in a left echelon peeling off each fighter as they passed over the field. They landed to the North, up slope toward the large, steel and concrete hangars. The squadron would not enter Available status with No.10 Group until tomorrow, and Brian started his 48-hour rest break at mid-day. The remainder of the day was spent getting settled into their spaces. No.609 Squadron was assigned to No.5 Hangar, the northeastern most hangar located behind No.4 Hangar in the V group of five massive concrete hangars only recently completed.

At the end of the day, several of the pilots wanted to go back to Andover to a new establishment called the Square Club. It was reported to be a more modern facility that featured music and dancing, which meant women. Brian still did not feel very well, and he really wanted to get a good night's rest so he could leave in the morning for his meeting with Mary Spencer in London. The fighter pilot's image demanded that he pretend the previous night's abuses had not fazed him in the slightest. Six of them including the two flying sergeants went to Andover.

The beer thrust into his hand nearly made him vomit although he had not even taken a sip. He fought hard and successfully against his nausea. Brian managed to only get past the first few sips when a rather tall, thin, attractive woman asked him to dance. The movement seemed to help, and the company of a woman made his pain disappear. She never introduced herself but would not let him go for several dances. She appeared to be more interested in his uniform than his name.

Brian never got a chance to finish his beer through the nearly constant stream of woman asking him to dance. He was thankful for the reprieve from alcohol and the nearness of the sweet floral perfumes of the women. Several wanted to dance more closely than normal, pressing their bodies against him. This was a fertile hunting ground if Brian had been in the mood. Several of the others disappeared into the night and the city streets leaving 'Fog' Johnson and Brian to return the Air Force sedan to RAF Middle Wallop.

Miles Johnson dropped Brian off at the Officer's Mess. He would return the automobile to the squadron parking area on his way to the Sergeant's Mess. The separation between the flying sergeants and the officers never gave Brian a good feeling. It was more like resentment he felt every time he was reminded of the difference. The thought did not last long as he went to his room and collapsed into bed. Tomorrow would be a big day, and he instinctively knew it would be full of surprises. He would not have to get up with the other pilots, but he would have to leave fairly early to catch the 08:37 train into London.

—

Saturday, 6.July.1940
Headquarters, Fighter Command
Bentley Priory
Stanmore, Middlesex, England
22:00 hours

The late night staff meeting and the chance of operations in the early morning, summer daylight would mean yet another night away from his home and his wife for John Spencer. There was satisfaction knowing that his personal sacrifice had value to the overall performance of Fighter Command.

While the Germans continued to probe the air defense system with reconnaissance flights, they had yet to conduct offensive operations. This meeting, as many of the previous meetings, would be devoted to intelligence. What did they know? What did they need to know?

Air Chief Marshal Dowding called the meeting to order at precisely 22:00. The head of the Intelligence Section, Air Commodore Hogan began his briefing referring to a large map of the English Channel, Southern England and Northern France.

"The build-up of German Air Force units along the coast from Cherbourg to Ostend continues with relative high intensity. They continue to resupply squadrons and stockpile materiel at all the aerodromes. There is little doubt left, the Germans are making final preparations for full-scale operations against the United Kingdom. The Air Ministry believes the initial primary targets must be Fighter Command in all respects in order to gain air superiority as quickly as possible.

"Aerial reconnaissance of French, Belgian and Dutch ports indicates a marked build-up of barge and transport vessels all along the coast. There can only be one purpose for these vessels – a general invasion of Great Britain. The build-up is too large, too broad, and too intense to be a faint. There are no signs in Norway that might suggest a northern invasion route. The War Cabinet and the Chiefs of Staff Committee estimate a possible invasion attempt as early as mid-August. Their available window is the six weeks from mid-August to the end of September when adverse weather conditions return. The preconditions for a cross-channel attempt must be naval dominance of the Channel approaches, air superiority over the landing area and adequate infantry and mechanized forces to conduct semi-self-sufficient operations in Southern England."

"What have we heard from the Y Section lads?" asked Air Marshal Leonard.

"They are still trying to determine the frequency sets. They have established the technique, but the exact intersections are still by luck."

"Have they seen any changes in the German's use of their *Knickebein* equipment?"

"Everything appears to be routine as far as their use of the device."

"I think we all might benefit from a report of the status of the Home Defense Force," suggested Air Chief Marshal Dowding.

"The War Office estimates it will take six months to a year to rebuild after the substantial loss of troops and equipment in the Battle of France."

"Let me add," Dowding said, "General Sir John Dill feels six months is the minimum time. Privately, the Army wants a year to rebuild. I might also say the Prime Minister has asked the War Office to prepare plans for offensive land operations on the Continent within two years."

There was soft laughter. "No one can say the Prime Minister does not have the bollocks to lead us through this mess," said Geoffrey Leonard for them all.

"While the colloquialism may be appropriate," Dowding continued, "I think it is important that we have things in perspective. This country is faced for the first time since 1588 with a serious invasion attempt. As you have heard, there is not much between the *Wehrmacht* and the heart of this country. The only obstacles to an invasion are the Royal Navy in the Channel and Fighter Command in the air." The somber note brought the staff back to business. "Air Commodore Hogan, if you would be so kind, please continue your briefing."

"The Air Ministry Intelligence Section published a summary of the *Luftwaffe* Intelligence. Various sources give us a view of their accuracy and thoroughness. An indication of the importance the *Luftwaffe* and *Reichsmarschall* Göring place on intelligence is the head of foreign intelligence for the German Air Force is a major, Major Josef Schmid. For your reference, his title is: *Befehlshaber, Fünfte Abteilung, Oberkommando der Luftwaffe.*"

"In English, James," said Air Marshal Leonard to everyone's laughter.

"Roughly translated, he is Head of Command, Fifth Department, Air Force High Command. The significance is . . . it is his department that is solely responsible for analyzing and disseminating intelligence on foreign air forces. It is the analysis of his department that guides the *Luftwaffe* in their operations against us."

"Are you feeling threatened, James?" asked Leonard with a joking tone. "Here you are an air commodore – a brigadier – and the Germans feel they can do your job with a major." More laughter filled the room.

John Spencer listened to the exchange with some resentment. James Hogan was one of the most engaged, energetic and enthusiastic intelligence officers he had ever known. He also knew there was a specific reason Hogan wanted to identify his German counterpart. John wanted to hear the remainder of the report.

"I do appreciate the humor, Air Marshal Leonard."

"Continue," commanded Dowding in his dry, calm, quiet manner.

Air Commodore Hogan nodded his head. "With SIS support and a variety of other sources, we have developed what we believe to be a rather good picture of the German view of the Royal Air Force and more specifically, Fighter Command.

"We managed to obtain a copy of Study Blue . . . ."

"The darkies have been quite busy," interjected Air Commodore Maple, Deputy Chief of Operations. Again, majority laughter. Most operational types, while they appreciated and depended upon them, were suspicious and somewhat distrustful of the intelligence professionals. Very few pilots really understood how the intelligence professionals actually worked, John Spencer told himself.

Air Commodore Hogan ignored the comment. "Study Blue was published by General Milch in July 1939, and established the itelligence basis for the invasion of the United Kingdom."

"I'll be damned. The bastards had all this worked out before they pulled the trigger," said Maple.

"Precisely. Study Blue, as well as other additional subsequent source materials, state that the RAF fighter resources are tied via radio-telephone to ground stations and controllers, and since ground stations are not mobile, the fighters are not mobile. According to the report, the German Air Force does not expect concentrated, strong, fighter interception at specific points and especially at short notice. The conclusion states they expect to gain sufficient air superiority in two to four weeks to enable a full scale invasion."

The conference room remained silent as each officer considered the information provided by Air Commodore Hogan. John had heard some versions of the elements although he did not know the information came from a presumably secret German study. He wondered how the RAF or the British had taken possession of such an important study. He also wondered if the report was true. Maybe it was planted, fabricated information designed by the German Minister of Information, Doctor Paul Joseph Goebbels.

"Is this thing true?" asked Maple voicing what John thought most of them felt.

"We have every reason to believe it is authentic. There are other bits of information which suggest it also reflects the general opinion of the German Air Force leadership."

"Then, I should think we can give them a good lesson in the cost of poor intelligence," said Air Marshal Leonard.

"One last item the Commander has asked me to brief ... sources indicate the Germans have decided an invasion of Great Britain is possible given air superiority and a few other conditions. An invasion date has not been set as far as intelligence sources can determine, however the War Cabinet supports an expected invasion date from mid-August to the end of September."

"As we have said many times," said Dowding, "our task has been established. The product of our labor will soon be realized. I want each and every one of us and indeed all of Fighter Command to be up to the task. The welfare of our citizens, the survival of our nation and quite possibly freedom itself will soon be left in our capable hands. Are there any questions?"

Group Captain John Spencer, Staff Secretary for Fighter Command, wanted to ask 'Stuffy' Dowding what tricks he had up his sleeve? What magic or miracles were waiting to help the inferior number of fighter pilots defeat an unbeaten German Air Force and the most successful fighter force in the world? Perseverance, courage and commitment had to be the key.

—

Chapter 11

Beauty is the lover's gift
--William Congreve

Sunday, 7.July.1940
Savoy Hotel
Strand, London, England

It had been many months since Pilot Officer Brian Drummond patronized the Savoy Grill. Fortunately, he told himself, the trains ran on time placing him at the requested location a half hour ahead of the appointed meeting time. The emotions Brian felt were a foul mixture of excitement, fear, lust and resentment. He hoped his perception of Mary Spencer's attraction to him was an absolute figment of his youthful imagination. Except for a few, what he thought were, suggestive words during his brief visit to the Spencer's house five months ago, Mary Spencer had always been a perfect lady. Brian actually wanted the sinful possibilities to be just his lustful imagination.

Brian looked casually and carefully around the moderate sized dining room. It was not quite half full before the lunch hour, which meant it would most likely fill up soon. He did not recognize a single sole. Three quarters of the men wore military uniforms, all British except for one American Army brigadier general who wore pilot's wings. He wondered what an Army Air Corps one-star general was doing in London? Brian did not possess the gregarious nature or curiosity needed to introduce himself.

As he concluded his second scan of the dining room, the delightfully proportioned figure of Mary Spencer entered the room, stopped to find Brian and smiled broadly as she spotted him. She wore a conservative, dark blue woman's suit with a simple white, silk blouse along with a modest blue hat and white wrist gloves. Even her walk broadcast elegance.

Brian stood as she approached. "Good afternoon, Brian." Mary extended her hand, which he accepted, and before he knew it, she leaned forward to kiss him warmly on the cheek.

Brian flushed slightly at the warmth of her closeness. "Good afternoon, Missus Spencer."

Her smile disappeared. "I forbid you to call me, Missus Spencer. I hope we can be on a more personal and intimate basis. I would also hope you will feel comfortable calling me by my given name."

"Certainly." Brian felt an incredible nervousness far beyond anything he felt in the air flying at high speed into certain combat. He willed his heart to slow its pounding.

"It is so good to finally see you again, Brian," she said with her soft delicate voice. "It has been far too long, and I have indeed missed you. I would like to thank you at the outset for agreeing to see me today. I hope you were not offended by my forwardness."

"No, ma'am. I mean, no, Mary," Brian stammered, unsuccessfully fighting his disquiet.

Mary laughed quietly with a bright, seductive quality in her dark brown eyes that made Brian even more uneasy. "I can see you are not a veteran at this game. Maybe it would be better if we ate our lunch in a more private setting." Brian could only nod and accept the control Mary exercised over all events around them. She gestured for the waiter's attention. "We would like to order our lunch and have it delivered to the Ambassador's Suite." Brian's heart nearly stopped at the thought of being alone with her in a hotel room. He wanted to say, no, but the word could not even rise to his lips. He had no air to breathe, let alone talk.

"Certainly, madam. What would the lady and the gentleman care to order?"

As Mary ordered without looking at the menu, Brian quickly searched the menu for something he recognized. He ordered a salad and potatoes.

"Shall we?" Mary said standing gracefully. Brian nodded as he stood with her, his heart pounding once again.

Brian followed her lead offering his left arm to her. Mary used their physical contact to guide Brian out of the dining room, down the wide corridor, through the lobby and to the elevators.

She drew him close pressing his arm against her breast. Thank God, the lift operator would not leave them alone. Brian could feel her stare as he concentrated on the ascending lighted numbers. The all too familiar caged feeling nearly caused him to command the operator to let him out of the small box. The helpless sensation, he felt several times before with women but never had the air choked him like this, kept him from gaining control of his emotions.

Mary must have sensed the anxiety, the tension, the uneasiness in him as they walked down the corridor keeping his arm pressed tightly to her breast. "Relax, Brian. I am not going to bite, and I am not leading you into eternal damnation."

Brian felt like a convicted criminal being led to his execution. He knew what was going to happen although he had never experienced it. In his growing collection of life experiences, he had never been with a married woman. He did not want to start now.

Once in the hotel room, Mary released Brian's arm as she allowed him to explore the large suite. Mary did not appear to be impressed with the fancy room. The suite was spacious, elegantly furnished with a separate large bedroom and adjoining bathroom with a dining room on the opposite side of the living room. The bed was one of the largest he had ever seen with four, dark, heavy wood posts and delicate lace canopy. Even the view out the floor-to-ceiling French doors and small balcony awed Pilot Officer Brian Drummond. The River Thames, Westminster Palace with its Big Ben bell and clock tower, the Tower Bridge and even the infamous Tower of London were visible from the suite balcony.

"I couldn't possibly pay for this, Mary," Brian protested.

She laughed without taking her eyes off him. "You are correct, my dear, but you are not paying for the room. I am."

"Won't Group Captain Spencer find out?"

Her expression turned serious. "First, Brian, I am wealthy in my own right. You have no need to worry about money. Second, I love my husband dearly. I will not allow anything to hurt him or our marriage. Third, I will ask you not to mention him, again. I know he his important to you, as he is to me in a different way, and I see no need to place him between us."

Brian felt certain her words were meant to ease his concerns, but to him they sounded like the executioner's song. His mind wanted to leave, but a powerful magnetic force kept him from doing what his mind told him to do. Nothing unseemly or improper had occurred, yet, and he still did not know why Mary Spencer wanted to see him in London this weekend.

As they both walked around the furniture and occasionally stepped out onto the balcony, they talked of his flying, which he had no reticence to do with anyone. He began rambling on about the experiences of the squadron over the Channel and France, about being shot down, and about the thrill of the hunt. Brian wanted to tell her about Jonathan's extraordinary experience flying the captured German fighter, but he honored his commitment to protect the information.

The knock at the door undoubtedly signaled the arrival of their late lunch that he had nearly forgotten. He opened the door to see a rather old, frail looking man in a waiter's uniform with a service cart.

"Your lunch, sir." Brian motioned for him to enter. The old man slowly pushed the cart toward the dining room.

"Would you mind setting the trolley by the window," said Mary. "The warm afternoon breeze, the delightful summer weather and the extraordinary view, are, I'm afraid, simply too divine to pass up."

"Certainly, madam," the old waiter said as he changed directions.

Mary Spencer pulled the remaining light, transparent curtains back from the open French doors. It was a beautiful day, Brian told himself. The old man placed the cart a yard inside the room, moved the various plates and ambiance items from the cart to the dining table, arranged the plates and service items, and placed two chairs to opposite sides of the table. Mary discretely placed two one pound coins in Brian's hand and motioned with her eyes as the old man completed his task. Brian passed the coins to the waiter as he started to leave.

"Thank you, sir. If you would be so kind, please ring the Grill when you are finished, and we shall remove the service trolley promptly."

"Certainly," Brian said.

When the waiter closed the door behind him, Mary Spencer motioned toward the table. "Shall we?" Brian helped her with her chair as a gentleman should, and then seated himself. *"Bon appétit,"* she said with delicate words. Before either of them ate a bite, Mary began what they both had waited for several days to complete. "I know you have wondered about what I thought was so important to take up your rest time from flying and to call you to London." Brian froze and did not respond. "It is my nature to be as absolutely honest and candid as I am able. My words may seem a bit blunt at least by European standards anyway." She smiled and looked deeply into Brian's searching eyes. "So . . . I will come directly to the point. I am afraid my reasons are quite personal and extraordinarily selfish. I freely admit that." She paused without taking her eyes off Brian as though she was waiting for some response from him. "I want to get to know you better than I do without all the other pressures which tend to be around us."

Brian finally moved, nodding his head. He decided since there was no earth shattering news or cataclysmic event to deal with, he would be candid and honest as well. "I am not sure exactly what you mean."

"Let me continue to be blunt. You are a very attractive man in many ways, and I know you find me attractive. I have seen your eyes many times. I am a lonely woman whose husband is absorbed in this damnable war. I need your company, Brian, and I believe you want mine."

She had not said anything about a physical facet to any relationship they might have, he told himself, although he felt the unseen pressure. At this instant, he remembered the stories his parents and his friends talked about regarding adulterous men and women in Wichita. He remembered reading, The Scarlet Letter, in school. He also thought about his benefactor, Group Captain John Spencer. This was not right. He wondered what Malcolm Bainbridge would say to him. The voice came to him. Malcolm would not be pleased.

In fact, Brian was certain, he would be angry. Would he be angry because she is John's wife or any man's wife?

"I cannot do this, Mary."

Disappointment filled her eyes. "Of course you can. It is easy and comes quite naturally between a man and a woman."

"I can't, and I really think I should leave."

Mary Spencer smiled. "I suspected you might react like this, so please let me continue." Brian stood up and started to retrieve his hat. "Wait!" she commanded rising and moving toward him. He took several steps backwards and she stopped. "No one need get hurt in this, Brian, that is the beauty of it. We both have every reason to be absolutely discreet for our own reasons." She paused looking for some reaction that she did not receive. "I know you will do everything to avoid offending my husband, and I can assure you I will do the same."

Brian thought of Anne Booth and Rosemary Kensington. "I have a girlfriend."

"And, I have a husband."

"This is wrong."

"It is wrong only if we make it wrong."

"It is wrong."

"Brian, listen. I need the company of a strong, virile, young man, and I can show you things you may never have experienced before in your young life. We can have fun together. Enjoy each other for the pleasure of it without forcing it to be anything other than pleasure, that is the beauty of what we can have together. That is all I ask."

Mary Spencer moved toward him again. He did not move. She grasped his hand lightly, lifting it to her breast. Brian found he could not resist the attraction of the full, soft flesh beneath her clothing. She reached for him and found what she wanted. Mary looked deeply into his eyes.

"No. No."

"Yes, Brian. Your body speaks for you."

"No."

Mary knelt before him, moving like a hummingbird until she had the stamen. The carnal magnet locked him in its powerful force field and held him in place. The attraction and passion between them broke through the constraints of mortal and moral concern. The natural progression took them through hours, and several respites to recover from the expenditure of life energy and into the evening. They eventually stopped long enough to eat their cold lunch that waited for the fires to subside enough to allow recognition of their hunger for food. The still warm early evening air and sufficient breeze cooled them just enough.

"Thank you, Brian."

"For what?"

"You are everything I had dreamed you would be. I can feel the struggle and disquiet I have caused you, but our pleasure does not have to injure anyone."

"Thank you, Mary."

"I hope you feel this is worth it," she said, with uncharacteristic hesitancy.

Brian considered telling her the complete truth but in the end decided for a partial truth. "Yes, I do," he said calmly.

They ate, exchanging communications without words as dusk began to cast its shadows over the city beyond their balcony. Brian, at a moment's lull, thought for the first time in hours about what happened and what consequences there might be. Mary sensed Brian's thoughts.

"Brian, I do not want you to feel guilty. You have simply given much needed pleasure to a lonely woman. You have probably helped your benefactor," she said, indirectly mentioning her husband for the first time. "You have relieved the pressure of his absence." Brian nodded his head in recognition. "You have made me a happy woman."

"I still feel bad for him."

"Don't Brian. He is doing what he loves. He is doing what the country needs him to do. You are doing what he cannot, and what I need you to do." Brian nodded again. "Think of it this way, you are helping the country." She laughed, and he chuckled not really knowing what she meant. "By keeping me satisfied, I should be less of a nuisance to John, thus allowing him to devote his complete attention to the war." They both laughed. "You must separate your relationship with him, and me for that matter, in a public or social environment, and the relationship we have in private."

"Not so easy."

"Sure it is. I have been around pilots and aviation most of my adult life. I know how pilots deal with danger, risk and death. They create this enormous chasm between flight and the rest of the world. It is exactly the same." She laughed in a more soft and delicate way. "Pretend you are flying me." She laughed more loudly and deeply. "Just separate what we do in bed from everything else."

"Maybe so."

"Sure. It will be easy, and we will have fun." She rose from the table and allowed her robe to fall to the floor. Brian absorbed the mature, full curves of her body. Mary smiled and giggled almost to herself. "Come with me, my lover. I want to make you a happy man."

They moved, touched, tickled and played between periods of inter-twined sleep. They never separated physically throughout the night for any reason. She touched or held him to her as he did with her. The feel of her embrace, the softness of her skin, her warmth, made all the brutality in the air disappear into the distant oblivion. She brought life, as every woman did, to his violent world. In the quiet moments between their exertion and sleep, Brian appreciated the difference he felt with Mary Spencer. For the first time since he recognized the attraction, Brian thought he might be able to do what Mary suggested. It just might work. He was helping her as she needed, he rationalized.

Mary and Brian continued on the roller coaster through his early morning bath and preparation until he had to leave for his return journey to RAF Middle Wallop. He had to be back on duty by noon, Monday. With the summer daylight, he might have one or more patrols or even a scramble before he could get a long, restful sleep. He wondered what the future held for him.

—

Monday, 8.July.1940
RAF Middle Wallop
Middle Wallop, Hampshire, England
19:15 hours

Sure to his suspicion, Green Section received an early evening patrol order. They took off with the Sun still above the western horizon. A convoy of merchant ships, eleven ships in all, was moving eastbound through the Channel and RDF apparently picked up some activity over Northern France.

The monotonous, long, racetrack, orbit patterns allowed Brian to think about other things. He remembered each of Mary Spencer's words. How could she possibly be right? They did have fun, and she understood pilots. Rosemary did not. Anne had accepted what he did and had not tried to understand, and she had said many times she did not need to understand. Mary did make him feel good in ways quite different from Anne and Rosemary. Maybe it could work. She certainly made him forget everything outside that suite at the Savoy Hotel. She helped him as he helped her.

They had been aloft 85 minutes when they received the recall command from Middle Wallop Sector Control. They had not seen any other aircraft, friendly or hostile. The ships made their stripes across the water without interference. The Sun descended behind some clouds to the west, although it was still above the horizon when they landed and taxied back to their area.

Brian had no squawks on his aircraft, and they had not fired their guns. Leading Aircraftman Bernie Gordon and the rest of the crew for Brian's PR-F aircraft were pleased they did not have any immediate work to do other than fuel the machine, and the aircraft continued to operate without deficiencies.

Flight Lieutenant Roger 'Jackstay' Beamish held back, motioning for 'Mongo' Strickland to go ahead back to Dispersal and for Brian to come to him. As Brian joined him, Beamish turned to walk away from the Dispersal building and the No.609 Squadron flight line.

"What the hell were you thinking about up there?" he asked with some anger.

"What do you mean?"

"You were not with us. You missed several turns, drifted from your position and were late responding to signals. I have never seen you fly like that before. Where were you?"

Beamish had never talked to him like that, and although he did not remember such transgressions, his section leader would not make them up just to harangue him. There were never any adequate excuses for a lack of attention in fighters or any aircraft for that matter. A moment's inattention would be more than sufficient time to be killed or to injure a comrade.

"I had a tough weekend. I am sorry."

Beamish turned to face Brian squarely. "You are damn bloody well right you're sorry, laddie. If I ever see you fly like that again, I will see to it you do not fly in Fighter Command. We were lucky we did not have to deal with any Germans, as lackadaisical as you were up there. Whatever it was that happened this weekend, put it aside, put it behind you. Forget everything except flying when you sit your arse in a fighter cockpit. Do you understand me?" he finished with a near growl.

"Yes, sir."

"Good," he said as his expression changed from steel to bubbles. "Now, let's go have a few beers."

Brian knew without exception that Flight Lieutenant Beamish was precisely correct. Malcolm Bainbridge had told him essentially the same thing too many times to count. Any distraction could be deadly in the air. Brian recommitted himself to not allow any interaction between the ground and the air. His survival and those of his squadron mates depended upon his concentration and focus. He would not fail, again.

—

Monday, 8.July.1940
Oval Office
The White House
Washington, District of Columbia, U.S.A.
16:10 hours

Secretary of State Cordell Hull was the last to arrive. Nearly confirmed Secretary of War Henry Stimson and Secretary of the Navy Frank Knox were already seated before the President, as was British Ambassador Lord Lothian. The ever-present Harry Hopkins hovered behind Franklin Roosevelt in proximity to the President's desk, as if some important paper might need instant retrieval. New to the group but not to the room or the President was a rather thin, academic-looking man dressed in a well-tailored three-piece, light grey suit.

"Nice that you could join us, Cordell," quipped Roosevelt.

"My apologies for the tardiness, Mister President."

"I believe you know everyone here with perhaps the exception of Vannevar 'Van' Bush," the President said. The two men shook hands, and then Hull sat on the couch on the other side of Stimson and opposite Knox. Hopkins took his seat next to the desk. "Van is the newly appointed Chairman of the National Defense Research Committee to coordinate and supervise defense research for the military departments and the government at large." The President did not expand his introduction to explain that the NRDC was created less than one month ago by his executive order, and that he expected the energetic and ambitious Bush to draw cohesion and direction to widely disparate defense research projects.

"Lord Lothian, if you would be so kind, you requested this audience."

"Thank you, Mister President," he acknowledged with a clear and sophisticated British accent.

"And, I was happy to oblige."

"I have been asked by His Majesty's Government and Prime Minister Churchill to officially place before you, Mister President, a proposal to transfer several dozen, secret defense technologies, as we have discussed informally before. Our scientific team continues to refine the list of included projects. Yet, we felt it time to open the planning effort in anticipation of executing the transfer as soon as possible."

"You chose the word 'transfer' rather than 'exchange,'" Franklin observed.

"Yes, Mister President. The specific word choice was Prime Minister Churchill's, I must say."

"Why so?"

"As you are quite aware, Great Britain is surrounded by Nazi Germany. The Battle of France strained our military services. With the deepest gratitude, we received the first shipment of military arms and equipment from your country, which we immediately distributed to refit the Army. The current estimate predicts the Germans will soon, within days, no more than a week or two, commence a comprehensive aerial attack on my country in preparation for an invasion of the British Isles before summer is out. We feel the window for the Germans is this summer. After that, the inclement weather will set in until next spring and our rearmament will be well underway by then, both of which will make invasion far more risky. That said, the War Cabinet wants to safeguard our vital defense secrets in the hands of our important and essential ally."

"Any questions, so far?" asked the President.

"You mentioned a list," Bush said.

"Yes. I have the current list for your review," Lothian answered, as he looked each man in the eyes. "As I mentioned, we are continuing to refine the included technologies from our perspective. We want to get the preliminary list before your experts to initiate a proper interaction regarding content, so that we might solidify the list and execute the plan within a few weeks."

"How would you propose we proceed, to that end?" Roosevelt asked.

"As I understand your new defense research committee, I would suggest Mister Bush meet as soon as possible with our military representatives. In anticipation of the question, our Air Attaché Air Commodore George Pirie has invited Mister Bush to join him and Army Attaché Brigadier Charles Lindemann tonight at his residence for dinner and detailed discussion of the list. I might add as well that Brigadier Lindemann is the brother of Professor Lindemann, the Prime Minister's science advisor."

"We should have representatives in these discussions," Stimson interjected.

"By all means."

"Do you have those names, Henry?" Roosevelt asked.

"No, Sir. Frank and I will need a day or so to select the correct officer to represent our respective departments."

"As soon as you have those names, please notify Van and Lord Lothian so that they can join and participate." Stimson and Knox nodded their acceptance.

"Can give us some representative examples of what is on the list?" asked Bush.

"Certainly. Frank Whittle's turbine engine, the Rolls-Royce Merlin engine, the cavity magnetron that is critical to making radio direction finding equipment small enough for aircraft, new explosive compositions, and I might add here, we wish to transfer our research to date on the potential uranium explosive work our physicists have done."

"Well, that is a broad range," Bush responded.

"Yes, as you will see tonight, the listed technologies are much broader than the few I have offered."

"What do you expect in return?" the President asked.

The 11th Marquess of Lothian, as he was more properly known, smiled and said, "Put these items to good use, as Prime Minister Churchill told us."

"The generosity of His Majesty's Government is overwhelming. First, we shall endeavor mightily to fulfill the Prime Minister's charge. Second, and I say to our benefactor," President Roosevelt said, as he motioned to the others, "we shall reciprocate in good faith and in kind."

"You are most gracious and generous, Mister President."

"Van, you have your charge."

"Yes, Mister President."

"Once the exchange program is finalized and we execute the plan, I would like a briefing on the full list, if you would be so kind."

"At your command, sir."

"Fine, now one last item while we have you with us, Lord Lothian." The Ambassador nodded his acceptance. "I expect Congress to confirm both Frank and Henry tomorrow. They will take the oath of office as soon thereafter as proper arrangements can be made. As we discussed a week or so ago, it is my intention to send Colonel Bill Donovan, as the unofficial representative of the Secretary of the Navy," he said and smiled at Frank Knox as though they were secret co-conspirators, "on a fact-finding tour of England. I believe all the appropriate arrangements have been put in place. His *prima facie* mission is to study and learn from British Fifth Column countermeasures. We have had our share of Nazi infiltrators and we need to learn quickly how to deal with them."

"Yes, Sir. Colonel Donovan will be welcomed with open arm and given *carte blaanche* with our military and security services. As you accurately note, all the arrangements are set for his visit, from the King and Prime Minister on down."

"Excellent." The President turned to Frank Knox. "What are his travel plans, Frank?"

"Once my nomination is confirmed and I am sworn in, we will have our last *bon voyage* meeting with Bill. He will go immediately by rail to New York to join up with Bill Stephenson, and then together they will take a Pan Am Clipper to England. They should arrive in London early next week."

"I shall inform the Prime Minister and the Government."

"Is there anything else we need to discuss?"

"I think not, Mister President. On behalf of His Majesty's Government, thank you so much for your precious time and invaluable support."

"Kick the snot out of those damnable Nazis," the President added in an uncharacteristic venacular.

The Americans chuckled, which somewhat surprised Lothian. "We shall do our best, Mister President."

They all shook hands and departed, except for Harry Hopkins as usual. As Harry pushed Roosevelt back to his desk, he said, "I think history was just made, Franklin."

"You may well be correct, Harry."

———

Tuesday, 9.July.1940
RAF Middle Wallop
Middle Wallop, Hampshire, England

"This sure does look like we are returning to the boredom and frustration of the Phony War days, after that little spurt in France," observed 'Mongo' Strickland, as he reclined with his eyes closed in an acquired beach chair.

Brian saw several pilots nod their heads in nonverbal agreement. The squadron had bounced from Available to Readiness to one short stint at Standby without a single launch all day. They had been at Dispersal since 06:30 and the waiting continued to have its corrosive effect on their nerves. Only a section of Hurricanes from No.257 Squadron had taken to the air in the early afternoon, and they returned an hour later with their gunport tapes still intact.

"Maybe we are making peace with our German brothers," said 'Fog' Johnson, also with his eyes shut while basking in the late afternoon sun.

Brian wanted a launch to prove he had not lost his skills after yesterday's admonition from 'Jackstay' Beamish. He needed to prove something to himself as well. Mary Spencer still occupied an enormous portion of his idle thought. He had even felt the urge to talk to someone. He still had the issue of Anne's betrayal that he had not come to grips with, and now, he had this affair with Mary Spencer. He had thought he might find some time to see Jeremy Morrison while he was in London, but Mary filled every moment. Even his best friend, Jonathan Kensington, noticed a distraction in Brian since his return from London. He had something to prove to everyone. Where were the Germans when he needed them?

The disturbing ring of the telephone terminated all their thoughts. The message did not take long to be received. "Scramble Green Section," stated Corporal Jennifer Warren.

Beamish, Strickland and Drummond sprang to their feet, grabbed their flight equipment and raced to their fighters. Brian glanced at the Dispersal room clock – 18:32. Two of the three fighter engines were already running at idle by the time they reached their aircraft. 'Mongo' Strickland's crew was last again, as they usually were.

Their takeoff was routine as the trio climbed at maximum performance. As they stablized in their climb headed south, 'Jackstay' Beamish radioed Sector Control. "Bandy, this is Sorbo Green, heading one eight oh, climbing through angels two."

"Sorbo Green, this is Bandy. Vector two three oh. Ten plus bandits at angels one two. Take angels one five."

'Jackstay' gradually altered their heading 50 degrees to the right with the reassuring roar of the engine. Brian, completed his pre-engagement checks. His sight was lit and set, the guns armed and charged with the gun camera switch on, and the engine in perfect performance. Brian was ready. His instincts told him this would be his first actual engagement in a month.

"Roger, Bandy. Listening, out."

They leveled off at 15,000 feet and accelerated to maximum speed as they headed toward their perch. Everything remained normal in his cockpit. Brian continued to scan the entire sky for any movement, anything other than clouds.

"Sorbo Green, this is Bandy. Vector one eight oh for intercept."

"Roger, Bandy."

Brian knew there were three sets of eyes searching for the German intruders. He concentrated his scanning forward and below of his left wing. The controller tried to put them between the incoming raid and the Sun that was well to the West. Something moved below them. It took another few seconds for Brian to identify the movement.

"Sorbo Green Leader, Sorbo Green Three, tally ho, tally ho, ten o'clock low, a flight of eight Stukas." It was the first time Brian had seen the Junkers 87 *Sturzkampfflugzeug*, the infamous screaming dive-bomber that had gained notoriety in the Spanish Civil War and had demonstrated devastating accuracy and effectiveness in Poland, France and the Low Countries.

"Bandy, Sorbo Green. Tally ho. Eight Stukas right were they should be. Right lads, let's keep an eye out for the fighters."

None of the Green Section pilots could find any fighters among the clouds as 'Jackstay' rolled to begin the engagement. As 'Mongo' began his roll, Brian found the fighters.

"Leader, Three. Fighters eleven o'clock level." Brian watched Beamish continue his attack. He held his wings level watching for any reaction by the German fighters. Brian quickly estimated the number of escorting fighters at 12, half Bf109s and half, the twin-engine, two-seat, Bf110, known as the Destroyer. Brian had seen the illustrations, photographs and films of the twin-engine German fighter, but this was his first encounter with the aircraft as well. "About twelve. Half One Oh Nines and half One Tens. They're holding back."

"Stay with 'em, 'Hunter.' Bandy, we could use some help."

"Sorbo Green, this is Bandy. Sorbo is airborne. Junior Blue, vector two six oh, angels one seven. Twenty bandits, ten miles at angels twelve and fifteen. Sorbo Green engaging."

"Bandy, Junior Blue. Tally ho, the bandits at twelve."

"Fighters diving to engage." Brian observed the Bf110 diving toward 'Jackstay' and 'Mongo.'

"Sorbo Green, break off for fighters. We'll take the fighters."

The other two Spitfires pulled up into a climb to face the diving Bf110s head-on. Brian pushed his throttle through the emergency gate to close on the ensuing tangle of fighters. He kept a close eye on the Bf109s still holding at altitude.

"This is Junior Leader. Tally ho. We have the Stukas. Red Leader, you take the back end. We'll take the front."

Brian took a brief glance to see the Hurricanes from No.238 Squadron breaking up the formation of German dive-bombers. As the three Spitfires mixed it up with the twin-engine intruders, the Bf110s formed into a fighting circle to concentrate the fire of their tail gunners.

"One Oh Nines are coming down."

"Sorbo Green, break it off, climb," commanded 'Jackstay' Beamish.

"Sorbo Leader, we're five minutes out. Stay with 'em, 'Jackstay.'"

Beamish did not answer as the three Green Section Spitfires left the Bf110 defensive circle to engage the now diving Bf109s.

"Stukas are diving on the Portland harbor shipping."

"Tighten up, lads. Let's keep the Stukas off the ships."

"Sorbo Leader. Tally ho."

The view of four white nose Bf109s diving directly at them did not leave Brian with a feeling of comfort. The Germans opened fire first. The bright flashes on the wings and nose told him bullets were on the way toward him. Brian lined up his sight on the leader, quickly glanced to check his slip ball. Half ball out the right. He pushed lightly on the right rudder pedal and squeezed the trigger. The reassuring chatter of the guns erupted from his wings. It felt like all eight guns were firing. No indications of any hits by either side.

The fighters passed in an instant. Brian rolled still holding the nose up as he strained to bring his fighter around and gain precious altitude. He felt his hand pushing on the throttle that was already past the emergency gate wire. He had all the 1,030 horsepower the Merlin III engine could deliver, and she was still humming smoothly.

Brian strained his neck to look over both shoulders trying to find his targets. He found one of the Spitfires, and then several of the Bf109s. He rolled a little more and released some of the backpressure on the stick to extend his perch toward a group of two 109s. Then, he saw what the two Germans were after.

"'Mongo,' you've got two on your tail. Break hard!"

Brian pulled his nose down hard, felt his airplane shake and shudder near maneuvering stall. He released a little pressure. The fighter rolled to line up on the attacking Germans.

"Hang on, 'Mongo.' I've got 'em."

"I'm hit."

"Johnny, get out of there."

Brian ignored the confusing broadcast words and concentrated on his line-up. The lead attacker steadied up for a few seconds.

"My God, he's exploded."

Brian squeezed the trigger. The wings erupted. He saw flashes on the Bf109 and parts of the right wing flew off as Brian passed. He pulled back hard as he rolled to get his nose back around to his targets. He saw smoke streaming from a descending Spitfire. Fortunately, Strickland's Spitfire had not exploded. Maybe it had just been a large flash fire. Another white nose Bf109 rolled to engage the wounded Spitfire. Brian pushed harder on the throttle, but it did not move as he pulled back harder on the stick. The aircraft bucked and threw him off his rolling turn. No stall, he told himself, as he let up a little to keep the nose coming. He rolled out with a good intercept line on the Bf109, but the German was closer to his target. Brian quickly looked over both shoulders to see if he had anyone on his tail. Nothing he could see. As he closed to firing range, he could see the distinctive whitish-gray smoke

. . . the German was firing. Line-up good. Fire. The wings erupted again. Brian kept his firing button down until he practically flew threw the German. Multiple hits all over his adversary.

Brian pulled his throttle completely back to idle. The engine responded falling silent against the rush of the air outside. He pulled back slightly, rolled the fighter past 90°, and pushed hard on his right rudder. The maneuver dissipated his excess speed allowing him to pull his nose through a rapid arc. He pulled back a little harder and rolled the aircraft completely through something that might have oddly looked like a mutated, squashed barrel roll.

The smoking Spitfire continued its gradual descent with wings level. Fire was clearly visible from the nose. The Bf109 also trailing smoke maneuvered gently to reattack the wounded Spitfire. Fortunately for Brian and his injured comrade, he had more turning energy than the German. He fired again. Parts flew off the German fighter. Fire erupted. The attacker had become the prey. His nose pulled up sharply as the German rolled sharply into what became a smoking corkscrew to the ground.

Brian checked his tail again. Nothing. He pushed his throttle forward to catch the wounded Spitfire. PR-J. It was 'Mongo.' He pulled up on his wing. Brian could not see a head in the cockpit and the canopy was still closed. 'Mongo' had not bailed out of his stricken machine. Brian moved up slightly to look down into his comrade's cockpit. He was slumped forward against his harness straps.

"Get out, 'Mongo.'" Brian shouted over the radio. No response. No movement in the burning Spitfire. They were passing 1,500 feet. Brian checked his tail. He was alone with his dying comrade. "'Mongo.'" Nothing. Brian pulled up to level off and rolled to keep his mate in his sight. The PR-J Spitfire impacted in a stand of trees and burst into flames.

Brian pushed his throttle full forward and pulled his nose up to return to the fight above. He took the moment's respite to check his gauges. +6¼ inches of boost. The Rolls-Royce Merlin III engine was putting out 1,030 horsepower. Coolant temperature approached the red line. He needed the cooler air above. Oil pressure and temperature were OK. He had not felt any hits on his aircraft, and the bird was still performing well. Numerous spinning or smoking aircraft fell from the sky. Brian counted two Stukas. One Hurricane. Two Bf110s and another Bf109. Nothing around him, yet.

Brian looked down to Portland Harbor. One ship was burning. Several white circles in the water marked the bomb explosions.

He searched the sky above. The tangle of fighters jumped out at him. He scanned the sky to find any strays. Another Stuka fell.

"They're running."

"Let's stay on 'em, lads, as long as we can."

Brian tried to find a lower target he could pick up and attack. His climbing speed was not enough to make up the altitude and distance. Another Stuka fell.

"Let's break it off, lads."

"Junior, join up, and return to base."

"Sorbo, join up, and return to base."

"Bandy, Junior Leader calling. I have several limpers. I will be landing at Bandy Three."

"Junior, Sorbo. Do you need any assistance?"

"Sorbo, thanks just the same. No, we're OK."

"Roger. Bandy, Sorbo. We'll land at Bandy One."

"This is Bandy, understood."

The loose formation of Spitfires heading northeast toward RAF Middle Wallop was an easy find. Brian looked for PR-D, Beamish's aircraft. He found his leader on the far side of the flight and joined up on the left wing, his position. The missing aircraft became more obvious even though Brian had watched Stephen Strickland's aircraft crash.

The return to RAF Middle Wallop was anticlimactic after the intensity of the aerial combat. The ground crews knew of the loss before they landed. There were no words only solemn, committed expressions of perseverance.

The debriefings took longer than usual reflecting the confused situation overhead Portland Harbor. Brian was given credit for his second full victory and his first since a partial win last winter. The first aircraft he hit could not be confirmed by anyone else even though he had caused grievous damage. Roger Beamish received his fourth victory, and Johnson and Carrolton, the two flying sergeants, each received their first victories.

By the time the debriefings were complete, the squadron was released. Few words passed between any members of the squadron. They all gathered at the Officer's Mess bar. The two flying sergeants were invited to join the officers which they did, in an unusual gesture to their fallen comrade. They each drew a beer.

"We shall raise our glasses and toast our valiant comrade," Squadron Leader Darling said. "God Almighty has his immortal soul. May he rest in peace." They drank to Steve Strickland.

Several pilots chose not to eat in the Mess. Brian ate and went to his room. He wanted to talk about what he had seen and experienced. He knew Group Captain Spencer had been through experiences like this, but he could not talk to him. Mary was still too close. He called Rosemary Kensington. He waited several minutes for someone to find her and get her to the telephone. Her soothing voice was like a cold drink on a hot day. In the end, he did not mention the loss of Pilot Officer Stephen 'Mongo' Strickland.

—

Wednesday, 10.July.1940
RAF Middle Wallop
Middle Wallop, Hampshire, England

As the Sun approached its zenith, the pilots of No.609 Squadron began to talk about the events of yesterday. The clouds that confused yesterday's engagement were clearing nicely and the warm summer sun allowed the pilots some relaxed time before lunch.

Despite Steve Strickland's antagonism and his often-dark view of events, Brian missed his mate. This particular loss remained vivid and close. Listening to Rosemary on the telephone last night helped Brian put events in perspective even though she did not know of Strickland's death.

Just before lunch, word arrived via the efficient grapevine communications line that No.11 Group involved three squadrons in an engagement near Dover over a large westbound convoy. Nearly fifty fighters, Brian reflected to himself, mixing it up in the skies. How on earth was anyone going to keep things straight with engagements that large?

"What do you think, Skipper?" asked Flying Officer George 'Angle' Ashcroft. "That convoy is headed our direction. Maybe we will get one of these ball-of-yarn engagements?"

"Hard to say, actually," answered Squadron Leader Horatio 'Spike' Darling. "Things do seem to be heating up a smidgen."

"It will come to us soon enough," added Flight Lieutenant Robert 'Sparky' Morrow, the number two officer in the squadron.

The telephone bell did not affect the group as it usually did. "Squadron to Readiness," announced Corporal Jennifer Warren.

"Something may be brewing," chuckled Flight Lieutenant Roger 'Jackstay' Beamish.

"Now, at least, we will have lunch brought to us," said Flying Sergeant Miles 'Fog' Johnson. Everyone laughed for the first time since yesterday's loss.

The squadron was now one pilot short and Squadron Leader Darling said he had no replacement notification. It could be a few days, or a few weeks or more before another pilot checked into the squadron. Neither Darling nor Beamish had yet moved Brian to the number two, right wing, position of Green

Section although he did wonder whether it might happen. Brian guessed they would wait to see who reported into the squadron to replace Stephen Strickland.

One of the twin engine, Blenheim night fighters of No.604 Squadron took off immediately turning toward the North as his undercarriage began retracting. Probably a maintenance check flight, Brian said to himself, although the pilot did look as if he was in a hurry. Brian met one of the pilots, John 'Cat's Eyes' Cunningham, at the Officer's Mess bar a few nights ago and had just started to ask some questions about his sister squadron before some interruption. No.604 Squadron was one of the few designated night fighter squadrons deployed to deal with night intruders. Brian was fascinated by the enormity of the interception problem at night, and he wanted to know how they did it. Everyone made jokes about trying to be a blind hunter and most of the pilots were glad it was not them. Day fights were hard enough. Night fights had to be impossible.

"Lunch is here, gentlemen," announced one of the mess corporals, as two men pushed a trolley of sandwiches along with an urn of pre-brewed tea, an oddity for them.

Everyone helped themselves with Corporal Warren leading the way. Squadron Leader Darling waited until everyone had their first helping before taking a few sandwiches. While the meal was not as good as those served in the Mess, the food was still good and the tea was just right.

The telephone rang again. Corporal Warren put down her half eaten sandwich to answer. Several pilots continued to eat. "Scramble the squadron. Vector one eight oh. Angels one two."

Sandwiches and plates flew, and tea spilled on the ground as the pilots jumped to grab their flying equipment and run to their aircraft. Several engines started up as they approached. The entire squadron, less one, was airborne within minutes. Darling checked in with Sector Control and received their initial instructions and confirmation plus additional tactical information.

An inbound raid of 100+ appeared to be headed for Convoy BREAD, a large westbound group of ships. Three other squadrons were also climbing to engage. No.43 Squadron, Rooster, Hurricanes from RAF Tangmere; No.145 Squadron, Patin, Hurricanes from RAF Westhampnett; and No.64 Squadron, Freema, Spitfires from RAF Kenley. Tangmere Sector Control, Horse, would provide instructions for the engagement.

Many thoughts raced through Brian's head as he completed his pre-engagement checks. No.43 Squadron, the Fighting Cocks, was the same squadron that Malcolm Bainbridge and John Spencer served in during the Great War. The circle was now nearly complete. Brian was certain they were all thinking about the size of this engagement. None of the No.609 Squadron pilots had ever seen anything this big. Maybe this was the beginning of the German invasion attempt everyone talked about for weeks? This was the beginning of the real war for England.

"Freema, this is Horse. Vector two two oh. Angels one five. You will have the escort along with Sorbo."

"Freema Leader. Roger. Listening out."

"Sorbo, this is Horse. Vector now one seven five. Angels now one six. You will be with Freema."

"Sorbo Leader, Roger."

"Patin, this is Horse. Vector now one two five. Angels one two. You will have the main body with Rooster."

"Patin Leader. Roger. Listening out."

"Rooster, this is Horse. Vector now one three oh. Angels one two. You will be with Patin."

"Rooster Leader. Roger. Listening out."

Brian tried to remember his visit earlier in the year to Turnhouse Sector Control at RAF Edinburgh. The image of the huge map board with the annotated blocks identifying the hostile and friendly aircraft being pushed over the map by the croupier armed women and the controllers perched above the board looking down on the scene gave Brian all the confidence he needed. They knew how to keep things straight.

As they leveled off at 16,000 feet still at full power, Brian rechecked his guns. Everything was ready. Clouds were building up rapidly over the English Channel and would make this interception task more difficult.

"Sorbo, this is Horse. Bandits five miles, should be off your right wing."

"Sorbo Leader. Roger. No joy. We have some build-ups around us. We are looking for them."

The controllers at Tangmere Sector Control patiently and methodically worked the sixty plus RAF fighters in a converging pattern toward the hostile raid they marked on the RDF scopes and plotting board. Brian listened intently to the various instructions keeping a clear mental picture of what the situation looked like around him. His head and eyes moved constantly trying to find the bad guys and more importantly to keep them from surprising him or his squadron.

Rooster Blue Three broadcast the first tally-ho. Down through the breaks in the clouds, Brian saw what had to be an on-going attack on a group of twenty or more ships maneuvering to avoid the bombs, to avoid colliding with themselves and whatever other evil lurked near them. He felt the temptation to dive into the growing fracas below him, but their assignment involved the fighter escort.

"Sorbo Leader, this is Sorbo Red Leader. Tally-ho. Fighters nine o'clock low. They are after the Hurris."

"Horse, Sorbo Leader. We have some of the fighters. Engaging. Sorbo Red, keep 'B' Flight up here until Freema arrives. There are more fighters about, keep them off our backs. 'A' Flight, let's go get 'em," Darling said as he rolled his PR-A Spitfire nearly inverted and pulled the nose down.

The other fighters in the first two sections followed suit with Brian diving last. He watched the Spitfires in front of him pick their first targets. He found a Bf110 in a climbing turn trying to reattack, lined up his sights to track his target, and glanced over his left shoulder, then right shoulder. Two diving Bf109s diving on his leader.

"One Oh Nines, five o'clock diving on you, 'Jackstay'," Brian radioed as he rolled and pulled his nose through to intercept the two single seat fighters.

Brian squeezed off a quick burst in front of them hoping to distract them. Either they did not see his tracers, or they were seasoned enough to recognize the burst was not close. He lined up on the leader. Closing range. Ball centered. In range. Brian pressed the red button on his stick.

The burst cut through the tail of the Bf109 just aft of the cockpit. The high speed of the dive supplied the force to sever the tail completely causing the remains to spin, twist and gyrate wildly. Brian pulled up immediately into a steep climb. He sensed the German's wingman would be on his tail.

As airspeed bled off quickly with the nose high in the air, Brian quickly looked over both shoulders. His worst nightmare bore in on him. Two red nose Bf109s held on his tail. The bright flash from the nose and wings told him one of the Germans had pressed his firing trigger.

Bright red flaming balls passed very close to his cockpit as he rolled his Spitfire onto her back and pulled as hard as he could. The 20mm cannon tracers looked enormous so close. He tried to get into a steep dive remembering Jonathan's experience with the captured Bf109E-3. Brian felt very alone, deserted, with two angry men running after him intending to do him injury.

He wanted to call for help, but did not feel he had the time to talk. Brian's speed exceeded 400 mph. The entire aircraft screamed and groaned. They were both back there although not as close and more importantly, they were not firing. A large cloud rose to his left. Brian turned to head directly into it. The size of the cloud meant it would be rough inside. He took one last look back. They still pursued him. He entered the cloud and focused his complete mental attention on the instrument panel in front of him as he pulled steadily back on the stick.

Without visual orientation outside the tiny confines of his cockpit, the added acceleration of the positive g's made his head wrench and spin violently. Brian tried to steady the wings somewhere near level although they kept rocking back and forth as he fought to maintain the control he wanted. The internal turbulence of the cloud buffeted the fighter and shook the instrument panel. He tried to keep his nose pointed up about 30°, but the vertigo disorientation combined with the strong turbulence inside the cloud made the task nearly impossible. The airspeed continued to wind down passing 150 mph while the altimeter wound up through 10,000 feet. He wanted out of the cloud. He tried to lower his nose to hold his airspeed, but the turbulence kept flailing him inside the abused fighter. He wondered if he would ever come out of the cloud, and then as if spit from the massive cloud, he was in clear air.

Brian had blue sky around him although there were still towering columns of cloud above and near him. He found a relatively open gap between two large clouds, leveled the wings and lowered the nose to the horizon – what he could see of it. Brian's equilibrium had been severely shaken, as the world seemed to continue spinning and twisting around him although the scene outside the cockpit told him otherwise. He fought with his brain trying to keep the fighter level. He was soaked in sweat, and his gut churned with nausea. He tried to look back on his tail to see if there were any Germans, but the motion of his head made his vertigo worse. He had to take sometime to settle his equilibrium before he could fight again. Very slowly he turned his head. He could not see another aircraft.

For the first time since being jumped by the two Germans, Brian listened for radio activity. Silence. "Sorbo Green Leader, this is Sorbo Green Three." Pilot Officer Brian Drummond waited for a response. None came, but his vertigo began dissipating. "Sorbo Green Leader, this is Sorbo Green Three." Silence. "Sorbo Leader, this is Sorbo Green Three."

"Sorbo Green Three, this is Horse. How do you hear this transmitter?"

"Loud and clear, Horse."

"Sorbo Green Three, what is your location?"

"I have clouds all around me and water below."

"Sorbo Green Three, this is Horse. Hit your Pipsqueak."

Brian looked down slowly and pushed the button marked, ID, on the panel just aft of his radio control box three short times. The special transmitter broadcast a coded signal that was displayed on the RDF scopes. It would take a few minutes to establish his location using RDF, telephone the information to Fighter Command, and then back down to the controller at RAF Tangmere.

Brian felt better. He turned his aircraft. He checked his fuel gauge. Ten gallons of fuel remaining. Instinctively, Brian pulled his throttle back to conserve fuel. Ten gallons meant twenty minutes of flight time, maybe a little longer. He was at 11,600 feet, so pulling off a little more throttle would save more fuel. He began a gradual descent.

"Sorbo Green Three, this is Horse. We have you about 35 miles due south of Wothing. How is your fuel?"

"Ten gallons."

The controller did their calculations. Brian pulled out his map made his own rough plot. He adjusted his heading 40° to the west. He thought he could make RAF Middle Wallop although several closer airfields would be safer. He could make home if he was careful.

"Sorbo Green Three. What are your intentions?"

"I think I can make it home."

"Sorbo Green Three, this is Horse. Suggest vector three three five for home."

Brian shifted left another five degrees. The Sun was now quite low on the Western horizon. He continually checked the sky around him looking for enemy fighters that might be lurking about as he updated his fuel usage and progress toward RAF Middle Wallop. The coastline appeared between the clouds giving him some added confidence. Soon, Brian recognized the characteristic shape of the Isle of Wight that formed the Solent estuary for the approaches to Southampton. He knew exactly where he was now. In a few more minutes, he was over the desired terrain a few miles from RAF Middle Wallop.

"Horse, this is Sorbo Green Three. I have home. Thank you for your assistance."

"Sorbo Green Three, this is Horse. Good mission. Glad to help. Out."

Brian landed without incident and taxied to his spot with his fuel gauge showing a needle width above empty, but the engine was still running. He saw the smiling face of Leading Aircraftman Bernie Gordon running toward him.

"You had us worried, sir," Gordon said when Brian shut down the engine.

"Not to worry, Bernie. I had a bit of a close call up there," he said motioning with his head to the South as he removed his headgear, oxygen mask and gloves.

"The Skipper reported you missing."

Brian laughed. "For a while, I thought I was missing."

"Good to have you back, sir. Any squawks?"

"None, other than dry tanks."

"We will give her a good look see, nonetheless."

As Pilot Officer Brian Drummond stood up to get out of his fighter, immediately, he noticed the deep ache in all his joints and muscles. The solidity of the ground injected him with fatigue. Only Squadron Leader Darling, Pilot Officer Kensington and Corporal Warren remained in the Dispersal building. Only Darling failed to smile.

"We reported you missing."

"Sorry, sir."

"What happened?"

"I dropped the leader of a section of One Oh Nines lining up on you and the rest of A Flight. I picked up his two wingmen and had trouble shaking them. I went into a big cloud that apparently took me much longer than I thought to come out the other side. RDF plotted me 35 miles out over the water to the East."

"You did not answer any of our radio calls. We thought they got you," said Jonathan.

"We shall get you debriefed in the morning. The squadron was released forty minutes ago. Good to have you back, Brian."

"Thank you, sir."

"Let's close it up, Corporal Warren."

"Yes, sir."

Brian recounted more detail to Jonathan as they walked back to the Officer's Mess. He told the story many more times in various versions through evening meal and in the bar until fatigue took the last of his strength. Brian Drummond did not fail to recognize the close call. He had already been shot down once, but this one felt closer to being lethal.

He eventually made it to his room and was soon into a deep sleep.

—

Chapter 12

No one can guarantee success in war,
but only deserve it.
-- Winston Churchill

Thursday, 11.July.1940
RAF Middle Wallop
Middle Wallop, Hampshire, England
06:45 hours

Brian and Jonathan were among the first group of four pilots to greet Corporal Jennifer Warren. The relatively low overcast meant it would probably be a slow day. The rest of the squadron would trickle into the No.609 Squadron Dispersal building over the next fifteen minutes. The squadron was scheduled to be at Readiness status at 07:00. Squadron Leader Darling would probably be the next to arrive.

"Good morning, Corporal Warren."

"Mornin' Jennifer."

"Good morning, sirs. No messages as yet."

"Thank God for small favors," Brian said without thinking.

"Close call got to ya, did it now," joked Flight Lieutenant John 'Waggle' Davies.

"T'was nothin,' actually," Brian responded with the best British accent he could conjure up.

"Becoming quite the citizen, are we now, Brian?" said Flying Sergeant Miles 'Fog' Johnson as he joined the group.

Squadron Leader Horatio 'Spike' Darling arrived next, true to form. "Good morning, gentlemen. Corporal Warren."

"Looks like we may have a slow one today, Skipper," said Davies.

"I don't know after the last two days. Things seem to be heating up."

Before Darling could enter his office to address the morning paperwork, the telephone rang. The wall clock showed seven o'clock straight up. Everyone stopped and turned to Corporal Warren as she lifted the receiver.

"Damn Gerries are starting early this morning," chuckled Miles Johnson.

"Scramble the squadron. Vector two oh oh. Angels ten."

"Warren run, retrieve the rest of the bloody squadron," barked Darling as they all stumbled to grab their gear.

"I was just kidding," protested Johnson as they ran from the building.

None of the fighters had completed their morning engine runs although they all had been properly preflight checked the night before. Darling, Drummond, Kensington, Davies, Johnson and Foxworth sat in their cockpits waiting for the other pilots. Brian knew the Skipper had to be going crazy with the delay getting his squadron in the air. While it was the first time they received a scramble command so early in the morning and just as they were supposed to come to Readiness, he knew there would be changes. The squadrons took pride in the quickness they could launch their fighters. Brian checked his watch as they started their takeoff roll – nearly 13 minutes, four times their normal response time. There would be changes.

Squadron Leader Darling did not wait for the join up as he executed a maximum performance climb into the overcast. They would join up on top of the cloud layer. He must have known or sensed it was only a thousand feet thick. They broke out into bright clear skies at 2,200 feet. The soft, white blanket below them left nothing for navigation. They turned to 200° as they climbed.

Brian stayed tight to Beamish's left wing. The right wing position remained empty. They were notified of a twenty plus raid on shipping near Portland. They were scrambled to assist No.501 Squadron, Hurricanes, out of RAF Warmwell. They apparently ran into more fighters than expected. Another mixed bag of dive-bombers and fighters. The radio calls gave a clear sign of the intensity of this early morning engagement. They would arrive east of the fight, so they could use the Sun to advantage. The cloud layer broke up over the coast and Channel.

"Sorbo Leader, this is Bandy. Mandrel feels he has the fighters, if you would take the Stukas."

"Roger Bandy. Tally ho, the bombers. Let's go get 'em, lads."

The others had to feel the same excitement Brian felt. This would be the first time they were given the opportunity to mix it up with the much slower, less maneuverable, lightly armed, lumbering, gull-winged, dive-bombers. Darling dove into the group of ten plus Ju87s with the rest of his squadron behind him. Two ships were already on fire and numerous bomb explosion circles pocked the water around the other ships.

The bombers terminated their attack in a desperate effort to protect themselves against the vastly superior Spitfires. Two of the Ju87s fell quickly. Several more were smoking as they tried to escape by diving very close to the water. Brian saw one well ahead of him. He pushed the throttle through the emergency gate for the extra power to catch his prey quickly.

It had been many months since Brian had flown so close to the Earth. He concentrated on his flying and his target.

"'Hunter,' pull up. You've got a bandit on your tail."

Brian did not look as he pulled his stick back sharply and hard. The Spitfire responded. He kept the nose nearly straight up until his airspeed rapidly passed 60 mph. He pushed in full right rudder swinging the tail around turning into his attacker. Surprised by the maneuver, the German pulled his nose off using the last of his airspeed. Brian squeezed off a quick burst that was not well aimed. They traded places. Brian was now the hunter and the German, the prey.

The German expertly moved his fighter to make Brian's aiming problem considerably more difficult. Brian managed to squeeze off two short bursts without effect. The distance between them began to increase. Brian pushed a little harder on his throttle and checked his engine – +6¼ inches of boost. He had all the power the Merlin III could give him. This had to be one of the newer Bf109E-4 aircraft. The German had slightly more speed from his 1,150 horsepower DB601C, fuel-injected engine.

When it became painfully obvious he was not going to catch the German, Brian pulled up smoothly into a Half Cuban Eight to reverse his course and head back to the fight. He saw several of the surviving Ju87s heading south beyond his practical reach. Brian rejoined the fighter engagement just as he saw a Spitfire explode into fragments. He lined up on another German who maneuvered smartly. A good long burst drew flashes of sparks and a few small pieces from the German fighter. He settled into a perfect firing position and squeezed the trigger only to hear the loud report of bullets hitting his aircraft.

Brian pulled back and rolled left. He saw the white nose Bf109 close on his tail. He pushed and pulled on the stick with his throttle fully forward. He looked back again only to see the German fire again. Cannon shells ripped through his aircraft. He felt a searing slash across his upper left arm. The pain was excruciating as he bit hard on his lip. Smoke filled his cockpit as fingers of flames lashed out at him. In an instant, he pulled his canopy back and released his seat straps. He pushed forward on the stick. The negative g shot him from the dying Spitfire. He could not move his left arm. Brian groped with his right hand across his chest until he found the steel ripcord handle and pulled it. The shock of the parachute opening while slicing the crotch straps into his groin gave him a stab of pain and a profound sense of relief.

Brian looked around above him to see what was happening. The rattle of friendly guns was heard several more times as well as the heavy thuds of the German cannon. The roar of engines gradually grew more faint as he descended. He was going for another swim, which he did not look forward to in the least. He saw a small boat with numerous men heading directly toward him. At least he would be picked up quickly and would not have to be in the water for long.

The pain in his left arm drew his attention. He pulled his oxygen mask away only to find blood coating the inside. He had bitten his lip. His tunic sleeve was ripped open across the outer portion of his upper arm. His blood soaked his left sleeve. Brian grasped his left arm to slow down the bleeding. The pain nearly rendered him unconscious.

With his focus on his wound, he did not notice the approaching water. Brian plunged into the sea. The salt water sent another bolt of enormous pain from his left arm through the rest of his body. He struggled to release his parachute harness. The shroud and canopy had already begun to sink enveloping him. His lungs began to burn demanding air. Brian finally released his harness and found his way through the tangle of parachute shrouds. When he knew he was clear, he pulled the lanyard on his Mae West that inflated and popped him to the surface like a cork. He nearly hit the boat and saw a man dive into the cold water.

The rescue crew quickly plucked Brian from the water and retrieved their swimmer. They noticed his still bleeding arm wound and promptly wrapped his arm with a tight bandage.

In the boat were three sea rescue men, one Home Defense soldier with his rifle pointed at two German pilots. Both appeared to be young, uninjured, grim and now captive. Brian was not certain of his German Air Force rank insignia, but he thought one was a lieutenant and the other a sergeant.

"Stuka crew," said the boat captain. Brian nodded.

He wanted to hit them as the personification of his enemy but remembered the etiquette taught him by Malcolm Bainbridge. Brian raised his right hand in a salute to his adversary. The two Germans started to stand but thought better of it when the soldier raised his rifle. They straightened their backs and returned the salute.

Armed guards took the Germans away undoubtedly to an interrogation and then a prisoner of war camp somewhere in Great Britain. Brian was transported by ambulance to the Weymouth hospital where he was stitched and bandaged. The wounds looked worse than they were. Except for some pain, stiffness and tingling, his left arm, hand and fingers all worked normally. He had bitten his lip but not seriously. Once completely checked over, the nurses put him in an automobile and whisked him back to RAF Middle Wallop, a three-hour drive to cover fifty miles. Numerous roadblocks, checkpoints and suspicious guards, quite ready to shoot at the slightest provocation, made the journey far more torturous than Brian needed.

The left wing of Green Section arrived back at No.609 Squadron Dispersal to find a grim, reduced number of his mates. He quickly searched the room. His colleagues acknowledged his return with a strange subdued apprehension.

"Ashcroft and Carrolton," said Roger Beamish acknowledging Brian's searching eyes.

"Lost?"

"Confirmed."

Brian sank into the mire with the rest of the squadron. They were down to nine pilots.

"Are you all right?" asked Darling.

"Just a scratch."

"From the looks of that sleeve, it looks a bit more than a scratch."

"The surgeon returned me to duty."

"Yes but are you fit to fly?"

"I think so."

"Somehow, I have my doubts. That uniform is a total loss. Would you like to change?"

"I'll wait, if you don't mind, sir. The nurses dried me out fairly well."

"I'll bet they did," said Beamish offering the only smile although quite brief.

"As you wish. We remain at Available status. They cannot release us, yet. You better give your details to Royster, first. When we heard you had been picked up, we got a reserve bird from base. I think Gordon is painting her for you, but she is ready."

Pilot Officer Brian Drummond found the intelligence officer assigned to his squadron. The debriefing took forty minutes, long by routine standards. The hits on the Bf109 were not sufficient to give him a victory or even a fraction. The exploded Spitfire was Ashcroft's aircraft. Carrolton failed to recover from an escape dive.

Brian returned to Dispersal. The room felt exactly as he had found it upon his return.

"Are you OK?" asked Jonathan.

"Yeah. Just some pain. They chewed me up pretty bad. I was just about to finish a One Oh Nine when I got hit. A lot of pain and I couldn't move my arm at first, but it is OK now."

"How long were you in the water?"

"Minutes, I guess. Rescue boat picked up a German crew, and then saw my chute. When I finally got back to the surface, they snatched me up."

"You seem to be making this parachuting business your specialty."

"Damn Germans are everywhere."

"The spooks estimate twenty J U Eight Sevens and forty M E One Oh Nines."

"Underestimated the raid, I guess."

"Indeed."

The telephone rang again. Several stood with their flight gear and started for the door as if to get a jump on the scramble command.

"Squadron Leader, for you, sir."

He took the handset from Corporal Warren. "Darling here, sir." He listened. "Yes, sir. Thank you, sir." He nodded his head, and then shook his head. "A bit down, sir. We lost two pilots and four aircraft, one pilot wounded but back on duty." Darling listened as all the pilots stared at him looking for any signs. "Yes, sir. Thank you again, sir," he said and hung up. He straightened his tunic, drew back his shoulders and placed his hands on his hips. "Air Vice Marshal Brand offers his condolences for our loss, and his congratulations on our successful engagement of this morning's raid. It was apparently the largest raid to date, and although our losses were grievous, the enemy's losses were far greater." Darling looked at the clock over his shoulder. "He also said the PM will broadcast a message at the top of the hour."

"Five minutes," someone muttered.

Brian leaned toward Jonathan and whispered. "Who else lost an aircraft?"

"Johnson. He got shot up pretty bad and had to jump, but he was over land."

"Good for him. I don't quite like this swimming crap."

They chuckled quietly.

"Corporal Warren, if you would be so kind, please tune up the BBC on the box. The squadron is released." No one left.

Some unrecognized music came to an end as she moved away from the radio. Light static filled the gap.

"This is BBC London Radio. Please standby for a broadcast by the Prime Minister, Mister Churchill."

"Good afternoon, ladies and gentlemen," said the clear, distinctive, lisping voice of Winston Churchill. "I come to you at a very serious hour in the history of our island nation and indeed the Empire. As many in the South are aware, German air activity against our shipping and the port cities along the Channel as well as against our air defenses has increased.

"I should take this opportunity to tell you, we are waiting for the long-promised invasion," he paused leaving everyone on edge, "so are the fishes." Churchill paused again to allow the bravado to work its magic. Dispersal echoed with laughter. "And now it has come to us to stand alone in the breach, and face the worst that the tyrant's might and enmity can deliver. Bearing ourselves humbly before God, but conscious that we serve an unfolding purpose, we are ready to defend our native land against the invasion by which it is threatened." He paused again to slow the tempo of his delivery and lower his voice. "We are fighting by ourselves alone; but we are not fighting for ourselves alone. Here in this strong city of refuge, which enshrines the title-deeds of human progress and is of deep consequence to Christian civilization; here, girt about by the seas and oceans where the Navy reigns; shielded from above by the prowess and devotion of our airmen – we await undismayed the impending assault. Perhaps it will come tonight. Perhaps it will come next week. Perhaps it will never come."

"Damnation," said Flight Lieutenant Morrow. "He does know how to stoke the furnace."

"Indeed."

"So," said Beamish. "It comes down to the Navy and us." No one said anything as the music returned to the radio. "From the last few days, I would say the battle is joined."

"Shall we retire to the Mess to pay tribute to our fallen comrades?" asked Darling. Only the sounds of foot steps, rustling clothing and the clink of metal fittings filled the room as they hung their flight equipment on their assigned pegs. They walked slowly and quietly along the base streets, out the gate, across the carriageway and into the stately Officer's Mess building. They all turned to the right, walked down the hallway and into the bar. They paid a solemn, respectful tribute to Flying Officer George Ashcroft and Flying Sergeant James Carrolton, and then toasted the memory of their other fallen friends.

—

Thursday, 11.July.1940
Headquarters, Fighter Command
Bentley Priory
Stanmore, Middlesex, England
20:45 hours

"I shall be surely damned, John, if good fortune does not at least come to us occasionally," said Air Commodore Hogan as he entered the office of the Staff Secretary, Group Captain John Spencer.

"What is it this time?"

"We just received confirmation that an M E One One Oh belly landed near Wareham in Dorset. Our lads did in both engines and the crew apparently did not want to take to the silk."

"Is the aircraft shot up rather badly?"

"Word from the site is, the aircraft is in rather good shape, a C Four model is our guess so far. We will need two new Daimler-Benz engines and airscrews, plus a few patches on some unsightly holes, but other than that, it is in good shape."

"Smashing."

"Quite. It would appear we will add another peculiar horse to our growing stable."

John thought of the other German aircraft in the hangar at RAE Farnborough, a Heinkel He111P-2 complete with operating *Knickebein* radio night bombing equipment, a Messerschmitt Bf109E-3 fighter, and now a Messerschmitt Bf110C-4 twin-engine, two-seat, fighter. Even he could fly this one once the exploitation crew is complete. At least Brian's friend, Pilot Officer Jonathan Kensington had a new machine to fly along with the other operational evaluation pilots.

"Have you told the boss?"

"No. Not as yet."

"Shall we?" John said, motioning toward the door. "Is the boss available?" asked John as they approached Dowding's personal secretary's desk.

"I will check for you, sir." She lifted the handset and pushed the appropriate lever on the interphone box. "Air Commodore Hogan and Group Captain Spencer to see you, sir." She listened. "Certainly, sir." She returned the handset to its cradle. "He will see you now, sirs."

"Good evening, Sir Hugh."

"Good evening, James, John." He looked back down to his papers. The single desk lamp with the blackout curtains eliminating any remaining exterior light made the elegant office seem uncharacteristically cold and cavernous. "What bad news do you bring me this time?"

"Now, why would you say such a thing?" joked James Hogan.

'Stuffy' Dowding looked up and gave them a rare smile. "It seems as though, since the invasion of Denmark, every time I see your faces in my office at night, I see the twin faces of the grim reaper."

"Now, it cannot be that bad, sir."

"Perhaps not."

"This time I think we have good news," said John Spencer. "The large engagement this morning near Portland has brought us what may be a flyable M E One One Oh C Four."

"So, you may get to fly one of their fighters after all, ay John?"

They all laughed. John questioned himself, was he really that predictable? Maybe that was a good way to be predictable. He simply loved to fly and did not get to do as much as he wanted and needed. "Am I that predictable, sir?"

"Actually, John, you are, however I am enormously thankful for that particular predictability."

"Thank you, sir."

"So, we have another captured aeroplane for our growing captive air force."

"We shall have the RAE blokes on the machine tomorrow," said Hogan.

"Very good. I have some news myself. The Air Ministry passed from the War Cabinet a summary, which you will have on your desk tomorrow, James that indicates Hitler may have lost his patience with us. We have quote 'failed to come to terms with our hopeless military situation' unquote was the way they put it. The activity we have seen this week is probably the best clear indicator substantiating the assessment."

"Any other details, sir?" asked Hogan.

"The popular opinion is, the Battle of Britain has begun," Dowding said with considerable solemnity.

"I think we have all suspected as much with the big raids over the Channel this week," John said.

"As we have discussed several times of late, the next few months are going to be difficult. We simply must find a way to make it to the relative shelter of the autumn weather patterns. Two months . . . maybe a little more."

They all knew the estimates, analysis, studies and opinions. This was the moment in history they all feared, and they recognized the inexorable advance of Nazi transgressions. It was now Great Britain's turn under the German guns and bombs. They all wondered, but no one said it aloud, whether the battered and beleaguered armed forces of the United Kingdom would be up to the challenge. They all knew they had no choice . . . they had to be.

—

Thursday, 11.July.1940
Oval Office
The White House
Washington, District of Columbia, U.S.A.
16:45 hours

The new Secretary of the Navy Frank Knox and Colonel Bill Donovan joined the President, who was focused on papers before him on the large desk. The President was alone in the Oval Office, without the usual presence of Harry Hopkins. Roosevelt motioned for the two men to be seated. When he finished his reading, Roosevelt wheeled himself to a position between the two couches and the two men.

"Well, good afternoon to you both. It seems our defined moment has arrived."

"Good afternoon, Mister President," Knox and Donovan said in unison.

"As we discussed three weeks ago, Frank, you are going to send Bill here on a special mission to London for us."

"Yes, sir. I believe all the arrangements have been made. Bill, if you will . . ."

"Thank you for the opportunity to serve, Mister President."

"You may not be so thankful when this gets going, Bill."

"Nonsense, we must do what must be done, Mister President. I am honored to serve."

"As you did on those bloody fields in France?"

"If necessary, yes, sir."

"I have full confidence in you, Bill. Now, I think our little conspiracy must be clear. You are travelling to England under the aegis of Frank, as the newly sworn Secretary of the Navy. Your outward mission is fact finding wtih our British colleagues regarding their fifth column, counter-espionage efforts. Churchill just replaced his director general of MI5, so things may be a little unsettled at the moment, but that cannot be helped and we may not have much time.

"I am certain you are aware of the Rumrich espionage case two years ago. The FBI is working several on-going investigations regarding potential

German spies in this country. There is plenty of public evidence and more classified material to justify your mission and visit.

"Your greater purpose must not be divulged beyond our little conspiratorial group." Both men nodded their agreement. "Churchill is pushing for our assistance. We have carried out secret, personal communications since he became First Lord of the Admiralty again, last year, and especially when he became Prime Minister in May. The British need our help, and we need them to hold the line at the Channel against the Germans. We have already delivered one shipload of arms and I have ordered further shipment preparations, but I am walking a very thin, misty line regarding the law, and we cannot afford a misstep with Congress or the American people. Further, I have an incomprehensible array of widely divergent and confusing counselors who do nothing but muddy the waters further. Bill, I need a trusted, first hand, thorough assessment of the British situation and most importantly their capacity to survive what is certain to be a German invasion in the next month or so."

"Yes, sir. I understand fully."

"I hope so, because this all might come down to your able shoulders and evaluation."

"Yes, sir."

"I have assurances from Churchill that you shall be given *carte blanche* for your work. He has opened the government for your examination. I expect you to meet with him and the King shortly after your arrival."

"Yes, sir. I have met with Bill Stephenson in New York numerous times in preparation for this mission."

"Stephenson . . . good man . . . he should be quite helpful."

"He already has been, Mister President. I leave here by rail tonight, after we conclude whatever prepatory discussions you need me to know, and I will join up with Stephenson tomorrow. We are both booked on the PanAm Yankee Clipper to Lisbon this coming Sunday, and then by RAF transport to London. The agenda is quite full and I shall endeavor to keep up."

"You shall perform admirably, Bill. The critical question for me is, will the British hold on? I am quite reticent to send any further arms aid to the British, especially in the shadows of the Neutrality Act and these damnable America Firsters led by Lindbergh. The Germans already suspect we are helping the British, but if they were to obtain physical proof upon a successful invasion, I might actually face impeachment. I need to know they can hold the line."

"Understood, Mister President."

"Any questions for me?" asked Roosevelt.

"No, sir. I think I know what you need, and I will obtain it for you, sir."

"Thank you, Bill. I shall wish you *bon voyage*. We shall gather again in a few weeks upon your return, to hear your assessment. Now, if there is anything I can do to assist you on this mission, please do not hesitate to call. Because of the arrangements here, you must work through Frank to maintain appearances, but if you cannot reach Frank for some reason, you must contact me."

"As you command, Mister President."

"Very well, then, Colonel Donovan, godspeed and following winds on your journey."

—

Friday, 12.July.1940
RAF Middle Wallop
Middle Wallop, Hampshire, England

The No.609 (West Riding of Yorkshire) Squadron woke up to a thick, foggy, quiet morning. The seriously reduced visibility meant the RAF Middle Wallop squadrons would not take part in any aerial engagements until the fog cleared a little for sufficient visibility to safely take off. They needed to at least see the other side of the takeoff and landing area. From their Dispersal building near Hangar No.5, their marker was a tree covered large mound with an ancient circle of stones among the trees just beyond the airfield perimeter. As they reported to Dispersal, they could barely see beyond the line of Spitfires in front of them.

"I trust we will not hear another comment about a slow day, 'Waggle,'" teased 'Jackstay' Beamish.

"After yesterday's result, not on your life," answered Davies.

The group of pilots laughed for the first time since their losses the day before. Laughter always felt good. It was the Lord's medicine, Brian told himself, repeating the words of his grandparents. They would not be able to bring back their lost comrades, no more than Brian could bring Malcolm back. Look forward . . . do not look back, he repeated Malcolm's words to himself.

"You would think Group would release us with soup like this," said Flying Sergeant Miles 'Fog' Johnson.

"Why? This is your weather, 'Fog,'" answered Flight Lieutenant 'Sparky' Morrow referring to Miles' several crashes trying to land various airplanes in foggy conditions.

Again, the pilots laughed.

"What would you do if they did release us?"

"Sleep."

"You do that anyway," said Beamish instigating more laughter.

A few pilots walked along the flight line. Some talked while others napped. This time they waited for the weather instead of the enemy. Brian and Jonathan sat in lawn chairs outside in the mist. They both had 24-hour passes this coming Sunday, from 12:00 Sunday to 12:00 Monday. The two friends decided they would go to London for different reasons. Jonathan sought the embrace of Linda Mason. Brian would imply a meeting with Anne Booth, but would use the time to talk to Jeremy about Anne and Virginia. Assuming he could get the answers he needed from Jeremy, Brian decided the time had come to confide in Jonathan. It was becoming too difficult to keep the situation hidden from his best friend.

"Maybe if the weather holds like this, the Skipper will let us off early, and we can get to the city for lunch with the ladies," Jonathan said.

"It would be nice, but I've given up thinking about the weather. It will be what it will be, and then we'll deal with it." Brian hoped he would not have to face the issue of Anne with Jonathan until after he had talked to Jeremy. The urge to call Flight Lieutenant Lord Jeremy 'Mud' Morrison grew rapidly. He wanted to ensure Jeremy would be available for their little chat.

"Of course, you twit. I was just thinking aloud."

"Well, then, we could always have a major raid, and the Skipper can't spare us."

"Now, that is a sodding bright thought."

The sound of numerous Merlin engines at relatively low power penetrated the lightening fog as a group of aircraft passed nearly overhead southbound. Brian and Jonathan looked up as if they might see something. Several other pilots came out and looked up as well.

"Some bloody bastard has those poor sods out in weather like this. Now, the blokes're tryin' to find a patch upon which to alight," Davies said.

"Maybe its One Five Two Squadron, Spits out of Acklington," offered Johnson. "A base chap at the Sergeant's Mess last night said we were supposed to get another Spit squadron. He thought it was One Five Two."

"Is that so?"

"That's what he said. Maybe they took off thinking the weather would break."

The small gathering laughed. "That is what got you into trouble a couple times, right 'Fog?'" joked Davies.

"Righty ho," he answered with a smile.

The squadron remained at Available status. Squadron Leader Darling sent everyone to the Mess for lunch. Corporal Warren was relieved by another corporal. Available status meant they could not leave the airfield. If the fog persisted past the lunch hour, they all expected to be released.

No one rushed through lunch. They tried to joke about anything that seemed like an appropriate target. Even the Prime Minister received his share. The topic that got the most attention was war. The signs continued to mount up, leading toward an invasion. The Prime Minister's radio broadcast the previous day tried to sound upbeat but carried a very somber message. Moving squadrons south foretold the expectations of probably the War Cabinet, the Air Ministry and particularly 'Stuffy' Dowding. The German air activity over the English side of the Channel told them quite a lot, as well. It had been the most intense combat week since the peak of Dunkirk, and it was certainly the closest to home.

As they left the Mess, everyone noticed the clearing fog. By the time they returned to their Dispersal, the marker mound, as they called it, was faintly visible. They might get an afternoon mission of some sort. Squadron Leader Darling telephoned Control, which was actually only several short blocks away near the northern boundary of the airfield.

"We have been raised to Readiness," he reported.

Nothing changed other than none of the pilots ventured very far from Dispersal. Just as most of the pilots began to nod off with a full stomach, the distinctive tone of the Merlins returned. This time they saw the characteristic shapes of a squadron of Spitfires pass over the field at relatively low altitude, peel off in rapid succession and make the circuit to land.

The aircraft taxied across the field toward Hangar No.1. The lead aircraft had UM-C markings.

"That's them. One Five Two is, Uncle's Monkey," said Johnson using the RAF phonetic alphabet.

"Smashing," Davies said. "What a call sign. Uncle's Monkey."

"Actually, they are Maida."

"How disappointing. Maybe we could change it, *de facto*, maybe."

"Now we have two Spits, one Hurri and a bloody night fighter Blenheim squadron. We are practically stacking them up here."

"As someone said at lunch, they are moving squadrons south because the Germans are coming," said Davies.

"And here we are practically on the bloody coast."

"Well, then, lads, looks like we have a fairly simple task to perform," Darling interjected. "All we have to do is keep Gerry from controlling the air, and they won't come visit."

"Now, you are talking like Churchill," said Beamish.

The last of the No.152 Squadron Spitfires taxied to their new area and shutdown when a fresh looking, average build, pilot officer walked into the Dispersal building looking rather lost.

"Is there a Squadron Leader," he paused to glance at a piece of paper he was holding, "Darling, here?"

"Another bloody Yank," observed 'Sparky' Morrow.

"I am Darling."

"I am 'Hank' Maxwell. I was told to report to you as a replacement pilot. I guess someone decided they'd had enough, huh?"

The room fell deathly silent. Brian winced in resentment of the crass comment by the only other American. He acted as if he could not sense the implicit reaction. Brian caught several expressions of disgust thrown his way as if he were responsible for his fellow countryman.

"May I see your orders?" Darling said without further comment. He scanned the papers quickly. "Your orders indicate your given names are: Melvyn Henry."

"Yeah, but I go by 'Hank.'"

"Well, then, 'Hank,' is it?" he said nearly spitting the man's nickname. "I think you should know, we have lost three pilots, three close friends, in the last two days of combat, and you are our first replacement pilot."

"Hey, I'm sorry. I meant no offense."

"Then, none will be taken. Let me introduce you to the other chaps in the squadron."

Squadron Leader Darling properly introduced each pilot, including his flying callsign and flight position. He did not introduce Brian as an American, simply one of the pilots. Brian appreciated the courtesy and respect Darling showed him by doing so.

"If you would be so kind, while we are still on alert, 'Hank,' please tell us a little about yourself."

Brian felt a set up given the rather coarse introduction. He grimaced a little inside and wondered what the new American was going to say. He hoped he would not say anything of an abrasive nature.

"I'm from a small town in Pennsylvania, near Philadelphia. I've been a pilot for six years flying mostly mail and sometimes people. I have just over 3,000 hours, which were very hard to come by, while I worked for my degree from the University of Pennsylvania."

"Why are you here?" asked 'Waggle' Davies noting as they all did the lack of any conviction to the current struggle.

"I want to fly."

"Mister Maxwell," Darling said, "there are far easier, less injurious, piloting jobs than flying fighters for the RAF at the beginning of what will certainly be the Battle of Britain."

"Nonsense. This is where it is happening, and I want to be a part of it."

"At least we will have another hand for the beer," said 'Sparky' Morrow. "If even for a brief moment."

"Right, then. You will be my number three, left wing. We are due two new Spits this afternoon. You will pick up the first one. Corporal Warren, if you call the Chief, we will give Mister Maxwell the Nuts designator."

Brian did not recall the squadron leader ever assigning tail designators. Usually, the maintenance crew took care to that task.

"Nuts?" asked Maxwell.

"N, as in Nuts, the tail designator for your assigned aircraft."

"Oh, yeah, sure, I understand."

"Now, if you will come with me. We will get you started on your checklist, and you should finish at the Officer's Mess across the carriageway probably about the time we are released from alert. We shall have a beer to welcome you properly." Everyone laughed with several little quips mixed into the words. "Assuming your aircraft arrives and is in proper order, we will fly an orientation flight tomorrow, weather permitting, before we put you on the board."

"Great. No problem."

Darling took him to the Operations building next to Dispersal. One of the administrative clerks would be tasked with assisting Maxwell with his check-in procedures.

The squadron pilots poked at Brian for the rough edges of his country-man, but were thankful to finally get a replacement pilot. They still needed two more before they would be able to launch a full squadron. Maxwell's bumpy arrival gave everyone something to joke about and certainly gave everyone a motive to add his contribution to welcome him in the squadron tradition.

Before the evening's festivities, Brian called Jeremy Morrison. He did not have the same break as Brian. He said he would try to change it, but at a minimum, he would meet Brian at Shepherds Pub in Mayfair after he was released from duty. RAF Hornchurch was a short Underground ride from Mayfair. Jeremy sounded pleased but noticeably subdued from his normal ebullient personality.

—

Saturday, 13.July.1940
RAF Middle Wallop
Middle Wallop, Hampshire, England

"**M**aybe we'll make it through the whole summer with this fog," Pilot Officer Brian Drummond said to his friend.

"If the last week is any indication," answered Pilot Officer Jonathan Kensington, as they sat in their usual lawn chairs outside in the clearing mist. "Another hour and we shall have the mound."

"I have to admit, I've become kinda partial to the fog. It has a protective quality to it."

Jonathan laughed. "I have never quite thought of fog that way, but now that you mention it, you may have a point."

"We only had a few foggy days a year in Kansas."

Jonathan nodded and looked off into the distance as if he were trying to find a thought. He looked around to see who might be close by and able to hear them. "Speaking of America, what do you think of our new American?"

"Maybe he's a likable guy, but he seems a bit crude to me."

"I don't know many Americans, Brian. In fact, I only know two. You are quite different from 'Hank' Maxwell."

"I'll take that as a compliment," Brian said with a chuckle, causing Jonathan to laugh.

"Does he know you are the other American?"

"He hasn't said anything to me, so I don't know."

The crystalline ring of the telephone broke all conversations and naps. Brian found himself growing to despise the sound. Those telephone calls controlled his life more than anything else.

"We are up to Readiness, lads," announced Squadron Leader Darling. "Convoy BREAD again, I'm afraid."

"The bastards are having one hell of a time getting through the bloody Channel," someone said inside the Dispersal building.

"Why didn't they go around the North instead of through the damn Channel with the sodding Gerries all about."

"Submarines."

Darling stepped outside. "Looks like the mound out there, would you say, 'Hunter?'" he asked.

"Yes, sir. Enough to go fly."

"Right, then." Darling leaned over near Brian's ear. "We won't hold it against you, but your countryman may have a time of it."

"Maybe he was just nervous or something."

"Maybe, but I shall give him a good run through nonetheless."

"Yes, sir."

Darling stood straight and walked to the Dispersal building door. "Mister Maxwell, are you ready to fly?"

"Sure."

"'Sparky,' you have the squadron while I am aloft with 'Hank' here."

"Righty ho, Skipper."

The two men walked off toward one of the new Spitfires delivered late yesterday. Just as Darling had indicated, the tail was clearly marked, PR-N. As Squadron Leader Darling had done for him nine months ago, he introduced Maxwell to his ground crew and gave him a quick checkout on the Spitfire Mark IA. They took their time getting airborne, but the dissipation of the melodic tones of the Merlin engines did not take long.

Brian Drummond sat alone outside for a few minutes enjoying the relative quiet of the early afternoon. Corporal Warren eventually came outside to stand beside his chair, took a few deep breaths and arched her back as if she needed to stretch her frame.

"Would you care for some tea and a biscuit, Mister Drummond?"

"No, thank you, Jennifer," he said looking up at her and smiling.

He wondered if she was going to make a comment about Melvyn Henry Maxwell, also. The thought passed, as she seemed content to simply enjoy the relative peace of the summer afternoon. The telephone startled both of them and made her spring back into Dispersal.

"Mister Morrow," she called.

They all waited for some indication of purpose for the call. They did not have to wait long.

"B Flight to Standby. Bandy will launch Junior in a few minutes. B Flight will escort them. Control is expecting a repeat of the last few days, and they want us overhead Convoy BREAD."

The Red and Yellow Section pilots walked casually toward their aircraft. They would sit all strapped into their fighters until the launch command was passed. In the case of B Flight, No.609 Squadron, they would follow the entire complement of Hurricanes from No.238 Squadron. Jonathan nodded and smiled to Brian as he made his way to his PR-K Spitfire.

Brian watched five pilots prepare themselves for the impending mission. He wanted to be with them, but he did not want to be with them. He loved the flying, the challenge, the excitement of fighter aviation, but the progressively closer cold of death dampened his enthusiasm. He knew Jonathan felt the same. Brian could not avoid the horrible thought, watching his best friend, Jonathan Kensington, settle into the Spitfire.

The sound of Merlins starting up behind the hangars gave him a pre-view. Those were most likely the Hurricanes of No.238 Squadron. A leading aircraftman in dark blue overalls ran up to Morrow's PR-B Spitfire. His right hand with two fingers extended rose from the cockpit scribing a circle in the air – their signal to start. The entire squadron of Hurricanes took off en masse toward the South with five Spitfires taking off together right behind them. With Darling and Maxwell out on the evaluation flight and the second half of the squadron flying South to probably another combat engagement, only 'Jackstay' Beamish, 'Boxer' Stockard and 'Hunter' Drummond remained behind with Corporal Jennifer Warren.

Stockard was probably sound asleep inside when Beamish came outside to sit next to Brian. "What is with this Maxwell fellow?"

"'Jackstay,' if you will forgive me, he is not my brother. I'm sorry he seems to be such an odd ball, but I don't like him any more than anyone else."

"My, my, aren't we testy today."

"I'm sorry, but everyone is saying something or asking something about Maxwell, as though I may have the answers. I don't. He's just another bloke as far as I'm concerned."

"I see what you mean. I suppose I was not aware you had become the focus of our thoughts regarding our replacement pilot. It isn't fair." He paused to collect his words. "I am simply curious. He is only the second American I have met."

"That is what 'Harness' said."

"Yes, well, nonetheless, he is still a curiosity."

"If you want to know my opinion," Brian said looking at Beamish for a nod that he received. "I think he just doesn't know. He seems fairly smart. He graduated from a university which I haven't done."

"Education does not make you a good person, Brian."

"I know that, but he has accomplished more than I have."

"Don't sell yourself short. You know how good you are with a stick between your legs, and a throttle and trigger in your hands."

"I suppose."

"You have credit for three and a half enemy aircraft. Another one and a half and you will be an ace. You are an important member of this squadron and contributor to the defense of freedom. What has he done?"

"Enough 'Jackstay,' I'm all right. I guess I'm just a bit sensitive because I'm not particularly proud of him as an American. I hope that changes, and he settles in better."

"We all do, 'Hunter.' We all do."

The sounds of Merlin engines took their attention skyward. Through the haze and scattered clouds emerged the returning Hurricanes of No.238 Squadron followed by a mile distance, the five No.609 Squadron Spitfires. Brian immediately thought of Darling and Maxwell. They were still out which meant the Skipper really was running him through the wringer.

"How did it go?" Brian asked Jonathan as the pilots returned to Dispersal.

"All we found was a circle of One Tens. The bastards are like turtles pulling into their defensive circle anytime real fighters show up. With a squadron and a half out there we took quite a few shots, got some hits but no kills I could see. They managed to find some clouds and ran for it."

"No bombers, ay?"

"None we could find," said Jonathan. "The hapless Convoy BREAD is past Plymouth by now, so maybe they have run the gauntlet successfully."

"'Sparky' brought all of 'em back, that's what counts."

"Precisely. I had better let the spooks have me before I attract their wrath."

The debriefing took an average amount of time for each of the B Flight pilots. As the first few began to return, Darling and Maxwell landed. Brian noted without expression Maxwell's darkened, perspiration soaked uniform and drooping posture as they walked toward Dispersal. The Skipper motioned for him to precede him into the building.

Squadron Leader Darling leaned over to Brian again. "No where near the stick you are, lad. The poor bastard may not survive the first few missions." He stood up and smiled before he turned to enter the Dispersal building for the debriefing of the squadron's newest pilot. Darling stopped at the door and looked over his shoulder. "By the way, I want you to take two days starting tomorrow."

Brian felt an odd sadness intermingled among surges of satisfaction. He resented the feelings, but he also knew they were feelings of life, like watching a turkey being slaughtered for Thanksgiving supper. Life was bright and dark . . . that was life.

—

Chapter 13

Friends share all things.

--Pythagoras

Sunday, 14.July.1940
RAF Middle Wallop
Middle Wallop, Hampshire, England
07:00 hours

As they assembled at Dispersal, the pilots of No.609 Squadron could have passed for seasoned coal miners gathering for their descent into the dark, damp depths of the Earth. There were no words, no smiles, or gestures of appreciation. The grim business of their profession slowly sucked out the enjoyment of life. Pilot Officer Brian Drummond struggled, as others did, with the fatal loss of friends and comrades in the previous week. The bright, near cloudless sky along with the early morning freshness and rich, fertile aroma of the nearby fields could not be enjoyed with the specter of death behind them and in front of them.

"Another glorious day in which to serve," shouted Flight Lieutenant Robert Morrow as though he was trying to speak to God.

"You will get yours," mumbled Flight Lieutenant John Davies.

Soft laughter punctuated the calm. Brian knew the laughter was important. Malcolm had told him many times, no matter how bad events may seem an aviator had to retain his humor, his ability to laugh at desperate times.

"The combination of this good weather and the renewed interest of the Germans in our little emerald isle probably means we will have a busy day," offered Flight Lieutenant Roger Beamish. "Does anyone know if Convoy BREAD finally made it out of the Channel, or whether there are any more convoys tempting the Germans?"

"Do we look like the bloody Admiralty, Roger?" barked Davies.

Beamish ignored the challenge. "Anticipation is all."

"Right, then. Now, let us finish off what sleep we missed before the action starts," said Davies, as he settled into a lawn, lounge chair squarely placed facing the Sun.

"Rough night last night, ay 'Waggle?'" poked Morrow.

Davies had already closed his eyes. "The spirits and dolly-birds are the only things keeping the demons at bay," he said quietly, as if he was saying it to himself as he was falling off to sleep.

They left him alone. Brian knew, as they all did, exactly what John Davies was talking about relative to taking every available moment for rest.

The early flying in Scotland against the occasional small raid of bombers contrasted like night and day to the sky full of fighters twisting, turning, diving and shooting. The intensity of last week's combat left a marked injury on everyone's thoughts. Brian returned to the stories from Malcolm Bainbridge, John Spencer and others – combat was everything they said it would be and worse. Each one of them reacted to stress differently, but they all reacted. The worst part continued to be the sure knowledge the aerial conflict would continue to grow more intense, more consuming and more lethal. They all knew it, but none of them acknowledged the thoughts aloud to one another. Brian and Jonathan came the closest, but even they seemed to be placing some strange distance between them like a moat against the heathen hoards.

Brian also thought of 'Hank' Maxwell. He was thankful the new, American pilot had not tried to join the conversation. Brian glanced over his shoulder to find Maxwell standing alone by the corner of the building staring off to some distant place. He looked alone. Brian felt sorry for him. He must have recognized his early misstep upon joining the squadron. After Darling's hard check flight, he probably was questioning the wisdom of his decision to join the RAF at war. Brian thought about going over to him.

The dreaded telephone rang before they could all settle into their chairs. "Squadron to Readiness," announced Corporal Jennifer Warren.

No one moved a muscle other than maybe to relax their stomach knots as best they could. Readiness meant they had to remain at Dispersal with their flight equipment close at hand. It also meant as Brian recalled, the RDF screens were beginning to light up with activity from the south. There was no certainty No.609 Squadron would be involved in any action, but it most assuredly brought them one step closer to combat.

Brian chose to relax in the sun and think of the two-day pass he would start at noon given that he was not on a mission at the time. He anticipated and yet feared his planned meeting with his former flight instructor and erstwhile friend, Flight Lieutenant Lord Jeremy 'Mud' Morrison. Brian thought he wanted to know as much as Jeremy knew about Anne, Virginia and the spy ring, but he knew none of it would be pleasant news. The burning question in his gut was not about the loss of his lover but about the threat to his dream. Could this entire affair affect his ability to fly the fastest, sleekest aircraft in this pure test of skill, luck and will?

It seemed only seconds to Brian when the telephone rang again. "Squadron to Standby."

"Here we go, lads," said Squadron Leader Darling. "Let's get ready for business."

All the pilots gathered up their helmets, oxygen masks, gloves and Mae West floatation vests, and walked casually, calmly and quietly toward their aircraft.

"Mornin,' Bernie," Brian greeted his crew chief. "Where is the rest of the crew?"

"Good morning to you, sir. Flight Sergeant pulled both Jordan and Colin for some other work detail after we completed our morning checks. The bird's ready."

"They brought us to Standby. No telling how long we will be here before we go."

"She's ready. I'll stay with you until you launch."

"Thanks, Bernie."

Pilot Officer Brian Drummond strapped into his PR-F fighter, ran through his pre-start checks, and then leaned his head back to wait for the launch order. Nothing happened at RAF Middle Wallop for a half hour. Sitting in a fighter cockpit waiting to launch like the cocked hammer of a pistol had its own peculiar brand of tension and strain. The urge to start the engine and push the throttle forward grew with each minute. Brian tried to think of the controller working some complex task on the map board, juggling several squadrons as well as other resources. An attempt at empathy did little to relieve the tension, but it did help. The pilots passed hand signals between them and talked with their crew chiefs.

Corporal Warren ran out to Darling's aircraft to pass a message. The squadron leader unstrapped, stood up and gave the cut signal. They withdrew from Standby status.

"We have returned to Readiness status," announced Darling once they all gathered at Dispersal.

"Why did they pull back the bow?" asked 'Waggle' Davies.

"They apparently had some confused situation to the east. That is all I have."

Each pilot took his own action to relieve the tension of Standby. Some had a cup of tea. Others joked, and a few tried to drift into sleep.

The morning continued along a tumultuous roller-coaster ride as they rose to Standby two more times only to stand down again. Fortunately, as the pilots joked, the later alerts were shorter.

Brian began to look at the clock anticipating 12:00, when he was scheduled to be released from duty. He needed the break as each of them did. Flying Officer Reginald Foxworth would be returning from his two-day break as Brian started his respite. 'Organ' Foxworth had not returned, yet. The image and memories of Jeremy Morrison again reentered Brian's consciousness. He realized he had not seen Jeremy since the real war burst into full flame three months ago. No.74 Squadron, Jeremy's unit, was still at RAF Hornchurch and had been involved in several notable engagements with good success. Jeremy's name had not appeared on any casualty lists, so he was undoubtedly still alive.

"Scramble the squadron," shouted Squadron Leader Darling.

For an instant, Brian thought it was a joke. His watch indicated, 11:37. This could not be real. The telephone had not rung. The blur of arms, legs and bodies convinced him it was not some infantile prank.

No.609 Squadron launched in short order. They were directed to the East of the Isle of Wight to relieve No.64 Squadron that needed to disengage for fuel. The ball of fighters popped out at them as they approached. Darling positioned them to enter the fight straight on without the usual preparation. The No.64 Squadron SH Spitfires turned north as Darling lined up the squadron. The German leader of a large flight of Bf110s, spotting the approaching squadron of Spitfires, decided withdrawal was in order. Almost simultaneously, twenty plus, twin-engine, German fighters turned south and dove to gain speed quickly. Darling led the squadron in the chase, but the reduced weight of the Bf110s gave them just enough speed to keep the Spitfires from closing the distance in time.

Satisfied the sky was clear of Germans in their area, Squadron Leader Darling led his group of fighters back to RAF Middle Wallop with their gunport tapes still in place. By the time they landed, debriefed and checked their status, it was 13:42. Brian waited patiently, trying not to show any enthusiasm or expectation, for his release from duty. Foxworth had been waiting for them when they landed, and he was back in harness a little worse for the wear. Darling appeared to be quite busy making several telephone calls and occasionally appeared to be quite agitated about something. It was 14:21, and Brian started to resign himself to a shortened or nonexistent break if Darling ever released him from duty.

Squadron Leader Darling appeared outside the Dispersal building. "Sorry, 'Hunter,'" he said as though he had to cancel Brian's pass. "I was rather wrapped up with Group. 'Organ' is back. You are released for your two day-er. By the way, I might add I received word the American Olympian Billy Fiske made it out of France and has been assigned to Six Oh One Squadron at Tangmere."

"Hurricanes?"

"Yes. It seems a handful of other Americans were in France, flying for *Le Armée de l'Air*, and are now being integrated into Fighter Command, so with Maxwell and the others, you are no longer the lone American in our merry little band of fly-boys.”

“Thanks, Skipper.”

“Say hello to Linda, if you see her,” Jonathan Kensington said. “Tell her I will try to get into London for my next break.”

Brian knew he would not see Linda since Anne was in prison. With others within hearing distance, Brian could not tell Jonathan he would not see her. Such a statement would only instigate additional questions. “Thursday?”

“That’s it, unless something changes of course.”

“Right. No problem. Now, if you will excuse me, my friend. I shall be off.”

“Enjoy,” Jonathan said with a wink. “See you day after tomorrow.”

Brian left the squadron and returned to the Officer’s Mess. He took a shower, changed uniforms, and then called Jeremy Morrison. His former instructor was still trying to figure out if he could break away. Jeremy said he had a 24-hour pass tomorrow that would coincide with Brian’s last day. They agreed to meet tomorrow at a minimum. Brian was to go to London, take a room at one of the hotels, and then call Jeremy again.

—

Sunday, 14.July.1940
Carlton Hotel
Mayfair, London, England
17:45 hours

The journey into London and through the Underground to Green Park Station had taken the better part of the remaining afternoon. Instead of the Savoy on The Strand, Brian had decided to try the Carlton in Mayfair. It was closer to Shepherds Pub, anyway. At first, the desk clerk had not been able to offer him a room. They had been fully booked, but thought they might have a few cancellations. Brian had waited only 25 minutes before he had been given a pleasant room near the top floor overlooking the east end of Hyde Park. It was a modest size, well-appointed room, not small like the room he had at the Savoy when he first arrived in England, or spacious and opulent like the suite Mary reserved for them last Sunday. He remembered the night with Mary, and then placed her back into his memory.

Brian called Jeremy. His source of answers would not be able to make it into London until tomorrow afternoon or evening, but he committed to the date. Jeremy said he would leave a message with a time and place for their meeting. Brian stood at the window feeling the sun on his face. He removed his tunic and loosened his tie as he scanned the city before him. He had nearly 24 hours before he would see Jeremy. Normally, he would have been with Anne by now, but that was no longer a possibility.

Brian knew he did not want to be alone. He could go to Shepherds in a few hours to see if he could latch onto one of the unattached women that usually frequented the fighter pilots' favorite haunt in London, but the effort did not appeal to him. Mary Spencer was the closest, but he quickly put that thought out of his mind. Rosemary Kensington was at Oxford. The venerable university town was about an hour away by train. Maybe she could skip a few classes.

The process of tracking her down took much longer than he expected. The telephone operators who assisted him were even becoming frustrated and annoyed with the chore, or maybe it was his persistence. Finally, he heard her voice.

"Rosemary, this is Brian."

"Where are you?"

"London."

"And, you want me to come to you."

Her forwardness continued to take his breath away. He always tried to prepare himself for her, but it never worked. "It was my thought, actually."

"You are beginning to sound British. Don't," she said as a command. "Keep your American charm, Brian."

"Sure."

"This is a historic occasion, I do believe. This is the first time you called me since Tuesday. How could I refuse?"

"Then, you will come to London?"

"Not so fast, my knight. I have several important classes tomorrow. We have our semester final examinations this month, you know."

"I'm sorry. I didn't mean to interfere."

Rosemary giggled, more to herself than for Brian. "You are so quaint. I shall need a little time to arrange things here, and if I recall the rail schedules, I could be in London within a few hours. Let us assume all shall be right with the world. Where should I meet you?"

"I have a room at the Carlton in Mayfair."

"Brilliant. That should suit our purpose quite nicely."

Brian felt a flush of embarrassment knowing exactly what she meant. "Then, I'll meet you in the lobby in say three hours."

"Lobby, my dear Brian? Unless you plan for both of us to be arrested for public indecency, I would suggest our meeting in your room. Which is . . . ?"

"One one zero seven."

"I shall see you in roughly two to three hours in room double one oh seven."

"Yes."

"Be ready, my love. I shall see you soon."

Before he could answer, she disconnected. Brian sat at the small desk for several minutes. How did Jonathan's sister become so bold, brash and blunt? Often times, he thought she could pass for a fighter pilot. She shared her bluntness with her brother, but Jonathan always presented a refined, more subdued character than Rosemary. Both were certainly strong willed, which was probably a worthy attribute in these times.

Brian decided to use the summer daylight to walk through Hyde Park. It reminded him of his walks with Anne, but the fresh air, the warm breeze and the rustle of the trees would be a good tonic for his anticipation of what was to come.

The presence of the police in larger numbers as well as small clutches of older men in civilian clothes drilling with wooden rifles or farm implements left no doubt of the expectation ahead. The Local Defense Volunteers, LDV, as they called them, displayed how thin the home defense forces were, but it also demonstrated the collective resolve not to succumb to the same fate as the French. The people believed what Churchill said in his speeches, or maybe Churchill was saying what the people believed. Either way, the result was the same. This would be a fight to the end.

The walk served its purpose. Brian felt relaxed and calm when he returned to the hotel. He had plenty of time before Rosemary was supposed to arrive. He removed his tunic once more and lay down on the bed for a quick nap. With Rosemary, there was no way to predict what might happen.

It seemed like only a few minutes when a knock at the door returned him to alertness. He stood, straightened his shirt and necktie, smoothed the bedspread and went to the door. He opened the door to see the joyous smile of Rosemary Kensington. Her seductive blue eyes burned with her blond hair draped across her shoulders. The light, wool pants suit she wore brought a more country flavor to the city. She slowly moved forward forcing Brian back like the opposite pole of a magnet. She closed the door behind her.

"Dear God, Brian, it is smashing to see you again. I have been so worried about you." Rosemary whispered, as if someone might be listening.

They embraced, kissed passionately several times, then Rosemary drew back slightly as though she needed to look at him again.

"I'm OK," said Brian.

"I can see that now," she said standing back further and removing her light coat, "but the newspapers told us about the air fighting over the Channel shipping. They never tell us what squadrons are involved, so I never know whether your name will appear on the casualty list."

"Jonathan would call you, if something happened to me."

"Yes, yes, enough of this for now. We have business to tend to, first."

"Is that so?" Brian said with a smile thinking he knew what she meant.

"I need to feel you, Brian, all of you," she said smiling coyly and grasping his hand again leading him.

Brian started their usual headlong rush into the throes of passion, but this time Rosemary slowed the tempo of their dance as if to savor each stage, view and touch. She was intent upon undressing him completely, so she could see his reaction to her. As she removed his shirt, the bandage covering his wounded left arm sprang out at her.

"Oh Brian, what happened?" she asked, as the feather touch of her fingers caressed him above and below the bandage.

"A small cut."

"Brian," she reacted, "they do not put dressings like this on minor cuts. Now, what happened?"

"My aircraft took several hits a few days ago, and I was wounded by the shrapnel."

Rosemary quickly undressed the rest of him and carefully examined his body like a nurse trying to find other wounds to patch. She left him standing and moved beyond arm's length in front of Brian.

"It is dangerous, isn't it?"

Brian nodded his head, not wanting to say the words he felt. She moved further back and sat in an elegant stuffed chair. He wanted to go to her, but he stayed like an accused man in a courtroom dock although being stark naked was quite unusual for him.

"Brian, this whole business worries me. I could lose you in a flash, couldn't I?"

He again nodded his head. Mortality or the intensity of aerial combat were not exactly topics he wanted to discuss with Rosemary at the moment. He wanted to change the subject, to communicate on a different plain. His instincts told him that she needed some time to recover. Brian began to fidget slightly feeling, for the first time in his relationship with Rosemary, the urge to cover himself. He felt exposed, distant and vulnerable, not sensations he found enjoyable.

Then, as though some great force stiffened Rosemary, she stood, smiled and held out her arms for a hug. She turned her head to look into his eyes. "Enough morbidity," she whispered. "You are the one defending this country. It, therefore, becomes my weight to bear, and I must do my part to keep you healthy and focused upon your task."

Rosemary stepped back several paces, again beyond arm's reach. She allowed a mischievous twinkle to illuminate her eyes as she unbuttoned her blouse. She giggled and wiggled seeing the response in Brian. Rosemary kicked her shoes off, and then dropped her pants and removed her undergarments displaying her unadorned body in full glory. Brian's heart rate and breathing quickened substantially seeing what he had suspected.

Rosemary took command of their union. Groaning with pleasure, she mounted him, accommodating the size she had grown to truly love. She spoke to him describing her feelings in abundant, intimate and loving detail until she recognized the approaching summit in her lover. Her movement became more intense and purposeful until she achieved exactly what she sought from him.

The sensations blurred into the insidious accumulation of fatigue, tension, fear, and salvation. Brian lost his grip on reality as he gave way to the total exorcism of the demons he had kept within him. Rosemary let him go sensing his most basic needs.

The ring of the telephone shocked Brian from his semi-slumber. He bolted out of bed. His reaction startled Rosemary causing her to knock the telephone off its cradle. Several seconds elapsed before Brian could regain his orientation and location. He felt foolish and yet relieved. It was not 'the' telephone.

Rosemary quickly regained her composure and answered the call. She responded with a thank you, and then hung up and turned to Brian. Rosemary touched Brian's cheek with a sympathetic touch. "Somehow, I think this war business is far worse than you are telling me."

"I am truly sorry, Rosemary. I apologize for scaring you. It is an unfortunate reaction."

"To what?"

"We get our scramble commands by the telephone. The ring tends to mean we have to go fight the Germans."

"Scramble?"

"It is the word we use for an immediate launch like we have to scramble to get in the air as quickly as possible. We run to our fighters and take off as quickly as we can. It doesn't give us much time to think. We simply react."

"I see," Rosemary answered, lapsing into her thought.

"Who was that on the phone?"

"It was the front desk. They have a message for you from Flight Lieutenant Morrison. He also said the Prime Minister is giving another speech, and we might want to tune the radio to the BBC World Service."

"Great."

Brian watched with obvious appreciation as she walked without the slightest sign of self-consciousness across the room to turn on the radio. The return trip gave him equal pleasure. It was not until Rosemary snuggled up laying her head on his chest that Brian became aware of the words from the radio and the Prime Minister's distinctive voice.

"We await undismayed the impending assault. Perhaps it will never come. We must show ourselves equally capable of meeting a sudden violent shock or – which is perhaps a harder test – a prolonged vigil. But, be the ordeal sharp or long, or both, we shall seek no terms – we shall tolerate no parley – we may show mercy – we shall ask for none."

The BBC announcer returned to provide additional news. Brian dwelled on the words. The somber tones reflected the gravity of the military situation while his words echoed a confident, resolute and purposeful resistance. Independent of the war, or maybe colored by the war, Brian enjoyed listening to Churchill. The peculiarities of his speech and melodic ring of his words, like a giant bell, gave strength and concentration.

Rosemary rose on one elbow remaining close to Brian. "Which do you think it will be?" she asked.

"What do you mean?"

"Violent shock or prolonged vigil?"

Brian knew what he thought it would be. He looked away from her. The opening shots of the violent shock had already been fired. All the pilots expected the violence to increase rapidly to a conclusion of some sort.

Rosemary touched his wounded left arm. "Violent shock," she whispered. Brian nodded his agreement. She rose from the bed again to turn off the radio.

He did not want to tell her the details of what had just happened last week. There was no point giving her more reasons to worry. He suspected she already had enough. Rosemary took the non-verbal communication and decided to change the mood in her bedroom. Her magic quickly transformed the room filling it with laughter, warmth and passion.

At the next lull in their pleasure, Brian remembered the telephone call. "You said there was a message from Jeremy Morrison."

"Yes. Apparently, he intends to meet you at eight tomorrow evening in the hotel lobby."

"Good."

"Do you have tomorrow night off as well?"

"Yes."

"Then, what about us?"

Without hesitation, even knowing what the conversation with Jeremy would be about, Brian said, "You can come, too."

"Is this business?"

"In a manner of speaking."

"Then, I shall pass. How long do you think your meeting will take? Should I stay here?"

Brian looked deeply into her eyes and smiled. "I'd like you to stay."

"We shall cross that bridge tomorrow. Tonight, we have other business," she giggled.

—

Monday, 15.July.1940
Carlton Hotel
Mayfair, London, England

"**B**rian . . . Brian, wake up," Rosemary said, bringing him back to consciousness.

The worried expression on her lovely face told Brian something had happened. "What?"

"You were having a nightmare."

"What happened?"

"First, you scared the bloody hell out of me. You started shouting, 'fire.' I nearly wet the bed."

There was a waft of humor in her words, but he knew he could not laugh. He tried to remember, if it was a dream. Nothing came to him.

"You are soaking wet. You were saying things I could not quite understand . . . something about . . . what was it . . . fingers melting, getting out, can't get out. Do you remember?"

Brian did not remember, but her words brought back images that had been present from time to time over the last few months. His two bail outs from disabled fighters. The fire from his engine. Watching Stephen Strickland's burning airplane crash into the forest. This was the first time anyone told him he had been talking in his sleep. He wondered if his nocturnal, dream-sleep, words had been spoken in the pilot's residence. Had some of his mates heard him talking in his sleep?

"Brian, I want to know what is really happening up there," she said, softly stroking his damp hair.

"No, you don't."

"Brian, please, as painful as it may be, it will help you. I want to help you."

"I can't."

"Why?"

"It's too ugly."

"All the more reason you should release that venom."

"You are so beautiful, and you make me feel alive."

"Stop trying to change the subject. Tell me."

"Rosemary, people die up there. We lost three pilots just this last week," he said, adding as much weight to his words as he could, hoping it might stop her inquisitiveness.

"I know, but it is war after all."

Brian got out of bed. "I don't want to talk about the war." He looked back at the smooth, round curves of her reclined body. Her lack of any self-consciousness about her body never failed to give Brian a warm, easy feeling through his entire frame. "I'm going to take a bath."

"Good idea. I shall take one with you . . . and, I promise no more talk of war," she said, and then added with almost a whisper, "for the time being."

The private bath, like the bedroom, was moderately spacious and luxuriously appointed. The bath had an extraordinarily large tub with sloped ends permitting two people to fit comfortably and semi-recline facing each other. She took an extended time to demonstrate the pleasures of the joint bath.

After a casual but sensuously eaten breakfast, the two lovers decided to take a long walk. The overcast sky offered a pleasant coolness even better for a walk than yesterday. Across Park Lane and down Serpentine Road they walked into the depths of Hyde Park and on the Western side, Kensington Gardens. They talked, laughed, hugged, kissed and walked silently with no direction or purpose other than to enjoy their closeness. They walked past Kensington Palace, and they laughed some more about Brian's naiveté regarding the naming of her home, Carlingon Castle. He remembered asking Jonathan last Christmas during his visit, why they had not called it, Kensington Castle. Now, he knew why.

They ate a light lunch at a small pub along the way, and then continued their leisurely excursion. Brian marveled how Rosemary always seemed to keep him off balance and alert. She was energy and youth personified.

On the way back to Park Lane, Rosemary stopped at a bench and motioned for them to sit. She held his arm tightly not really wanting to talk, just be close to Brian. After several minutes, she looked toward him. "Do you want me to stay the night?"

Brian smiled into her eyes. "Yes, if you can."

"I can."

"Great. You do make me forget the war."

"Then, I am good for something, aren't I?" she laughed.

They laughed together talking about the birds in the trees or peculiar people within sight. They were having fun together. Gradually, they made their way back to the hotel. There were two hours to his planned meeting with Jeremy. Brian thought about Rosemary being with them. She was going to hear the story eventually. Tonight was as good a time as any. If she changed her mind, he would tell her what they would be talking about tonight. In the end, she remained with her earlier decision. Rosemary would remain patiently in their room and have something from room service.

Brian saw Flight Lieutenant Morrison as he entered the hotel lobby. "Jeremy," shouted Brian.

"Brian, you old dog."

Brian extended his hand, but Jeremy passed it to embrace his friend. "I have truly missed you, my friend."

"And, I have missed you. So much has happened in the last two months."

Jeremy's smile disappeared. "I dare say, a rather serious understatement, my man."

"Yeah."

"I know a small, quiet restaurant not far from here. I might suggest, since we are both without our women, I am certain I could find us some companionship."

"That's OK." Brian knew Rosemary's presence upstairs would make Jeremy uncomfortable and possibly truncate their discussion.

"Then, so be it. Let's walk, shall we," Jeremy said, motioning toward the door.

They began walking, acknowledging the greetings of anonymous citizens, without words between them. As they headed down a narrow side street, the citizenry disappeared leaving them to their footsteps.

"Say 'Hunter,' I hear you had to make your second jump this week," Jeremy said strongly.

"We were in a tangle. I was on a few Germans, and one of them got a lucky shot."

"Isn't that the way it always is? It is always the one you don't see that gets you."

"Something like that."

"If it is any comfort, you are not the only one to be shot down. Al Deere has lost a few aircraft. Even 'Bobby' Tuck has had his close calls, as well. You are in good company, Brian. You manage to walk away from these incidents. As you are, I am certain, painfully aware, not everyone does."

"Yeah. We lost three last week."

"I know. Ah, here we are."

They entered a small, nondescript establishment. Jeremy was true to his suggestion. It was quiet. Several, well cushioned, semi-private booths lined one wall. A few other tables were positioned so they did not intrude on the booths. Jeremy and Brian were the only patrons visible. Jeremy knew the owner as well as the service staff. They were well treated and taken care of by the staff. With the amenities along with the appetizer, salad and main course behind them, Jeremy took them to the anticipated topic.

"We both know why we are here, so I will not beat around the bush. First, how terribly sorry I am that you were caught up in this sordid affair. You must understand, I never even remotely considered the possibility. I most humbly offer my sincerest and heartfelt apology to you for all this."

"Apology accepted, but why, Jeremy? Why?"

Jeremy Morrison nodded his head. "I shall tell you what I know. I was interrogated by Scotland Yard and the darkies for nearly a full day."

"Darkies?"

"Intelligence blokes, actually counterintelligence, I do believe. MI5, I think it is."

"That's who questioned me as well."

"Anyway, the best I have been able to determine is, a rather sophisticated spy ring was developed by the Germans through a foolish fascist, William Joyce, many refer to him as Lord Haw-Haw, but he is a traitor, nonetheless. They were able to recruit a half dozen or so prostitutes, some would call them courtesans, since their clientele were specifically and almost exclusively the rich, powerful, influential or important men in government, industry or the military. I know I have not seen all the names, but the ones I have seen are staggering. Virginia and Anne fell victim to various devices, but mostly,

I believe they were too naive. They began trading information as if it were gossip. They apparently were well rewarded for their services, however they will pay the ultimate price for their naiveté."

"What will happen to them?"

"There is no easy way to say it, Brian. They will hang."

"Jesus," Brian gasped as if stabbed.

"Quite. This ring also involved an American by the name of Tyler Gatewood Kent. He worked at the American Embassy as a cipher clerk, apparently. It also involved several individuals at the Foreign Office. The long and short of it was, our dolly-birds stepped into a rather odoriferous pile of dung, and they shall not survive it."

"I knew it was bad when these goons questioned me. They had a woman lure me into their trap at Anne's home. They also told me not to talk to anyone, but I just had to know. When is their trial? Can I talk to Anne?"

"I must say, Brian, justice is very swift when it comes to treason in war time. Their trials, or at least Virginia's and Anne's, both separate, were held just over a fortnight ago. It took less than a day to convict them. Anne is scheduled to hang on the 8th of August; Virginia one week later. The appeal process will be equally swift. Now, there is more bad news, you will not be able to talk to them. They are being held incommunicado from everyone."

"They must be scared to death," Brian said, and instantly regretted his choice of words.

"I did use my station and my brother's connections to get a short meeting with Virginia before her trial. It was intimately supervised by Scotland Yard."

"How was she?"

"Deeply remorseful and scared out of her skin."

"Poor girl."

"They did what they did with their eyes open, Brian. They fell victim to Joyce's siren song. They thought they were helping their country and world peace. They believed what he told them. Hell, Joyce probably believed it, as well. It seemed so right to them at the time. I can remember several conversations in retrospect where I think Virginia was asking me how I felt about the situation on the Continent, as if she were sounding me."

"The police said nothing would happen to me. How about you?"

"I shall land on my feet. I am only guilty of seeking pleasure. I might add, I did work very hard to clear you of any duplicity."

"Thanks. Apparently everything checked. They said there would be no further action against me."

"Excellent."

"They scared the hell out of me, though. The American Government tried to deport me earlier this year for being over here in the first place. With all this spy crap, I could see the wolves drooling at the gate."

"They shall not have you, my boy."

"I hope not."

They ordered a small sweet for dessert. Jeremy asked for brandy to seal the meal, as he put it. It was an excellent meal despite the vile topic.

"You said they specialized in the rich and powerful, so why me?"

Jeremy laughed. "I could say the same thing. I think there is only one word – love. I suspect I would have taken Virginia out of her business at some point, maybe when the war was over. I know Anne loved you, Brian. She truly loved you. You were very special to her. She became attached to you from that very first night at Troscadero's. Remember?"

"I remember," Brian answered and smiled. He had been so innocent and immature.

"It was fun while it lasted."

"She taught me a lot. She made me feel so good."

"They were both excellent at what they did. Frankly, they loved sex."

"Yeah, they did."

They drank the remainder of their brandy. Jeremy paid the bill.

"What do you say we go back to Troscadero's as a tribute?"

Brian instantly reminded himself that Rosemary Kensington waited for him. "I'll have to pass."

"Why? Do you have a date?"

"As a matter of fact, I have a woman waiting in my room."

"Why you sly little devil. Why didn't you invite her, so I could enjoy her as well?"

"I did invite her. I told her it was business, and she chose to remain in the hotel."

"Quite. Where did you find this one?"

"She is the sister of my best friend. I met her last Christmas when I visited their home in Newcastle."

"She came quite someway to see you, then."

"She's a medical student at Oxford."

"And, a brainy dolly-bird, as well."

"She is fun."

"Yes, right you are then. Let's get you back to the hotel."

Jeremy walked with Brian back to the Carlton. They laughed and joked about the variety of flying incidents they knew about between them. It was the aviator's version of small talk. Jeremy was a good sport about the evening. Brian thanked him for the meal, the information and his friendship. He watched Jeremy swagger off down the street.

It was nearly midnight when Brian joined Rosemary. She did not question him in the slightest. She skillfully and promptly returned them to their primary shared endeavor.

—

Tuesday, 16.July.1940
Carlton Hotel
Mayfair, London, England
05:30 hours

Brian Drummond stood at the window staring out at the rain soaked city street and the heavy gray sky releasing its moisture. He had to be back on duty at RAF Middle Wallop by noon, which meant he would have to leave the warmth of Rosemary's company within the hour. His thoughts could not escape the question of what lay ahead. Would this week be even more intense than last week? Would there be more losses? Would the Germans move inland with their bombing campaign? When would the invasion come? The questions kept flooding to him.

"Is everything all right?" asked Rosemary with her inquisitive but soft voice.

Brian turned to her, feeling completely uninhibited about his nakedness. He considered sharing his thoughts but discounted the urge. There was nothing to be gained by adding to the burden he was certain Rosemary already felt.

"Sure. I was just enjoying the rain. It is a nice, steady, even rain. I thought about calling back to the squadron. With a rain like this, Group may release us, which would mean another day in London with you."

Rosemary smiled and pulled the sheet off her. "Then, by all means call and come back to me."

He placed the call reaching Corporal Warren. It was raining the same in Hampshire, and the weather forecasters predicted rain all day. She asked Squadron Leader Darling who believed they would be released, and then he heard the distinctive ring of the operational telephone. Even the nearly 100 miles distance did not prevent the quickening of his heart. Warren returned to Brian to tell him the squadron had indeed been released for the day. Brian asked her to tell Jonathan Kensington he was going to remain in London for another day.

"So, you are able to stay?"

"Yes."

Rosemary pulled the sheet over her head as Brian joined her.

"Before we get started again," said Rosemary, "I am afraid I must get back to Oxford, or I shall be in a dreadfully difficult predicament."

"I understand. I really should be getting back as well."

"But, we have plenty of time for more pleasure," she said, as she reached for him.

Brian felt the urge growing. Another urge grew faster. "Rosemary, I want to tell you about my meeting last night."

"Why?"

"I want you to hear it from me, not someone else."

The words conveyed an element of seriousness that had the desired effect. Rosemary listened as Brian told her about Anne, and his relationship with the now convicted and sentenced spy and traitor. He did not delve into the intimacy between them, but he did try to be honest about his feelings for her. Rosemary asked a few questions – natural understandable questions. She did not appear to be particularly concerned about what had happened.

"Thank you for sharing your troubles with me," she said.

"I hope I have not become repulsive to you."

"On the contrary. Quite the opposite, actually. All of us make mistakes. That's what makes life so ... well ... intriguing. Mistakes are experience. It sounds like you loved the woman, and she loved you. That is good. It is unfortunate she did what she did, but that's life too. What matters to me is, what is between us."

Rosemary returned to her more carnal activities as their minds moved into a new episode. Her resiliency never ceased to amaze Brian.

They enjoyed each other until mid-day. They cleaned each other, dressed each other and ate lunch before taking the Underground to Paddington Station. They separated with smiles on their faces and a pleasant ache in their bodies.

—

Tuesday, 16.July.1940
No.10 Downing Street
Whitehall, London, England
23:00 hours

"Prime Minister, may I introduce Colonel William Joseph 'Bill' Donovan," said Bill Stephenson motioning toward the tall, well-built man in a medium gray suit.

"My apologies for the late hour, Colonel Donovan. I am afraid the pressing affairs of State and a protracted War Cabinet meeting this evening delayed our introduction."

"I am a night person, Prime Minister, so no problem for me."

"As you may know, I have a reputation for being somewhat of a night owl myself."

"Your modesty does not diminish the perception."

"Thank you, Bill. May I call you, Bill?"

"By all means, sir."

"Then, I must insist you call me, Winston, or some other term of familiarity. I should think we are embarking upon a long journey together."

"As you wish, Winston."

"I understand you have much the same relationship with President Roosevelt as Bill, here, does with me."

"I suppose you could say that. We were classmates at Columbia Law School, and we have stayed in touch, although we are of different political parties, I'm afraid, so our circle of friends and colleagues are different."

"War does make strange bed fellows."

Donovan chuckled. "Perhaps an understatement."

"Two Bills. Let me see." Winston scratched his knee in contemplation. "In deference to your size, I should think we should refer to you as, Big Bill, and 'Intrepid' here, we should call, Little Bill, to distinguish each of you when you are not present." The three laughed at the identification. "Is my information correct . . . you have sacrificed your lucrative Wall Street law practice to join our little struggle?"

"First, I will maintain my law practice until we enter the war, and second, I do not consider it particularly lucrative although it does keep me in pocket change."

All three men laughed. "Pocket change, indeed!" exclaimed Churchill.

"I have asked Admiral Pike, with whom I believe you are acquainted, to join us, as well as Colonel Menzies and Brigadier Harker."

"I have known Admiral Pike for several years, and hope he would agree, we are friends. I am amply aware of Colonel Menzies' position as 'C,' although I have not met him nor Brigadier Harker, as yet."

"Excellent, then when they arrive, we shall make the proper introductions."

"I eagerly await that moment."

"Am I properly informed that both of you made the journey across the Atlantic by aeroplane?"

"Yes, Sir. The PanAm Yankee Clipper, a Boeing Model 314 flying boat, is a rather elegant and expeditious transport from New York to Lisbon. Twenty-seven hours certainly beats seven to ten days by ship. A BOAC Hudson was waiting for us and brought us to London, so I certainly thank you for that swift transport."

"I really must try that means of transport. I do enjoy flying."

"Am I properly informed . . . you are a pilot as well, Prime Minister?"

"Please, Bill, Winston is sufficient between us, and Bill," he said nodding to Stephenson, "and I have been friends since before the Great War. And, yes, you are properly informed. I have always enjoyed flight and wiggling the stick as the real pilots say."

"Then, you would enjoy the Boeing 314 flying boat."

I suspect we will need air transport to expand the special relationship between our two nations."

"Yes, sir, quite so," Donovan responded. The pause left a moment for the American to gather his thoughts. "As you know, sir, I have been asked by Secretary of the Navy Knox to learn as much as I can from your security services regarding their methods in dealing with Fifth Column activities."

Churchill smiled. He knew Donovan's mission was and had to be much greater than the stated purpose, but truth be told, he did not care what reason was used or who sponsored the visit. Winston intended to make sure His Majesty's Government provided whatever assistance was needed for Donovan's full mission. "I can assure you, Bill, the full resources and facilities of His Majesty's Government are available to you. I wanted to spend a little time with you before the professionals arrive. As you may know, I recently appointed Brigadier Harker to be Director General, Security Services – MI5 as we say in our shorthand. He should be fully prepared to assist you, and I expect him to be enthusiastically cooperative. The King has asked to meet with you. We have scheduled an audience for ten o'clock tomorrow morning."

"Thank you, Prime Minister."

Churchill nodded his head in acknowledgement. "I took the liberty of including the Director General, Secret Intelligence Service, MI6 if you will, and the Director, Navy Intelligence, as they work directly with MI5, which is primarily our internal security apparatus. Now that I think of it, you should probably meet with the Commissioner, Metropolitan Police, Air Vice Marshal

Sir Philip Game, as it is his constables who generally carry out arrests and prosecutions for MI5."

"I would be honored to meet with anyone you deem appropriate to my mission," Donovan said.

"To be frank, Bill, considering our position in this war and President Roosevelt's predicament with Congress and the American people, I would like you to meet with our defense ministers and service chiefs and absorb as much of our defense preparations as you are able during your stay. As part of that latter process, I have one personal request."

"By all means, Winston, whatever you wish."

"We have a young American pilot serving in the RAF, who has been with us since before the war. He flies Spitfires with Six Oh Nine Squadron. He has proven to be an exceptional young man and a magnificent fighter pilot. I also understand President Roosevelt issued him a full pardon from the Neutrality Act."

"I have no idea, Winston," Donovan responded. "That is beyond my knowledge."

"Regardless, I thought to arrange a dual purpose visit one afternoon. You can get a good look at the Spitfire fighter and meet your countryman, young Pilot Officer Brian Drummond."

"It would be my pleasure, sir."

"Very well, then," Churchill said. "We shall arrange it. I had an extended lunch with him at Chartwell. I think you will be impressed. I would like you to spend some time with the First Lord A.V. Alexander and the First Sea Lord Sir Dudley Pound to gain a clear view of our situation in the Battle of the Atlantic. We need your surplus destroyers to augment the Royal Navy in convoy escort duty. I have repeatedly conveyed our needs to President Roosevelt, and I know he is doing what he can, but I would greatly appreciate your gaining first hand knowledge to assist him in moving the destroyer transfer along. The post-war disarmament nonsense has left us woefully short. Those destroyers are one of Bill's primary objectives in his liaison work."

"I have no expectation of office, but I have asked the President how I may be of service. I have even offered to go back to the line in uniform."

"I know the feeling, and you would be well received. After all, did you not receive your country's highest award for combat valor during the Meuse-Argonne Offensive just prior to the Armistice?"

"The Medal of Honor," added Stephenson.

"Yes, sir. Helluva fight, I must say."

"I served on the line as well, so . . . ."

The knock at the door interrupted their conversation. "Yes," said Winston.

Churchill's assistant private secretary Jock Colville entered and announced, "Vice Admiral Sir Geoffrey Pike, Brigadier Harker and Colonel Menzies are here to see you, Prime Minister."

"Please show them into the Cabinet Room, Jock. There will be too many for my office. Shall we," Churchill motioned for his guests to follow Colville.

Winston and the two Bills entered the Cabinet Room. The three chief intelligence leaders were standing just inside the door. As Churchill entered, Colville closed the door behind him, and then seated himself by the door in case he was needed.

"Good to see you again, Bill." said Sir Geoffrey, pumping Donovan's hand. "Good evening to you, Winston . . . Bill."

"Rear Admiral Anderson sends his best, Admiral Pike."

"How is Walter?" Admiral Pike turned to Winston. "Admiral Walter Anderson is my counterpart, Director of Naval Intelligence for the Americans." Winston nodded.

"He seems to be enjoying himself, although events in the Atlantic as well as the Pacific keep him virtually cloistered at the Navy Department."

"It would appear to be contagious, these days," added Winston Churchill.

Introductions were dispatched promptly.

"Shall we be seated," offered Winston. Once everyone was settled, Churchill began the late night meeting, actually early morning since it was after midnight. "This is a historic occasion that will most likely not be recorded in the history books, but significant nonetheless. Colonel Donovan is here on a fact-finding mission on behalf of Secretary of the Navy Frank Knox to help us forge the mighty keel of what will soon become a most awesome ship of war. The President and I share the view that Hitler's rabid tyranny must be exterminated no matter what the cost. The essential, if not crucial, element of our endeavor will be the collective strength of our cooperative intelligence services. As such, this is the first meeting of what will remain an exclusive group, and as the President and I have agreed, we will share all material and information, with proper safeguards, to ensure we are victorious." The others nodded their agreement. "In the nature of free and open communications, please allow me to set the stage for Colonel Donovan's visit. His primary focus is on Fifth Column countermeasures, as such Brigadier Harker, if you would be so kind to host our distinquished guest. I trust you are fully prepared to address whatever inquiries Colonel Donovan may have."

"Yes, Sir. We are ready."

"I also think it prudent for you two to sit down with Sir Phillip, to ensure Colonel Donovan fully appreciates the relationship between your Security Service and the Metropolitan Police."

"By all means."

"Excellent. Colonel Donovan has gratiously consented to broadened discussions regarding our strategic and operational intelligence processes. President Roosevelt voiced his frustration to me, regarding the unity of purpose in his intelligence services, so I thought it might be useful to him for Colonel Donovan to carry back some direct information with respect to our experience, thus my invitation to you," he said, nodding to Menzies and Pike. "While our formation of the Special Operations Executive will not be formally established until next week, I would like Colonel Donovan to spend some time with Hugh Dalton," Churchill added, referring to the Minister of Economic Warfare, who was preparing for the creation of SOE and clandestine operatons on the Continent to disrupt the German occupation as well as future actions to liberate the occupied countries. Bill," he said, speaking to Stephenson, "please make the appropriate arrangements for Colonel Donovan as we have discussed and ensure he gets everything he needs."

"Yes, sir. It would be my pleasure," Stephenson responded.

"I want it clearly understood by everyone, Colonel Donovan is the guest of His Majesty's Government and he is to be treated as my personal representative. If there are any problems whatsoever, you are to contact my office directly and promptly. I trust that charter is clear enough."

Everyone responded in the affirmative and without any need for clarification.

"In light of the late hour and looming events," said the Prime Minister, "might I ask that we adjourn for what is left of the night. I am certain Colonel Donovan would appreciate some rest. I should think I can leave the professional exchange in your capable hands." Winston motioned to the four intelligence professionals.

"Our apologies, Prime Minister. Of course, you can," answered Menzies.

"One item I would like to hear and Colonel Donovan may benefit is the status of our search for Lord Haw Haw."

Harker gave Donovan the abridged version of the counterintelligence work of MI5. "We have confirmed Joyce's escape. He is currently ensconced in Germany under the watchful eye of Heydrich himself. We suspect Heydrich and that pint-size, pipsqueak Goebbels will find a way to use the wayward traitor in their propaganda schemes. I'm afraid we have not heard the last of Lord Haw Haw. And, I'm terribly sorry we could not capture him when he was in hand."

"He will one day face his reckoning," said Churchill.

"I am familiar with Joyce's activities in the pre-war years," Donovan said. "I am sorry to say we have many more like him in the United States. J. Edgar Hoover and his FBI have been keeping a close eye on our wayward sons as well. Thank you for the update."

Winston considered a short discussion about Joseph Kennedy but decided to postpone that topic until another time. "With the introductions complete, I pray you will use Colonel Donovan's time to the utmost. It is truly an honor and a pleasure to make your acquaintance, finally, Colonel Donovan, or should I say, 'Big Bill.'"

"Likewise, sir."

"Stewart, if you and 'Jumper' would ensure the other topics are covered to Colonel Donovan's satisfaction. Let us take this opportunity to solidify the Allied intelligence community and enhance our ability to vanquish the enemy."

"Certainly," answered Bill Stephenson.

"Yes, sir," Admiral Pike responded while Colonel Menzies nodded his head in agreement.

"Excellent, then, are we adjourned for this evening, or should I say for this morning?" Churchill chuckled looking at the wall clock showing a quarter past one o'clock in the morning.

The appropriate salutations completed the late night meeting. As the four men departed No.10 Downing Street, Winston Churchill turned to his administrative task of dictating his notes, thoughts, directives and suggestions to the several stenographers waiting, as usual, for him to start. Nearly every night of his professional life, Winston tended to the recording and documentation of events surrounding him as well as the leadership of the National Coalition Government. This night would end as so many did in the near dawn hours.

—

Chapter 14

They live ill who expect to live always.

-- Pubilius Syrus

Wednesday, 17.July.1940
RAF Middle Wallop
Middle Wallop, Hampshire, England

"**M**akes you wonder if God has started the second flood," joked Pilot Officer Brian Drummond. The heavy blanket of the rain added to the slow, lethargic mood of the pilots. They knew they would not fly in the current inclement weather, but unless they were lucky again as they were yesterday, they would remain on duty, just in case.

"Maybe Group will let us go early," said Flying Officer Foxworth.

"So far . . . knock wood," Miles Johnson interjected, "this week has been the exact opposite of last week. Here it is, the middle of the week, and this is the third rain day."

"Second."

"OK. Two and a half."

They all laughed and joked about the strange but vital struggle with time. They also knew each minute of peace was precious and most probably the quiet before the storm. The passing minutes without the pressure of the alert became like a glorious sunset, or an exquisitely prepared, succulent meal, or the bursting fragrance of a blooming rose garden on a calm spring day – a moment to be cherished.

The telephone rang with its instant physiological and mental reactions. Brian looked outside. It was still raining rather heavily, and the mound was not visible. They could not launch the fighters, which meant they were perhaps going to release them. Squadron Leader Darling listened for the longest time to the one-sided conversation nodding his head numerous times.

"Well, gentlemen," Darling began, "we are released." General applause, cheers and announcements of entertainment intentions punctuated the squadron leader's words. "However, we are not going anywhere." Then, groans and curses. "The Group Commander intends to visit our little paradise."

"How long do we have to wait for this, Skipper?" asked John Davies.

"A few hours. He wants to meet each of the squadrons before lunch, and then sit down to sup with us. The visit should be complete by early afternoon." More groans. "By the way, Weather predicts rain through tonight."

"All of my efforts will be indoors," chuckled Robert Morrow. Others joined in with their agreement. Brian thought of Rosemary and wished he was in London, or even Oxford, with her. Jonathan could only shake his head probably thinking the same thing.

Squadron Leader Darling told them to straighten things up including their uniforms. A couple of pilots decided to change their uniforms. Brian and Jonathan were among those who put on fresh uniforms this morning. None of the pilots seemed to be the slightest concerned about the visit of their commander, a senior officer in the RAF. He was just another bloke with more dark blue stripes on his tunic sleeves.

Word came to them when he arrived. They would be the last unit he would visit. He started with Sector Control in their bunkered building at the North end of the facility. Not quite two hours passed before Air Vice-Marshal Sir Quintin Brand, Air Officer Commanding-in-Chief, No.10 Group, walked through the rain toward the No.609 Squadron Dispersal building.

Squadron Leader Darling introduced the pilots and officers of the squadron to their commander. As a decorated and accomplished Great War fighter pilot, Brand commanded their respect. Except for his uniform, Sir Quintin's quiet personal manner, unassuming attitude, and dark hair, mustache, round face and modest frame made him seem like a visiting father checking on his son.

They listened and talked with their group commander as fellow pilots. He wanted to know how operations were going from their perspective, what they needed to perform their mission better, what they thought could be improved on their aircraft. He shared his views of the military situation although Brian felt certain the senior officer withheld some of the more bleak information – information that would only serve to distract or weaken the young fighter pilots.

The flying officer who had been taking notes of the comments touched his commander's left elbow. Brand nodded. "I am afraid the clock continues to tick," Sir Quintin said. "I thank you for taking the time to talk with me. I hope I shall see you at Mess."

"Thank you, sir," the pilots said virtually in unison. He nodded his acknowledgment.

"Good luck, lads, and good hunting." Several pilots joked about having the Germans precisely where they wanted them – in their sights. "Mister Drummond, may I have a word with you." Brian expected jeers from his comrades but the room remained quiet.

Brand looked first to the squadron leader's office, and then looked outside. The rain stopped although the roof still dripped. The senior officer motioned to the exterior. Brian followed.

"My apologies for any embarrassment, but I am not certain when I may have another opportunity to talk with you." Brian nodded, unable to avoid the questions about the personal attention. "I hear from Group Captain Spencer, you had a rather famous flight instructor." Brian thought of Jeremy Morrison, probably his most notable RAF flight instructor. The curious expression humored Sir Quintin. "If my information is correct, your first flight instructor was, Malcolm Bainbridge." Brian nodded, trying to control the instant flood of emotions. "I knew him in France. I was in a sister squadron. He managed to get himself shot down near our aerodrome. My condolences for your loss. He was a good man."

Brian swallowed hard, struggling with his memories.

"I am terribly sorry, Brian. I know he must have been very special to you."

"He was, sir. He taught me to fly and inspired me to join the RAF." Brian felt his eyes well up.

Sir Quintin placed a fatherly hand on Brian's shoulder. "He was important to us, as well. I am certain he would be most proud of your commitment to our struggle and your performance. Three and a half victories are very respectable, especially when this battle has only just begun."

"Thank you, sir." Brian felt a flush of pride that such a senior officer would know about his performance.

"My very best to you, young man. We shall do our utmost to provide the best information and guidance to you and your fellow pilots. We will keep an eye on you, so try not to feel you are alone in this."

Pilot Officer Brian Drummond deeply appreciated the extra concern from the No.10 Group Commander. He knew he would do his part to win this conflict. Air Vice-Marshal Brand departed for at least one other stop before the RAF Middle Wallop officers ate lunch with him.

The luncheon with their commander filled every available space of the large dining room. He made a few general comments on his observations as well as words of encouragement. Most of the pilots felt their commander understood what they were doing and told them in broad terms what lay ahead. Brian had an inner respect for the senior officer. After lunch, Air Vice-Marshal Brand returned to No.10 Group Headquarters in Box, Wiltshire, and the pilots dispersed to enjoy another respite from combat.

—

Thursday, 18.July.1940
RAF Middle Wallop
Middle Wallop, Hampshire, England

No.609 Squadron had been overhead an eastbound convoy of some twenty vessels near Portland for 30 minutes. Control told them to expect an enemy raid although it was evident nothing had shown up on the RDF scopes, yet. The tail end of the large storm that affected the early part of the week left enough layers of scattered clouds to make the target acquisition and general search process more difficult.

Pilot Officer Brian Drummond still marveled about the sensation of power he felt looking out the tight confines of his cockpit with nine other Vickers Supermarine Spitfire Mark IA fighters gathered around him. The brown leather helmets, oxygen masks and goggles made all the heads he could see appear menacing and formidable. They were still missing two replacement pilots. The aircraft arrived ahead of the pilots. The new guys might even be waiting for them when they returned.

"Sorbo Leader, this is Bandy calling."

"Bandy, this is Sorbo Leader, go ahead."

"Sorbo Leader, we have possible bandits, twenty plus, angels one five. Take vector one five five, angels one eight."

"Understood, Bandy."

Squadron Leader Darling turned the flight to the proper heading and started a slow descent from their patrol altitude. Brian rechecked his cockpit – ready for action. The Merlin continued to purr in the nose of his fighter. Darling kept their speed down to an easy 280 miles per hour as they moved to their projected intercept point. The clouds remained a problem although they continued to thin.

"Tally-ho," Darling broadcast. "We have a gaggle of Stukas with an equal number of One Oh Nines. 'Sparky,' you take 'B' Flight on the Stukas. 'A' Flight, we have the fighters." Brian's headset was silent as the controllers would listen for now while the fighters did what they were designed to do. "Here we go, lads. Let's have at them."

Two separate streams of Spitfires dove on the Germans. Ten against what looked like 20 Ju87 dive-bombers and 20 Bf109 fighters. Not bad odds, Brian said to himself as he rechecked everything ready for the fight.

In an instant, the sky was alive with words of attention, warning and happenings. Guns could be heard over the radio as the two groups of orderly aircraft fell into total disorder churning to obtain the advantage of position and energy.

Brian worked hard to keep track of what was happening around him. Fleeting targets crossed his sights, several within range, and Brian squeezed off the proper number of machine gun bursts. The broadcast words between them seemed to be more dense and intense than most of the previous engagements. Everyone seemed to have fighters engaged. Maybe there had been another group of German fighters waiting for the RAF pilots to commit to an engagement.

Each shot Brian took brought a concomitant requirement for immediate action to deal with a bandit bearing down on him. German fighters were everywhere. The urge to extricate himself from the growing intensity of the furball bloomed rapidly. He quickly looked for a cloud to help him reinitialize the fight – a good one was not close enough. Carefully, Brian worked his way toward the coalesced mass of several clouds maneuvering aggressively against potential antagonists. Many minutes and a few close calls passed when he finally entered the cloud.

Every fraction of his concentration funneled into his instruments as he fought against the usual vertigo climbing at maximum performance. The wings rocked and the nose jumped perilously near stall. Brian began to question the wisdom of his decision when he popped out of the cloud with the nose nearly twenty degrees above the horizon.

Brian instinctively pushed the spade forward to lower the nose. The engine choked. "Shit!" he shouted as he pulled back gently on the stick. He needed more airspeed. The absence of the comforting purr of the Merlin gave Brian a most immediate problem. He pulled the stick to the right stop.

The right wing of the Spitfire dropped pulling the nose down as well. As the long nose, dropped below the horizon, airspeed began to build and positive g returned. The windmilling propeller kept the engine turning over. As soon as the carburetor float dropped, fuel flow returned, and the engine roared back to life.

The Spitfire jumped like an angry tiger. Reorientation took only an instant. Brian found the furball, and quickly assessed where the gray and black camouflaged, brutish looking fighters were. Like a hungry lone wolf, Brian picked his prey and descended on his target from out of the Sun. The PR-F Spitfire closed smoothly on the rabbit. Brian pushed the red button on his control spade. The exciting eruption disintegrated the German aircraft. The ensuing fireball directly in front of him dramatically altered the fuel-air ratio, again choking the fire from the engine. Loud bangs registered the shrapnel impacts on his aircraft. Once clear of his latest victim, he promptly got the engine relit, and then evaluated the integrity of his fighter. Everything OK.

Fighters. His buddies would be trying to avenge the loss of one of theirs. Sure enough. A white nose, Bf109 was turning hard well behind him. Brian pushed harder on the throttle already against the maximum stop, rolled sharply and pulled back hard turning into this potential attacker. He denied any shot. The two fighters passed canopy to canopy at very close range. Brian rolled to wings level and pulled the nose straight up into an Immelmann turn as he had done so many times over the Great Plains of Kansas. Rolling the aircraft to point the left wing at the water below him, Brian searched first for any potential attacker then for a target.

A little voice told him to look to the lower right corner of his instrument panel. Eleven gallons of fuel. He rolled out of his turn heading north. He would have enough fuel to make it back to RAF Middle Wallop.

"Sorbo Green Leader, Sorbo Green Three." He waited for a few moments and started to press the transmit button again.

"'Hunter,' this is 'Jackstay.' We are to refuel and rearm at our alternate for a rapid turn about."

"Thanks, 'Jackstay.'"

Brian altered his heading to the west, pulled the throttle back, and started his high-speed descent toward RAF Warmwell. He spotted several other Spitfires to his right. The large white PR letters told him it was his squadron. A flight of three led by PR-H – 'Waggle' Davies and Yellow Section. Then, he saw the PR-D Spitfire that he moved toward and joined up on the left wing of 'Jackstay' Beamish. He saw Roger look over his shoulder and nod his acknowledgment of Brian's position.

Landing at RAF Warmwell was uneventful. They taxied past the VK Hurricanes of No.238 Squadron. The ground crews of their sister squadron leapt into action refueling and rearming the Spitfires. Brian unplugged his communications cords and his oxygen connection. He walked around his aircraft to evaluate the damage to his machine. Several ugly, jagged holes marred the underside of his wing and fuselage. The leading aircraftman assigned to him promptly evaluated the holes judging them insignificant, and said he would bend in the curled edges and put an adhesive patch over the holes.

Darling gathered the pilots. There were only eight. Whom did we lose, Brian asked himself quickly scanning the seven faces. 'Harness' and 'Organ.'

Pilot Officer Brian Drummond could not ignore the shaking in his legs. He found 'Sparky' Morrow asking the question without words. The 'B' Flight, Red Section leader held up his hand.

"'Harness' was under the silk. He waved so he was OK. I saw the rescue boats, but had to deal with those pesky Germans."

"I don't think 'Organ' made it," said 'Waggle' Davies solemnly. "He was shot up, on fire, and then exploded."

Eight heads hung low with no words as each pilot dealt with his own thoughts.

"We are in a nasty business, lads. Shake it off. Control wants us back up as soon as we are reloaded. Does anyone have damage that might keep them down?"

"I took some shrapnel, Skipper," Brian answered, "but my crew chief says it will fly."

"I took some hits as well," added 'Sparky' Morrow.

Several others had hits although no one thought the damage would keep them out of the sky. Darling looked toward the row of Spitfires triggering a cascade of turning faces and attentive eyes.

"Looks like the crews are nearly complete. Let's mount up and get back in the fight." The group started to break up. "Remember," shouted Darling, "find a target and shoot the bastard down. Don't look back. Don't follow your target."

Squadron Leader Darling waited until he saw eight crewmen in front of the Spitfires indicating readiness to start. He raised his right arm and scribed a circle in the air. The groan of the electric starters filled the air followed promptly by the resonant rumble of the Merlin engines firing off. Only the time needed to allow the coolant and oil temperatures to return to the normal range kept the eight from jumping back into the air.

As the ground dropped away, the radio chatter returned. It took several minutes listening to the calls of direction, desperation, anger, frustration, success and failure to ascertain they were en route to join No.64 Squadron. Finding the aerial contest did not take much effort. Brian began the mental process of tracking the gray fighters among the outnumbered green and brown machines.

They positioned themselves to reengage the intruders. The German leader must have seen the approaching squadron of Spitfires and matched that information with his dwindling fuel and ammunition, and changing odds. They all dove virtually simultaneously toward the south. The Spitfires gave chase. The nearly empty Bf109 fighters had the speed advantage to make a successful escape.

Sorbo took the protective position allowing the Freema Spitfires to return with their fuel levels fairly low. The return to RAF Middle Wallop brought welcome relief from the tension of combat. Brian pointed out the temporary repairs on the PR-F Spitfire. More permanent repairs began before Brian reached Dispersal.

Pilot Officer Jonathan Kensington waited at the door. "What took you so long?" he said.

"What happened?"

"I thought I would try your return mode." Jonathan laughed.

Brian did not. "Very funny.

"I just finished off a German when his wingman got me. Stopped the engine, and I could not make it to land, so I went for a summer swim."

"Did they pick you up right away?"

"I was in the water maybe 20 minutes – long enough to get cold."

"Any injuries?"

"None other than my pride."

"I guess that's part of the job."

The debriefing took much longer than most of the previous events. The Germans demonstrated more tenacity than previous engagements. Davies received credit for one Ju87 before the dive-bombers retreated and the escorting fighters remained to fight a protracted, pitched battle over the English Channel near Portland. The tally finished at one Ju87 and four Bf109s downed with several damaged versus two Spitfires lost including one pilot. Jonathan was credited with one Bf109, and Brian with another German fighter.

None of the projected replacement pilots arrived as they mourned the loss of Flying Officer Reginald 'Organ' Foxworth. The traditional toast to their fallen comrade brought the usual solemnity. Realization that they had numerous women to inform of their loss presented a daunting but modestly humorous task. They remembered him as a good pilot and devoted womanizer.

Jonathan's replacement aircraft would be properly painted and ready for tomorrow's operations. They were back down to nine pilots. No one wanted to think about the future. They could only think about the moment.

—

Friday, 19.July.1940
RAF Middle Wallop
Middle Wallop, Hampshire, England

Two long patrols and the gunport patches had not been broken. Between missions, Pilot Officer Brian Drummond and the other pilots of No.609 Squadron heard about some action over yesterday's convoy, now in the Dover Straight. They did not like monotonous, inconsequential patrols, but they were thankful for the interlude. They could only get just over half the squadron airborne. The losses of the last few weeks substantially weakened the squadron although none of them complained. The pilots joked about the Sector controller thinking they were launching an entire squadron when it was only half, and the engagement odds becoming less reasonable with fewer RAF fighters and more *Luftwaffe* guns.

"When are we to receive our replacement pilots, Skipper?" asked Pilot Officer Roland 'Boxer' Stockard.

"Two days ago." The flippant answer added to the laughter.

"Right, I think I did see the blokes wandering around Number Two Hangar and Six Oh Four Squadron," added Roger Beamish to more laughter.

"We need a night of drunken debauchery," shouted 'Waggle' Davies, causing a crimson blush in the otherwise stoic Corporal Jennifer Warren.

"No difference for you," responded Morrow.

"I am trying to be serious."

"Certainly you are."

"You degenerates might like to know the name of our convoy in the Western approaches," Darling offered.

"By all means."

"Convoy BOSOM."

"And, an ample bosom at that," said Davies.

"Where on Earth do they dream up these names?" asked Flying Sergeant Miles 'Fog' Johnson.

The telephone rang. "Here we go again," someone muttered. The speaker was right. They launched again, this time with ten SD Hurricanes of No.501 Squadron. The Hurricanes were directed against an equal number of Ju87 dive-bombers while the nine operable Spitfires of No. 609 went after twice as many Bf110 fighters.

The Germans, on this day, did not demonstrate any enthusiasm for the fight. The dive-bombers dropped their loads into the open sea, turned and ran as fast as they could. The twin-engine fighters occupied the British long enough to enable the escape of their flock, and then they ran as well. Several pilots managed to break their gunport tapes although none of the belligerents appeared to be hit – another engagement without consequence.

"Three sorties in one day," said 'Jackstay' Beamish. "Business appears to be picking up."

"We launched, Roger, but we did not accomplish anything," answered 'Sparky' Morrow.

"Right, we launch with half as many aircraft, therefore we must fly twice as much, or fight twice as many Gerries," added 'Waggle' Davies. His remark touched off the deluge of laughter, jokes, jabs, although the humor took on a noticeably darker tone.

Headquarters, No.10 Group, waited another hour after their debriefing to release No.609 Squadron from alert duty. It was mid-afternoon, leaving four hours of daylight. They still did not have any replacement pilots. Maybe Group felt sorry for their plight, and decided to give them a few extra hours off duty. Whatever the reason for the early release, the pilots did not complain.

"I have several pieces of leadership information," said Darling, "I know you will be interested to know, it was announced this afternoon General Sir Alan Brooke will become General Officer Commanding, Home Forces, replacing General Sir Edmund Ironside who is retiring."

"Must be nice taking to the garden in the middle of a bloody war," Morrow responded.

"You may recall General Sir John Dill replaced Sir Edmund two months ago as Chief Imperial General Staff," Darling continued. "It seem General Ironside was not in favor."

"Brutal at the top," added Maxwell.

"Thought you ought to know."

"What say we all trundle up to the Mucky Ducky," suggested 'Waggle' Davies.

"Smashing idea. The bird hunting seems to be particularly bountiful in Andover these days," said 'Boxer' Stockard.

"Right, then, might I suggest we take our sustenance at Mess. That should allow enough time for an ample bevy of beautisimus dolly-birds to gather for our picking."

The cheers acknowledged Davies' exposition. Without words, Brian knew they needed a squadron night away from the war. Both Brian and Jonathan recognized this had to be a boy's night out. While normal people in normal times would have the next two days of a weekend off work, they would face another day of aerial combat.

Flight Lieutenant Roger Beamish took what was left of his 48-hour pass. Squadron Leader Darling begged off as the only married officer among them having his companionship predetermined. The seven remaining pilots found two automobiles and headed up the A343 carriageway toward the village of Andover.

The Black Swan pub was the largest and appeared to be the most prosperous community establishment in the village. The station house, so the locals said, dated back several centuries, and possessed a colorful ribald history that many wanted to ensure continued into the future. The proprietor served a wide variety of liquor and beer as well as a respectable range of sandwiches, potpies, soups and traditional dishes. An old Victrola provided the music when dancing was desired although occasionally a small band and an adequate singer provided live entertainment. The half dozen available rooms for hire gave the public house even more attraction.

The doors and windows were open to the fresh summer air. Enjoyment could be heard well before the small band of fighter pilots entered the pub.

"This is going to be a good night," said Miles Johnson.

"You ought to wait outside for an hour to give the rest of us a head start," jabbed John Davies. Johnson's section leader usually led the pack in a chorus of indirect references to his striking, Nordic good looks, boyish mannerisms and magnetic success in attracting the attentions of the best looking women in the vicinity. Only Brian Drummond and Reggie Foxworth rivaled Miles in his demonstrated desirability to the female gender, but Reggie was no longer with them. His loss yesterday and the clarity of Brian's memory of him took a good portion of the fire from his engine.

The pilots were welcomed as conquering heroes. The stories and mythology surrounding the aerial contest over the Channel began to spread and grow among the populace. Patrons of all ages asked questions, made comments and added to the mystique of these intrepid aviators. The beer began to flow freely allowing the pilots to forget the trials, losses and close calls of the last few weeks. The words were strong and taunting toward the Germans and specifically the leadership of Germany and more pointedly, the *Luftwaffe*.

Men still outnumbered women and most of those were older, attached women. At a lull in the festivities, Hank Maxwell worked his way toward Brian and Jonathan. His smile flushed like a toilet from his face.

"Why didn't you tell me you were an American when I joined?" he challenged.

Brian looked at Jonathan, who stayed neutral, and then back to Maxwell. "Because while I'm in Fighter Command, I want to be British."

"Are you embarrassed to be American?"

"I'm proud to be an American, but America is not in this fight, and I need to be British."

"How old are you anyway?"

"Nineteen."

"You're just a kid. What the hell are you doin' here?"

"He is killing Germans," Jonathan interjected, trying to establish some distance between the two Americans. "And, doing quite well at it, I might add."

"You shouldn't forget where you come from, boy."

"I won't, Hank, but I would suggest you should start thinking British."

"Ah, screw you," he said and turned away.

"He must have a nettle up his bum," said Jonathan. They laughed. "We do think of you as British, Brian, and we are glad to have you."

"Thanks."

Brian and Jonathan danced and flirted with several young women enjoying the conversation, but neither aviator could shake off the losses of the last two weeks and their relationships. They considered several times walking to the railway station for a quick journey to the women they loved, but gave up the notion in favor of staying close to their comrades. True to form, Miles Johnson ascended the stairs with a reasonably attractive woman quite a few years older than him. They smiled, toasted their brethren and drank another beer.

A minor commotion started at the far end of the bar near the entrance door. They observed the growing clump of people. 'Sparky' Morrow's face and left arm waved them closer. The unattached and now wobbling remaining pilots of No.609 Squadron gathered around Morrow.

"The gentleman here," 'Sparky' began, pointing over the intervening people to an elderly man in the center of the group, "heard the broadcast of an unofficial, but apparently popular response to Hitler's so called, 'peace offering.' It seems Sefton Delmer . . . you may recall the correspondent with the *Daily Express* . . . flung a rather banal insult back at him . . . something about hurling it right back into his evil-smelling teeth, or some such."

"That's it," said 'Waggle' Davies, "this has been far too easy so far. Let's see if we can make the bastard really angry and make this a real contest."

"What are we to do, John, break out the white flags and surrender to the bloody Gerries?"

"The friggin' bloody bastards are probably going to invade anyway. The elder gentleman also heard a subsequent bit of news on the BBC at the top of the hour . . . Hitler made a speech at the Berlin Opera House along the lines of, he could not allow the British to threaten the peaceful German nation, and he had no choice but to prepare for the invasion of Great Britain."

"The demented, sodding corporal must think he is trying to save us from Churchill, or ourselves, for God's sake," said Roland Stockard.

Hank Maxwell appeared to lose color as he listened to the bravado. Brian wondered if his strident words and his first few combat missions made him return to the question of the wisdom of his actions. The evening soon tipped over the edge. This would be a drink night as opposed to a woman night. Several of the dolly-birds would go home alone without the male companionship they sought. None of the No.609 Squadron pilots were coherent when they arrived at the RAF Middle Wallop Officer's Mess after depositing Miles Johnson at the Sergeant's Mess in the wee hours of the morning.

—

Saturday, 20.July.1940
RAF Middle Wallop
Middle Wallop, Hampshire, England
14:00 hours

Many of the pilots including Pilot Officer Brian Drummond thanked the Germans for focusing their attention to the east on Convoy BOSOM, now in the vicinity of Dover. The Squadron stood at exactly half strength with Flight Lieutenant Roger Beamish on his well-deserved two-day break from the fighting. As they picked up fragments of the nearly continuous action in the Dover Straight, at least two of the pilots, Stockard and Maxwell, continued to vomit as their bodies tried to rid themselves of the excess alcohol. None of them felt ready to fly and fortunately they stayed at Available status through the lunch hour.

"Dear God, what possessed us to do this to ourselves?" Jonathan said. He looked a little piqued like Brian felt.

Brian was not particularly certain he would be able to hold down his lunch. Hank Maxwell did not as he got up far more quickly than he sat down and ran around the far end of the Dispersal building. The reduced physical state explained the nearly unconscious, semi-recumbent condition of the pilots. Squadron Leader Darling knew without asking what had happened to his pilots and chose to let nature leach out the residual poison.

"When is all this madness going to end?" asked 'Boxer' Stockard as he lay flat on the ground with his eyes closed.

"Sooner or later," said 'Sparky' Morrow in nearly the same position.

The telephone rang sending Maxwell around the corner again.

"We are up to Readiness," announced Darling.

"What is out there, Skip?"

"Another convoy entering the Channel. This one is named, PEEWIT."

Several of the pilots chuckled showing the first signs of recovery. "PEEWIT. That is a hell of a frigging name. What is happening with BOSOM?"

"Control indicated One One Group is having a fairly successful day. They managed to trap the Ju87s to keep them from escaping and are chewing them up – less fighters than we have seen."

"They get all the luck."

"How many in this PEEWIT?" asked Morrow.

"Control says about thirty or so."

"Now, that will be a ripe tomato for the picking. Gerry won't be able to pass on this PEEWIT group," said 'Waggle' Davies.

The telephone rang again, causing Maxwell to sit up straight although he managed to hold his nausea. They all had to feel nauseous although most fought the indications.

"We are up to Standby," said Darling. "Let's gather up our kit and mount up. 'Hunter,' you will be with 'Sparky' and Red Section."

Brian and the others did as they were told. As he walked to the aircraft, Brian scanned the southern sky. Broken clouds kept him from seeing a clear view. Bernie Gordon had the PR-F fighter ready. She was fully armed and fueled with all items checked and double-checked. He would be flying with Morrow and Kensington. There would be no Green Section for this mission and Yellow Section was still short one pilot.

The launch command did not take long coming. Brian had just finished strapping into his Spitfire. They headed southwest toward Lyme Bay, west of the Portland promontory. Control provided no indication the half squadron would have any assistance from a sister squadron. Trails of dark smoke like a thin set of stalks rose into the sky to the east. Other squadrons were busy as well.

The ships of Convoy PEEWIT were easier to find than their attackers as they churned up the sea in zigzag patterns. The occasional expanding circles of foam meant bombs. The tally-ho call brought Brian's attention to a new sight. A group of Messerschmitt twin-engine, Bf110 fighters were dropping bombs on the ships, fortunately without much apparent effectiveness. As the Spitfires dove on the aggressors, Brian along with his comrades scanned the sky for the single seat fighters they suspected of lurking about. None could be found.

The remaining German fighter-bombers dropped their bombs indiscriminately to lighten their load and face the British defenders. The characteristic tactic of Göring's prize Destroyer fighters was to form a defensive circle to enable the rear seat gunners to inter-lace their machine gun fire for mutual protection.

The eight Spitfires enveloped the ten German fighter-bombers as they slashed, darted, dove and fired on the strange circle of aircraft. It reminded Brian of the pioneers circling the wagons in the Old West against a marauding band of Pawnee warriors. He wondered if the Germans took the idea from the American West.

Brian managed to achieve a few hits on the Germans although he did not produce a victory. Several other pilots accomplished the same thing, but the engagement concluded with the Germans making an escape break, diving toward the water for a dash to the French coast.

The return to RAF Middle Wallop was silent, peaceful and uneventful. Brian felt no satisfaction although they had accomplished their mission. None of the Convoy PEEWIT shipping had been hit or damaged.

Squadron Leader Darling waited until the debriefing was completely finished before he gave a stern but positive admonition to his pilots. They did not appear to possess the same level of aggressiveness and enthusiasm they had displayed so many times before. If they were going to drink and carouse, they had damn well better perform, or there would be no opportunities for pleasurable diversions. The message got through.

"He's right," Brian whispered to Jonathan.

"Of course, he is right. We have dealt with those Destroyer circles more effectively many times before."

Brian remembered the previous night as well as other nights before. "Why does everyone want to drink so much?"

Jonathan rose from his chair to lead Brian in a casual stroll toward the aircraft. "Brian, how do you deal with your fear?"

"I concentrate on what I am doing and try to ignore the danger."

"Well put, my friend, but you have been shot down twice and nearly shot down more times than that. You must feel fear when you find a One Oh Nine slicing into your tail, and you can't seem to shake him. You must feel fear."

"I feel fear at night when I think about what happened, but at the moment, all I feel is the bird and making her do what I need."

Jonathan twisted in frustration with his friend. "Maybe you are different, but most of the rest of us feel that into-the-bones, tear-your-innards-out, cold sweat fear and want to erase it. Alcohol is an easy means to eradicate the nausea that stays with you. That is why some of us drink too much."

Brian absorbed the images Jonathan created. They had talked about fear before but never in such graphic and intimate terms. "Do you feel that kind of fear?"

"Yes. Yes, I do, but I try to ignore it like you. I thought I was going to die when my engine was shot out Thursday. I nearly shit my knickers."

Brian placed an arm around Jonathan's shoulders and squeezed. He knew he had never felt that kind of deep fear, but he had his own demons. He remembered the flash of the Seaver's dog, the instant numbing chill of inevitability, and cartwheeling Malcolm's Stearman. Brian also remembered

Malcolm's words like an angel talking to his subconscious mind. Fear served no purpose beyond focusing one's concentration like a powerful lens. Only skill, instinct and action could deal with adversity.

"I am sorry, Jonathan."

"No need to be sorry. I simply wanted to answer your question. At the end of the day, it is simply coping . . . coping with your fear."

"But, like today, it dulls the edge."

"Brian, getting pissed is the only thing that keeps the sword from breaking for some people."

The young American knew his friend was precisely correct. He had seen it in others like Jeremy Morrison after the Battle of Barking Creek. "Maybe."

"It is more than maybe; it is the way things are, I'm afraid."

The stories of Malcolm Bainbridge painted a clear picture in Brian's mind. The way Malcolm described the pallor of death in the trenches and skies of France during the War to End All Wars came to him. His mentor dealt with it in the same way he had been taught. Concentrate. Focus. Never give in to the emotions, especially fear. Never, ever, panic. Control. Control your emotions, control your aircraft, control the situation. It was always the same.

The conversation was too dark. Brian thought about a proper diversion. "Do you want to make a run into London?"

Jonathan laughed which made Brian brighten as well. "Excellent stroke," Jonathan said, slapping Brian on the back. "Too morose, so you change the subject. London, ay. We would spend most of our few precious night hours on the train."

"Yeah, but we could have some fun. It would be worth it."

"I am afraid, once again, my friend, Linda and I do not share the same bawdy basis as you and Anne." This time Brian's levity instantly disappeared. Jonathan noticed the change. "What is the matter?   Something happen between you and Anne?"

Brian knew this was the time to confide in his friend. After all, he had already told the story to Jonathan's sister. Brian looked around to ensure no one else was listening. "In a manner of speaking."

"What?"

Brian told Jonathan the complete story from his interrogation by Inspector Dunwoody to his conversation with Jeremy Morrison. He did not tell Jonathan about the two nights with his sister. Jonathan felt bad for his friend, but good that nothing was apparently going to happen to Brian.

"This is probably for the better, anyway," Jonathan said.

"How so?"

Jonathan stopped to face his friend. The broad smile and twinkle in his eyes broadcast his mood. "Sometimes, you and Anne reminded me of two dogs in season. Have you seen it?"

Brian remembered the farm scenes and more than just dogs. "We weren't that bad," he protested without objection.

"You bloody well were," he said, moving his hands and hips in perfect imitation. "Like two bloody, fucking dogs, I'd say." They both laughed hard and looked around to see who might be watching. Fortunately, they saw no one. "Enough of this tawdry behavior. At any rate, no, I don't think we should make a run, as you call it, into London."

"No guts, no glory." They laughed again, harder and more uncontrollably.

"Are you trying to build your reputation as a swordsman or a steely eyed, hunter, fighter pilot?" They laughed some more. "Besides, Group will probably keep us on alert until dusk, and you know we will be back out here at dawn. Furthermore, the summer months don't give us much nighttime, so no London, at least not tonight."

"All right, you can be the stick in the mud."

"Right you are, my friend. I will be the stick in the mud. We will eat our supper, have a beer with the lads in the bar and call it an early night. I am still trying to recover from last night's foray."

"As you say, then," said Brian, as he returned to Dispersal.

True to Jonathan's prediction, they remained on alert through a brief, late afternoon shower. Only Miles Johnson did not share Jonathan's plan for the night. The young flying sergeant headed back up to Andover in his continuing search for heavenly delights.

—

Saturday, 20.July.1940
Cabinet Room
No.10 Downing Street
Whitehall, London, England
16:30 hours

"We have good news from the States I thought important enough to share with you this Saturday afternoon," Prime Minister Churchill told the War Cabinet, less Neville Chamberlain, who was becoming progressively more ill. Only the four ministers plus Sir Edward Bridges made it to the unscheduled meeting. "We received confirmation from Lord Lothian," Winston continued, as Lord Halifax nodded his concurrence, "that President Roosevelt signed into law a major new naval rearmament bill yesterday."

"A bit late to the game," Attlee interjected.

"Quite so, yet, I am certain we can all agree, better late than never. I know the President and his supporters have been campaigning hard for the new authorization. To our capacity, this new law is virtually an unbounded expansion, and it is one more clue the Americans are coming around to the reality they will be in this fight soon enough.

"Another piece of excellent news, the President broadcast over radio his acceptance of the Democratic Party nomination as their candidate for the Fall election. Roosevelt knows the score. He is navigating shoals of a forbidding coastline. He is the best friend we have in a treacherous world with few friends still standing. I sent a quick supportive telegram after listening to his acceptance speech early this morning."

"Do you really think the Americans will come around, Winston?" Clement asked.

"Based on what the President has accomplished so far in a hostile, isolationist arena, I think he will be successful in turning American opinion to help us fight this war. The new naval rearmament law should relieve some of the pressure on the President."

"We need their men, not just their guns and ships," Greenwood added.

"Quite so, I am afraid, which is all the more reason we must ensure Donovan collects up all the evidence he can absorb to help the President. He has already met with the intelligence chiefs, including Sir Phillip at Scotland Yard. So far, the visit is going quite well, despite our dire predicament. Hugh Dalton goes live with the new SOE on Monday, and he has met with Donovan at least once already, and he expects further discussions."

"A bit premature, don't you think?" asked Arthur Greenwood.

"I think not. Hugh has a good handle on our vision for the unconventional warfare business. I think Donovan sees the very real need for a similar organization. Pike and Menzies have been impressed with his grasp of the strategic intelligence task as well as the need for a master intelligence apparatus in Washington. If he is successful with just part of these necessary changes, it will be most helpful to our cause. With less than four months to their elections, I cannot imagine Franklin being able to take such a drastic reorganization. However, we can help him prepare the ground by educating Donovan with everything we have to offer. Unfortunately, the risk is it might all be for naught if Roosevelt is not re-elected." Churchill looked to Lord

Halifax. "Ed, what is Lord Lothian's assessment regarding the likelihood of Roosevelt's re-election?" he asked, using the viscount's given name.

"Based on our discussions to date, the President appears to be on firm ground. Philip hears a lot of 'don't change horses' reasoning, which would be supportive of the President's re-election. However, the real concern is Congress. The isolationists hold significant numbers of supporters in both parties, actually. If they were to gain more seats, they could make any moves by the President rather moot. President Roosevelt pulled off a masterful political jump with his appointment of Frank Knox and Henry Stimson, both staunch and influential Republicans, I must add. Philip is continuing his efforts to refine his election assessment, but realistically we will not get a good view until after the respective party conventions and active campaign season begins in September."

"I know I do not need to say it, but please convey to Lord Lothian the need for his utmost attention on the election prospects."

"Indeed, no need to say it, but I will certainly ensure he appreciates the importance."

"Could we use the technical exchange program you have been considering to indirectly support Roosevelt?" asked Attlee.

"How so?"

"Leave the impression we are giving up our most secret technical equipment, projects and developmental work as a measure of our trust in him as the American president."

"Interesting proposal, Clement. You might well have something there. Why don't you explore the potential with Lothian to see how we could use the exchange program to ancillary advantage? You might discuss this with Bill Stephenson. The family of Bill's wife, Mary, are quite influential and attuned, so he may have complementary advice as well."

Churchill thought for a moment, and then decided to move on. "I wish to report to the War Cabinet, I have had numerous discussions with Hugh Dalton on the new SOE organization. He has a good grasp on his structure and already laid the groundwork for recruitment. He is tasked with taking offensive action behind enemy lines to disrupt their logistics, set ablaze their material and war-fighting capacity, stimulate resistance movements in the occupied countries, and in short, cause mayhem on the Continent and elsewhere."

"How will this play with 'C's collection and analysis efforts?" asked Lord Halifax.

"I see the processes as predominately exclusive – MI6 listens and watches, SOE will act. Occasional intersections may occur, but we must trust Menzies and Dalton to be coordinated and mutually supportive."

"I guess we must see how it goes. Perhaps I should discuss my concerns for interference with Hugh before he gets too far long."

"As you wish, Ed, but make it soon. Hugh is moving out smartly to get underway, and we need those disruption operations as the Germans prepare for their invasion." Lord Halifax nodded his agreement. Churchill looked to Bridges. "Sir Edward, would you be so kind to add the Donovan mission to the Cabinet agenda for tomorrow afternoon's meeting?"

"Yes, sir, by all means."

"Lastly," Churchill continued, "I must inform the War Cabinet . . . yesterday, Lieutenant General Sir Alan Brooke replaced General Ironside as Commander-in-Chief, Home Forces, effective immediately. Sir Edmund has agreed to retire. He will be promoted to field marshal, and the recommendation to raise him to a barony will be presented to the King for his New Year honors. We are grateful for his service."

Lieutenant General Sir Alan Francis Brooke, KCB, DSO & Bar, gained considerable reputation as the commanding general of II Corps during the Battle of France and the retrograde defense of Dunkirk during Operation DYNAMO. Churchill believed Brooke was more attuned to the demands of modern, combined arms, highly mobile, combat operations that the *Wehrmacht* demonstrated so expertly and well. General Brooke was certainly more current, having most recently faced the Germans.

"Was there some particular reason for such a sudden change at such a crucial time?" Attlee asked.

"We needed a younger, more vigorous man with a more progressive approach to our home defense preparations."

Clement Attlee stared at Churchill, and then only nodded his head in acceptance.

"Any other questions on the Brooke appointment?"

The ministers shook their heads in the negative.

"With that, unless there is any new business," Churchill said, and then looked to each minister to receive a negative gesture, "let us call it a day."

—

Chapter 15

The block of granite which is an obstacle
in the pathway of the weak,
becomes a stepping-stone
in the pathway of the strong.
-- Thomas Carlyle

Sunday, 21.July.1940
RAF Middle Wallop
Middle Wallop, Hampshire, England

Pilot Officers Brian Drummond and Jonathan Kensington walked slowly in the early morning light from the Mess through the orthogonal streets of the fighter base. The morning activity swirling around them demonstrated the normalcy of the day. There were no ways to tell this was a weekend day, the Lord's day. The business of national defense continued unabated.

"I think I could go back to bed and sleep for a week," Brian said.

"I agree."

"You know, I still feel less than bright and shiny."

"You are not alone," Jonathan responded. "We all could use a break."

They turned the corner of the Dispersal building.

"We are up to Readiness," said Flying Sergeant Miles 'Fog' Johnson, matter of factly, as the two friends approached.

John Davies came out of Dispersal.

"Oh great," Brian answered. "We can't even sit down, and they're putting us on alert."

"I knew something was missing," said Davies. "Group forgot to check with our man Drummond."

"I was just . . ."

Davies held up his right hand. "Ah, ah. No need to explain."

"Oh, gee, thanks, 'Waggle.'"

The telephone brought them to Standby. Brian retrieved his flying kit from his peg as the other pilots did. They checked their aircraft, joked with their ground crews, strapped themselves into their aircraft and prepared for combat. They did not have to wait long.

As the squadron climbed for altitude through the scattered clouds, Brian could not avoid the question of whether this was simply an interim step on an inextricable and inescapable descent into the abyss. Would their numbers continue to erode, as they were in other squadrons, until there were no fighter pilots left to defend the country? Every engagement so far for No.609 Squadron resulted in a better than parity outcome, but they were still half as strong as they were just three months ago. Was the outcome of this battle already determined? Brian shook off the thoughts as he rechecked his guns, camera, reflex sight and engine instruments. The fighter was ready.

Their target was easily located – a flight of about twenty Ju87 Stuka dive-bombers. Convoy PEEWIT was farther east than yesterday, but it was still the intended objective of the German intruders. Darling waited as they searched the sky above, behind and around the bombers looking for their fighter escort. The thickening and billowing clouds made the escort acquisition very difficult. They watched the first Stukas roll into their characteristic steep diving attacks. Darling knew they could not wait any longer.

"Let's go to work, lads. Keep your eyes out for the shooters."

The Spitfires dove on the determined German dive-bombers. As they closed rapidly with their targets, Brian saw the first explosion – a direct hit on one of the merchant ships. Other bombs fell – several misses and then another hit. Brian forced his attention over his shoulder. Still no fighters. He picked out his first target, checked the slip ball, near perfect alignment, centered up his sight reticle on the cockpit and waited for the correct moment. Flashes from the aft compartment told him the German gunner was firing at him. He squeezed the trigger.

Sparks, flashes and fragments of the German aircraft filled his wind-screen as he pulled up and rolled left. Brian scanned the sky above him. Only the angry hornets swarm of Spitfires enveloping the hapless German dive-bombers could be seen. Brian looked over his shoulder to see the black smoke trail streaming from his target, now spinning wildly toward the sea.

As Brian pulled his fighter through the topside of a lazy loop perching for his next attack, a bright flash of light above him and near a cloud caught his attention. He rolled completely back upright. Another flash. Canopy glint. It had to be German fighters.

Instinctively, Brian pushed harder on his throttle to get all the power the Merlin engine could give him. He maneuvered his fighter directly into the area of light flashes, and then he saw the dark, angled shapes.

"Fighters," Brian broadcast to alert his comrades. The sky seemed to fill with German fighters. Brian thought maybe twenty or more. His fighter strained in the high power climb as the closure rate became painfully obvious. "Twenty bandits above," he said.

"Bandy, this is Sorbo Leader calling. We could use some help," Darling broadcast.

"Sorbo, this is Bandy, help is on the way."

Brian lined up his sight reticle on the lead Bf109. He did not wait for the German to fill the range gap. He opened fire, felt the reassuring shudder of his guns firing, and then saw the flashes of the German guns. Brian passed through the diving Germans in an instant. No hits either way. He rolled his fighter through a half roll, and then pulled the nose down looking out the top of his canopy searching for a target. The sky was soon a ball of fighters twisting and turning.

Words of warning, direction and alert filled the spaces between the outnumbered Spitfires. Several Bf109s turned into Brian. They split taking away any easy firing sequence for Brian. "Clever little devils," Brian said into his oxygen mask. He picked the closest German, lined his sight up and fired as they passed again. He pulled hard turning into the second fighter, but could not get a shot off before they passed.

The nose of the Spitfire came up sharply as he tried to climb into his attackers. They, in turn, maneuvered expertly for their re-attack. One of the Germans shallowed his turn giving Brian just the angle he needed. He maneuvered his Spitfire for the intercept. The German must have lost sight of him. Brian looked quickly over his shoulder. The other German was too far away, but obviously recognized the situation. One of his compatriots must have broadcast a warning, or the unfortunate one saw the closing Spitfire. He jerked his aircraft sharply into a dive. Brian had the angle and adjusted his intercept. The German twitched and jinked trying to spoil Brian's shot. As he closed on his firing range, Brian looked for the other German . . . seven o'clock and still well out of range. He returned to his target, adjusted his slip for a good line up and fired a long burst. Numerous hits, but nothing conclusive. Brian passed his target and turned his attention to the other German. The nose of the PR-F Spitfire lined up on the other fighter. Brian held the trigger button down moving the gunsight reticle over his target. The two adversaries fired long bursts.

Brian heard several loud bangs before they passed. Several more loud bangs told him another fighter was engaging him. The fighter began to vibrate and shake. He jerked the stick back and right. He was still flying. The hits had not damaged anything vital. Brian scanned the sky below him, no immediate threats, and then turned over to check above, still no immediate threats.

He quickly checked his instruments. Coolant and oil temperatures still good. Oil pressure normal. The melodic purr of the Rolls-Royce Merlin III engine confirmed the instrument indications. The vibration remained steady, which meant his condition was not getting worse.

Brian found another target, but before he could close on his target, one of his comrades came to his rescue. He had to break off his attack and turn into his attacker. Good alignment. Brian pressed his trigger button. The long burst began and then stopped. All guns stopped. He was out of ammunition.

"Oh, great," Brian said aloud.

His best chance was straight ahead. More bangs on his aircraft. The Spitfire shuddered momentarily but kept flying as they passed.

"'Hunter's dry," he broadcast, as he climbed away from the fight.

No Germans followed him. As soon as he was clear of the fight, the Germans broke off the attack, probably low on fuel or ammunition, or both.

Squadron Leader Darling collected up his reduced squadron and checked his fighters. Several others had run out of ammunition. All of them had taken hits and yet none of them had been seriously damaged. An entire squadron of Spitfires passed above them in the opposite direction. They would have protection from any further attack. Darling led the squadron back to RAF Middle Wallop.

"Looks like you got chewed up pretty good, Mister Drummond," Bernie Gordon reported, as Brian was unstrapping from his fighter. "Control brought us down to Available for the moment."

"How bad?"

"A couple of leading edge hits curled the aluminum. One of the airscrew blades lost a chunk. Several hits on the fuse, maybe more."

"Complete fire out," shouted Aircraftman Colin Jenkins, his armorer, indicating all his ammunition was expended.

"We jumped a gaggle of Stukas, and then got bounced by twenty or more One Oh Nines. It was a hell of a fight."

"Looks like it. Some of the others were hit, too."

"According to our radio check, all of us got hit."

Gordon smiled. "We'll get her back in shape in a jiffy."

Brian surveyed the damage to his aircraft before joining the other pilots for the debriefing. The Spitfire did not look very pretty, all chewed up like a torn and bloody dog limping back from a violent fight.

The debriefing took longer than usual. The gun camera film would be used to confirm the claims, but according to the intelligence blokes, Darling and Drummond downed a Stuka each and Beamish, Johnson and Kensington each got a Bf109. It had been a successful, but costly engagement. With the air cover occupied with the fighters, the dive-bombers achieved several more hits on Convoy PEEWIT. One ship sank and two more had to divert to

Southampton for repairs. Two of the Spitfires had serious damage that would take a day or more to repair.

As they returned to Dispersal, four pilots in fresh RAF pilot officer's uniforms stood outside. Squadron Leader Darling checked their papers, and then made the introductions. "When it rains, it pours," he said and then smiled. "These gentlemen are here to join our happy little group. Pilot Officers Frank Burns and Stanley Koenig, both Americans, and Janus," he paused to look at the papers, "Kradilcek, is it?" The medium build, blond haired, blue eyed man nodded. "And, Kormer Mansek, both formerly of the Czech Air Force." Each of the squadron pilots was in turn introduced by Squadron Leader Darling. Brian considered if he should try to avoid the disclosure problem by declaring his nationality but decided to stay with his desire to 'think British.'

"Back up to strength," observed Flight Lieutenant John Davies.

"We've some trainin' to do, I'd say," Flight Lieutenant Roger Beamish added.

"Right," said Darling with a pensive tone. "I should call Group to see about the plans. If you gentlemen would be so kind," he nodded toward the replacement pilots, "please tell us a little about yourselves while I telephone Group." Darling went to his office.

The metallic sounds of the aircraft repairs did not skip a beat despite the onset of a light drizzle. The group of pilots joined Corporal Jennifer Warren inside the Dispersal building.

"This is Corporal Warren," said Flight Lieutenant Robert Morrow, the B Flight Leader and number two in command, "our operations clark." She nodded her head in recognition. "As Squadron Leader Darling suggested, please tell us where you come from and a little about your flight experience."

"I'm Frank Burns. I'm from Dayton, Ohio and a graduate of Ohio State University. I've been flyin' for the better part of five years. All four of us were flyin' with *le Armée de l'Air*," he said with an excellent French pronunciation, "east of Paris. After the collapse, I managed to make my way here through Marseilles, Gibraltar and Liverpool on a merchant ship. I don't know how many combat missions I flew, but I managed to rack up four victories before the surrender."

"My name's Stan Koenig. I'm from Bakersfield, California, and I was in a different squadron from Frank. I was near the Ardennes when the Krauts invaded. I got out through Brest. I only have one victory, so far."

"Name . . . Janus Kradilcek," the handsome one said. "I . . . I am captain in Czechoslovak Air Force. I kill eight aircraft," he said holding the appropriate fingers to emphasize the numbers, "five bombers, three fighters and twenty-three Germans," he growled, displaying four fists full and three fingers. "I here from Bratislava. I fight in Poland and France. I hate Germans. They kill my family, and now I kill them." He smiled, as if to say he was not consumed by hate.

"My name is, Kormer Mansek," the smaller, darker man said in better English. "I am from Prague and the University. I am also in Czech Air Force with rank of lieutenant. I fought with the French and have three confirmed credits."

"It is good to have you with us," said 'Sparky' Morrow.

They all shook hands and began the social conversation of pilots. Jokes sprang up about an RAF squadron in the defense of the homeland that had barely half British pilots. If the count was narrowed to the English, they were less than half with Beamish from Scotland and Davies from Wales. Hank Maxwell made quick work of announcing his nationality as well as Brian's, which the younger American did not appreciate. The three other Americans were college graduates, older, but less experienced than Brian.

Squadron Leader Darling returned. "If I may have your attention, please." He waited for silence and all eyes directed at him. "Through a combination of several factors not least of which are the recent losses of the squadron, the influx of replacement pilots and expected increase in the intensity of the air war, the squadron will be standing down from combat operations for several days." Good-humored remarks about intended actions interrupted his words. "Leadership has its price. As such, the section leaders and I shall remain along with the replacement pilots including Mister Maxwell to conduct some much-needed training. The rest of you, although only four in number, will remove yourselves from this facility not to return until sixteen hundred hours on Wednesday, at which time we shall rejoin this sorry little war."

"Skipper, I would just as soon stay," Brian said.

"Me as well," added 'Fog' Johnson.

"So sorry, Mister Drummond and Sergeant Johnson. I am afraid you do not have a choice."

"We can help, Skipper," Brian said, deciding to press the point.

"I am not in the habit of repeating myself, and I will certainly not begin now. Any other questions or comments?" No one said a word. "Smashing. Corporal Warren, if you would be so kind, please report the squadron as Unavailable."

"Yes, sir."

"Now, if there are no other questions, we are finished for the day. Section leaders and our new pilots are to be back here by 10 o'clock tomorrow morning. We will be on half days."

The four released pilots looked at one another as if some divine guidance might appear in the eyes of one of them. None of them moved until almost in unison they looked back to their leaders who motioned with his head for them to leave. Normalcy returned as they stowed their flight equipment. The four veterans started walking together until the point where Miles Johnson needed to break off for the Sergeant's Mess.

"What are you going to do, Roland?" asked Jonathan.

"I thought I would spend some time with me P & M. They live not far from Coventry."

"How about you, Brian?" Jonathan asked. The American smiled broadly. Jonathan fained disgust. "Outside of giving into your lustful urges, come with me to Newcastle. Some peace and quiet should do us both good."

Brian regretted his failure to ask Rosemary Kensington when she would be finished with school. He wondered whether she might be at Carlingon Castle. He hoped that she would be there, but regardless, it would be peaceful and quiet as Jonathan said – both elements being highly desirable at this point in their lives. Whether Rosemary was present or not, it would probably be a good idea for him to go with Jonathan.

"OK. Let's do it."

"Brilliant. I shall telephone my parents from the Mess, and then we shall be off. Are you going into London for the train?" Jonathan asked Roland Stockard. "We can ride together."

"That is the easiest route."

"Excellent, then let us be off."

With the arrangements made and a small bag of spare clothing and accouterments, the three pilots hitched a ride on a supply truck to the Andover railway station. They would ride together to Waterloo Station, and then split with Roland going to Euston Station, and Jonathan and Brian going to King's Cross Station. The journey to Newcastle would take most of the day. They expected to arrive at Carlingon Castle around sunset. The wood, cloth and leather interior of the railcar brought a sense of relief and relaxation. All three dozed through the many stops into London's Waterloo Station.

—

Sunday, 21.July.1940
No.10 Downing Street
Whitehall, London, England

Winston Churchill continued his professional reading until the War Cabinet Secretary, Sir Edward Bridges knocked on his private office door. "The War Cabinet plus the others you requested are assembled."

"Thank you, Sir Edward."

Winston followed the cabinet secretary into the Cabinet Room. Chamberlain, Attlee, Lord Halifax, Greenwood, and the Cabinet Secretariat occupied their usual seats. Neville Chamberlain continued to deteriorate in his health and appearance. He was not well, but he at least attended this meeting. Joining the War Cabinet for this early evening meeting were the service secretaries – Alexander, Eden, and Sinclair – along with service chiefs – Pound, Dill and Newall. Sir Edward took his seat next to the prime minister.

"We have a matter of utmost urgency to discuss, however before we address this item, are there any matters of pressing old business?" asked the Prime Minister. The forms of negative reply varied but were unanimous in their conclusion. "Excellent. Then, permit me to begin.

"We have received information from highly reliable sources," Winston paused to allow the importance of the ULTRA information to sink in, although he had agreed not to divulge the actual source, "*Herr* Göring will soon host a gathering of German Air Force leaders at his Karinhall estate outside Berlin. Our information indicates most of the commanders are arriving tonight with the principal meetings over the next two days."

"Where on Earth did such information come from?" asked Arthur Greenwood, the minister without portfolio and deputy Labor Party leader.

Several of the other men knew of ULTRA but most did not. The more seasoned cabinet members or officers knew protected sources had to be involved and recognized they most probably needed to be protected.

Winston Churchill patiently responded. "Let it suffice, Arthur, sources of the utmost importance to our country are involved and by their nature must be safeguarded."

"As members of the War Cabinet, we do not deserve to know these sources?"

"Knowledge of the sources will not alter the conclusion we may reach with the information. We have professionals whose task it is to measure, judge, control and protect this type of most sensitive information. Now, if there are no other peripheral questions, I should like to discuss this latest gem from the intelligence community. I would be most pleased to hear your opinions regarding the significance and purpose of this meeting."

Secretary of State for Air Sir Archibald Sinclair, the closest British counterpart to *Reichsmarschal* Göring, after scanning the room, chose to answer first. "In his place," he paused to clear his throat, "I should think it might indicate the need for resolution of some serious problem, or more likely, a change in strategy."

"I share Sir Archibald's assessment," added Anthony Eden, Secretary of State for War and cabinet minister head of the Army.

"What a perfect target," Air Chief Marshal Newall muttered, "if our information is correct."

"What was that you said, Sir Cyril?" asked Winston.

"Pardon me, Prime Minister. I just thought aloud, Karinhall would make the perfect target for Bomber Command."

"Good that you should bring up the point, which I would like to debate. However, before we address the issue of potential action, I would like to appreciate the meaning."

"It could be simply a routine gathering or even a social occasion such as a celebration of their victory in France," said Lord Halifax.

"Could be but not likely considering the early stages of the Battle for Britain and any invasion attempt," offered General Dill. "The Germans are rather fastidious and predictable in their devotion to a mission. I would agree with Sir Archibald's assessment, and furthermore, since we are unaware of any difficulties that might warrant such a gathering, I believe this may be an understandable strategic planning session – a proper prelude to their invasion attempt."

The nodding heads confirmed Winston's thoughts. "Our intelligence experts agree, which is why I thought we should address the issue," Churchill said. "It has been suggested by Sir Cyril and others, we might want to seize the opportunity to eliminate the leadership of the *Luftwaffe* at this critical juncture of the war."

"It would undoubtedly be a very costly raid, even if we could pull it off," answered Newall.

"It would most likely confirm our access to most secret German information," added Sinclair.

"Therein lies the crux of the question . . . is it worth the risk?" asked the Prime Minister.

"The opportunity to eliminate or at least severely shake up the leadership of the German Air Force at this stage of the air battle is worth a substantial risk," said Sir Archibald Sinclair.

"I would agree with the minister," added Air Chief Marshal Newall.

"Is it worth losing one or more of our most important intelligence sources?" Winston paused and leaned forward over the table. "Sources that could yield equally if not more important information in the future."

"If we cannot use the information, then we must ask what is the information good for?" asked Arthur Greenwood.

The Right Honorable Clement Attlee, Lord Privy Seal and leader of the Labor Party, leaned forward. "The Prime Minister's first question to us is the reason. We may not be able to take offensive action, but we can certainly use the information to understand, anticipate, project and maybe outmaneuver the enemy. I say, the information sources are more important."

"I agree," added Lord Halifax.

Neville Chamberlain remained distant and unanimated in this vital discussion. Winston could not avoid the sallow and strained appearance of his face. Although he had been one of his most outspoken critics, Winston still had considerable respect for the integrity, wisdom and moral strength of this now weakened elder statesman of the Conservative Party. He wanted to ask Chamberlain for his opinion, but in the end decided to leave the venerable gentleman of politics to his own thoughts.

"I should like to remind the War Cabinet what we at the Air Ministry believe lies just ahead for us on this island," said Sinclair, straining against his own knowledge, imagination and convictions. "Although the enemy has confined himself to Channel shipping, for the most part, we estimate they will soon begin an unrestrained air offensive against our aerodromes and specifically the resources of Fighter Command, as well as concentrated attacks on our industrial base. I know I do not need to remind this august assembly that should the enemy overwhelm Fighter Command the likelihood of a full scale invasion becomes immensely more probable."

"Not with the Royal Navy in the Channel," stated Admiral Pound.

"Quite so, I am certain, Sir Dudley. However . . . how long can the Royal Navy remain in the Channel if the *Luftwaffe* controls the skies?"

"Do you actually think they can overcome our air defense system?"

Sinclair twisted in his chair and leaned forward onto his elbows. "Let us take stock of the situation, shall we? Our best estimates place their fighter strength at double, if not treble our numbers. Bomber strength nearly four times. The initial forays against our shipping and coastal targets have been a mere fractional preview of what will most certainly come upon us, soon."

"But, we have this RDF equipment and our communications network," offered Greenwood.

"Right you are, Arthur, however, we are already short of our most valuable and critical resource . . . our oh so young fighter pilots."

"Our losses in the last few weeks have been alarming, to say the least," Newall added to complement his minister's remarks.

"Then, are you suggesting we should risk our sources?" asked Attlee.

"It is worth considering," answered Sinclair.

Winston Churchill absorbed the dialogue. He admitted to himself the urge, the temptation to strike hard at the brains of the German Air Force. It was indeed a tempting target. "Does anyone feel, given complete success of such a mission, the course of the Nawzee aggression would change?"

"It could very well have the opposite effect from what we desire," suggested Lord Halifax.

"It is possible, maybe even probable," offered Chamberlain for the first time.

"Even with full success," said Attlee, "it might only buy us a little time, if any."

"Certainly, time is of the essence in our efforts to rearm the Army and equip the Home Defense Forces. Any time would help," stated Eden.

"I agree," said Winston. "We could use the time, but in the end, is whatever precious time we might gain worth the possibility of losing valuable sources?"

Every man in the room withdrew into their thoughts considering the most vital question and dilemma. Winston was sure most of the Cabinet shared his personal feelings as well as his positional opinion. The Enigma device could remain of incalculable value throughout the war, if they protected its existence and product. Winston knew the only answer they could reach, but he needed the War Cabinet to share the burden.

"Think of the value to morale at home of such a bold mission," said Sir Archibald Sinclair without answering the questions and holding on to his opinion to strike.

"Yes, but the question, if you please."

The Prime Minister looked each man in the eyes until he received their answer. Most shook their heads. The risk was too great placed against the potential gain. Several ministers, none of which had direct access to ULTRA, voiced or indicated their acceptance of the risk.

"It would appear we have a less than unanimous agreement to protect our sources. Is there any other discussion on this issue?" Silence provided the answer. "Sir Edward, if you would, please ensure the record does not contain any specific references to the target we considered . . . simply a specific attractive target was considered and rejected."

"As you wish."

"Excellent. Then, shall we proceed to the more mundane business at hand," Churchill said, as they turned to the papers before them. Winston briefed the War Cabinet on the counter-espionage, information collection mission of William Donovan, as he repeatedly emphasized the importance of a positive outcome. The ministers were unanimous in their support. They carried a more contentious debate about Hitler's "peace offering" to the British people. True to form, Chamberlain and Halifax thought the gesture from the German leader would this time be meaningful and genuine. Churchill, Attlee and Greenwood emphatically did not agree; as they saw the offering just another hollow placation from the German leader. This time, Churchill wanted the appeaser Lord Halifax to deliver the clear, concise, public reply to Hitler. The remainder of the War Cabinet meeting would deal with the resupply of the Army, the impending arrival of several shiploads of 0.303 caliber rifles from the United States, courtesy of President Roosevelt and General Marshall. Winston noted to himself for the first time in several months the unmistakable wafts of optimism. They might actually make it through the current storm. The traditional inclement weather of the autumn season was now their nearest and closest ally.

—

Monday, 22.July.1940
Carlingon Castle
Newcastle-upon-Tyne, Tyne & Wear, England

The elegantly renovated old castle lay quiet as Brian rose, washed and descended the stairs. Theona Kensington and her son sat around the kitchen table talking and picking apart an occasional piece of toast.

"Good morning to you, Brian," said Missus Kensington. "You must have had a good sleep."

"Yes, ma'am, I certainly did. I guess I needed it."

"From what little Jonathan has told me, it sounds as though you both needed a good rest." Brian could only guess how much his friend may have told his mother. He surely did not tell her about being shot down or wounded. "So, a rest you shall have."

"Where is Mister Kensington, if I may ask?"

"He was off to work hours ago . . . before either of you regained consciousness."

The two RAF fighter pilots laughed at the description of their undisturbed slumber. They arrived shortly after midnight and did not waste time finding their beds. The clock on the wall indicated 10:27. It had been many months since either of them had been able to sleep through most of the morning. It produced the desired effect.

"Tell me, Brian, what trouble have the two of you gotten into lately? How bad are things in the South?"

Brian looked to Jonathan who only stared back at him. There was no guidance from his friend. He thought he sensed a yearning for the story to be told but no willingness to open the grim topic. Would he tell his mother about the experiences of the last few weeks?

"I am not sure what Jonathan may have told you, but I think it is going OK. The Germans have confined their attacks to shipping in the Channel, and we have managed to chase off the bastards. Oh, excuse me, Missus Kensington. I did not mean to curse."

She smiled. "It is quite all right, Brian. I think they are bastards as well for what they are doing in Europe."

"We will hold them off, Mother."

"I am sure you will, Son. I just do not want anything dreadful to happen to you."

"We will be OK, as Brian says. Don't worry."

Missus Kensington searched her son's eyes, and then returned to her unspoken inquisition of Brian. He knew he had to meet her eyes, not look away and show no signs.

"I think you two are lying to me. You do not want me to know what is really happening. Maybe I should just find out for myself."

"Mother, please. We are doing what the country needs us to do, and we are doing a good job. Worrying about things will not alter the outcome. Only our skills, endurance and persistence will get the task done."

"You make it sound so simple. I just worry about you whether you think I should or not."

"I know, Mother, but your worry won't keep the bullets out."

"Jonathan," protested Brian. The clash of frustration and empathy sparked the Kensington scion to launch himself out the kitchen door to the bright summer day. Theona Kensington started to follow her son, and then sat back down and looked inquisitively to Brian Drummond.

Brian knew all too well the fear his friend felt. Somehow Brian need-ed to help his friend with the catharsis he had found with Anne. Jonathan could not keep these horrors locked up inside him, or they might ultimately consume him.

"Missus Kensington," Brian began not quite knowing what he should say, "we have had a difficult few weeks. We lost four pilots in the last two weeks, which is why they gave us a few days away. The squadron is training some new pilots." Brian considered telling her about them both bailing out of their damaged fighters, but he could not see how that information would help a concerned mother. "We are doing rather well, I must say, and if you will allow me to be candid," he paused for her confirmation, "your worry and concern for him, just makes it more difficult."

"I think I understand."

"We have a saying which we think describes what I am trying to say. 'A wife and children knocks you down a notch.' What it means is, when a fighter pilot worries about those who love him, it makes him more cautious and therefore more exposed. This may not be the right thing to say, but I know how Jonathan feels. I hope you can understand."

"Let me be equally candid with you, Brian. If mothers had their way, their children would never venture away from home. They instinctively want to protect their children. The thought of my son locked in mortal combat, no matter how important or necessary for the defense of this country, is almost more than this mother can bear."

"I appreciate your point, but Jonathan needs your support, your cour-age, your strength. It is sometimes all that sustains us."

Rosemary Kensington floated into the room wearing a very thin, nearly transparent, red ankle length nightgown with matching light robe flow-ing behind her. The details of her slender body beneath her bedroom attire grabbed Brian's eyes like powerful magnets. As soon as she recognized Brian, she jumped into his arms without the slightest hesitation or embarrassment.

"Rosemary Alice Kensington, have you no shame," Theona Kensington admonished.

"He has seen it all before," Rosemary giggled, and then kissed Brian deeply.

"Dear Lord above, you are a disgrace." Rosemary waved her hand as if she was trying to discourage an annoying, pesky insect without separating from Brian. "You must go upstairs at once, young lady, and not come down until you are properly attired."

"As you wish, Mother." She looked back into Brian's eyes signaling what was about to come. "Brian, come help me get dressed."

"Damn you, Rosemary Alice. Stop this disgusting display at once and get your bum to your room."

Rosemary winked at Brian and left him to deal with his own embarrassing affliction. Brian waited for Theona's daughter to leave and for her back to turn toward him, and he bolted for the door. Fortunately, no one was in sight. Brian walked across the lawn toward the nearest tree. Leaning against the sturdy trunk, the young American gazed out beyond the trees to the picturesque valley. It was as he remembered – an idyllic place – even more green, lush and soft.

Rosemary bewildered Brian. He simply did not know how to deal with a woman so open, uninhibited and effervescent. She intrigued him, more from wondering what she was going to do next than from what she had done.

"Sometimes I do not know what I should say or not say." Brian turned to see Jonathan walking toward him with his hands clasped behind his back. "You want to tell people what it is like, but you are afraid of how they might react, like they might feel sorry for you."

"You hit the nail on the head. You want to tell people, but you can't."

"Talking with Anne helped me to unload some stuff, Jonathan. Maybe you should talk to Linda, or even Rosemary."

Jonathan Kensington laughed as though Brian told an incredible joke. "You must be kidding. My sister." He turned instantly serious. "You had better not say a bloody word to her."

"Not me," Brian fibbed, knowing he had already confided in her.

"She would go absolutely ape, especially with her feelings for you."

Brian raised his hands in surrender. "I won't say a word, Jonathan."

His mood changed just as quickly as a few moments ago. "Maybe Linda, although I am not certain she could handle the intensity."

"I think you could talk to Linda. She could deal with our business. I also think Rosemary can as well."

"We shall see."

The sound of a door closing attracted their attention. Rosemary, now dressed in riding trousers, high, polished, brown boots and a frilly, white blouse, bounded across the lawn toward them.

"What could be so serious?"

"What do you mean?"

"Mum and I saw the two of you locked in some serious conversation, so I thought I would lighten it up a smidgen."

"Nothing important."

"You mean nothing you would tell me."

"All right, then, nothing we would tell you."

"What are you doing home anyway, don't you have school?" asked Jonathan.

"Finished for the semester. It is the holiday period before the autumn session."

"Smashing," responded Jonathan in a less than excited tone.

Rosemary ignored her brother's mood. "Let's go for a ride," she offered.

"Not me."

"Come on, Jonathan," Brian pleaded, not quite ready for being alone with Rosemary so close to her family.

"No. I'll talk to Mum. You two go ahead."

Brian acquiesced. They saddled their horses and headed west toward the higher mountains. The small, puffy clouds lazily passing through the light, summer haze made the day feel warmer than it was. The rich mixture of pine scent and floral fragrances carried well on the light breeze. The weather was as idyllic as the scenery.

They talked about things as far removed from the war as possible. Rosemary enjoyed the university, the challenge, and the knowledge. She acted as though they had not met last week. Brian could only marvel at her words since he did not share her same love of school learning. For him, aviation was everything. He loved flying.

He allowed the questions and comparisons between her appreciation of Oxford University with his enjoyment of flight. He tried several times to describe the excitement associated with making a machine do precisely what he wanted it to do. Rosemary sincerely tried to understand, but in the end, gave up the attempt.

They came to a thick stand of conifer and deciduous trees. Rosemary directed her horse through the thick vegetation. Brian followed. Both of them leaned forward to allow the horses to move the branches. In perhaps ten to fifteen yards, they broke out into a nearly circular meadow. The tall grass gave the ground a deep, soft carpet. The gentle gurgling sounds of the brook over the rocks slicing through the middle of the meadow added an almost dream like quality to the scene.

Rosemary dismounted and walked toward a majestic solo oak tree in the center of the meadow. Brian followed her lead, again. She pulled a large blanket from behind her saddle. She spread the blanket out in the shade of the large tree near the stream. Inside the roll, Rosemary had wrapped a bottle of red wine, a long loaf of French bread and a block of cheese.

Lying down on the blanket resting on her right elbow, Rosemary Kensington patted the spot next to her. Brian looked around, as if someone might be watching.

"It is quite all right, Brian. We own this land, and no one comes up here."

"You never know," he laughed.

"Sure, I do." She lay back, resting her head on both hands. "I used to come up here when I was a child. Whenever I had problems, they usually got sorted out in this place. My brother has been here a few times but never seemed to appreciate its magic."

Brian reclined next to Rosemary, not quite an arm's length from her and raised on his left elbow. "What problems do you have?"

She looked puzzled. "What do you mean?"

"You said you come up here when you have problems."

Rosemary smiled and looked up into the tree branches. Her striking blue eyes captivated him. They sparkled and yet possessed an inner peace. "It is not just a place to solve problems. It is also a place to enjoy and get away from the world." She looked deep into his eyes. "You need this place, Brian."

She held him with her eyes. "It is beautiful," he answered. She wet her lips with the delicate tip of her tongue.

Their passion and need for each other took control. Brian carefully restrained his own excitement to give her the pleasure she sought. She rose to remove every item of clothing slowly and deliberately before he joined her. They lay together entwined looking to distant places. He gently stroked the soft skin of her shoulder, back and hip as she moved to ensure as much of their skin touched as humanly possible.

"This place can exorcise your demons, Brian, if you let it."

"You have given me far more than this place, but I know you're right."

Rosemary became so still, Brian wondered if she continued to breathe. He tried to see her eyes, but she stared off to some far away place. "I remember vividly you telling me at Brighton Beach about being shot down. I can see the same strain within Jonathan. Although I have not told Mum what you told me, she senses the danger."

Brian pulled her tightly to him. "I don't want to talk about the war."

She stroked his chest. "I want to make all the pain go away."

"You have."

"Somehow, I don't think so, but let's give it a go." She sat up, turning toward him, and crossed her legs. Her back straightened as she pulled her shoulders back. His eyes moved to the modest, conical mounds of flesh on her chest. She cupped them. "They are nice, aren't they?"

"Jesus, Rosemary. You're embarrassing me."

Her head flipped back like a howling wolf as she laughed deep and hard. "You are supposed to have fun with the flesh." She jiggled her breasts. "These are for your pleasure and mine," she paused lowering her eyes coyly, "at least until a baby needs them."

Brian rolled onto his back and looked away from her. "Sometimes, I do not know what to do with you or around you."

"Just enjoy life, Brian, just enjoy life."

"That is certainly working."

"Come now. Sit up. Let's break this bread together."

He did as he was commanded. Brian marveled at the lack of inhibition in Rosemary and the sense of freedom he felt with her in the middle of this idyllic meadow. Sitting on a blanket in the middle of a mountain meadow like two innocent, unashamed children enjoying the summer sun brought its own soothing curative powers.

They laughed, touched, talked, fondled, played and enjoyed the pleasure of each other's company. They were alone in the entire world. There was no war, no death, no struggle, no interference, no tension – only the sounds of nature and their enjoyment. There were no stones to hurt their bare feet as they frolicked like two yearling deer through the grass, the stream and among the abundant wildflowers.

"We should be going," Rosemary said with some sadness as she noticed the descending Sun.

"I don't want to leave this place. I have never felt so carefree and peaceful."

"Did I not tell you this was a magical place?"

"You did, and I believe." Brian reached for her shoulders and drew her close. He kissed her gently and yet passionately. "I shall never forget this moment."

"I should hope not. Now, we really must be going. Even in the summer months, the mountain air becomes quite chilly when the Sun sets. And we, without a stitch of clothing, will surely catch our death of cold."

They took many pauses as they dressed, as if they would not be able to touch once they were fully clothed. The laughter continued as they found more things to laugh about around them. The ambling return ride to Carlingon

Castle was filled with words of love and pleasure. The scenery was overpowering. The skies to the east were absolutely crystal clear. For the first time, Brian saw the North Sea many miles beyond the lush, green landscape of the Kensington land.

"We were beginning to worry about you," Missus Kensington said as they entered the kitchen.

"We took a long ride through the mountains," Rosemary answered with incredible innocence and without the slightest hint they had been naked most of the afternoon. "I wanted to show Brian some of our best scenery."

"Like your precious meadow," taunted Jonathan.

"Of course."

"Well, then, I suppose you have seen it all, I should think," Jonathan added.

"Why don't you children freshen up before your father returns. I think we will have an earlier supper tonight. The BBC announced that Lord Halifax will broadcast the government's response to Hitler's peace offering tonight at eight o'clock, and I know your father will insist we listen."

As Brian cleaned himself and changed uniforms, he jumped from the image of the afternoon's relaxation to the expectation of Rosemary's entrance at any moment. She did not come to him, and he longed for her presence. He waited as long as he thought prudent and descended the stairs.

Mister Kensington arrived shortly after Brian had joined Theona and Jonathan in the kitchen once again. The meal preparation was well underway, and they tried to stay out of the way. There was a noticeable connection between the Kensingtons and their help. They enjoyed a cup of tea while the work continued. As the activity began to intensify, Theona Kensington suggested they move to the living room.

The conversation remained lively and enthusiastic. Although he had not seen the Kensingtons since the previous Christmas holiday, there was an undeniable increase in confidence as though there was less uncertainty ahead. The Kensingtons seemed to reflect what many Britons presented. Events were being decided. There was no more waiting.

The evening meal topics avoided politics, the war, and any other unpleasantness. Reminiscences of the Kensington children's youthful experiences as well as good-natured interrogations of Brian Drummond's childhood mixed well with the personal observations of the landscape of North England.

At the appropriate time, they gathered in the living room, as they had for the King's Christmas message, to listen to His Majesty's Foreign Minister,

Lord Halifax, deliver a succinct, purposeful reply to the German leader. The announcer made the introduction.

"Many of you will have read two days ago," the calm, strong voice of Lord Halifax began, "the speech in which *Herr* Hitler summoned Great Britain to capitulate to his will. I will not waste your time by dealing with his distortions of almost every main event since the War began. He says he has no desire to destroy the British Empire, but there was in his speech no suggestion that peace must be based on justice, no word of recognition that the other nations of Europe had any right to self-determination, the principle that he has so often invoked for Germans. His only appeal was to the base instinct of fear, and his only arguments were threats."

"Give it to 'em," interjected George Kensington.

"Father, please," objected Jonathan, as he strained to hear the words.

"Hitler has now made it plain that he is preparing to direct the whole weight of German might against this country. That is why in every part of Britain there is only one spirit, a spirit of indomitable resolve."

Brian thought of another spirit of indomitable resolve as he looked into the waiting eyes of Rosemary Kensington. She winked her recognition.

"Nor has anyone any doubt that if Hitler were to succeed it would be the end, for many besides ourselves, of all those things that make life worth living. We realize that the struggle may cost us everything, but just because the things we are defending are worth any sacrifice, it is a noble privilege to be defenders of things so precious. We never wanted the War; certainly no one here wants the War to go on for a day longer than is necessary. But, we shall not stop fighting until freedom, for ourselves and others, is secure."

It was not until the announcer returned to confirm the conclusion of the Foreign Minister's message that anyone in Carlingon Castle recognized the conclusion of the speech. They looked from one to another.

"Amen," said George Kensington, as though he had just heard a sermon.

Several heads nodded, and a few chuckles passed. They talked about the content of the short response. Even Rosemary joined the dialogue in earnest. Brian knew they believed what the Foreign Minister said. The reflection of their inner confidence and resistance gave Brian strength and determination to endure and overcome any obstacle to succeed. In his gut, he understood and accepted that they must win.

As the house eventually drifted into the silence of the night, Brian went to Rosemary who had waited patiently for her lover to arrive. They enjoyed each other again before they accepted the envelope of sleep.

—

Tuesday, 23.July.1940
Carlingon Castle
Newcastle-upon-Tyne, Tyne & Wear, England
05:00 hours

Brian woke early with the Sun. He slowly and gently extricated himself from the clutches of Rosemary Kensington. Much to his good fortune, no one else appeared to be moving about the house. He could easily return to bed for another few hours of sleep, but chose to clean up, put his uniform on less his tunic, and moved to the kitchen. The distinctive smell of bacon greeted him as he moved down the stairs.

Theona Kensington sat at the kitchen table with a large cup of tea or coffee reading a book and talking to the staff. "Good morning, Missus Kensington," Brian said with a cheery voice. She looked up and smiled.

"I trust you had a good sleep, Brian," she half stated, half asked, and then winked at him.

A flush of embarrassment forced him to look away and find something for his attention. Did she know about his relationship with her daughter? How could she know unless Rosemary told her? Did she enter Rosemary's room during the night to find them as they were . . . entwined, sated and peaceful? All the questions and possibilities clouded his senses. The longer he waited to answer the more suspicious or confirmatory his actions would become.

"Excellent, I'd say," Brian said, trying to sound calm, casual and as unembarrassed as he could.

"Smashing. Would you like some tea or coffee?"

"Tea, please."

"Tea and toast for Mister Drummond, if you would, Betty."

George Kensington, followed shortly thereafter by Jonathan Kensington, joined them. They all marveled at the sparkling, crystalline reflections from the dew on the grass and shrubbery. It looked like another gorgeous day. The tranquility of Northern England, Carlingon Castle and the Kensington estate intensified Brian's longing to stay. Rosemary had been precisely correct – the mountain meadow was indeed a magical place. Despite the presence of Rosemary wrapped around him, he slept more restfully than at any time in the last several months. Even Anne Booth's comfort did not work as well as this place.

Surprising everyone, Rosemary entered the kitchen before George Kensington had to leave for Newcastle. Her blond hair flowed behind her as she bounced into the room. The modest, floral print dress effectively hid what Brian knew lay underneath.

"Good morning all," she nearly shouted.

"No need to ask how your night's sleep was," joked George Kensington.

"Extraordinary," she gushed looking directly at Brian. "Simply extraordinary. Don't know when I have ever slept better."

"It must be the glorious summer day that greets us," said George.

Brian broke his eyes free from Rosemary's control to find Jonathan just staring at him. He thought about leaving the room to avoid any further perceived embarrassment.

"I think it must be chemistry or magic," chuckled Theona.

"How's that, you say?"

"Just a thought, George. Just a thought."

"Whatever," he answered in frustration. "I really must be off. Big day at the office, you know."

"What are your plans, Jonathan?" asked Missus Kensington.

"We must be off as well, I'm afraid." Jonathan looked at Brian. "We are due back at the squadron this afternoon and our train to London leaves in about an hour."

Brian nodded his head in agreement although he wanted to stay. There was no war here, but his best friend was correct.

"Don't go," pleaded Rosemary. "Call your leader and ask for another day at least."

"That is not possible, Rose. They need us, and we were only given two days."

"But, I do not want you to go," she cooed and squirmed as though she had an intimate itch that could not be scratched.

"Really, Rosemary Alice. Must you make such a spectacle of yourself?" protested Mister Kensington. "We simply must be off, now, if I am to deposit our two intrepid aviators at the railway station."

Brian followed Jonathan upstairs. He quickly packed his clothing and accouterments. Rosemary entered the room before he could finish. She walked toward him with sadness in her eyes, wrapped her arms around him and buried her face in his shoulder.

"I don't want you to go," she whispered.

"I know. I don't want to go, either." They held each other motionless and silent. "You were right. This is a magical place."

Rosemary Kensington pulled back just enough to look into his eyes. Excitement replaced the sadness. "I can show you much more magic, if you stay."

He kissed and caressed her. "Lord knows I would but duty calls."

"Duty may call," she purred like a cat about to pounce, "but, I can touch you," she finished as she grabbed him causing him to suck in a large breath of air.

"You are absolutely incorrigible," Brian said as he lifted her completely off the floor allowing her to wrap her legs around him.

"Brian, are you ready?" called Jonathan from the hall and fortunately not his doorway.

"Coming," Brian said.

"I wish," Rosemary whispered.

"Jesus, Rosemary."

"You love it when I do nasty things, don't you?"

Brian smiled. "They are exciting, I must admit."

"You remember that when you are off playing birdman."

"Absolutely," he lied.

Brian gathered the last of his things and started for the door. He turned to take one last look at a tall, slender, well-proportioned, blond haired, young woman he was becoming attached to in more than physical terms. He waved and turned.

"I love you, Brian," she said softly, as if she were embarrassed by the words. He nodded his head and left.

The ride into Newcastle seemed quiet although Mister Kensington talked about the war as seen from the North. Jonathan did not say a word and just looked out the window. Jonathan's father wished them the best of luck and shook hands with Brian, and gave his son a hug. They stepped onto the railway platform twenty minutes before the train was due to arrive. Jonathan stood straight and proud with his hands clasped behind his back obviously not wanting to talk. Brian did not feel an urge to talk either as his mind returned to the mountain meadow.

It was an hour outside Newcastle when the only other occupant of their compartment, an elderly man, left them alone that Jonathan said his first words after leaving Carlingon Castle. He jerked his head away from the window to find his friend's inquisitive eyes. "You are indeed bonking my sister, aren't you?"

he barked. Brian looked out the window at the passing terrain that he could not see and away from his friend. "Aren't you?" Jonathan continued to press.

Brian knew the issue had come up before when they left RAF Drem to move south when the Germans invaded France. He told himself he would come clean with Jonathan when they arrived at RAF Northolt, but the rapid, intense events of the war intervened. Now was not the time, either, except if he reacted badly it would taint an otherwise extraordinary respite from the war.

He looked back to the waiting eyes of his best friend. "Yes," he said.

"I suspected as much at Drem when she practically wrapped herself around you. Then, after watching that little *tête-à-tête d'amour* this morning, I remembered." He paused to let his stern face transform into a smile. "I just wanted to give you a start," he laughed.

"Well, my friend, you did. I thought you were on the verge of taking my head off."

"I can't do that. You are my protector."

"What do you mean?"

"I have had the dream many times since the war started. When it becomes a nightmare and something dreadful happens to me, you or your likeness is always there to pull my bacon out of the fire, as it were."

"Naw."

"Well, yes, actually, but none of that. I wanted to tell you I talked to Rosemary yesterday." Brian nodded, waiting for the rest of the story. "When the two of you disappeared for the afternoon and especially after she said she showed you her meadow, I virtually knew the truth. I asked her nonetheless, and she confirmed what I suspected. I must tell you I have never seen her happier . . .in her entire life, I might add. She loves you, Brian."

Embarrassment surged through him, again. He had never heard another man use those words with him. "She is an incredible woman, and I think I love her."

"My only caution is, be careful. She can be a wild one, and she has always been one of the most headstrong people I know."

"Tell me about it. She has practically swallowed me alive."

Jonathan held up his hand and lowered his head. "Wait now. I do believe proper decorum dictates . . . I do not need the sordid details."

Once more, embarrassment took Brian. "I mean . . . I tried to avoid any relationship, but she made it impossible."

"There you go, that is my baby sister. What she wants, she is relentless in her pursuit. Kind of like you when you are hunting Germans." They laughed and diverted their conversation when the elderly man returned to the compartment.

They waited for several miles before Brian motioned for them to leave the compartment. He wanted to talk. Jonathan led them back to the dining car. It was just after lunch and nearly empty. They asked for some tea and biscuits.

"To be straight, Jonathan, I am angry and confused."

"Angry?"

"Why did Anne do those things?"

"Brian, only she knows. You must let go of that. No matter how good she was between the sheets, she betrayed her country."

"And me."

"Forget her."

"I know," Brian answered as he thought of Anne and Rosemary.

"So, why confused?"

Brian asked himself whether he actually wanted to continue. Maybe it was not the right thing to talk about even with his best friend. What the hell, he told himself. "I'm not sure exactly how to say this, but I felt safe, comfortable with Anne. Rosemary keeps me on edge all the time." Jonathan laughed a hearty laugh, clearly amused by Brian's revelation. "I never know what she is going to do next."

"I am not surprised."

"I like her. We have fun together. She makes me feel really alive, kinda like Anne did, but I feel like I'm on the edge of maneuvering stall – one twitch from out-of-control."

Jonathan continued to chuckle, amused with his friend's plight. "Don't worry about me or my parents. If something develops between you and Rose, then so be it. If something does not, enjoy the moment. You appear to be good for each other. Flow with the river."

Brian nodded his head. Jonathan's reasoning made sense to him, and he could relax knowing unwanted expectations were not growing. They spent the remainder of the rail journey enjoying the countryside, the people, the support from strangers and things removed from the war, women and even flying.

The British railway system ran precisely on time this day and as fate would have it, an Air Force truck was waiting at the Andover rail station to retrieve some material for their air station. They arrived at the Officer's Mess an hour earlier than required. After depositing their bags, they walked to the squadron dispersal hut.

—

Wednesday, 15.July.1940
RAF Middle Wallop
Middle Wallop, Hampshire, England
17:45 hours

Jonathan and Brian were the last two members of the newly constituted No.609 Squadron to return from the break. Laughter and joviality marked each and every pilot including the otherwise troubled Pilot Officer Hank Maxwell. As they talked, they learned the training had gone exceptionally well with no interference by the war. Even the two Czech pilots seemed to speak better English than when they arrived.

As the minute hand on the wall clock indicated 18:00, the telephone rang returning the group to reality. "Squadron to Readiness," announced Corporal Warren in her soft, but authoritative voice.

"We can expect a patrol, at a minimum. Yet another convoy has entered the Channel toward London," said Squadron Leader Darling.

Within minutes, a full squadron of twelve Spitfires was climbing to the southwest. Brian could not escape the comparison of the tight formations they used six months earlier during the Phony War to the more spread out formations they used today. They learned from their opponents. The Germans called their formations, *schwarm*, literally, flights, but the German word had a different connotation in English. The pilots of Fighter Command referred to the German formations as, swarms or sometimes finger four, since it looked like the stagger of four fingers of one hand held together.

Brian rechecked his guns and switches. The radio communications portrayed a developing situation that could result in combat over the English Channel just south of Portland. They leveled off at 20,000 feet overhead the gaggle of some fifteen ships and throttled back to loiter, waiting for the approaching enemy.

As they waited and the radio calls began to dissolve the threat, Brian's thoughts turned to Jonathan's dreams and feelings of premonition. How could he possibly be Jonathan's protector? Aerial combat quickly degenerated into survival. You tried to help your mates, but most of the time you were either defending yourself or singling out the closest target. In the skies these days, there were only two types of aircraft – shooters and targets. Each of the pilots worked as hard as they could to be more of the former than the latter. Maybe Jonathan had seen the future?

"Sorbo Leader, this is Bandy calling. Return to base."

"Understood, Bandy. There you have it lads, let's go home."

The late afternoon sun among the distant thin clouds off his left wing provided an enticing prelude to what should be a grand sunset, Brian imagined as the wide V of five, large, concrete hangars appeared out his forward windscreen. As Squadron Leader Darling continued their gradual descent through 1,000 feet, Brian safed his guns and prepared his Spitfire for landing. They would be landing straight ahead toward the north. He waited for his section leader, Flight Lieutenant Roger Beamish to lower his landing gear and flaps, then he followed each step. It was good to be back in the saddle, Brian told himself as he adjusted his position, rechecked his landing gear down and locked, and scanned his airspeed indicator as the throttle came back to idle making the Merlin pop, sputter and protest. The differences in the sound of the Merlin III engine at idle and high power never ceased to amaze him. The Rolls-Royce aeroengine loved to produce horsepower.

The debriefing did not take long as Flying Officer James Royster gathered the minimum information required to record the mission. No one complained about the uneventful nature of the sortie. The words could have come from a group of farmers, or coal miners, or railway workers at the end of their workday. For the first time in a long time, this group of pilots did not talk about aviation, airplanes or flying.

It was the spare pilot Kormer Mansek that broke the moment. "I hear from other pilots, we got first night kill."

"Really," responded John Davies with the sparked curiosity each of them felt.

"Who?" asked Robert Morrow.

"I do not know who."

"I will call over to the Six Oh Four chaps," Davies said.

As the call was made, the speculation began in earnest. The problem of night interception of bombers or any other aircraft for that matter remained a long-term enigma to the fighter pilots. No.604 (County of Middlesex) Squadron, a sister squadron at RAF Middle Wallop, used the twin-engine, Blenheim fighters configured with various bulges, antennae and other warts in an attempt to develop a night intercept technique. Hearing the beating, out-of-synchronization, twin-engine, reconnaissance aircraft of the German Air Force overhead during the nighttime hours did not sit well with any of the fighter pilots. They felt impotent to stop the intrusions, and they were. The night fighter pilots could barely contain their own frustration and anger. The one emotion that flowed freely was the terror of flying in the ink well, trying to find another larger aircraft also flying in the ink well and trying to maneuver within a few hundred feet for a good gun shot. The tales of nighttime attempts sent chills into every single pilot who listened and imagined.

"It was 'Cat's Eyes' Cunningham," Davies reported. "He got one with that RDF kit on the nose they have been testing. They don't even know what the bloody thing was."

"How do they know it wasn't one of ours?"

"Apparently, they did not have a Pipsqueak, so no Pipsqueak equals enemy."

"What's a Pipsqueak?" asked Stan Koenig, one of the new American pilots.

"Small device that tells the RDF blokes we're friendly," answered Morrow.

"There will be a celebration at the Mess tonight, now that the night crawlers bagged one," joked John Davies.

Squadron Leader Darling called into Sector Control. "We are released, lads. Good to have everyone back together and a good first day back. Now, let us go have some beer with 'Cat's Eyes' and hear the tale."

They laughed and began the process of creating the jokes that would soon become the mythology of the night fighters. Every pilot could smile this night, even Hank Maxwell. Brian and Jonathan compared impressions and both felt, this was a changed, more resolute and determined squadron than existed three days ago.

—

Chapter 16

Those who restrain Desire,
do so because
theirs is weak enough to be restrained.

-- William Blake

Wednesday, 24.July.1940
Headquarters, Fighter Command
Bentley Priory
Stanmore, Middlesex, England

The spates of rain and the thick, multi-layered clouds over the South kept the enemy bomber activity to a minimum. The slow, dreary day allowed Group Captain John Spencer to gain ground in his never-ending struggle with paperwork. The progressing hour gave him the excuse he needed to descend the 80 steps into the underground bunker that was the Operations Center of Fighter Command.

John Spencer entered the gallery overlooking the enormous map of Great Britain and the few markers designated hostile. The information indicated solo reconnaissance aircraft at high altitude. The controllers decided the weather added too much risk. The intruders were not likely to see anything of significance, if they ever did find the ground.

"Not much business today, John," said Air Marshal Leonard, Chief of Operations.

"No sir. Maybe we can take a breather this day."

Leonard glanced at the clock that displayed the late afternoon hour. "You may be just on the money, I suspect."

The diminutive and balding figure of Air Commodore Hogan, Chief of Air Intelligence, entered the gallery. He looked down upon the map board as they all did. "Not much, ay?"

"Not today. How are you, James?" asked Leonard.

"Couldn't be better."

"You must have another gem for us."

"I certainly do. The Y Section lads have finally confirmed their ability to jam up this damnable German broken leg night bombing signal."

"What do you mean . . . jam up?"

John Spencer listened as the two senior officers began the discussion several of them had waited for in frustration. The *Luftwaffe Knickebein*, or broken leg, system was a simple, effective method of intersecting radio beams pinpointing the release point for bombers at night or during bad weather. The

RAF discovered and operated a captured system for months in an attempt to find a countermeasure. Since it was a passive system onboard the German bombers receiving coded radio signals broadcast from Europe, their only means of defeating the system was to confuse the receivers.

"It is a term the Y blokes coined like putting jam into a precision watch mechanism . . . it mucks up the equipment . . . like jam in the works."

"It is radio equipment," protested Leonard, rejecting the analogy.

"Truly. It is also a figure of speech. As I understand the process, they find the frequency being used and broadcast a powerful signal on the same frequency, thus blocking the receiver making it impossible to receive the proper signal."

"I see, and they can do this with consistency?"

"So they say. The hard part was developing the equipment to find the selected frequency for a given night. Foul weather forecast for the next few days should give us a good test. I suspect Gerry will try a night mission."

All three officers looked down to the map board for any preliminary indications of what might be coming. None of the intruders appeared to be bombing missions.

"Do the Germans have the system switched on?" asked John Spencer.

"Yes . . . nearly two hours ago."

"Then, we wait."

The tall, slim, stoic figure of their commander Air Chief Marshal Sir Hugh Dowding joined the group. Although he did not smile, John Spencer thought he could detect a slight sparkle in his eyes. Sir Hugh arrived at the same conclusion as the others regarding the state of operations over the United Kingdom. James Hogan briefed the commander on the information from the electronic operations section of the Air Ministry. The news added to his pleasure and actually brought a modest smile to his face.

"I also have good news," he began. "Sir Cyril just rang through with word from the War Cabinet. The President of the United States has approved the sale of thousands of aircraft. Of the lot, we shall receive a thousand and a half of P-40 Warhawk pursuit planes."

"When?" asked Leonard.

"Unfortunately, the first shipment will not arrive until early winter."

"So, we are still on our own," said Leonard.

"I am afraid so, but it is a heartening sign we shall soon have a bountiful source of fighter aeroplanes in the near future."

"It is excellent news, sir," interjected Group Captain Spencer, "however, as I recall, the P-40 is not as capable as the Spitfire, or the Hurricane for that matter."

"Quite right, John, but they are better than Defiants and Gladiators."

"Absolutely."

"Then, we shall rejoice in the accomplishment, shan't we?"

"Indeed, sir."

Dowding looked down on the map board. "It would appear we may have a slow evening. When was the last time any of you were home for supper with your families?"

The grumbles and grunts told most of the story. John Spencer could not remember the last time he ate supper with Mary. If he reached home at all, it was late at night and invariably Mary was asleep when he arrived and when he had to return to Headquarters. They had gone days and weeks since the invasion of Denmark without saying a word to each other. John knew the demands of the war were having a toll on him as well as Mary, but the defense of the country placed greater demands on his time, energy and efforts. Mary Spencer would simply have to understand the sacrifices they all had to make to defeat Hitler and his marauding armies.

"I think His Majesty can spare each of you for the evening. The duty crew can handle the few intruders we may suffer. Take the time and go home," Dowding said.

"You should take your own medicine, Sir Hugh," said Leonard.

They all laughed. It was good to see the normally reserved character of their commander crack just enough to see the man beneath the stoic exterior. "Quite right, Geoffrey. Quite right. Each of us shall try, then."

The group of four senior officers followed their commander out of the gallery. Hogan returned to his subterranean office while the other three officers followed Dowding up the poorly lit, long stairway back to the surface. They dispersed to their respective offices while John trailed him down the western wing of the old but restored monastery.

The dark exterior and now steady light rain compounded the urge to leave the business of war and go home to his wife. Group Captain Spencer looked at the small mountain of paper calling him to deal with the Command's business. He told himself only another hour would be needed to put a healthy dent in the mountain.

More than an hour passed when Air Chief Marshal Dowding knocked lightly on the door and leaned into John Spencer's office. He stood in recognition of Sir Hugh's rank and the respect he felt for the accomplished and decorated officer.

"I thought I told you to go home, John. It is a drippy night, and the paper will wait."

"Yes, sir, but even more will face me tomorrow."

"Go home to Mary, John. She needs you."

The image of Mary Spencer flashed into John's consciousness. Mary never seemed to 'need' him although they did have fun together. The demands on his time especially since the end of the Phony War were a constant irritant between them, but she seemed to be tolerating the loneliness and inconvenience. "Thank you, sir. Shortly, if you don't mind. Just a few more critical items and I will call it a night."

"You are insufferable, John, but I shall acquiesce. Have a good night. I shall see you in the morning."

"Good night, Sir Hugh."

John waited for the slow gait footsteps to drift away, and then he sat back down at his desk. The image of Mary sitting at home having a light supper while reading a book kept him from the papers on his desk. He longed for her company, but the last he wanted was anyone even suggesting he was not devoted 100% to his portion of the war effort. Many people depended upon his productivity to keep things moving. He would not let them down.

The Staff Secretary to Fighter Command refocused his attention to the spectrum of paper before him. The hours dissolved past him until fatigue overcame him. With his eyes shut for the last time in the losing battle, John Spencer's head slowly descended to the desk before him. Another night would pass without relief.

—

Thursday, 25.July.1940
RAF Middle Wallop
Middle Wallop, Hampshire, England
07:30 hours

Pilot Officer Brian Drummond, along with his fellow pilots, looked up from their various seated or reclined positions on the early sunny morning to their leader, Squadron Leader Horatio Darling, as he joined them after the first telephone call of the morning. They waited for what would undoubtedly become the first of maybe several patrols. Such a beautiful day with light winds, nearly clear skies and moderate temperature meant the German Air Force would most likely avail themselves of the classic flying weather conditions and the several plump convoy targets in the Channel. For Pilot Officer Jonathan Kensington, the day would be spent at RAE Farnborough as their guest for another series of evaluation flights.

"Well, lads, here we have it. We will mount up for the short journey to Warmwell and will operate out of there for the day." Darling looked directly into Jonathan's eyes. "Since you will not be with us today," he turned to the spare Czech aviator, "Pilot Officer Mansek will take your place."

Darling allowed the hoots, hollers and jokes for Jonathan's temporary reassignment. Brian could tell his best friend was not particularly excited about leaving the squadron even for a day. Pilot Officer Kormer Mansek would be flying Jonathan's PR-K Spitfire. Jonathan Kensington would wait for a lumbering Anson to transport him to his task after the rest of the squadron departed for RAF Warmwell. They would have to wait to hear what new experience pulled one of their pilots away.

"Low level, Skipper?" asked Flying Sergeant Miles 'Fog' Johnson.

It had been more than a month since they were able to enjoy the thrill of flying close to the terrain. Nearly every pilot took great pleasure being among the trees and hills. The general populace appeared to appreciate the visible signs of an active defense. The rare redeployment gave them an opportunity to show the flag, so to speak, to broadcast the sounds of freedom across the countryside.

"Smashing, then let's hop to it," Darling said.

With the first of the morning checks complete and everyone showing a thumbs up signal, Darling asked for a squadron takeoff and was given permission by the tower. Twelve Spitfires bounced down the inclined grass field toward the south. The full squadron stayed low, barely high enough to retract the wheels, and cleared the trees at the far end by only a few feet. The Spitfires would hold full power for the entire ten-minute flight across the Hampshire and Dorset countryside without overheating the engines. The distinctive spire of Salisbury Cathedral marked their path slightly north of the historic city.

As they approached RAF Warmwell, northwest of Weymouth and Portland harbor, the squadron reformed into a left echelon with Darling initiating the peel off break over the airfield. They landed one behind the other, taxied to their dispersal area marked by two large, general purpose, Army tents as they had seen during their original area orientation flight earlier in the month. One was their Dispersal tent while the other served as the maintenance crew tent. Several of the ground crews waited for them as they stopped their engines. The others would arrive shortly.

The tent conveyed a lack of permanence that made the rustic, rudimentary accommodations more tolerable. A simple, moderate size desk, two telephones and a dozen straight back chairs comprised the full extent of the available furniture. A few of the pilots complained about the lack of a decent place to sit but quickly resigned themselves to lying on the grass. Just as a majority of the pilots began to drift off to sleep basking in the warm southern sun, their first call came in over the telephone.

Flight Lieutenant Robert 'Sparky' Morrow's 'B' Flight took to the air first. Squadron Leader Darling's 'A' Flight received orders to follow within fifteen minutes. As Brian prepared his aircraft for combat, he remembered the rarity of launching half the squadron, and then followed shortly thereafter by the other half of the squadron. The handful of occurrences resulted in a large engagement. He readied his fighter and his mind for what he felt certain would be yet another large engagement. As they climbed in a large spiral over their dispersal airfield, the white trails of the ships' wakes just to the west of Portland identified the bait. If German bombers were headed north from France, they would have no difficulty finding the ripe target of twenty plus merchant ships.

As they continued their climb through 15,000 feet, 'B' flight joined up to reform No.609 Squadron. Off to the east several miles, a squadron of Hurricanes was climbing for position as well. As they converged, the UF tail designator identified No.601 (County of London) Squadron, the millionaire's squadron as they joked in Fighter Command because of the wealth of several of the assigned pilots. Their callsign, 'Weapon,' fit them, as well. Brian also remembered that one of the millionaires in the squadron was the American, Billy Fiske, who had something to do with the cinema industry.

They spotted their target far off on the horizon. A large number of bombers, maybe thirty or more, were headed directly toward them. The escorting swarm of fighters did not become visible for several minutes. The bombers appeared to be split between He111 and Do17 types. Brian remembered they had not seen the German medium bombers in nearly two months.

The Hurricanes leveled off while the Spitfires continued to climb. The RAF fighters would divide the Germans in the usual manner – Hurricanes on the bombers and Spitfires to handle the fighters. The No.609 Squadron Spitfires slowly began to spread out as they picked out their first targets. There would be no element of surprise with this engagement. It would soon be a free-for-all fight.

The air battle lasted for forty minutes until the Germans broke off the fight. The fighters fought to a draw with no airplanes lost on either side.

The Hurricanes of No.601 Squadron had better luck, downing four bombers without a loss. Three burning ships beneath them marked the success of the German attack.

Before they landed, the controllers instructed them to refuel and rearm as quickly as possible. All the pilots had not reached the tent when Squadron Leader Darling reemerged signaling them back to their aircraft. The squadron launched on its second sortie as soon as the aircraft were ready.

No.609 Squadron flew three combat sorties and two transit flights this day. The Germans kept nearly constant pressure on Fighter Command throughout the entire day. No.10 Group was fully occupied protecting shipping in the western approaches while No.11 Group had an even more difficult time over the Dover Straight. For the first time since the Battle of Britain began, anchored shipping and harbor facilities were attacked all along the southern coast from Plymouth to Maidstone. As the intelligence specialists constructed the picture, the *Luftwaffe* lost 18 aircraft, mostly bombers, while Fighter Command lost seven precious fighters, but the real tragedy came from the sea with the depths claiming 11 ships and their valuable cargo.

Pilot Officer Jonathan Kensington waited for them at Dispersal when they returned to Middle Wallop. "What was it this time, 'Harness'?" asked his section leader, Flight Lieutenant Robert 'Sparky' Morrow.

"Messerschmitt One One Oh, I'm afraid."

"Oh dear," joked 'Waggle' Davies, "stepping down a bit, aren't they."

"How was it?" asked Brian.

"Fairly fast machine although not particularly maneuverable, as we already know. It is no wonder why they round up into those bloody circles when we approach. Even the Defiant can out turn Göring's Destroyer."

"You mean you were able to fly an M E One Ten," said Frank Burns, the oldest of the Americans and seemingly the most knowledgeable.

"Quite so, actually."

"How did we get one of their fighters?"

"Poor bloke had a forced landing."

"He's already flown the One Oh Nine," added Brian Drummond.

"I'll be damned," said Burns.

"We should hope not," answered Davies, instigating a good laugh by all.

"In fact, from what we know, Farnborough also has a Heinkel One One One and most of a Dornier One Seven."

"Quite a little air force," added Morrow.

"How is the visibility from the seat?" asked Miles Johnson.

"Bad, to say the least. All this structure around you with a larger cockpit which makes the obstructions even worse than the One Oh Nine."

"How does it handle?"

"Like a sled. I sure wouldn't want to fight in the machine."

"Kind of makes you want to go out and chew up a few, doesn't it," said Roger 'Jackstay' Beamish.

They continued to compare notes about the twin-engine fighter while the debriefings were completed, and they told Jonathan about the action he had missed. It had not been a good day for Fighter Command. It was also the hardest the Germans had fought since Dunkirk. Events were happening on a more rapid pace that gave all of them the impression the Germans were getting serious about the invasion preparations. This day gave them plenty to talk about after the evening meal and before fatigue captured the remainder of their strength.

—

Thursday, 25.July.1940
Cabinet Room
No.10 Downing Street
Whitehall, London, England
16:00 hours

"Shall we begin, gentlemen," announced Sir Edward. "Sir John, you are first up."

Home Secretary Sir John Anderson removed a small stack of papers from his leather, carrying case, and behind him to hand the papers to Lieutenant Colonel Vivian Dyke of the Secretrariat Staff. "One to each minister, if you will, and the remainder to me."

Dyke distributed a single sheet from the stack to each sitting minister in His Majesty's Government, including those not officially members of the War Cabinet, and returning the remainder to the Home Secretary.

MOST SECRET - RAINBOW

```
Gift to the Americans
-- Gun Turrets in Aircraft,
-- R.D.F,
-- Rocket Defence of Ships,
-- Multiple Pom-Pom,
-- Armour Plate,
```

```
-- Light A.A. Guns,
-- Chemical Warfare,
-- Explosives,
-- Gyro Predictor Gun-Sight,
-- Petrol Injection Engines,
-- Jet Propulsion Engines & Internal
   Combustion Turbines
-- Automatic Oxygen Separator,
-- Martin Baker Barrage Cable Cutters,
-- D.P.L. Scheme,
-- P.A.C. Scheme,
-- Long Aerial Mines,
-- Magnetic Mines (Naval),
-- Gliding Torpedoes,
-- Radio Navigation,
-- Compass,
-- Self Sealing Petrol Tanks,
-- 1/2" Gun for Aircraft.
```

MOST SECRET - RAINBOW

"I must remind everyone that this discussion is considered most secret and must be protected accordingly. You have before you the final listing of technology items to be shipped to the United States. We have negotiated this listing with the services. Everyone short of the War Cabinet is in agreement."

"What is the significance of 'Rainbow'?" asked Prime Minister Churchill.

"A little tongue in cheek, I'm afraid," answered Sir John. "The pot of gold at the end of the rainbow."

"Gift to the Americans?"

"Likewise."

"That shall not survive this day. This is difficult enough without any antagonism of our American cousins. It is important we discuss and agree to your listing, John, but this is not a social exercise." Churchill was clearly not pleased and seemd to be winding himself up. A slight, flushed scowl grew upon his distinctive, round face as he raised and pointed his right index finger at everyone in the room. "The War Cabinet has not yet formally approved this exchange, but this had better be taken seriously – deadly seriously. We are faced with mounting evidence across the Channel the Nawzees intend to invade our precious island," he pounded his fist on the table, "within a month, two at the outside. We need the bloody Americans in this fight. Without them, our struggle to defend our island home and ultimately to liberate Europe will be much longer, and more costly in precious lives of this generation and His Majesty's treasure. If there is but one person involved with this technical exchange program who cannot approach this task with the reverence it deserves, I want him removed immediately and confined *incommunicado* for the duration of the war."

"Winston, you cannot do that," interjected Greenwood.

"I most assuredly can, Arthur . . . under the Emergency Powers Act . . . as such a person is a direct threat to the security of the Empire."

"Dear God," mumbled Lord Halifax.

"Am I perfectly clear in this matter?" The Prime Minister waited for an affirmative response or gesture from each man in the Cabinet Room.

"Very well, then . . . Sir John, please proceed."

Anderson cleared his throat. "We will retrieve each of these copies and remove the offending title tonight."

"Thank you."

"To continue, are there any questions, or any discussion?"

"Chemical warfare?" Lord Halifax asked.

Anthony Eden leaned forward. "That is the Army's, I'm afraid. It is as much the intelligence we have collected from the Germans as it is our research and development at Porton Down. Included in our materials for transfer are the chemical formulae as well as manufacturing, storage and delivery processes developed by Porton Down for various choking, irritant, blistering and nerve agents. We believe this work is more advanced than the Americans have been able to carry out."

"Hopefully, those chemicals never see the light of day," Halifax said.

"Yes, well, I.G. Farben has been under the heavy thumb of their Nawzee masters," added Churchill. "The Americans need to know where we are and more importantly where the Germans are in this disgusting arena of warfare. Allow me to ask, I presume we are including our atomic work to date in the explosive group."

"Yes," Anderson responded. "In addition to the chemistry and production of plastic explosives as well as the high order weapons explosives for bombs, torpedos and such, we will ensure the latest work by George Thompson's committee will be included. We have also agreed to assign John Cockcroft to the exchange team as the representative of the MAUD Committee."

Churchill nodded his agreement.

"I am familiar with most of these items, except for P.A.C. Scheme," Attlee said.

Sir Archie Sinclair answered this one. "It is the Parachute And Cable device that uses a rocket to deploy a long cable with a parachute to keep the cable airborne longer. We expect an air defense artillery unit to launch the device into the path of oncoming bombers to damage the wing, foul control surfaces, or drag one of Professor Lindemann's aerial mines into the bomber."

Attlee nodded.

"As we discussed before, we will include the Rolls Royce engine but not Whittle's prototype, correct?" asked Churchill.

"Yes," answered Sinclair. "A complete Merlin Mark III engine will be shipped along with a complete set of design and tooling drawings. Group Captain Pearce has been assigned to the team and he will be prepared to discuss the engineering drawings for Whittle's turbine engine, but all the prototype units are needed for development."

"Yes, well, the Germans are ahead of us there, so the drawings will have to suffice for now," Winston said.

After a brief pause, Sir John said, "If there are no further questions . . ."

"I have a few more. Has this list," Churchill said, holding up the paper, "been shared with Colonel Donovan?"

"Yes," answered Sir John. "I met with him two days ago. I knew it would be a continuing topic, and as we are approaching the execution stage, I took it upon myself to brief Colonel Donovan."

"Excellent . . . quite appropriate."

"Lord Lothian has had the preliminary list for several days with verbal instructions to discuss the items in general but not divulge the list until approved by the War Cabinet," added Lord Halifax.

"Excellent as well. I am still not convinced we should do this, or at least not at this critical time," Churchill said. "On one hand, I know it must be done, to protect our most secret weapons work and to hopefully convince the Americans about our alliance with them. Yet, on the other hand, my gut keeps telling me no for reasons I am not able to articulate, which I acknowledge is most unusual for me."

Several of the ministers chuckle in familiar recognition.

"What are the reasons we should not do this?" the Prime Minister asked.

Air Archibald Sinclair looked around the room nervously.

"Let's have it, Archie."

"Well, Winston, I think I speak for most of us, our primary, if not paramount, concern is the risk that these most sensitive technologies to our defense efforts will find their way into German hands. The Americans just do not seem to be as concerned or as capable of dealing with German spies as we would like. We have seen too much evidence of German success and the failure of American counter-espionage efforts, for what they are."

"That is exactly why Colonel Donovan is here, now," responded Churchill.

"Colonel Donovan cannot plug the leaks in the dike by himself. He holds no office or authority. We are talking about now, not a year from now."

"If the Germans invade," interjected Lord Halifax, "we will not have time, and most likely not capacity either, to share these items with the Americans, so that they can continue the fight. This is insurance against invasion."

"There is that aspect," Winston said. "Anything else?" Churchill motioned toward each man, as if to say, speak now or forever hold your peace. He looked to Lord Halifax. "Please message Lord Lothian to gain his counsel on this critical question of information security as Archie has raised it."

"Very well."

"Lastly, do we have a price on this list?" he asked, placing his right index finger on the paper.

"No," responded Sir John.

"I will convey our concerns as diplomatically as possible to President Roosevelt in a private and personal message and seek his perspective. He knows are intentions are good, and I am certain he recognizes the validity of our concerns. While we are doing these last few items, please do your best to generate a cost or value for the proposed exchange program, if you would, Sir John. I do not yet know what benefit such a number will be, yet better to have it than not."

"It might frighten us, Winston."

Several ministers chuckled, as did Churchill. "Quite so." The Prime Minister turned to Sir Edward. "Let us postpone the remainder of the agenda to tomorrow's meeting."

"Very well, sir. We are adjourned, gentlemen. Have a good evening."

—

Friday, 26.July.1940
RAF Middle Wallop
Middle Wallop, Hampshire, England

A light rain fell as the pilots of No.609 Squadron left morning meal at the Mess. For Pilot Officer Brian Drummond, the characteristic moderation of the rain in England contrasted vividly with the violent thunderstorms, tornadoes, hail and deluge rain events he was quite familiar with on the plains of Kansas. The rain actually felt good and strangely warm. Maybe it was the lull in the war the rain usually caused that made Brian appreciate the precipitation so much, or maybe it was just the plethora of green the rain produced. All he truly knew was he loved the English rain.

"Someone said the cloud chasers forecasted this as the leading edge of a large storm," said Jonathan, as they walked with the two Czech pilots. "Maybe they will give us a break."

"*Ja* needing no break." ," growled Kradilcek, the former Czech Air Force captain and ace. "*Ja* needing dead Nemci!" The hatred in his voice gave Brian a chill.

"Janus, you say, 'I do not need a break. I need dead Germans!'" corrected Mansek, emphasizing the missing words.

"My countryman has no love of our enemy," Mansek said to Brian and Jonathan.

"We share his feelings," Jonathan answered.

The two Czech pilots had seen more combat than most of the squadron. The stories of the aerial combat in Poland and France intrigued most of the pilots. Although they fought Germans over the beaches of Northern France, they fought more as equals. The Czech and Polish aircraft were no match for the *Luftwaffe* and that made the fight appreciably different.

The squadron was reported Available. The pilots had just settled into their usual wait for the call when the six Hurricanes of No.238 Squadron's A Flight took to the air, and No.609 Squadron was brought to Readiness. The six aluminum, wood and fabric Hurricanes quickly disappeared into the gathering clouds to the west. The weather forecasters predicted thunderstorms and heavy weather later in the day.

"Looks like we may have a contest between Gerry and the weather for what will give us the most trouble today," said Flight Lieutenant John Davies.

"Spot on, I'd say," added Flight Lieutenant Robert Morrow.

The speculation about the weather occupied the conversation of those who chose to remain awake while they waited. The six No.238 Squadron Hurricanes returned an hour later with their gunport tapes intact – no engagement. The clouds continued to grow and move closer adding to the anticipation they might get an early release.

Stories of the heavy action in No.11 Group over the Dover Straight and along the Southern coast to the east of Southampton gave the pilots more to talk about. Their sister group covering the southeast corner of England carried the brunt of the German assault so far. The same names continued to pop up in the story telling amplifying the stature of a dozen leaders among the pilots of Fighter Command. Lord Jeremy Morrison's name came out several times. His squadron, No.74 Squadron, led by the quiet but methodically efficient South African, 'Sailor' Malan, gained substantial reputation with their successes. According to word-of-mouth, Lord Jeremy was now an ace with five victories. It was good to know he was still doing well.

The squadron was released in early afternoon due to the growing storm billowing to the southwest and the lack of enemy activity. Johnson and Stockard departed at a near run trying to reach their girlfriends before the rain. Burns, Koenig and Maxwell wanted Brian to join them for a run into London. The thought of seeing friends and maybe a few women tempted the young American, but he decided against the effort in deference to the limited time available and the potential inquisition he undoubtedly would be submitted to, by the three older countrymen. Brian and Jonathan walked casually back to the Mess with the two Czech pilots. Kradilcek grumbled some more about being denied another opportunity to kill Germans.

"Mister Drummond, sir," called out one of the mess corporals. "You have a lady visitor in the lounge."

Brian's mind raced through the possibilities. The most probable was Rosemary Kensington. She was certainly the most impulsive and forward. Brian glanced at Jonathan and shrugged his shoulders as the two Czech pilots continued to the wide staircase to the first floor rooms. Jonathan must have thought it was his sister as well following Brian into the lounge.

An elegantly dressed woman sat with her back to the entry. Hearing the footsteps, she stood and turned to face the two pilots. The shocked expression on Brian's face brought a smile to her face.

"I don't suppose you expected to see me here," said Mary Spencer.

Brian swallowed hard and eventually looked to his best friend who could only return an intense expression of curiosity. Brian looked back to Mary and then Jonathan before he gathered his composure to speak. "Is something wrong?"

"No, no, quite the contrary. Everything is simply brilliant." She looked to Jonathan. "Aren't you going to introduce me to your colleague?" she asked extending her right hand.

Brian froze stuttering a few sounds. What would he say?

"I'm Mary Spencer," she said, grasping Jonathan's hand firmly.

"Pleased to meet you, Miss Spencer. My name is Jonathan Kensington."

"Pleased to meet you, I am sure."

Brian's heart raced. He tried to think of an action, some way to extricate himself from this embarrassing situation. Jonathan had to recognize her name and his stammering inability to respond.

"If you would excuse us, Miss Spencer. We have a few chores to tend to upstairs. Brian shan't be a moment."

"Certainly."

Brian nodded his head and submitted to the guiding hand grasping his right elbow. The two pilots walked up the wide staircase and down the right corridor to Brian's room. Once inside, Jonathan turned to face his friend.

"You are bonking her as well, aren't you?"

Brian swallowed hard again. He tried to think of something disarming to say but could not find the words. He remained frozen before his best friend, his eyes searching for help.

"Dear God almighty, Brian. If my guess is correct, that woman downstairs is THE Mary Spencer, as in Missus Group Captain John Spencer." Brian reluctantly nodded his head. "Are you out of your fucking mind. She is the wife of your benefactor, the man who changed your squadron assignment so you could fly Spitfires, and the man who introduced you to Winston bloody Churchill, himself. Are you out of your frigging, sodding mind?" he nearly shouted.

Brian felt like a worm or worse yet a child being chastised for some ridiculous act. He knew Jonathan was correct. His best friend was only trying to be a best friend. How could he possibly explain the circumstances behind the situation? There probably was no explanation, only factors or clues.

"What the hell are you going to do?" asked Jonathan with anger still in his voice.

Roger Beamish pushed the door open. "What seems to be the problem here? Most of your words have echoed and intrigued more than I am certain you would want to know."

"Sorry, sir," said Jonathan with Brian feeling even more embarrassment. Beamish closed the door behind him. Jonathan turned back to Brian. "Well?"

"Well, what?"

"You know frigging well what."

"I don't know what she wants."

"Dear God above, are you that naive? She has sex written in big bold letters in those dark eyes of hers. You cannot do this, Brian."

"That's what got me into this in the first place."

"Now, what does that mean?"

"She said she would tell her husband we were having an affair even if we weren't. She said she was lonely because he was never home, and all she wanted was some companionship."

"Some companionship. You never answered my question, you are bonking her, aren't you?"

"Only a couple of times."

Jonathan sat on the bed and placed his face in his hands. Brian waited patiently for his friend to consider his next action, the words he might use or even whether he would respond. The longer he waited, the more Brian began to feel resentment at the admonishment from Jonathan.

"Jonathan, I don't have to justify myself to you, and I thought, as my friend, you would understand my situation. I'm not asking you to agree with me, but I do expect you to be a friend."

Pilot Officer Kensington looked up at Brian. "Please don't tell me you haven't done anything wrong."

"Look, Jonathan, I know this isn't right. If anything, I feel like she forced me into the affair. I like her, but the thought of risking my relationship with her husband sends chills through me. I couldn't find a way out. What do you think I should do?"

"End it, Brian. End it, now."

"What if she follows through with her threat to tell her husband?"

Jonathan Kensington stood up to face his friend. "Do you actually think she would do that?"

"I don't know, and I'm sure I don't want to know."

"Haven't you considered the risk of Group Captain Spencer finding out?"

Now, Brian sank, feeling the walls closing in on him. "Of course, I've thought about that."

Flames of anger burst into Jonathan's eyes. "Are you going to fuck every woman in the British Isles?"

The sword blow sliced through his core draining the warmth of life from Brian. He could only open his mouth. No air came out. Brian staggered backward a few steps feeling a combination of repulsion and remorse.

What could he say? What should he say? Was Jonathan simply observing reality and expressing what had to be true? He had been in Great Britain just over a year, and he had been with more than a handful of women including a convicted and sentenced prostitute-spy, the wife of his benefactor and the sister of his best friend. He felt like a victim rather than the predator Jonathan implied he was.

Jonathan recognized the reaction to his words. "I am sorry, Brian. I did not mean for it to sound quite like that. I know these affairs are not entirely your doing. Maybe I am wrong in this."

"I never meant to hurt anyone."

"I know." Jonathan began to pace like a caged big cat. "Look, we have been up here entirely too long, and your important guest has been waiting, undoubtedly not patiently, standing in the lobby. Go to her, see what she wants, and just be as careful and discreet as you can."

Brian nodded his head, gathered his composure and checked his appearance in the bureau mirror. He walked to the door and turned to check his friend for any last sign. Jonathan swung a fist toward him as a figurative, brotherly blow and smiled.

"Be careful."

"I will. Thanks, Jonathan."

Brian checked his uniform one last time in the hallway mirror before descending the stairs. He took a deep breath to relieve some of the tension he felt as he entered the lounge.

"I was wondering if something happened to you," Mary said with genuine concern.

"Jonathan and I had a few things that had to be taken care of upstairs."

"I trust everything is now as it should be."

"Yes."

"Shall we go then?"

Brian hesitated with the feeling of the still warm admonishment from Jonathan. He felt some safety and strength in the exposed and quasi-public place. "Go where?"

Mary leaned forward toward his left ear. "I need you, Brian, in the most desperate way."

His heart nearly exploded in his chest. He felt a strange urge to run, but engulfing flames of lust and physical pleasure drew him closer to the vortex. Jonathan tried to help him see the error of his relationship with

Mary Spencer, but the pleasure of her embrace made the acceptance too easy.

The illicit lovers drove to a quaint, picturesque country village inn for a night of passion, release and fulfillment. They gave to the other precisely what each of them needed, wanted and craved. There were very few discernible words between them as they banished the outside world.

Brian justified his contribution with thoughts of helping Mary, making life easier for her, and he tried desperately to eliminate any vision of Jonathan Kensington or John Spencer. He refused to believe anything so wonderful could be wrong.

—

Saturday, 27.July.1940
RAF Middle Wallop
Middle Wallop, Hampshire, England

Brian had not considered the means of his return to the airbase. The lightening sky of the early morning hours signaled the urgency Brian felt. Against the protestation of his lover, Brian left a satisfied and content Mary Spencer despite her repeated but feeble attempts to lure him back to her appreciative embrace.

Brian quickly realized there were no taxis in the country. He considered asking Mary to return him as she had taken him, but the continued temptation would probably be more than he could resist. Finally, he woke the innkeeper who was none too happy about the intrusion, but in the end, the older man's country generosity and good-natured spirit overcame the irritation. The innkeeper dropped Brian off at the front gate across from the Officer's Mess barely 15 minutes prior to their normal duty time of 06:00. The guards grinned and snickered as yet another crazy pilot returned from a night's foray into the countryside.

Brian arrived at Dispersal without the benefit of a morning shower, shave, meal or a refreshing night's sleep, but with a smile on his face, nonetheless. He was the next to last to reach their duty station. Jonathan Kensington chose to only shake his head in knowing dissatisfaction with his friend's choice of actions while others gave seemingly knowing winks. Fortunately, Brian told himself, no one appeared to know whom the attractive, older woman was who snatched him up and took him away, but most of his comrades could recognize a lover.

"We weren't quite sure if you were going to make it back from your night of heavenly bliss," joked 'Red' Burns, adding a few extra hoots for good measure.

"No problem."

"I'll bet," added 'Slim' Koenig.

Squadron Leader Darling returned from the Operations building. "All right, lads. Leave loverboy to his memories and gather up your flying kit, we are off to Warmwell for another day's work."

Before the squadron launched, a section of three VK Hurricanes from No.238 Squadron took off toward the south undoubtedly on an early morning mission. Halfway to Warmwell, the squadron received a call from Middle Wallop Sector Control diverting them directly to assist the element of their sister squadron. The three Hurricanes jumped into a flight of Ju87 dive-bombers only to be bounced by a squadron of Bf109 fighters. The No.609 Squadron Spitfires quickly evened up the numbers as the bombers promptly deposited their explosive loads in the vicinity of Convoy BACON without effect. The furball of fighters lasted nearly half an hour, long after the Stuka dive-bombers had escaped.

Brian noted several thick, black smoke trails heading to the water below. He could not tell whether they were friend or foe, but knew in time they would find out, to what side they belonged. Brian was able to get numerous hits but nothing conclusive before he ran out of ammunition and had to extricate himself from the fight.

When the fight was over, they turned westward, landing at RAF Warmwell. Once at the Dispersal tent, Brian learned one of the smoke trails belonged to one of his countrymen. Pilot Officer Henry 'Hank' Maxwell did not survive the engagement. 'Boxer' Stockard saw Maxwell's aircraft explode before he could turn to assist him. Johnson and Koenig both scored solo victories during the engagement.

The squadron flew one more sortie protecting Convoy BACON before returning to RAF Middle Wallop. The boiling, towering Cumulonimbus clouds spread thunder, hail and heavy rain across Southern England. The sights and sounds of the approaching storms reminded Brian Drummond of his native Kansas, as the pilots marveled at the sight and joked about the relief mother-nature gave them.

After the requisite debriefing, the pilots were released for the day due to the heavy weather. They barely reached the shelter of the Officer's Mess when the storms reached them. Brian retired to his room, closed the door, doffed his clothes and fell into bed. Within seconds, he became oblivious to the violent storm outside his window and the several knocks on his door.

The rumbles and flashes had stopped although a steady rain continued when Brian awoke from his afternoon recovery slumber. It was nearly time for the evening meal. He casually cleaned himself, changed uniforms and descended the stairs. He entered the crowded, smoke-filled, and raucous Officer's Mess bar. Brian recognized pilots and other officers from all three of the Middle Wallop squadrons.

"Good of you to join us, old boy," shouted John 'Waggle' Davies, as Brian made his way to the bar for a pint of bitter. "We have already toasted our lost comrade."

"Several of us thought you might have died, you were sleeping so hard," said Roger 'Jackstay' Beamish.

"I didn't get much sleep last night," Brian answered without thinking.

"So you had a fun filled night with your rather comely lass, did ya now, laddie," laughed Beamish, as several of the pilots added their own taunts.

The two other Americans, Frank Burns and Stan Koenig, joined the small group. Brian noticed Jonathan at the far end of the long room. He apparently wanted a little distance from his adulterous friend. Brian decided to let Jonathan come around when he was ready.

"We were talking earlier about the news from Eleven Group," said the diminutive Stan Koenig. "Seems the Krauts have started using Messerschmitt's for dropping bombs, then they become fighters. Pretty nifty, huh?"

"We've managed to chew up those damn Stukas rather nicely, I'd say," added Davies.

"Can't imagine fighter pilots dropping bombs worth a damn," said Burns.

"Maybe not, but they managed to sink the HMS *Wren*, a rather capable Royal Navy destroyer, so they can't be that bad."

"Lucky shot."

"Lucky or not, if memory serves, the *Wren* is the first Navy ship sunk since this battle began, and it was done in by a bloody, friggin' One Oh Nine bloke," said Davies.

"The most disturbing aspect of the fight so far must be our loss of pilots, and the damnable Germans have only gone after the bloody shipping in the Channel. They haven't even started on the aerodromes and factories," said Beamish pulling a dark cloud of realism over the conversation.

For Brian, the combination of the potential consequences of his affair with Mary Spencer, Jonathan's strong disapproval of his actions and the loss of the squadron's fifth pilot gave him every excuse he needed to drown the emotions into numbness. The young American was not alone as numerous others with near equal representation from the three resident squadrons joined him. They tried to laugh about the precarious situation around them and the grim image of the future. None of the pilots would acknowledge the dire prospects, but they all felt them. Pilot Officer Brian Drummond, left wing of Green Section, No.609 (West Riding of Yorkshire) Squadron was the first to fall this Saturday night. His section leader, Flight Lieutenant Roger Beamish, caught his fall, recognized the condition and called the new right wingman, Pilot Officer Janus Kradilcek, to help him carry the young American to his room with as much dignity as could be provided an unconscious, large man.

—

Chapter 17

Better to be lucky than good.

-- The Aviator's Mantra

Sunday, 28.July.1940
RAF Middle Wallop
Middle Wallop, Hampshire, England

The summer mornings began to blur into the same homogeneous mass of routine from the wake-up call of the mess corporal, a breakfast be-grudgingly eaten, the walk across A343, through the well-guarded gate and multitudinous buildings of an RAF sector control station to Hangar No.5, and check-in with Corporal Warren. This warm day moved to the same rhythm. The pilots gathered at Dispersal while either Squadron Leader Darling or Corporal Warren called Sector Control with the availability of No.609 Squadron. More often than not, the squadron was brought to Available status although the incidents of jumping directly to Readiness or Standby were increasing. The pilots took a collective sigh when Corporal Warren announced this day they were at Available status. Although cloud cover above Southern England was multilayered and prevalent, the weather was not particularly bad by British weather standards, but apparently it was enough to keep the Germans slowed down from their pace.

Brian stayed within his usual routine. Collecting his flying kit, he walked to his PR-F Spitfire and his crew. The aircraft was fully loaded and ready to leap into action at the instant of command. Bernie ran through the few out-standing squawks, snags as he called them – as yet uncorrected maintenance problems. The gun camera needed a small replacement electrical connector. Several cowling latches had to be replaced. They were still waiting for the parts. None of the discrepancies would affect the combat performance of the Spitfire Mark IA although the intelligence folks would not obtain the reel of film they used to record aerial combat engagements.

Brian returned to the lounging pilots outside the Dispersal building. "Who's due back at noon?" Brian asked of Jonathan Kensington.

"'Waggle' is due back today. 'Fog' has another day."

"Who's next?"

"Boxer.'"

"When's your next break?" Brian asked as his thoughts jumped to Jonathan's sister.

"I do believe I am scheduled for a one day this Friday. Why?"

Brian leaned his chair back against the wall and raised his face to the sky as if the Sun would warm his face. He closed his eyes although the cloud cover hid the Sun. The trips to London and his time with Anne Booth continued to haunt him. He could not adequately explain the growing attraction to Rosemary Kensington. It felt like he was grabbing for a life ring in the water. The struggle with Anne's crimes and her betrayal stuck with him. Fortunately, Rosemary's blooming influence diluted Brian's conscious thoughts of Anne.

"What is on your mind, Brian?" asked Jonathan with an edge of concern.

Brian sat up and looked around. A few of the other pilots who were outside appeared to be absorbed in some discussion. "Nothing, really."

"Why don't I believe you?"

"I was just wondering when we would have a break together."

"Rose, is it then?"

Brian reacted to the reality of Jonathan's recognition. He did not want him to be correct although he knew his best friend saw his thought quite clearly. "Naw. I was just thinkin' about London," Brian lied.

Jonathan was not to be swayed. "Now, now, Brian. It is all over your face."

The flush of embarrassment heated him. He quickly saw the situation as lost and decided to change the subject. "Did you see the gun camera films from last Sunday's mission?"

"Good show," laughed Jonathan in response to the overt attempt at redirection. "Yes, I did. What was your point?"

"Some great flying, huh?"

"Yes, Brian. It was splendid flying."

Jonathan was perceptive enough to recognize the conflict within Brian. He pushed his chair back against the wall as Brian had done earlier.

Pilot Officer Brian Drummond was silently thankful for the respite. He wanted to talk about Anne's betrayal and the newly ignited attraction to Jonathan's sister, to seek Jonathan's advice and counsel. It was the slow times that bothered him the most. He asked himself the same questions Inspector Dunwoody asked him regarding his relationship with Anne. He wanted answers, but none seemed to be forthcoming.

The telephone rang and Brian's attention along with all the other pilots focused on the next set of words. "Squadron to Readiness," announced Corporal Warren.

Brian visualized the hostile raid blocks beginning to appear and move across the map board at Fighter Command. One or more of those blocks were undoubtedly moving across the Sector Control map board in the bunker at the North end of the airfield.

"Another convoy must be in harm's way," said 'Sparky' Morrow.

"Damn Gerries must think they are going to sink the Navy," added 'Boxer' Stockard.

"Just maybe the bloody Gerries are drawing us out, setting a trap," 'Jackstay' Beamish contributed as he left the Dispersal building to join the growing number of pilots waiting outside.

Brian immediately returned to the September day nearly two years ago when Malcolm Bainbridge exposed him to his first mock aerial combat. The Germans did indeed continue to increase their attacks on merchant and naval ships in the English Channel, but to their knowledge they had yet to attack England itself. All the overflights had been reconnaissance flights or inconsequential aerial combat near the coast. Were the Germans toying with Fighter Command like a cat playing with a mouse caught in the open? Were they trying to slowly bleed the air defense system until it could no longer maintain air superiority – most probably a prerequisite for the Germans to attempt an invasion?

"We are next, I'm afraid," 'Sparky' Morrow said.

"We'll simply have to keep the damn Krauts outta here," said 'Red' Burns.

"Easier said than done, I should think," added Morrow.

The telephone rang again bringing the squadron to Standby. Brian headed toward his PR-F Spitfire. He refused to believe they were the mice. Their situation might not look the brightest, but they had demonstrated their skills against the best German fighters. He kept reminding himself of the lessons taught to him by Malcolm. Keep your eyes on the horizon. Take any long journey one step at a time. Wise advice it seemed.

"We are to Standby," said Bernie Gordon, as he joined his pilot at the aircraft.

"Yep."

Brian checked his helmet, oxygen mask, goggles and gloves on the instrument panel, and the connection of his headphones and mask. A quick visual scan of the cockpit told him everything was ready for takeoff. He leaned against the trailing edge of the wing.

"Had enough waiting?" asked Gordon.

"That's a way of saying it. Too many negative thoughts. A lotta folks seem to be worried about what lies ahead."

"Aren't you?"

"I suppose, but I'm only going to think about winning the next fight."

"How do you do this every day?"

Brian thought about the question. It was certainly not something he spent much time thinking about. "The waiting is worse than combat, I think."

"Aye, but how do you take the pressure?"

"Ignore it."

Bernie Gordon laughed and rocked against the wing. "I guess that would work."

Brian laughed with his crew chief. "It does for me."

Horatio Darling and Roger Beamish as well as the other pilots of Blue and Green Sections walked toward the flight line. The casual walking pace told him they were probably being launched on a routine patrol over some convoy. Brian stood and waited for his section leader to join him.

"We've a convoy to watch over, again, laddie," said Beamish. "Nothing new."

Brian nodded his head in response and waited for his section leader to turn toward his own aircraft, and then climbed into the cockpit. He moved smoothly and efficiently through his pre-start actions.

"Clear," commanded Brian.

"Clear," responded Gordon telling Brian the propeller arc was free of any obstructions, animate or otherwise.

Brian cracked the throttle open and pushed the starter button. With three blades passing the vertical position, Brian switched the magnetos to BOTH and the Merlin fired off promptly producing a black cloud of fuel rich smoke. The big engine roared to life as Brian pulled the throttle back. The popping and sputtering conveyed the engine's protest at being left at idle. He pushed the throttle forward just enough to give him a smooth running engine.

The launch process took a lazy eight minutes since they had not been given a scramble command, and no one was under attack. Finding the convoy below the clouds took a little longer than expected, but the thirty plus ships of various sizes moved in a straight easterly direction. They were near the coast and surely were within sight of the Southern shore of England. The radio remained strangely quiet until it was time for the six Spitfires to return to Middle Wallop.

Squadron Leader Darling led the six fighters in a graceful descent toward the convoy. He signaled for Flight Lieutenant Beamish to split off toward the North. They were going to make a low pass down either side of the convoy. The maneuver, while great for the morale of the seamen, was dangerous. All it would take is one trigger happy gunner to ruin their whole day.

They spread out across the Channel surface barely a few yards above the gentle waves. Beamish advanced his throttle to full open to allow the deep, rich purr of the Merlin engines to complement the sight. Even though Brian was the farthest from the ships, he could see men along the railings waving and undoubtedly cheering the passing fighters. They turned north, rejoined as a flight of six and headed for home. Darling kept the flight low all the way back to Middle Wallop.

Darling asked for and received permission for a low pass over the hangars before they peeled off for landing. The high speed Spitfires had the same effect on the jaded airmen and pilots. Everyone loved the demonstration of power and grace.

"So, you blokes thought you would put on a little show for us earthbound malcontents, did ya now," joked 'Sparky' Morrow, as they walked back to Dispersal.

"We certainly did not have a smidgen of excitement on that patrol, so why not," responded Beamish.

"All the gunport tapes are still intact, so it had to be a bore," added 'Red' Burns.

The remainder of the afternoon seemed to slow even more. Only one Hurricane from No.238 Squadron took off to the North on what had to be a maintenance check flight. The night fighters of No.604 Squadron were beginning their preparatory engine run-ups when the squadron was finally released for the evening.

Walking back to the Mess without the sounds of war while the Sun was still above the horizon even though it was nearly eight o'clock in the evening gave Brian a vivid image of the summer one year ago. The varied melody of many birds added the feel of Hyde Park and the casual walk with Rosemary.

Brian looked to his best friend as they walked toward the main gate. "Let's go into the Mucky Ducky," he said.

"It is Sunday evening, Brian."

"I know, but I don't want to get drunk in the Mess. Not tonight."

"Getting pissed won't make her go away."

"Are you going or not?"

Jonathan considered the urgency in Brian's voice. Against his better judgment, the left wing of Red Section consented to the journey. "Someone will have to keep you out of trouble. I suppose I'm elected."

The two young pilots skipped the evening meal, borrowed an automobile and made it the ten miles up the A343 to Andover and the Black Swan Pub. As was often the case, the patronage was on the light side, which suited

Brian. It only took a few pints of near black, heavy, earthy Guinness to loosen Brian's tongue. The two friends drank, talked, drank and talked until the world around Brian began to blur along with his speech. Jonathan shared his friend's pain, helped to put events in perspective and limited his intoxication, to transport Brian back to his bed at the RAF Middle Wallop Officer's Mess.

—

Monday, 29.July.1940
RAF Middle Wallop
Middle Wallop, Hampshire, England

"**D**on't you look like a pile of fresh dung," said 'Sparky' Morrow, as Brian and Jonathan joined the squadron at the Dispersal building.

Brian felt worse than the comparison. He knew Squadron Leader Darling would not be happy with his diminished state, which is only one of many reasons Brian passed up breakfast. Jonathan reluctantly and begrudgingly did his part to protect his young American compatriot from the merciless taunts of the pilots. The ritual came with the profession. They lived near the edge, and they enjoyed reminding each other where the edge was whether it was alcohol, women, automobiles or airplanes. It was a private connection between them, a bond among brothers.

"Uh," was all Brian could grunt.

"What was the reason this time?" asked Roland Stockard.

"Women."

"The woman," said 'Waggle' Davies, now back from his two-day break.

"Ah, leave him alone," responded Jonathan. The defense rarely worked. Often, it simply incited the frenzy.

"Now, we have something," 'Sparky' Morrow said. "What woman, pray tell." He sounded like an old woman at afternoon tea seeking the latest society gossip.

"I managed, with the assistance of a friend, to put this mysterious puzzle together."

"Do tell."

"It seems our young buck got himself tangled up with a prostitute-spy. The woman was convicted and is soon to be executed by the hangman, so the word has it."

Brian felt a bone-shaking nausea swallow his body. He could not tell whether it was the hangover or the discovery that made him feel so bad. In a flash, Brian disappeared around the corner of the building to vomit in a strangely violent manner like his insides would explode. Squadron Leader Darling waited outside with the others when he returned.

"Mister Drummond, in my office now!"

Brian felt worse than 'Sparky' Morrow's description. His efforts to avoid detection failed. He knew the speech that loomed before him. Brian pulled his shoulders back, fought the rumbling nausea that saturated his body and tried to put his best face on for his commander.

"It won't help there mate," taunted Morrow. "Skipper's got you on the mucky side."

Brian tried to smile as he entered the Dispersal building. Corporal Warren smiled at him, as if to bolster his spirits. It did not work. He felt an overwhelming urge to run outside and vomit again but fought hard against the urge. The door closed behind him.

"How many times do I have to tell you about this?"

"Sorry, sir."

"Sorry, my arse. I am disposed to ground you for the day or maybe more."

"I'll be all right before we launch."

"The hell you will. We are at Available as we speak. We could get a scramble order at any moment, and you sure as hell are not ready to fly." He paused to stare at Brian although the American could not look his commander in the eyes. "What was it this time?"

Brian considered the question. He did not particularly want to share his misfortune and internal conflict with his commander. He wanted all this to go away. Part of him wished he had never met Anne Booth, and he cursed Jeremy Morrison for introducing him, but the other part loved her in a unique, strange way. He felt the need for his own exorcism.

"It's a woman, sir."

"What?" shouted Darling.

"A woman I know was arrested for spying, tried for treason, convicted and sentenced to be executed, next week I think."

Darling's facial expression changed in an instant. The tension and anger evaporated. "Oh, that. I was wondering when you might be ready to talk."

"You mean you know?"

"Yes, Brian. Our counterintelligence blokes are pretty damn thorough. They have absolved you of any wrongdoing."

"Yes, sir, but I can't let go of it. I keep asking myself the same question, why?"

"How did you get mixed up with her?"

"Jeremy Morrison introduced us."

"Lord Morrison. 'Mud' Morrison?"

"Yes, sir."

"You do run with an interesting crowd, my boy. Did you tell her anything that might hurt us?"

"The investigator's asked me the same question God only knows how many times and ways," Brian answered pausing to think again. "I don't think so. I didn't like to talk about what we do."

"I'll bet," Darling said with a snide tone and expression.

"This is extremely embarrassing, sir, but the real hurtful part is, I had strong feelings for her. She was special in so many ways. She always made the pain and nightmares go away."

"She was a prostitute, for Christ's sake. That's what she did for a living, Brian."

Pilot Officer Drummond felt the hot surge of anger overcome the nausea. He had tried hard to suppress his knowledge of Anne's profession. He never really thought of her as a prostitute, at least not when they were alone. "Not with me she wasn't," he responded with the most subdued voice he could muster.

"What does that mean?"

"She wasn't a prostitute with me."

"You mean she did not charge you the going fare for her services?"

"No, sir."

"Did she ask you for information?"

"I've asked myself that question and so many others continuously. She always treated me as a close friend and to the best of my recollection, she never asked me about the service."

Darling thought about Brian's words. "Brian, I am truly sorry this has happened to you, but life goes on. You have been cleared of any wrongdoing. You are one of our best fighter pilots. You are an important part of our defense effort to keep the Germans off this island. You simply must put this unfortunate episode behind you."

"Yes, sir."

"You have heard my speech many times. You know deep inside you cannot let this nonsense bring you down. You know as well as anyone, distraction up there will get you killed and maybe others as well."

"Yes, sir."

"You are on the hook until 'Fog' Johnson returns at mid-day, and then maybe I can let you go sleep it off. You best pray to God the Gerries don't decide to invade today."

"Yes, sir."

"Now, get the hell out of my office," Darling barked more in jest than earnest.

As Brian returned outside to the friendly teasing of his compatriots, the distinctive sounds of several Merlin engines starting provided the backdrop when the telephone rang. They all waited.

"Squadron to Standby," announced Corporal Warren.

No.238 Squadron Hurricanes took to the air en masse. Something was beginning to happen over the Channel that meant the Spitfires of No.609 Squadron were probably next in line. Waves of nausea flooded back over Brian as he thought of engaging in mortal combat when he felt so terrible. The telephone seemed to continue to ring all morning as their alert state was dropped to Readiness, then Available, and back to Readiness. The Hurricanes landed after being airborne a little more than an hour. The gunport tapes were still intact.

"Maybe Gerry is taking the day off for divine worship," joked 'Boxer' Stockard.

"Bloody hell, you say," interjected 'Sparky' Morrow. "The bloody bastards don't believe in God. How could they justify doing what they are doing if they believed in the Holy Father?"

"Here, here."

"Isn't today Monday?" asked 'Red' Burns quite innocently.

"What?"

Stockard went into the Dispersal building and reemerged a few moments later. "'Red's bloody well right, it is Monday."

"I'll be damned," said 'Jackstay' Beamish. "We're havin' ourselves too much fun. We're forgettin' the bleedin' days."

They all laughed at the confusion nearly constant alert was causing on the sense of time for the pilots. Although the clouds over Southern England were not particularly threatening, apparently the weather over the Channel gave the Germans little opportunity to find targets. Brian thanked the Lord to himself for whatever reason kept them on the ground.

As Flying Sergeant Miles 'Fog' Johnson returned to the Squadron with a string of innuendoes about his nocturnal exploits in Andover, a messenger delivered an official envelope to Squadron Leader Darling. It took several minutes before their commander joined them.

"I would like each of you to read this Ministry order," he said.

Brian watched the eyes and faces of each pilot as the single sheet of paper was passed hand-to-hand. It was an important piece of paper. Several of the pilots showed no reaction whatsoever, while others shook their heads with expressions of disgust.

"What the hell are they thinkin' up there?" asked 'Jackstay' Beamish.

Squadron Leader Darling chose not to respond until each of the pilots read the order. Brian was the last to receive the message.

```
ZZZZ/7143GGF5728/AM-AC/4431291/TEKSI/554/ZZZZ
DATE:  29.07.40, 0300 HOURS
FROM:  AIR MINISTRY
TO:  ALL COMMANDS
SUBJECT:  AMO 1254
BREAK
ENEMY USING AIR/SEA RESCUE FLOAT AEROPLANES
FOR RECONNAISSANCE AND TARGETING PURPOSES.
AEROPLANES DISTINCTIVELY MARKED, PAINTED
GENERALLY WHITE WITH LARGE RED CROSSES.
OVERWHELMING EVIDENCE REGRETTABLY INDICATES
INFORMATION COLLECTED BY THE ENEMY FLOAT
AEROPLANES REPEATEDLY USED TO ENGAGE WARSHIPS
OF ROYAL NAVY AS WELL AS UNARMED MERCHANTS
SHIPPING.  BREAK
ADMIRALTY ISSUED NOTICE TO MARINERS AND
FO NOTIFIED THE GERMAN GOVERNMENT FURTHER
ABUSES OF HUMANITARIAN MARKINGS WILL NOT BE
TOLERATED.  BREAK
EFFECTIVE IMMEDIATELY, GERMAN HE59 FLOAT
AEROPLANES, REGARDLESS OF MARKINGS, WILL NOT
BE PERMITTED TO OVERFLY OR OPERATE WITHIN 10
MILES OF ALLIED SHIPPING, NOR WITHIN 10 MILES
OF UK COASTLINE.  AMBULANCE AIRCRAFT THAT DO
NOT COMPLY WITH THIS REQUIREMENT WILL DO SO AT
THEIR OWN RISK AND PERIL.  BREAK
ALL UNITS AND ELEMENTS OF FC HEREBY INSTRUCTED
TO ENGAGE ENEMY AMBULANCE FLOAT AEROPLANES
```

```
REGARDLESS OF POSITION OR ACTIVITY IF PROPER
COMMAND IS RECEIVED FROM SECTOR CONTROL
OR COMMAND WARSHIPS OF ROYAL NAVY, OR THE
AMBULANCE FLOAT AEROPLANES OBSERVED IN
VIOLATION OF THIS ORDER.  BREAK
IF SUCH ENGAGEMENTS OCCUR, PILOTS MUST
REPORT TYPE AEROPLANE, ACTIVITY, LOCATION
AND CONSEQUENCES AS WELL AS ANY ADDITIONAL
PERTINENT INFORMATION TO AIR INTELLIGENCE
BRANCH.  BREAK
IT IS WITH PROFOUND REGRET THIS ORDER MUST BE
ISSUED.  HOWEVER, THE ENEMY CANNOT BE ALLOWED
TO UTILISE THE MARKINGS OF INTERNATIONAL
HUMANITARIAN SERVICES TO CONDUCT COMBAT
RECONNAISSANCE ACTIVITY.  THIS ORDER SHALL
REMAIN IN EFFECT UNTIL FURTHER NOTICE.
END
ZZZZ/7143GGF5728/AM-AC/4431291/TEKSI/554/ZZZZ
```

"There you have it, lads. Any questions?" asked Darling.

"What the hell are they thinkin' up there?" 'Jackstay' Beamish repeated his rhetorical question.

"'Jackstay's right, skipper," added 'Sparky' Morrow. "Sure, those damn Heinkel Five Nines are savin' Gerries so they can fight another day but bloody hell. Lord knows, we want to eliminate as many of them as possible, but this is a bit on the extreme side."

"They're painted white and they've got friggin' red crosses on 'em, for Christ's sake," Jonathan contributed.

Darling held up his right hand. They all stopped talking and looked to him. "I called both Sector and Group for clarification. First, the order is genuine. Second, there has been more than one report the Germans are using the float aeroplanes for reconnaissance, not just air/sea rescue. A variety of ships have reported spotting a Heinkel Five Nine close by, and then faced a determined attack a short time later. At first, they considered the incidents merely a coincidence. According to Group, they have other evidence that confirms the additional reconnaissance mission for these aeroplanes. The bottom line here is, we have our orders."

"Bloody hell, skipper," protested 'Sparky' Morrow. "Sure, we are fighting for our proverbial lives here, but isn't there any civility left?"

"Pretty soon, the damn Germans will be shooting at our rescue boats," 'Fog' Johnson said.

"And, then our blokes hangin' under the silk," added 'Jackstay' Beamish.

"To keep things in perspective," said Darling, "let us remember the blokes in One One Group are far busier than we are at the moment. The enemy has bombed ships at anchor in Dover Harbor. Hell, 'Sailor' Malan's Seven Four Squadron had a very tough day. Word has it he nearly bagged Mölders, the German ace. The bastard barely made it to the French coast and had to belly in. 'Sailor' got chased off by a whole bloody squadron of One Oh Nines. This is a serious fight we are in, lads, and this is only the beginning. They don't issue orders like this for the hell of it. We do not know all the reasons, but I am certain they are real. Let us just do our job."

"But, skipper . . . ," protested 'Fog' Johnson until Squadron Leader Darling held up his hand.

"The boss is right," added 'Sparky' Morrow. "We've a job to do. Let's get on with it."

"This is going to be a helluva war," said 'Slim' Koenig, more to himself than the others.

Even in the fog of his hangover, Brian recognized the seriousness of the order from the Air Ministry. Engaging an unarmed, conspicuously marked, rescue, floatplane would be hard for any of them, but he tried to see the rationale. The Germans were using rescue craft to locate and clearly define targets for the bombers. Many more lives would undoubtedly be lost in making the targeting information more accurate. The thought of shooting at bright white airplanes with large red crosses painted all over them brought back Brian's nausea. This was not what he imagined those many months ago, talking to Malcolm Bainbridge at a country airfield near Wichita, Kansas. His teacher never told him about this part of combat. Maybe he never faced anything so harsh? Maybe he did and just could not tell the story? Brian wanted the nightmare to end, but he knew it was only just beginning.

The pilots of No.609 Squadron suffered the tension of further changes in their alert status as they discussed, struggled with and came to grips with the reality and consequences of the AMO 1254 message. The order seemed to mark the beginning of a darker, uglier phase of what had become known as the Battle of Britain.

A courier delivered a large, carrier envelope to Corporal Warren and departed without waiting for a response. The despersal clerk opened the tied envelope, extracted a single sheet of paper, and quickly took it into Darling's office. As exited his office and returned to her desk, Warren said, "Mister Drummond, if you will," as she motioned to the squadron leader's office. No one reacted this time.

"Yes, sir," Brian said, as he came to attention before Darling's desk.

The squadron leader simply handed the paper to Brian.

```
ZZZZ/2347TMG9901/AM-AC/511357/HGETT/278/ZZZZ
DATE:  29.07.40, 1612 HOURS
FROM:  AIR MINISTRY
TO:  CO NO.609 SQDN
COPY: FIGHTER COMMAND AND NO.10 GROUP
SUBJECT:  SPECIAL MISSION
BREAK
PILOT OFFICER B. DRUMMOND IS HEREBY ORDERED TO
FLY HIS SPITFIRE TO RAF NORTHOLT TO BE PARKED
AND STANDING BESIDE HIS AIRCRAFT NO LATER THAN
0800 HOURS, TUESDAY 30 JULY 1940.  BREAK
PO B. DRUMMOND WILL BE MET BY A DISTINGUISHED
AMERICAN VISITOR AND HIS ESCORT.  BREAK
PO B. DRUMMOND IS DIRECTED TO BRIEF THE
VISITOR ON HIS AIRCRAFT AND ANSWER ANY AND ALL
QUESTIONS POSED BY THE VISITOR.  BREAK
PO B. DRUMMOND IS TO REMAIN AT THE SERVICE OF
THE VISITOR UNTIL RELEASED AT WHICH TIME HE IS
TO RETURN TO SQDN AND NORMAL DUTIES.  BREAK
ANY QUESTIONS OR CONCERNS WILL BE DIRECTED TO
COAS IMMEDIATELY.
END
ZZZZ/2347TMG9901/AM-AC/511357/HGETT/278/ZZZZ
```

"What does this mean, Skipper?" Brian asked.

"I think it is fairly plain and direct."

"Who is this American visitor?"

"The Air Ministry most likely did not want his name in an open message, and if they wanted you to know, they would have told us. Further, it says answer questions, not have a conversation with the man, so I strongly urge you to speak only when spoken to, and you are not permitted to ask questions."

"Who is COAS?"

"Chief of the Air Staff, Air Chief Marshal Sir Cyril Newall."

"So I am supposed to fly to Northolt to answer this guy's questions about the Spitfire?"

"That is what the message says, does it not."

"Yes, sir. But . . ."

"No, buts, 'Hunter.' You have your orders. It should take you 30 minutes to get there, so I would suggest you alert Leading Aircraftman Gordon that you must be wheels up by 07:00 hours tomorrow."

"Yes, sir. Very well, sir. Anything else, sir?"

"No. I eagerly await the story of your experience. This is a rather unusual request. Now, you are released from alert duty. I strongly encourage you to eat a nice meal, take no alcohol, and for God's sake, get a good night's sleep."

"Yes, sir. I will tell Bernie the plan, and then head direct to the Mess for the rest of the day and evening."

Darling nodded his head and gestured as if shooing a fly.

Brian found Gordon and his crew as they were painting over the permanent patches to replace the temporary ones from previous battle damage. Gordon had somehow been informed of tomorrow's special mission and directly to make the PR-F fighter look as good as possible. They had done an excellent job, as they always did. Brian's crew did not ask him about the special mission, and he did not offer what little he did know.

—

Tuesday, 30.July.1940
RAF Northolt
Northolt, London, England
07:35 hours

Pilot Officer Brian Drummond landed his PR-F Spitfire smoothly and taxied toward the aerodrome operations building and control tower. The flight from Middle Wallop had been smooth and uneventful. Before he reached a parking spot, a ground crewman directed him toward the far end of the flight line away from the other assorted aircraft. Brian parked his aircraft where he was told, checked his instruments to make sure all was well with his mount, and then shutdown his engine. He removed his leather helmet, left it connected, and wedged his headgear between the windscreen and glareshield, and then removed and place his flight gloves on top of his helmet. The ground crew-man had chocked his wheels and opened his access door as he unstrapped and extricated himself from the tight cockpit. Lastly, once on the ground, Brian removed his flotation vest, placed it on his seat, and then straightened his tie and uniform tunic.

"Will you need petrol, sir?" asked the ground crewman.

"Fuel in the bowser has no purpose, aircraftman. Yes, please, top off my tanks while we wait."

"Yes, sir."

The crewman had finished fueling his aircraft and cleaning his can-opy when a medium green, 1939 Austin Model HR B Saloon automobile approached. The driver in a dark suit and bowtie stopped behind the tail of Brian's Spitfire, quickly got out, opened the rear passenger door, and ran around in an attempt to open the other rear passenger door, but he did not make it in time. Two men exited the car. The taller man, nearest Brian, wore a light gray suit with solid, royal blue tie. He waited for his companion. The shorter man rounded the rear of the car. He wore a medium blue suit with a rather odd brown, forest print tie. The short man approached Brian first and extended his right hand, which Brian shook.

"You must be Pilot Officer Brian Drummond," he said.

"Yes, sir."

"My name is Stephenson, Bill Stephenson, from the Foreign Office. Nice to meet you. May I present Colonel William J. Donovan, a countryman of yours."

"Brian Drummond, sir," Brian said, as he shook Donovan's extended hand.

"The pleasure is mine, young man."

"Thank you, sir."

Stephenson began, "We were informed that you would brief Colonel Donovan on the features of your aeroplane and answer any questions he might have."

"Those are my orders, sir. I am at your service."

"Where are you from, Brian?" asked Donovan.

"From RAF Middle Wallop, sir."

Donovan laughed. "No, where are you from in the States?"

Brian instantly felt the jaws of a trap and probably showed it. "Sir, I do not want any trouble. I have a letter of pardon from President Roosevelt."

Donovan laughed again, this time much more robustly. "Ah, yes, the Neutrality Act. Brian, please forgive me, if I caused you any apprehension, and I certainly apologize for not thinking of that particular aspect of meeting with you. I am a simple lawyer from New York City on an unofficial mission for the Secretary of the Navy Frank Knox. I am not here for the Justice Department or any other law enforcement organization. Prime Minister Churchill suggested I meet with you, as you made an exceptional impression on him, and he thought I might benefit from our discussion."

"I only met Mister Churchill once for lunch at his house."

Donovan chuckled, again. "Then, you made an even greater impression on him. So, back to my original question, where are you from in the States?"

"Wichita, Kansas, sir."

"The middle of the Great Plains."

"Yes, sir."

"How did you wind up here, Brian?"

The young American fighter pilot in his British air force uniform recounted his journey from Wichita to England. Donovan and Stephenson appeared distinctly interested in Brian's story. Even Stephenson asked a few questions, mostly about Malcolm's service in the RFC during the Great War and his influence on Brian.

"Well, the Prime Minister wanted me to meet you and learn about your fighter airplane. Before we get started, I must tell you, I am not an aviator, although I do have a keen appreciation for the value of aviation on the battlefield and in commerce."

"Don't let him fool you, Brian," added Stephenson. "He is much more than he seems. He won the Medal of Honor in France."

"Nonsense, Bill. The Medal is not a prize. You are awarded the Medal with humility, for doing what had to be done."

"Congratuations, sir."

"Think nothing of it. It is the past. Let's hear what you have to tell us."

Brian carried out a thorough, walk-around briefing on the features and capabilities of his Supermarine Spitfire Mark IA. Both Donovan and Stephenson were surprisingly knowledgeable about the Spitfire, and the Hurricane fighter for that matter. They noted some of the aircraft's quirky limitations as well – the narrow undercarriage and crosswind sensitivity, the normally aspirated Merlin engine that made it susceptible to negative 'g' cutout, and undersized 0.303 caliber machine guns versus the German 20mm cannon.

"Have you seen combat with your Spitfire?" Donovan asked.

"Yes, sir. You can see the repaired bullet holes," Brian answered, as he pointed to the freshly patched and painted spots on the tail of his aircraft. "My crew worked hard to make her as pretty as possible, sir."

"Please congratulate your crew. They did a bang up job."

"I will, sir."

"How does she do in combat?"

"She's a killer – fast, agile and deadly."

". . . in the hands of an expert pilot," added Donovan.

"Perhaps."

"What have you flown against?"

"We have had to deal with just about every aircraft in their frontline service, but we mostly work against their best fighter – the Messerschmidt One Oh Nine. They have been using mostly E4 and some E3 models. It is a very capable machine with a helluva bite, I might add. With the larger raids we are facing now, the Hurris usually take the lower bombers, while we try to keep the fighters occupied."

"Hurris?"

"Hawker Hurricane fighters – our sister ship."

"How many victories do you have so far, Brian?"

"I believe I have been credited with five and a half so far."

"Then, you are an ace."

"I try not to think about that sort of stuff. I am focused on winning the next engagement and surviving the next sortie."

"Quite understandable. Is there anything else you would like to show me?"

"I would love to take you for a flight, so you can see first hand what a magnificent machine she is."

Donovan laughed again. "I shall take your word for it, Brian. I would be very much out of my depth in a fighter aircraft like your Spitfire. If there is nothing else, would you mind spending a little more time with me? I understand the base commander has a conference room we can use for an hour or so."

"I am at your service, sir."

"Let's walk," Donovan said.

Brian saw Stephenson motion for their driver to follow them, as they walked down the backside of the flight line, past a squadron of Hurricanes, several Blenheims, a couple of Defiants and a Hudson parked in front of the base operations building. A WAAF corporal met them at the entrance and led them to a small, modestly appointed, room clearly labeled as the commander's conference room. The rectangular, solid burch table had eight chairs, four per long side. As they entered the room, Stephenson asked the corporal for tea and biscuits. They took chairs with Brian on one side and the two Bills on the other. The refreshments arrived promptly, and the door closed. Stephenson poured each of them a cup of tea and passed the plate of small, sugar cookies.

"Let me ask, Brian, do you think the Germans will invade England?"

This time it was Brian's turn to laugh. "Excuse me, I did not mean to laugh. I have no idea, sir. I am just one fighter pilot. I go where I am pointed and I try to shoot down whomever is not supposed to be there."

Donovan showed no reaction and pressed on. "Yes, but you surely have an opinion, and I am certain you and your colleagues have discussed the possibilities."

Brian's smile disappeared. "Yes, sir, we have. I think they have no choice. If they do not subdue Great Britain, they will ultimately be defeated. I believe what Mister Churchill says."

"Do you think you can stop them, if they do attempt an invasion?"

"They will not get past us, sir. My mates are a rather determined lot, I should say, and we are holding our own."

"So it appears." Donovan decided to change directions. "Earlier, you indicated you left home and went to Canada to join the RAF. If my information is correct, you were just a few months past your eighteenth birthday, last year."

"Yes, sir."

"Knowing what you know now and what you have experienced so far and what is undoubtedly ahead of you, would you do it again?"

"Absolutely . . . without question."

"Why?"

"I feel this is what I was meant to do. I have loved flying since I was a boy, and there is no airplane on the planet as good as my Spitfire. I am honored that the British would have me and allow me to join them in this fight. I know for a fact that if we do not stop the Nazis here, we will face them in Kansas. I must do my part to beat them here."

"Fact?"

"My apologies, sir. I got carried away. I do not know what Hitler intends to do or how this fight will turn out, but I do know that we cannot take a chance with that outcome."

"We?"

"The United States, sir."

"I understand you were the lone American in the RAF for nearly a year, and there are other Americans with you now."

"About a half dozen were flying with the French. They arrived last month. Several have already died in combat. There should be many more Americans over here."

"Yes, well, I suspect you have heard of the American Firsters. The isolationist mood in our country is quite strong."

"Oh, yes sir, I do understand that. My parents are among them. They tried everything to get me home. I am most grateful for the presidential pardon that ended that worry for me."

"Do you have that letter with you? I would like to see it."

"No, sir. It is safe in my footlocker back at Middle Wallop. I can produce it for you, if you need to read it."

"No, that is not necessary. I was just curious."

"Who requested the pardon for you?"

"I have no idea, sir. It just arrived a few months ago. I do not even know whether the President knew who I was or what I was doing."

"He does now, and I will certainly tell him of our meeting."

"Would you be so kind to thank him for me? That letter made a very big worry of mine go away in an instant, and I need no distractions while I am doing what I am doing."

"You can count on it, Brian. You mentioned earlier, you believe Mister Churchill. Why so? What makes you believe him?"

"He understands. He knows what we are doing and why. I had heard stories from Malcolm and Group Captain Spencer that just struck the bell for me. I think he is straight with us. He tells us the way things are, even though we may not like it. He seems to know exactly what to say."

"He is quite good with words."

"Yes, sir, that he is."

"Do you have any questions for me, Brian?"

"I am not supposed to ask questions, sir."

"Nonsense. It is just us. Bill here will certainly not tell on us."

Brian thought about Squadron Leader Darling's instructions. He looked to Bill Stephenson, who nodded his head in agreement. Donovan waited patiently.

"If I may say so, you are too old to fight. Why are you here, sir?"

Donovan laughed, again. "Well, I do not think I am too old, but I shall not argue the point. I am here to learn what I can from our British cousins to help us prepare for what appears to be the inevitable war, as you say."

"I will add," interjected Stephenson, "that he is here to assess our ability to defend this island."

"That is not my stated mission, but I shall not argue that point, either."

"You asked me what I thought about the invasion. What do you think?"

"Fair question. I agree with you precisely, Brian. I think the Germans must subjugate the British to have any hope of retaining what they have conquered. I must also say, not to flatter you, but you represent exactly why they will not be successful if or when they do attempt a cross-Channel invasion. I am impressed with your selflessness and courage. You defied federal law to fulfill your duty, as you saw it. You deserve nothing but praise and respect from all the rest of us not under arms."

"Thank you, sir."

Donovan looked at his expensive wristwatch. "Unfortunately, I am afraid we must be going. I only have a few more days before my return to the States, and we have more stops to make."

"Thank you for listening, sir."

"Thank you, Brian, for taking the time from your duties to show me your fighter airplane. I shall certainly convey my gratitude to Prime Minister Churchill for arranging our meeting, and I shall inform President Roosevelt that his faith in you is very well placed. And, if you will permit me, I would like to inform your parents that you are well and in high spirits."

"Thank you very much, sir. I would be most grateful."

"Give 'em hell, Brian."

They shook hands. The two Bills followed Brian outside. Pilot Officer Drummond turned to face Donovan and Stephenson, and then rendered a crisp salute. Both men came to attention and returned his salute. As Brian turned behind the tail of his aircraft, he glanced back to see both men standing where he left them. The car and driver had pulled up and waited on them. There were apparently waiting for him to depart.

Brian strapped in, started up, called for taxi, moved to his takeoff point, turned into the wind, completed his checks, and called for permission to takeoff, including a low pass on the field. The tower controller indicated no traffic in the area and surprisingly permission was granted. The PR-F Spitfire roared past the tower. He was airborne, retracted his undercarriage and intentionally kept the aircraft low to build up speed. At the far end of the field, he pulled up smoothly, kept the throttle up against the emergency gate, and executed a graceful wingover. Brian flew a tight circuit, returned to the wind line, and dove his aircraft to the ground. His speed built-up rapidly as he leveled his Spitfire with his propeller tips just a few feet above the grass. He was doing better than 400 miles per hour as he passed the tower and saw the two men waving to him. Brian pulled up, waved his wings twice, and then rolled the aircraft twice, before turning sharply to the southwest for his return flight to Middle Wallop. The flight was uneventful, giving him time to think about the morning event. He wished he had asked if it was all right for him to talk to his mates about the meeting. In the end, he thought so, since no one told him otherwise.

—

Tuesday, 30.July.1940
Headquarters, Secret Intelligence Service
No.21 Queen Anne's Gate
Westminster, London, England
15:15 hours

To the Chief, things had not looked good for a long time. This particular day started poorly and appeared to be getting worse by the moment. For Colonel Stewart 'C' Menzies, the loss of a field agent never set well no matter how much they understood the risks. The value, and some would say, the success of the SIS had always been its agents, its human intelligence, and its ability to develop an understanding of special events.

The rapidity of the German invasion of the Low Countries and France, and the temptation to leave agents in place behind combat lines left several key operatives on the Continent. This morning, Agent Stone transmitted a protracted dash, in mid-message as his last defiant act upon his surprise discovery most probably by the Gestapo. If he was not killed outright, the Germans would keep him alive just long enough to confirm the limit of their interrogation. He would most likely be dead within a week, maybe two at the most.

Agent Stone had been well placed in Paris. He was more French than the French. The initial assessment of his capture told them the Germans probably employed a sophisticated, far more efficient radio direction finding set of equipment to locate his transmitter in the large city. The Special Equipment Section redoubled their efforts to improve transmission security for field agents. If the Germans did have better direction finders, the improved communications security procedures or equipment had suddenly become mandatory – an absolute necessity. They needed the shards of human developed intelligence that only a determined agent could obtain.

What worried 'C' the most was that 'Stone' was the eighth agent in six weeks to be discovered and the one SIS thought was the most secure . . . if there ever was such a thing as secure for field agents?

The buzzer on 'C's desktop interphone box broke his thoughts. He pressed the appropriate lever.

"Mister Denniston to see you, sir," announced his highly capable and often underestimated secretary.

"Yes, by all means. Do show him in. Thank you."

Alastair Denniston, Head of the Government Code and Cypher School at Bletchley Park, entered the room as devoid of expression as ever, but with a slowness to his gait. 'C' judged his chief code breaker brought bad news in the case manacled to his left wrist.

"Good afternoon, Alastair. And, how are you this fine summer's day?" asked 'C' trying to be as cheery as he could.

Denniston would not be swayed. "Terrible since you ask, sir."

"What have you?"

As he opened the case, he said, "this came in two days ago. We broke it just this morning." He handed a single sheet of paper to Menzies. "As you can see, I thought it important enough to make the journey myself."

MOST SECRET - ULTRA

```
SECRET
DATE: 28 JULY 1940
TO: ALL AIR FORCE COMMANDS
FROM: CINC
BREAK
OUR MOST GLORIOUS DAY IS NEAR.  YOU ARE
INSTRUCTED IMMEDIATELY AND WITH GREAT HASTE
TO PREPARE FOR THE GREAT BATTLE OF THE
GERMAN AIR FORCE AGAINST ENGLAND.  UNITS OF
AIR FLEETS TWO, THREE AND FIVE SHOULD BE
PREPARED TO COMMENCE LARGE SCALE OPERATIONS
WITH A MAXIMUM NOTICE OF TWELVE HOURS.  OUR
LEADER HAS DIRECTED FINAL PREPARATIONS
FOR OPERATION SEALION.  IN VIEW OF THE
FORTHCOMING OPERATION, DAMAGE TO SOUTH COAST
PORT FACILITIES MUST BE KEPT TO A MINIMUM.
DETAILED ORDERS WILL BE ISSUED AS APPROPRIATE.
END
SECRET
```

MOST SECRET - ULTRA

'C' looked up from the paper. "Who is CINC?"

"My apologies, sir. It is shorthand for commander-in-chief. This message is from Göring himself."

"I see." Menzies looked at the message one more time quickly. "It would appear our adversaries have decided to get serious about this little war. Dear God above, I hope Fighter Command is up to the task."

"Indeed."

"We will need to get this information to the Prime Minister."

"I have taken the liberty," Denniston said, reaching back into his case, "to prepare a general message for the War Cabinet."

'C' took the second piece of paper.

MOST SECRET – OFFICER ONLY

Information has been received from reliable
sources that air attacks can be expected
all along the Southern coast and Channel.
Large-scale bombardment is anticipated.
Appropriate defensive measures should be taken
immediately. Enemy air operations may be a
prelude to an invasion attempt.

This message must be treated as OFFICER ONLY
and should not be transmitted by telephone.
War Office, Air Ministry and Admiralty are in
possession of this information.
H. Pritchard
M.I.14. Lieut.Colonel. G.S.
1040 hrs.
30.7.40.
Distribution:
D.D.M.I.(I). (for D.M.I.).
G.H.Q. Home Forces.
G.H.Q. (Adv.) (I), Home Forces.
M.O.3.
File.

MOST SECRET – OFFICER ONLY

"I am not so sure I like the last sentence. Strikes me as inciteful."

"I can redo the notice here at Headquarters," offered Denniston.

Colonel Menzies considered the suggestion. The Enigma message along with the most recent photographic aerial reconnaissance of Northern France and Belgium confirmed the conclusions in Denniston's notice. Maybe it was time for everyone to face the reality of what lay ahead. The one obstacle was the prime minister's penchant for optimism in the face of adversity or calamity. In the end, he decided to test the limit, again. "I shall take it as is." He raised both pieces of paper. "Leave these with me. I shall brief the Prime Minister myself. Let us see what he wants to do."

"Very well, sir. Then, I should be off to Bletchley. Our intercept traffic is definitely picking up. I shall endeavor to keep you fully informed as we progress. These damn codes are frustrating to say the least, and our productivity on breaking them is far too spotty."

"Thank you, Alastair. Please convey my sincerest appreciation for the exemplary work of your crew. This well spring may yet sustain us all through this crisis."

"Indeed."

"If you do not hear back from me this evening, you may consider your suggestion accepted by the War Cabinet. We are still testing the waters with this class of information."

"Yes, sir. If there is nothing else, I shall be off."

"Safe journey and thank you once again, Alastair."

"Certainly, sir," Denniston said, as he turned and departed.

Stewart reread both messages several times as he placed the information in the context of all they knew about German intentions. He was sorely tempted to ask several of his remaining agents on the Continent to visit the coastal area. Having first hand agent observations could prove to be invaluable in fully appreciating the Enigma source. He nodded his head as if he were reluctantly agreeing with one of his department heads. He gathered the proper carrying case, deposited the two sheets of paper and informed his secretary of his destination.

—

Wednesday, 31.July.1940
RAF Middle Wallop
Middle Wallop, Hampshire, England
09:00 hours

"This is going to be a helluva war," offered Frank Burns, as the squadron waited at Available status.

"How right you are, 'Red,'" answered Robert Morrow. "If we are not low on pilots, we are low on aircraft."

"And, such fine weather," said 'Boxer' Stockard. "The passing clumps of clouds are just enough to keep Gerry from getting too busy, but today looks nearly perfect over the Channel."

"We shall be busy this day," said 'Waggle' Davies.

For Pilot Officer Brian Drummond, the aerial combat of the last few days meant he and half of the other pilots would have to fly without the full weight of the squadron. No.609 Squadron lost two aircraft, yet to be replaced, and had four other machines seriously damaged requiring extensive repairs. None of the pilots liked flying short handed whether due to aircraft or pilots to fly them, but they faced the shortage of flyable fighters as they did any other impediment – with distant, dry humor and acceptance.

Since most of the damaged aircraft came from 'B' Flight, the remaining aircraft would flush up 'A' Flight. Jonathan took the right wing position of Beamish's Green Section with Brian flying left wing. Janus Kradilcek joined the 'jumpers' club yesterday when a German fighter started a fire in his machine. Several of the mountless fighter pilots were given one- or two-days rest passes and would rotate until the replacement aircraft arrived.

The reduced squadron did not have to wait long for the call.

"Scramble," shouted Corporal Warren.

The wheels retracted into the wings as they broke ground. They climbed for altitude within two minutes of the call. Brian used the transit time, as the others did, to prepare his machine for combat. The guns, engine and gun camera were ready.

This engagement was going to be interesting. Other squadrons in the vicinity of Southampton and the South Central coast were either already committed to other engagements or returning to rearm and refuel. Their half strength squadron was going to face a German raid of twenty plus aircraft. Unfortunately, the vital RDF equipment could not tell them what types of aircraft made up the raid. Facing twenty or more fighters would be harder than half those many but would not alter their actions.

This mission began like all the others of July. The German raid headed directly for another Channel convoy – today's name, AGENT. They spotted the ten plump, slower Junkers 87, *Sturzkampfflugzeug*, Stuka dive-bombers, but Squadron Leader Darling chose to wait until they found the fighters. They did not wait long. Two layers of fighters were spread out behind the bombers.

The lower group of ten Bf110, twin-engine fighters flew behind and several thousand feet above the bombers. Above and behind them were an equal number of Bf109 fighters. Darling continued at altitude trying to position for an up-sun perch. None of the Germans appeared to react to their presence. Maybe they had not been spotted, yet? Any little advantage would help.

"Bandy, this is Sorbo Leader calling. Tally-ho. We have a dozen Stukas, plus twice as many One One Oh and One Oh Nine fighters. We could use some help, when you can manage."

"Sorbo Leader, we will try to find some support."

"There you have it, lads. Gerry's waiting. Let's get to work. Green Leader, you take the twins. We shall take the singles."

"Roger," was all Beamish broadcast in response

"Yee-haw," came the recently added punctuation of 'Red' Burns, as they rolled toward the fighter escort.

The single engine fighters did not wait to respond as they immediately turned to engage. Brian watched 'Spike' Darling lead Blue Section into the Bf109s. The twin engine Bf110s formed their usual defensive circle and waited for the three Spitfires to close within range of their guns.

'Jackstay' picked a target on the near side of the circle. 'Harness' took a right side aircraft while Brian chose a Bf110 fighter on the far side of the circle.

Brian aligned his sight to give adequate lead as he closed with his target. The Bf110 was in a moderate right turn that presented Brian with a nearly top planform shot. Several impacts flashed on the tail telling him there was insufficient lead. He adjusted quickly moving his target further to the left of his sight reticle. Hits began to scatter over the wing and cockpit as he passed over the top.

The PR-F Spitfire banked right as the nose rose over the horizon. Brian manipulated the controls to give him a line of sight to his wounded target and position his fighter for another pass at the stricken intruder. The German, twin engine, fighter continued in the defensive circle although a thin trail of light smoke from the right engine identified his target.

With the adjustments in position, Brian's fighter lined up on his target. The rhythmic flashes from the rear cockpit meant the German gunner was still working to defend his aircraft. Brian concentrated on his alignment and lead sight position as he squeezed the firing button allowing all eight Browning machine guns to erupt in response. The aim was perfect. Impact flashes spotted over nearly the entire aircraft. The gunfire from the rear seat stopped as parts of the Bf110 flew away. The right engine seemed to explode as the aircraft rolled sharply to the right with heavy, black smoke marking its path toward the sea below.

Brian rolled back in a climbing left turn toward another perch position. He scanned the sky around him. The radio calls announced the arrival of No.43 Squadron Hurricanes with B Flight bouncing the unopposed dive-bombers and A Flight joining the fighter engagement. The bombers and hapless Bf110 fighters recognized their disadvantaged situation and tried to escape back to France.

"'Hunter,' on your tail!"

Brian twisted in his seat as he pulled the nose hard, jammed the throttle through the emergency power gate wire and saw two, side-by-side, Bf109 fighters open fire on him. No hits. He rolled inverted and pulled his nose down well below the horizon. The scream of air rushing by his canopy became a deafening roar. His two antagonists persisted as he used both arms to fight the enormous control forces of high-speed flight.

The green and brown of Southern England rushing toward him changed in his defense. With both arms, Brian fought the control spade as he pulled back and the nose slowly responded. As the nose rose above the horizon and the roar of high-speed air decreased, Brian looked over his shoulder only to find the two Germans bobbing in their efforts for another firing solution.

"Hang on, 'Hunter,'" Roger Beamish radioed.

Speed had not worked. Turning would only improve the angles for his attackers. Brian pulled his throttle completely back causing the Merlin to spit and sputter as it was choked for air. The deceleration threw him against his straps causing one of his attackers to overshoot. He rolled hard, pulled his nose down and slammed the throttle forward. The Merlin groaned in protest but leapt to full power pushing Brian back into his seat.

The distinctive and sickening bang of bullets hitting the aluminum skin of his Spitfire gave him the adrenaline rush of fear as he redoubled his straining effort to spoil the shot. The other Bf109 passed in front of his nose. Brian pressed his firing button for a quick hip shot. No effect. He pulled as hard as he could back on the spade causing him to fight against the heavy 'g' forces.

More bangs on his aircraft from yet another unseen attacker spurred him to demand even more from his endangered machine. An instant, all encompassing, brilliant, white flash ended Brian's consciousness.

—

Wednesday, 31.July.1940
Standing Oak Farm
Winchester, Hampshire, England
09:40 hours

The confused summer sky seemed no different from any other mid-year seasonal day. The incessant work required on the farm kept Charlotte Palmer's mind focused on the day's chores. The morning milking of the cows was now three hours behind her and the afternoon milking was less than eight hours away. With her two, long-term employees volunteered and off to the Army, Charlotte now relied on the assistance of two elderly men, Lionel Bridges and Horace Morgan. Mister Morgan was the father of one of her lost hands, Ian Morgan. The daily care of the farm's garden was behind her. The last significant activity prior to the afternoon milking entailed the repair of several fences damaged by a fallen tree limb from the high winds of the strong thunderstorms several days ago.

Lionel returned to the city to purchase some spare spruce rails while Horace tried to find the appropriate tools for the task. Charlotte took a moment to inhale deeply to absorb the rich smell of the earth and grass around her. She looked over her shoulder across the large pond to the old stone house and wooden barn. Horace Morgan had not begun the return journey from the barn, and Lionel Bridges in the farm lorry would not be expected for another half hour at least. She accepted some time ago the slower pace of her older employees although she still wanted to move more quickly. Charlotte Palmer sat down on the full grass and lay back with her arms behind her head. The scattered clouds and warm afternoon sun made her flannel shirt, gray wool trousers and heavy boots feel a little warmer than she needed.

The first oddity on the day came with the distant, strange, intermittent buzz in the sky to the south. She scanned the southern horizon. The bursts became louder as other sounds mixed in with the flurry of buzzing. Then, she saw the source.

Several small airplanes twisting and turning moved toward her position. A smooth, curvy, greenish-brown aircraft was being chased by two, gray, angled aircraft. As the sounds became louder, Charlotte determined the cause of the buzzing when she saw streams of smoke coming from the wings. The aircraft had to be air force fighters and the buzzing must be the guns firing from the wings. Black, thick smoke erupted from the lead aircraft. It stopped turning heading directly toward her. More buzzing preceded the bright flash and disintegrating explosion of the injured aircraft. Flaming chunks of the aircraft fell in an odd arc past her. Charlotte shot to her feet fearing for her house. The pieces of the fighter continued beyond the house and barn hitting the ground behind her on the far side of the hill.

The two chasing aircraft groaned as they turned to face several other curvy aircraft. They moved away toward the south. Charlotte looked back toward the house and could not see either of her helpers despite the commotion above them. Just as she sat back down, she noticed something move above her. She looked up to see a white, semi-spherical canopy with the limp figure of a human beneath it descending from the sky. There were no sounds as the man drifted toward her. It looked like the man would land in the pond in a few minutes.

Charlotte stood again wondering what she should do. The man under the canopy appeared lifeless as he entered the pond.

"Horace," she yelled as loudly as she could. "Horace Morgan, come quickly."

No response could be detected. The white canopy covered the surface of the water. Charlotte knew without question the man would surely drown if he was not dead already. She cursed the age and diminished capacity of Horace Morgan, and then ran down the hill toward the pond. There were no longer any choices if the man would have any chance of survival.

Charlotte Palmer waded into the pond and swam to the sinking canopy. The body floated face down under the soaked material, for the moment. The man would not have much time. She fought with the heavy, white, nearly transparent material and then realized she still had her mud boots on her feet. The shrouds attaching the canopy to the man acted like a large bowl of unbreakable spaghetti noodles. Charlotte knew there was not much time left if she was going to save the man.

She uncovered his left arm just enough to grab his uniform sleeve. Pulling, tugging and fighting to untangle the man from the shrouds exhausted Charlotte causing her to gasp for air and to have some difficulty keeping her head above water. For the first moment since she saw the man enter the water, she questioned the wisdom of jumping into the pond without help and whether she needed to abandon the rescue to save her life. She swallowed a mouthful of water forcing her to cough, sputter and claw for air. Charlotte Palmer feared for her life as her limbs and body fatigued near immobility. As she struggled for air, she left the man trying to make the shore before she drowned. She lay on her back to give herself a moment's recovery before she stroked to the shore. Her chest heaved violently.

From behind the southern hill, an airplane flew by at high speed and very low with his right wing nearly striking the hilltop. She could clearly see the masked face looking down directly at the man in the pond and her. The sleek, curvaceous airplane had distinctive, large letter, PR-D, tail markings. The roar of the engine startled Charlotte as she watched the machine roll back onto the opposite wing and pull up sharply into a looping turn. The pilot must have been looking for his mate and having found him was coming back around to see if he was OK. The event spurred Charlotte to a renewed effort to save the man. She simply could not bear the thought of facing one of those courageous RAF pilots without saving the man.

She returned to the injured pilot, struggled to turn him over, and fought with the last few shrouds holding him. Miraculously, the man pulled free. She held his head above water ripping at his mask and goggles only to reveal a pale, near colorless, boyish face. Charlotte kicked her feet and stroked with her spare arm as she cradled the man's head in her arm.

The heavy, water laden, canopy acted like an anchor. She flailed at his straps trying to detach the parachute. The only things Charlotte accomplished was adding to her fatigue. She needed to move quickly, or the sinking canopy would soon pull him under. She swam as hard as she could toward the shore trying to keep his head above the water surface.

The fighter returned several times before she reached the shore. His head rested in the mud as she tried to raise herself onto her hands and knees, and collapsed onto her shoulder, and then rolled onto her back. The air was not coming to her lungs fast enough. Her muscles burned and screamed at her, defying her will to continue. Charlotte's entire body shook from exhaustion. She raised her head to look across the pond.

"Horace," she tried to yell, but could not muster up enough force. Charlotte watched the Spitfire come directly at her gunning his engine several times, and then wagging his wings before he pulled up and pushed his engine to full power. The aircraft strangely had different tail markings – PR-K. Was there more than one pilot interested in the fallen one? She forced herself to take several very deep breaths, and then screamed. "Help." She gasped several more times. "Help me."

Without waiting for any sign of a response, Charlotte gathered up some strength from somewhere to check the unconscious man lying next to her. He was not breathing and beginning to turn blue. She had to get him to breathe.

Charlotte Palmer began to race through actions that might help the man. She pulled his leather helmet off, pulled his necktie apart and opened his collar. She slapped him several times trying to shock him to life and pushed on his chest several times trying to nudge him into breathing without apparent effect.

"What is it, Missus Palmer?" asked Horace Morgan, somewhat breathless himself.

"Go quickly and call the Emergency Services," she gasped. "Tell them, we have a seriously injured pilot." Charlotte continued to fight for replenishing air. "Go quickly, Horace, we must save his life."

As the old man turned and ambled off as quickly as his old legs would take him, Charlotte returned to the pilot. Her thoughts raced through any actions that might save the man's life. She slapped him twice more without the desired effect. She was running out of ideas leaving her with one choice. If he could not breathe on his own, then maybe she would breathe for him.

Charlotte Palmer leaned over his head, wondering what she was getting into, pulled his mouth open, took a deep breath and pushed her exhalation into him. His chest rose, which made her feel better. She repeated the exchange several times, but his body would not breathe on its own. She placed her ear to his chest and could not hear a heart beat. She pounded her fist on his chest several times, and then breathed into him several more times.

"Breathe damn you," she admonished the unconscious pilot.

Although he was not breathing on his own, he did not seem to be getting any worse. Charlotte kept trying to breathe for him. She had no idea how long she tried to revive him, but her efforts were rewarded when she felt resistance to her supporting breath. His chest began to move regularly and his heartbeat could be clearly heard. Color flushed through his face although he remained unconscious.

Charlotte Palmer looked up to the heavens. "Thank you, Lord. Thank you."

With the most immediate threat apparently resolved, Charlotte searched for any sign of help. Would she have to find the strength to carry the man to the house? Nothing could be seen moving anywhere. She needed to pull him from the pond, at least. Grasping his shoulders, she dragged him from the pond's muddy fringe to the grass. She needed to check him for other injuries.

His uniform jacket and trousers had numerous tears and dark, blood soaked spots, but nothing that seemed to be serious. The helmet, mask and eye goggles that covered his face when she reached him in the water must have protected his boyish, good-looking face. The man was so young to be going through such deadly events.

"The Emergency Services say," Horace Morgan gasped, "they shall be here shortly, Missus Palmer." The old man was obviously not used to the quick actions this incident required. She turned her concern to the health of her helper. "Is he alive?"

"I think so, but he needs a proper surgeon to determine that, but at least he is breathing on his own, now."

The slow movement of Mister Morgan gave the ambulance time to arrive from Winchester. The large, red cross, festooned lorry arrived with precarious speed. Two men ran toward her with a stretcher led by another man in a white coat. They immediately took charge of the situation as if Charlotte Palmer and Horace Morgan were not present. The physician worked quickly to assess the condition of the pilot.

"Missus Palmer, saved this man," said Horace.

The two men unbuckled and released the pilot's harness.

"Is that so? What happened?" asked the doctor.

"Nothing much, actually."

"Come, now, Missus Palmer." Horace Morgan turned to the doctor. "She nearly drowned pulling him from the pond, and she breathed life into him. She saved his life."

"He stopped breathing?" asked the physician.

"Yes."

"And you literally breathed into his lungs?"

"Yes."

"Did he have a heart beat?"

"No."

"How did you get his heart beat to return?"

"I did not know what to do, actually, so I pounded on his chest. I think his body just decided to keep going."

"Well, Missus Palmer, you have no need for modesty. You have truly saved one of our fighter pilots. He should recover, good Lord willing."

They lifted him onto the stretcher and quickly carried him to the ambulance. The doctor waved, as he joined his patient. The medical truck departed not quite as quickly as it arrived.

Charlotte Palmer waited until the ambulance disappeared over the far horizon, and then she sank to the ground as the combination of relief, fatigue and tension sapped the last of her strength. She could not believe she just lived through the afternoon's events. Horace Morgan sat down next to his employer until Lionel Bridges returned with the wooden rails and a growing curiosity about the ambulance he passed on the return to Standing Oak Farm.

—

Chapter 18

It is the logic of our times,
No subject for immortal verse –
That we who lived by honest dreams
Defend the bad against the worse.

-- C. Day-Lewis

Thursday, 1.August.1940
No.10 Downing Street
Whitehall, London, England

The gentle knock at the door startled Winston Churchill from his deep thoughts. In the evenings, the annoying grind of the interphone buzzer was replaced by the door knock to lessen the irritation. The increasing frequency of U-boat sightings and attacks occupied his concentration this particular evening. He still had to remind himself that the business of governance never ceases, and as a servant of the people, his time now belonged to the people and their government.

"Yes," Winston responded, trying to contain his irritation.

The door opened just enough for half the body and extremities of Jock Colville to appear. "Sorry to disturb you, Prime Minister. Colonel Menzies to see you, sir. He indicates it is urgent he see you."

"By all means. Please show him in." Winston chose to remain seated behind his large desk scattered with the reports and maps that occupied his thoughts. "Good evening, Stewart."

"Good evening to you, Prime Minister. My apologies for disturbing you so late in the evening, but I do believe you will soon appreciate the urgency."

"Quite all right. I was just consumed by these damnable U-boats. The reports seem to indicate that despicable mad-man is making his move to choke us off."

"Yes, sir. Well, I am afraid I do not bring good news."

"What is it?"

Colonel Menzies retrieved two sheets of paper from his case, one ordinary white paper and the other a bright yellow paper. "Our analysts reached a streak of good fortune today. We received this message early this morning," he paused to hold up the paper, "and they managed to break it late this afternoon."

Winston extended his left hand signaling Menzies to give him the decrypted message. The white paper passed between them. The unusual bright yellow paper Menzies retained intrigued Winston. "Most unusual paper," he said nodding and looking toward the other paper in Menzies hand.

"Yes, sir. This is the next topic. You may have received reports regarding leaflets dropped by the enemy. The Home Forces retrieved several green and yellow samples. I thought you might enjoy this latest present from our adversary."

"Quite. But, first . . ." The Prime Minister turned his attention to the decoded German message in his hand.

MOST SECRET - ULTRA

```
SECRET
DATE: 1 AUGUST 1940
TO: OKH. OKM, OKL
FROM: OKW
BREAK
THE LEADER'S DIRECTIVE NUMBER 17
OPERATION SEALION IS TO PROCEED AS SOON AS THE
APPROPRIATE ARRANGEMENTS CAN BE COMPLETED. IN
ORDER TO ESTABLISH THE NECESSARY CONDITIONS
FOR THE FINAL CONQUEST OF ENGLAND THE AIR
FORCE IS INSTRUCTED TO OVERPOWER THE ENGLISH
AIR FORCE WITH ALL THE FORCES AT ITS COMMAND
IN THE SHORTEST POSSIBLE TIME.  AIR ATTACKS
WILL BE DIRECTED PRIMARILY AGAINST FLYING
UNITS, THEIR GROUND INSTALLATIONS AND THEIR
SUPPLY ORGANIZATION, ALSO AGAINST THE AIRCRAFT
INDUSTRY, INCLUDING THAT MANUFACTURING ANTI-
AIRCRAFT EQUIPMENT.  AFTER ACHIEVING LOCAL
AIR SUPERIORITY, THE AIR FORCE WILL ATTACK
ONLY LIGHTLY PORTS ON SOUTH COAST IN VIEW OF
OUR OWN FORTHCOMING OPERATIONS.  I RESERVE TO
MYSELF THE RIGHT TO DECIDE ON TERROR ATTACKS
AS A MEASURE OF REPRISAL.  THE INTENSIFICATION
OF THE AIR WAR MAY BEGIN ON OR AFTER 5 AUGUST.
THE EXACT TIME IS TO BE DECIDED BY THE AIR
FORCE AFTER THE COMPLETION OF PREPARATIONS AND
IN THE LIGHT OF THE WEATHER.
END
SECRET
```

MOST SECRET - ULTRA

"Brilliant," Winston said. The strained expression of confusion and curiosity on Menzies face produced a slight chuckle from the Prime Minister. "I suppose that was a rather odd response to such a grim message. I must say, Stew, the acquisition of that Enigma device may very well be our salvation. While it does not offer up any more bullets or cannon shells, it has eliminated some of the uncertainty of war. At least, we know what that vile and abhorrent bastard's intentions are."

"Indeed. I might add Prime Minister, while the captured box as well as the experience of the Polish experts has been invaluable, a great deal of credit must be given to the analysts who must find the proper wheel and plug sequences each day in order to break down the messages."

"Please pass my sincerest appreciation for their work as well as the gratitude of an unknowing nation."

"I shall, Winston." The lull in conversation encouraged Menzies to add one additional point. "We have a far better understanding why the Germans are so arrogant about their codes. The Enigma is an exceptional piece of work to be admired for its simplicity and sophistication. The decoding task is taking a terrible toll on our people, but the analysts invariably, and I do believe unanimously, profess their respect for the device."

"Evil genius," Winston said with some disgust and irritation.

"It does confirm the intractable requirement for us to protect this source at any cost."

"I do absolutely agree, Stewart. You have my unwavering support to that end."

"Thank you."

Winston extended his left hand again. His curiosity regarding the bright yellow paper needed to be satisfied.

Menzies handed over the leaflet. "These were dropped last night over Hampshire and Somerset. So, they are being treated with humor and disdain."

PEACE

The leader of the German people wishes to bring a message of peace to the inhabitants of Great Britain.

Recent events have brought an unfortunate change of circumstance for many citizens in Europe. While these events have been most regrettable, they have been justified. The Leader wants to assure the citizens of England that he has the utmost respect and admiration for the English, and he has no desire to continue this unfortunate conflict. However, further provocation of Germany must be properly dealt with to protect the sovereignty of the German state. The Leader extends his hand of friendship to the English people and encourages them to change the adversarial and war-like attitudes of their government. The attacks on German ships, aircraft and people simply must stop if there is to be peace. The German Government has made innumerable attempts to reconcile any differences, but has been answered with violence. The Leader has shown remarkable patience and tolerance, but this must be considered a last appeal to reason. The English and German people should join together in peace. Let us all have peace.

PEACE

"Audacious bastards, aren't they?" said Winston.

"I do believe this would qualify."

"If we could only show the people the evidence we have before us."

"Indeed." Menzies allowed a long pause as Winston reread the leaflet. When he looked up without words, he continued. "What do you want to do?"

The response came immediately. "First, I shall brief the War Cabinet tomorrow. Second, I believe we should issue an invasion alert based on the reconnaissance evidence from Northern France. And third," Winston paused to consider his words, "I am inclined to engage the press, say *The Times*, to expose Hitler's duplicity."

"Prime Minister, Denniston drafted an invasion alert message, which I have with me, but if I may be so bold, I would suggest an invasion alert in light of this leaflet might be confusing to the citizenry, and public discussion of the invasion potential might be counter-productive. I must say, I also have concerns relative to drawing any suspicion in the minds of the German leadership regarding the integrity of their communications."

"I am not going to make any reference to our intelligence," Winston responded with an edge of irritation.

"No, sir, but I might add, to the Germans, they have extended an open hand. We should have no knowledge of Directive One Seven. What made us believe an open hand meant invasion?"

"Ah, yes, quite right, Stewart, as always. Then, I shall seek the counsel of the War Cabinet and recommend we let it lay for a bit."

"As you say. It would be prudent to raise the level of readiness of our forces simply based on the photographic reconnaissance."

"Yes so it would. Anything else, Stew?"

"No, sir."

'C' retrieved the ULTRA message and allowed the Prime Minister to retain the leaflet. The two men exchanged pleasantries for several minutes before Colonel Menzies departed. Winston remained thankful he had a friend and highly competent professional as his Chief of the Secret Intelligence Service. The relationships gave the Prime Minister the confidence he needed to ensure he received timely, accurate and properly analyzed intelligence. The British intelligence services had an unfortunate reputation for being somewhat fractious at times. This was absolutely not the time for discordance.

Winston was even more thankful for the Enigma box. The value of having access to secret enemy communications could not be calculated. While his insistence on seeing the raw decyphered messages remained a grave concern to SIS and GCCS, he refused to give up that access. He was one of the few people outside GCCS that saw the original decyphered messages, and he would insist the arrangement not be altered.

Winston remained motionless and lost in his thoughts as he considered the actions for the next War Cabinet meeting tomorrow morning. Anthony Eden, at the War Office, would undoubtedly bring a sample of the Nazi leaflet as well as announce the accumulated information regarding the enemy propaganda. Winston concluded that he could not predict how the War Cabinet members might respond to the information he would convey, but he did agree with 'C.' The United Kingdom needed to finalize its preparations for the invasion. Time was rapidly running out, and Winston Churchill did not want to be the first leader of the British people since medieval times to suffer subjugation.

Winston began to feel the nibble of impatience. He wanted to keep the worst from happening, but if it was going to happen, he wanted to get on with it. In his heart, Winston was convinced the engulfing conflagration would not be won by preparation or strength but by will. Either side would do what it had to do. The real question was, what did the leadership, the government, the armed forces, the people want to achieve? Winston chuckled to himself, having the most and best fighters, ships, men and resources would not hurt the cause a bit.

The Prime Minister rose from his chair to tell Colville to retrieve on of the night duty stenographers. He dictated several letters, notes and messages earlier in the evening. He wanted to transmit one message in particular. "Do you have the note to President Roosevelt?" he said to the young, rather plain woman. The young ones always got the nighttime duty.

"Yes, sir," she said leafing through a stack of papers. "Here it is." She pulled the single piece of paper from the stack and handed it to the Prime Minister.

MOST SECRET AND PERSONAL

```
56
1.VIII.40
TO:  POTUS
FIRST, I MUST THANK YOU FOR YOUR EFFORTS ON
OUR BEHALF.  I RECOGNISE THE GREAT POLITICAL
RISK YOU TAKE.  ONE DAY, THE BRITISH PEOPLE
WILL BE ABLE TO SHOW THE GRATITUDE THEY WILL
FEEL.  BY THE WAY, THE FIRST SHIPMENT OF YOUR
0.3006 CALIBRE SPRINGFIELD RIFLES ARRIVED
SEVERAL DAYS AGO.  WE ANXIOUSLY AWAIT THE
OTHER SHIPMENTS.
RECENT INDICATIONS POINT TOWARD A PROBABLE
INVASION ATTEMPT BY THE NAZIS WITHIN THE NEXT
TWO MONTHS.  WE HAVE SEEN GROWING MOBILE
BARGE TRAFFIC ALL ALONG THE OPPOSITE COAST AS
WELL AS INTENSIFIED AERIAL COMBAT OVER THE
CHANNEL AREA.  IF THEY ARE TO MAKE AN ATTEMPT
```

THIS YEAR, THEY MUST DO IT BEFORE THE ONSET OF
FOUL WEATHER IN THE AUTUMN. THE WEATHER WILL
BE OUR ALLY DURING THE WINTER MONTHS.
WE HAVE ALSO EXPERIENCED, AS WELL AS GATHERED
OTHER INTELLIGENCE REGARDING, THE INCREASED
OFFENSIVE PRESSURE FROM ENEMY U-BOATS. IT
SEEMS CLEAR THAT IF THEY ARE UNSUCCESSFUL WITH
AN INVASION, THEY INTEND TO BLOCKADE OUR LINES
OF SUPPLY.
I RESPECTFULLY RENEW MY REQUEST, ON BEHALF
OF THE BRITISH PEOPLE, A PURCHASE OR LOAN OF
40-50 OF YOUR OLDEST DESTROYERS TO SUPPLEMENT
THE ROYAL NAVY. WE MUST PROTECT THE CHANNEL
APPROACHES. FURTHERMORE, WE MUST GIRD
OURSELVES AGAINST THE INEVITABLE CHOKE HOLD
THE NAZI U-BOATS WILL ADMINISTER IN THE NEAR
FUTURE.
WE ARE IN RECEIPT OF YOUR LIST OF TECHNICAL
EXCHANGE ITEMS. OUR TEAM IS REVIEWING THE
LIST AS WE SPEAK. I EXPECT WE CAN FINALIZE
THE EXCHANGE IN THE NEXT FEW WEEKS. I THANK
YOU FOR YOUR SUPPORT.
LASTLY, WILD BILL VISIT HAS BEEN MOST
PRODUCTIVE I DO BELIEVE. I EXPECT TO MEET
WITH HIM ONE LAST TIME TOMORROW. HIS
SCHEDULED DEPARTURE IS SATURDAY, 3 AUGUST. I
BELIEVE HE WILL BRING WHAT YOU NEED.
SIGNED,
FORMER NAVAL PERSON

MOST SECRET AND PERSONAL

"Very good, thank you," Winston said, as he returned to his office.

Churchill reread the message and considered several changes. He decided against them and directed Colville to send the message immediately. He would see Bill Stephenson in the morning, before meeting for the last time with Bill Donovan. He would prepare Stephenson for the inevitable discussions with Donovan on their return flight to New York. The British relationship with the American military would soon become vital. General Marshall had already proved to be essential in obtaining nearly a million Springfield rifles to rearm the decimated Army after the losses of the British Expeditionary Force in France.

Churchill believed the British would be able to defend their island nation from the Germans at least this summer. He also believed they would not be able to defeat the Germans and restore freedom in Europe without the Americans. Winston convinced himself many times over that victory belonged to a grand alliance between the British and Americans, just as it did in 1918.

—

Friday, 2.August.1940
Headquarters, Fighter Command
Bentley Priory
Stanmore, Middlesex, England
15:20 hours

Group Captain John Spencer stared out the window that usually stayed to his back. The tall, grand windows of the old monastery offered an attractive view. The clear, hazy and nearly cloudless skies above the conifer treeline to the north told him this was likely to be a busy day for Fighter Command. He considered passing across the hall to the Commander's conference room to use the southerly facing windows for a better assessment of the weather but decided against it. He returned his attention to the papers on his desk just as a soft couple of knocks preceded the door opening.

His WAAF clerk entered the office carrying a small stack of papers and a strained expression. "Excuse me, sir, but if I recall, you were rather fond of a young American pilot by the name of Drummond, Brian Drummond, were you not?"

"Yes."

"Well, sir, I just noticed Mister Drummond's name on the casualty listing from Wednesday."

John's heart skipped a few beats as he grasped the words. He opened his mouth to speak, but no words would come as he sank back in his chair.

"Oh, oh, not to worry, sir. He was listed as serious."

"Where is he?" he asked, interrupting her before she could finish her description.

"Says here, he is in Hampshire Central in Winchester."

"Would you be so kind to call down there to check on his condition as well as find out how long he may be hospitalized."

"Yes, sir. Right away," she said, as she turned to the door.

God, he hated this damnable war, he told himself. Losing Malcolm four months ago in that freak accident and now possibly losing his only connection with Malcolm bore down on him like some prehistoric monster bird waiting to devour him.

John Spencer pushed himself back into his paperwork. He feverishly attacked the reading and action annotations that characterized his duties to the staff of Fighter Command partially to redirect his thoughts as well as get as much done as possible. If Brian was still in the hospital, he had to make the journey to the city just north of Southampton to visit the young man.

The door opened again. "He is still in the hospital. According to the ward nurse, he had a severe concussion and nearly drowned. Apparently, his parachute landed in a farmer's pond, and he was saved by the farmer. He was unconscious for more than a day but appears to be recovering. The doctors estimate he should be released in a day or so, but should not return to flying for at least a week, perhaps longer."

"Anything else?"

"That is the extent of the information I could coax from her, sir."

"Excellent. Very well done. I think I shall try to get down there to visit him tonight or tomorrow."

"Do you want me to make any arrangements, sir?"

"No, thank you. I should be able to find a seat on the coach from Waterloo to Winchester, thank you just the same."

"Very well, sir," she said and left.

A clear vision of broken and wounded pilots in the field hospitals of Northeastern France two decades earlier came to him. How many of his friends and mates had he seen in those beds with doctors and nurses dressed in often blood spattered white clothing running about? Too many. Now, it was beginning again. Although he had never been to the hospital in Winchester, he knew the scene all too well. The only difference would be the building instead of a tent. Brian's business was a game of living and dying. John could only hope and pray he and as many of his mates as possible survived the onslaught.

John looked up to the wall clock on the adjacent wall to his right. It was 16:37. He had at least several hours work ahead of him. He might be able to make the last train to Southampton if no more paperwork entered his office. John thought about calling Mary but hesitated. He could tell her before he took the Underground to Waterloo Station. Knowing her, she might want to accompany him to Winchester. She seemed to reflect his concern for the young American volunteer.

A hard knock on the door told him a man was about to enter. As he raised his head in response, Air Commodore Hogan entered his office and closed the door behind him. "Well, John, we seem to be getting closer by the day."

"What this time?"

"The Air Ministry just issued an upgraded invasion alert. The War Cabinet decided this afternoon that invasion is now probable within the next few weeks . . . before the end of summer."

"What do you know?"

"First, the photo recce evidence shows substantial build-ups all along the Channel coast from Bremerhaven to Brest. Second, the German aerial attacks have been moving progressively closer to the south coast. Just yesterday, they attacked every convoy in the Channel from west to east including the two big ones, AGENT and ARENA, as well as numerous ships at anchor including several Royal Navy warships in virtually every major harbor. Third, other intelligence sources indicate a rapid move toward offensive land operations. The opinions as to what it means are essentially unanimous. The only debate is when."

John Spencer thought of Brian. Maybe luck would keep him in the hospital or at least out of the air until the worst of it was over. Assuming they survived the juggernaut, he told himself.

"That is not all, I might add."

"What else could there be?"

"The Admiralty reports an unprecedented number of U-boat sightings in the North Sea and North Atlantic. They believe Dönitz is preparing the noose in case the initial invasion attempt falters or fails."

"Any other bright news, Air Commodore?"

"Only the boss just asked for a night conference to consider the latest developments. The group commanders are en route."

"Damn, so much for that," muttered John.

"What?"

"Oh, I just received word my young American volunteer was shot down two days ago."

"Did he survive?"

"Yes. The report lists him as serious in hospital at Winchester."

"This is your best friend's son?"

John smiled at the thought. "Practically, but no . . . just a prize student."

"And you were going to visit him in the hospital."

"Yes."

"Well, you could ask the boss to give you a day pass."

John Spencer considered the suggestion for several moments. "No, if something is going to happen, 'Stuffy' will need me here."

"We all will, John. We all will."

John contemplated his options. "Maybe I should just call Mary and ask her to visit Brian?"

"She knows him doesn't she?"

"Yes. That may work."

"Then I shall leave you to it," Hogan said, and turned to leave John alone in his office.

He knew Mary would not be happy. Yet another day and night, and he would not be able to join her even for an evening meal. He wanted to check on his young protégé, as that is how he thought of Brian, but James Hogan was correct as usual. Things were beginning to happen at a much faster pace, now, and the success or failure of Fighter Command and the Royal Air Force depended on vigilance, focus and commitment.

"Bushey Heath Two Four Seven One," Mary Spencer answered the telephone call.

"Mary, this is John."

"Not again, John," she responded with a foul concoction of irritation, frustration, confusion and anger. "I have not seen you in nearly a week, and you are less than ten miles away."

John felt his own irritation level mounting. Why didn't she understand the burdens of war? Why couldn't she accept the demands and pressures upon him and so many others? He told her numerous times about the growing signs of invasion. He could not bring himself to tell her how close the country was to the edge of the precipice. There could be no value in scaring her. But, why couldn't she see the signs for herself? Everything seemed to be collapsing around them, and yet she could barely contain herself regarding the demands on his time. Why couldn't she understand?

"Mary, we have been through this too many times. There is a real war on."

"John," she interjected her protestation.

"Look Mary, I did not call to argue about the demands on my time."

"Then what did you call about?"

"Brian Drummond was shot down two days ago."

"Dear God," Mary expelled the words.

"Mary, he is OK. He is in a hospital and is expected to recover."

"How serious?"

"A concussion," John answered withholding the adjective, severe. "I called to suggest you visit him in the hospital. He is in Winchester Central for at least another couple of days. I thought about going, but we have a rather sticky situation at the moment."

A long pause of hissing silence filled the space as Mary mulled over John's suggestion. "I shall make arrangements to go down to Winchester tomorrow. I will pass your concerns and thoughts for his quick recovery."

"Thank you, Mary. I am worried about him. He lost Malcolm several months ago, and I want him to know he is not alone. I want him to survive this nastiness."

"I will be sure to tell him."

"I shall try to get home as soon as I can, Mary. Please understand."

"I will try, John. I will try. Now, you take care and defend us from the heathens."

"I will. Good night."

The telephone went dead as the connection was broken. John did not have much time to be with his thoughts. His presence was requested in the conference room for a preliminary discussion with Air Vice-Marshal Park regarding the most recent changes in German tactics. The work of defense continued.

—

Friday, 2.August.1940
No.10 Downing Street
Whitehall, London, England
17:00 hours

"Misters Stephenson and Donovan have arrived for your scheduled debriefing," announced Colville.

"Thank you, Jock. Please clear my calendar until tomorrow morning," commanded Prime Minister Churchill.

"Yes sir. I have already done so. I must remind you, Missus Landemare has a private dinner planned for you and your guests at eight, I do believe."

"That should be sufficient. I suspect we shall make a night of it, as I understand they are due to depart tomorrow morning."

"That is my understanding as well, sir."

"Very well. Please show them in, if they are ready, and I do not want to be disturbed, except for some operational emergency."

"Yes, sir."

Colville left and returned a few minutes later. "Misters Stephenson and Donovan, sir."

Churchill rose from his chair to greet his guests. Colville closed the door behind him. As Churchil and Donovan settled into their plush, ample, leather chairs, Stephenson poured a glass of scotch for each man, and then sat with his friends.

"So I do not get crosswise with Missus Landemare, she has dinner planned for us at eight, and I trust you will be able to remain my guests this evening. It is my understanding both of you leave tomorrow morning, so it would be easiest for you to stay here."

"That is the plan, Winston," Little Bill answered.

"Excellent. Then, let us begin with a toast to President Roosevelt and our Grand Alliance," Churchill said, as he raised his glass to the others. After clinking glasses and taking a healthy sip, Winston continued, "I eagerly await your assessment of our situation."

"Most humbly, Winston, I am but one man, and a little over two weeks was hardly sufficient time for a proper assessment. However, I can safely say it has been a uniquely informative visit. I must begin by conveying my utmost gratitude for the extraordinary welcome and access you allowed me. I do believe the Secretary of the Navy will be quite pleased with the results."

"Excellent . . . and the President, I should think."

"I would presume so, but that is not my place or charter."

"Yes, yes, quite so. Please continue."

"Also, I must tell you that having Bill," Donovan said, motioning to Stephenson, "with me throughout my tour was a godsend, and I cannot thank you, both of you, enough for allowing him to be away from his important and pressing duties so long to escort me and clear the way for me to learn."

"Nonsense," Churchill said, waving his hand. "The relationship with your president and your country is of paramount importance to us, and there can be no reserve in such a relationship. We must trust each other, implicitly." Donovan bowed his head in recognition. "Now, please do continue," he said with mounting impatience.

"I was able to spend considerable time with 'C' and his MI6 staff, with 'K' and his staff at MI5, as well as with Sir Philip and his chiefs at the Metropolitan Police. I truly appreciate the extra time they spent to educate me on their organizational structure and combined operating procedures. I was also quite impressed with your combined services interrogation center at Trent Park. MI5, MI9 and MI19 have an ingenius site and operational plans that should become a bountiful source as the war progresses. We have nothing even remotely like their capability and that is truly sad with a looming world war. Witnessing their very close coordination and cooperation was most illuminating to me, and I believe will be quite useful to us, assuming we are able to overcome the bureaucratic morass that exists between our various intelligence agencies."

"I know that is one of Franklin's greatest concerns," Churchill said.

"And, rightly so. The state of our intelligence services is, quite frankly, embarrassing."

"You will help the President overcome those shortcomings."

"If he wishes me to assist."

"Again, nonsense, he will. I have confidence." Churchill gestured for Donovan to continue.

"I also was able to spend a fair amount of time with Hugh Dalton and learned of his plans to carry out his charge from the War Cabinet with unconventional warfare on the Continent with his Special Operations Executive . . . most informative, I must say. I laud your commitment to take the fight to the enemy, especially in the light of their conquests. While I think Brigadier Harker would readily admit, there are no perfect processes. Yet, your successes against fifth column infiltrators have been far more accomplished than anything our FBI has been able to do so far. You set the bar very high for us, I have noted."

"Hopefully, you have good notes to help your countrymen plug those gaps and sufficient contacts within His Majesty's Government to sustain you during the formative months as well as advance our mutual cooperation to defeat our common enemy."

"I believe I can safely say I have accomplished the mission with which I was charged."

"Excellent. Now, what of your other observations."

"The armed forces ministries and chiefs of staff were all most generous with their time and surprisingly candid in their communications with me. I met with General Ironside, and then General Brooke, who gratiously showed me the defense in depth preparations along the Channel coast and inland approaches. We, also," said Donovan, nodding his head to Bill Stephenson, "had a delightful, extended, lunch discussion with Admiral Ramsay, now Sir Bertram I understand, who offered a thorough briefing on the Royal Navy's operation plans for the defense of the Channel approaches for the expected invasion attempt later this summer. I must say, in all candor, the captivating part of the discussion was his recounting of the miracle of Dunkirk."

"Yes, quite so, I am certain, but as I have cautioned my countrymen, victories are not won by evacuation."

"Most assuredly, however, the accomplishment of those little boats in such a short span of time and against such daunting obstacles has to be seen as one of the most miraculous military achievements in all of history."

"Considerable credit must go to Sir Bertram and his Dover Approaches staff for the planning and supervision of Operation DYNAMO," added the Prime Minister.

"I know Secretary Knox and President Roosevelt will be as enthralled as I was by the achievement . . . a third of a million men withdrawn from a hostile beach is unprecedented is all of history, to my knowledge."

"Yes, well, my experience with evacuations has not been all that stellar prior to Dunkirk."

"Now, Winston," interjected Stephenson, "you must not continue to flagellate yourself over Gallipoli. Admiral Carden's timidity and failure to execute what was a brilliant campaign plan lost that battle, not you."

"Yes, well, whatever the reason, that debacle cost us more than a quarter of a million casualties at a time when we could ill-afford such losses and got me sacked as First Lord."

"Winston, please!" protested Stephenson.

Churchill waved his hand dismissively, and then nodded his head to Donovan to continue with his report.

"A.V. Alexander, Admiral Pound and Admiral Pike took me through a thorough briefing in the Admiralty's Situation Room, regarding the status of forces, the enemy's known order of battle, and the immense challenges they face securing the oceanic supply lines. They certainly made the case for the destroyers you have requested from President Roosevelt. I was also intrigued by your underwater and airborne detection research to deal with the U-boat menace. The accomplishments of Dönitz and his U-boat service are quite frightening."

"Vermin, plain and simple . . . vermin of the sea."

"I must confess my awestruck amazement with Air Chief Marshal Dowding's Air Defense of Great Britain system, operations plan and performance to date. I can see the basis of your confidence in defending England. My visit to Bawdsey Manor with its Chain Home station along with the detailed briefing by Doctor Watson-Watt on your radio detection research was quite eye-opening to say the least. We have so much to learn. I also had the honor to meet and have lunch with your nephew Group Captain John Spencer, a unique character I must say. He has a grasp of things far beyond his rank. I suspect he has a very bright future ahead of him in the air force. Again, I must thank you for insisting that I meet with Pilot Officer Brian Drummond. He is quite enamored with his Spitfire fighter and is among good company in Fighter Command."

"When did you meet with him?"

"Last Tuesday, I do believe," Donovan answered, looking to Stephenson for a confirmatory head nod.

"Quite fortuitous, it seems," said Churchill. "I was given a report yesterday, that he was shot down the next day, and saved from certain death by a rather heroic young woman. The information of the episode remains sketchy at the moment, but I understand he was somehow thrown clear unconscious from his damaged aircraft, apparently his parachute deployed by some unknown means, and he landed in the good size pond on her farm. She dove into the pond and nearly drowned pulling him to land, and then she managed to get him breathing again before the ambulance service arrived. Most heroic, I must say, and a very lucky young man. My report indicates he is recovering nicely in hospital and should be able to return to duty soon. We certainly need pilots like him, especially in the next two months."

"War is nasty business."

"Indeed!"

"I wish I had time to visit him, but we are scheduled to depart tomorrow morning."

"I will ensure your condolences are sent to him."

"Thank you, Winston."

Churchill nodded. "Were you able to talk to Sir John?"

"Home Secretary Sir John Anderson?" Winston nodded his confirmation. "Yes, we met several times. He briefed me on the technical exchange list he has been working on. I believe I understand each of the line items, to at least convey their importance. Sir John also facilitated another series of visits and meetings. I understand the necessity for the work at Porton Down, but the specter of chemical and biological warfare are beyond comprehension."

"We have no choice, given work we know is going on in Germany."

"I understand that, Winston, but still . . . how barbaric will we become in this war?"

"I truly hope the Hun does not resort to use of those substances they are developing and producing. We both survived their dreadful deployment in the last war. We cannot allow them that advantage."

"Understood, but still . . ." Donovan's voice trailed off into contemplation.

"What else?" Churchill asked with a tone of impatience.

Donovan recognized the Prime Minister's mood and picked up the lance. "Sir John also generously arranged an afternoon meeting with George Thompson and his MAUD Committee. To be frank, I had no idea the science had progressed this far. Clearly, we need to catalogue all of the known uranium supplies and somehow gain control of those supplies."

"Were you able to discuss that particular topic with Colonel Menzies?" the Prime Minister asked.

"Actually, no, we ran out of time."

"Once you have completed your mission with Frank Knox, I think you will agree MI6 is ready to compare notes and to make a joint plan to accomplish that important objective. As soon as the President designates an intelligence objective, we are ready, willing and able. The most problematic today is Czechoslovakia, as their mines are already under German control."

"Perhaps an appropriate target for Hugh Dalton's SOE."

"Perhaps."

A couplet knock broke the discussion. All three men looked to the door, as the door opened slightly and Jock Colville's face appeared. "My apologies, Prime Minister, but I must remind you dinner is planned for eight."

"Thank you, Jock. You are a savior." Churchill looked to Donovan and Stephenson. "We must not disappoint Missus Landemare, and we can continue our discussions at dinner and after . . . at least until you must depart for home. Shall we?" Churchill motioned toward the door.

Colville led the three men to the State Dining Room. The vast, elegant room hardly seemed appropriate for three men, however the Prime Minister wanted to make a final point for his guest. Dinner was served on time and took them two hours to complete, not because of slow service, but stretched by focused words and the transition to the more personal relationship elements that would sustain them both professionally and socially. Churchill coaxed the discussion to the potential and need for a master intelligence service in the United States, and how such an organization might be constructed and operated. They would not retire for some rest until nearly 02:00 the following morning and after the consumption of considerable drink.

—

Brian began the day just as the previous few days and nights had begun, with pain. He continued to feel like a fresh melon in a large vice clamp. No matter what the doctors tried, the pain persisted and remained undiminished. In the occasional lull between the storms of pain, Brian struggled to remember what had happened. He lost nearly two days from Wednesday afternoon to Friday. The air combat and the two or maybe three German fighters chasing him slowly returned. The nurses kept working with him to fill in the blanks.

The story of his rescue gained detail and embellishment, he told himself, with each telling. Several key elements retained their consistency. Numerous people witnessed the flaming explosion of his Spitfire. Several saw his parachute. No one could explain how he got out of the destroyed aircraft or how his parachute had been deployed. The only sequence Brian thought plausible was somehow as the aircraft broke up his seat straps were detached, he was thrown clear, and his ripcord had been snagged on the way out. It did sound incredible. He actually did not care how; he was just thankful luck was on his side again.

According to the nurses, a prominent female farmer in the area saved him from drowning in a large pond. He knew he would have to find a way to thank her. Several versions of the rescue story indicated the woman nearly drowned trying to save him.

"You have a visitor," announced the ward nurse.

Brian looked around to see Jonathan Kensington's smiling, fresh face. "I was beginning to wonder if you were going to come see me," said Brian with lightness and humor to his voice.

"You simply must stop this game, 'Hunter.' You keep trying to find new ways of seeking sympathy. One of these days you may go too far."

"Real nice. My best friend comes to insult me."

"No, just to check on you," Jonathan paused to scan Brian's covered body. "Does not look like anything serious."

"Right you are, except for this pounding in my head and a few cuts, scrapes and bruises."

"What do you remember?" asked Jonathan.

"Nothing for a couple of days. I remember the fight, being chased, and then a blurry haze in this hospital bed. The nurses have told me about some of the things in between."

"Did they tell you about an attractive young woman saving your silly little arse from drowning?"

"Yes, but how would you know she was attractive?"

"'Jackstay' and I made several low passes until she pulled you out of the water."

"And, I suppose you were low enough to see her face."

"That is roughly about right."

"She is a prominent farmer in the area, so they tell me."

"Is that so? I do declare, my good friend, you have more luck than sense, but I guess that is better than vice versa."

"'Spike' and 'Jackstay' came down to see you yesterday morning, but you were incoherent."

"Please thank them for checking on me. I don't remember a thing until sometime yesterday afternoon and even that is fuzzy."

"The doctors say you are going to be OK. Should be another few days in the hospital. You must have taken a rather good bump to the head when your fighter came apart. 'Jackstay' was rolling to help you when it exploded. You had three bloody One Oh Nines on your tail. Almost like you were spit out of the fireball, 'Jackstay' says your chute popped you out."

"I've been trying to figure that out."

"Somehow as the aircraft broke up, you must have been released from your seat and something pulled your ripcord."

"I'll be damned."

"Quite."

"Other than this pounding headache, I'm ready to get back up there. How are things going?"

Jonathan Kensington wondered how much he should tell his friend. The invasion alert, the increased number and size of the raids especially to the east, none of it would help his friend recover. "Business as usual."

"You lie. I can see it in your eyes."

"Forget about the war for now. You just concentrate on your recovery so you can get back in the saddle."

"No problem."

"Smashing. Now, I simply must be getting back to Middle Wallop. 'Spike' only gave me the morning to come see you."

"Thanks for coming, Jonathan. I'll be back soon."

"Certainly. Cheers," he said, as he turned and left.

Brian watched his best friend leave the hospital ward. As he thought about what Jonathan did not want to tell him, Brian returned his attention to the large room. Thirty beds nearly half full mostly with pilots from everything he could gather. His own bed was in the far left corner as you entered the ward. He remembered they brought three wounded fighter pilots in late yesterday. Maybe the war was picking up the pace. Maybe the Germans have already landed on English soil. No, he told himself that could not be. That would be the singular topic of discussion, if it was true.

Three women in colorful dresses walked into the ward, asked the nurse something, presumably where a patient was, and walked to a bed at the far end of the room. The muffled words carried a tone of concern, but soon transitioned to humor. Laughter filled the room that made Brian feel better. The melodious tones of the female visitors relaxed Brian. He began to drift off toward sleep until he heard the footfalls, determined steps of a man. A squadron leader with his cap tucked under his left arm entered, looked around, found the person he was looking for and moved slowly toward the far end of the room. He did not recognize the officer.

The man must have singled out his objective. Brian watched him move directly toward the three women. All three turned to look at the approaching officer and the woman in the bright red, floral print dress must have recognized the ominous expression on his face. She began to shake her head. The woman staggered backward until she hit the wall.

Brian could clearly hear her pleas of protest, and then the most God-awful, blood-curdling scream. The tortured, agonizing screams continued bringing a half dozen nurses scrambling to ascertain the problem and remedy the situation. The confusion, turmoil and beehive of activity along with the distinct punctuation of cries from the woman told Brian she had probably just been notified that her boyfriend, fiancé, lover or husband had just been killed in action.

The character of the woman's agony etched itself in Brian's memory. He had never heard anything like it before, and he hoped he would never hear it again. It was worse than any pain he had ever felt.

They escorted the slumping and writhing woman from the room. Her cries could be heard for sometime through the doors and walls. Several nurses remained to quickly and efficiently evaluate the effects on each one of their patients.

"How are you feeling Mister Drummond?" asked a middle-aged, matronly nurse.

"I suppose I'm OK. What happened?"

"I am afraid the Air Force chose a very inopportune time and place to notify the woman that she was now a widow."

"That was the worst scream I've ever heard."

"The pain of dreadful loss, I'm afraid."

"I'd say," Brian said in staunch agreement.

The nurse moved closer to him looking deeply into her patient's eyes. "My original question was more than pleasantry. How are your headaches?"

"OK," he lied, thinking he might be able to return to the squadron earlier.

"Mister Drummond, please, you don't have to be a man with me. I am asking you a serious and concerned question as to your health."

Brian laughed at her frankness, which made his head hurt more. He reached up to grasp his forehead, as if it might fall away.

"Still rather bad, I'd say," she observed.

Brian nodded his head very slowly feeling the effort to speak would cause more pain than slight movement. She added a pillow behind him and gently nudged him to lie back against the mound of pillows.

"Now, do you think you can describe how you feel, Mister Drummond?"

"The pain is all over, but it's the worst across the front. I've never felt a headache like this."

"You have suffered a severe concussion which means your brain got bashed around in your noggin. It is bruised and swollen. As with all bruises, they take time to heal and relieve themselves. The next few days are critical to your long-term health, Mister Drummond. We simply must know what is happening inside your skull, and you are the only one who can tell us."

"I understand."

"Do you?"

"Yes."

"Excellent," she said, as she walked away. "Then, we shall get along in smashing fashion."

She was modestly plump, but she still knew how to walk. At least the power of observation has not failed me, Brian said to himself, proud that he could notice such things despite the headache.

Brian's thoughts returned to the woman's screams and cries. He told himself he must never forget those screams, and yet, he knew he had to put them in their proper place. His mission, his objective, his dream was in the air. He had to concentrate on recovering his health and rejoining his compatriots. He needed them, and he felt certain they needed him. Brian focused on relaxing his entire body and ignoring the pain in his head. Soon, the soothing release of sleep enveloped him.

Gradually, an awareness of his surroundings crept back to him. As he opened his eyes with a slight blur to his vision, Brian was startled to see a woman sitting in a chair next to his bed. As his vision cleared, the smiling but apprehensive face of Mary Spencer came closer to him. Her light, loose, airy, medium green dress complemented the elegance of her appearance. She gently touched his head. Her soft, smooth, warm hand seemed to extract the pain from his skull.

"How are you, my dear Brian?" she said with her feathery, concerned voice.

"What are you doing here?"

"Brian, I am hurt. If I did not know better, your query would suggest I am not the person you wanted to see."

"I'm sorry, Mary. I just didn't expect to see you down here."

"John told me you had been shot down and were in the hospital. He asked me to visit you and convey his concern and best wishes for a speedy recovery. Frankly, I hope you do not recover."

"What?"

"I did not mean that as it sounded. I simply wish you did not return to the cockpit and that danger."

Brian appreciated the concern he felt from Mary Spencer but wondered about what other reasons she showed up at this Winchester hospital. He did not doubt his injury worried Mary. He just could not imagine her making the journey because he was in the hospital. Brian slowly nodded his head in response.

"What happened?"

Brian told her what he knew from his memory as well as what others had told him about events surrounding his downing. Mary did not ask many questions, which made Brian feel the topic probably made her uncomfortable. What she did ask revolved around his medical condition that he relayed as best he could.

"How is your head, now" she asked as she continued to stroke his forehead. The soothing of her touch tempted him to ask for her to stay until he recovered.

"Better," was his succinct answer.

As they continued to discuss his medical condition, Brian noticed the duty ward nurse enter the room with another woman and point toward him. He watched the new woman walk confidently toward him. The woman had a young, almost doll like face with nearly gray, speckled hair pulled back into a tight bun at the back of her head. The most unusual element of her appearance was the light brown slacks, red checker shirt with sleeves rolled up to her elbows. She seemed to be rather tall, slender and carried herself in a straight, assured manner.

"Pardon me," she said to Brian, and then to Mary. She had the coolest, blue-gray eyes that seemed to dominate the room. "Are you Pilot Officer Drummond?"

"Yes."

Brian and Mary looked, maybe some would say stared, at the woman as they waited for her to continue.

She extended her hand to him. "My name is Charlotte Palmer." Brian took her warm hand, nodded his head slowly to acknowledge her name and wanted to know more. What was she here for? Did she bring bad news like the earlier incident? He felt her pull her hand from his. She then extended her hand to Mary.

"I am Mary Spencer, a friend of Brian's," she said.

"Pleased to meet you both." She looked back to Brian with a strange, inquisitive expression in her eyes. "I am the one who pulled you from my pond."

Brian felt a rush of gratitude and appreciation. From everything he had been told, this woman was the thin line between life and death. Her subtle beauty sharpened to a deep, rich depth. Brian could not explain the attraction he felt toward Charlotte Palmer but was unable to differentiate between his thankfulness for her rescue or her earthy elegance.

"I'll be," exhaled Mary.

"They tell me you saved my life."

"I do not know about that," she responded with humility. "You landed in my pond and you needed help. Fortunately, I was working on my fence near the pond."

Brian could not think of anything to say and simply attached his gaze to the blue-gray pools looking back at him. She smiled, but soon began to convey her discomfort. "Can you tell me what happened?" he finally asked.

"I will do my best." She looked around the room for another chair. "May I?"

"By all means," he said, as he tried to get up to move a chair. His head pounded against his sense of courtesy.

"No, no, please stay put," Charlotte Palmer said, as she quickly retrieved a small chair from the other side of the ward. Mary and Brian waited for her to settle into position near the foot of the bed.

"As I said earlier, I was working near the pond at my farm when I became aware of sounds of aircraft straining as well as gunfire. I heard an explosion, looked up and saw a large black cloud and parts of an airplane falling beyond my farm. The fighting continued as your mates kept after your attackers. Sometime later, I saw your white parachute. You were completely limp. I could not determine whether you were alive or dead when you landed in my pond. Something told me I needed to pull you out. I nearly drowned. I must say several of your mates flew low to check on you, which inspired me to redouble my efforts. From there, the Emergency Services took over."

Brian had so many questions he did not know where to start. Mary sat looking at Charlotte as if she was in a trance. The stories the nurses told him focused his curiosity on this woman's effort to keep him alive. "The nurses tell me you did more than just pull me from the water."

"I did not think," Charlotte said, as she looked away and shifted her position several times. "I simply reacted to the situation."

"What exactly did you do?" asked Mary with somewhat of an edge to her voice.

Charlotte Palmer glanced at Mary, and then looked back to Brian. "You were not breathing, and I could not detect a heart beat. I breathed into your lungs and pounded on your chest."

"So, it's true."

"What do you mean?" asked Charlotte.

"They told me you did some extraordinary things to bring me back to life. They also said, if you hadn't done what you did, I would most probably have died."

"Then," Mary interjected, "we all owe you a debt of gratitude."

"Nonsense."

"I agree but more," said Brian, "I owe you my life."

Mary Spencer stood up and looked at Brian. He thought he could see anger in her eyes. What could possibly make her angry? Brian started to ask what was bothering her, but decided he might be wrong.

"I must be going," Mary said. Brian did not offer any resistance. "I came to check on you and pass along the best wishes of both John and myself. I am so happy you are recovering well."

"Thank you for coming, Mary. Please thank Group Captain Spencer for me as well."

"I shall." She leaned over and kissed Brian on the forehead. "Please be careful up there," she said motioning with her head to the sky above. "It was a pleasure meeting you, Miss Palmer. Thank you for saving our Brian's life."

"The honor was mine," responded Charlotte. "My apologies, Missus Spencer. I did not mean to interfere. I shall leave."

"No, please stay, Miss Palmer. I have so many questions," Brian said, and then looked back to Mary Spencer. "I will be as careful as I can, and thanks again Mary for your concern."

Mary Spencer turned and walked gracefully to the exit. Brian could not resist watching her hips sway subtly and the seam of her hosiery accentuate the curves of her lower legs as she walked away.

"I am so sorry, Mister Drummond. I did not mean to interfere."

"No problem."

"If I may be so bold, Madam Spencer did not appear to be particularly pleased with my presence. I suspect I have strained your relationship with her."

Brian instantly jumped into many questions. Could she tell Mary and he were lovers? Did she know Mary was married to Group Captain John Spencer? What did she think of Mary? What did she think of him? The questions continued to come with no answers. Brian thought about trying to briefly explain his relationship with Mary, but realized there could be no succinct description.

"She is used to getting her way. She'll get over it. I didn't know if I would ever be able to meet you. I know there is no way I can ever thank you sufficiently for saving my life."

"Nonsense. It was my privilege to contribute to the war effort. Judging from the interest of your mates, I believe you fly Spitfire aeroplanes, is that correct?"

"It certainly is . . . since last October. I fly with Six Oh Nine Squadron out of Middle Wallop."

"That is just up the carriageway then?"

"Yes, it is."

The ward nurse announced the approaching termination of visiting hours. Brian felt like a zoo animal in his cage at closing time. They were about to be fed and tended to by their keepers. He did not want Charlotte Palmer to leave.

Miss Palmer changed to a more animated and warm expression like a schoolgirl who has come to some realization and wants to confirm her observation. "I have never had the opportunity to meet, let alone talk to, a fighter pilot. What is it like?"

That was the only cue Pilot Officer Brian Drummond needed. "Like the most glorious freedom you can ever imagine."

"Really?"

Brian felt a genuine exuberance he had not felt in many months. He finally had a fresh, inquisitive, interested person to talk to, and he owed her for his life. "It is right up there with great sex," he said with youthful vigor and without forethought. Instantly, he noticed Charlotte's expression withdraw from his immodest exposition. "I'm sorry, Miss Palmer. I didn't mean to embarrass you." He started to get up, but his head immediately convinced him not to move any further. He lay back down on his pillows. "Being around other pilots, high-speed fighters and the dangers of aerial combat sometimes make you forget about other people's feelings. I truly am sorry, if I offended you."

"It is quite all right, Mister Drummond. Apology accepted. I supposed I am not quite accustomed to such ribald enthusiasm."

Brian did not know what that meant exactly, but he thought he could figure it out. The last thing he wanted at this moment was to offend his savior. Plus, as each minute passed, he became progressively more appreciative of her common beauty. She wore no make-up of any kind he could detect, and yet her full lips, petite nose, and naturally rosy color belied any need for adornment. Brian kept being drawn back into her eyes. The most exquisite eyes he had ever seen. They became progressively more magnetic. The sweeping, gentle curves of the perfect almond shaped eyes, and those deep, blue-gray pools that kept him riveted. Brian soon became aware that Charlotte Palmer's eyes were rapidly becoming the sole focus of his attention. The incessant pain disappeared.

Charlotte Palmer let her eyes communicate her mounting discomfort with his attention. "My husband was a naval officer."

"You said, 'husband' and 'was.' I am sorry for your loss."

She lowered her eyes to break the connection. "Thank you, Mr. Drummond. Ian was a Royal Navy lieutenant on HMS *Glorious*."

"I'll be damned. The *Glorious*. I lost a friend as well. He was one of those crazy guys that landed their fighters on the *Glorious* to save the aircraft from capture in Norway only to be sunk by the *Scharnhorst*." Brian finally remembered his manners. "My apologies again, Missus Palmer. I forgot myself. I offer my sincerest sympathies for your loss. This war has seemed to touch all of us in one way or another."

"Thank you for your sentiments, Mister Drummond. My condolences for your loss as well."

Brian nodded but did not want to talk about death any more. "May I call you, Charlotte. I would really prefer to be called, Brian."

"As you wish, Brian."

"Thank you, Charlotte," he said, as her name rolled off his tongue. Her given name complemented her simple beauty.

Brian noticed the ward nurse walking toward them with a more determined look in her eyes. He held up a hand trying to signal her to stop.
Unfortunately, the gesture did not work.

"I am afraid I must insist that you leave at once, madam," she said.

Charlotte Palmer turned toward the nurse. "Yes, certainly," she said,
and then turned back to Brian. "I am so pleased you are recovering, Mister .
. . excuse me, I should say, Brian. My prayers will be with you."

"Thank you once again, Charlotte. My debt to your courage is bound-
less."

"Good day, then."

Brian did not want her to leave. "May I call on you sometime?"

"I am still in mourning, Brian. I do not think it would be proper."

"I don't mean it that way. I would like to see your pond and hear some
more about the events of that afternoon."

"Excuse me," she said, as she stood to leave. "Please let me know
when you would like to visit. I would be happy to show you my pond," she
added with a soft chuckle.

Brian watched Charlotte Palmer walk out of the ward with long, confident strides. She impressed him as a strong woman with a hidden fragile
edge. While all the English women he knew were confident and self-assured,
Charlotte possessed a strength he had only noticed in Jackie Cochran, the
famous female aviator.

The evening meal of fish potpie, peas and new potatoes did not seem
to bother Brian as it usually did. The evening examination by the doctors
and nurses passed without objection or interest. Brian remained intrigued by
Charlotte. He wanted to know more about her. He wanted to understand
who she was. Most importantly, he had to find a way to thank her, to convey
his deepest, most sincere appreciation for what she had done for him.

The overhead lights went out at 22:00 hours sharp. The sanctuary
of sleep gradually enveloped him as he pondered, wondered and imagined
Charlotte Palmer. He felt a smile even if there was not one on his face. He
was soon sound asleep.

"Brian." He heard in the distance. Was he dreaming? "Brian." The
voice seemed closer and more familiar.

"Uhhh," he groaned.

"Brian, it's me.

He began to return to consciousness. "What time is it?" he asked from
his groggy state, convinced it was not a dream, and somewhat irritated the

nurse would be waking him in the middle of the night. But, the nurse never said, 'It's me,' an expression of familiarity.

"It is after midnight. Are you awake?"

He recognized the voice as his eyes opened in the dim light of the nighttime hospital ward. "Rosemary, what are you doing here at this time of night?" Brian asked a little too loudly.

"Shhhh," she whispered with her right index finger across her lips.

"How did you get in?"

"I had a problem with the railway from Oxford. I needed to see you today. I must be back up there for a special meeting, so I could not wait for visiting hours tomorrow. I had to sneak in after most of the staff went home for the evening. The night nurse was busy doing something else."

"You're incredible, Rosemary."

"Aren't I though. How are you, Brian?" she said as she began to feel his hands, arms, feet, legs and chest as she searched for injuries.

"It's my head, Rosemary."

"Your head?" she asked as she felt his skull.

"Inside."

Rosemary Kensington began to gently kiss his forehead working her way down to his lips. Without any resistance, protestation or indication of pain, she kissed him on the lips moving quickly to a more passionate level. Brian reached to embrace her. She withdrew. Her light colored, airy dress made her seem to float next to his bed.

"You scared the bloody hell out of me."

"Things happen, Rosemary. I can assure you, it was not by design."

"How do you feel otherwise?"

"I still have a little pain."

"Where?"

"Headaches."

Rosemary kissed him several more times. "No broken bones, wounds or other injuries?"

"Just scratches and bruises."

"What happened?"

"I got in a fight, and my fighter came apart."

"Oh, Brian," she whined softly.

"It's all right."

"This time, but how many more of these . . . these . . . incidents are there going to be? Brian, why do you have to do this?"

"You know why, Rosemary. You know why. It is my duty."

She stood quietly beside the bed stroking his forehead ever so softly as she dealt with her thoughts. Brian wanted to know what she was thinking but did not want to get into a protracted discussion about the risks he took while flying. Rosemary must have satisfied herself with the state of her thoughts. A smile slowly washed over her face. She looked over her shoulder to scan the room. Brian did the same. Everyone appeared to be asleep or out of the room. The ward was cool with an evening breeze blowing through the ward and not the slightest movement or sound other than a several snoring patients. Rosemary carefully pulled several standing privacy screens to block any view of the room. The beds on the opposite side of the room were empty, so she did not bother with screens at the foot of the bed.

Returning to Brian's head after her effort, she kissed him passionately and deeply. "I hope nothing else is broken," she purred, as she moved her left hand smoothly down his torso.

"Rosemary," Brian tried to protest, but inside the excitement took hold.

"Relax, Brian. I just want to make sure you are not injured or impaired elsewhere." Her voice picked up a pixy like giggle he remembered from nearly every meeting they had enjoyed.

"Someone might come in."

"After midnight," Rosemary objected, "really? Surely you jest? Not to worry. I shall be discreet." She achieved the result she wanted. "Anyway, I came prepared."

She pulled the sheet back and climbed onto the bed straddling Brian's torso. Ever so slowly Rosemary Kensington descended onto him. She was as ready as he was and probably just as hungry. It made him feel so alive, so free, to be with her. Rosemary carefully spread her skirt around them to cover their union. Brian fought to control the powerful urges he felt and allowed her to control the pace of their movements. Rosemary moved with an exquisite rhythm and purpose as she tried to achieve her own satisfaction as well as Brian's.

"Thank God, these are stiff beds," she whispered somewhat breathlessly.

Brian nodded with an enormous smile on his face. She was absolutely right. Their nocturnal intimacy made very little sound as they both worked to control their exhalations of ecstasy.

Something moved behind his lover. Brian looked with his eyes trying not to distract Rosemary. A young, night shift nurse he had seen before stood just beyond the privacy screen at the foot of the bed. She had a smile on her face, and she winked at Brian, and then left them alone. Brian took a deep breath and looked back into Rosemary's eyes. She did not seem to be focused on anything as her eyes opened and closed as her mind flew off to some far away place.

The shudders, choppy heaves of her chest and distinctive contractions gave Brian the confirmation of her pinnacle. She struggled to keep going. The excitement and sensations worked their magic as he soon joined her.

"Ah, yes," were the only words she said, as she savored the moment gradually coming down from the peak. She lowered her head to his shoulder allowing him to embrace her. Her chest was heaving, as her breathing remained heavy and deep. Her face was damp and cool against his cheek.

They stayed that way well into sleep. They were awakened by the young night shift nurse sometime before dawn as they lay side-by-side. "You will need to leave before the shift change, miss."

"Oh, dear. We must have fallen asleep," said Rosemary.

"I do believe so," answered the nurse.

Rosemary Kensington waited for the nurse to leave them so she could rise and adjust her clothing without any more embarrassment, if she felt any. The process took only a minute or two, and she looked like she had just come into the room.

"I hope you feel better, Brian."

"After last night, I think I'm fully recovered. Thanks, Rosemary."

"I should thank you. You have always brought me pleasure."

"You did all the work," laughed Brian.

"Nonetheless, it was true pleasure."

"None better, I'd say."

"Smashing. Then, you won't forget what awaits you, so don't let this happen again. Next time, you might not be so lucky."

"Not to worry."

She laughed a sarcastic, doubtful laugh. "I'll bet."

"You know I'm going to do my best. The rest is up to the Lord."

"As you say. What time is it?"

Brian could not see the clock over the entrance. He pointed in the correct direction. She stepped to the foot of the bed so she could see. "Quarter past four and it is starting to pinken outside. I really must be going."

They kissed as lovers. She departed. Brian kept his smile.

—

Cap Parlier

Author

—

Cap and his wife, Jeanne, live on the Great Plains of Kansas, along with three dogs and a cat. Their four children have begun their families as well as producing grandchildren – the rewards of long life. He is a graduate of the U.S. Naval Academy, a retired Marine aviator, a Vietnam veteran and an experimental test pilot. Cap has retired from the corporate world and can now fully indulge his passion for the story. He has numerous other projects completed, but not yet published, and others in development, including screenplays, historical novels and a couple of history books.

—

Interested readers may wish to visit his website at http://www.Parlier.com for his essays and other items, or subscribe to his weekly Blog: *"Update from the Heartland."* Cap can be reached at: Cap@SaintGaudensPress.com.

Books by Cap Parlier:

—

<u>Anod series</u>
The Phoenix Seduction (1995)
Anod's Seduction (2004) [reprint of The Phoenix Seduction]
Anod's Redemption (2004)

—

Sacrifice (2000)

—

<u>To So Few series</u>
To So Few – In the Beginning (2014)
To So Few – The Prelude (2014)
To So Few – Explosion (2015)

—

<u>and with **Kevin E. Ready:**</u>
TWA 800 - Accident or Incident? (1998)

—

Coming soon from Cap Parlier, **To So Few – The Trial**, the fourth book of the series novel of flight and a warrior's life.

—

These and other great books available from Saint Gaudens Press

Post Office Box 405
Solvang, CA 93463-0405
URL: http://www.saintgaudenspress.com
Visit Cap Parlier's Web Site at: http://www.parlier.com

—

Saint Gaudens, Saint Gaudens Press and the Winged Liberty colophon are trademarks of Saint Gaudens Press

www.ingramcontent.com/pod-product-compliance
Lightning Source LLC
Chambersburg PA
CBHW061327050726
47504CB00013B/433